PRAISE FOR DONALD E. McQUINN'S EPIC SAGA OF COURAGE AND SURVIVAL IN A SAVAGE WORLD OF THE FUTURE:

By Donald E. McQuinn:

TARGETS
WAKE IN DARKNESS
SHADOW OF LIES

WARRIOR*
WANDERER*
WITCH*

*Published by Del Rey Books

WANDERER

Donald E. McQuinn

A Del Rey® Book
BALLANTINE BOOKS • NEW YORK

To those who completed the circle
—Betsy, Alison, and Robin
—with love and great pride.

A Del Rey® Book
Published by Ballantine Books

Copyright © 1993 by Donald E. McQuinn
Map copyright © 1993 by Carol McQuinn

Library of Congress Catalog Card Number: 93-90153

ISBN 0-345-39018-0

Manufactured in the United States of America

First Trade Edition: November 1993
First Mass Market Edition: September 1994

10 9 8 7 6 5 4 3 2 1

ACKNOWLEDGMENT

With thanks to my friend Brett Carroll, Director of Lecture Demonstrations, at the Department of Physics, University of Washington, a man who knows the magic of science and understands the importance of teaching it as part of life.

ACKNOWLEDGMENT

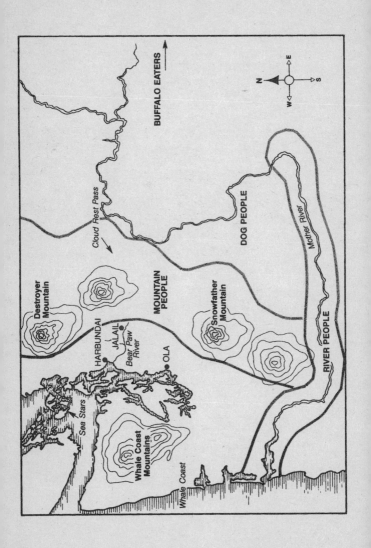

PROLOGUE

The sun was at its highest in a faultless sky. Its brilliance scourged the barren mountainside with a light as pitiless as truth. Erratic winds pressed one way, then another, swirling away all the heat, except for that hoarded in the tumbled boulders.

Labored breathing rasped from the throats of the three figures struggling up the steep path to the mountain's blunt summit. Dressed in heavy black robes that reached to the ground, cowls drawn over their heads, their progress was halting, unsteady.

Far below that trio, a straggling group of other black-clad figures huddled in protecting crannies. Downhill farther yet, the black-green wall that was the edge of the forest pulsed to the wind's insistent music. The first pale tips of spring's new growth was an almost festive wash of color against the weatherbeaten sobriety of older pines.

Three large curtain-enclosed litters rested on the ground near the waiting group. Startling against the muted tones of the mountain, they were painted in bright colors and festooned with flowers. Occasionally the wind worked free a soft, bright petal. Tossed aloft, each had a translucent beauty that sparkled in the grasp of the air's rough playfulness. Inevitably, however, they all were crushed to earth and lost among the rocks.

There were flashes of color on the black robes of the three climbers, as well. Piping of silver and gold, the stripes no wider than a finger, marked the edges of the sleeves, skirt, and cowl on the leading figure. The other two featured different colors, and the trim was twice as wide. Each inner part of the cowl was

1

lined in the same colors as the outer decoration. One wore a pattern of stylized long green leaves against a blue that exactly matched the sky. The third wore two entwined shades of diffident dark brown that seemed to meld into the soft black of the robe.

Groaning, the leader stepped onto the mountain's crown. Almost flat, the entire expanse stood revealed. Clear of any rock larger than a man's fist, the plateau was perhaps one hundred long paces from end to end, and half that wide. At the southern end, there was a temple. It was hut-sized, but the sophistication of its immaculately dressed stone, precise architecture, and gabled roof shocked the eye.

The gray iron door was firmly closed. Its metal blankness questioned: Did it shield whoever—whatever—dwelt there? Or did it confine danger?

Or both?

The robed figures threw back their hoods and raised their faces to the sun. They were women, into the years of graying hair. The one wearing gold and silver trim was eldest. All made three-signs, making a fist, using the thumb knuckle to touch forehead, mouth, left eye, and right eye. All bowed heads in prayer.

Self-consciously adjusting their robes, they then closed toward each other and replaced the hoods. They advanced on the building in step, gold and silver on the right, brown in the center, blue and green on the left. In spite of all that, there was imbalance. Two showed reluctance in their gait and in the way they constantly sought physical contact with a companion. The third, she of blue and green, strode with determination.

The door swung open.

The wind steadied from the south. It whisked away puffs of dust raised by the women's footsteps.

Beyond the plateau, the world stretched away in bold mountains and canyons. Crystalline air brought rivers, forests, and small villages so close one expected to hear the call of birds and children's laughter. Something in the depths of the soul made it known, however, that such simple joys never touched this place. Here was mystery. Here the wordless wind warned of power that transcended what humans called reality.

When the women reached the building they knelt before the stone slab doorstep. From inside their robes, they produced offerings. The elder placed a kernel of corn and a grain of wheat on the step. The woman of brown poured salt from a leather pouch into a dish. Her second contribution was a finger-sized ingot of steel. Lastly, the woman of blue and green set down another saucerlike dish and filled it with water from a flask. Beside that, she placed a tuft of wool. Her hands were the only ones that didn't tremble.

As much felt as heard, the rhythm of a huge, unseen drum pushed against the women. The minor-major double beat of a heart grew louder and louder. In a reverberating crescendo, it seized the women. They became earth, stone, mountain. And then the rhythm retreated, fading back to subliminal pressure.

Softly, dry as ashes, a voice echoed hollowly from within the stone walls. "One knows why you come, Sister Mother."

A nervous tremor turned the eldest woman's formal nod into a spasmodic twitch. She tried to speak, but managed only a weak, crying note.

The woman of blue and green pushed back her hood. Pale lips were drawn tight. Her eyes slitted in concentration. She said, "We come to beg your help."

The dry voice intoned, "Sister Mother speaks here, Harvester. Not you. One knows where your mind has taken you. One prays you find your way back."

The Harvester lifted her chin. "My soul, my heart, my mind— all are sworn only to Church's service."

The double-beat thundered. Sister Mother prostrated herself on the step-altar. The woman of brown fell over, curled in a fetal ball. Only the Harvester remained in position, and even she grimaced, eyes closed. The rhythm trailed off. The voice went on in cold, rustling fury. "You dare lie to One. You think to enlist me in your schemes. You, Sister Mother, hear. You need strength, as never before. You, Gleaner; your spies are Sister Mother's eyes and ears and must know all. The beast that stalks Church is ever new and ancient beyond the beginning. Small enough to hide in any place, powerful enough to have obliterated the giants and their slaves. What comes makes evil of the purest. All that can save Church is the rarest of treasures. Church must produce it. With it, she guides. Without it, she dies. In no case can Church ever be the same."

Still facedown, Sister Mother pleaded. "Help me. Tell me what to do, whom to trust."

Rough laughter scraped through the doorway. "Church would

do well to trust her enemies; they have the virtue of dependability." Then, sternly, "One cannot do for Sister Mother what she must do for herself. One can only warn. New empires are a-borning; fear not only their might. The long-feared blossoming of Sylah of the Iris stirs. The force to destroy Church shall come forth with the first life of next spring. You have exactly one year to prepare. The Flower will be brought to glory by the white and black, by all-powerful magic that creates beauty and destruction, peace and war."

The door swung to half-closed. Nearly hysterical, Sister Mother edged forward. "Must Church strike Sylah? One of our own? You are the Seer of Seers! What is the treasure? Tell me what to do."

Inch by inch, the door continued its movement. "One never sees all. One never completely understands all that One sees. Still, I have something else to say. For you, Harvester: I have changed and tranced many times lately, trying to plumb this matter. Always, I find you waiting in my Seeing. At the edge, you understand? Not clearly visible, but a presence. And I feel death. What does that suggest, sister?"

Heavy sobs from the unmoving Sister Mother punctuated the long pause while the Harvester considered her answer. "Perhaps that I will fight for Church. It must survive. There will be violence, as there has been already. As for me, I have no fear of death in Church's name."

"Admirably said. May Church at least change, then?" The voice was patient.

"Church is immortal, immutable."

"You sadden." The door swiftly closed. Through it, the voice was amazingly clear. "Beware, Sister Mother, of deceit, of unbelievers. Beware most of all the truest of the true. Therein lies perversion."

A small man wrapped in a cloak the color of the surrounding rocks watched carefully from a hiding place at the lip of the plateau as the women filed off the opposite edge. When the Harvester stepped down, she turned and pushed back her cowl, then replaced it. Immediately, she followed her companions and was lost to sight.

The man sped to the small building. Stepping over the offerings, he drew a thick-bladed short sword and knocked on the door with its butt. He poised to strike.

4

There was no response.

Gripping the door handle, he yanked. It swung open easily. The sword stabbed reflexively at empty air. Slowly, eyes bulged with fear, he entered the room. On the floor, a small stone pot held a glowing coal of incense, its wispy smoke rising to enshroud the wizened face of an old, old woman. Through the shimmering pall she glared contempt that clashed with a voice as soft as a caress. "Aahh, you come. Brave warrior. One commends."

She gestured at two pieces of cloth next to the censer. The movement sent tendrils of smoke coiling at the man. He flinched. Her face cracked in a twisted, pitying smile. "Pick them up," she said, and as he did, she went on, "You will give these to the Harvester. Tell her this: 'It grieves One to have seen that you will have other victories, some as important as this one.'"

He managed a nod.

"Then strike," she commanded. "It is as it must be."

Shivering violently, the man made a three-sign. He hugged himself.

"Strike!" She shrieked it. "Now, or by the word of the One in All, One will tell you of your own death. Strike, coward, as you must."

And so he did, his own desperate scream overriding any cry the Seer might have made.

The heartsound roared. The man choked, dropped his sword, and covered his ears. The noise throbbed along every bloodpath in his body, tearing at flesh and bone. Whimpering like a beaten child, he stumbled backward out of the room. Once in the sunlight, he ran.

Some time later, at a rest stop amid the pines of the lower slope, the man sidled close to the blue and green litter of the Harvester. Peering through the semitransparent screen, the woman saw him. After a quick glance around, she ordered her bearers to leave. When she was quite alone, she gestured the thin figure forward. As soon as he knelt outside, she asked, "Is it done?"

Eyes averted, he said, "Yes, Harvester."

The tone roused her suspicion. She pushed the screening aside. "She spoke, didn't she?"

The man blindly extended the articles. The Harvester's face

5

tightened at the sight of her own belt, missing over a year. The second was a patch of Church robe, with the small embroidered iris emblem of that order's Chosens. The Harvester threw them both to the foot of the litter. She listened stonily to the Seer's message, then sat back to think.

The emblem had to be from the child Sylah. A grown woman, now; a War Healer. It was a warning, then. Everyone knew One was a friend of the crack-brained old Iris Abbess in the far north, she of the hysteric dreams of the Door. And Sylah was her favorite. Together, the articles proved One used personal possessions to work her predictions. That was a sin. She was a fraud, as well. No one who saw the future would wait so calmly to be murdered.

Still, she'd been absolutely accurate about many things for as long as anyone could remember. What she said about victories indicated she saw *something*. Old fool.

Suddenly, the Harvester sat bold upright. Of course. Victories. The Seeing told One who won the coming conflict. The witch couldn't bear knowing, *wanted* to die.

She leaned out of the litter to address the man. "You're sure she's dead? Where's your sword?"

Cringing, the man backed away, still kneeling. "May the One in All help me, I did it. Then I heard her dead heart beating. I left the weapon. It hurt my hand. Hurt. Cold, Harvester. Like ice. I can't get warm. What have we done?"

"We?" The Harvester dropped the cloth between them. "You trespassed on holy ground. You killed the Seer of Seers. Pray I'll continue to favor you and find a penance that will let you save your soul. Now, get away from me."

The man fled.

Musing, the Harvester said, "Next spring, she said. A year from now. Not much time. If that fool's allowed to seek the Door, she'll create division among us all. If she finds something . . ." That didn't bear thinking about. She stared off into space, then spoke decisively. "The Seer of Seers knew. And I understand."

The Harvester looked toward the gold and silver litter. She smiled. Slowly, it waned. Only the most practiced, the most observant, could have detected the tightening facial muscles that betrayed suppressed emotion. Then, control rejected, the Harvester abandoned herself to expression. Her lips pulled back from clenched teeth. Her eyes narrowed. She breathed deeply, rapidly.

6

Her breast rose and fell as if she struggled with an inner demon almost too strong to contain.

"Sylah," she said, and the name was a sigh of hatred. "Sylah."

BOOK I

THE PATH
OF MISTAKES

CHAPTER 1

Anxious fingers of light reached out from the crackling flames in the fireplace. Their nervous search fondled grim walls and a floor of rough stone. Unable to reach the full extent of the room, they carved out a fitful, shifting island of ruddy illumination. When the last remaining log collapsed into a muddle of whispering coals, there was a startled, answering movement at the line where firelight broke on solid blackness.

There was a chair, a thing of leather and wood, so darkened by age that it suggested a tangible structure of the night itself. Again, there was movement. It defined a seated figure, cowled in Church's black robe.

The change in position was unhurried. The surprise occasioned by the falling log was obviously past. Nevertheless, there was a sense of irritation in the room now, and disappointment, as though the person had been immersed in some deep reverie and resented return to reality.

A languid hand appeared from inside one of the spacious sleeves, soft white against the wool. It stroked the cloth in a preoccupied rhythm for a few moments before sweeping up decisively to brush back the cowl. Gold glinted boldly, a massive bracelet and a ring. The facial features were sculpted in lines of determination so uncompromising they threatened to overwhelm the woman's beauty. Ebony hair celebrated release in a shining cascade.

Rising smoothly, she moved to throw more wood on the fire. She stopped, head cocked, listening. Rain beat against the thick wood shutters holding out the night. Wind moaned deep in the chimney's throat.

11

She was certain she'd heard something else. Distant shouts? And sharp, hard noises. Hoofbeats?

It made no sense. Gan Moondark would never schedule troop movements inside the walls of the castle—not without warning everyone who lived there. It couldn't be an attack. The troops manning the battle walks would be shouting, battering the huge alarm gongs to fill the night with brazen thunder.

A shiver touched the small of her back, skittered up her spine to cower under the hair on the nape of her neck. Memories flooded her present.

Once there had been another night of unexplained presence. A child sensed its danger, a heavy, menacing force outside her home. That home was a hut, not a castle.

Men had made the sounds; the child had heard them. Now she was grown; Rose Priestess, War Healer, Sylah. Wife to Clas na Bale, who was Gan Moondark's true friend.

The little girl's name wasn't Sylah when those men came and killed her family while she watched. Neither did the men care what became of her after Church chose her, thereby saving her from death or slavery. Church named her, as was Church's right and obligation.

The child survived because she'd learned to keep her memories buried. A Chosen had no memory of any childhood except Church. Or she disappeared. Forever. It was the way. The Apocalypse Testament said it: "To be chosen to serve Church best, one denies all that has passed and once was. Past is dead is death is killing. Now and tomorrow, those called Chosen are Church's most treasured instruments, the living proof that all are meant to live in peace with the earth."

She heard sounds again, muffled by the wind and rain. Angry, confused, she told herself there was nothing to fear here. Hadn't she, herself, participated in creating this sanctuary?

Sanctuary. The word rattled through her mind, ringing bitter discord.

Gan Moondark's sanctuary, after he'd united the barons of Harbundai and overthrown Altanar, the king of what had been considered invincible Ola. Now Gan ruled the Three Territories; Harbundai, Ola, and the vast lands of his own seminomadic Dog People living to the east of the Enemy Mountains. It was Gan who asked Clas na Bale to lead the Dog People in his stead, and so deprived her of her husband. *Sanctuary.*

Without Clas no place was any less lonely than any other.

Torchlight slipped under her door, a sinister blazon that grew brighter as the source progressed down the hall toward her. The fiery glow licked the stone floor, searched all the way to her feet.

This section of the castle was empty, waiting for a new group of girls to be trained as War Healers. No one would hear if she screamed.

A man whispered something indistinguishable, the words rapid and hoarse. Suppressed laughter followed, more frightening than the hushed words. Quick footsteps retreated. The torchlight remained.

The latch crept slowly upward. There was no way to bar the entry. The door's heavy timbers were falsely impressive. King Altanar had decreed that no rooms inside his walls, except his own, could ever be barred against himself and those called his protectors.

Sylah drew herself erect. Her right hand sought the comforting shape of the shortknife up her sleeve. She reminded herself that she was Church, and holy. Anyone who deliberately killed her became the required victim of every soul who owed allegiance to Church.

But there were those whose need for power outstripped fear of death or eternal damnation.

They tried to kill her before. Clas saved her. If she must fight alone now, so be it. She would not plead.

"I know you're there," she said warningly, and the movement of the latch stopped. Then it jerked upward. The door flew open to boom against the opposite wall with a force that set it to shivering like a chilled hand. The man who'd done it stood bent forward, the torch raised above his head so his face was in shadow.

Sylah needed no closer look. "Clas!" The voice that had firmly rejected fear moments before squeaked embarrassingly, then babbled, "It's you! What are you doing here? You're supposed to be with your tribe! The pass. The snows. It's too dangerous."

He stepped in and pitched the torch at the fireplace. It spun away, the flames making a low ruffle until it landed on the grate. Scooping her lightly into his arms, he kicked the door shut behind him and carried her farther into the room. He kissed her, and she responded wildly, half crying, half laughing, then pulled away. Interrupting her inchoate, tumbling questions, he said, "No. Tonight we speak only of tonight. Tomorrow Church can have you back— for this cursed search you will have that takes you from me. Tomorrow we can talk of that, or passes and snows, or anything else. Tonight is ours. Mine. Your husband's."

The assurance of it, the self-certain *possession*, jolted her. No

13

one spoke to her like that. No one claimed her, called her *mine*. She felt the involuntary stiffening of her muscles, the coldness welling deep inside.

He put his mouth to her hair, caressed it with his lips. He said, "I had to come. I had to see you once more before you leave. Life's only another duty for me until you finish this thing you must do and come back to me. I love you, Sylah. My Sylah."

Her head sagged forward to rest in the space between his jaw and chest. A pulse in his neck throbbed against her cheek, mimicked the sudden racing of her heart. She bit him gently, teasing the skin between her teeth, then said, "And I love you. My Clas."

CHAPTER 2

Sylah automatically rose at her accustomed time the next morning. Squinting sleepily, wrapping her nakedness in a heavy robe, she was pushing open the shutters to a brittle gray dawn before she was truly awake. Below her, the bleak surface of the Inland Sea stretched away to the forested base of the Whale Coast mountains. Clouds the color of raw iron masked the snowy peaks.

A flicker of movement on the water caught her eye. Flashing oars stroked a slim, low-slung hull vessel toward Ola's docks. Its sail was furled in the still air. Sylah grimaced. The design was unmistakable. A sharker, the notorious craft of the Skan people from the far north, men who were raiders by choice, traders if outnumbered. They roamed and ravaged wherever the Great Sea allowed. Some people bought slaves to row similar ships, hoping they could outrun the Skan if attacked. Few managed.

No Skans had come to Ola since Gan Moondark conquered it just the previous summer.

She shivered, only partly from the cold.

Gan Moondark. Last summer. Sometimes it seemed a thousand years ago.

His destiny had snared them all. They'd benefited. At a cost.

Clas na Bale had been the honored fighting instructor of the Dog tribe, and Gan was one of his students, a Nightwatcher. Then Faldar Yan had tried to usurp the position of War Chief from Gan's father. In the ensuing turmoil, Gan killed Faldar Yan in a duel. More treachery made it look as though Gan had violated the tribe's code of honor. With the Moondarks forced to flee, Clas joined in the escape. Faldar Yan's successor was his son, Bay. He died suspiciously, leaving a man named Likat to become War Chief. He tried to ally the Dog People with King Altanar in an attempt to conquer the nation of Harbundai. When the Dog People realized Gan had fought his way to leadership of Harbundai's army, they rejected Likat. Now Clas was War Chief, at Gan's request, freeing Gan to consolidate the Three Territories.

The last point reminded her of the peculiar foreigners who'd also been pulled into Gan's fate.

What would have become of her—or Gan and Clas—without those strange people? Such good fortune could attract equally bad luck.

Bad luck, she thought in a flash of bitterness; *that* would fall to others, not Gan.

Hadn't she lived without Clas through an entire fall and winter, preparing for a quest that couldn't include him because of Gan? And who could guess how long the journey would keep her separated from Clas?

Gan. For all the challenges facing him, he was together with his wife, Neela. He had her support and comfort. He had their child. Their son.

Grim depression pushed at her.

She reminded herself that because she'd been caught up in Gan's destiny, she was within striking distance of her obsession with Church's deepest secret, the fabled Door.

But it wasn't obsession. Something called her. She didn't know exactly what she sought, wasn't even certain of its existence. She only knew she must *go*.

Turning, she looked at her husband. He was still facedown, an arm flung across the bed where she'd just been. She thought of the harsh discipline of her childhood that still jerked her from sleep every morning whether she was rested or exhausted. Oddly, this morning she was physically quite tired, although her mind sparkled with secret happiness. Remembrances of the night churned in her thoughts. Her face warmed alarmingly.

She threw her robe aside to burrow under the quilted down cover. Clas rolled onto his side. She pressed against his back, savoring the play of muscle and bone when he sighed deeply.

A sense of completion filled her. We *are* one, she thought, surprised and then amused by her own sudden, unexpected fierceness.

Or was *desperation* the more accurate word?

There were things they should discuss. When she pulled back

15

to study him, he was so relaxed she couldn't bring herself to disturb him. Her mind wandered. She thought of how he must have struggled to cross the mountains this early in the spring. So dangerous. And he'd be on the return trip that afternoon.

Once he was gone, time would be measured in terms of returning to him.

Her eyes traced the slope of his shoulder, stopping at the grooved scar just where the muscle curved up to connect with his neck. It always made her think of a plowed furrow.

How could she have fallen so totally in love with a man whose life was combat? How could she separate herself from him?

Power. *If* it existed, the Door was power. The acknowledgment that she needed it so terribly shamed her. Why couldn't she be satisfied with what she'd accomplished? Why did she need more than Clas' love?

Could the need for power have driven the Teachers? Church history said that generations ago, the branch of Church calling themselves Teachers had claimed to have discovered the secret of the Door. They offered to share it with all who accepted Church, in exchange for sexual equality. For their presumption, men exterminated them. And all knowledge of the Door.

Sylah willed her fists to relax and open. She thought of them cradling whatever secret warranted the Teachers' bold bid.

Clas would never understand.

He was a warrior. He knew fighting and killing. Risk. He knew what it was to be tortured.

He knew nothing of being property.

She was a Chosen, and Chosens were Church things. Owned.

That was being too harsh, she thought: Church's women fought constantly for independence. Without male protection, a non-Church woman was no more than a child-bearing utensil.

I will be free. There is no truth so strong it allows one person to possess another.

The words rang so loudly in her mind she started, afraid she'd actually spoken.

Calming herself, she told herself she would make it true. With the Door's power no one could threaten her, ever again. All women would rise to their proper place.

Clas stirred, half turning. He frowned darkly, then settled. She ran her fingertips across his bristled, close-cropped hair. It was a new trim. The realization he'd had it done just for this trip, for her, touched her.

Suddenly, so swiftly she had no time to react, he spun to face

16

her, grabbing her wrist. She gasped her surprise, and when she got her breath, her words came in a sputter. "You were awake all along!"

His laughter rumbled. "How could I sleep? You think too loudly."

It was a small joke, but the coincidence was a shock. She tried to push him back as he hovered over her, braced on one elbow. It was like pushing the wall.

"Get away." She feigned indignation. "Look, it's near full sunrise. We have many things to do, and . . ."

He clamped his hands on her at the bottom of her rib cage and rolled onto his back. Effortlessly, he lifted her. The covers draped over her created a small, dark tent for them. Her pretended anger broke against his sheer pleasure in her, in his own strength, in the joy of being. She laughed down at him, cupping his face in her hands, covering the black square tattoo over the welted scar on his cheek.

Even though he continued to smile, his eyes took on an intensity that made them glass bright. His voice thickened. He said, "Let the sun rise as it will. There's only one thing in the world we have to do." Slowly, as he might bring a fruit-laden branch within reach, he lowered her to him, burying his face between her breasts.

Her breath caught in her throat. She had no thoughts for the day. The moment was the world.

Hours later the cloud cover was broken into scattered white heaps that bumbled across the sky like fat puppies. Bright sunshine warmed the rutted road leading to the docks. Beyond the stone jetties shielding the small harbor, it struck dazzling bursts of light from the tops of chopping waves.

Sylah held Clas' arm as they walked. When she glanced up at him, her idle comment died unspoken, checked by the severity of his frown. She asked what troubled him.

Uncharacteristically, he hesitated. More, his answer had a defensive note. "Conway. Tate. There on the dock. You said no one would come to the docks to make these Skan raiders welcome, but there they are. I wish you had Dog warriors traveling with you instead of those strangers."

It startled her so greatly she stopped. His momentum pulled her arm free before he turned to face her. She said, "Strangers? They've fought beside you and Gan. Since the day you left they've worked to make my quest theirs. They've learned to ride

17

and handle a murdat well. And they have the lightning weapons; that alone makes them invaluable companions."

"Lightning weapons. Faw! That's the sort of thing that bothers me." His jaw jutted stubbornly. "It's not natural to kill a man so far away you can't recognize him. That thing they call a wipe—the long tube that uses those little copper darts—is bad enough. The fat tube under it, the boop—that'll kill a dozen men with one loud bang. I'm grateful for their help. I like them. But . . ." He floundered for words, then burst out, "You should've seen them in that Devil ambush. You know, when Gan and I saved them. They acted like they'd never seen a real fight. Aside from Tate—and Conway, I guess—they still do. They're not just strangers, they're *strange*."

He stopped to glare at the Whale Coast mountains as if blaming them for his uncertainty.

Sylah opened her mouth to argue, then shut it again. There was nothing anyone could say to him when he was in this mood.

It wasn't as if there was anything actually troublesome about the strangers. Of course, one kept coming back to the point that no one had any idea where they came from. Even the Peddlers, those tribeless ones who wandered everywhere, never heard of them. Further, the strangers steadfastly claimed they'd traveled between their homeland and the Enemy Mountains without ever being observed until the Devil ambush. That was simply unbelievable.

And no one seeing the woman named Donnacee Tate was likely to forget her. Not only was she black, she'd impressed Gan and the other warriors enough to rise to be one of the army's senior leaders. Legends said some of the giants who ruled the world before the beginning were black. Or yellow, like the Nion traders from across the Great Sea. It disturbed Sylah that she'd never heard of anyone who'd seen another black person, be they giant or anything else.

Then there was the matter of the man called Jones.

Eight strangers survived the Devil ambush Clas referred to. One, named Falconer, died in Ola's castle while Altanar still ruled. Jones betrayed them all. *Moondancer.* He knew when the Jalail barons meant to kidnap her and Gan's wife, Neela. He allowed it to happen. Her hand went to her stomach in an unconscious gesture as a wave of mourning and loss tried to drown her. Almost imperceptibly, she bent forward, as though she could turn back time and still shelter the child that had died within her because of Jones' treachery.

Clas was staring at her, his face like something carved of glacier ice. "Were you thinking of them? Of the Jones one? He's why I worry about them all. Even Tate, though we shared blood."

She attempted to speak, and he cut her off with a gesture. "You won't change my mind." He reached to stroke her cheek, and she marveled that such hardness could permit so tender a touch. He said, "Nor will I change yours, my Priestess. I know I can't hold you by force. That means I must trust your judgment."

She covered his hand with hers. He looked away, made a noise in his throat. "I didn't say I like your judgment. Don't look at me that way. It's not fair."

"Like the strangers' weapons?" She turned his hand, kissed the palm, teased him with her eyes.

"Exactly." He laughed, pulling her to him.

Linking an arm through his again, she resumed their walk down toward the dock and the tied-up sharker. She felt his ongoing suspicion, and determined not to let it erode her confidence in her friends. They were honest, helpful people. The man called Louis Leclerc, who everyone said understood tools the way warriors understood their weapons, was a perfect example: He created the black, smelly powder stuff that knocked down the gates of Altanar's castle, didn't he? Without that, her own life would have been ended. If the other three women—Kate Bernhardt, Sue Anspach, and Janet Carter—were afraid to fight like Tate, and knew practically nothing of Healing or Church, that was only because they were from a different place, wasn't it?

She swallowed a smile. Different place, indeed. They read. And *wrote*. They'd actually had the courage to show young Chosens how to do it, and, wonder of wonders, let the children display their ability to Gan. Because they convinced him such skill could help him direct his warriors more effectively, he directed the women to show *all* Chosens. For the first time anywhere, someone besides the most favored males and Church women were being shown letters and numbers.

This time she did smile, embarrassed at her fear of even thinking the word *teach*.

The three foreign women wore Church clothes, did what they did for the benefit of all, she told herself, then made a surreptitious three-sign to ward off danger. For safety's sake.

Clothes. That made her think of Conway. He was the one who suffered visibly at the loss of even the smallest piece of anything he'd brought from his homeland. Some sorrow was natural; their possessions were marvelous—outerwear that shed water like duck

19

feathers without stewing the person wearing it, boots made of material that wore like iron and dried out while leather still squished with each step. But it was just clothing, after all. Ugly brown and green splotches without any pattern. Superb craftsmanship, but no concept of design or ornamentation or dramatic effect. Why would a man be emotional about stuff like that?

Clas was right, after all: They *were* strange.

On the dock, Conway told Tate, "I don't look forward to talking to this captain. He's got a rotten mouth."

Tate nodded. "I understand. I knew a colonel like him once. Dumb. Never learned the difference between tough and nasty."

Conway pulled a face, pretending great surprise. "An incompetent Marine? You admit it?"

"Oh, sure. Thing is, in the Corps, he stood out. In the Army, who'd have noticed?"

"You never quit, do you?" He laughed easily. "I wonder what your leaders would say if they knew their indoctrination survived five centuries of cryogenic life suspension?"

"They'd be on me like a coat of paint if they thought it didn't. They'd say if any part of me made it through, it better be the esprit de corps."

Both fell quiet after their exchange, and Conway was sure Tate's silence was filled with the same bittersweet tang as his.

They lived. The world they knew was gone.

Political determination in it had degenerated to nothing more than constant, escalating terrorism. Ever-increasing populations crowded themselves into madness. The same expansion destroyed forests, polluted rivers, seas. Climate skewed, became as insane as the thrashing humans. Inevitably, with no one precisely sure how it started or with any ability to stop it, war crept across the globe. Every nation, ethnic group, or association of any description demanded room. At any cost. Neutrality was interpreted as covert support for one enemy or another. Everyone literally struck out at everyone with gas, germs, radiation, nuclear weapons.

A religio-ecological sect calling themselves Williamsites had anticipated just such a cataclysm. Using the most advanced biological techniques, they set out from their worldwide network of Ecotemples to repopulate the earth's remnant natural habitats with breeding stocks of animal, insect, and plant species. Simultaneously, there came a call in what was left of the United States for volunteers to go into cryogenic crèches. Their mission was to emerge healthy and assist in restoring their damaged country.

Conway, Tate, and over a thousand others were assigned to the crèche in the Cascade Mountains of the Pacific Northwest.

While the outside survivors of the apocalypse abandoned their disease-riddled, radiation-soaked, chemically lethal centers of civilization and sank into struggling savagery, the crèche, hidden in a deep, natural cave further enhanced by technological safeguards, ticked off the centuries. Tended by a virtually eternal nuclear engine and robots, the frozen humans waited in their thousands. Not dead, not alive, utterly forgotten. Adrift on a sea of time, they were rescued by an earthquake that shattered the cave and tricked the machine controls into believing the rejuvenation order had been issued.

Twelve initially survived.

Now they were seven, one of them a brain-damaged religious madman.

Educated billions, reduced to four women and three men. Technocrats, trying to survive in a place where forging steel was the peak of technology.

Without their weapons, they were as helpless—and useless—as babies.

Irony of ironies. They had survived apocalypse and had no value, except to continue the killing.

Unless another crèche existed, still waiting for a rejuvenation signal from a dead world.

The Door? Sylah's Door? What if . . . ?

A hoarse shout from the ship's captain intruded on Conway's thoughts. Watching the slim ship rock on what used to be Puget Sound and was now the Inland Sea, he felt once more the burden of his alienness. Pirate vessels of wood, sail, and oars where there had once been steel hulls and nuclear engines. Up on the hill behind him, the stone castle of the kingdom of Ola brooded over sparsely settled countryside that once was home and workplace to teeming numbers. Some of the castle's rocks gleamed whiter than others. They were cement or marble, materials from buildings and highways so far beyond these people's comprehension that they believed those things had been designed by giants and built by ordinary humans who were their slaves. They called the forgotten, buried sites godkills, when they found them, and they were mined by slaves because they were still feared as death itself.

Conway imagined one of the original survivors of the world's collapse hovering over a fire, telling the next generation they must keep to the forests and fields because all the places where men had lived before hid unseen things that killed.

21

Some would test his tales. When the skeptics developed disease, or began to rot from radiation or chemicals, no one would question further.

Conway looked across the Inland Sea to the Whale Coast mountains—the Olympic range—and wondered what the Adirondacks, the Smokies, the Rockies were called.

America.

A beautiful country. Magnificent. It stood for things. Good things.

There was no sense thinking about it. Everything he'd known and loved was gone. The other world took his wife. His child. Their murders had been someone's political statement.

Somewhere there was probably a grave or plaque with his own name on it.

A memorial.

To the south, the Glass Cliffs gleamed mocking agreement. They were a constant, brutal reminder of what man could accomplish. A nuclear blast of unimaginable heat had fused the earth itself there, leaving a glittering scar where, centuries later, the only life that dared its defiled ground was a scattering of leprous plants.

A voice whispered sweet seduction, asked why he should continue to hope. All that was left for him was to wait for this savage place to send him along to join those who'd been like him.

No!

Denial exploded deep inside him.

All the disappointment, the loss, the baffled, uncomprehending anger of his two lives in two worlds, coalesced in a single moment of decision. The force of it closed out everything around him.

He would fight.

The wars that obliterated his time had spared him. To wonder why was as foolish as those wars had been. To surrender to depression was as wasteful. He was here, in this time. A different place, a different man.

Alive. Able to touch, to understand.

He tore his gaze from the obscenity of the Glass Cliffs. Down the long, shining reach of the Inland Sea the pristine head of Snowfather Mountain reared against the sky. A sensation of relief, almost of peace, filled him, as though he'd arrived at a long-sought refuge.

He had, he told himself. This was home. Perhaps he'd belonged in that first life, perhaps not. Fate had brought him to this one. In

22

the end, its fierce integrity must claim his life. He accepted that. Better than accept, he would challenge, measure his strength against whatever it had to offer. Until he lost, Matt Conway would *live*.

CHAPTER 3

Tate watched Sylah approach with Clas. The castle, as well as the town laid out around it, had been bubbling with gossip over his arrival in the night. She smiled at the brighter, livelier look of Sylah on this morning. Robed in her customary flowing black, she appeared to float along the dock's rough, splintered timbers. Above her left breast, the embroidered flower of her Rose Priestess rank glowed blood-red. Beauty and bearing drew the eye; character created a distance between herself and everyone but Clas. Even the sailors' initial leers turned to surreptitious glances, then slid away.

Returning Clas' wave of greeting, Tate wondered how many of those sailors' looks might be abbreviated by his presence. There, she thought, is a man who understates. Plain, right down to the wooden scabbard of his murdat and its worn wood handle. Unadorned buckskin shirt and trousers. Still, two things about him cried out to all—the square black tattoo on his cheek that covered the puckered scar there without disguising it, and the triple-ringed steel necklace with the small white objects dangling from each ring. The things appeared as sinister as cherry pits, until one learned they were the first bone of a human little finger. Each— and only one—was taken from a man personally killed in combat. The whisper of the dozens of tiny trophies on the cold metal said as much about Clas na Bale as most people were willing to learn.

Tate compared her own brilliant costume to the couple's austerity. She knew she was striking. Knee-high boots, with soft doeskin trousers tucked into the tops, and the loose, bright red wool blouse made an effective combination. A handwoven facsimile of her government-issue equipment belt replaced the original. A tooled leather scabbard held her murdat, the spearhead-shaped fighting blade of the Dog People. It was on her left hip, and the hand on that side rested naturally on its handle, a whale tooth carved in the shape of a springing tiger. Less conspicuous, her pistol was holstered on the right. Ammunition gleamed from green and white striped cloth bandoliers crisscrossing her chest.

Her thoughts centered on her friend Sylah, this time with the unpleasant tang of accepted realization: as much as she loved her, she also envied her. She didn't resent her, nor did she want Clas. She merely wished she had the least touch of what she thought of as Sylah's heart-calm.

Clas broke through her moral puzzling by sweeping her off her feet in a rib-cracking hug. In spite of her firm resolve not to do so, she groaned aloud, nearly masking his welcoming "I know you, my blood companion." He put her down and stepped away to hold her at arm's length. "I've missed you. I could have used you to help get my Dog People reunited after all the damage Faldar Yan did."

Tate said, "I know you, Clas na Bale. I've missed you, too. What's this about damage? I thought that was all over. I understood those who supported Faldar Yan and Likat repented everything."

"They did, but many resisted him and his warriors. There were arguments. Injuries. A few died. We've had more duels in the past months than in my entire life. But it's over now. The healing's taking hold." He turned to grasp Conway by hand and elbow. "I know you, Matt Conway. I spoke to Gan last night; he said you've been invaluable."

After exchanging greetings, Conway animatedly related what he and Tate had gleaned from travelers and Peddlers about the lands to the south. Clas listened carefully, occasionally asking a brief question. Finally, he said, "I have to be blunt. I know no other way. You'll never be more than a few days' ride from the unknown. Even Peddlers call the country between here and Kos the Empty Lands. There are predators, men and animals. Much of the territory west of the mountains is dominated by Kos. Kos itself is a shadowy, unknown land, where many unwary travelers have disappeared. And now we have Peddlers' tales of new forces coming from the east."

Conway said, "There's more than one path. We've been assured travelers to Church Home are seldom disturbed."

Tate turned away from the ongoing discussion. Despite its importance and her concern over the dangers, she felt peculiarly distracted. Undefinable restlessness pulsed in her.

At least she had some idea what was driving Conway to break free of Ola and its memories. Tee, the rebellious slave woman who'd led him to the anti-Altanar forces, was primary. She remembered how shattered Conway was when, after being freed, the woman rejected him. Conway would never understand. Any woman would.

As a gift-woman from her tribe to Altanar, she was expected to bear the king's child. Tee refused. The result of her courage was her presentation to Altanar's protectors for their amusement. A bitter taste rose in Tate's throat. "Protectors" was what they called Altanar's white-clad palace guard; torturers and murderers, all. After years of them, poor Tee felt herself degraded beyond love's capacity to salvage.

If anyone were ever to save her, it would have to be Tee herself. People said she'd joined a ship's crew and taken to a sea-trader's life.

Tate wandered down the dock toward the ship.

A flock of brant, hundreds strong, passed overhead. Prim black and white, their plumage accented subtlety of design where their larger, regal cousins, the Canada geese, favored drama. The rush of their wings deluged her with sound. They landed in the shallows, breasting the cold, green clarity into curls of silver. Quick, taut, they gabbled anxiously, craning to look away north, to their distant breeding grounds. Need to renew stirred in their chemistry. Home called more urgently with every movement of the sun.

Tate saw that, and ached with mute, unformed questions. She walked farther, watching the ship's captain supervise arrangements for offloading. He was short, thickly muscled, harsh in his commands. She estimated the crew at about thirty. Many were shirtless, exposing dark red and blue tattoos of geometric motif. Most bared torsos showed at least one scarified wound. Every man wore a knife.

The captain's imperious shout ended her inspection.

A small boy literally sprang out of a cargo hatch, vaulted a bale of furs, and raced to present himself. He was about twelve, thin, with a head too large for his body. His ears were flat against his skull, as if the need for speed pressed them down. Sharp features twisted into a knot of concentration, the eyes gleamed beacon-bright. Filthy leather shorts and shirt hung on him, so ragged they were a travesty of protection. Still, when he shivered, Tate knew it was from no chill. She felt his fear as he did. Involuntarily, she tensed in expectation of a blow. "Yes, Master?" the boy asked.

The captain raised his fist. The boy flinched and dodged, which made him totally unprepared for the swift strike of the other hand. The slap staggered him.

The captain said, "Get me a drink."

25

The boy ran for the hatch. When he reached it, he halted, as a small animal will pause sometimes before escaping down a hole. He'd given no previous sign he even knew Tate existed, yet now his eyes went straight to hers. The weight of that impenetrable, indecipherable look threatened to crush her.

Dazed, she stared at the yawning hatch for several moments before making her way to Conway with uncertain steps she couldn't properly blame on the rough dock. She pulled him aside, unconcerned for the rudeness that widened the eyes of Sylah and Clas. She was desperate to share her new knowledge.

"That boy," she said, straining at the words. "I have to talk to him."

Sylah overheard, and spoke up while Conway was gathering his wits. "If you mean someone from that ship, I advise against it. The Skan bought and sold slaves here when Altanar ruled. That's why the dock is deserted. They're foul men. In fact, I was just telling Conway we should leave now."

"You don't understand." She answered Sylah, but her gaze remained fixed on Conway. Dragging him closer to the ship, she shook with excitement. Several controlled breaths afforded her a measure of calmness. She said, "I have to talk to him, Matt. You know why. You understand." It was a plea.

"Understand what? What boy?"

Angry, disbelieving, she said, "The *boy*. On the ship. The one the captain hit."

"I didn't see that. Where's he now? I don't think . . ."

The boy reappeared on deck with the captain's drink in a pottery cup. Tate turned away, watching from the corner of her eye, lowering her voice. A knowing smile tugged at the corners of her mouth. She said, "He's black, Matt. Mother or father. A grandparent, at the very least. I've got to know where he's from."

Conway studied him. After a bit, he sighed. "Donnacee, there's nothing there. He's a little darker than I am, but a lot lighter than plenty of people. You're worrying too much about that sort of thing."

Tate winced.

A surflike roar in her ears drowned out the familiar chatter of the brant, the hoarse cries and commands from the ship.

Conway's familiar, trusted image wavered, lost its definition.

Her friend's face was gone, replaced by a white, featureless nothing.

She was smothering.

Remembered voices drifted into the emptiness. Hating voices, that had left invisible, never-healing wounds.

Words seared her throat, words she wanted to scream at him to make him experience scorn. Slurs. Worse than that, let him feel true loneliness. Let him learn what it was like to have your life soiled by sly looks, whispers, with unexplained smirks that turned away when faced.

Let him learn how that hurt.

Then maybe he'd partially understand why this boy had to have her help. *Her* help. No one else could fully grasp his need for his beginnings. No more than they could understand her need to know her own continuity. Her belonging place.

CHAPTER 4

She raged, face thrust into Conway's. "You telling me I don't know my own race, my own blood? Or don't you care? That's it, isn't it? Everyone here's so mixed they look like one kind of white or another. No blacks? No loss. *You're* here, your kind. You—"

He grabbed her elbow, squeezing so hard the last word collapsed into a hiss of pain. He said, "Shut up." The command was hushed, heavy with outrage. He went on, "We've been over this before. Maybe there're places where blacks didn't get completely assimilated. If that's so, maybe we'll find them when we go with Sylah." She broke off the glaring contest, the wrath in her features slacking. He relented, as well. "Look, I'm not going to tell you I know how you feel, 'cause no one can. I know it's bad." He shifted his hand to hers, holding it lightly, trying to be reassuring.

Muttering, she said, "They make me feel like a freak. Want to know if I'm real. Try to rub color off. At least before, back where we came from . . ." She stopped. Her chin came up. "They make me crazy here, too, Matt, but they still haven't made me blind. Or foolish."

Stiffly, she marched back to the ship. The squeal of braided leather rigging was like derisive laughter. The rearing bowsprit, a carved representation of an attacking bull seal, seemed to rock with malicious amusement. Up close, she could peer past the fencelike raised oars and over the wooden wall that protected the wooden benches. The barrier was notched and scarred by arrow and axe strikes. There were two open cargo hatches where collapsible derricks presently hoisted bales of furs up from the cold. No shelter broke the sweep of the single deck, and Tate shivered at the thought of men on those exposed benches when a winter storm dropped on them.

A cruel existence that bred cruelty into its survivors.

She put her hands on the upper edge of the shielding wall. Small swells moved the slender, sinuous hull; it, in turn, pushed against her with a silent message of eagerness.

She called to the captain. "Hello! I have a favor to ask."

Chatter dwindled to nothing. She gathered herself before saying, "I'd like to talk to the young boy on your ship. Are any of you related to him?"

Loud laughter greeted the question, fading as the captain approached to stand opposite her. He said, "They told me this Gan Moondark had strange people in his lands. I heard about you. The black witch. Magic weapons. Gives orders to men." He winked. "Women's market talk doesn't frighten me. The boy cost me a white bearskin. He's not for sale. Or rent."

"Where's he from?" Behind her, she heard her friends muttering concern. She couldn't stop. There had to be someone, somewhere, to at least remind her of kin, another person to provide the consolation of *likeness*.

Part of her mind scolded, forced her to admit there was nothing about the boy she could point to and claim it was a black characteristic.

Yet she was so *sure*.

Calling the boy to him, the captain put a hand on his shoulder. The boy stared off into the distance.

A thin edge of doubt cut at her determination.

The captain inched closer. Tate took a step away, and immediately regretted falling into his trap. He'd wanted to force her back. It established his control, and it put him in position to inspect her. Stony, calculating eyes ranged her body, conjured images of auction blocks and obscene indignities. Only pride held her fast. Finally, feigning innocent curiosity, he asked, "Are you really a woman?"

The insult set off a rumble from Conway and Clas. Tate gestured them to be quiet.

"You said you've heard of me," she answered. "Either you know exactly who and what I am, or you lie. I never heard of you, but I know the truth of you—a thing who owns a boy. No man at all."

28

He answered her taunt by swinging the boy around in front of him. Muscles bunched and swelled in his arms. He lifted the scrawny child clear of the deck. Writhing, kicking, the boy clawed ineffectually at the ropelike fingers choking him. He opened his mouth, for complaint or mercy, no one could know; the only sound that escaped was a wheezing rasp.

Tate gathered herself to attack, then noted the forefingers moving up onto the boy's jawbone, the thumbs braced against his skull just below the ears. If she moved, the man would merely twist his massive wrists and snap the boy's neck like a chicken's. In her heart, she understood he was teaching her her place. He expected her to beg, humble herself. Then he'd kill the child.

She bit her lip and waited, hoping her pretended callousness wouldn't simply goad him.

Tiring of his failed game, the captain threw the boy aside. He landed in a heap, quickly struggling to a sitting position. His look at his master showed no sign of surrender. Rather, as he sucked in huge gulps of air and rubbed his neck, Tate saw the quick glow of hatred. Then he was expressionless again.

The captain said, "Still think I'm not a man? Stay the night with me. Tomorrow you can talk to the boy all you want. If you're woman enough to satisfy me."

Drawing herself to full height, she spat. Like a lazy silver coin in the sun, the gobbet arced to strike him full in the face. Stunned, he crossed his eyes comically to watch the frothy mess drip from his nose. Then he roared, scrubbing at his face as he charged onto the dock.

Tate skipped backward, and Conway was chilled to see she'd drawn her murdat, rather than her pistol. He practically screamed at her, "Shoot him! Shoot!"

She ignored him. "We fight for the boy," she said to her foe.

"Agreed." Wasting no time or words, he advanced.

Conway didn't know what to do. Tate had deliberately provoked the fight, and chosen a weapon that gave her opponent every advantage. He wondered if she'd surrendered to something like a death wish.

As she circled, the movement put her between himself and the ship. His gaze traveled beyond her, through a gap in the crowd of sailors leaping to the dock. The boy was still where he'd landed, but now his wiry body was coiled in a tight spring of excitement. Something flickered across the engrossed face. Swift, subtle, it wasn't really an expression, but more like the revelation of a hidden thought. Whatever it was, Conway would have sworn that in some bizarre way, the boy was amused.

Conway had his pistol out and aimed at the captain even as the incident passed. Clas stepped in front of him, forcing the weapon downward. There was agony in his expression, but his voice was firm. "She exchanged blood with me, Matt Conway. Our honor is one. She challenged him. I can't let you fight for her."

A sense of danger warned the captain of the dialogue. He paused, his suspicious glances darting between Tate and her friends.

Conway struggled to break free. Clas said, "Don't. You would shame her, me, my people. Her life would be without value. Let her fight honorably."

For long moments they were static, Conway uselessly pressing against Clas' great strength. Finally, Conway let his arm go limp. He said, "Honor! If she dies, I'll find a way to make you pay, you hear me?"

"I hear." Sadness ached in the words. Clas released Conway's weapon and turned away.

The captain leapt to the attack, pounding at Tate's defense. She gave ground, bending away from the ringing blows.

A vicious cross-body swipe by the captain appeared certain to finish her. Somehow, she ducked under it. Then, with the swiftness of reflex, she slashed up. The captain yelled pain and surprise; the point of her murdat slit his left sleeve and the flesh under it from elbow to shoulder.

Conway cheered wildly. Clas said, "His wound looks far worse than it is. She must be very careful."

Embarrassment and fury contorted the captain's face. Inexorably, he drove Tate toward the shoreline. Conway, Clas, and Sylah had to retreat hurriedly to avoid her. Sailors bayed for a killing.

Suddenly, Tate whirled away from a long, spearing thrust. Coming full circle, she struck down across the captain's front at the extended arm. Countering, he drove his left shoulder into her, destroying leverage and timing. Her blow, robbed of its power, hacked his right wrist. It was enough to make him drop his sword. He clubbed at her awkwardly with the bloodied left arm. Sheer strength sent her sprawling.

She scrambled to her feet as he reached for his weapon.

Exhaustion filled her lungs with fire. When she ran at him, the weight of her raised murdat threatened to topple her, and her aching, boneless knees buckled dangerously. Scalding tears tried to smear her vision; she blinked them back.

Bending, he cried, "Wait!" raising the slashed left arm in supplication. The single word sounded as if dragged from his guts.

Tate blinked, surprised. He remained in his awkward attitude.

"Kill him." Clas' voice was a whipcrack. "Strike. *Strike.*"

Tate stopped less than a body length away. Her murdat sagged.

With a motion that was little more than a twitch, the captain threw his sword.

Tate had no chance to dodge. The heavy metal handle hit her across the eyes. Automatically, she raised her hands to them.

He drove a fist into her stomach, then a knee to her face when she doubled over. The mournful clang of her fallen murdat as it slipped between timbers drowned in the water below.

He slowed, watching, seeing that all her energy was necessary to keep upright. He picked up his sword at her feet almost lazily.

Once again, Clas locked Conway's gun hand in his own.

The captain struck with the flat of the blade, the sound of it against her head an ugly thud. She groaned, staggering sideways. Repeating the blow on the backswing, he kept her from falling off the dock, hammering her back the way she'd come.

Again. Then again.

And she refused to fall.

Until he drove his right hand, still holding the sword handle, directly into her face. It spun her completely around, and she dropped facedown, her head hanging off the edge of the dock, arms extended, the submerged hands weirdly distorted by the shifting surface of the water. Small fish lanced hungrily through the swirled clouds formed by her blood. Finding nothing substantial, they nipped each other in frustration.

Waving his sword at his crew, the captain shouted over his shoulder. "Do I kill her now, or do you want her?"

Clas said, "You've beaten her. You'll spare her or kill her. Nothing else."

Flushed with victory, the captain faced him. "We'll do what we want."

Clas let go of Conway's hand, saying, "This is not allowed. Conway, I've wanted to watch the lightning weapons up close for a long time. If this shamelessness continues, please kill him."

The courtly formality brought hysterical laughter clawing up Conway's throat. He nodded, not trusting his voice, not trusting his rage to betray him by making him shout his determination to kill the captain long before any more harm came to Tate.

Consciousness passed through Tate's mind in short, bright

31

surges, exactly like the small waves sliding past her blurred gaze. Pain accompanied each moment of awareness.

She didn't want to die. Tomorrow—all the tomorrows—waited for her. It was wrong to lose them on a scabby dock.

Angrily, she tried to resume the fight. Her stomach rolled sickeningly, stole her strength.

She needed time. Just a little. A minute. That wasn't so very much, not for a life. She listened to each beat of her heart. So precious.

Why didn't he end it?

Movement. Under the water, just within the peripheral range of the eye that still functioned. Something deep, not in rhythm with the waves.

Coming toward her. At her.

Pale. Getting larger.

A face. A horror.

She tried to scream at the walling eyes, the bloated cheeks, the lank, streaming hair.

And then the boy was surfacing, directly under her, so close she could have kissed him, could see the fine black specks in his pale green irises. Shivering violently, he extended a hand to hers, under the water. It held her murdat. She had to concentrate to wrap her fingers around the grip.

He continued to stare into her eyes as he slowly sank out of sight into greenness. For the second time she felt him take hold of some buried, visceral part of her.

One of the sailors shouted, "Give her to us."

The clack of a round being jacked into a pistol chamber was unknown to the captain, but there was a terminal authority to the sound that snapped his head around to Conway.

Tate gritted her teeth and rolled over, stabbing upward.

Screaming, leaping clumsily, the captain bent to clutch at his crotch. He turned with pained, dainty steps, keening eerily, and only then could Conway see the upraised murdat in Tate's hand, and the thick, viscous stain expanding from his groin. It appeared he might straighten, but he only managed a last, agonized bellow before he collapsed.

Conway and Clas reached Tate simultaneously, each scooping a hand under an arm. They hurried away while the shocked crew milled about, leaderless. Shouts from up the hill announced the fight had been observed and a rush of help was on the way. The sailors leapt to the mooring lines and rigging. One vaulted the crawling captain, then, after coolly appraising the distance the descending crowd had to cover, grabbed a beseeching arm and dragged him to the ship.

By then the foursome was off the dock and onto the road, Sylah's gentle hands and practiced eye examining. She had Conway take Tate's feet while Clas held her at the shoulders to carry her, saying, "I think nothing's broken. She'll heal."

They moved rapidly up the hill, watching over their shoulders as the ship made sail. The crowd slowed its hurry toward them. Clas said, "It's good you didn't have to use the weapon."

Conway said, "I would have. I see no sense in anyone dying just for honor."

"No?" Clas seemed as sad as surprised. "Everyone dies, Matt Conway. To die for your honor, or that of your tribe or family or friends, is to use death; it assures that a man wins at least part of his last fight. There's a good memory in it, so it's not necessary for those left behind to hate. Any other end is just an end, unless there's dishonor. To die dishonored is tragedy. That's our view. I never knew before today that your code demands the death of whoever kills a friend, even at risk of your own life. Your customs are fiercer than I thought." His sudden laughter was harsh. "We're all prisoners, aren't we?"

Briskly, Sylah interrupted. "Enough. Tate may wake, and I want her hearing no foolishness of war or fighting. Especially not this mad thing of yours, this honor, with its hundred faces, that lives only for dying."

Like chastened boys, they hung their heads and marched on in silence. Sylah bent over Tate, fussing with her injuries, the better to hide un-Healerlike tears.

The crowd greeted them as heroes. So preoccupied, no one saw a sodden figure slip out of the water where the dock joined the shore. Doubled over, all joints and angles, the ship's boy was across the sand in a whirling flurry, diving into the protective brush at the high water mark. Never visible for longer than the blink of an eye, he darted from cover to cover in their wake up the hill. He shook uncontrollably. His lips were drawn back from bone-white, chattering teeth.

The expression was certainly a function of the cold. Yet he could have been smiling. Either way, it was a visage as malevolent as the snarl of a cat.

CHAPTER 5

Shadows and spears of light played across the neatly tended ground beneath the trees. The tiny woman walking there was oblivious to the beauty of the constantly changing patterns.

Her Church robe featured an embroidered purple and white violet at her left shoulder. It gleamed with the luster of new acquisition. Shyly, almost disbelievingly, she raised a hand to trace its stitched edges.

A pair of squabbling robins swooped wildly across her path, so close she felt their passage. Startled, she stopped abruptly, trying to follow the headlong flight. The thick trunks of the trees defeated her. They were very old, planted in strict lines, gnarled by time and weather. Each was sawn off at the general height of a tall man's head, leaving only a few heavy branches spanning horizontally toward the other trees in the grove. A thicket of green shoots rose from each branch, creating a thick, swaying canopy. Some of the withes bore long white stripes where bark had been carefully peeled.

The willows were a sacred grove. Rigorously pruned, the ancient trunks faithfully produced new growth every year, and it was from that that Church manufactured one of its most efficacious medicines. Extract of willow bark had wondrous pain-relieving qualities, either taken orally or mixed with soothing oil and applied directly to burns or wounds.

Like all sacred herb gardens and groves, this one was far removed from human habitation. Sometimes Healers needed great distance from those they served. Whenever War Healers discussed their Healer sisters, anyone acknowledged the superhuman courage the latter exhibited in the face of disease. That was an outgrowth of the virulent plagues that swept all populations from time to time. Any sickness, no matter how mild, was treated as deadly. Only Healers stood firm to face it, conducting their healing houses with a serenity that dumbfounded anyone who watched. Nevertheless, in confidence, War Healers questioned their sisters' almost sacrilegious willingness to experiment with such unproven nostrums as willowbark extract to prevent failure of the heart. No one confronted them, however. After all, one might fall ill, and goodwill should not be needlessly tested.

34

Looking about her, Lanta was reminded that her visit to the grove had its own secretive need. She smiled wryly at the thought. Newly declared Violet Priestess Lanta—proud, humble, joyous, frightened—had sought the grove for its nonmedical healing properties: its soft silence, its rich smells of earth and growth and renewal. She felt the ponderous tree trunks excluding the world. She touched the new violet again, setting off delicious memories of the moment Gan Moondark told the violet Abbess that Priestess Lanta had earned the gratitude of the Murdat, Ruler of the Three Territories. He requested her promotion.

She unconsciously dropped her head as she peered around, afraid someone might be watching, and no observer would fail to see her shameless pleasure.

She sought one of the wooden chairs provided for just the sort of contemplative solitude she needed. The seat was large for a normal person. For Lanta, it was a retreat. Snuggled against the high back, she pulled her feet up under her and seemed to blend into the thick cedar slabs.

Not even the delight in her new rank could wholly dispel the purposelessness that had seized her in recent weeks. The onset of spring had filled her with a dissatisfaction that refused to be identified. Alternately listless or driven to frenetic activity, she irritated those around her and embarrassed herself.

Until now, she had resisted the urge to use the trance of concentration. All Priestesses were taught the technique of chant, of inward withdrawal. The resulting calm peacefulness was so pleasant that Church warned against the technique. There were sinister rumors that many Priestesses had become enslaved by their ability to lose themselves in self-induced bliss.

She had particular reason to dread the trance as a treacherous friend.

She was a Seer, and sometimes when she willed herself to complete relaxation, the wondrous, terrible thing that enabled her to see beyond the veil of time penetrated her ease. Then came messages, sometimes bright joy, sometimes counterbalancing tragedy.

Some called her blessed. Her Abbess called her "our gift," and battled fiercely to keep her in the local abbey, rejecting all offers by Church Home to call her to them. Sometimes Lanta wondered if the Land Under held any curse worse than being secretly feared by all.

Now she had to make a choice. To use the trance was to risk violation. Yet she could think of no other way to probe for an answer to her persistent restlessness.

It took several adjustments for her to find a proper position on the chair. Finally, hands decorously clasped in her lap, tiny feet dangling, she sealed her senses against the outside world and drifted on the tides of her body. Her features softened by imperceptible degrees until they were utterly slack. Oddly, the expression wasn't neutral. A watcher would have said she hadn't withdrawn from the world, but disdained it. Pulses trembled softly at her temples and throat. There was an aura of hidden alertness in her repose, as a small bird drowses, ever poised for flight.

A hand fell away to her side. It lay palm up, fingers curled inward like the petals of a thirsting flower.

Her mind refused her. It bolted from image to image, settling on nothing, giving her no chance at isolation.

Someone else was in the grove.

Troubled, like herself. The air vibrated with their mingled tensions.

She opened her eyes. For a heartbeat, they were out of focus, so that her first impression was of an out-of-place green that had nothing to do with the verdant grove. As her vision cleared, she recognized the cloak lining of the approaching Violet Abbess. With a man, a stranger.

Measured steps precise, bony back stiff as any hop pole, the older woman advanced with her mouth bent in the smile that always made Lanta think of a painted shield. Behind her, rain clouds streamed across the sky framed by a natural break in the willows. The scene reminded Lanta of the tapestry in the abbey. The Abbess liked to stand in front of it when she had a disciplinary matter to discuss. The pictures were drawn from the Apocalypse Testament, the passage that declared, "Life is the flame that consumes us all, and by flame we are cleansed and released to renewal. Whatsoever may be most foul, so fire shall cleanse and free its spirit."

The tapestry was dark, fat with rolling boils of smoke and the angular char of burned trees and buildings. Here and there, sharp red and yellow teeth of flames scavenged what was left.

Lanta disliked the tapestry. She disliked the quotation, although she never confessed it; a beating was the least she could expect for such impertinence.

Lanta rose to greet them.

Without any return greeting, the Abbess said, "This is a Messenger. From Sister Mother to me. You must hear."

Lanta cringed inwardly. What could she have done to warrant the attention of Sister Mother?

36

And a Messenger? The very name made people nervous. A tight, self-contained band, Messengers were most people's sole method of long-distance communication in a world where writing was regarded as a profane art. They were expensive. And inviolate. If a Messenger was interfered with in any way, even offered a bribe, the offending tribe was refused all service until the guilty party was punished and the Messengers were compensated. Normally forbidden to reveal anything that might harm their clients, they willingly told all they knew of those under such a sentence. It was a dire penalty. Unable to communicate with neighbors, such a tribe was blind, deaf, mute. Unable to negotiate alliances, they stood alone. And fell quickly.

Messengers were treated with regard, but little liking. The wicked smile this one sent Lanta, while keeping it carefully hidden from the Abbess, did nothing to improve her opinion of them.

Sweeping off her cloak, the Abbess assumed Lanta's chair. She fanned her face with a corner of the material, the violet lining and the green outerwork alternating like a butterfly wing. At her command, "Speak," the Messenger began. As was required, he imitated his client. Lanta marveled at the aged, cracked voice, the feminine cast to the words. She was afraid to look away, afraid that when she looked back, it would be Sister Mother herself.

"My words will reach you a year after the death of the One, the Seer of Seers. As our treasured sister, Abbess of the Violet Abbey of Ola, you have the honor of sending the Priestess Lanta to Church Home. She will be examined and tested as a replacement for our departed One. Please express our joy in anticipating Lanta's arrival, as we know you experience your own joy in seeing her selected."

The Abbess' words came as if she had sand on her teeth. "We're proud of you, my child. One of us, a Chosen. Our gift, and now recognized by Sister Mother herself. You bring honor to the abbey."

Lanta murmured modest thanks. The Abbess continued, "You're relieved of all your duties. Prepare to go. I suggest you isolate yourself and pray. You have a problem with pride."

"Yes, Abbess." Covering her unease, Lanta fell back on the safety of catechism. " 'We are all Chosen of Mother Church. She is past and future.' "

Rising to leave, the Abbess patted her on the head. Her thick, two-fingered ring of gold and amethyst hit with enough force to hurt. Lanta almost giggled; the symbol of the Abbess' office had its hidden dangers.

The Abbess said, "The Messenger has more information for us, intended for all Church in Ola. There will be a meeting after the evening meal."

Lanta barely got through the good-byes. Church Home. Sister Mother. The answer to her restlessness.

There was no future for her in the Three Territories. There never had been. During King Altanar's time there was repression, intrigue, and the struggle to protect Church. That gave motion and excitement to life, but not fulfillment. Now that the Three Territories were united in Gan's hands, peace would give Church the opportunity to grow and provide ever-better service to her people. The Violet Abbess would always seek more power. She was probably capable of conniving with the unwashed barons who secretly longed for Altanar's return.

Lanta made a hurried three-sign to protect herself from the wrath of the One in All for impiety. Or impoliteness.

There would be great challenge in maintaining Gan's peace. But Violet Priestess Lanta would toil in a very small, very insignificant corner. The Abbess would continue to use her. If Lanta was successful in all her efforts, she could hope to replace the Violet Abbess in the distant future. If the old schemer didn't outwit death itself.

Lanta considered another three-sign and ruefully decided she'd need stronger medicine; a special prayer after dinner might help.

She hopped back in the chair, pressed against the back, hugged herself with delight.

The other mind, full of troubles and fears. Still present.

The first words of the voice came so softly Lanta was afraid it was the Seeing. The touch of ice tingled on her flesh. When the words came again, she realized the voice was human. "Don't turn around, Priestess Lanta. I have no wish to be seen by you, or anyone else. Our meeting must remain unobserved."

A woman. Eyes straight ahead, Lanta said, "Who are you, to be so certain we're not watched?"

Laughter rustled like a small creature breasting dead grass, then, "It is my business . . . no, my life, to be unseen. The violet flourishes best where unobserved. The Tender of your order has words for you."

"From the Tender? Herself? You have permission from my Abess? You're another Messenger?" Lanta bit down on the questions an instant ahead of harsh interruption.

"That swaggering fool? You insult. I raced him. The snows trapped us, but I left first. I speak to you alone. *Listen.* Church is

38

in the greatest danger since the purge of the Teachers. A force has risen in the east. It grows stronger with each conquest. It advances, bringing Moondance. To survive, Church must lose no opportunity, deny no weapon. You understand?"

"Yes." She hardly heard herself.

The unseen speaker continued. "Our Tender, guardian of our souls, is concerned about the Rose Priestess called Sylah. Her search for the legendary Door suggests sacrilege. The Door is only rumor, a tale for children. Nothing more. That being true, why does not the Iris Tender forbid this waste? The Violet Tender suspects a plot. The Violet Tender fears that Sister Mother will refuse to pursue accommodation with the one named Katallon, the leader of this new force. Church must ensnare this evil before she can destroy it."

Lanta's throat worked convulsively, fighting against welling nausea.

Church was splitting.

The speaker waited, knowing questions must come.

Reluctantly, Lanta forced herself to address the central issue. "What does the Tender wish?"

"Ahhh." The unexpected relief in the deep sigh surprised Lanta, but before she could ponder it, the voice went on, "They said you were as obedient as you are . . . gifted." There was a pause both before and after the last word, a silence that raised the hair on Lanta's neck. Then, "You have helped this Sylah before, Priestess. She trusts you. You will go to Church Home as Sister Mother orders. Accompany Sylah. Assure that whatever she learns of the Door is known to you. The Violet Tender *must* have that information as soon as the devious, aggressive Iris sisters."

Desperately, knowing it was a useless ploy, Lanta pretended suspicion. "I don't even know you're who you say you are."

A fist from behind appeared above Lanta's head. The robe sleeve pulled back from the wrist, exposing a bracelet of woven gold wire, its mesh enfolding several small, spherical amethysts. It was a decoration afforded the highest priestesses of the Violet order, and Lanta was certain its exposure was no accident. The fist, at the upper limits of her vision, opened. Something large on a golden chain fell free to gyrate just inches from her nose. Lanta gasped recognition as the movement slowed, and the speaker chuckled softly. "You have heard of the True Stone? Then see it, and believe. Look deep, child, and see what you serve. See our heart."

It was a large, irregular amethyst, unworked, save for one polished surface. The prime talisman of the order; Lanta had never heard of it leaving Church Home. As it stopped moving, Lanta felt her whole being focus on that flawless, beckoning smoothness. Her gaze went into it, ever deeper, until it seemed she must flow, like water, to its scintillating mystic center. There was the marvel, just as legend told. A resistant corner of her mind knew the phenomenon was no more than a juxtaposition of crystals and light. What her heart and spirit saw was the cross, the holiest and most forbidden symbol in all Church. Men had used it to kill the One Who Is Two, and were eternally shamed. No woman was allowed to even mention His name or the cross. The very existence of the True Stone was a peril to the entire Violet Abbey.

She blinked.

Stone, chain, and fist were gone. Before she could turn, the voice behind her hissed warning. Lanta slumped in the chair. She said, "What you ask is impossible. How can I persuade Sylah to let me accompany her? How would I even get a message to the Tender? Does she require me to See? I am not allowed—"

"Obey your instructions. All else will be attended to. Never tell anyone of our meeting. Now, from the lips of the Tender herself: Fail, and Violet will find cause to cast you out. You will live, but only as an object lesson to others who would reject Church's needs. Your life will be an unending prayer for release. Am I understood?"

"Yes." Lanta barely heard herself. The sun moved quite far before she assumed she was alone.

A moment later, however, she rose quickly, the motion firm and controlled. After all, before all this happened, wasn't she complaining to herself that she had no future in the Three Territories? And the speaker wasn't as clever as she thought; twice she called her Priestess, when her proper rank was Violet Priestess. A small gap in the armor of all-knowingness, but welcome.

She had taken no more than three steps when the false self-confidence collapsed. She leaned heavily against one of the old, comforting trees.

Everything she'd been taught about the sanctity and unity of Church—her Mother, her only family—had been thrown into doubt.

A single word stole through the pathways of her mind, fouling all it touched.

Betrayal.

CHAPTER 6

Sylah stood beside her horse and watched with amusement as her tiny companion lowered herself cautiously from stirrup to ground. The last part of the maneuver was practically a jump. When the elfin face turned up to hers, Sylah tried to hide a grin, but Lanta spied her difficulty and responded with her own laughter.

Sylah apologized as best she could. "It's not right to laugh, Lanta, but you make it impossible. I'm not used to watching someone climb down off a horse."

Lanta feigned indignation, drew herself to her full height. The pose brought her head to a point inches below Sylah's chin. She said, "A small arrow will fell the largest tiger."

Sylah's edgy look around was sincere. "Don't make jokes about tigers. We're too far from any help for that sort of humor."

Lanta was unconcerned. "They prefer brushier country, not old forest." Her gesture dismissed endless ranks of massive trees. They'd dismounted on a long straight stretch of the main southbound road. Fir branches intermingled in a vaulted green ceiling that filtered sunlight to a pale luminescence. The air was a near-liquid richness of sharp resin and damp loam. When the horses whickered, the sound seemed to hover, caged in stillness.

In fact, until the matter of Lanta's dismount, the pressure of the brooding woods had contributed mightily to Sylah's general discomfort. Lanta had not been a pleasant companion. For that matter, it was unlikely anyone in Church was on this day. The Messenger had shocked them all. Still, Church trained her sisters to observe the unconscious movements and mannerisms by which all people signaled their deeper thoughts. They were equally well-schooled in containing much of their own reaction. Much of Sylah's unease came from the way Lanta's troubled state broke past the barriers.

Unless—most troublesome thought of all—Lanta was pretending distress.

The feeling of some sort of game in progress had cloaked their meeting from the beginning. Sylah decided to confront the problem. "You puzzle me. I speak of tigers and you wave them off, yet you were far from calm when you insisted on this meeting."

41

It was Lanta's turn to be concerned. "Did I seem nervous? Could anyone else notice?"

"Who could notice? We were alone." Once again, Sylah glanced around. "Not as alone as we are out here, I grant you. Why this secrecy? Is it about your call to Church Home?"

"Guesses that accurate will have people saying it's you who Sees, instead of me." A twitchy smile moved her features.

The pace of the game had quickened. Sylah said, "If you can be ready soon enough, you could travel with us. It might be safer."

Lanta's nod was bird-quick. Her eyes, so dark a green they made Sylah think of the surrounding forest, never wavered. "The Messenger talked to the Violet Abbess about the nomads and their leader, Katallon." Lanta took a deep breath. When she spoke, her gaze slid away from Sylah, set their focus on the distance. "The Messenger said none of his craft will go near the nomads, so he was willing to talk about them. He says that a few years ago, a Peddler came to Church Home with tales of a new nation of nomads to the east and south. Sister Mother honored my Violet Order with the opportunity to bring them truth and healing. Five Priestesses were sent, three Healers and two War Healers. Our sisters were accepted and sent a Messenger to say they were being treated well. In time, Sister Mother sent the customary replacements. They rode into open hostility. For several moons they continued east, always watched, never contacted. Finally, they were met by the original five Priestesses, who refused to return to Church Home. They gave no reason, but told the others to leave and never come back. Sister Mother sent a second group. Several moons passed before a Peddler brought news of them."

Lanta's hand drifted upward awkwardly, blindly seeking her horse's reins. She squeezed them until her knuckles were bone white. "The nomad leader, the Katallon one, gave the Peddler a box to deliver to Sister Mother. A gift, he said. Sister Mother opened it in front of the Councillors and all the Tenders of the Orders—Violet, Iris, Lily, Daisy—and all the rest. It was salt. They thought it was symbolic, like our spring offering to the Seer of Seers. Then Sister Mother tipped it onto the table. There was a head. Preserved. One of *us*."

For a moment Sylah was too stunned to react. She said, "No," disbelieving. Retribution was certain. Everyone knew that.

Lanta said, "There was a note. Between her teeth. It said two of the first sisters still lived, and that Church was doomed. Katallon will destroy her."

She stopped. The shining pink tip of her tongue was a startling, darting contrast to her dry, bloodless lips. "Moondance, Sylah. Katallon crushes all who resist, absorbs all who surrender and accept Moondance. The note bragged: 'Where Katallon steps, only my followers live.' "

"What's been done? Why is this a secret?"

"Fear. Church Home is paralyzed. Some advise Sister Mother to make whatever peace she can with Katallon, saying that our skills will make us indispensable. Others demand resistance, whatever the cost. Church is split."

"Split? *Split?* Church is whole, now and always! We fight among ourselves, but we are *one*."

"No. The threat is too great. If Church chooses the wrong path, she dies."

"Why have I heard nothing of this?"

"Moondance knows of the division within Church. Sister Mother has placed a ban on any talk outside Church Home. Even now, priestesses from both factions travel everywhere, demanding that leaders take one side or the other. Moondancers search for them, plot against them."

Sylah sagged. Was this the game? To frighten her away from her quest? To force her to choose sides? Lanta was Violet, just as the priestesses who went to Katallon's nomads. Surely Violet would want the power of the Door to come to them.

For the briefest instant, she feared the small woman and her unknowable power. The thought passed immediately. Lanta was a friend. A sister. She looked deep into the small face, wishing she could soothe away the confusion there.

Lanta said, "I don't know anyone else who'd do what you just did."

"Did? What did I do?"

"Met my eyes. You always have. You trust me."

"Don't praise me too highly." Sylah found a smile. "You have to use the trance to generate Seeing. I know that."

"Everyone knows it. But they won't look me in the eye. Or touch me. Can you imagine what it's like when I reach for someone?" Suddenly belligerent, she extended a hand. She dared.

Sylah hesitated, not out of concern, but in amazement at the rush of contradictory emotions tearing at her friend.

She took Lanta's hand. The small woman withdrew it. For several heartbeats, she stared up at the taller Sylah. Her voice trembled. "Long ago, I lied to Altanar about what I saw in your future.

43

I gave you your life. I claim fair return now. I'm trusting you with my soul."

Sylah nodded. Her heart was racing. The game had changed again, and she was lost. Too many directions, too many uncertainties.

Lanta said, "The Tender of the Violet Order instructs me to accompany you on your quest. I am to offer my services to you, do anything I can to help you find the Door."

Relieved, Sylah smiled. "That's all? To repay what you did for me? Your Tender's no bargainer, my friend. I'd agree to that just for the pleasure of your company."

Lanta's shrill laughter abused the purity of the forest. "My Abbess is breaking her knees in constant prayer, hoping I will be chosen the One, and influence decisions as the new Seer of Seers. In the meantime, if you discover the Door, whatever you find must be shared with the Violet Order. First."

Sylah flared. "I seek the Door for Church, for all women. My findings will be my secret. No one will decide how to use what I discover. I can eliminate your problem: don't come with me."

She spread her hands in sudden entreaty. The bitter, twisted arrogance shattered, to be revealed as empty despair. "I must. I must inform on you. Or be cast out. You're the only person who never treated me as a witch. Please, please don't tell them. If you do, or refuse to let me come with you, I'll understand. I hope I can be strong about it. I know I did the right thing by warning you. I only wish . . ."

Embracing her, Sylah held her tight. Her skin tightened at the contact, and she racked her brain for words to describe the feeling. Not exactly fear or apprehension. More a sense of something that *could* endanger. It was the incomprehension in an animal's eyes when it sees fire.

Lanta was not fire. She was a person, a friend who had, as she said, given Sylah her life.

She continued to hold her arm around Lanta until the smaller woman had a foot in the stirrup and was mounted. Sylah got on her own horse, leading the way back toward the city of Ola.

She was glad Lanta was so subdued. She needed to think.

Church at war with itself. Inconceivable.

Her quest—compromised, watched. The Violet Order. Greedy, plotting minds, waiting. All of them? Could there be unknown allies in that group? Who?

Lanta.

A small doubt surfaced in her mind. She imagined it, squirming, feeding, like the grubs that live in the hollow stems of the squash. They ate far from the flower, yet eventually they destroyed the vine's ability to nourish. The lovely, forming fruit languished, turned to a slimy, rotten mass before one even knew there was a problem.

Sylah tasted bile.

If a note accompanied Katallon's obscene "gift," wasn't it probable that another priestess wrote it? A Violet. Why hadn't Lanta mentioned that? Was the schism in Church already so desperate that murder was merely another weapon? Could the Violet Order speak of accommodation while seeking alliance?

Lanta. What better way to assure her acceptance than to "confess" her weakness, then appeal for understanding and mercy from the one she meant to victimize?

All those emotional signals—were they fake?

Where was the truth? Had Lanta spoken any?

What of Tate and Conway? What made them always so evasive?

During the quest, who would be her confidant when the inevitable doubts came, when her resources waned? Who should she trust the most?

Who should she trust at all?

CHAPTER 7

"We should have stayed on the west side of the mountains."

Altanar sawed on the reins of his mount to force it off the trail, then jerked it to an abrupt halt. Jones stopped beside him, casually easing his horse into Altanar's, pressuring him into cover on the uphill side of a screening juniper. They'd seen no one on the gentle land stretching off to the east, which seemed the most likely direction from which to expect danger. To the west, the ground rose steeply to become the Enemy Mountains. As Jones scanned the lower reaches, a sleek magpie, its white wing patches startling against each black stroke, flew away. In seeming agreement with Jones' caution, it dodged erratically through the shrubby trees.

Jones wished he could properly relax. He liked this country. The scented air stimulated him with its redolence of junipers and the flinty tang of rock-strewn earth. And the clarity! Vision reached forever, aware of vastness, of white-fanged mountaintops declining to rolling, arid hills that etched the far horizon. Jones felt good with the mountains at his back, with the whole continent before him. The land that touched what the savages called the Great Sea was pinned between it and the same mountains. Too narrow. Here was where he belonged, confronting the greater mass of those who needed the salvation he could offer.

Only he understood. It was a lonely thought.

Gratingly, Altanar continued his complaint. "The wind's a knife here. I taste snow in it. We shouldn't have followed the Mother River upstream so far before starting south. We should turn now, find a pass back to the west." He huddled inside a sealskin parka, peering from the depths of the hood like a cornered badger. The formerly luxurious fur of the garment was travel-worn. There were near-bare patches where his elbows rubbed his sides. It was grimy, and a seam at one shoulder gaped. Similarly, the ornately stitched boots extending from under the coat were stirrup-scarred, unkempt.

Jones took a long drink from his canteen, the smoothness of its nylon camouflage cover in contrast to his prickly tan-and-white cowhide jacket and gray homespun trousers. When he opened the jacket to pull out a handkerchief, a shining silver pendant on a silver chain came with it. The rear guard of the party—seven of the total of fourteen heavily armed men—were coming abreast by then. Their garb was equally rough, giving them all a lumpy, brutish appearance. Most of their coats were ill-fitting, and sported clumsily stitched rips and suspicious stains. They all still wore scraps of the all-white uniform that marked them as protectors, Altanar's elite personal guard. Now the material was tattered and so soiled it seemed to be trying to deny that shameful past.

One man caught the sudden appearance of Jones' disk and started. His hand flew to touch his forehead with a bent forefinger. It was the first gesture of his tribe's three-sign, and when he saw Jones' bird-bright eyes watching, he blanched. Instantly, he lowered his hand to his brow as if scratching an itch.

Jones winked and looked benign. Once the man was past, Jones glanced at Altanar. The fool saw nothing. Of course. Ever since they'd left Ola a mere day ahead of one of Gan Moondark's patrols, he'd been deteriorating. Yet he continued to bark his asinine orders at these straggling survivors. A fool. The men understood who was their true leader.

Still, it was Altanar's name that originally drew these scum. There was a lesson there, Jones told himself: If you were going to depend on men to risk their lives for you, they had to be totally loyal or totally corrupt.

Loyalty was for fools.

Self-interest was man's primal thought, and its natural expression was treachery. A natural man understood that all were like himself; anxious to be bribed, willing to betray, constantly seeking advantage. Such a man protected his leader because he knew the hand of every other man was against him. Such a man never knew who was watching, waiting to inform on him if his dedication ever faltered.

It was a perfect, self-perpetuating relationship.

Altanar's protectors had nowhere better to go. Until now.

One day there would be a hundred—yes, a thousand—for each of these. They would wear armor with gold trim, and . . .

Jerking upright, Jones scolded himself for daydreaming.

Altanar was saying, "Are you listening? I said the weather's warmer near the sea."

"And every narrow forest track will have its watchers, looking for us."

"That can't happen here?"

Jones sighed. Only months ago, Altanar's sarcasm had sharpness. Venom. Now it was merely the sour whine of an old woman complaining about cool tea. Jones took care to sound reasonable. "There may be watchers here. Not so many, though, and we're not so tightly confined to trails. From a distance, we're just another hunting party."

Altanar gave up the argument. He spurred his horse viciously, startling it into a leap that nearly unseated him. In response, he battered its head with his riding crop. The horse was one of the barely broken animals they'd stolen from the River People, and Altanar's combination of indignities tore away its veneer of training. Leaping vertically, it came down with its back arched. Legs stiff as posts rammed the earth in a spine-jarring, head-snapping series of hops that had Altanar grabbing with everything but his teeth. Frightened cries exploded from him at each landing.

It never occurred to Jones to try to rescue him. He lacked the horsemanship, for one thing, and any hint of violent activity was his cue to move away. Unconsciously, his hand went to his head. Creeping fingers stole under his fur cap, their touch icy against the hot, pulsating pink circle of scar tissue.

Sylah's mark. Where she'd sliced open his flesh, cut out pieces of the skull shattered by a Mountain warrior's slingstone. Exposed his brain.

47

Her. Inside his head. Smirking, prying eyes, watching him think, seeing terror and agony play across the vulnerable soft gray folds and wrinkles. Soft, knowing hands; probing, touching his thoughts, playing with his dreams. His secrets.

He imagined her under the pounding, tearing hooves of Altanar's mount.

A protector rode to help. Altanar welcomed him by throwing himself bodily at him, bowling the man backward out of his saddle. Both landed with a bone-rattling thud, Altanar on top. He rolled off in a stumbling panic, gesticulating wildly. "Kill it! It tried to kill me."

Several of the approaching riders nervously fingered the bows slung across their backs, but none moved to carry out the order. Meanwhile, the horse, either belatedly aware of its freedom or sensing Altanar's hatred, bolted.

For a moment, Jones wondered why the men hesitated to obey. The reason occurred to him when he saw the fallen rescuer rise and indicate silently for two men to pursue the runaway. Counting himself and Altanar, they were sixteen men with twenty horses. Four horses were needed to pack gear. A lost animal meant one man afoot until a replacement was found.

The little drama, and his analysis, pleased Jones. It proved Altanar's men were already weighing his authority against their own interests.

A shout from one of the pair chasing the escaped horse interrupted his thoughts. He was thinking that it was good they'd caught it so quickly when a finger of doubt touched his spine. It was an uncertain pressure, gone so quickly it created more confusion than concern. A quick look around showed no one else disturbed, so he said nothing.

He listened, however, and as Altanar mounted a commandeered horse, he scanned the area around them intently. There was no movement. Nor any sound.

Not even from the men who'd ridden out.

After they'd been under way a while, he asked a protector what was keeping them.

The man shrugged. "A horse can hide pretty good in this mess. It may be a while before they rejoin us."

"I want scouts out ahead," Altanar said, riding up to join them.

"And the flanks?" the man asked.

"No. They slow us down. Don't worry about a rear guard, either. If the River People were still after us, we'd know it. Concentrate on what's ahead."

Jones and Altanar continued together silently in the middle of the loose column.

Jones admitted to himself that they were simply adrift. He had no hope of improving his position without more manpower, yet once he began to gain fighting strength, Church and any local ruler would seek him out to destroy him or force him to flee. Moondance cult members would keep this small group fed. Shelter was a different proposition. Whenever they stopped with other humans, they courted capture.

It was useless to plan.

But he *must* have a stronghold, a rallying point. Then he could grow.

Where? *How?*

Suddenly, chillingly, that same dank finger of unidentifiable concern touched him again. It was so startling he gave a muffled exclamation. Altanar looked at him curiously, and Jones managed a faint noncommittal smile. Altanar dismissed him. Jones strained to see or hear something. Anything.

And then the brush came alive.

Whole bushes raced toward him, shrieking. An arrow flew from some of the charging greenery, its sibilance growing louder, louder, until he actually felt the hum of the vibrating shaft touch his ear. Behind him, a man screamed. The sound jolted Jones out of his immobility. He whirled to see the arrow sticking out of the victim's eye socket. The other eye stared terror at the gray feathers even as death's glaze swept it.

It was over in seconds. Men with faces painted to resemble skull-white, black-eyed, bloody-mouthed fiends were among them, on them, pulling the stupefied protectors from their mounts. Those still alive dropped their weapons and raised their hands. One writhed and screamed on the ground, pinned there by a thick-shafted spear. Jones was thinking how he resembled nothing so much as a fly skewered by a nasty child when a branch-covered warrior raised a massive club over the man. When it fell, it crushed the screaming with a finality that made Jones clammy and faint.

A voice shouted over the rest. "Kill no more! I want them alive!"

Jones looked to Altanar. His companion was grinning foolishly, as if the attack were a minor accident, the dead men a regrettable, but easily overlooked, inconvenience. He was nodding by the time the approaching warrior who gave the order was within ten yards, already agreeing to anything the other man said.

The warrior inspected them without speaking the whole time he stripped off his remaining camouflage. Mountain People, the blood enemies of Gan Moondark's Dog People. Several carried sodals, the lancelike swords they favored for mounted engagements. All were armed with the ma, the shorter, heavy blades for close combat.

Jones noticed something else about them; their unwashed bodies and filthy clothes stank riotously.

Slowly, almost lazily, the warrior in charge unbuckled the straps holding the halves of his torso armor together. The outer covering was thick hide; it covered an interior frame of woven willow wands. Under the shell, the man was lean and muscular.

The lurid painted face bent toward Altanar. Inside the wide black circles, the warrior's bloodshot eyes still danced with the fire of combat. His words trembled with barely controlled violence. "I know you, King Altanar. My name is Fox Eleven. I am a Manhunter of the Mountain People. Because we helped you in your war against the Dog People, they scattered us. We starved this winter. Have you ever seen a child die, sucking at the breast of a mother who has no milk because she starves, as well? I've dreamed of your death. It will be slow. My dead will hear you coming."

Altanar looked around, eyes walling. The survivors of his force were herded into a mass. All avoided looking at their captors. Altanar fumbled at his neck, produced the massive diamond called the King's Badge. He dangled it before him. His shaking hand increased the dash of light from its facets. Around them, Jones heard a collective sigh like the passing of a soft wind. For the first time, he saw the full numbers of Fox's ambush party, now surrounding them.

Beseeching, Altanar displayed the jewel. "This will buy you food, clothing, horses—even a safe place to live. You can grow strong again, protect yourselves against all your enemies. Soon you can even strike back at Moondark. Just let me go."

Fox made a show of looking at the other captives. "And these?"

"They serve me. If they must be sacrificed for me, that is the way."

"Your pretty stone already belongs to me," Fox said. "The only thing you have that I want is your pain. These creatures did your torturing for you. Now I want them to practice on this Moondancer, the Jones one. You'll watch. Anticipate. Then comes your turn." He turned to the cowed protectors. "As long as these

50

two live, you live. Keep Jones, then Altanar alive long enough . . ." he shrugged, "maybe I kill you quickly. Entertain me well, and you may even go free."

Jones heard something. He turned to see Altanar sliding sideways off his horse. His eyes were rolled up so that only the whites showed, and he flowed, boneless, to the ground.

Fox watched coldly. When he turned to the protectors, he said, "I don't expect either of these weaklings to stand up well to your skills. Hope I'm wrong, or you have little time left in this world."

CHAPTER 8

Jones lay flat on his back, his head propped against a tree. His features were harsh strokes across skin stretched taut and pale. Unblinking eyes stared emptily at the dawn, seemingly unaware of the world, yet—eerily—they wept. Stubbled wet whiskers caught the light in sparkling glints.

His feet burned below the leather binding securing his ankles. All feeling had left his hands, similarly lashed under him. A thin piece of sinew held his neck to the tree. The binding was tight enough to burrow into the flesh. Swollen blood vessels pulsed against the barrier.

Sunrise colors blurred through the tears, creating a shifting whirl of fragmented images that might have been memories, but which he admitted could just as easily be madness.

Fires. Bright flashes, far away, searing death-kisses against a dawn like this one. Burned, burning bodies. Rubble, stretching to the horizon, coiling smoke to the sky. *Blood.* Amputations. Yawning wounds. Sores from microbes known only to laboratories. *Prayers.* Pleas for the strength to survive and forgive, pleas for air safe to breathe, pleas to the God of Battles to deliver friend to victory and foe to vengeance.

Someone laughed. He rolled his eyes toward the sound. Three small boys and a girl in ragged, filthy skin clothing shifted uncomfortably at his look, but held their ground. Finally the largest boy said, "Are you dying?" When Jones failed to answer, he frowned, a comic effort to appear adult. He dared a kick to Jones' side. "Do you still hurt?"

The girl giggled.

Jones closed his eyes.

After three days of travel, dragging his prize prisoners along on foot behind horses, Fox finally felt his group was secure enough to enjoy an afternoon's sport. The protectors stripped Jones and hung him by the wrists from a branch. They spread his feet until his hips threatened to dislocate, holding them apart by tying them to a stout branch. Exposed, spinning idiotically, he ignored the stretching muscles and cracking joints to beg them to cover his nakedness. They laughed. And brought out the blindfolded children. One at a time, each was led under him and allowed three swings at him with a sturdy pole. Jones was surprised and dismayed to discover how much pain he could absorb before fainting.

A day passed before he became aware of his surroundings again. The Mountain People were patient; they waited once more for him to regain some strength. Today, he knew, they would be amused further. He wept because he still lived.

The bold boy kicked him harder. "My mother says you're weak. She says you're no fun."

Such disrespect for his suffering touched the remaining glow of spirit in Jones. "I hope they torture her," he said. The bold boy cocked his head, considering the merits of the idea. The smallest boy was more sentimental. He punched Jones with all his might and bent to scream in his face, "No one's going to hurt our mother!"

Jones strained to move. The girl suddenly pointed, excited. "Look! Look at the thing on his head! See how red? It's moving!"

The boys stared at the livid circular scar, fascinated. The larger one said, "You're afraid to touch it." The girl squealed and backed away. The smallest boy was unimpressed. "So are you."

Challenged, the large one swallowed hard. Jones squirmed, grinding his teeth. Froth flew from his lips. Rough, dirty fingers violated him, shaming him worse than the nudity of his torture. He screamed outrage, and was astounded to see the boy levitate across him, eyes and mouth rounded with surprise. Crashing to earth with a howl, his tormentor crabbed away on all fours before coming upright to sprint off, never looking back. Wincing at the pressure of the sinew, Jones turned the other way to see Fox methodically slapping the three children until they staggered. He said, "Everyone was told to keep away from this one. Go to your fathers. Tell them to come to my tent."

Fox turned to Jones as the children fled. He said, "If anyone bothers you, you should call for help."

Jones sneered. "To stay alive? So you can torture me longer? You think I'm as great a fool as you?"

"Be careful; you still live."

"I'll say what I want. Why fear you?"

Fox sneered. "Because you can't escape. You'll suffer as long as it pleases me to watch." At Jones' burgeoning retort, Fox waved him to silence. "Of course you don't deserve it. Your pain's nothing to me, you understand? It takes my people's minds off their troubles. And it terrifies Altanar. You help me hurt him. Until you're used up."

He walked away. Jones tried to follow him with his eyes, and that's when he saw a protector lounging against a tree in the distance. Intent on Fox, the man affected disinterest until the Mountain leader was screened by trees. Immediately, he hurried to Jones and offered him a drink from a gourd canteen crudely decorated with incised stars. Jones gulped greedily, spilling as much as he got. He objected angrily when his benefactor pulled the gourd away, but quieted at the offer of a bite of dried meat. While he chewed, he glared hatred.

The man said, "In your place, I'd feel exactly as you. You understand my position, though?"

"More meat. Water."

That provided, the protector went on. "I'm honestly sorry you got caught up in this. Altanar . . ." He grimaced. "I won't mind working on him. He deserves it."

"If you're so sorry, help me escape."

The man shook his head, and Jones barked laughter. The movement forced the sinew to bite deeper. Wiping Jones' neck with some leaves, the man continued to speak soothingly while loosening the cord. "Fox can track anything anywhere. We'd have no chance. You think I haven't thought about running? As soon as you and Altanar are finished, us protectors are next. He'll never let us go."

"How very sad."

"More for you than me." The man yanked the neck sinew tight again. Ignoring Jones' yelp, he straightened and went on, "When my time comes, I'll go quick. You think of that, later."

"I'm old. My heart . . ."

"I know what I'm doing, Moondancer. Your heart'll last for days."

"No! You can't. I never hurt you. Why?"

"Because I want to live as long as I can, that's why. While I'm alive, I can hope." .

"Then give us both hope. They won't come after us. They have Altanar. He's the one they hate." The true wisdom of this logic didn't strike Jones until the words were out of his mouth, and in his enthusiasm, he strained against his neck binding until he choked. He continued, regardless. "You can steal horses. Food. Sneak out to me in the dark—"

Interrupting harshly, the man said, "They tie us up at night. Anyhow, after tomorrow you won't be able to sit a horse. Or walk."

Sometimes, in the high forest, when the air is unmoving on an overcast day, the clouds will split and sunlight will lance through to the earth. That swift touch of heat can be enough to make the earth sigh. It's such a delicate breath that only the aspen leaves react. A sound as soft as that slipped past Jones' lips, yet the terror in it was thunder-strong. When he forced words out, they rattled against each other. "What are you saying?"

"It's Fox. He says we have to frighten Altanar more." He turned to go. "I'm sorry. I truly am."

"Wait. Wait!" Jones squirmed. "It's Altanar! Not me! No more. Please, *please*."

The man paused. "If it'll help you stand what's coming, remember: they'll do the same to us as we're doing to you."

"You lie. You said you'd go quickly. You won't suffer. Only me. Just me. Why is it me?"

"I've got to go."

"Come back," Jones begged, straining to keep him in sight, continuing to call piteously after he disappeared. When the man returned, he sobbed relief. Beseeching, he said, "Do it for me. Do what you'll do for yourself."

"Impossible. They'd know."

"They won't. We both know it's only a question of time before . . . before I . . ." The word wouldn't come. He swallowed. "You know. What I mean is, you could . . . slip. Something. Don't hurt me any more."

"It has to look right." The man squatted beside him again and jabbed stiff fingers into his shoulders. "You've got to help me fight to live. If they learn I mean to help you, they'll kill me, and they'll keep you alive for weeks. Every day worse than the last. Don't betray me. I'll end your pain as soon as I can."

Jones was too overcome to answer. He continued to mumble gratitude long after his new friend was gone. Pleasure even seeped into his feelings; he'd deny Fox most of the entertainment he expected.

They came for him soon after nightfall and within minutes he was drowned in a maelstrom of torment. He lost track of time. Whenever he opened his eyes it was a surprise to discover daylight or darkness. Sometimes his mind rejected the enormity of his suffering, and he laughed along with the crowd. Sometimes he outsmarted them and hid inside the agony, letting it saturate him until nothing they did affected him.

There were two constants in his life; pain and the protector, bathing the wounds he'd just created, repairing damage, whispering, "As soon as I can. Next time. We'll fool them."

And then Jones woke in a still peacefulness that shimmered with silvering moonlight. For a moment, he was terrified that this was death. Then, he sensed he was conscious for the first time in a long while. That was even more terrifying; had the Mountains nursed him back to reasonable health in order to start on him again?

Mistily, shards of a remembered dream came to him. He saw himself climbing a sheer rock face, running sweat. Sharp rock tore flesh from clutching fingers. Below, a monster shrieked rage, hunger, frustration. Above, the rock disappeared into the sky. Its surface rippled with heat waves from a burning sun. When a shadow passed over him, he feared, and looked up. Two sinuous, scaly creatures descended toward him. Eyeless, they sought him with red, dripping tongues that stuttered past daggerlike fangs.

He knew he must attack. Hanging by the fingertips of one hand, he grappled with the closest horror, drew it to him and sank his teeth in its throat. It screamed and thrashed wildly. He was ready to leap into space, taking it with him to a mutual death, when he realized it was shrinking. Again, something deep inside him, something more basic than instinct, told him exactly what to do. He forced the loathsome dream-thing into his mouth, gagging, choking on its rough skin. He swallowed until it was gone. Strength filled him like breath expanding a drowning man's lungs. He scrambled after the other creature, dealt with it the same way.

Then, without warning, he was atop the cliff, facedown on a plateau barely large enough to hold him. Rising, he looked about. There was nothing. A hollow, blue void surrounded him.

There had been words then; he remembered. Now they refused to come back. But they had been prophecy. He didn't understand how he knew that, but he didn't question.

Back in the dream, he was alone on the pinnacle. Unchallenged. Undefeatable.

Godlike.

In the dream, he stepped into the air to drift back to the body in the camp of the Mountain People. The body that housed his new, mature spirit.

Now, fully conscious, fully in the present, he luxuriated in mysterious comfort. He was released. Purified. Pain of all descriptions clawed his body; his mind scorned it.

He looked directly up into the orb of a full moon, felt its sterile chill touch his flesh like a seeking benefice. Turning his gaze on himself, he saw he was unbound, naked to the open sky. Stiffly, he forced his head to the side. Among the trees, he made out a vague shape. He drew a rib-cracking breath. He said, "Fox. Come here."

There was the sharp hiss of intaken breath. The shadowy figure jerked. Jones repeated his order. Fox came. His eyes were huge.

Jones said, "How long have I lain here?"

"You still live?"

"How long?"

"Two full days. We threw you here to die."

"Why?"

"Your spirit left you. No matter what the protectors did, you only stared. Then you spoke in a language no one could understand. I knew you were talking to other spirits in the Land Beyond. I told them we must let your spirit come back, that if you died without it, it would haunt us."

Jones *smelled* the fear on Fox. He felt stronger for it. He told Fox to help him to his feet. Fox said, "You'll never stand. Your spirit only came back so you could die properly."

"Then why are you here while everyone else sleeps? What brought you to me?"

Fox shivered. "I don't know. I had to be here. Watch."

"You came to me. You're the first to see how faith heals. *My* faith. Now, help me up."

It was slow work, with pauses while burned skin stretched or abused joints and muscles adjusted to movement and weight. Through it all, Fox's breath whistled as if he had been running, and his only comment was a constantly repeated, "You can't do this. You can't do this."

By the time Jones was fully erect, steadied against a tree trunk, the sun was risen. He closed his eyes for what seemed only a moment, yet when he opened them he found the whole camp gathered around him and he wore a skirtlike skin draped from his waist. The talk of the crowd was a low mumble, pregnant with dread. He pretended to be completely unaware.

The sun felt good on his body.

In his body.

A ripple of amazement ran through the gathering as he lifted an arm. He pointed where the full moon still held a place in the sky, defying the brighter sun. "See the moon." The words were blurry. His tongue hurt, filled his mouth with pain. He repeated himself, adding, "My spirit was driven out. I went to speak to my mother, Moon. She has sent me back for Sun to give me warmth." Several listeners dropped to their knees. He felt his facial wounds crack open when he smiled. He went on. "You threw me down to die. Moon gave me life."

Keening rose here and there, muffled, as if those making the sound couldn't stop yet dared not draw attention to themselves. Jones went on. "I am to you as the moon that is born, grows, ages, dies, and returns. I am to other men as the snake is to animals. My old skin falls away and I am renewed." His words needed no thought. Whispers within his brain *demanded* to be spoken.

He pointed at a large rock outcrop some distance away. "I will go there. You and you," he indicated two warriors, "will carry me."

The remaining eight protectors and Altanar stood at a distance within a circle of Mountain warriors. The latter held mas, anxiously anticipating the order to slaughter those who'd tortured the gaunt apparition that now ordered them about. Jones wanted to spit on them; they believed killing the protectors would appease him.

They had much to learn.

He gestured to the circle of guard. "Follow," he instructed them, then, "Fox. Beside me."

At the site, he had Fox support him while he went from rock to rock, feeling, listening. Finally, he indicated a particular boulder. "Roll it aside," he ordered, and men crowded to obey. They leapt away with equal speed when they uncovered the heaving, writhing mass of rattlesnakes nested in a hollow under it.

Jones said, "These know I am one who dies and returns. You have seen. Now, see more." He stepped to the edge of the pit, where the disturbed reptiles were beginning to seek escape. A small one crawled across his bare foot. The belly scales plucked at his scabbed flesh. The sensation triggered a mental image of a familiar man shuddering in panic at the sight of a snake. Why did he feel such contempt for that person?

For a moment, he hesitated. Powers so primal he couldn't identify them warred in him. Then, swiftly, he reached into the mass, fighting to hold back joyous, confident laughter.

He held up two massive, buzzing snakes for all to see. He draped them over his shoulders, twined them around his neck. Their darting, glistening tongues tapped his cheeks as he kissed the tops of their heads. Then he extended his forearms, palms upraised, resting his elbows on his hipbones. The fat bodies, almost as thick as their support, each coiled as much length as possible on a hand. Glitter-eyed, they scanned the stunned crowd with imperious disdain.

"Protectors," he said in a whisper. "They served me well. Bring them."

There were screams and fighting, but soon all were in a line facing him. They still wore the leather bonds they slept in. The snakes remained nestled on Jones' palms, and they stared coldly at the horrified prisoners while Jones paraded back and forth in front of them.

He stopped. One of the two men in front of him was the fool who'd almost made a three-sign in his presence. The other was his benefactor. He said, "The greatest honor of the new Moondance is yours."

Before the pair could do more than look relieved, Jones extended his hands. The snakes struck.

Choking, screaming, the men jerked at their bound wrists, twisting away from their guards. Venom injected directly into their throats reached their brains in seconds. Shrieking, they collapsed in convulsions.

Jones watched. He felt a barrier growing around himself and the writhing men; he could almost touch it, a smoky haze that closed out everyone else. Then it shrank, and he understood the wall was their life force, coming into him. For an instant, it was tight, binding, like an obligation. Finally, it entered him.

Ecstasy.

He spoke across the bodies. "The spirits of those who die by my order will wait in paradise to be reborn, as you have seen me reborn. Their spirits will come at my call to serve me until I must, once more, return to my mother, Moon. When I rejoin my followers here, so will they, restored, better in every way. Those who resist me will die and be dead forever. Who here questions?"

He sought Fox with a gaze as hard and sure as steel. The warrior, bone-pale with shock, met it only long enough to acknowledge submission. Far in the back of the crowd, Jones spotted

Altanar, trussed like a pig for market. He wondered what use he could find for him.

A wave of pain suddenly swept through him, a sensory memory of flame and knife and bludgeon. He felt himself sway. Stepping back, he managed to brace against a rock.

It was a warning. He understood it. Only that which advanced his cause could be tolerated. The new must feed on the old.

CHAPTER 9

During the long months of Clas' absence, Sylah had taken to long walks to isolate herself and her unruly mind from the company of others. On one such occasion, random footsteps led her to the seaward wall of Ola. Gan was there. Alone, he stared out at the Inland Sea, lost in thought. His great dog, Shara, alerted him to another presence. He welcomed Sylah, and for a while they sat together, talking of the future, of hopes and fears, as only tested friends can.

She had never fully realized the resentment—even rebellion— that seethed under the placid surface of his reign. Most troublemakers had fled his Wolves to live harried, nomadic lives wherever they could outside the Three Territories. Covert whisperers, spies, and malcontents remained, an infection that refused to be treated.

Sylah listened, and heard the sadness of a man who'd discovered that evil isn't an enemy to be met and defeated, but a seductive presence in the lives of all.

She'd nearly forgotten how very young he was. The poignancy of his education tore at her heart.

He also confided to her his fascination with the sea. "I can sit here for hours and my only objection is the Whale Coast mountains blocking my view of what's beyond. I dream of what's out there. Freedom, where a man can go in any direction he wants. Why do I feel walled in by these mountains? They stand there, looking down at me. They're a trap. I know how foolish that sounds, but it's how I feel. The sea—that openness, like the prairie—is escape."

Sylah said, "I think I understand, but given a choice, I'll take solid earth under my feet, thank you very much. Think of your poor seasick dog. And your horse."

He laughed. "That's my dark secret, you know. Sometimes I sit here, and I see a ship slashing through the water, balancebar knifing, and I see whole troops of ships, with archers, grappling lines, boarding hooks. I see the feint and charge of we Dog People, only with boats instead of horses. It's an exciting thing."

Holding her silence, she was waiting for him when he cut his eyes sideways at her. A small, sheepish grin tried for her sympathy. He said, "You don't see that, do you?"

"Absolutely not," she snapped.

They laughed then, appreciating each other, relishing the differences between them, enjoying the similarities. The rest of that day had passed in soft-voiced sharing of memories.

Watching the sea also became one of Sylah's great pleasures. Stormy or peaceful, there was always activity. It temporarily distracted her from never-ending doubts and concerns.

For a few days after Clas' return to the Dog People, the excitement of watching Conway exercise the Dog war-horses and dogs he'd brought for them occupied her adequately. On this morning, however, she sought the lonely solace of the west-facing ramparts.

She was watching when a fat merchantman made port. There was a southwind chop that day, and it took the beamy vessel almost broadside when it headed east, turning her attempts at dignified progress into waddling comedy. Twin masts whipped side to side, clutching at empty air. Crewmen skipped across her deck, quick as weasels, grabbing lines and projections to halt or change directions. Their agility brought her to her moorings without damage. Once the balancebar swiveled to vertical, she came to rest with a squeal of wood on wood. When she continued to push and grunt against the dock, Sylah could only think of an old hog scratching at a fence.

A gangplank was lowered. A figure appeared from the low deckhouse at the stern. Sylah sat bolt upright, clutching the edges of her bench.

The woman who strode onto the dock had hair as white as silver, a glaring contrast to her black robe trimmed with blue and green. Once off the ship, she drew up her cowl, momentarily exposing a lining in the same blue and green.

"The Harvester." Sylah breathed the words aloud. She'd never seen any Church official senior to her own beloved Iris Abbess. The Harvester selected those who would become Abbess, supervised their initiation into deeper secrets of Church. It was unknown for one to leave Church Home.

Sylah literally ran to the dock to greet her. The tall figure stopped, raising a commanding hand. The simple movement was a transformation. Her robe, swirling in the hard wind off the sea, took away any physical clue of a human form. The warding hand hid everything but a pair of deep-set eyes that burned down at Sylah from within the dark of the enveloping cowl.

When the woman bared her head, however, she smiled broadly, a generous mouth in an angular, strong face that carried age with ease. Sylah blushed with pleasure at the Harvester's words. "You're Sylah. I'm sure of it. The descriptions all mentioned your beauty. And good work. None said you were so prompt, though. What a grand coincidence to find you here to meet me. Let's call it our omen, to share. It means we're to be very close, we two. I hoped we would be. Our wonderful sister, your Abbess, spoke of you constantly in her dealings with Church Home. Always with love." The Harvester's voice was a resonant alto. Sylah winced, thinking how the Iris Abbess' voice had a similar timbre.

"I am Sylah, Harvester. Forgive our lack of welcome. We had no idea . . ."

"Nor I, sister, nor I." The Harvester chuckled, then went on, "I'll explain later. I long to soak in hot water. My nose and lungs crave the scent of herbs and essences to smother the stink of unwashed men and bilge. My ears ache from the squeal of tortured wood and the moan of rigging. And the truly amazing inventiveness of sailors' tongues. My dear sister, I have heard simple pulleys showered with obscenities a normal human being wouldn't use on a fiend who'd just disemboweled his parents. Save me. I beg you."

Sylah stifled an undignified giggle and took the Harvester's arm. "Right away, Harvester. Come."

"My name is Odeel. Hold that arm tightly, and explain why your country rolls and plunges under my feet the same as that miserable boat. Protect us from a land that swoops and wobbles. Whoops! That rock moved deliberately. Tell me of Gan Moondark. I must speak to him when I'm human again."

Later, Gan was equally intrigued by her. In the room he used as a meeting place, he sat behind a table with legs carved to represent leaping salmon. The surface was painted with stylized black and white images of the same fish. The chairs in the room were low-slung forms that supported the body on leather webbing and cushions. All were built to seat one person, except for a long, bench-backed piece that could handle four.

Gan's wife, Neela, and her princeling, Coldar na Bale Moondark, sat on one end of the long piece, with Sylah on the other. The Harvester was directly across the room. After one look at her, Coldar insisted on closer involvement. Odeel extended her smile and her hands to him. In a moment, he was in her lap, happily playing with the bejeweled gold sickle on its gold chain that was her badge of rank.

Neela excused herself and returned with delicacies—honey-glazed hazelnuts, sweet cookies with berry jam, square bars of a dried confection made of sunflower seeds, apple pulp, and honey. Coldar discovered the jam and instantly lost interest in gold playthings. Neela had to move quickly to rescue the Harvester's robe from the suddenly grubby, sticky child. There were also several herb teas. Each was contained in its own ceramic jar. The containers and accompanying cups gleamed in a bright semicircle around the small charcoal brazier and its pot of hot brewing water. The tray was an oval of satin-glowing copper, with tubular jade grips. The steel teaspoons had bone handles, carved into fanciful animal figures.

Gan was quick to explain that all of it was left over from the deposed Altanar. He apologized for what he called the extravagance of the utensils. Sylah was disappointed by the covert look of amused disbelief sent her by the Harvester. The tall woman compounded that cynical response by answering, "Display is good. It makes the ruled understand that rulers are, indeed, different. Display spurs obedience."

She paused to stir her tea. "I'll be direct, Gan Moondark, out of respect for your youth. Old ones such as I sometimes prefer the game to the goal. Youth is impatient, has no time for useless maneuver. Directly, then: We're concerned about our sister, Sylah."

Gan's features tightened. Neela reached to take Sylah's hand. Gan said, "She risked casting out for Church."

"Unquestioned truth. But far removed from the problem."

"Yes?" The tone betrayed nothing. Nevertheless, Sylah wanted to warn her sister. The Harvester didn't know how this man watched and waited, as patient and invisible as any wolf.

Odeel said, "The foulness called Moondance rises, worse than a war, worse than a plague. There have been attacks on Church. The holy ban against taking our lives is trampled."

Outside, the sun was setting, and a growing darkness weighted the unlit room. Neela got to her feet and lit candles. Odeel rose and paced. The unsteady illumination contributed to the sense of difference, of *stranger*, surrounding the Harvester.

Odeel went on. "There's more. As a friend of Church, I ask you to swear none of what is said in here will be repeated."

"No." Gan leaned forward, fists on the table. "I keep my options open, Harvester. I won't be bound to any blind oath."

There was a slight pause, and Sylah wondered if Gan realized exactly how telling a blow he'd struck. The Harvester wouldn't be accustomed to anyone rejecting her opening, especially a man she regarded as a simple warrior king. Sylah could almost hear the older woman's brain working to realign her argument.

Total surrender was a shock. Odeel bowed her head, saying, "I was rude. If we're to help each other, there must be complete truth and openness. Very well. Since the beginning, the kingdom of Kos has kept the Empty Lands essentially unpopulated, a gap between itself and all other people. They're secretive. They know much of you. You are feared, Gan Moondark. You've created a strong force with the Wolves of your Three Territories, and Kos is wary."

"Pity Kos," Gan interrupted dryly. "They worry for nothing. Kos is more than two moons' fast travel from here. I have no interest in them, unless we can arrange trade."

"Kos is very rich. Such people never rest easy. Sylah's goal of finding the Door of Church legend creates a unique problem. Kos wars constantly with the Hents, to the south. Now Kos fears the nomads pressing against the Enemy Mountains from the east. The nomads are Moondance's greatest champions, and, as such, worry that the secret of the Door may give Church advantage in the conflict between the two religions. Their leader is named Katallon. He promises to respect Kos' borders if the search for the Door is prohibited."

Sylah fought to keep her voice calm. "I'll avoid the Kossiars and the nomads. I *will* find the Door."

Odeel ignored Sylah, spoke to Gan. "I am instructed to return with Sylah, that she be trained, then returned to you with a retinue of Healers, War Healers, and administrators. She will be Iris Abbess of the Three Territories."

"Iris Abbess?" Gan smiled at Sylah. "A great honor. And I've been against this quest of yours all along. I've made no secret of that."

Odeel smiled.

Gan continued, "Nor have I made any secret of my intention to support you in whatever you choose to do."

Odeel's expression took on a hard glaze. Imperiously, she raised her chin before pulling her cowl over her head, walling herself off. "You reject Church?"

Gan said, "I reject pressure, Harvester. My friend's quest is hers. She stood by me and Clas na Bale and Neela and Tate when any misstep by one meant death for all. I will do all I can for Church. Church will not tell me what I must do to Sylah."

Sylah had heard such a silence as now filled the room only once. When she and her companions were fleeing the Mountain People, there had been a time when a snow cornice threatened them. It was a thing of deadly quiet, but with the force of mountains in it. Gan and the Harvester made her think of that elemental conflict, gravity tirelessly straining against unremitting cold.

On that occasion, it was Gan's fate that drew everyone into jeopardy. Now it was her own.

What right had she to risk others?

Neela took the opportunity to try to ease the tension. "Please try to understand, Harvester; Sylah's quest is for all of us. Our women here have more freedom, more sense of accomplish—"

Odeel's interruption cracked like a whip. "Church knows you corrupt Chosens. You have strangers—aliens, non-Church women—making those innocent children learn. The forbidden word *teach* has been whispered. The Apocalypse Testament says, 'Wisdom is the control of man's knowledge. Man's learning is the most destructive force known, even unto destroying man.' Church is the guardian of wisdom and knowledge. Not you, Gan Moondark."

The Harvester put down her cup, sweeping her robe around in an angry billow, flinging off the cowl. The material stirred breezes, staggering the candle flames. The white hair, so immaculately groomed before, now burst wildly from her head. Her voice vibrated with emotion as she strode to the door.

"I leave for now. Rose Priestess Sylah: If you persist in this idiot's quest without Church blessing, you will be no more a priestess."

Sylah's throat locked. She clutched at it, forced it to open. "I search in Church's name, in the name of all women. How . . . ?" The question trailed to nothing.

"What Church sees is false hope, at best. Crude ambition, at worst. The former Iris Abbess missed no opportunity to tell us at Church Home of your so-called 'destiny.' If your search fails, the enemies of Church will say you found nothing because we preach only tales and legends. An attempt to find the Door brings the fury of the nomads on us. If your search succeeds, if there is such a thing and you actually find it, you unleash unknown powers. The Seer of Seers said so; she declared that Church will be destroyed, can never again be what it was or is."

64

A slight movement of Odeel's hand might have been a bid for personal contact. She failed to complete it. "You cause us all great grief with your selfishness. I am ordered to warn you, nevertheless. You will not be allowed to destroy Church. In the name of love, if it must be so, Church will hate. In the name of life, if it must be so, Church will kill. *You must not destroy Church.*"

The rumbling close of the door behind the Harvester echoed the devastation of Sylah's heart.

CHAPTER 10

Alone in her room the next morning, Sylah idly drew invisible pictures with her fingertip on the polished surface of her table. Occasionally she sipped from a mug of steaming tea. On the last occasion, her nose wrinkled in disappointment, and she busied herself pouring some hot water in the mug to rinse it, then brewing a fresh batch.

A small charcoal brazier on the table was her heat source. It was a rectangular ceramic box, with blocky ceramic legs. Glazed dark-earth brown, it was decorated with random flecks of deep blue. There was enough room between the bottom of the brazier and the table to prevent scorching. Additionally, the legs ended in wooden feet, carved to resemble cat faces; they were obviously designed to prevent heat transference. The sides of the brazier featured U-shaped tubes that provided air for combustion while acting as a baffle to discourage escaping sparks.

A metal top plate was equipped with handles for lifting. When Sylah raised it to add charcoal, the scriptlike wriggles of black and red across the glowing chunks were like tantalizing, indecipherable messages. She replaced the lid, poured a fresh drink, and put the pot back on. Her vision fixed on the twisting, disappearing wisps of steam.

Reason demanded she ignore the Harvester. The quest was good. It was for women, and Church was the only refuge women had; how could anyone believe she'd harm Church? Even if the secret of the door placed power in her hands, was that necessarily evil?

Men would say so. Men said anything that weakened their total dominance was evil.

Why, then, when she finally found her way clear of the images of the Harvester's fury, did her mind fly to Clas, to a man?

Everything changed when he came into her life. She knew the tenderness behind his iron will. She saw character where others saw only the black tattoo. Sylah, his wife; she saw the shyness and bold desire. She knew things about herself she'd never suspected. Emotional things. Physical. Exciting.

She clenched her fists, squeezed until her fingers were like embers in her palms.

Why did being right have to hurt?

Tendrils of steam slipped across her cheek like small, warm sighs.

Clas' breath felt like that. The steam was scented with raspberry, though. His breath was heavier. Compelling. There were times, just before sleep, when that rhythmic touch and smell filled her, and she had no need of other senses.

No need.

She lifted the mug, drank deeply.

Need. There were many kinds of need.

Her breasts seemed to swell, strain against a robe suddenly binding, confining. Her loins warmed, and a familiar languor flowed in her blood, touched her with soft fire wherever it roamed.

She jerked to her feet. Gracelessly, she cocked her arm and flung the inoffensive mug. Streaming dregs, it crashed into the stone wall at the back of the fireplace, fell in wet pieces that sizzled and spat on the near-dead coals.

Scooping kindling out of a basket, she determinedly started a proper fire. In time, as the flames moved across the small sticks and onto the larger billets of wood, the sharp pain of her loneliness subsided to its routine dull ache. As a result, she was composed, if a bit surprised, when the knock came on her door.

The Harvester stood there when she opened it.

Unwilling to trust her voice, Sylah stepped back, gesturing invitation. The tall woman swept past her, then turned. With a wry smile, she said, "I overspoke myself earlier today. They train us to read the faces and bodies of those around us, yet our own feelings escape to expose us. I'm sorry I threatened." When Sylah opened her mouth to reply, Odeel was too quick for her. "Nevertheless, what I said was true. Your quest could be the final tap on the wedge that splits Church forever. Or worse. You have no idea of the power of Moondance. I again urge you to abandon this search."

Sylah looked at the floor. "Harvester, I cannot. I'd go mad. Something drives me." Her enthusiasm strengthened her, and she raised her head, confronted Odeel. "I've told no one this, not even Clas. I have been selected. Fate tests and shapes us all, so I know that what I accomplish will test and shape Church. I will gift my sisters, not just those in Church, but everywhere. I am *meant* to seek."

"Would you speak of giving fire to a child as a gift? Would you speak of shattering hundreds of years of tradition as accomplishment? Would you speak of self-importance as selection? Can't you see you're possessed by ambition? You reject us all."

"Never that." It was a cry for help. "No. What I do is for all; I need you all." Emboldened by desire to make the other woman understand, Sylah took a step forward, put her hand on Odeel's arm.

The Harvester's stare at the presumptuous touch was almost palpable. Sylah's hand dropped to dangle awkwardly. Only then did the Harvester continue. "Every move, every word, that affects Church must be controlled."

"I must go."

In the long silence that followed, the Harvester grew rigid with anger. Then, blessedly, there was a gradual softening. Disapproval remained heavy on her, but resignation eased it. She sighed, and reached to take Sylah's chin in her hand. "I admire your tenacity, dear Sylah. I sorrow that I can't agree with it. I leave you as soon as the ship can get under way. I'll see to it that Church offers you no help. I assure you that you will never rise higher in Church than Rose Priestess. Still, I shall pray always for your personal safety. Now, I ask the third time, as you know I must: Do you continue to deny me?"

Numbing cold swept Sylah. The ritual of the three denials was old, some said ancient beyond even the beginning. It was usually a preliminary to casting out. The dispassionate demand that they both acknowledge such formality shook her resolve as no argument could have. Still, she found voice. "I deny, Harvester. I thank you for your prayers. I know that you, too, do what you must."

Odeel gestured at the brazier. "I have a long walk back to the dock, and this wet wind cuts me like a whip. May I trouble you for some tea to warm my way?"

Sylah bustled, getting fresh water, adding charcoal to the brazier. The Harvester insisted on helping, emptying and rinsing Sylah's mug, fetching one for herself. Relieved by the rekindled

67

warmth of her guest, Sylah never saw the swift movement that brought a leather pouch out of the Harvester's deep pocket. Nor did she see the yellowish powder that poured from the sack into one of the cups.

All the while, Odeel chattered, the smooth, distracting patter of the devious. While Sylah laughed merrily, she calmly assumed the task of pouring.

They drank slowly, carefully neutral. Sylah felt the Harvester was anxious to avoid any more argument. Time sped past. They had yet another cup of tea.

Odeel insisted she rinse the cups, continued on in the role of pourer. Seated once more, another side of her crept into their quiet talk. "My father was a godkill digger." She said it with a touch of wonder. Sylah understood that well she might. The godkills were all that was left of the communities where the slaves lived when the giants who ruled the world destroyed it. There was no more dangerous job. No one still believed the ancient tales that godkills harbored incurable disease or the flesh-eating radeath. Still and all, digging was normally the province of slaves or human scavengers. Or Peddlers.

Odeel continued. "Father lost our farm to a merchant. We were Kossiars. In Kos, desperate men can hire themselves out to dig godkills. It's not pleasant, knowing your father is the only free-man in the village looked down on by the slaves. Still, he fed and clothed us." She excused herself, went to the window. Returning to the table, she resumed her story. "The day after Mother's burning, I presented myself to the abbey. My tenth year, I reckon. The Sisters took me in. I never saw my father or any of my family again. Church is my world, my soul. As Church gave me life, so I gladly give life for Church."

Sylah said, "We both know bitterness."

Odeel's smile had a peculiar, almost cruel twist. "All women are harshly bound. You seek to change that. I know they must live within the bonds. It's a lesson we all learn, Sylah. Some with more difficulty than others."

A searing twinge in her stomach cut off Sylah's response. The pain faded slightly, only to return like the twist of a blade. The Harvester gripped Sylah's wrist. "What's wrong?"

"It's nothing," Sylah managed. The pain mounted steadily. Her head felt stuffed, as if it were swelling. She had a sudden mad fear that it might split. Her mouth was dry, and she reached clumsily for her mug.

The Harvester stopped her. "No more tea. Fresh water's what

68

you need." She hurried to fill the mug from the large urn by the fireplace.

Sylah drained it. In seconds, she felt better. Much better. Oddly, the pounding pain remained, but it seemed ... What? Pointless. That was the word. Nothing was important. Everything was nice. Soft.

The Harvester put gentle fingers to Sylah's throat pulse, studied her face, fingertips, ears. "What do you feel, Sylah? Tell me." She took Sylah's hands in her own. Sylah was startled by the heat of the Harvester's touch. Or was it because her own hands were cold? Her feet certainly were. And her nose.

Sylah said, "It's cold." She couldn't imagine why the Harvester was so completely unmoved by the massive import of that news. She merely pressed the cup on Sylah again, demanding she drink.

The Harvester rested against the edge of the table for another few moments, then suddenly walked away to stand with her back to the window.

"Come to me," she said. *"Now."*

An order.

Sylah's mind fragmented. She heard commands shouted at Chosens. There were punishments for being slow or—terrible thought—disobedient. She struggled out of the chair.

One step away from the steadying table finished her. She pitched forward, reaching out to the Harvester. Crashing into the stone wall, staggering backward, hands flung out for balance, she cried out for help. The sound was a faint mewing. Blurry, wavering eyes found the Harvester. The tall woman seemed far away, a force that loomed like Snowfather Mountain, cold and forbidding. She looked down at Sylah on the floor.

And smiled triumph.

CHAPTER 11

When Sylah woke she was prone, with no idea how long she'd been that way. The glow from embers in the nearby fireplace burned her eyes. Blinking back tears that owed as much to fright as to pain, she turned her head. The tiny flame of the room's single candle now was needling brightness. She moaned, shut her eyes. Struggling, she forced herself to all fours, only to collapse and roll onto her back.

Framed in the window, glittering stars swirled madly across the sky. Suddenly, they stopped. Instead, she spun, a terrified, nauseated speck in the vastness of night. She was attached to nothing, bathed in coiling trails of light. She gagged, twisting away.

Then it was over. She was still. The stars were in place. Silence—menacing, suggestive—filled the world.

A darkness at the topmost edge of her vision loomed over her, ever larger, blotting out the stars. A voice said, "And so it ends, poor fool. 'The truest of the true' you may be, but you'll *not* destroy my Church."

Squinting against the pain-bringing light, Sylah tried to wipe tears away. Her muscles refused to comply.

Lassitude swept her. She didn't care about the rebellious muscles.

Nothing mattered. She drifted in carefree warmth.

Softness. That feeling had happened to her before.

At the table. Drinking tea with the Harvester.

Now she was separated from everything. Alone.

Fight. Embrace the pain, the nausea. Recognize them as reality.

No. Everything was all right.

Helpless. Echoing, echoing.

It didn't matter. Everyone was helpless.

She tried to concentrate, pinched her lip between her teeth. Something crunched. The salt taste of blood startled her. It also seemed to spur her mind to clarity.

The Harvester.

Sylah managed to sit up, then slump back against the stone wall. Its chill indifference seemed to drain her resolve. A wavering, tremulous thought tried to remind her that she must protest something. But what? Protest to whom? There was no one but the Harvester, and she was authority.

Everything was all right.

She was losing herself again.

Fight!

Something swallowed her mind, something dark and evil, living inside her.

Everything was all right.

The Harvester gripped Sylah's hair, lifting. The crack of the other hand across her cheek sounded like a distant branch breaking. Pain came as a slow, breaking wave that crashed and retreated in a confused welter of thoughts and reactions. Sylah knew she should cry out. It didn't seem worth the effort. She braced with her hands on the floor, tried to focus on Odeel's face. It was almost touching her own.

"That's better, then," the older woman said. "You shouldn't have the will or the strength to sit up. Your eyes are correct, though; no fear, no recognition. Dear, dear Sylah. You have no idea how distasteful it is to look into such eyes."

The Harvester shivered slightly as she turned her attention to the golden sickle at her breast. The surface of the piece was etched with crisscross lines, creating myriad facets on the mirror bright surface that caught every glimmer from the candle. The effect on Sylah's sensitized eyes was a swaying, demanding dazzle. The Harvester commanded her to watch. Watch.

Sylah's eyelids grew heavy, as the Harvester's voice said they must. She wanted to sleep.

No, not sleep. Escape. Get away from the pressing, cold-voiced orders, the will-crushing gleam of the sickle on its chain.

Suddenly the Harvester's face was in front of her again. There was a hint of admiration in her voice. "You're very strong. You resist my little toy as well as my drugs. It's over, though. Your mind is mine to command now, a stilled pool, waiting for whatever ripples I choose to create there. From what I'm told, it's not an unpleasant state. I could almost envy you."

Sylah forced a sound past the straining muscles of her throat. She willed the Harvester to *feel* her rage, the determination to regain control of herself. Her fingers curled, scratched at the stone floor.

The Harvester took a half step backward. "Incredible. You saw? You heard? I've never . . ."

She broke off, decisive once again. "Stand. Stand, Sylah!"

The sickle swayed, gleamed, lured. Sylah rose.

Other orders followed. Sylah walked, sat, stood again.

Secure in her victory, the Harvester gloated. "Once I've had time to work with you, you'll be a great asset to Church. You're far too headstrong, presently. You must understand that I am Church, now, Sylah. All your training, your indoctrination is centered in me. I am Mother. I *am* Church." Odeel repeated the latter statement over and over, bringing out the sickle again, swinging it in a gentle arc in front of Sylah's fixed, dull eyes.

Odeel finally stepped away, gazed out the window. "Church needs you Sylah. You'll come with me on the ship, back to Kos, then to Church Home, where we'll pursue your quest for the Door. Together. Church will help you. You remember your catechism; are you sworn?"

"I am sworn to Mother, the Healer."

"Exactly. And who is Mother, Sylah? At the word *Mother*, whom do you see?"

"The Harvester. Odeel. You."

"And Church? Who is Church?"

"You. Mother."

Softly, the older woman said, "Oh, excellent, excellent. You worried me for a while, my dear, yes you did. No one's resisted my potion the way you did. No one who lived." Then, briskly, "This is the time when you normally call on the black one, Tate; we'll do that. Remember, you're exactly the person you always were, except now you serve Church through me. Your new way to pursue your quest is a Church secret, and you must protect it. You understand?"

Sylah nodded, then followed the Harvester out of the room, docile, unconcerned.

At Tate's quarters, Odeel ordered the attendant Chosen to wait outside. With the girl out of the way, Odeel moved to where Tate lay flat on her back in bed. She was packed in poultices from waist to scalp. At the sound of visitors, she reached up with painful slowness to lift the bandages from her face.

Bending over to look directly down at her, Odeel said, "I know you, Donnacee Tate. Our friend Sylah speaks highly of you."

The battered features managed a grotesque smile. The effort impressed Odeel. One eye was completely closed by massive swelling. The other was a mere slit. The lips were split, round and swollen like broken fingers. A thick aroma of herbs rose from dark skin that gleamed with a mix of sweat and moisture from the hot packs. A trick of the light caused a gleam, like a sputtering candle, in Tate's good eye.

Halting, her voice a husked croak, Tate spoke. "I know you, Harvester. Gan was here. Said you want stop Sylah's quest for Door."

Odeel worked to understand the distorted words, but her primary effort was directed at reading any signals sent by Tate's features and movements. The dark complexion added intrigue, and the terrible injuries created almost-insurmountable challenge.

Still, Odeel was certain she'd seen resentment and a touch of smugness. A reasonable assumption was that the upstart Gan had bragged to her about putting the Harvester in her place.

Gan would learn about places.

There was more, though. *Fear.* Why would Tate be afraid?

Unless the Door was as important to her as to Sylah. Unless Tate knew something.

Strangers. Secretive. Claiming no particular purpose for their wanderings, claiming to be from a land that knew Church, but had no actual Church contact.

Tate was saying, ". . . 'specting Conway, my friend. Going with Sylah, too. We help her."

Before Odeel could respond, the young Chosen opened the door. "Matt Conway, Donnacee. He's coming."

"Just in time." Tate raised her head from the bed, twisted it gingerly from side to side, obviously seeking. "Sylah?" The word was concerned, almost plaintive. "You so quiet. You here?"

Quickly, Sylah was at the bedside, taking her friend's hand in hers. Odeel stepped back, chagrined; she hadn't realized how near blind Tate was. She'd been so busy looking for hidden things she'd overlooked a major vulnerability. She resolved to do better. Once the initial greetings were over, she eased away from the trio, observing while Sylah and Conway entertained Tate.

Everything about them spoke of unity. Unconsciously, Conway moved to partially overlap Sylah, a position that shielded her, as well as Tate, from the interloper, the stranger. Odeel was certain it was quite unconscious on his part. He wasn't that clever.

They both hovered over Tate protectively. Their voices were warm, consoling—and too soft to be understood beyond the bed. Odeel heard Tate, however. Concerned, puzzled. "You all right, honey?" She reached to close slow fingers around Sylah's wrist. "You sound funny. What's wrong?"

Sylah murmured. Tension remained in Tate's stiff attitude, the continued grip on Sylah's wrist.

It all irritated Odeel. And disturbed her. The black woman's perception that Sylah was somehow different was obviously intuitive, rather than intelligent. That fact alone clearly revealed the bond between them. The man Conway was a fool, but loyal. When they found Sylah gone, they'd be very angry. There could be pursuit.

They couldn't possibly catch up before Sylah was safely inside Church Home. They'd never rescue her from there.

Still, they'd come from somewhere far away and survived to reach Ola. They had marvelous weapons.

Conway turned and walked to her, smiling brightly. She waited amusedly for his attempt to surprise her. He was so disingenuous, the way he revealed himself even before he spoke, his head involuntarily inclined toward Sylah. "I know you oppose Sylah's

73

search. I suspect a lot of the opposition is because Church is afraid for her. So are Tate and myself, so is Gan. You see, even though we represent a potent weapon for him, he's glad to see us leave with her, because he knows we intend to protect her."

He paused, glancing around.

It really was ludicrous. He was going to confide in her. She tingled with delight, already envisioning the faces at Church Home when she told the story.

Conway said, "There's more to it than that. I think someone should explore the Empty Lands for a better route to Kos. If we can open up a trade route between Ola and Kos, we're a step closer to some sort of alliance. Church should welcome that, what with all the reports of nomads stirring to the east."

"They're not just stirring, young man. They're swarming across the land. You can be sure Church will be most interested in what you say. Tell me, what does Gan think of your plan?"

"He doesn't know." Odeel thought how his diffidence gave him a certain engaging quality. For a moment she pitied his naive unawareness of exactly how dangerously he'd just changed his position in the game. Conway went on, "Once Tate's well, we'll need very little time to prepare for the trip. Clas na Bale brought war-horses for Tate and myself—Dog war-horses, the best in the world—and a pair of dogs for each of us. Until she's better, I ride out beyond the settled area into the hills and work them every day. I can't wait for Tate to be able to join me."

"You do this alone?"

Conway grinned, boyish. "I don't think of myself as alone. The horse and the dogs are better company than most men."

"That's been my experience."

He laughed. A good laugh, she thought; robust, brimful of living.

Such a pity.

CHAPTER 12

Tentatively, Conway dropped the war-horse's reins. Its jet black ears twitched forward at the touch of the straps on the back of its neck. Light pressure from Conway's heels and knees sent them on a random course through the huge trees. With a growing sense of unity they played games that one day might save their lives.

Behind them, one on each side, two huge dogs duplicated every maneuver. Long-legged, rough-coated, they loped silently through the forest. The grizzled gray female, Mikka, had to weigh at least one hundred and thirty pounds. The rawboned male, Karda, was a rich black, and by far the gawkier of the two. Conway estimated his weight already at a good hundred and fifty pounds, and obviously destined to grow to fit now-floppy feet and oversized lazy ears.

Thinking of Shara, Gan's mature war dog, Conway grinned at Karda's attempts at seriousness. Just now, faced with a dead branch in his way, the youngster approached boldly, never breaking stride. He launched himself into the air with a sort of violent grace, and snagged a hind foot. He landed running, but in a flustered scramble, and a genuinely hangdog look at his master.

Still, he kept up with the trotting horse.

A few moments later, they broke free of the forest onto a vast cattle pasture, and Conway heeled the horse to a gallop.

A product of centuries of selective breeding and training, the Dog war-horse was born for open ground. At Conway's urge, it stretched its neck as if to catch time in its teeth. Ears back, eyes wide with excitement, it reached forward with eager hooves, driving, pounding, racing so hard it seemed about to soar.

Bent forward, chin almost resting on the streaming mane, Conway gripped the reins. A glance over his shoulder assured Karda and Mikka were hurtling after, white fangs gleaming against tongue-lolling grins.

The smell of horse blended with the sharp tang of firs from the towering mountains and the crushed grasses of the meadow. The warm sun that bathed him was suddenly so pure it almost hurt, and he whooped delight at myriad shades of burgeoning green, earthen browns, brilliances of early wildflowers.

He reined in where the pasture ended at a wall of timber. The ground sloped away sharply. From somewhere deep inside the forest's darkness the heavy rumble of a hidden waterfall reached for him.

Conway pressed ahead, eager to be searching out the new and different. He wished Tate could share in it.

There was a certain irony in that. He genuinely enjoyed being alone with his team. He used them as an excuse, actually. But frequently the new Conway was bad company. Despite his general eagerness to meet and test himself against the unknown world awaiting him, there were times when he was depressed to a state of near immobility.

75

Tee was usually at the base of it. He missed her with an ache he'd never known before. She'd saved him. More than his life, she'd saved the part of him that made him fully alive.

Then she left him, because she was a slave, a woman who'd been used by any who wanted her, and couldn't believe anyone could love her.

There was another memory that wouldn't leave him alone. Burl Falconer, the Army colonel who committed suicide because he was afraid his delirium would lead him to reveal to Altanar the secrets of their origin and their weapons. Falconer knew—they all knew—that people in this world who claimed to be from a five-hundred-year-dead past would be called witches and killed. More than that, Falconer feared he might babble something revealing about their weapons. If Altanar, or someone like him, ever learned how to use them, that person would eliminate them immediately.

Horribly, it was that old world that had killed Falconer even as he dreamed of what this one could be. Bacteriological warfare, they called it. A frightening phrase. Compared to the reality, the words were timid. Test-tube diseases, genetically altered to strike down humans and leave animals unscathed. Viruses that attacked only certain blood types. Things that sought one race to the exclusion of others.

Hellish inventions that mutated to circle back and fall on their creators.

A miserable little insect that transmitted something into Falconer's blood that was no more than a minor itch to the now-resistant people who might very well be his own descendants.

Conway never ceased asking himself if he had Falconer's courage. It was a question as seductive as it was frightening.

The horse tossed its head and tiptoed sideways. It steadied at Conway's touch. Nevertheless, as they picked their way down the hill, its ears continued to flick, searching. The dogs were alert, too, their noses high.

Soon Conway glimpsed the waterfall through the trees. A little later, they left the slope to enter onto a brush-choked floodplain. The horse picked its way carefully across the cobbled surface. The dogs crowded close. If Conway signaled them away with gesture, voice, or the silver whistle on its chain around his neck, they'd obey instantly. By choice, they maintained visual contact with their master.

The team forged out of the cover and Conway stopped in awe. The drop of the silvered cascade wasn't high, but the volume of water was immense. It fell into a near-circular pool, churning up a frothing wildness. Thunder radiated from it, bored through the earth to set bones trembling. The stream leading away lapped greedily at the stone beach. Spindly brush on the banks trembled as if in dread. Sticks and twigs lodged in the higher branches proclaimed flood levels; snapped trunks boasted of power.

Cold still held most of that strength fast to the mountains. Up there, ice and snowmass waited. Already the sun was playing across the peaks for a few extra minutes every day. Soon it would force winter's grip.

Conway dismounted, leading the horse, calling the dogs to him so he could ruffle the heavy ears and coarse coats. They wagged tails like axe handles. He stepped into the frigid shallows to scoop up water and splash his face, then threw a stick for the dogs. They carefully followed its arc and then turned wide, unbelieving eyes on him. He would have sworn they were shocked. For the first time, he understood exactly what they were. Companions, even friends, they weren't pets. If he wanted them to go get the stick and bring it back, that could be arranged, they seemed to say, but condescending games were best left for *mere* dogs.

Conway bowed from the waist. "My error, sir. And madam. Let us all be patient with each other, shall we?"

He patted their heads. They wagged tails again. All was forgiven.

After a drink, he rode downstream. Occasionally the form of the riverbank required they either forge through the brush or pick their way through the shallows. The horse particularly enjoyed the latter, prancing and smacking hooves down through the rippling surface to clash on the submerged rocks.

Once they saw a huge salmon roll, the polished silver back and shining dorsal fin startling. It was gone in an instant, a silent notice that soon the small river would be a ferment of breeding activity. Thousands of fish would strain upstream to the spawning beds. Conway was sure it was no coincidence that they discovered bear sign soon afterward. Huge pigeon-toed tracks in a muddy stretch of bank sent a quick chill up his spine. It was something of a relief to him to see the way the dogs also bristled. They sniffed the prints, growling softly. When they resumed their progress downstream, Karda dropped behind and angled off, keeping to cover. Nearly every time Conway checked, the big male was practically slinking along through the brush. Mikka held place between Karda and her master.

The proximity of the bear was still strongly on Conway's mind when he heard something. The dogs were troubled. Every few steps, one or the other stopped, cocking its head from side to side, fixing the direction. Conway's first impulse was to dismiss the sound as a bird's call, but as they advanced, the notes resolved into the haunting song of a flute. The music swelled and faded, a partner to every breeze, an eerily ventriloquial effect. Conway smiled at the puzzlement of the dogs. Their heads swiveled constantly, always returning to him for expected instructions.

Conway pressed forward slowly, until he realized with a start he was at the edge of a carefully tended grove of very old willows. At the same time, he saw movement, back away from the riverbank. Dismounting in order to see under the thicket of thrusting new growth, he watched a black-clad figure wander among the thick trunks. Her aimless wandering through the interfering growth explained the ghostly distortions of her song. Conway stood entranced. The small figure stopped abruptly. When she whirled to face him, she threw back the cowl to stare with wide, dark eyes. She clutched the flute in front of her with both hands, as if to parry a blow.

Conway waved, feeling clumsy. "I know you, Priestess Lanta. I didn't mean to frighten you."

Her laughter was nervous. "I know you, Matt Conway. I didn't expect anyone else to be out here."

Instinctively, he knew he shouldn't enter the grove. He took a step backward as he explained his presence. She came forward to join him outside the boundaries. When he complimented her playing, she blushed, quickly shifting the conversation to the grove and its purpose, pointing out the spring in the distance, with its adjoining small healing house. Both facilities were outside the limits of the willows, confirming Conway's impression of a sanctified site.

In unspoken accord, they retreated to the riverbank. The dogs loitered behind. They seemed uneasy. There had been no more bear sign. Conway wondered if they were too young for this sort of experience, but before he could dwell on the matter, Lanta was saying, "I come here as often as I can. There's no place so peaceful. I can just walk. Be by myself."

"And play your flute."

She colored again, gesturing with the instrument. Conway reached for it, and she let it go. It was of walnut, the holes artfully rimmed with silver. The mouthpiece was an inset ivory oval. Wire-thin silver inlay vined round and round the instrument's length, and there were beautifully carved tiny amethysts set into the very end of the piece, creating a ring of violets.

Returning the instrument, Conway said, "It's almost as beautiful as the music you make with it. It must be very soothing to be able to walk alone in this grove, hearing only your own thoughts, your own music. I wish I could."

She smiled. There was a layer of reserve immediately behind it. Conway thought of her song, melodiously light, yet achingly sad. She said, "That's an interesting coincidence. I was thinking of you galloping on your horse, working with your dogs. All of you a team, enjoying companionship without complications. I wish I could do that."

Side by side, they walked farther downstream. The river was wider here, flat; Conway skipped a rock across the surface. He said, "Seeing must be a terrible burden."

"We don't speak of it."

Ignoring her stiffness, he said, "Just as well. It doesn't seem to work."

"What?" She stopped, glaring. "You doubt?"

He grinned down at the small fury before him. "I was only thinking that if you knew the future, you'd have known I was going to bring up the Seeing, and you'd have warned me not to. Or gone somewhere else today. Or something. We could have avoided the whole thing."

Watching her features go from anger to disbelief almost made him laugh again, but he controlled it. She said, "You're joking. About the Seeing. No one does that."

"It's time someone did, then. Too much seriousness is as deadly as carelessness. I know. Tell me, how's it work? Do you see events, or what?"

Still a bit in shock, Lanta answered readily. "Words. I see words, all in flames. They tell me."

"Is that why you were allowed to learn to read?"

She nodded. "Priestesses are allowed. I was given special help."

"You can't control it, can you? I mean, you can't avoid it."

"True. I can almost always bring it. We have a way. I hate to use it. Sometimes it comes by itself, though." She shivered, closed her eyes for a moment. Her expression afterward was studiously composed. She asked, "You aren't afraid of Seeing? Do you have it?"

"No, no; not me. I'm not afraid of it, but I'm glad I don't have it. Seems like a lot of responsibility. If I did have it, though, I'd be the richest gambler you ever saw."

She laughed. Happily. For a moment the veil of separation that always cloaked her was torn. Nevertheless, it was back even as she was tapping him playfully on the shoulder with the flute. She said, "No one's ever teased me about the Seeing. They fear. I think you'd laugh at a curse as easily as a blessing."

"It's especially important to laugh at the curses. It steals their power."

The levity was gone instantly. Her eyes rounded, and she made a rapid three-sign. "Be careful, Matt Conway. There are powers . . ."

At first he meant to joke. Her concern was too genuine, too deep, for that. Instead, he said, "The only powers I truly fear come from other people. When it's my turn for bad luck, magic won't be any part of it."

For a long moment, she held his gaze, and then she broke off and turned away, headed back the way they'd come. He followed, waiting for her to reopen the conversation. They were at the edge of the grove before she did. Keeping her eyes fixed on the far shore, she said, "I will tell you a thing, Matt Conway. Not as a Seer. As another person. A woman. I've watched you since Altanar first brought you to Ola. You came here a man without a purpose. Now you want a goal, but you don't know what it is. You chase yourself through the mists of fate."

"You're very sure of yourself."

"Of course. Every woman knows how to use a mirror." She stepped into the grove, then turned to face him. The delicate features were unrevealing as stone. With a quick move, she pulled her cowl forward, and it was as if she disappeared entirely. She turned away with a slow, lingering grace. His last view of her was of a shapeless black figure gliding in and out of sight among the gnarled trunks.

Her soft, trembling music followed him back upstream, fading until no effort of concentration would bring him another note.

Across the river, well back in the trees, the Harvester and a spade-bearded man in metal-barred leather armor sat on horses and watched Conway's progress. The woman spoke. "Are you going to let him ride away?"

The man said, "The ones who followed him are in position, Harvester." He waved.

An answering wave came from the brush on the opposite bank, upstream between Conway and the waterfall.

Turning back to the Harvester, the man said, "We can leave now."

"Not yet."

"They're going to kill him. You don't want—"

She rounded on him, yet her expression was soft, undisturbed. "Never, *never* presume to tell me what I want, Baron. It's quite rude. And possibly dangerous, if you take my point. I'm not one of your affrighted little Olan chickens. I rode out here to see the Matt Conway one die. And so I shall."

CHAPTER 13

It was Mikka's odd behavior that brought Conway out of his preoccupation. He was following a relatively straight stretch of the river, and the grizzled female had ranged far ahead. Karda was halfway between her and Conway. Suddenly, Mikka was in full flight back downstream. Rocks flew up behind her from the force of her effort. Karda joined her retreat as she came abreast of him. Together they raced to take positions on Conway's flanks. By then the horse was jerking its head up and down, snorting heavily.

The first arrow came from the brush to their rear. It fell short, steel head clashing against rocks, striking sparks. Mikka stepped aside nimbly as the second came at her. It hit the stones, clattering to a stop at the water's edge.

Conway rose in his stirrups and turned that way. He held his hands over his head, forefingers and thumbs joined in the universally understood sign of the sun, the peace symbol. "Don't shoot!" he shouted. "Who are you?"

Unspeaking, an armored man carrying a stubby, recurved bow rode out from the bushes. He carried an arrow in the same hand. Upstream, two more men trotted into sight around the bend.

The lone man notched the arrow, drew it back.

"No!" Conway whirled to face him. "What're you doing? I'm not—"

Before he could finish—or dodge—he heard a hot sound, as if someone were broiling bacon in a very hot pan. Something plucked at his jacket. His side burned. He looked down at the ripped cloth, watched it grow bright red. The wound was immediately above where his pistol should have been. If he'd worn it.

Thunder rolled through Conway's head. All his frustrations, his uncertainties, his depression, focused on this moment, this identifiable source of *challenge*.

Wind rushed in Conway's face as he charged. He flung himself to the side, saw the flicker of the arrow where he'd been an instant before.

The growing fear in the bowman's eyes was like a beacon. Conway drew his knife from its scabbard at his calf and came upright in the saddle. The blade was a foot long, made of a complex steel alloy unknown on earth for half a millennium. It was a full quarter-inch thick, with a dished nose. The inside curve and the cutting length gleamed bright with sharpening. The five-inch handle filled his hand. Every morning he shaved with the weapon. He'd never used it in anger.

His attacker dropped his bow, stood upright in the stirrups, a sword in hand. As Conway closed, his opponent struck in a sweeping, ground-paralleling blow. Conway fell back, flat along the horse's back. The blade blurred above him. The impact of Conway's own counterstrike nearly pulled the knife out of his grip.

Skidding to a halt, the war-horse reared into a full turn.

The bowman clutched at the junction of leg and torso, just below his armor. Arterial blood fountained between his fingers.

The dogs hit him simultaneously from the same side. Combined mass and speed tumbled him out of the saddle and into a thrashing mess. The echoes of the man's final, horrified cry were already sighing from the forest across the river before Conway could call them off. He replaced his knife and scooped up the dead man's sword. The other two riders galloped toward him, iron-shod hooves sparking on the stones.

On whistled command, the dogs engaged the rider closest to the river. Conway shouted to his mount to attack. Teeth bared, it screamed its own challenge. Crouched low, Conway presented the sword like a lance.

Armor deflected Conway's sword point. In return, he took a blow across his chest. Dazed, he slumped in his saddle. Cold fear knotted his guts at the sight of his jacket sliced open, his whole front sodden from chest to crotch. The sword dangled from weakening, shocked fingers. He wasn't sure he could raise it again.

The horse saved him. It had been commanded to attack, and it was the order it was bred for. Whirling, it struck at its enemies. The other animal was never trained to withstand such fury. It reared, defended itself, effectively destroying its rider's ability to fight.

When his opponent's mount fell, dismounting him, Conway found the strength to lean outward and thrust. Through a mist of red, he parried a blow, thrust again. Then there was a twitching body on the ground. He rode to assist his dogs.

The last man had taken his mount belly-deep into the river. The maneuver escaped the dogs; it kept him out of the fight. Conway gathered strength to go after him. With one last look at the raging hounds, the man sheathed his weapon. He raised his hands, made the peace sign.

Conway was dizzy. He dismounted gingerly. The shock of the knee-deep cold water sent a burst of renewed energy through him. It lasted only a moment. He wished he'd stayed mounted.

Leaning against his horse, he ordered the dogs to get back and be quiet so he could hear. Something downstream caught his eye. Lanta. Running. Too late, he thought. By the time she gets here, this one'll be as dead as his friends. But first I need answers.

Part of his mind told him that what he planned was barbaric, unforgivable. The part he heard most clearly said he was entitled to whatever vengeance he could effect.

"Who sent you? Why?" The words rang like metal. Echoed. Odd.

"Baron Steelarm, subject of King Altanar of Ola."

"Impossible. Steelarm ran south, into the Empty Lands between here and Kos; one of their patrols got him and all his people."

"He lives. Many of us with him. We're bandits now."

"Why try to kill me?" The man seemed to drift shoreward, then back out into the river. A function of the sun on the water, Conway decided. Still, it wouldn't hurt to be alert for tricks. He looped an arm through the stirrup. Just for a little extra support. The chest was hurting more, a heavy sort of ache. Had he seen Lanta? He glanced downstream. She was still there. Closer. That was good. He looked down. The water around his feet was bloody. She was probably going to be upset.

The man was saying, ". . . the Door. The Baron said kill you and the Black Lightning, because you're her main support. Please, that's all I know."

"Drop your sword. Get off the horse. Come here." Now the words were mushy. Where'd the metallic echo go?

The man cocked his head. He seemed to be scrutinizing Conway, but his words were placating as the horse edged shoreward. "You won't kill me? I'm throwing away the sword. I'm your prisoner." He drew the weapon. And charged, war cry rising.

Conway's horse reared in response. The stirrup jerked Conway almost off his feet. From the corner of his eye, he saw the dogs hurtle past. The rider's sword swept down, struck Conway's horse. Conway threw his sword as hard as he could, and then he was being trampled, flung aside.

Unbearable weight bore him down. Water—icy, black—swept over him. He couldn't breathe, couldn't call out.

It hurt to move. He *had* to move. He was drowning.

Drowned.

The world turned red. Black.

Empty.

Lanta swept past the confused, threatening dogs as if they didn't exist. More from surprise than comprehension, they permitted her to wrestle their coughing, gagging master from under the dead man and drag him ashore.

Stiff-legged, Karda advanced to look down on the body. He snarled and crouched as a wave nudged it into the current. The sword jutting from the throat glittered in the sun until the water deepened, and then the body rolled facedown. It was gaining speed as Lanta went to work on Conway.

His breathing was very shallow. The pulse at his neck fluttered.

With his knife, she slit his rough woolen shirt to expose his wounds. The arrow had cut deeply, but no organs were affected. The slash across his upper body was uglier. The flesh hung open like obscene lips, and where the heavy blade struck hardest, it broke two ribs.

His eyelids twitched, popped open. He wore a startled, foolish look. Lanta was as taken aback by her own reaction as by his sudden consciousness. Exasperation. Relief. She wanted to tongue-lash him until he cringed. She never got the chance. As clearly as if he were making ordinary conversation, he said, "Fix the horse first." Then his eyes rolled back in his head. Her hand flew to pull the lids over the terrible emptiness of the naked whites.

She had no needle, no thread, no way to treat him against the dangers of dirt creatures and unseens. Rinsing his shirt in the river, she used it to bind the wounds.

More treatment was necessary. If she left him alone to get equipment, there was great danger. The small black bears wouldn't confront the dogs, but one of the great silverbacks wouldn't hesitate. Wolves prowled these forests. Tigers.

Taking the sword, she rushed to the brushy growth edging the beach. It took a while for her to find what she wanted, but she managed to put together a two-pole litter. Clothes and belts from the two dead attackers provided the carrying platform between the poles and lashings to hold them to Conway's horse. Straining, almost weeping with exhaustion and the pain of soft hands blistered raw from wielding the sword as an axe, she managed to get him onto the litter.

She scrabbled into the saddle. The horse, as if understanding the situation, waited patiently for her. Under way, he behaved as gently as an old plowhorse. The dogs flanked their master, frequently edging close to sniff at the bandages.

When they reached the grove, Lanta bathed his wounds at the spring. There was ointment in the healing house, pine resin infused with extract of willow bark and garlic oil. Opening the jar's beeswax seal sent the dogs away sneezing and rubbing their noses in the dirt. Lanta rather liked the zest; she smeared her patient lavishly. The medicine eased pain. Sometimes it actually eliminated infections. Bandages from a cedar cabinet replaced the ruined shirt, which she unceremoniously dumped in the nearby latrine.

Her gaze fell on the horse. It watched her. Its shoulder and foreleg glistened red. The huge brown eyes accused. Sighing, she led it to the spring, where she soon had his wound cleaned and treated with the same salve.

With all that done, she checked Conway's pulse again, and was pleased to note it was stronger. His bleeding was stopped, and his breathing seemed easier. Pallor still lay on his features.

She elected to walk beside Conway as they left. He grew agitated as he jounced along. Lanta was glad she'd had the foresight to lash him down. Shortly, he was trying to shout, his features taking on some color as they contorted in alternating expressions of fear and anger. He was so weak it all came out as loud muttering. Lanta bent to him to listen.

He was speaking language, but not exactly *correctly*. Some words she was sure she'd never heard before, in any guise; they were nonsense things. What could "gi-ger counter" mean? Did he count gi-gers in his home country? And what did it mean when he said "Everyone! Quick! The bomb shelter!" What was a bomb? Why was it so important to shelter one?

The demanding question was, Why did he talk with such a distorted accent? Most of it was completely unintelligible.

As suddenly as he'd started to babble, he fell silent. Lanta was dumbfounded to see tears easing under his tightly closed eyelids. The silent grief was unnerving.

She wondered what could have driven him to leave his lands. Something so strong he couldn't deny it. Or refuse. Orders?

She studied his features. Nothing particularly distinguishing. Except character. Even now, he had an air of quiet determination.

Widely spaced eyes; that was a plus, especially when they were bright with amusement. She remembered how he'd teased her about the Seeing. Like a mischievous boy. He'd gone too far, though, mocking the unknown powers.

Still and all, he had a considerable attraction. His long journey with the other strangers probably had its roots in some man–woman conflict. Lanta imagined the thin-faced nagging female that made his life miserable.

At least the slave girl, Tee, treated him well. Before she left. Some people never knew when they were well off.

Lanta wished she knew more about his people, the background he and his friends were so secretive about. There was a natural kindness and consideration in him that she'd never seen before. Some said it was effeminate. If they'd seen this morning's work, they'd know better. As she did.

How was it that she felt she knew him well, when in truth she knew hardly anything about him? Very contradictory.

She brushed his hair back where a sheen of perspiration slicked it to his forehead, then rearranged the chest bandage. His breathing was slower. His muscles were butter-soft. She smelled the sweat lingering on her fingertips. The bitter tang was a bad sign, but the musty, thick undertone dismayed her. It was a scent that grew stronger and stronger on her diseased patients as death tightened its grip.

Sylah was selfish, thoughtless, even to consider letting him join in her search for the Door. This attack proved that.

Sudden, improper burning touched the back of her eyes. She hurried to climb into the surprised horse's saddle, urging more speed. She wouldn't cry. A Healer learned not to weep for her charges; the good died as readily as the evil.

A pudgy little bird flitted onto a branch just ahead. Russet-breasted, with a dark collar, it cocked its head, peering at Lanta from a bright eye surmounted by a pale stripe like an oversized brow. Its two-note call was a lonely, lilting minor, almost unbearably sweet.

That was when Lanta's tears came.

CHAPTER 14

The Harvester's horse staggered to a halt in the courtyard when she heaved back on the reins. The bit cut cruelly, but the animal was so near collapse it offered no protest. As she slipped to the ground, the horse shuddered, spreading its legs, dropping its head. A wide-eyed boy ran from the stables. The Harvester glared at him, seemed ready to speak, then wheeled to enter the building that included Sylah's quarters. The boy watched until she was safely out of sight before turning back to the horse. Soapy sweat lathered its coat. The thick veins on the belly and muzzle throbbed.

At the sound of the Harvester's voice, the boy jumped like a rabbit.

"Don't stand there, you lazy scum! Have two fresh horses here by the time I come back with Rose Priestess Sylah, or I'll have the living meat flogged off your worthless back. *Run!*"

Gone before he could move, her words hung in the air. When the stunned boy could react, he sprinted, yelling for the stablemaster.

The Harvester flung open the door to Sylah's room and strode in.

To emptiness.

Unbelieving, pale, the tall woman stood as if frozen. Slowly, woodenly, she turned her head, unwilling to accept what her eyes told her.

Sylah was gone.

Head back, mouth agape, the Harvester closed her throat against the scream of rage searing her throat. First Conway. Now this. Her deserved reward for so much careful planning, for all her travels and bold action. Gone. How? *Where?*

Picking up a chair, she sent it spinning across the room to smash the cedar chest. Crockery and utensils spilled out of the broken doors. There was solace in the destruction. The Harvester picked up the fire poker, raised it like a club. Slowly, breast heaving, she lowered it, leaned on it.

Think, she told herself. Even if Lanta keeps Conway alive and they reach help, there's still time to find Sylah. And escape.

The Harvester ran down the stairs, back into the courtyard. The boy was just leading two saddled mounts to the hitching rail. When the Harvester flew out the door, he stopped in his tracks. The animals tossed their heads in nervous sympathy.

Ignoring all of that, the Harvester rushed to grab the boy by the shirt. "Sylah," she said, and was aware of the rasping demand in the single word. She released him, spoke slowly. Pleasantly. "Did you see Rose Priestess Sylah leave?"

The boy nodded, mouth open.

"How long ago? Which way did she go? Was she with anyone?"

Sweating, the boy made sounds. The Harvester ached with the need to beat intelligible words out of him. Sweetly, she said, "I frightened you before, didn't I? I was afraid for her. Just another silly woman; you know how excitable and helpless we are. Please, help me. Tell me what you saw."

Not completely reassured, the boy said, "She left just before you rode in. That way. By herself. Like every day."

The Harvester straightened, closed her eyes. Every day. She repeated the words in her head, cursing herself. What had she told Sylah? "Behave exactly as you always do." And what did Sylah do every day? She visited Tate.

The Harvester snatched the reins and swung into the saddle. The woolen half-trousers under the robe were still damp from her previous ride. She gritted her teeth at the clammy contact and swatted her mount's rump, jerking the riderless horse along behind her.

The door to Tate's room was open. Sylah stood with her back to it. A Chosen stood in the hallway. One look, one gesture from the Harvester, and the child was running away.

Tate's husking voice was saying, "I don' unnerstand. Never seen you like this. You still upset over what that old woman said, aren't you? Foolish. You, and the old Iris Abbess, you stood up to Altanar. Set things up so women of the Three Territories have some rights, and so the li'l Chosens all learn to read. More than old Harvester ever did. If was me, tell her what to do. So should you." Exertion brought her breath in labored gusts.

The Harvester concentrated on Sylah. From behind, she watched with excitement and mingled amazement as Sylah's sleek, black hair swayed and trembled as she fought against the mind controls. In the end, the answer was acceptable, if stiff. "The Harvester is Church, and Church must be obeyed. I am sworn to Mother, the Healer."

Tate's rough whisper was worried. "That's second time you told me that 'sworn' thing. I said before, that's no answer at all. What is *wrong* with you?"

"Oh, there you are." The Harvester swept into the room, linked a proprietary arm with Sylah's unresponsive one. Turning, moving a bit forward, the Harvester looked back into Sylah's face. The features were slack, pallid. The lips were dry and cracked. Only her eyes were alive, and they were frenetic. Constantly in motion, pupils dilated, they contradicted everything else about the woman.

Such resistance, such strength. The Harvester was sick with disappointment that she couldn't share this accomplishment with someone. To Tate, she said, "Poor dear. She's been under a terrible strain. Would you mind if I took her back to her quarters? She needs rest; some hot soup. Perhaps massage."

Tate squinted her one good eye, trying to see more clearly. Formally, she said, "I know you, Harvester. She need help?"

"Help." Sylah repeated the word, less than a whisper. To the Harvester, it was thunder. It was impossible.

Tate twisted her features even tighter. "What? You say something, Sylah?"

"She's so weak," the Harvester said. "She agreed with you."

"Agreed what? I asked her—"

"And she answered you. If you could see better, you'd know how weak she looks."

"Don't have to see. Sick because you brought her trouble. Sylah, you want to go home, go. You don't, you stay here with me."

Tate coughed. The Harvester stepped in front of Sylah, turned her back on the woman in bed. Hands on Sylah's shoulders, she said, "Tate's right. You decide. Look at me. *Look at me*, and tell us what you must do."

Ignoring the rustle of the bedclothes as Tate squirmed about behind her, the Harvester kept her gaze fastened on Sylah's frenzied eyes. Little by little, they slowed. The Harvester thought of caged birds battering themselves into stupor. As Sylah sagged, leaning her weight into the hands bracing her shoulders, the Harvester spoke again. "Tell us, Sylah. Say what you know is true."

A freshet of sweat suddenly poured down Sylah's face, slicked her hair to her temples and forehead. Almost imperceptibly, she pulled back from the Harvester's touch, forcing the older woman to stretch to maintain it. Sylah's words were a groan. "I am sworn to Mother, the Healer. I obey." Then she blinked. "Help," she repeated.

Behind the Harvester, Tate was too agitated to ignore any longer. As the Harvester turned to face the injured woman, she said, "I'm taking Sylah home. As her friend, as well as a Healer, I know what's best for her."

"Friend," Sylah said. Jerkily, she turned to Tate. "Friend."

Tate said, "Call Chosen. Give you a hand, take Sylah healing house."

"An excellent idea. Yes. But there's no need. Anyhow, the Chosen seems to be missing." As she spoke, the Harvester linked arms with Sylah again, edging her toward the door.

Sylah resisted. "Friend help," she said.

"That does it." Tate worked a bandaged hand free of the covering blanket, pointed at the Harvester. "We all wait for Chosen."

The Harvester examined Tate. The good eye watered copiously. When Tate moved the pointing finger to wipe it, the hand shook.

"We wait for nothing." Saying it felt as good as song. "There are great things to be done. You'll not interfere. Sylah is mine. Mine to command, mine to use. She will seek the Door. For me. For the greater glory of Church."

Edging closer to Tate, the Harvester smiled at the way the injured woman cowered, seeking the farthest edge of the bed. The other, the Conway one, might survive, thanks to the ineptitude of idiots. This Tate one could snarl defiance, but not escape. From inside a voluminous sleeve, the Harvester drew a shortknife. Softly, caressingly, she said, "The Apocalypse Testament warns that we must resist evil. I'll pray for your misguided soul."

Tate said, "Best look before leap, old woman. See what's under blanket."

A pointed mound rose at Tate's right side. A vigorous move, and a blue-black metal thing slid free of the covers. There was a hole in the end of it, and it sought the Harvester like a malevolent eye. Tate said, "Drop knife. Back off."

The Harvester smiled. "Is that one of your lightning weapons? It doesn't impress. Kill me, and all Church will avenge me. You know that."

Tate smiled back. Bruises turned it into an ugly burlesque. "You dead, for sure. Maybe I just blow away arm? Or both arms? What then? You want tell people what you did Sylah? How 'bout it—death before dishonor? Your pick."

With great dignity, the Harvester handled the knife back up her sleeve. Arms folded, she backed toward the door. Sylah watched her with the vacant stare of mindlessness.

Tate struggled up to one elbow. "Hold it." The attempt to shout set off explosive coughing. The pistol jerked about like something on the end of a wind-whipped branch.

The Harvester clutched Sylah's waist from behind, dragged her toward the door. "You can't even cry for help. Unleash your lightning, if you dare."

Gasping with pain, Tate forced herself to a sitting position. She extended the pistol in both hands. "Sylah?" she called. "Sylah! Fight!"

Tears of frustration blinded Tate completely. Sounds of struggle came to her. Muffled, terrible sounds. Tate wiped her eye on her shoulder. For a heartbeat the front sight post was clear, a tiny black tombstone. Swimming above it, Sylah's face. Wet with sweat. Expressionless.

Tate swung the pistol to the side of that face. Squeezed the trigger.

In the stone confines of the room, the report was like being inside thunder. The bullet ricocheted with a mad scream, struck another wall, changed its tone to a wolflike howl. A human screamed.

And then silence.

Finally, Tate found the courage to call. "Sylah? Sylah, you there? God's sake, answer me. Please!"

Crying. Brokenhearted sobs. "Here, my friend." The crying went on. Tate struggled to get up, fell back.

Sylah came to her. They embraced, sharing tears. Sylah said, "What happened? I feel empty. As if I died. But I'm alive. I know you gave me my life, but I don't understand how. What happened to me?"

"It's all right," Tate soothed. "We're all right. Where she— Harvester?"

"She's gone. There's blood. *Blood?* The *Harvester*? What have I done, Donnacee? Our souls. What have I done?"

CHAPTER 15

"I'm telling you, he's here. The boy's alive, and he's in Ola." The setting sun painted the small courtyard with a dim, fireplace glow that deepened the lines of bafflement at the corners of Tate's eyes. Muscles bunched in her jaws.

Anxious to avoid antagonizing her friend, Sylah affected a

calmness she no longer felt. Their small benches faced each other, and she turned sideways on hers, anxious to compromise Tate's confrontational posture.

Tate's physical healing was coming well. Both eyes functioned as well as ever, her voice was back, albeit still a trifle husky. There seemed to be no lingering effects. Except in her mind. It was inner disturbance that troubled Sylah.

The root of the problem was the fight on the dock. Sylah had seen similar reactions to a death-fight. For many, it burned their minds the way farmers burned their marks on the flanks of cattle. Some hungered ever after to relive the mad thrill or were haunted by what they'd done. A smaller number became haters. Or visionaries.

Sylah couldn't identify the exact change in Tate, but she feared it. Since the fight, her friend's attention drew ever closer to that single subject. Losing the boy practically dominated Tate's conversation. She even treated the incident with the Harvester as a minor matter.

That disturbed Sylah more than she dared admit. The minimal concern for religion displayed by Tate and the rest of the strangers was one thing. To deliberately wound a Church leader, a Harvester, was a vast sin. The local abbeys were rent with argument over it. No one argued the Harvester's guilt; not everyone agreed Tate had a right to interfere, much less use force. The Harvester's successful flight dampened some of the passion in the Three Territories. What would happen when the woman reached Kos and Church Home to relate her version of events was too dismaying to dwell on.

At least she and Conway were healing well. Conway. There was another complication, another reaction to excitement. Sylah carried one central image of him, his hand resting on the bandages on his chest. There was something possessive about the way he did it. That was all she needed, she thought sourly; a man who'd go out of his way to find combat, rather than avoid it. Worse, the general consensus, from Gan down to the average Wolf, was that Conway had been lucky beyond belief. Good fortune made a sorry platform for a warrior to stand on.

Tate had fallen into a sulky silence. Rather than intrude on it, Sylah pretended interest in the courtyard. Conway had introduced her to it. At any other time, it would be a welcome haven, with its walled-in solitude, waterfall, and pool.

A hummingbird appeared. Swift, erratic, utterly confident of its aerial mastery, it was a welcome distraction. Shining green, it made her think of a wet, storm-thrown leaf. When it faced the sun, the incredible amethyst gorget on its chest blazed a retort. Magically, it whirred from flower to flower, hiding its fiery jewel and then exposing it in a game that defied her eyes to keep pace.

Tate broke the silence to drive her argument forward. "I know you and Conway think I'm crazy, but I'm sure the boy came to me when I was still in bed. There were a lot of dreams; I admit that. But I know I woke up once in the night, and he was standing there looking down at me. He stayed until I had to close my eyes, and when I opened them again, he was gone."

"Surely, though, you see why I have trouble accepting what you say. The castle's guarded day and night, inside as well as out. No one—I mean, no one else—has seen the boy since that first day. I *want* to believe you . . ." Sylah's voice trailed off in apology.

"But you don't." Waving away Sylah's attempt to respond, Tate continued, "He'll come. He's afraid, that's all."

Nodding a bit too eagerly, Sylah said, "That must be it. He's so small. Everything's so strange. He'd want to be sure of his welcome."

"Welcome? I fought for him."

"And for me. What would have happened to me without your belief in me?"

"You'd have been all right. That old hag drugged you."

"She meant to take me away with her. She did something to my mind. I had to do what she said. Say what she told me to say. I can't get her out of my head." Suddenly, Sylah felt weak. It had happened before. When she thought of the Harvester fouling her dreams, controlling her life, nausea swept her. Oddly, she felt a surge of strength at the same time. It was as if mind and body were erecting inner barriers. This time, however, Tate was there immediately, steadying her. Leaning on her friend, Sylah said, "You see, I do understand. Things happen to us all, things we can't explain."

Tate looked shocked. "That's it. Same thing. I mean, I can see; he's not a pretty child. But there's something there."

"It's like the Door. People hate me for wanting it, think I'm crazy. But just when I'm ready to agree with them, it's as if I can hear the Iris Abbess, supporting me, telling me I mustn't give up. And I *want* to go."

Shaking her head, Tate laughed softly. "We're a pair, we are. Couple of weirdos."

"Weirdo? What a perfect word." Sylah hugged her.

93

Tate pulled away gently, went back to her bench, worried that the dishonesty in her thoughts might show in her face. There was no way to explain to Sylah that she believed the boy offered a link to the world where that "perfect word" died at least five centuries ago.

A world that threw her up here, a total misfit.

Her inadequacy shamed her. Not one of the crèche survivors had the practical expertise to re-create algebra, calculus, geometry. Who'd needed any of that, when computers knew it all and used it with such efficiency? Of all the people to survive the cryogenic crèche, only Leclerc had any mechanical skills. They all understood that if Leclerc "invented" too much too fast, he'd be accused of witchcraft. He'd already reproduced black powder and coke ovens; everyone respected him. But when he walked by, mothers hid their children, making surreptitious three-signs and mumbling prayers.

So here was Donnacee Tate, world-class loser. Twice. With an obsession.

Sylah broke in on Tate's brooding. "What if the boy blames himself for what happened? Maybe he's afraid you blame him too."

"I should have thought of that. I wish I could just talk to him for a minute, reassure him."

"Be patient. Try not to become too upset." The words were clumsy with the concern that tries to mask doubt.

Suddenly, Tate stiffened. Her fists jerked to her breast. Her gaze, directed past Sylah, took on feverish intensity. Sylah knew better than to move. Fear insisted she turn, but an even stronger force told her to let Tate dictate the action.

"Don't go," Tate said.

When Tate's expression and position remained unchanged, Sylah understood that a crisis had passed. She turned slowly, taking her cue from Tate's caution.

The boy greeted her with a steady stare. The last horizontal rays of the sun gave his eyes a strange luminosity.

Tate almost choked. "Don't run away! We won't hurt you. I won't let anyone hurt you. I want to talk to you." She stepped away from Sylah, extended hands that pleaded to touch him. "How'd you get here?"

"There's a place over there where you can climb over. It's easy." His small gesture reminded Sylah of the hummingbird's swiftness. His shirt and shorts were worse than before, rags hanging from the bone-rack body. "Are you angry? My master hurt you worse than he ever hurt me. Your friends saw what happened. They'll beat me, give me back to him."

"Never. You're free. And I need your help."

"Me?" Disbelieving, he retreated. Tate leaned forward, desperately trying to regain the distance. Sylah stepped aside. The movement sent him into a tense crouch. Despite the facial expression that gave every evidence of apprehension and a posture that was a readiness to flee, Sylah had no *sense* of fear.

Tate advanced, continuing to speak soothingly. With his attention focused on her friend, Sylah again felt that what she saw contradicted what was actually happening. Try as she might, she couldn't rid herself of the sensation that he stalked Tate. It made her irritable, and she chided herself: What harm could there be in such a small, skinny child? He was a living definition of helplessness.

Tate reached to touch his head, stroked the tangled hair. His eyes flicked toward Sylah. Tate saw it. She said, "Sylah's my very good friend. She likes you, just like I do."

The boy's head moved in a small negative shake. "None of them do. I'm just a slave. They like you. They don't like me."

Tate said, "Now that's not so. Don't ever call yourself a slave again. You're free. And even if you weren't, all my friends would still like you."

"No. Promise you won't let them hurt me."

"Of course I promise, because they don't want to hurt you. They want to help you. We all do."

Again, he looked to Sylah. "Will you help me?" It was more challenge than request. Sylah's skin tightened, as at the touch of a dank wind. Bumps rose on her arms. Choosing her words deliberately, she said, "The friend of my friend will always have my help."

Nodding, the boy faced Tate again. "I wanted to come to you. You were brave. My master wanted to kill you. He's killed other people. I saw."

Tate lowered her hand to his shoulder, and he shied out of reach. "My name is Tate," she said, "and this is Sylah. She's a War Healer, a Rose Priestess."

He nodded. "A Chosen," he said, and Sylah stiffened. Hinted contempt oozed in the words, a reminder that she, too, knew about being used like any other utensil.

"That's right." Sylah meant to continue, but he cut her off, turning away with cool dismissal to face Tate once more. "And you're Donnacee Tate, one of Gan Moondark's Six Strangers.

They call you the Black Lightning. The Matt Conway one they call the White Thunder."

"Well." Tate was a bit taken aback. She recovered quickly. "How did you learn so much about us?"

"Old women will always feed a hungry boy. If you listen to their silly gossip, they feed you more. And talk more."

"Learned to use your wits, haven't you?" Tate laughed. "To-night, though, it's you who'll do the talking. What's your name?"

"Which one? Masters gave me names. Called me names." His lips were full and sensuous in the thin, pointed face. They made an empty smile.

"The first one you had."

"Dodoy."

Tate jerked. She reached to put her hand on Dodoy's shoulder. He made no effort to avoid her this time. Tate's voice remained calm. "There's a familiar sound to that. Were you here in the castle? When I was ill?"

His laughter was high-pitched, harsh. "I thought the guards would kill me today, just getting here. Inside?" He laughed again.

To Sylah, Tate said, "I have to get him something to eat, some better clothes," and led him away without looking to see if Sylah followed.

Dodoy looked, however. With Tate's guiding hand still on his shoulder, he turned to peer past her arm. His face was coldly in-animate, the eyes like closed doors. Still, she knew she was being warned that he was a factor in her life now.

CHAPTER 16

Tate marveled at the change in Kate Bernhardt, Sue Anspach, and Janet Carter. They wore their Church dress with apparent ease. Her friends had clearly made their peace with this environment.

Everything in their manner spoke of fulfillment; in Carter's case, that was little short of miraculous. Tate still smiled when she thought of the fiery Carter as a teacher of small children. Yet she loved it, as did Anspach. Bernhardt was an agronomist, was im-mersed in the uses of the land. She was already famous among the locals—and any travelers who came her way—for her ques-tions and voluminous notes. She was respected for what she could teach farmers. What endeared her to them was her ability to learn from them, and spread knowledge wherever she went.

As they settled into chairs in the castle's conference room, Tate's major emotion was sorrow. She wished the three of them understood her.

Even in their own world, they were women who were uncomfortable with the notion of female warriors. Tate knew she'd projected herself out of their circle. She mourned the loss of her friends' closeness. But there was no turning back.

Donnacee Tate had also made her peace with this environment. Only, in her case, it was more like war.

Ironically, they all sought the same things. The other three, as women who'd lived in a world where they expected and demanded equality, brought to their new life as much activism as was practical. Their influence extended throughout Gan's domain, largely because they were his official link with the wives of his soldiers. They acted as the business managers for the weaving, pottery, and leatherwork that came from those women's cooperative factories. Already, women in towns and villages were starting similar factories.

That had been Tate's function, once. Hers and Sylah's when they lived in Jalail, creating the units now called the Wolves. It had hurt to watch the other three take over more and more of her functions dealing with the wives. At least she'd avoided the confrontation on the matter of male orphans.

Tate was there the day the trio presented their requisitions for food, housing, and care personnel; Gan approved everything. Except for the disposition of orphaned boys. He declared them ward of the Three Territories until sixteen years of age, when they'd serve in the army in some capacity until twenty-four. They were free to exit to civilian life then, if they chose.

In spite of her anger over Gan's arbitrary and unreasonable attitude, Tate had truly enjoyed seeing Janet Carter's temper explode. Just like old times.

Later, there had been secretive mutterings among the four of them about fascist pigs and imperialist adventurers. None of it served any purpose. The boys were being raised to soldier.

By the standards of Gan's world, the program was radical social adventure. Slavery or instant death was the normal fate of captured male infants. Gan's solution to the problem of freed or abandoned young slaves and the unadopted sons created by the war with Altanar might lack elegance, but it answered most needs of the children and his new state.

Today, however, that issue was at rest. Kate, Susan, and Janet all looked like cats filled with canaries. Something was up.

When Conway came in with Sylah and Lanta, they stirred impatiently in their chairs, straightening robes that were already immaculately in place. Conway grinned crookedly at all of them, but when his gaze fell on Tate, he laughed out loud, then winced and groaned. When he'd recovered, he said, "Ah, Donnacee, it's good to know you're here. And that you're still so wonderfully beat up. I was afraid I'd be the ugliest person in the room, but now I can relax."

Feigning anger, she shook her fist at him. "If you were healthy enough to make it interesting, I'd put ugly on you. If there was anyplace didn't already have a full ration. Who you calling beat up?"

Carter interrupted as soon as Sylah and Lanta were seated. Her tight, precise voice fired words more rapidly than usual. "We have a going-away present for you, Sylah. For all of you, really. Ever since you told us how the Iris Abbess had studied the Door matter all your life, we've been convinced she wrote down *something* about it."

Carter paused, and Anspach, on cue, reached inside a voluminous robe pocket. She hauled out a roll of parchment, opening it with a flourish.

Bernhardt leaned forward eagerly. "It was under the stones of the hearth. Janet was tapping, and we all heard the hollow sound . . ."

". . . and we found this," Anspach finished. Looking about, blushing, she added, "Yes, we were searching for hiding places. It was Janet's idea."

Carter interrupted. "It wasn't. We all agreed."

Tate snickered. Carter heard. For a moment, the famous temper flared. Then she was giggling. She said, "So we sound like giddy little kids; we found it. It's so *exciting.* Anspach said, 'Think: Where do they always hide stuff in the movies?' and we looked, and bingo!"

Sylah said, "Movies?"

Lanta said, "Bingo?"

Anspach shook the paper so it rustled. Rushing, she said, "Listen to what it says:

'It is my conclusion, based on many interviews over many years, that the Door is truly lost to Church. I do not believe, as some do, that its existence or its purpose is a secret. It is a mystery. Possibly a false one. But I think

98

not. Perhaps my reasons are romantic foolishness, but I choose to believe that our beloved and honored Teachers did not die for nothing. There are too many tales from too many sources of their never-revealed sanctuary. The tales are too consistent. Of course, I dismiss entirely the superstitious foolishness about roaring iron monsters that guard the sanctuary and kill intruders with a blink of the eyes. Nor do I accept spirits of thunder and lightning either.' "

Anspach paused, looking up from the document. "There's a star added to it here, and a note on the margin. It goes on:

'I may have to reconsider this last remark. These new people have come among us with weapons that are clearly the power of thunder and lightning. There is more to this than I understand, and far, far more to them than they are willing to explain. I trust them entirely, yet there is something about them that I fear more than any of their weapons.' "

Redfaced, Anspach kept her eyes on the parchment. She said, "The original document continues, then.

'I have carefully and secretly analyzed every rumor and story about the Door that has come to my attention. I have participated in many Church conferences about it, some of them secret to all but we select few. Three things are remarkably consistent: A claim of a hidden city in the mountains (this is where the iron monsters usually enter the narrative). The description of that city as a place where *the giants decreed there should never be darkness*—the phrase is unusual, yet the folk legends of every culture known to me insist that the giants turned night to day at will. The location. *Near Church Home, across a destroying desert and a devouring river, south of the country where the sun can kill and the place where the sun can never shine.*' "

All eyes went to Sylah. She beamed. "My Abbess. From the Land Beyond, she comes to me." She rose with swift grace, rushing to hug each of the women. Coming to Conway, she deferred to his wounds, kissing his cheek in a more sedate celebration. Swirling, making a whirling rustle with her robe, almost dancing back to her chair, she sat back down. "I'm going to find it. My friends. My dear, precious friends. I'm going to find it."

They all cheered, then clustered, overflowing with enthusiasm and congratulations.

After one final leap, Dodoy sank to the floor of the dank, dark passage behind the wall. He was exhausted from his attempts to see through the inconveniently high peephole. He hit the cold stone with his fist, wishing it was the pasty face of one of the three cows who brought such information so unexpectedly. If they'd had the sense to give anyone a hint they had really important news, he'd have brought something to stand on. Now all he had was bits and snatches of what the old Abbess said.

He was glad she was dead. It served her right.

Still, he knew something. Not far from Church Home, whatever that was. Something about a desert. That was a place where there wasn't any water; he knew that. He seemed to remember being hot and thirsty as a child. And what was that about a river? Maybe he hadn't heard that correctly, but he was sure the old witch's paper said, "A city where there should never be darkness."

He had no need of a torch to make his way. There were metal fittings for lights along the walls, but the network of secret passages was his playground. Dim light from peepholes occasionally leaked into the gloom, and it was all he needed. The others suspected the existence of the spyways, but he was the only one who'd discovered a way into them. Cold and dampness troubled him, at first, but now he welcomed it. Even if someone else discovered the passages and came in after him, they'd move cautiously, repelled by those things, as well as the spiders.

That meant the spiders were his friends. So was the clammy stone and the dead air. A slave understood: Whatever or whoever helped you get what you wanted was a friend. So long as the help continued. Or was needed.

Again, he thought of the Abbess' message and scowled. He'd heard much less than everything. Still, if he used what he knew properly, they'd tell him the rest.

Running his fingers across the stone until he found a suitably dry spot, he leaned against the wall to think. Soon he was humming softly.

He must control Tate, and they all must continue to believe he was afraid.

Tate was easy.

The others . . . They weren't friends.

CHAPTER 17

Conway waited at the thick-planked table in the castle's conference room. To his right, tall rectangular archer's slits pierced the granite of the south and west walls. Blades of afternoon sunlight lanced through them and down across the interior, where their angularity softened into pools of warmth on the floor. Crystalline inclusions within the stone glinted. The light also picked out the vivid colors of the magnificent Dog blanket that covered the tabletop. Its bright yellow circle and surmounting yellow winged vee on a scarlet background was Gan Moondark's family crest.

Shifting the beaded shoulder bag that held his outdoor boots, Conway wondered why the use of soft indoor shoes was one of the Olan cultural quirks Gan hadn't changed. On improving sanitation and personal cleanliness up to Dog standards, he was inflexible. The Olans were just beginning to realize the benefits.

Conway appreciatively sniffed the herb-scented atmosphere in the room. Prior to frequent scrubbings and the introduction of incense burners and treated candles, the castle had always reminded him of a chill, malodorous cave. Altanar and his forebears had practically littered it with art and treasures, but they had little interest in soap.

Unlike the Olans and the Mountain People, Gan's tribe considered cleanliness integral to religion. Somehow, they'd made the connection between washing and "dirt creatures" and "unseens." Conway thought of the meticulousness of the War Healers who'd treated his wounds.

Then there was the matter of alcohol. Church knew how to make it. When he recognized the smell and asked where it came from, he created a minor scandal. Shocked Chosens avoided him for days. It was Lanta who finally took it on herself to explain to him that what she called "clear-clean" was a secret potion, known to be good for the outside of people, but deadly inside.

He accepted that as a rational, if arbitrary, analysis.

He also wished he had a gallon of clear-clean quietly aging in a charred oak keg.

Sylah's entry interrupted his musings. She carried a rolled parchment. Using it to salute Conway, she strode to stand on the opposite side of the table. She glanced at his chest. "How are your wounds? I spoke to Tate this morning. She's ready."

He tapped himself, not too hard. "Fine. I've been exercising—sword drill, riding. Between us, we've delayed things at least two weeks. I apologize for both of us." He wondered if she heard the contradictions in his voice, the eagerness and the uncertainty.

She gave no sign as she spread the parchment flat. "The important thing is that you healed well. We'll be on our way in two days. That's why I wanted you to see this. The best map Altanar was able to create," she said. "The result of spies, Peddlers, careless words dropped by Messengers, and from Church."

"Church?"

"Yes. Healers and War Healers. Kos was once a Church stronghold. There was a plague. Church was blamed and banned for many generations. There are three abbeys; Rose, Violet, and Lily. The sisters are closely watched, confined to the abbey grounds, but otherwise treated very well. Kos is generous with gifts of appreciation to Church."

"How do you know all this? Why haven't I heard any of it before?"

"Some of my earliest recollections concern this quest." She put both hands on the table, leaning forward, projecting intensity. "I woke nights, sweating from dreams of unbearable heat. I'd be so thirsty I couldn't cry out. I dreamed of snow-capped mountains, of canyons that seemed to split the world. And always I understood, without knowing why, that my dreaming was a search for a thing called the Door. When I told the Abbess—she wasn't the Abbess then, of course—she made me swear I'd tell no one. For the rest of her life, she helped me get information about the world beyond Ola." She stopped abruptly, dropping her head. The silence was thick with grief. Conway wanted to speak to it. There was nothing to be said, however, and he knew it.

Sylah resumed. "Legend says the Teachers flourished in Kos before the great purge. We may find clues there. Now, everyone who deals with Kos says it's full of intrigue. It's a society of caste and privilege, opulence and oppression. Slavery's a mainstay of the economy, cruelty the backbone of social control."

Placing a hand on the thick parchment, she moved it slowly southward, across the blue scrawl of the Mother River, across the land between high peaks and the sea. The mapmaker indicated passes and rivers, trails and man-made features. Two mountain tops were painted red and decorated with plumes of smoke. Black curlicues on the slopes were, presumably, lava flows. About

102

where Conway vaguely remembered a peak called Mt. Hood, the artist had penned in a neat, snowclad cone. The fact inspired a faint hope that there might be some accuracy in the portrayal. Then Conway noticed Sylah's moving hand uncover the picture of a whale off the coast. It was swallowing a boat, complete with a crew of ten.

Conway wondered what Mt. Hood *really* looked like. Whatever it was called now.

He already had some knowledge of the Empty Lands. No settlements approached Ola's size, or even Jalail's. A mere handful had so much as a central fort for protection during times of attack. The mountain reaches were home to tribes similar to the Mountain People of the Enemy Mountains between Ola and the land of the Dog People, but not as bloodthirsty.

Sylah drew a finger from mountains to sea about a third of the way between Ola and the deep bay of Kos. "Kossiars patrol this far north and as far east as the sunrise slopes of the Enemy Mountains. No one knows how far south they reach. The patrols enforce tribute, raid the uncooperative."

Conway said, "Tate and I heard other stories about Kos; a godkill site that seems to go on forever, strange animals. It's said even the Skan fear the place. Peddlers have to stop and trade at its borders. Messengers are blindfolded and escorted. Sea traders told us they can only come ashore on an island, that the Kossiars kill anyone on their lands without the right tattoos or official badges."

"We avoid Kos by crossing the Enemy Mountains about here." She pointed to a place marked He Watches Pass, glancing at Conway. "You remember we discussed it before?"

"Right, because it's far north of the main trade route between Kos and the east side of the mountains, the country everyone calls the Dry. I spoke to a Peddler who said He Watches isn't hard to follow."

Without taking her eyes from the map, Sylah said, "What else did he tell you?"

Conway heard the amusement in her question. "He also said there's only one acceptable road running south from the Mother River to Kos. There are a few maintained trails between settlements not on that road, and no inns anywhere. According to him, the best thing about the Empty Lands is that it's easy to get lost; if you're lost, the Kossiar patrols may not find you."

"He felt the patrols are the only real danger?" She was smiling at him, challenging.

103

"Not exactly. He also mentioned tigers, bears, wolves, and a population that's likely to turn you over to the Kossiars for a reward. Unless they think you have something worth stealing, in which case they'll just kill you and rob you."

Sylah rolled up the map. "You didn't mention Church as a danger."

He felt his face grow warm. "I didn't think it was a good idea."

She shook her head irritably. "No. Never do that again. I need your mind, Matt Conway. Your thoughts and opinions. Unreserved. We know the Harvester will tell her version of what happened here. Most will believe her. My life guarantees were weakened by the division in Church. Thanks to Odeel, they're worth even less." She reached for his hand. "Our greatest danger is treachery. You see why I must know you are honest with me at all times? At any cost?"

Conway squeezed her hand, released it. "Sorry. It won't happen again." He paused, then blurted the question he dreaded. "What about Tate? Not Tate, exactly, but that kid, Dodoy. He's all she thinks about. You know about people's minds, about women; what're we going to do?"

"Trust her. We can't pull her to us. We can push her away. Patience, my friend. Compassion."

Conway made a sound he hoped was noncommittal. In spite of his better judgment, he went on. "She knew this was the last time we'd be meeting, checking the map. You know why she's not here? She had to take Dodoy to the market. He needs shoes. I'm worried about her, Sylah. She's fixated."

A frown knifed lines across her forehead. "I don't know that word, *fixated*. It sounds very bad. I worry about her, too. We must give her time. She'll always be our Donnacee. We know that."

"Yes, that's so. Look, she was going to go with me to the military stables and make one last equipment check and work out the horses and the dogs. Join me?"

Smiling once more, she left the chart on the table, coming around to take his arm. They were chattering like schoolchildren as they left the gray, stone room.

Conway wondered if she was really as excitedly sure as she seemed. His own mind was clouded, ashamed. Sylah had said, ". . . I must know you're honest with me at all times." Then he'd let her believe he was sure Tate would be all right.

The first lie had come in less than a minute. And it had come easily.

Tate hurried up as Sylah and Conway stepped outside. "I'm

sorry I'm late." The apology was breathless. "Dodoy had to have better boots. The others pinched him."

Sylah said, "I thought they were new."

Tate grimaced. "Isn't it awful? The man measured him all wrong. Dodoy hated them."

"Where is he now?"

"At the stables. He's going to wait for us while we exercise the war-horses, and then help with the last supply check. He was so excited when he told me. He's so darling when he gets like that. Bursts with life."

Conway was surprised. "Did you tell him why you want him along?"

"Absolutely not. If I told him now, he'd think I was using him."

Sylah resisted the urge to tell her that she was doing exactly. that.

Riding through the city, Sylah took part in the conversation, at first. In a while, her mind ranged beyond the bricks and stone of the confining city. She let Tate and Conway drift ahead.

Passing out through Sunrise Gate, she eased off to the side to trail her fingers across the polished brass plates of the huge door. A wavering image mocked her. The face was distorted, unrecognizable.

She heard the Harvester, whispering. "I *am* Church. At the word *Mother*, whom do you see? Answer, Sylah. Answer Mother."

There was another voice. Loving.

I will not be owned.

The words boomed.

When her eyes flew open, she discovered herself well clear of the gate. She hurried to rejoin the others.

Nothing happened, she told herself. I heard nothing. Imagination.

It took quite a while to reach the military stables. Tate chattered the entire distance about Dodoy. Sylah risked one eye-rolling look at Conway, and was rewarded by a quick grin of complicity.

The war-horses had no names. The Dog People who bred and trained them never named them, feeling it was bad luck. Sylah's horse wasn't a war-horse. He was named Copper, for his lustrous coat.

Dodoy appeared, creeping through a door as warily as a barn cat. He sped to Tate's side. Even as she tousled his hair, he watched Sylah and Conway. When the other adults greeted him, he nodded silently, continuing to stare bluntly.

Lifting his face toward Tate, he said, "The soldiers say there's a storm coming. Can we wait until it's over before we leave? We'll get all wet. What if I get sick? Sylah's just a War Healer; she wouldn't know what to do if I got really sick."

Yes I would, Sylah thought grimly, but she put on her most duplicitous smile. Through the smile, however, she sent thoughts at Dodoy that should have knocked him down.

The boy went on. "What if the wind blew over a tree? And somebody got hurt? We'd just have to come right back here, wouldn't we?"

Patiently, Tate explained and soothed. Sylah and Conway mounted their horses, leaving her to follow when she was ready. Once at a safe distance, Conway said, "He's going to drive me crazy. She can't convince him we won't hurt him."

Sylah nodded. "Sometimes it's a great temptation to prove him correct. Look, he isolates her. We're here. She's back there with him. In an emergency her first concern will always be the boy."

"Tate's too intelligent to lose sight of what's important. She's the best partner anyone could want."

Sylah let the unconscious irony of the statement pass. Conway's loyalty wouldn't tolerate any more criticism than she'd already offered. She decided to try another approach.

"Has she learned any more about his birthplace?"

"Only that it's to the south." He frowned, and she waited patiently. Conway's features were peppered with doubt and concern. Soon, words burst free. "She says she doesn't want to rush their relationship. What she won't see is how he manipulates her."

"Wait for me!" Tate's shout brought him erect in the saddle, face aflame. His eyes begged Sylah, who merely said, "We're of a mind, Matt Conway. Be alert."

CHAPTER 18

A quick shiver ran through Copper. Sylah turned his rump to the wind and stroked his neck. She wondered if the horse reacted to the weather or a premonition.

Downhill, perhaps a quarter of a mile away from the field where the group bunched together, the Mother River surged seaward. Upstream to the left, it swung round a bend, clawing at the bouldered shore. Stained with runoff, spring-burdened with everything from twigs to trees, it slid past in silent, awesome urgency.

To the west its course was almost dead straight, until it disappeared into an advancing mass of mist. Swirling, smoky weather tumbled up the broad canyon, absorbing the great river almost contemptuously.

Sylah's stomach tightened at the sudden, unwelcome thought that the water similarly enveloped whatever prey fell its way.

She shrugged herself further into her otterskin robe.

The wind driving the mist upriver snatched at irregularities in the current's surface until it created a wave. Then, with childish cruelty, it tore away the crest. The spew of white droplets somehow twisted itself around in Sylah's mind so that she found herself thinking of executions conducted by Altanar's white-garbed protectors.

Another example of her morbid frame of mind, she thought, glancing at the diminutive Lanta as she did. The other priestess' attention was firmly locked on the ugly ferry waiting for them.

There was ample reason for Lanta's apprehension. The vessel had the esthetic appeal of a brick, barely curved at either bow or stern. Propulsion came from two sails, presently furled on their long booms. The latter yanked and jerked angrily against restraining lines and the thick masts sunk into the boat's deck thrashed back and forth. The forward boom would barely clear the head of a horse standing in the well-like deck space between the masts. A particularly heavy gust of wind made the boat stagger awkwardly at the limits of the thick chains that ran to the scarred trees that were her mooring posts.

When Sylah looked away, Conway's smile caught her eye. Droplets of mist spangled his face like sweat. He said, "This is where the adventure begins."

Tate said, "What do you call the past few days, the other rivers we crossed? Holiday time? I haven't been dry since the day we left. Won't this weather ever break?"

"They were just rivers." Conway was disdainful. "Across there is mystery."

Sharply, Lanta said, "If we get there. This is no young warrior's ride for new and interesting sights. There's more danger than you seem to realize."

He continued to smile as he rode off a short distance. In response to his whistles, all four dogs materialized uphill, where the forest bordered the field. Tate's pair of brown females stood close to each other; they were never far apart, unless ordered. His own black male, Karda, hung back, still watching the back trail. Mikka, her lighter gray blending eerily with the mist, advanced farther into the tall grass. Conway called his pair. They ran, and he thrilled at the fierce magic in their long-striding silence, a power that always beckoned him to join with them, more than the other way around. There was no question that he was the leader, the giver of commands. Still, when he worked with them, there was a feeling of wholeness that put them beyond other men, other animals. Conway thought of it as awareness beyond men's senses, intelligence beyond dogs' comprehension.

Tate rode up beside him, and he included her in his thoughts, gesturing at the arriving dogs. "What would our friends from before think of this scene? Imagine those two in a world where only married couples with a license for two children are allowed a pet dog—to weigh no more than thirty pounds."

"I knew a guy who was a dog breeder." Tate grinned at his surprise. "The family owned the breeders' licenses together. Turned down a fortune for it, many times. And what about horses? What was it—a ten-year waiting list just to get your name into the national annual recreational ownership lottery? Remember? And if you weren't one of the 'lucky thousand' in your year, you could register again and wait for another decade."

Conway sobered, thinking back to people lined up for their meat ration, bread ration. Sugar. Fats. Millions of people, packed into their rotting, polluted cities.

"You hear me?" Tate's sharpness rasped across his introspection. He turned quickly.

"Not a word. Daydreaming, I guess." They were alone, the others having started for the ferryman's small hut.

Tate whistled in Tanno and Oshu, then said, "I asked you if you ever wondered why these populations are so small. And isolated. They're all hostile, so fighting explains some of it. We know they started with small numbers. They've had at least five centuries to build up, though. I think I know what's wrong. You've seen how sickness scares them?"

He said, "Plague," and she nodded grimly. He went on. "I believe you're right. The things the lab people turned loose way back then must mutate like crazy. Seems logical they'd build that into their bugs. To defeat inoculations."

"Logical." The word became condemnation. Suddenly, she laughed aloud. "So what? Germs, arrows, whatever. Let's make a mark, Matt. You with me?"

Reaching out together, they joined hands. Neither spoke. When they separated, they galloped forward, whooping, celebrating, exulting.

Sylah and Lanta watched them come with head-shaking bemusement.

When they rejoined the two women, Sylah was bargaining for passage. The ferryman, a large, gnarled man, held out until she offered more than he could refuse.

"We'll end at the bottom of the river, probably," he grumbled, pulling on a quilted coat with a wide, flared skirt that reached to his ankles. Its palm-sized buttons puzzled Conway, until he realized they could be easily manipulated with numbed hands for a quick escape if the wearer found himself in the water. A poncho went over the coat, draping below his waist. It was made of narrow strips of a semitransparent material. Whoever created it cunningly joined the horizontal bands with lapped seams for maximum waterproofing. Seeing Conway's interest, the man held it out for inspection. "Seal guts," he said. "We trade grain with the downriver Whalers for waterproofs like this. Stops rain and wind like nothing else. With this duck-down coat under it, I don't care if the weather comes straight from the Land Under." His glance jerked to the Priestesses. "Your pardons."

Sylah said, "You know this river too well to let it take us to the Land Under. You just want to raise the price for the trip."

"You're a tough one. Not like the other."

"Other?" Sylah asked the question, but they all paused.

The man shifted nervously. "The other Priestess. Six, seven days ago. Come at first light. Hid inside that hood thing. Wouldn't look at the water until we reached the other side. Wasn't near so rough as now. Paid my first price without arguing. Bad scared, like she knew the river could kill her, even if no man could."

"She was alone?"

He relaxed into a confiding grin. "That's what she wanted me to think. Never said nothing about friends. After I got back, though, I had to go hunt for our milk cow. We got this gate, see, with this latch . . ."

Conway said, "Just the facts, please," and Tate made a strangling sound. The piece of dialogue was an integral part of every TV 101 (usually titled something like Beginnings and Formulae) course in any university; his use of it in the midst of growing tension nearly sent her into giggles. The ferryman looked aggrieved for a moment before continuing. "She came with a half-dozen

109

men. I found their tracks where they all left the road and milled around. She rode alone toward my place. The rest went west."

"How do you know they were men? And with her?" Sylah asked.

"Gossip. Man passing through told me about six men he saw at an inn the night before she showed up here. Two was rich; he called them barons. I don't believe that, but he said they give all the orders and the other four jumped. Anyhow, the priestess stayed at the inn, too. They never talked to each other. She left a little bit behind them. Joined up on the road, I guess; seven horses waited in the woods on my land."

Sylah said, "You've been very helpful. Someday perhaps I can repay you."

He looked away, almost shyly, then went on hesitantly, "If I knew something else, would you keep it to yourself? Your friends, too?"

"Of course. That's why they're my friends."

"There was another rider. Man, woman, I can't say. I asked, but no one saw this one. I found other tracks where someone could've sat and watched everything I told you about. I can't guarantee it happened that way. I'm no tracker. But that's how it looked."

"Someone watching the watchers?" Tate's tone challenged. "Why?"

"If you'd watch how close you're all listening to me, you'd probably think you was the ones could best answer that." The man flashed Tate a shrewd smile.

"The other rider never came to your ferry?" she continued.

"Stayed this side of the river." At their uncertainty, he explained. "It's two days' ride to the next ferry, and no one swims the Mother. If he stole a boat or paid someone else to get him across, I'd hear about it. I don't suppose there's anything you want to tell me about any of this, is there?"

She said, "There's nothing to tell. We're just travelers, on our way south."

Moving to the door, he said, "Oh, I believe that, Rose Priestess. Now come along, and you can watch me hook up the team of ducks that'll pull us across the river."

Laughing at his own wit, he led the way to the ferry. Supervising the tying of the horses in the open hold, however, he was all business. His crewman cast off the mooring chains. The ferryman angled the unwieldy craft out. Playing current against the wind, he strained mightily at his tiller. The crewman eased one sail, tightened the other, anticipated most commands. Nevertheless, they

110

rolled frighteningly several times, and spray from the downwind side was a constant discomfort.

Landfall was a skillful display of rivercraft. With the sure hand of experience, the ferryman eased into an eddy. Two men ashore raced to catch thrown lines. Once the ferry was secure, they replaced the cordage with chains identical to those on the northern bank.

The dogs bounded ashore happily, but it took several minutes for Conway and the crew to wrestle the drenched, frightened horses ashore. The disciplined war-horses were a bit easier than the pack animals, all of which had worked their loads into disarray. While he worked on repositioning and lashings, Conway was impressed by the furtive behavior of the people watching from the doorways of the small collection of board-and-hide huts. Even the children dodged out of sight rather than face eye contact. The mingled stinks of wood smoke and dead fish added nothing to the sodden look of the place. The only interesting things around were the sailboards leaning against the huts. They were made of wood and leather, with hand-painted sails that appeared to be canvas. An unfinished example rested on a pair of sawhorses. The exposed construction of ribs and stringers suggested the limber bones of a fish. Coiled lines, large hooks, and snubbing cleats on the hulls indicated that the owners went after fish of great weight.

As soon as they'd ridden out of earshot, Tate asked, "What do you make of this other priestess the ferryman was talking about? Part of the faction problem?"

Lanta answered, "There's no doubt," and Sylah added, "It also tells us that Gan's opposition is more active than we knew. The two rich men were barons, I'm sure of it."

Dodoy said, "We should go back to Ola. The barons are after us. We're only here because of Sylah's Door."

Tate pulled him to her. "Hush, now. It's going to be all right."

He opened his mouth to continue, but a shout from behind interrupted him. They all turned to see the ferryman pounding along the road on an unsaddled horse. He was breathing hard when he stopped. "I came as fast as I could. There's something you have to know," he said. "One of my linehandlers was telling me a man upstream had a boat stole. Couple nights ago." He pointed at the fog-shrouded cliffs. Their hazy proximity made the narrow strip of land seem even more threatened by the hungry river. He said, "Same man saw a rider up there, day before yesterday. Didn't do nothing. Just looked. All day. There again this morning. Gone now."

Sylah asked, "You think the watcher and the man who stole the boat are the same?"

Her skepticism brought two bright spots of color to the man's cheeks. "You should hope not. Whoever it was picked up the boat and carried it to the water. A big boat. Whole family ten feet away in the house. Never heard. If that's all nothing to you, then I bothered you for no reason."

Before anyone could comment, he yanked his horse around and raced off the way he'd come. No one spoke for some time.

Conway was surprised by his own reaction. There was fear, but it was a distant, almost intellectual thing, brushed aside by a tingling eagerness. Surreptitiously, he flexed tense muscles. The sliding, bunching power and the lush relaxation that followed filled him with an almost sexual heat.

He looked at the others. Dodoy was excited, his hands wriggling up and down his reins, making his horse shuffle irritably. Tate watched the boy, concerned.

Lanta studied the cliffs, as if her gift might penetrate the misted forest. Then, as if startled by a sound, she twisted to catch him watching her. Prickling hair rose on Conway's nape as he remembered that this was a Seer, one who saw tomorrow's truths. She flashed a brief smile before she looked away, and he was lost again in the contradictory signals she always seemed to be sending him. He knew there was happiness in her, yet whenever it seemed most likely to break free, something pulled it back, shrouded it. Why was she so determinedly *apart*? The behavior embarrassed and confused him, as though he'd been caught trying to peek behind a mask.

There was no time to puzzle over it. He turned to Sylah, saying, "I'll take point with my dogs. Tate should take drag."

As they each moved to their positions, Lanta spoke to Sylah. "Do you think he's capable of riding point? You mustn't think of him the way you'd think of Clas."

Setting off in Conway's wake, Sylah chuckled. "I think of no man as I think of Clas. He and Tate have to learn. The dogs'll warn them of danger."

"I pray it's so."

It was a while before Sylah felt it was safe to turn to look at Lanta. When she did examine her companion, there was nothing to see. Sylah permitted herself a small grimace of frustration. There *had* been a tone . . . No, nothing that strong. An undercurrent. Yes, that was it, an undercurrent of emotion. Lanta's prayers

112

for Conway grew from more than concern for a traveling companion.

CHAPTER 19

Tate watched Dodoy picking up firewood. He visibly disliked the chore, but went about it with no outright dissent. She'd learned that that was his way. There seemed to be no little boy inside him. He suppressed anger until it exploded. Childish games and amusements bored him. For something to truly entertain him, it had to have a bite, a touch of harshness.

She was sure she'd already seen changes for the better in him in the eight days since the river crossing.

There had certainly been changes in their surroundings. For the first two days, the road was wide enough for a pair of farm carts abreast. Muddy, potholed, it meandered through rich farming country. Sky-darkening clouds of starlings braved the dismal early spring, wheeling, whistling, chattering. Their thousands combined to smother most other sounds. Occasionally, however, they were brushed aside by massive flights of geese or ducks. They all mingled in the fields, harvesting what they could from fresh-turned earth. Sometimes flocks of pigeons joined them. Hawks and eagles patrolled the edges of the masses, hurtling down to strike the careless or weak.

In the fields that were already seeded, children worked ropes controlling scarecrows or dashed across the fields slashing at the trespassers with long, thin poles. They invariably paused to watch the mounted group pass. Shy dreams of other horizons shone in their eyes.

The road ended with jarring abruptness. It plunged into the forest at the limit of the last farm like a lost arrow, becoming a narrow rut winding through towering firs. From that point, it was five days before they saw any sign of human life, except for the path itself. Yesterday they'd found a campfire site, so old a dandelion sprouted in the charred circle. They'd dismounted to inspect it, treating it as a great discovery. Today had been more of the same. Endless, unbroken forest. Tate leaned back, yearning for sunshine.

Sylah chose that moment to join her, putting down a leather sheet to protect against the damp ground before settling beside her. She offered Tate a wooden mug filled with a steaming liquid, saying, "This is a soup we haven't tried before—duck and apple, with some potato. You can hardly tell it's a dried mix."

Uncertainly, Tate took it, reflecting that most of her dining experiences since surviving the crèche had been satisfactory. With notable exceptions. She'd seen things served as food that nearly sent her screaming from the scene. The smell of this soup, however, snapped her eyes wide open.

"There's—there's *orange* in this. I haven't tasted orange in—oh, my, how long?"

Sylah smiled her pleasure. "I was as surprised as you. A nice touch from the army wives who put up the dried rations. I wonder where they got it? So little of the powder comes into Ola or Harbundai."

"Those ladies are getting to be truly considerable traders." Tate took a healthy sip from the mug and sighed. "Whoever did this has my eternal heart." She handed the cup back.

Sylah shook her head. "Keep it. Lanta's got enough for all of us. I should take some to Conway; he's graining the horses and rubbing them down."

"Oh." Tate exclaimed distress, starting to rise. "I meant to help him offload. Is he done already?"

"He said he wanted you to have some time to yourself. He didn't mind, really."

Tate said, "I'll take care of it next time. You know, he's enjoying himself. He's becoming quite trailwise."

Sylah chuckled, turning away with a gesture of embarrassment. When Tate insisted she say why, she looked around carefully. "I was only thinking how glad I am that he has his lightning weapons. Have you seen him with a bow?"

"No. Why?"

"He's awful. He tries so hard, and it's just sad. Arrows go everywhere. The Wolves were calling him Cloudkiller."

They laughed together, rocking back and forth, and Tate confessed that she'd used a bow and arrow exactly once. "The time the bear came after Clas and me, remember? We were so lucky."

"I was the lucky one. My husband and my friend survived." Scanning around them, she grew contemplative. "I was thinking today how this reminds me of the camp we made during our escape from Bay Yan and Likat after Gan killed Faldar Yan—the small stream over there, campfire smells. If I let myself think about it, I can believe there's someone watching from behind every tree, waiting around every bend of the path."

114

"I get the same feeling. I never said anything, but I even dream about it."

"Dream?" Surprise burst from Sylah. Nervous laughter started, stopped abruptly. She leaned closer. "I do too. Not just the trail. Sometimes it's the Abbess. It's always the same. She tells me she believes in me, tells me to keep on. I wish you'd known her longer."

"She was a wonderful woman. And she's right about you."

"You mean that? After all that's happened?"

Puzzled, Tate stared. Sylah hurried on. "The Harvester, I mean. The other things. I didn't do anything wrong. I truly believe that. But Conway was hurt. Church will be angry with you. So many things. Because I won't stop looking for the Door. My fault."

"That's just flat wrong." Tate scolded; tone and manner exposed scorn. "You're just like me, so don't try that stuff. If there's something you have to do, you do it. You don't know how to quit, so don't even talk about it."

The words gladdened Sylah, and yet they struck her with a weird, confusing power. The sensation passed in a breath, but it left her oddly lightheaded. Above all, however, she was reassured. Her hand went to Tate's arm. "You do understand."

"I told you; we're alike. And we're all tense and tired. It's so quiet. And dark. Miserable rain—it's not even a decent downpour, just this constant wet that gets all over everything." A jay squalled in the distance. Her head snapped up. "Where's Dodoy? I don't see him." She rose, calling softly.

The boy appeared from behind a tree. "Is it time to eat?"

"Not quite. Did you get enough wood?"

He nodded, his attention fixed on the remainder of the soup. Tate sat back down and offered it. "Sylah brought it. Wasn't that a nice surprise?"

He drained the mug, extending it to Sylah.

Sylah said, "You can wash it when you wash for dinner."

Instead of moving toward the nearby stream, he said, "You always say I don't wash enough. I think I know why I don't like it as much as all of you. When I was real little, someone told me we didn't have enough water to be clean like other people. The only place we could get water was the river. She was afraid of it. She said it would hurt you. Something like that."

Tate said, "Think, Dodoy. It's important. Exactly what did she say? Did she say it would drown you?"

"That wasn't it."

"Did she say it would eat you? Devour you?"

115

Slowly, as if preoccupied, he fumbled in the leather sack holding his belongings where it lay beside Tate. Hauling out a fire drill and its accompanying flat board, he wound the string around the shaft. When he had the stick twirling, he went on. "I'm not sure. What was the last thing you said?"

"Devour? That word?"

"I think so. That means eat, right?"

Eagerly, Tate faced Sylah. "You heard. The same word the Iris Abbess' letter used to describe the river. Exactly. There's a connection. There has to be."

Sylah found a smile. "If I hadn't seen and heard, I wouldn't have believed." A wisp of smoke curled up from Dodoy's board. He built a small cup of tow around it. Absorbed in his work, he was equally oblivious to Tate's joy and the cold speculation in Sylah's eyes.

Lanta called, "Everything's ready. We can eat now."

Tate said, "I can't wait to tell the others. He's got childhood memories of a desert land. It has to be near Church Home. When he sees it, he'll remember more. He can be our guide. It's wonderful."

"Wonderful," Sylah agreed, hurrying to catch up as Tate led the boy off.

Conway had erected a fly so Lanta could cook and they could all eat under cover, and halfway to it, Sylah realized her mug was back where Dodoy dropped it. Retrieving it, she continued to wonder about *devour*.

A chill stopped her in her tracks. What if he was an incipient Seer? There were stories of those who had that capability and didn't comprehend what it was until a knowledgeable observer recognized it. Such power had to be nurtured, controlled. Or go wild.

The meal passed as usual, eaten rapidly, with little talk. They rode all day in a strange sort of tense boredom. By evening, physical and emotional energies were sapped. After a hot meal, renewed, that was when they normally enjoyed some light, relaxed conversation. Until nightfall.

Sylah marveled that Conway managed on as little sleep as he did. He'd assumed nightwatch, with its constant wakenings, as well as any small supportive tasks he noticed. He was careful to avoid any sign of outright control, however. She appreciated that. Now, with dinner finished, he reminded Dodoy it was his job to clean the dishes. Tate rose to help the boy.

Conway was enjoying the same scene, but he heaved to his feet with a sigh of resignation. He called to the others that he was moving out to nightwatch.

He wondered if they could imagine his two-edged sense of anticipation, this time when he felt most a warrior and most afraid that he might fail his companions.

Gan and Clas and all the others had taught him well; he knew that. He used the murdat capably. Maybe he was weak with a bow and arrow, but he had the wipe and the boop.

And the sniper's rifle.

Reaching for it, he stroked the waterproof sealskin cover of the plastic case lashed to his saddle. Every word of Falconer's lecture was still in his memory. "Don't try to outguess this solar-powered scope. And never even wonder about taking it off to use it for long-range viewing. You'd never get it back on properly. It's all automatic. Center the sighting dot on the target and push this button. The laser measures the distance, feeds the data into the computer, and it adjusts the sight picture. All you do is turn this little knob to add your estimated windage. *Squeeze* the trigger. You'll hit your man ninety-eight point five times out of a hundred. You're throwing approximately three-quarters of an ounce of copper-jacketed spent uranium. Don't worry what damage the slug does. Aim for the middle of the target. You won't have to shoot the same man twice."

Conway drew his murdat from its carved wooden scabbard, holding it out at arm's length. It had balance and form that pleased the eye. The pebbled sharkskin leather handle was not only good looking, it afforded a sure grip when wet. On the wood of the scabbard, a carved prairie bear rose on hind legs to threaten. It all reflected craftsmen's pride.

The wipe was ugly-honest, a tool for combat.

The rifle lied. Sleek, glossy, its stock of rare, genuine walnut and its blue steel barrel begged to be held. The solar panel and light-gathering optics dazzled with technical lordliness. Yet it reeked of cold killing. Falconer used it once. Across a distance of at least a half a mile. Sent a man spinning and tumbling into a broken heap. One shot.

Conway realized his hand was resting on the case again. As he pulled it free, a chill trembled along his spine. He told himself it was because it was going to be a wet night, and gathered up his Dog blanket, the one treated to resist water.

Karda and Mikka spanned out ahead of him, going downhill.

It was several hours later that the pressure of a paw on his right thigh brought Conway from sleep to full consciousness. Utterly

117

still, he studied the darkness. He'd trained himself to sleep sitting up, backed against a tree. Mikka always rested on his pistol side. Slowly, silently, he drew his wipe from its waterproof leather scabbard. There was already a round in the chamber; he needed only to flick off the safety. As he did, he touched the six-power scope mounted above the receiver and mourned the centuries-dead batteries that had once turned it into a night-vision device.

Distantly, there was a confused rustle. Horses. Several horses, downhill, scuffling along the dark trail, uncertain of their footing. Directly below him, a man coughed. The riders left a silence behind them that throbbed in Conway's breast.

For what seemed like hours, he puzzled over the group. Were they fleeing someone? Why else suffer the problems of a night march? He let the others sleep undisturbed. For himself, every question he asked generated ten more, each as unanswerable as the first. After much useless effort to sleep, he remembered the relaxation techniques taught him by Sylah. Silently, he thought the chant, the soothing repetitions of in-directed words that turned his mind on itself. He saw a meadow, the grass soft and fragrant. The man lying in the sun there was himself, as was the second man, who stood on guard. That man was alert, ready; he assured the sleeper rested silently and well.

He woke to Karda growling softly. Conway was instantly awake again, every sense straining. A predator attracted by the horses? He reminded himself to move nothing but his eyes, and to see from their corners. Stress made them water, and he risked a painfully slow reach to brush them away. The wipe in his hands felt useless against the unknown, unseen presence.

He put a hand on Karda's head to gauge the direction of the intruder. The dog was also confused. Slowly, however, like the turning of a wind, the tension left the animal. Conway sent him to investigate.

Sleep was out of the question until Karda returned. When he did, he was calm.

Mikka leaned away, broke contact with Conway. Karda snuffled, then lay flat with a soft exhalation. Not long after that, Conway sank back into sleep.

He woke to a hazy dawn and the sound of activity uphill at the campsite. Sylah and Lanta were just stepping from under their shelter, beginning their morning ritual. He rose easily, then rubbed his arms and chest briskly, warming his blood before trotting down to examine the trail.

There were fresh tracks in plenty. He wished he knew more

118

about reading them. Clues like scarred shoeprints convinced him there were at least four riders, and perhaps six.

No sign of life for days, then riders as well as stalking animals in the night, he thought. Good reason to be even more careful.

Still, in the light of day his level of fear seemed overwrought, even dangerous. He had much to learn about nightwatch.

Making his way back toward the others, he decided to wash up on the way. There was no hurry; the riders were long away, and the animal story was just another incident. He winced inwardly, already hearing in his imagination the teasing he'd take when he confessed how concerned he'd been.

The creek was in the direction Karda had pointed in the dark, and he wondered if the dogs would find any sign he could positively identify. Not likely, he told himself ruefully. He recognized only the most basic tracks.

He'd gone about thirty yards from his watch post when he came to the creek bend where an earlier overflow had thrown a sand deposit out of the streambed and across the forest floor.

Karda and Mikka rushed ahead to sniff and growl at the footprints there.

Human footprints.

CHAPTER 20

"It's a woman." Conway placed his own foot beside the print. The three women bent forward to examine the difference closely. Dodoy crowded in front of them, nearly walking on the tracks. Tate gently pushed him aside, where he squatted, sulking, like some small, angry bird.

Sylah said, "We can't tell how long it's been here. Since the last heavy rain; that sand would wash clean very easily."

"I can be more accurate than that," Conway said.

Tate bent to peer closely. "How?"

Conway pointed at the edges of the depression. "See how distinct it is? That's because it hasn't had a chance to dry out. This is compacted sand; as soon as it loses moisture, it'll crumble. Look at the configuration. She was practically tiptoeing. And here, both feet side by side; probably making sure she was downwind from where she expected me to be. I'll be more careful from now on. Even so, the dogs knew someone was here."

As if approving of his reasoning, Tanno and Oshu moved, stiff-legged, past Tate to sniff the footprints. They retreated to stand protectively beside their master, the ruff of fur around their necks standing out. She stroked their heads absently, concentrating on the tracks. Karda and Mikka, already finished with their investigations, sat at a distance.

Sylah glanced at them. "It's odd your dogs never challenged."

"They knew. They warned me. We were all three awake, even though the wind was from uphill and they had no proper scent."

Dodoy said, "Then how can you be so sure the footprint's new, or any of what you said? Maybe you dreamed the whole thing."

Tate grabbed the boy's shoulder and thrust him behind her. Eyes on Conway, she said, "Don't be rude, Dodoy. Matt knows what he's doing."

Unabashed, Dodoy peered around her. "He's not a real warrior, like Gan Moondark or Clas na Bale. Somebody's after us, and he doesn't know anything."

Sylah poised to intercede, but held her peace. Conway spoke to Tate. "He's right. I'm not a tracker. I learned some things, though. If you hadn't been so busy coddling your little friend, you might have, too."

For a long moment, they glared at each other. Both pairs of dogs shifted nervously. Mikka's uncertain whine was the only sound. Tate broke the tableau. She grabbed Dodoy by the back of the neck, hustling him uphill toward the campsite, saying, "We have to talk." Her dogs fell in behind her, looking back occasionally as if trying to understand the tension still tainting the air.

Sylah gestured at the retreating group. "I sympathize with the dogs. All they know is that they're supposed to protect us, all of us, and suddenly their masters are snarling at each other. How do we explain to them?"

Conway said, "How do I explain to her?"

Sylah and Lanta followed his gaze, where the small figure scuttled along in front of Tate. Lanta said, "Perhaps if you did as we do, spend time in meditation every morning."

Conway smiled wryly. "Learn to love him?"

Very seriously, Lanta shook her head. "Just learn to not hate him." When he opened his mouth to protest, she held up a hand. "You will, in time. He sees you as competition for Tate's affection. If he can make you appear to be his enemy, he'll steal her friendship from you. Be careful."

She was gone as soon as the words were said, leaving him to

turn awkwardly to Sylah. He said, "She's got it all figured out. Is she right?"

"Perhaps. I think so." She moved to return to the campsite, and he fell in beside her. He said, "Listen. While we're all confessing things here, don't you think it's time you tell us what you think is behind this Door?"

Startled, she stopped, faced him. A weak, confused gesture tried to dismiss him.

He persisted. "Come on. You must have an idea."

"No. Really. I don't."

"Then why?" He made a cutting gesture. "Oh. I've heard all about the Teachers and their supposed power and the massacre. But not a word about what this power might be. For that matter, if they were so strong, how'd men find a way to . . . to . . ."

"Butcher them?" Sylah bit off the words. "We're only tolerated at all because we're the life-bringers. The Teachers challenged that dominance. Our only defense is morality, and if that fails, we die. You know as well as any. For your information, my Abbess said only a few Teachers knew the location of the Door. Their identity was secret. When the killers couldn't find the ones they wanted, they killed all. It's said some actually taunted their executioners, saying that only another Teacher would ever open the Door, and when that happened, the descendants of the killers would curse them forever."

Conway stopped, and she turned to look back at him. Since he was downhill, they were eye to eye, and he fastened his stare on her as though he would see past muscle and bone to the center of her being. "You seek that power?" he asked.

"Of course." Then, hurriedly, "Not for myself. I wouldn't want it at all, if they hadn't made me want it. Power frightens me. I see it frightens you. But think of *equality*. For one like me. I'm grateful to Church for saving my life. But I am *hers*. Can you understand?"

"And if you have this power, you'll own yourself?"

"Not just me." She chopped the air angrily. "The power of the Teachers will help all women. All people."

"It won't corrupt you?"

"Certainly not. You offend."

"I mean to. I want you to think about what you're doing. I trust you. I'm your friend. That's why I'm telling you you're walking on the most dangerous ground a person can test. This power wasn't enough to save your Teachers, but it was important enough for them to die for without revealing its location. Do you honestly

121

believe it can't corrupt you? Will you protect it so faithfully? Do you have the strength to reject it if there's a danger it might fall into the wrong hands?"

Twisting away, she walked up the hill, unable to will the stiffness out of her back, the fury from her stride. How dare he doubt her? Her life, her soul, was the search for the Door. If the Iris Abbess thought her worthy, who was this stranger to wonder about her?

Who was he to examine the dark doubts that only she should know about?

Who was he to make her cry?

The first time he caught her sleeve, she pulled it free with a lunge that destroyed her balance. Without his quick grab at her arm, she would have fallen. Stumbling clumsily, she rounded on him. The sadness in his features stilled her harsh words. He said, "You understand being considered a possession, and I cannot. On the other hand, I can understand loss. I don't want to lose a friend again, Sylah. I see Tate slipping away from me. I'm worried about this Door thing coming between you and me. Would you think I was insane if I said I don't fear the death of my friends as much as I fear losing them? Does that make sense?"

Sylah wiped at her eyes with a handkerchief. Impulsively, she reached to touch his cheek. "You're a troublesome man," she said, then smiled crookedly. "I think 'troublesome' and 'man' in the same sentence may be one word more than necessary." They smiled at each other, seeking ever-firmer ground in the emotional morass between them. Sylah went on, "Seriously, life must be very difficult for you, separated from your own familiar world. If you'd rather leave, return there, I'd understand that. You see, I want my friends to think things through, too."

Conway laughed. It was a short, hurting sound. He said, "I think I'll stay where I am, thanks. Anyhow, I'm looking for something, too, Sylah. Me. As long as you find me helpful, I'll look with you. After that?" He shrugged.

Tate called, saying the porridge was ready. Sylah and Conway resumed their walk up the hill.

Lanta worked on a pack lashing, watching them come. She leaned back on the line, giving it a yank that squeezed a startled snort from the packhorse.

After filling her wooden bowl, Lanta casually retreated uphill from her companions. Pulling the cowl of her cloak over her head, she let steam waft up inside its cover, savoring the mix of cornmeal, oats, wheat, chopped hazelnuts and walnuts. She spooned honey into it. Bathed in that aromatic warmth, she ate. And peered out of her enveloping hood to watch Conway and Sylah.

No sidelong glances or meaningful sighs passed between them. In the first place, Sylah was too well trained to reveal any internal turmoil.

Suddenly, she was embarrassed by the way her mind was working. Not only was she attributing improper thoughts to Sylah, she was basing all her conclusions on a completely false premise. Of course Sylah wasn't giving off any of the normal behavior signs of a woman attracted to a man. She wasn't even aware of what was happening to her. Not yet. Now she only saw Conway as a good companion. Handsome, admittedly, with good shoulders and firm muscles. No physical match for Clas na Bale. Conway would never be competition for Clas in Sylah's mind.

What made the situation so very dangerous, then, was the romanticism of it. Everyone knew Conway had never recovered from the loss of Tee, and that he was accompanying Sylah because he hoped to drown his sadness in adventure. The smoldering hurt in his eyes could melt the heart of anyone who wasn't careful. He even moved like a man trying to find his way through a terrible, heavy world. Not that he was clumsy or graceless. On the contrary, his movements all indicated excellent strength and control, and he sat his horse as if fixed to the saddle. If one looked really closely, however, one couldn't miss the touching air of sad preoccupation.

That was the trap. His emotions were hidden, the way a river's quiet surface hid its bounty. The best fishermen always knew the secrets of the rivers because that was what they did, not just to eat. Women had an even greater curiosity, could never resist exploring the depths of men. Especially those like Conway.

The worst torment was knowing there was nothing she could say without making matters worse. They were both clearly blind to the thing about to fall on them.

Something sharp and unexpected caught at Lanta's thinking. Inexplicably, she found herself visualizing a rose's thorn, although the quick pain had been more of an ache. Sorrow, she decided, because Sylah was being so careless. Anger, too. Conway should be alert enough to realize his attractiveness was endangering a happily married woman. He wasn't the type who'd do something dishonorable intentionally. What was happening was no less dangerous for all that.

Something had to be done.

Lanta scraped the last cereal from the bottom of her bowl and licked the spoon. She continued to run her tongue across its textured wooden surface, watching the others. Contemplative, sleepy-eyed, she might have been a small cat, aloof, cleaning a paw while pretending no other interest whatsoever.

CHAPTER 21

When the meal was over, Conway said, "We should change the way we travel today," and everyone stopped to stare at him.

He went on, "I didn't want to mention it, but I've decided I have to tell you; other riders passed here in the night."

Questions crackled around him. He tried to gesture them away, finally calling for quiet. "The woman who left this morning's footprints isn't a very likely threat. What really troubles me is what the ferryman told us about that lone rider and the group he was watching. I have to wonder who's chasing whom."

Sylah asked, "What do you propose? If they're hunting us, they only have to backtrack to find us."

"If our information's correct—and if we haven't gotten off on a wrong trail—there's a village at the next river crossing, and that should be a short day's ride ahead. I'll scout. The rest of you follow halfway between now and second meal. If everything's normal, I'll be waiting for you at the village."

Lanta wished she could scoff aloud. Taking on the most dangerous role was exactly the sort of thing that would impress Sylah. Soon she'd be noticing his other qualities. Then it would be too late.

"We lose almost a half a day's travel," Lanta said.

"He's right, though," Sylah answered thoughtfully before turning to him to add, "but I don't want you going alone. I'm going with you. Tate, you and Lanta follow with the packhorses."

"No." Lanta's voice surprised everyone, including her. She forced words. "I mean, if they're after anyone, Sylah, it's you. Whoever means to stop you has no reason to hurt me. I'm Church, and I'm not seeking the Door."

"You're my friend, my traveling companion."

"I insist. I go with him, you ride in the safer position with our friend, Tate."

Anger wadded Tate's features. Sylah prevented any outburst by gripping her shoulder, saying, "If I need protection at all,

124

Donnacee, I'll need any warning Conway can provide, and I'll need your very best effort. Ride with me."

Tate managed a smile. She called Dodoy to her and walked toward the stream.

As Conway and Lanta saddled up, Sylah lent a hand. Wrapping Conway's blankets in the peculiar cloth manufactured by the people of the Whale Coast, she made a face and punched it irritably, saying, "How long does it take for the dead-fish stink to wash out of this stuff? I love the way it sheds water, and it's certainly strong enough, but that smell! Ugh!"

"If we didn't have it, we'd be using Dog blankets for shelter, and you know what they weigh."

Unimpressed, Sylah said, "Men. Sometimes I think you only have a nose to keep your eyes separated."

"No woman believes that. You're the ones who keep the perfume makers busy. For men."

Lanta squeezed her reins to stop the shaking of her hands. She dug her heel into her horse's ribs, startling it out of its lethargy and into an athletic sideways hop. Bumping into Conway's mount, it barely dodged a kick from the offended war-horse. The resultant whinnying and skipping about set Karda and Mikka into a growling, threatening crouch. By the time everything was calmed down, Lanta was feeling very pleased with herself.

On the way downhill to the trail, Conway reined up by the sand deposit and dismounted, indicating the footprints to the dogs. They sniffed, ears pricked up at the urgency in his voice.

To Lanta, he said, "I hope they understand that scent's important. It's not part of their training, unfortunately."

When she expressed surprise, he explained as he remounted, "Some are trackers, all right, but most are what Gan calls 'eye dogs,' meaning they rely more on sight." Karda was watching as if he understood every word, and when Conway laughed aloud, the big male heaved himself up on his hind legs, resting his forepaws on Conway's thigh. The dog was large enough that his rear feet were some distance away from the side of the horse, and his huge head was still even with Conway's elbow. Looking down into the panting maw, Conway noted that Karda's teeth seemed even larger than usual from that angle. He tousled the hand-sized ears, then had to do the same for the smaller Mikka, who demanded equal attention on the other flank.

Lanta said, "They love you. They want to do what you want them to do. They'll be looking for her."

"I wish I had your confidence."

They were the last words they exchanged for a long time.

For a while, the trail was as it had been for days, a narrow line snaking between towering evergreens. Morning mist drifted through the forest, pushed uphill by a sighing breeze. Sometimes it was low enough to obscure vision, sometimes rising to trickle through the higher branches. Wherever it touched the needles, it glossed them with a fine film, so the pair of riders moved through a soft, enveloping gleam. Ahead of them, almost as silent as the haze, the great dogs quartered back and forth, one or the other occasionally dropping back to look for signals, then lengthening stride to resume the scout.

Conway noted signs of recent passage; scuffed earth, broken fern fronds. A great many very large slugs had died messily under the horse's hooves. He wished he could estimate the number of riders. His lack of skill irritated him. Gan or Clas would know numbers, condition, the size of the riders. They'd read the trail the way a civilized man read a book.

Civilized.

He looked around him at the forest. In his world they paid security companies to provide round-the-clock protection for the scraps of unsettled land. Access to the remaining wilderness was strictly controlled. Primitive areas were treasured, because most "forests" were sterile plantations.

If they'd saved more natural land, kept the seas healthy, done something about the population growth that turned the whole earth into a screaming, starving rookery, would they have avoided the slow, interminable dance of small wars and retributive terror that led to the final convulsive collapse?

The piercing cry of a flicker broke his reveries, reminded him that arrows from ambush in this world were as lethal as nerve gases in the one he'd left behind.

Not long afterward, they found fresh horse droppings on the trail. Conway had no idea how fresh. The calmness of the dogs was some reassurance, however, and when they came to a fork in the trail and the unidentified riders had clearly gone west, Conway breathed more easily. Nevertheless, he kept his attention on the business at hand, and left off comparing his two worlds.

The sun was shortly past midpoint when they started up a slope. It developed into a lung-bursting climb that had Conway and Lanta struggling along on foot beside the horses as the latter scrambled for purchase. When they topped the ridge, they sagged against the same tree and stared in awe at a shallow, sea-green valley that stretched for hundreds of yards ahead of them and even farther to both flanks. Only a few widely separated trees studded the affected area. To the east, a broken cliff face blocked any passage by horseback. Conway debated exploring for a detour to the west, but abandoned the idea, reasoning that the trail wouldn't simply drive ahead through such an obstacle unless there was a necessity.

"How can this be?" Lanta asked. "Look, there can't be more than thirty or forty trees in the entire valley. It's awful. They look so isolated. It's blackberries, isn't it? Is it all blackberries?"

Conway said, "I think so. There must have been a burn; something let the vines get a solid foothold. Whatever happened here, we're on the wrong trail. It'll cost us days to go back and find our mistake. At least this route goes on south. It looks passable. I wonder who maintains it?"

"Church pays local people to clear trail in some places. Messengers, too. They add the cost to their fee. That's one reason why they can be so expensive. Sometimes rulers make their people do it, because it helps trade. This one has a bad feel; I think it's probably kept up by Peddlers and smugglers."

Conway stretched aching muscles. "I suppose this is what we get for keeping to the lesser-known routes. No one ever mentioned anything like this." He glanced at her from the corner of his eye as he spoke, searching for any suspicious reaction. Simultaneously, he cursed himself for not remembering exactly who suggested the route they'd been following for the past few days. Whoever told him of this trail never mentioned anything like this. Could it have been someone who wanted to deliberately delay them or endanger them?

If so, it had to be a result of the Church schism.

Sylah and Lanta were close as true sisters now, but what would happen when their different sects pressured them to regard each other as strayed? Conway had seen people divide themselves into true believers and the damned. They consumed each other.

Was he to watch that happen again?

He looked more closely at Lanta.

Seer. Violet Priestess. Healer. She was a tiny thing, but without any affected preciousness. Rather, there was a quality about her that made him think of the resilience of good steel.

Studying her so closely forced him to confess that he didn't like looking into her eyes. Attractive. *Beautiful* wasn't too strong a word. Such a deep green color, they had a trick of appearing darker. Especially when she drifted into that wan, lost sort of look. He wished he could know what she was thinking then. It'd be nice to say something to help, maybe even make her smile. She had a smile like sun on flowers. He was surprised at how clearly his memory conjured it up for him.

What if Church's feud forced her to be Sylah's enemy? His enemy? If she attacked Sylah or Tate, could he stop her? Kill her?

He made an involuntary sound deep in his chest, earning a questioning look from Lanta. To cover his confusion, he unfastened his canteen, took a long pull.

They stood on the crest of a ridge where the trail broke out of the forest. An outcropping of stone formed a downsloping approach to the blackberry tangle. At the point where the rock jumble ended, the path was reduced to a ragged cut in the canes.

Conway whistled the dogs ahead, following slowly. Inside the gap, the fresh growth seemed to reach for him, its new strength so eager the unhardened vine tips were translucent. In contrast, the ground was nearly dark. Thick, woody stems, living and dead, stood jammed against each other. Survivors strained to lift lifemaking leaves up to light. Conway slashed off the more aggressive intrusions. When the sun broke from cover, the tunneled path was suddenly a mosaic of shifting, dancing greens and golds.

Conway pulled first one foot, then the other, from the stirrups and up to the saddle. Carefully, gripping the pommel as long as he could, he rose to a standing position. From the animal's back he could barely see over the top of the jungle.

Progress was slow, but uneventful, for quite some time. They soon discovered that the man-made trail wasn't the only one in the sea of canes. Animals, large and small, created their own meandering paths, and these intersected the main route like streams feeding a river. Conway actually began to enjoy the novelty of the place. Each turn and bend offered some surprise. The dogs were far ahead, and the gap between them and the riders gave small animals time to resume their normal wanderings. The first rabbit to scamper across in front of Conway brought a delighted exclamation from Lanta. A little later, another one, caught out, dashed wildly ahead of them. The powderpuff tail winked agitation for several yards before it was able to leap away to the side. Several of the joining path entrances they passed were far larger than any rabbit's scurry. Looking from one of them to Lanta, Conway saw she was as concerned as he. There was no need for either of them to actually speak of tigers or bears.

When the huge boar suddenly appeared directly ahead, Conway's first thought was of anticlimax. He'd been worried about a fearsome, roaring predator. He estimated the thing in front of him was at least three feet tall at the shoulder and must weigh at least three hundred pounds. Impressive, by all means. But, after all, a pig.

The boar swung its head from side to side. Conway had never seen anything like the shining, curving tushes. It opened and closed its mouth rapidly, making a clacking rattle like eager shears. The bristled ruff around its neck rustled when it stamped the ground in warning. Conway noted the hooves. They were so tiny they seemed almost caricature. Clean, however. Shiny, in fact. And the animal's rough coat wasn't pig-dirty, either, but glowed with a robust luster.

Conway told himself it was a pig. Just a pig.

It stamped again. Clashed its teeth. Saliva flew. Fierce eyes widened and rolled.

Far, far away, a dog barked.

Conway cautiously kneed his horse into retreat, simultaneously easing the wipe around, trying to assure a clear shot. The horse backed, step by painfully slow step.

CHAPTER 22

For a space of several heartbeats, all went well.

Behind him, Conway heard the nervous whuffling of Lanta's horse as it, too, retreated. The stink of sweat-lathered animals clotted the humid air of the enclosed pathway.

The boar continued to threaten.

Hidden in the undergrowth off the trail, unobserved until that moment, one of a litter of piglets lost its nerve. Squealing falsetto terror, it erupted almost directly under Conway's mount's nose. After a quick jerk of surprise, the war-horse was back in control.

Not so the boar. It was charging even as the sow contributed her hysterical racket to the uproar and raced after the bolter with the rest of the litter.

Conway's horse half-reared, the flailing iron-shod forefeet fearsome weapons. The boar checked its rush, dancing from side to side, seeking an opening. Unable to bring the wipe to bear, Conway could only curse and hang on.

The great hounds bayed in the distance, hurrying to assist.

The boar seemed to understand exactly what that sound meant.

Abandoning all caution, he drove past the war-horse's wind-milling, trying to strike at the more-vulnerable hind legs.

He almost got them. The horse twisted sideways, landed far to the side of the path. Entangled momentarily in the clutching canes, it then seemed to rebound. The combination and swiftness of the moves was too much for Conway. He soared out of the saddle, falling heavily facedown in the matted growth. He watched in dismay as the wipe buried its muzzle deep in the soil, effectively transforming it into useless junk. Disregarding the tearing thorns, he pulled his murdat free of the scabbard.

The boar was no longer interested in Conway or the war-horse. With those enemies behind it, it focused its attention forward, aiming at Lanta's terrified mount. One buck served to pitch her from the saddle. Stampeded, her horse then vaulted over the back of the boar, directly into Conway's war-horse. The force of the collision dropped both horses into the thicket, one on each side of the trail.

The pair scrabbled wildly, noisily. Lanta's mount caught Conway's war-horse a crushing blow between the eyes with a hoof just before smashing into Conway's head with the same fore-leg.

The impact threw the man farther into the canes, thorns shredding clothes and flesh as he went. He ended on his knees, facing the trail, holding himself upright with his left hand. The murdat hung loosely in the right, the point in the earth. It was more of a prop than a weapon.

His horse was down. Blood poured from a jagged wound on its forehead.

Lanta screamed. It was a wordless, horrified plea.

Clumsily, Conway lurched forward. Tumbling onto the trail, he saw the boar between himself and Lanta. It was gathering itself for a charge when he shouted a hoarse challenge. The boar whirled, and, with a thick, heavy grunt, accepted the new contest. Conway knew he wasn't fast enough to draw his pistol. The boar would cut him to ribbons before he touched the holster.

In that same thought-instant, Conway knew he was secretly glad.

The murdat. Live or die, it would be by hand. Matt Conway. Not a machine. A man. Steel in fist.

Idiocy.

He dropped to his knees, extending the murdat in both hands.

The charging animal took the point an inch or so above his eyes. The impact bowled Conway over like a toy, but he held the blade rigid. It tore a furrow through hide and meat down to bone. More in surprise than pain, the boar stopped and retreated, shaking its head. Enraged, it came again. The noise from the clashing jaws was enormous. Blood and saliva flew from its snout in a constant spatter.

Repositioning himself, Conway lowered his point of aim, saw the tip of the murdat penetrate just below the throat. Glancing off bone, it nearly twisted out of his hand. And then it stopped. For a long instant, the two opponents were eye to eye, separated by little more than the length of the man's arms. Conway was shocked to realize the mad racket filling his ears wasn't just the animal. At least, not just the four-footed one. He was yelling and screaming himself, abandoned to the primal revelation of mortal combat. A searing, heady lust sang in him. Life was distilled to one moment, one test of strength and will.

The torn, bleeding man panted into the ripped, raging face of the red-eyed animal.

The boar screamed and pushed forward, slashing with the tusks. Sheer strength forced Conway backward. The buried sword kept the animal at bay.

Conway felt himself weakening. From fingertips to shoulder sockets, muscles melted with fatigue.

The boar came on, not caring that it was killing itself in its need to kill its tormentor.

A twist tore the murdat from Conway's hands. The boar staggered sideways at the unexpected loss of resistance. Falling to its side, it kicked the ridiculously tiny hoofs in the air, then rolled back, prepared to rise.

The dogs thundered down the narrow trail, fell on the thrashing boar in a snarling, snapping heap. Conway thought he heard Mikka yelp. There was so much blood and sweat in his eyes he couldn't see to be sure. There was another yelp as he wiped a forearm across his face to clear his vision. A blooded Karda and Mikka had the boar down. The handle of the murdat still protruded from the boar's chest. A length of exposed blade was almost as much a danger to the dogs as the pig.

Conway half rose, falling forward, dropping onto the sword with all his weight and the last bit of strength he could muster.

The boar screamed. And kicked. Its death throes sent Mikka spinning. Conway closed his eyes and hung onto the murdat as if it anchored him to life.

He was still clutching it when he recognized Lanta's voice.

131

"Let go now," she was saying. "It's over. I'll make you well, Matt Conway. I'll make everything fine. I'll tend to you."

Lovely words. Lovely voice. So sweet.

He felt himself flowing into unconsciousness, too weary to ask himself why he struggled against the languorous, seductive inner voice whispering, "Sleep. Believe. Surrender."

He was almost certain it was an inner voice.

CHAPTER 23

Opening his eyes, Conway jerked painfully.

Weak, gray light. Cold.

What was this dim, unwelcoming place?

The sea.

He strained to understand. How could that be?

Rain. The reek of a fishing boat. And movement. Slow, rolling movement. He needed solid bearings or he was going to be violently ill.

His head ached.

His horse. The dogs.

A boar.

Remembrance burst on him. He sat up, gritting his teeth against waves of pain.

He was on a bed of boughs and skins. Above the blanket that was now fallen to his waist, his body was a map of scratches. Most merely broke the skin; some could have been knife slashes. The flesh paralleling the worst of them rose in angry red welts. A large square bandage was held to his right temple by two leather thongs. The cloth was damp, earthy smelling. A poultice, then.

More examination showed he was naked under the blanket, and his legs had fared no better. In fact, there was another bandage on his right thigh. He lifted it carefully to peek at a nasty wound that could only have come from the boar's tusk. It had penetrated rather deeply. He had no idea how or when it got there.

The fish smell was from the translucent Whale Coast cloth that formed the roof and one wall of his quarters. Such as they were. He appeared to be in a shallow sort of grotto formed of three massive boulders. There was a ground-level entrance hole, a pinned-up fold in the cloth wall. He'd have to literally crawl through it.

While he considered that possibility, Lanta's head appeared there. When she was far enough advanced to look up, her surprise at seeing him sitting upright made Conway smile. The change of expression hurt enough to make him aware his face was scratched up, as well.

She flashed him an answering smile, hurrying forward. When she was in, she reached back for a thick-walled wooden bowl. Raindrops gleamed on its curved sides and steam curled out of it. At his first sniff, his stomach growled like an aroused dog.

Speech came hard. Finally, he managed, "You all right? Mikka. Where's Mikka? My horse?"

Lanta said, "I'm fine. Sylah sewed up Mikka and the horse. They're healing. You shouldn't be sitting up. You'll break open those scratches." She gestured with the bowl, and he remembered that only a blanket covered his nakedness. He clutched it around him, wincing again at the pull of torn skin.

Frowning, Lanta hurried to his side, putting down the bowl, pushing his hands away. "See, I told you," she said, scolding. "A lot are weeping again." She reached for the blanket. He flinched. Startled, she paused, then laughed aloud. "Shy? Now? Who do you think bathed and medicated you? I'm a Healer; I've spent my life at this."

"And nearly worried herself sick over you, nevertheless."

They both turned to see Sylah inside the shelter, getting to her feet, brushing her robe. Tate followed close behind. She was talking before she was completely inside. "I wish you could have seen yourself when we found Lanta working on you next to that boar hog. You looked like somebody tried to whittle you a whole new body. And the lump upside your head was on its way to being a famous eggplant. On top of that, we had to wrestle your horse. He was still groggy as a goat, but he was determined to protect you. Poor animal's getting a lot of practice looking at you lying in the dirt." The humor of the remarks failed to disguise her relief. She moved to touch his cheek, then kissed his forehead.

Lanta spooned stew and held it up to Conway. "Eat." It was an order. He complied eagerly.

Between bites, he said, "How long was I out?"

Sylah pointed upward, drew an arc. "Quite a while. A combination of too little sleep and the exertion. Not to mention the blow. I'm concerned about your horse. And Mikka's going to limp for a few days; a bad shoulder cut."

"My horse? What's wrong?"

"The head injury doesn't seem to be a problem. He's limping, though. Lanta's been applying baths and salves."

Looking at the small Priestess, who steadfastly kept her gaze concentrated on the soup, he was chagrined to notice how badly her exposed hands and wrists were scratched. Some of the injuries were as deep and ugly as his own. He said, "Lanta, I never asked about you. Are you all right? You're well enough to be doing all this?"

Coloring, she mumbled assurances. He went on, "I'm grateful. For all of us. I have to go see the animals. You understand."

Lanta opened her mouth to object, but Dodoy's scuffling entrance interrupted her. Once inside, the boy grimaced. "Phoo! This place stinks."

Tate said, "Don't say that. This is special cloth." She made him look at it, showed him the quiltlike composition. "No one knows how the people on the Whale Coast make it, but the story says a boy made the first piece. He wasn't strong enough to please his father, and he was small. But one day he learned how to use mussels from the sea and other secret things he discovered—all by himself—to make this material. No one can tear it. See, he showed his father you don't have to be big to be important and useful."

Dodoy said, "It's not just the smelly cloth. It's all the things she put on him, too. Is he going to die?"

"Sorry." Conway took the bowl from Lanta and drained it. "Maybe next time. For now, I'm going to check on Mikka and my horse. Lanta, I'll take over treating them, if you'll show me what to do."

The women all argued that he should stay in bed, but he shooed them all out so he could dress. It was harder work than he expected, but he thought of the new Matt Conway, the one who confronted challenges. It didn't seem to help much, but he finished dressing, anyhow.

Karda was waiting outside the entry hole, and he washed his master's face thoroughly before Conway could struggle to his feet. Shouted orders and protests, marred by laughter, went shamefully disobeyed as the dog cavorted around him like a monstrous puppy. When Conway had Karda calmed down, Lanta led them to a nearby cranny where the injured animals waited. On the way, she told how they'd explored and decided to establish camp there. "We've a stream a hundred yards or so that way," she said, gesturing, "and a small spring up the hill. We're well hidden, far off the trail. The rain's already erased our tracks. Sylah doesn't think you should be traveling for a day or two. The animals need rest, too."

The horse whickered softly at Conway's appearance, and Mikka got to her feet, limping to him to be fussed over. Karda watched, wagging his tail. The horse's injury was the most troublesome. He moved with great care, favoring the swollen leg, but carrying his head at a strange angle, as well. Lanta explained that the kick not only opened a wound, but seemed to have caused neck muscles to stiffen. She said, "I'm almost out of salve. I'll have to use less on him, if I'm to have enough for you and Mikka."

"Use it on them, I'm fine."

"That's not considerate, that's foolish." The words were clipped, sharp. "If you're not important to yourself, you're necessary to us. If you need the only salve I have left, so be it. There'll be no argument."

She ducked away from Conway, scurrying to a ceramic jar he hadn't noticed. Her face still tinged pink, she busied herself with Mikka. The dog's wounds were ugly, but, as Lanta medicated them, she explained, "They're clean. They don't threaten organs or mobility." She moved swiftly, hands sure, and then she was examining the horse. He turned his head when she lifted his foreleg, his luminous eyes speculative.

Speaking in a soft, comforting voice, she examined the fetlock carefully, saying, "There's still a bit of swelling here, but the heat's gone. I was worried about wind puff, but it seems all right."

"Wind puff? That's his ankle."

Lanta's startled confusion drove home the enormity of Conway's miscue. He wished he could pull the words, and their exposure of his ignorance, back.

She said, "We call it wind puff. You know, when they get a swelling or a separation around a tendon. What do you call it? Do your people always say ankle instead of fetlock?"

"Uh, no. Not everyone. We call that other thing a wind swelling. Yes. Mostly wind puff, but sometimes wind swelling." He was sweating. It got in the scratches, stung like fire.

Lanta turned back to the horse. "Now, let's see about that shoulder." She stepped in front of the animal and gripped the foreleg with both hands at the knee, lifting it, bending it forward. He tossed his head, sagging. She released him immediately, moving to stroke his neck. "Poor thing. I hurt that shoulder, didn't I? Well, we're going to make it all better." Easing the hand down his neck, she gestured for Conway to hand her the salve.

Looking in the jar, he saw the small amount left, and ladled up a large dollop on his fingers. Lanta took half of it. "The rest is for you," she said, glaring.

He recognized finality when he saw it. "Can't you make more salve?"

She was thoughtful. "I saw willows by the stream. And wild garlic. But I don't have anything for the salve, itself."

"We've got a pig; you use the lard, don't you?"

"From a wild boar? There wouldn't be much. And it's far away."

"I'll get it. It's still fresh."

She looked at him from the corner of her eye. "Fresh meat. I'm so tired of . . ." Shaking her head, she set her jaw. "No. You're not up to that. I'll get Tate. We'll do it."

"I can do it." He stopped petting Mikka. She butted his hand before turning away to lie down with a resigned sigh.

Lanta said, "We can do it. Together," and ended the discussion by walking away. He hurried after.

Butchering turned out to be more than hacking away with the murdat. Conway made as if to remove a ham, and Lanta practically screamed at him to stop. From then on, he followed directions. She had him cut circles around all four legs, just at the knee joints. Another cut circled the neck, a bit forward of the shoulders. From there, a slit the length of the body ended at the vent. Smaller lines were drawn from the leg cuts to join the body cut. Then she showed him how to slip a small knife under the hide, and, lifting a small section at a time, separate the two. When he asked why they needed the skin, when there was no time to tan it, "You'll see," was all she'd say.

Showing him where to cut, she had Conway open the body cavity. She had him remove the liver, producing a cloth for him to lay it on. With her shortknife, she cut away the leaf lard by the kidneys. As she'd said, there wasn't much. She examined it closely, holding it to the light. "Looks healthy. Springtime wild boar. Lean." She put it beside the liver.

When she was satisfied they had all the meat she wanted loaded on the pack horse, she made Conway pick up the offal and carry it away. She explained. "The animals will clean it up soon, but we're taking no chances. Anyone looking for us who found parts of a butchered animal would immediately pay more attention to this area. We leave nothing near the trail."

Rain started to fall. As they made their way back uphill, Conway remarked that it would help hide any sign of their activity. She favored him with the pleasantly surprised smile teachers reserved for slow learners who make a breakthrough. He didn't know if he should be proud or furious.

CHAPTER 24

They arrived in camp to find Sylah and Tate both glowering. "What do you think you're doing?" Tate demanded.

Conway waved at the horse. "Lanta needs lard for salve. We all need fresh meat. I went after it. She wouldn't let me go alone."

Sylah said, "I'd think not. You should have both stayed here."

"And let the meat go to waste?" Conway asked blandly.

It earned him a smile of mixed appreciation and exasperation. "I didn't say I wasn't glad you went. I said you shouldn't have."

Lanta visibly relaxed. She said, "I'll fix a broth with some of the meat. While it's cooking, I can make a salve."

Sylah agreed. "Whatever meat you don't use, I'll dry." She paused, studying Conway. "You. I want you to rest."

Tate heard the concern behind the sternness. She said, "I'll take nightwatch, Matt. Get some rest."

Conway wanted to argue. His body disagreed. He was asleep as soon as he stretched out.

The next morning, while Sylah and Tate constructed a drying oven, Lanta had Conway cut her four stout poles about three feet long and sharpen one end of each to a point. By the time he finished that, she had two fires going. One was a good deal smaller, several feet away from the larger. She showed him where to drive the poles into the earth; they formed a rectangle enclosing the larger fire. Next, she cut long strips from the green hide, using them to lash the truncated legs of the boar's skin to the posts. Sagging in the middle, it looked like a bloody, hairy hammock. Conway watched in frank horror as she poured water into it and added vegetables. When she began cutting chunks of meat and pitching them into the mix, he couldn't remain silent.

"You're going to *cook* that way?"

She continued, unconcerned. "As you said, we have no need for the hide. A low fire keeps it from burning through, the meat cooks slowly, and all the fat next to the skin enriches the stew. You'll like it."

He swallowed noisily. The hair was already frizzling. An unfor-

137

tunate shift in the wind sent the smoke billowing around him, and he moved with a speed and grace that stressed every scratch and ache of his body. And that he ignored in his haste.

Lanta was already arranging rocks to provide footing for a metal pot over the smaller fire, which was declining to a bed of coals.

She said, "This fire needs to be small, as well, or it destroys the power of the salve ingredients. Heat's the enemy of many medicines."

Leaving him alone to watch the stew, she returned quickly with a leather bag. Scrambling around in its depths, she retrieved a bundle of rather grubby looking sticks and a squat ceramic jug with a wooden plug. Conway was assigned the task of cutting up a few pieces of the bundle, which, it developed, were strips of willow bark. For a moment he considered the dichotomy of using his blade, a metal of such technical advance, to make Bronze Age medicine. Then Lanta's work demanded his attention. The jug held garlic. She crushed it to a pulp with a small mortar and pestle. Willow shavings and garlic went into the pot with the lard.

Conway thought he saw a flicker of uncertainty touch her features for a moment before she rummaged in the bag once more. This time she produced a box as long and wide as her hand and about two fingers deep. It held a flour-fine powder. Measuring carefully, frowning with concentration, she added it to the mixture. Seeing Conway's curiosity, she said, "Valerian. Some call it heal-all. It relaxes the muscles."

"Do I seem all that tense?"

Laughing, she rose. "Not you. Poor Mikka, though. And the horse."

It was his turn to laugh. "So I get relaxed because my animals are overwrought, is that it? Great."

She made a face at him and turned her attention back to the pot. She stirred the melted lard, sniffing judiciously, tasting once. Conway watched in silence to match hers, a quiet so companionable the aching and burning of his injuries slipped away unnoticed. He nodded off once, recovering with a start, finding himself lightheaded. The sensation passed quickly, leaving a faint nausea and a warm flush that lingered until he got to his feet.

Lanta arranged the melted fat to sit near the coals, then rose. "This needs to steep a while. Come, let's see what Sylah and Tate are doing."

He caught her arm, causing her to turn to him. Her surprise seemed almost fearful, and he spoke quickly to allay it. "I want you to do something for me." She continued to look up at him, still unspeaking. If anything, she seemed more apprehensive. He hurried on. "Just now you said 'the horse.' I want him to have a name."

Even though she shook her head, she seemed relieved. She said, "The Dog People believe that's bad luck."

"I know. He's with me now, not them. I want you to name him."

"Me?"

"You healed his shoulder before, and these new injuries. I want him to have a name, and you've earned the right to give it to him. Please?"

Protesting, she sped over the rocky ground toward Sylah and Tate. Conway followed, refusing to be denied. At last she stopped, back against a huge boulder. She was blushing. "I named him long ago. I couldn't tell you. You're not angry?"

"I'm very happy. Tell me."

"Stormracer."

He repeated it, testing it. She watched him anxiously. "You don't like it?"

"It's a good name. Why, though? What made you think of that?"

The blush deepened. "Oh, I don't know. But it fits him. He's so black, and strong. When he gallops, his hooves make thunder. It seems like he can outrun the wind."

For a long moment he stared at her, not quite smiling, not quite serious. He said, "That's more poetic than anything I'd have thought of. Maybe that's why I like it so much. Thank you, Lanta. Stormracer he is."

She murmured thanks, and then he had to hurry to catch up to her once again.

A little while later, they were examining Sylah and Tate's handiwork. A two-layered affair of stone, the lower section was a firebox, the upper a drying compartment. Tate said, "We can do this as long as the wind's from the west. It wouldn't do to have the smell of cooking meat blowing downhill to any riders who might be checking that trail."

Sylah added, "The cuts I mean to smoke are soaking now. I don't have enough salt for a brine, so I've made a hot pickle."

Conway looked to Tate, who sent him a knowing grin. He turned to Sylah. "You laced it with peppers, didn't you?"

"Lots." She laughed. "It preserves the meat."

"Where is this poison?"

She pointed at a waterproof basket. Conway lifted the lid cautiously, sniffed the brew inside. Gasping, he stepped back and clapped the lid on again. "Murder," he breathed.

Archly, Sylah dipped a finger in the liquid, tasted it. She blinked rapidly, then sighed. "Ooh, good. Just right." Her eyes sparkled. Conway knew it was as much from tears as high spirits.

"It's even hot for you. It'll fry the rest of us."

Tate said, "Maybe. But what a way to go, right?"

Sylah added, "There's mint on the banks of the creek. And I found some thyme. It's not just peppers. You'll love it."

"Sure." Conway's sarcasm sent the women into gales of laughter.

Lanta said, "We have to get back to my fires. I don't want to spoil the salve."

Dodoy was poking at the fire when they got there. Lanta explained what she was doing. The boy sidled off, not looking back.

"I don't understand him at all," Lanta said. "He's never *with* us."

"Don't waste your time on it." A heavy weariness swept over him. The gesture of dismissal he sent after the boy seemed to take a long time.

Lanta tested the salve once more. Satisfied, she strained the melted mixture through a fine cloth into a clean ceramic pot. Straightening, she faced Conway. Concern chased across her features. She cocked her head, reached to pull at the bottom of his eye socket, inspecting. Her other hand went to his wrist. "Fever," she said, and after a short pause, "Fast pulse. Too fast. Back to bed for you."

"I'm just tired." She pulled on his arm, and he stumbled. "Maybe a little dizzy."

She let go of him to scoop up the pot of salve where it was cooling, then she pulled him toward his quarters. There was little resistance.

Once inside the shelter, Conway unhesitatingly went to his bed and stretched, facedown. Lanta built a small fire on a makeshift hearth not far from his head. Folding back the cloth fly overhead, she created a draft hole for the wisping smoke. Wafting the pot back and forth over the flames, she stirred the mixture with a finger, testing the warmth. Immediately, the stone-enclosed room was pungent with garlic.

"Undress," she said, and when he looked questioningly at her, her expression dispelled further conversation. She turned her back, until he said, "I'm ready." She smiled at the discreet blanket drawn up almost to his shoulders and coolly flipped it down to his waist.

Her hands, laden with the warm salve, moved with a sure gentleness that turned Conway's wandering thoughts to bird wings or the gliding touch of a breeze. The irritating itch of the lacerations melted away. When she told him to roll over, he was so nearly asleep he hated to move.

Tee had warmed his flesh like that, exploring, defining hands drawing tension away. There were no physical wounds then. Tee simply understood that sometimes a man needs an inner healing. Herbs won't help him. Not even sex is powerful enough to effect a cure. Not by itself.

He wondered if Lanta knew any men who were special to her. Not likely, he decided. She was too involved in her work. Anyhow, who'd want anything to do with a Seer, who knew exactly what you were thinking and going to do—before you did?

That thought brought a smile.

Her hands now kneaded the muscles at the base of his neck, working slowly, deliciously down both sides of his spine. Her weight pressed down on him, bowed his ribs. His breath rhythm became her movement.

Through the scent of the salve, something very faint, elusively floral, teased him. It refused to be identified. Something she wore; he was sure of that. The other aroma should have overwhelmed the lighter fragrance, and yet he was much more aware of the latter. He had the strange sensation that the delicate scent was in his head, creating a film, isolating him.

His whole body was in flowing cooperation with Lanta's touch.

Was she humming? He tried to hear. His mind wouldn't focus.

Not exactly singing. Not a song. A musical repetition. Over and over.

When he opened his eyes, it was to the guilty suspicion he'd slept a long time. Sunshine passing through the cloth fly bathed the room in a warm glow. He was lying on his side, facing the rock that was the back wall of the room. A deep crack ran across it, a darker black line against the black basalt. He rolled over cautiously, and was pleased to discover how much of the pain was gone. Karda was lying beside him. The dog's expressive, dark eyes gleamed and the massive tail clubbed the ground. Conway reached to rub the dog's head, and Karda flopped and lolled happily. The drumbeat of the wagging tail doubled its pace.

Movement at the edge of his vision drew Conway's attention.

Even as he turned to see what it was, Karda was suddenly alert. Together they faced the entryway and watched Dodoy come in. Neither moved or made a sound while the boy edged close and took a seat on the ground. He drew his knees up to his nose, then wrapped his arms around his legs. A hand gripped each wrist. Apparently quite comfortable in his odd attitude, he gave the impression of being knotted in a sack, with nothing but the top of his head and peering eyes sticking out the top.

Conway rubbed a hand across his face. He was startled at the growth of beard there.

When it became apparent Conway was determined to wait him out, Dodoy spoke. "After Lanta said you were sick, Sylah never came in here. Tate, too; she told Sylah they should leave Lanta to heal you and let you catch up. Sylah said they need you and the lightning weapon."

The boy stopped there, watching, blinking rapidly. Again, Conway's determined silence revealed nothing, and Dodoy plunged on. "They were afraid. Sometimes I fear you. You're big, and I'm very small. People don't always know who's a friend and who isn't. If I knew something else that happened that you should know, and I told you that something, would you be my friend?"

Conway said, "I don't collect information on my friends, Dodoy. If you ever learn that, maybe you'll have friends of your own. You better leave."

Retreating back behind his knees, Dodoy said, "See how easily you forgive Sylah and Tate? But you're still mad at me. I know I don't understand everything, because I'm a child, but I don't care, because they need you. I'm afraid because if I don't tell you what I know, you can't save them."

"Save them?"

"There's a danger they don't know about. Neither do you. And I'm too weak to do anything."

Conway turned his back on the boy. Nausea crawled up and down his throat. His thoughts seemed to be liquid, uncontrollable.

His gaze came to rest on the meandering crack in the stone wall. An insignificant flaw in something so fundamentally sound, yet someday meltwater would drain down that face and fill it. Then the wind would shift. The running water would slow. Freeze. Ice would expand in the fissure. The rock would break. Not at once. Not with a roar. Slowly. Agonizingly. A tiny bit at a time.

Hating himself, Conway reached for his clothes where they were folded at the foot of his bed, saying, "If you've got something to tell me, Dodoy, say it and get back to your chores. I want to get dressed."

Dodoy studied Conway for several long breaths, then said, "Somebody made a chant two days ago, when you came in here to be sick. I heard."

Two days ago. So that was how long he'd been asleep. He said, "A chant? All Church women do that. It helps them relax, think more clearly. Is that all you wanted to tell me?" Conway remembered Lanta's lullabylike humming while she rubbed salve on his injuries. He said, "I think you heard Lanta. She was singing to herself while she was in here."

Dodoy loosened his hands, seemed to expand. "Sylah was here, too? Tate?"

"No. Just Lanta. Treating me."

Slowly, almost imperceptibly, a knowing grin spread across the thin, sharp face. "Treating," he said, stretching the two syllables into accusation. "She wasn't singing. I heard. She chanted."

"Well, who cares? If she thinks it helps her . . ."

Sliding backward toward the entry, Dodoy said, "I will be your friend, even if you don't want to be mine. I help you. I warn." He reached behind himself, holding the flap open. "There is special chanting. For Seers, for Seeing. She says nothing to the others, not even to you. When she treated you, Matt Conway, did you become very tired? Sleep? Why would a friend wish to See you? Or maybe you should wonder *whose* friend would wish to do it."

Dodoy disappeared through the entryway. Conway's final glimpse of the boy's shining bright grin was like watching a dagger slide into a scabbard.

With the boy gone, Conway and Karda remained unmoving until Conway finally had to change position. When he did, the dog shifted quickly, continuing to face the door, but leaning his great bulk against his master. Assured that the man couldn't move without his knowledge, Karda settled down, chin on forepaws. He watched where Dodoy had gone.

CHAPTER 25

Sylah shrugged out of her sleeping robe and pulled her everyday wear over her head. She shivered at the first cool touch of the wool as its encompassing length whispered down over her body.

143

The warmth she carried over from the snug comfort of bed asserted itself quickly. In the darkness, she bent to draw her fingertips across the tight weave of the Dog blankets, visualizing the imagery. The blankets of Clas' people. Would they ever be her people?

She was astonished to realize she'd never considered where they'd live when she returned from the search for the Door.

There was no point in considering it. Power would flow to her, and with that, responsibility. No one could anticipate the future created by power. It had a destiny of its own, and people were randomly blown dust. That was the way. Clas would understand.

Straightening once more, she frowned. In her mind, she saw the multicolored blanket tents of the Dog campsite, their bright concentric circles enlivening the prairie. She smelled the honest animals heaviness of horses, the fragrances of herbs, the aroma of cookfires. In the depth of her soul, she felt the vozun and pala drums. Above all that, she remembered how the free, happy children ran and shrieked laughter, playing as all children should.

As she did before the raiders stole her, stole her childhood.

As her first child never would. The child that died within her, lost in Altanar's dungeons.

Why? *Why?*

Because she was an object, something to be used, bargained for, traded.

A thing the Harvester would have degraded even more.

To the west, stars boldly decorated the still night. Those in the east glimmered their last. Kneeling at the spring, she hesitated before beginning her ritual wash to savor the crisp tang of the moist air. Tumbling over the lip of its small pool, the flow greeted her with sibilant chatter.

From one of the deep pockets of her robe, she took out her soap container and drying cloth and positioned them on the ground, drying cloth to left, soap to right. Head bowed, she made the morning three-sign of the Iris Abbey. The hand was formed to represent the leaves and corm of an iris; forefinger bent, covered by the thumb, the remaining three fingers spread apart. With the knuckle of the thumb, she touched her forehead, then a point centered on her chest. Next she touched her eyes, right followed by left. To pray, she joined both hands so the index fingers were at the tip of her nose. "May I see the truth and pursue it with a true heart and clear mind. May I see wrong and avoid it. May I see in all things the wonder and glory of the One in All and be ever grateful that He sends the sun to remind us of the One Who Is Two."

She picked up the soap container. It was an ornately carved box of red cedar that had belonged to the Iris Abbess when she was a girl. It was made in two halves; the bottom held the soap and the top fit over it. A leather strap, with a cunning silver buckle cast in a warty little toad's head, held it closed. The toad's tongue was the tongue of the buckle, and she could never open it without remembering the old Abbess' lecture that he was the cleverest of creatures, because although it had the quickest tongue of all, it used it only to catch food.

The wood of the box was dark and silky, impregnated with the oils of thousands of bars of soap. Visually, as well as by texture, it gave life to the carved images of flowers on the sides of the lid. On the larger surface at the top was a portrait of a sister at prayer. Directly behind her head, placed so it could be taken for a halo—were such a thing not forbidden to Church—was a golden sun disk.

Sylah scrubbed vigorously, enjoying the spur of ice-cold water. When she was through, she dried as briskly, then replaced her belongings in her pocket and sought a place to greet the day.

As she had the previous mornings at this camp, she went to a flat rock at the edge of a sharp drop into the blackberry valley. There was only a moment for her to wonder where Lanta was before the first edge of the sun became visible through a low space between the looming, black peaks of the Enemy Mountains. She raised her arms, held them out horizontally.

Men called the posture obscene, said it was meant to expose women's bodies. Women called it greeting the sun.

And laughed secretly, knowing it was a cross, forbidden to women by men.

A petty victory, some would say, rather like the sun disk on the soap box that every sister knew was a halo. Still, a victory, in a world where oppression was a tradition and defeat was constant.

Perhaps not so petty, after all.

It was a good sunrise. With her eyes closed, Sylah sensed the light, felt the first, tentative warmth on her chilled face. "The darkness passes," she intoned. "Light is. Life is."

When she turned to go back to camp, she saw Lanta coming toward her from higher up the slope. When the smaller woman was beside her, Sylah said, "I didn't hear you get up this morning."

Lanta said, "I wanted to be early. I noticed a place up there

145

yesterday. It's not a hard climb, and the view's much grander. I should've asked you to go with me."

"I understand. We get little privacy. Especially you. You've been with Conway almost constantly."

Lanta gestured a shade too casually. "You spent a great deal of time with him, too. And you did much more work on Stormracer and Mikka."

Sylah was about to make a remark about the division of labor when she heard the noise. She stopped abruptly, throwing back her cowl, the better to listen. When Lanta tried to ask what the problem was, Sylah stopped her with a sharp, chopping gesture. Together, they posed like deer scenting the air.

"There," Sylah said at last. "You hear?"

"Barely. An elk bugling?"

Sylah grimaced, continuing their walk. "It could have been a mountain lion. Listen: Can you hear it now?" Once more they stopped. Tauntingly, the breeze stirred branches and fir needles, set the forest to snickering at them. Saw-edged blackberry leaves rubbed against each other with a noise like rushing water.

Lanta said, "The wind makes it so hard . . ."

Sylah lied. "My imagination, I guess. We're all nervous. It's the sitting, doing nothing, that makes us that way. I'm glad we're moving today." She *had* heard something. Vainly, she scanned the area for some visual clue.

"I'm not glad we're breaking camp, not at all. It's going to be very hard on Conway."

Sylah forced the matter of the noises out of her mind. She patted Lanta's shoulder. "He has to learn to endure. I've watched him. He's a fighter, but I sense something different about him. If I didn't know how many adventures he must have had, finding his way to Ola, I'd say he was untested. The fever's an example. He wasn't terribly injured in the fight with boar; he was recovering exactly as we expected. Then, for no good reason, he's sick. Terribly, frighteningly sick. Have you ever seen a man drop so quickly, so completely?"

Lanta was angrily defensive. "Many times. In plagues and things. He's very strong. He's almost completely well. And he's a good patient."

Sylah answered with careful solemnity, pointing with her chin. "Right now I think he's worrying about his stomach."

Conway was outside his lean-to, moving carefully, but making steady progress toward the cookfire where Tate was preparing

146

porridge. Dodoy glanced up from poking the coals with a stick. Offering no greeting, he went back to it.

The meal passed smoothly, with everyone returning easily into the routine of breaking camp and loading the pack animals.

Tate was delighted to be on the move again, particularly since Conway's unsteadiness made her the only choice to ride point. Whistling up her dogs, she instructed Dodoy to stay with Conway, and left ahead of the others.

Even when it was time to follow Tanno and Oshu into the narrow gap through the blackberries, she felt only confidence. She admitted easily that an animal such as the boar would be no less a challenge for her than for Conway. Perhaps more so. Strength was what saved him, not skill or cunning.

She thought back to the fight with the Skan captain. She'd nearly gotten killed, but she'd learned she could fight well enough to stay with the best. Strength wasn't the answer for her, though. Most men would easily outmuscle her. So far, there'd been neither opportunity nor need to confide her close combat training to Conway or the others.

She didn't know why she hadn't made the opportunity. It wasn't as if she were keeping it a secret. Not really. Still and all, thinking about not sharing information made her feel grimy.

She shook her head free of niggling questions.

Thought. That had to be her primary weapon. Always thinking, being one step ahead of everyone else: that was survival. The best way to help Sylah, too, of course. Aloud, she said, "You take the king's shilling, you do the king's work." It was a phrase that had died with its world, at least five centuries ago, but it was a philosophy that would sell well in this world. In truth, she didn't care if anyone agreed with it or not. It was the way she saw herself. She was a professional, and she'd signed on to help Sylah through to the end.

On the other hand, there were things she couldn't do.

At that point in her mental wandering, she arrived where the fight had taken place. Crushed and broken canes marked the scene, although the rains had invigorated the growth. Recovery was already well under way. New, eager stalks and leaves bent into the battle-created gaps, reaching for light. With the under-structure broken and knocked awry, the higher reaches of the jungle also sagged inward. Aggressive vine tips twined and coiled about each other in the struggle to claim the sun. They hooked Tate's clothing, plucked at her sleeves like importuning beggars. She drew her murdat and punished them.

While she did, she irritably told herself that worrying about her integrity wasn't the same as making reservations about her relationship with Sylah. In the first place, Sylah wouldn't ask her to do anything out of line. The crunch would come if Dodoy began to remember landmarks and wanted to take a course different from Sylah's. Tate admitted to herself that she wasn't sure she could remain by Sylah's side in that case.

Breaking one's word wasn't just something. Not for Donnacee Tate.

Was it worth that to find her own people? What would she ever do if she abandoned Sylah and Conway to follow her own needs?

Hacking at more vines, she asked herself what right any of them had to question her goals. They all had their own agenda.

Reining up suddenly, she shook her head, then rubbed her temples. Aloud, she said, "Listen to yourself, Tate. You hear what you're doing? Some friend."

From deep in the thicket, a bird sang a long, complex response. A moment later, it flitted into sight, skipping from perch to perch with mercurial unpredictability. Tate was close enough to see the pinpoint glisten of its eyes. Its tail, board stiff and perkily upright, jerked continually.

There was a brief flutter of wings, and it was gone. A heavy silence settled on the path. Tate's horse blew through its nose softly, as if reacting against the quiet.

The swift change of atmosphere reminded Tate forcibly of exactly where she was, and how hostile the place could be. She heeled her horse forward. It seemed to her it responded more readily than usual. When Tanno peered back from around a distant bend, checking on her mistress, Tate was so glad to see her she smiled openly. The dog wagged her tail and went back to work.

The trail led generally south and west. By the time she reached the first trees of the forest on the far side of the vine-dominated valley, it was midmorning. The sun broke through the high overcast briefly, then was hidden as a rolling boil of heavy clouds lumbered across the sky. They brought a spatter of rain, and for a moment she debated wearing her Dog-woven poncho or wrapping herself in the quilted Whale Coast cloth. The latter was completely waterproof and lighter, but thinking of the smell persuaded her to choose the poncho. The wool soaked up some water and got heavy, but it was prettier. The black and brown rattlesnake patterns on the dark green background made for better camouflage.

Strange, she thought; there'd been nothing to suggest she might need camouflage. Still, the thought had come forcefully.

Whistling in the dogs, she examined them carefully when they came into sight. Aside from the fact they were obviously enjoying roaming the countryside, there was nothing remarkable in their behavior. In fact, when the rest of the party caught up and broke free of the blackberry tangle, all four dogs romped happily in greeting.

Sylah suggested they eat before continuing. They never cooked the midday meal, not wanting to take the time or risk the smoke. Everyone chose from the available food loaded on the packhorses. For this occasion, Sylah selected dried meat, sprinkling it liberally with a pepper vinegar. Tate and Conway made an elaborate show of choosing dried fruit. Lanta, belying her size, tucked away a large bowl of pakka, a combination of nuts, toasted grains, and pieces of chopped, dried fruit.

Finishing quickly, they chatted easily as they resumed the journey. Sylah suggested to Tate that she leave the point duty to the dogs so she could ride along with the group. Tate accepted the idea. In spite of the relaxed atmosphere, however, they individually turned to watch the blackberry hollow disappear as the ranks of fir closed it off from view.

The trail continued gently downhill, generally southwest. Through the trees ahead, however, loomed a mountain's sheer stone face. The trail angled to the left of that feature, cutting between it and the higher mountains to the east.

When Conway attempted to apologize because the village they'd expected to find obviously didn't exist, Sylah stopped him. "We accepted the probability of confused trails when we decided to avoid people as much as possible. It's not certain we took a wrong turn or misunderstood directions. More likely, we got bad information. We'll be fine."

Tate and Lanta chorused agreement, just as they exited the forest onto the graveled shore of a beautiful triangular lake. One of its points aimed directly at the adjacent stone face. The latter loomed, despite the fact that it was a good quarter of a mile distant.

A breeze rippled the lake's emerald waters. It came from the south, channeled through the pass they'd soon be riding into. At the southern limit of the lake was the edge of a fairly recent burn. Instead of sky-blocking ancient trees, there were dead black spikes everywhere. They pointed accusingly at the sky, blaming it for the lightning that had destroyed them. High above, an eagle

149

drifted on the wind, tilting from side to side. It screamed once, a shrill, descending note. Following its course, Sylah rose in her stirrups, turning almost completely around to watch its grace.

Reversing its course, the bird called again, paralleling the landmark rock face. It was so close it seemed its wingtip must brush it. Sylah decided that it must have been the bird's cries she heard at the morning greeting with Lanta.

They reached the southern end of the lake a short time later. Green, tangled new growth fought to reclaim the scorched land. Sylah estimated the damage to be about four years old. Erosion scars were angry, open sores in the earth. The sight was so dramatic that the scent of burned wood came to Sylah as if the fire still raged.

Her line of thought was abruptly canceled when Karda and Mikka suddenly rushed forward. Karda positioned himself a few yards in front of Conway's horse. They all reined up, just as Oshu came into sight, racing for Tate. Halting in front of her mistress, the dog looked over back the way she'd come, and growled. Then she looked back to Tate for instructions.

Tanno remained somewhere ahead of them, out of sight, silent.

Sylah said, "Lead us, Tate. Have the dog take us to what troubles her."

Tate nodded, then spoke to the dog. It immediately began retracing its steps, the long, swinging stride requiring the horses to break into a trot to keep up. To Sylah, Tate said, "Tanno's probably got another boar or something spotted on the trail. I think Oshu'd be more excited if there were people involved."

"Let's hope so," Sylah said.

Tate frowned at Sylah's uncertainty. Turning, she waved Dodoy further back.

They'd ridden only a short distance when Oshu turned right, leaving the trail. She looked over her shoulder to assure she was being followed, then continued.

Tate said, "What's this? Did they decide to hunt down a deer, or something? They know better than that."

Conway said, "Karda and Mikka seem unconcerned. If it was a chase, they'd be wanting in on it."

Oshu led them uphill, toward the rock face of the cliff. They were some distance from its base, but huge slabs of rock, fallen over the ages, littered the ground. Passing out of the burn, the group rode through forest again. It was sparse, but the protective shade seemed to soften the unspoken, growing tension. Trotting out from behind one of the house-sized boulders, they saw Tanno ahead. She waited patiently, lying down, head swiveling from the direction of the cliff to the approaching riders, then back again. Seeing Tate, she wagged her tail once, then concentrated on something to her front. Whatever it was, it remained hidden from the group by another massive rock.

When they could see past that obstacle, they stopped and stared as one. Sylah's first thought was of the sounds she'd heard earlier. She'd tried to make herself believe they were the sounds of nature. Her heart had known what her mind refused to accept. Now there was no argument.

Circling in the sighing breeze, a black robed sister of Church spun slowly in obscene dance, hanged by a rope slung over a tree limb.

CHAPTER 26

The smoke from the smoldering campfire rose around the sister in a gentling shroud. Perversely, the body twisted to expose the choked, distorted face deep within the cowl. A shift in the wind drew the smoke back over it. Through her horror, Sylah thought how appropriate that even nature should try to hide such a cruel and shameless crime. Behind her, she vaguely heard Lanta's painful retching.

Tate was frozen, staring, Conway white with shock.

Sylah forced herself erect, heeled her horse forward.

The woman wore the three violets of a Tender of the Violet Order embroidered on the right breast of her robe. Nightmare-slow, Sylah reached for the rope. The knot, drawn iron hard, was nearly buried in the flesh of the neck. Whoever did this thing knew how to tie such a knot, how to assure it would squeeze off air, blood, and, finally, pain. Not that the latter was a charity. No.

Altanar's protectors hanged people. They used such a knot. They didn't kill by snapping the neck. For Altanar and his protectors, the end of pain was paid for with the end of life. One bought that relief slowly, slowly.

Sylah's fingernails ripped on the knot, then Conway was roughly shoving her away. His murdat flashed. A heavy, wet sound—not the brisk chop she expected—and the rope parted. Before Sylah could dismount, Conway sliced the knot. Part of her mind registered how competently his hand searched for a pulse.

He knew it was useless, of course, but it was form. Just as it was form for her to acknowledge his negative shake of the head.

Conway saw Lanta approach, and hurriedly drew the cowl closed.

Lanta started at the embroidered insignia. "One of us," she said in a hoarse whisper.

At first, Sylah thought she might be ill again. Lanta swallowed noisily, however, then inspected the features. That done, she closed the cowl once more. To Sylah she said, "I can't be sure. The disfigurement . . . I don't think I ever saw her before."

Tate asked, "What's she doing out here all alone? I mean, a Tender—that's high rank, right? Wouldn't she travel with a group? A guide, or companion, at least? And why on this out-of-the-way trail?"

Sylah agreed. "It makes no sense. Unless the friction between orders is out of hand, and a woman of such rank feels it's necessary to travel as secretly as possible."

Conway pointed to the sister's left wrist. "Outlaws," he said. "That tear in her wrist happened when someone jerked a bracelet free. Look how her fingers on the right hand are ripped; there were rings there, you can bet on it." With stiff, brusque movements he jammed his hands into the deep robe pockets, turning them inside out. "Nothing," he said. "Everything's gone. I'll check the campsite, see if I can find her horse."

"I'll help you," Lanta said, then to Sylah, "We have to have a pyre, Sylah. If you don't want to delay more, I'll stay behind and do it alone. She's my order."

Sylah said, "We'll burn her properly. 'Fire cleanses.' "

" 'Fire purifies us all,' " Lanta responded. Each executed a three-sign. Lanta hurried to follow Conway.

As Tate and Sylah carried the sister's body between them, Sylah was struck, as always, by the looseness. Many times she'd wondered about the final liberty of death. The Tender's hand dragged across the soft forest duff, creating a shallow furrow. It made Sylah feel the dead woman scorned them, was showing them that although they could lift and move her, her true obligation now was only to the pull of the earth. She had discovered eternity, and mocked their transitory concept of dignity.

Searching for a proper cremation place, Sylah discovered a niche in some rocks. With Tate, she attacked a downed tree with their axe, lopping branches for firewood. They created several crisscross layers before placing the sister on top, then laid another half-dozen layers atop her. When they were done, both women were sweat-drenched, and the sister was visible only as something darker than the shadowy pyre interior.

That was when Tate discovered Dodoy wasn't with them. She dropped the axe, raced to pick up her wipe where it rested against a tree. "Matt! Where are you? Is Dodoy with you?" She repeated herself twice, growing more agitated each time. Conway, Lanta, and his two dogs trotted into view some distance away. Conway yelled back, "Not with us."

Tate ran to leap into the saddle, whistling for Tanno and Oshu; the dogs were already racing to her. Ignoring the pleas of the others for her to wait, she pounded back through the forest, yelling Dodoy's name as she went.

From his perch high in the rocks above the lake, Dodoy watched the excitement. To his immediate left rose the cliff wall, while behind and above him was a more manageable, although quite steep, grade leading west over the top of the small mountain. Below him was very sparse forest that had found purchase in the rocks. The mountain sloped away gently for some distance to his right before dropping off abruptly. That was the pass they'd been headed for. The wind coming through it stirred the trees, made the branches dance.

The people below him were dancing, too, Dodoy thought, smiling. He had a clear view of them. Good enough to let him see Tate almost run over Lanta with her horse. The small Priestess tripped, went sprawling, rolling over and over. He clamped both hands over his mouth. There was little chance they'd hear him laugh at this distance, but there was no sense in taking a chance.

Once, on board the Skan ship, he found a wooden box with the top and bottom knocked out. He'd put it on the deck and dropped cockroaches in it. When he poked at them with the end of a burning stick, they scuttled and darted wonderfully. That was what the people looked like. Especially Lanta. Black. Legs and arms jerking. Just like a bug.

This was even better, though; the cockroaches could only run around. The only noise they made was tiny scrabbling. People yelled. The voices reaching him were thin and unintelligible. He wished he could hear exactly what they were saying.

It served them right. Especially Tate. She gave too many orders. Like sending him back behind everyone. How was he supposed to see anything from there? Waved at him, like he was one of the stupid dogs. And as soon as she saw the stupid woman hanging from the tree, she forgot all about him.

What was so important about someone already dead? If Tate really liked him, she'd have come to him, told him not to be afraid of the way the ugly purple face looked at him with its nasty, popped-out eyes.

He shivered and sat down, tucking his elbows into his sides.

Instead of coming to him, when he really wanted her to, what'd she do? Ran to the dead woman. Stupid. What could she do for her?

He thought of the cockroaches again. Whenever one reached the top of the box and tried to escape over the edge, he whacked it with the burning stick.

It'd be fun to be able to shoot arrows at Sylah and all of them. Not hit them, because they might shoot back. He certainly couldn't kill any of them. The others would leave him. Alone. Probably even take his horse away, make him walk.

None of them liked him. Not even Tate. She said she did, but all she cared about was where he came from. Thought there was a reward, something like that. Talked about how he reminded her of somebody in her family. She must think he was really stupid. She was *black*. No one else had skin like that.

But he knew he was from someplace far to the south of Ola. South of Kos, even. The man who sold him to the Skan captain said so. And he was from someplace where there wasn't any ocean; the first sight of all that water scared him. When they actually made him get on the ship and go out on it, he was so afraid he cried and wet himself.

Unconsciously, he squirmed in his hiding place, thinking of the way the captain made it clear he wasn't to do either of those things again.

His hand stole to the scars across his buttocks. Then he smiled, hearing the captain's sounds when Tate stuck the murdat in his crotch.

A person could get even. Sometimes better than even, if the person was patient. If the person was smart.

Down below, Tate was almost all the way back to the blackberries.

At least she'd given him a chance to escape from the ship.

The others were chasing her. Conway's dogs were gaining on her.

If they rode back into the thicket, there could be an accident. All he'd be able to see would be leaves jerking around. That wouldn't be any fun. Anyhow, if someone got hurt, they'd have

154

to sit around and wait for them to get well. Like for stupid Conway after his fight with the pig.

He'd tell them looking at the dead old woman scared him, so he ran away. Tate would believe. She'd keep the rest away.

He stood up and took a deep breath to yell, started a wave.

Something wrapped around him, pinned his arms to his side, crushed his chest. He rose in the air. A hand as rough as tree bark covered his mouth. Someone swung him behind a rock, spun him around. A heavy bearded face lowered itself to his level. The eyes were blue glass. The bushy brown beard moved. A voice came through it. "Not one sound, little rat. Not one." A knife appeared in the man's hand. It slipped across Dodoy's throat. Its bite was like a hundred mosquitoes, all at once, all in a line.

He squealed.

The man's laugh was quiet, like soft drumbeats. The knife stayed in place. He said, "I see you understand. Turn around. Hold your hands behind you."

Dodoy obeyed instantly. With practiced swiftness, the man crossed the wrists and lashed them together, painfully tight. Next, the man grabbed a large clutch of Dodoy's hair. The other hand grasped his belt in the back. Dodoy rose once more. He thought his hair would pull right out of his head; his trousers tried to split him in two. He gritted his teeth: *Not a sound.*

The man slammed him down on a horse. Dodoy reached vainly for the stirrups. With his hands tied, the only way he could keep his seat was with his knees.

The man got on Dodoy's horse. He reached down to take the reins of the animal Dodoy was riding, saying, "You should feel honored, little rat. The last person to sit that saddle was a high-ranking Violet Priestess." Seeing Dodoy's reaction, he laughed again, the same muted drumming.

Dodoy started to cry.

The man said, "That's good. Very good. That'll help. You want to live, rat?"

"Yes! Yes. I'll do whatever you tell me. I promise."

Jerking the reins, pulling Dodoy's horse in trail, the man said, "I wouldn't trust your promise any more than I'd try to save a snowflake on my tongue. Just do as you're told and hope it works."

"I will. I do." Dodoy wanted to say more, but the man growled at him to be quiet.

Tears continued to stream down Dodoy's face. He cursed them all. Fools. Cockroaches. If they'd left him alone, none of this

155

would have happened. They were happy in Ola. That witch, Sylah. And Tate, stupid Tate, her and her stupid orders.

Now this. The man would sell him.

He hated them. All of them. Stupid dogs should have found him right away.

Lanta, Conway, Tate; they followed Sylah. Her fault. Their fault. All of them. Whatever happened, they deserved it.

CHAPTER 27

Conway whistled the dogs back to him, letting Tate plunge into the blackberries. It didn't make sense to him that Dodoy would wander back down the trail that far, nor could he believe he'd re-enter that thicket alone. Once over the shock of discovering the boy missing, Conway reasoned that their best chance of finding him was the dogs.

Karda and Mikka came to a stop in front of Stormracer and sat, waiting instructions. Conway pointed away from the blackberry thicket. "Karda. Mikka. Seek. Dodoy." At his *go* hand signal, they padded away purposefully.

The dogs soon left the trail for the mountain to the west. Conway called to Tate. There was no answer. Sylah and Lanta waved acknowledgment, galloping to rejoin him from the edge of the thicket. He waited for them, then called Tate one last time before following the dogs.

The trio proceeded slowly, scanning the ground for hoofprints. Occasionally one or the other would exclaim over some perceived mark, and they'd discuss it. In every case, they eventually admitted they were guessing. They were in one such conference when Conway looked up and was surprised to see Mikka hurrying toward him.

Conway had convinced himself Dodoy was simply off on some self-centered entertainment of his own. Now he wasn't sure. If the boy was so close, he certainly heard Tate's distressed calls. Conceding his dislike for Dodoy, Conway still didn't want to believe the boy would torment her.

The size and number of the boulders began to interfere with his progress. Mikka, unconcerned about a horse's ability to navigate narrow passages or scramble across haphazard rock piles, led Conway into three impassable situations in a row. Frustrated and

156

irritated, Conway had just turned around to ride back out of the last dead end when a bedraggled Tate pushed past the two Healers to confront him. She said, "Why are you going back? Aren't you going to help me look?"

He glared. "The horse can't fly, Donnacee. This gully's impassable a few yards beyond here. Of course, I intend to keep looking. If you get out of the way."

Tate scrambled clear. "Well, why aren't you calling him, reassuring him? The dog doesn't like him. The poor kid's scared to death, that brute staring—"

Conway jabbed his heels in Stormracer's ribs, drowned the rest of her complaint in the clatter of hooves on rock. Mikka, confused, dropped her tail and set about leading on yet another route. Conway wished he could make her understand that all she had to do was follow the track of Dodoy's horse, and everything would be fine. The dog, however, wanted only to take the most direct—dog direct—route to Karda.

Tate, distracted and afraid, rode so close to Conway that her horse crowded his. In turn, Stormracer kept trying to escape that pressure. Conway's neck grew redder with every step.

Lanta whispered to Sylah. "This is getting very bad. Can we do anything?"

Sylah shook her head. "Once Tate has the boy in hand, everything will calm down."

Lanta said, "She should leave Conway alone. She's going to make trouble, you watch."

Ahead of them, Conway gave a strangled shout as Stormracer reared and spun, determined to rid himself of the irritation from Tate's mount. Tate belatedly yanked at the reins as her horse dodged lashing hooves. Then Tate's dogs decided their mistress was threatened. They rushed at Conway. Tate's sharp command brought them back to her side, still bristling.

It was all over in moments. Nevertheless, the atmosphere was changed. Where there had been tension, now there was a sense of damage done.

Pungently, Conway suggested Tate practice some of the vaunted discipline she claimed to personify. "Start with yourself," he shouted over his shoulder, sending the still-skittish Stormracer after Mikka, adding, "and when you see some progress in that direction, you might want to give some thought to your horse, your dogs, and that kid, too."

"Just find your own dog," she answered. "Or else get out of the way and let me do it."

Her expression when she stole a glance at Sylah and Lanta proved she knew she'd been wrong. The sudden set of her shoulders was a clear statement that she had no intention of admitting it. Nervous fingers drumming the stock of her wipe, she waited for Sylah and Lanta to reach her side before following at a more discreet distance.

They all saw the man holding Dodoy simultaneously.

He stood atop a huge slabsided flat rock that jutted from the mountainside like an altar. The steep slope rose so it was an easy step to the ground at the back end. The front was too high to vault onto, and the man had a clear view of anyone attempting to flank him. Two steps off the rear of his stage would put him among shielding boulders that offered protection all the way to the crest. In a dark long-sleeved jacket and matching trousers, he waited, spread-legged, calm and composed. He wore a sword strapped to his back, the blade long enough to reach down his back to his buttocks, while the hilt projected over his left shoulder. A slung bow and the feathered butts of a quiver of arrows projected above the right.

Karda sheltered behind a rock off to the flank, only the crown of his head and eyes exposed, ears flattened to his skull. Instead of turning to look at Conway, the animal rolled his eyes as far as he could, then returned his attention to the man. Mikka took cover behind a tree, alternately watching Conway and the stranger.

The man held Dodoy in front of him, peering over the top of the boy's head. His left arm encircled Dodoy's waist. His right hand held the knife to Dodoy's throat. A wash of blood stained the boy's pale skin. When he struggled and attempted to call to them, the polished blade twitched and glared light directly into Tate's eyes. The shock broke her trancelike state. She screamed at the man.

"Let him go! You've cut him, damn you. Let him *go*."

Unruffled, the man addressed Conway. "I'll trade. The Iris one, Rose Priestess Sylah. The boy for her."

"No." Conway unobtrusively flicked off the wipe's safety, eased a round into the chamber. "Let him go."

"Ask the others. Ask the Black Lightning behind you. She says the boy is hers. We both know it's an escaped slave. By law, I should deliver the two of them to the rightful owner. Instead, I offer something the Tate one wants for someone who's nothing to you, the Rose Priestess Sylah."

Sylah moved forward, stopping beside Conway. He noticed she was careful to stay to his left, automatically staying clear of a

158

right-handed man's sword arm. Her voice reeked with scorn. "I know you, Protector. Who throws you bones since Altanar's fall? You think to find your disgraced king, give me to him?"

For the first time, the man reacted. Color flooded his cheeks. His eyes widened. It took a moment for him to regain control. "I serve whoever pays. I serve their gold well."

"You killed a Priestess. Your life is ended. What am I to you?"

He shook his head. To Conway, he said, "I do business with men. The boy for the woman."

By design, or by momentary lapse, Dodoy slipped. As the man moved to regain his grip, the knife pulled away from the boy's throat. Free of the blade, Dodoy screamed. "Give him Sylah! Donnacee! Mother! Make him let me go."

The protector replaced the knife. Dodoy quieted.

Tate broke into tears. When Conway turned to face her, she shook her head, refusing to meet his gaze.

Sylah said, "If I go . . ."

Conway shouldered his horse into hers, nearly spilling her. He said, "If he tries to take Dodoy away, I'll blow his feet off."

The exchange brought Tate forward. With one hand on Sylah's shoulder, she stared up at Dodoy, saying, "Don't shoot, Conway. He'll cut him sure."

Nodding, the man agreed. "I watched the Falconer one demonstrate your lightning weapon for Altanar. Kill me, and the knife still gets this one."

Conway said, "Just put him down. Leave. We won't come after you."

The man laughed, white teeth gleaming through the beard. "That's not good enough, Conway. My problem is, Church won't rest until its lovely ladies smell my burning. Unless I get the Rose Priestess, I have to take the boy with me to protect myself. That means your black friend'll never rest until she puts my guts on the ground. The Priestess is the key to my life." Dramatically, he hoisted Dodoy by the collar, dangling him as if peddling a rabbit in a market. "Trade, or look on this for the last time."

Tate was shaking violently. She braced herself on the saddle with both hands. "I'll find you. I'll track you down and I will kill you. Not for revenge. For the pleasure of seeing you die."

Soberly, the man said, "I know you'll try."

Sylah said, "Donnacee, my dear, dear friend. I'm so sorry. It's going to be all right." She reached to cover Tate's hands where they rested.

Tate flinched at the touch. Eyes closed, lips stretched over

159

clenched teeth, she said, "I don't want to hear it. I don't want to think about it. Your wonderful plans, your grand adventure. See what—"

Conway shouted at her. "Stop it! It's not her fault, Tate. Don't make things worse."

The protector was laughing again. He finally spoke, addressing Sylah. "Well, Priestess, see what love and respect your goodness has earned you. Is the black one your friend? Watch her, in the days to come. Every time she looks at you, she'll picture her darling pet cold and dead. Or digging in a godkill, not knowing the difference between life and death. I kill only to survive. She wants to kill me for the pleasure of it. Which of us is the better? Think about that. Think about her sleeping beside you." He sheathed the knife, adjusted his hold on Dodoy, took a step backward.

Grimly, Conway conceded that the only decent shot he'd get was if the man grew careless. He changed his grip on the wipe, tensing for a snap shot.

Tate moaned audibly as the man continued to retreat, step by wary step. She raised her weapon, but immediately lowered it. Her teeth worried at her lower lip, and tears ran unchecked down her cheeks.

Dodoy cried piteously, begged for Tate. His shrill hysteria unnerved her. She called his name. Tanno and Oshu crowded close to her horse, confused, and angry. Karda and Mikka, dark eyes fixed on the protector, rose to a crouch, ready to charge. Conway's soft command brought them to order.

Dodoy screamed.

Tate leapt from her horse and ran forward, Tanno and Oshu bounding beside her. Instantly, the protector stopped, and when he did, Dodoy shrieked at Tate to get back. "You made him cut me again. You let him get me, and he's hurting me. Save me. *Save me!*"

Tate flinched as if each word were a fist. She fell to her knees, hands outstretched. Wordless agony, almost a melody of pain, flowed from her open mouth.

The protector resumed his retreat, backing steadily closer toward the uphill slope and the protective warren formed by rocks and trees. He paused, offering one last taunt. "I'm leaving you the old Priestess' horse, Conway, and the boy's."

He half turned.

Conway actually heard the arrow before he saw it. The whir of its passage was an uncertainty in his mind, like a riddle whose answer he knew, but couldn't quite remember. Then, wondrously, terribly, the white shaft was growing out of the back of the protector's shoulder. The man stiffened. His hesitant steps forward were the self-conscious mincing of deep embarrassment. Dazed concern clouded his face.

The second arrow struck below the first, closer to the spine. It dropped him to his knees. His hands flopped to his sides.

Dodoy never looked back. Free of the encircling arm, he was sprinting off the short step at the back of the rock when his feet touched the ground.

Tate was waiting for him, scooping him up in midstride. Dodoy shouted at her to run, pummeling her back with his fist. She bent over him protectively and raced to shelter behind a convenient boulder. Belatedly, the rest of the group took cover, searching warily, unsure if they dealt with a benefactor or another raider.

On the top of the rock, the protector continued to sway back and forth.

Thinking aloud, Conway said, "He looks like he's mourning."

"He is," Sylah said.

When the man toppled, the quiet rustle was the only sound in the forest. Into that yawning silence, Sylah called up the mountain. "Hello! Who are you? I am Rose Priestess Sylah, a War Healer of the Iris Abbey." The stillness continued. When Sylah called again, it was a questioning, "Hello?"

Cautiously, Conway approached the body. Snowy arrow feathers on a white shaft twitched in the wind. Shielding his eyes, Conway peered uphill. "Are you a protector?"

The answer was laughter. Not scornful, or mocking; rich with satisfied amusement. The group exchanged nervous glances. The very lightheartedness of their benefactor made the situation all the more macabre.

A distant clatter of rocks spoke of departure.

Sylah advanced. She and Lanta moved the dead man to the edge of the flat-topped rock. Copper, scenting blood, pranced and jittered.

Conway rode up. "What're you doing?"

"He has to have a proper burning," Sylah said.

"Leave him. The other animals'll take care of him."

She glared. "You shame. He is not an animal. It is our duty."

He matched her stare as long as he could, then, muttering under his breath, he bent to the body and lifted it. Sylah steadied Copper and Conway slung the man across, lashing him in place.

There was no talk on the way back to the Tender's body. When Sylah asked Conway to place the protector on the same pyre, he simply grunted disapproval and did as bid. That done, he stalked off, ostensibly for more firewood.

Lanta aimlessly wandered to the Tender's campsite. She imagined the other woman, alone in this wilderness. Had her killer come skulking in the night? Or did he ride up boldly, full of friendly greeting and murderer's guile?

Lanta's skin was clammy. Pulse throbbed at her temples, in her throat. She sat down against a rock. Her hand, limp on the ground, found a stone. She brushed it away irritably. And gasped aloud as the purple fire of the True Stone skipped across a shaft of sunlight, trailing its gold chain.

As soon as she could move, Lanta scooped up the holy treasure, stuffed it into the inner pocket at the breast of her robe. The stone eliminated any question. The woman in the grove at Ola was the Tender herself.

The True Stone. How? Why? Images—disjointed, unrelated fragments—slashed across her inner vision.

"Lanta?" Someone was shaking her. It hurt. She squinted, made a mewing noise in her throat. The hands turned gentle, stroked her temples, rubbed her wrists. She opened her eyes to meet the deep blue of Sylah's worried look. Sylah said. "What's wrong? Are you ill?"

"Thinking about our sister," Lanta said, hiding behind the half truth of it. "I'm all right. Really." Hating her own slyness, she continued, "Why would one as important as a Tender be here? Have you any idea?"

Sylah shook her head, as much in wonder as denial. When she offered Lanta a hand, she accepted it gratefully. On her feet, gripping the Stone, she felt more secure. Still, when Sylah said, "It's time," she nearly broke down again. Mustering her strength, she fell in beside Sylah. They moved to the pyre.

Sylah struck the sparks, lighting the tow. Together, they recited the prayer for swift passage to the Land Above, not stopping until the ashes of Priestess and killer were mingled, indistinguishable from the fuel that consumed them.

Sylah rose slowly. She said, "We should make camp elsewhere, even if it means a night ride. We have to leave behind everything that happened here. Everything." Her voice trembled with sorrow, as well as with the unspoken fear that forgetting might be the one insurmountable task that could break them.

162

CHAPTER 28

Jones followed Fox. Flat on their stomachs, they inched the last few yards toward the juniper-crowned ridgeline that was their objective. At this altitude, the air was cool. The lowering sun at their backs contributed little warmth, and the crisp, tangy scents of sage and juniper seemed to promise even greater chill as dusk deepened. In tantalizing contrast, the evening sky was a horizon-to-horizon display of thick-bellied clouds that resonated warm shades of pink, orange, salmon.

The Mountain warrior moved farther up the slope, his headband sporting sprigs of brush and grass. Jones, similarly equipped, and dressed in identical leather shirt and jacket, waited until Fox reached the ridge before starting his own climb. When Fox turned to glare at the noise behind him, Jones had to look away to avoid laughing. The man looked like an angry shrub.

Continuing up, Jones put a finger on his wrist to check his pulse while he reflected on what was about to happen. The beat was steady and sure. A surge of pride swelled his heart. Not many men in history—in either world—had been called on to make the decisions that were calling out to him almost daily.

He refocused on Fox. There was a good example of his leadership problems. A perfect savage; superstitious, absolutely group oriented. Impervious to pain, ambition, enticement. Integrated into his environment with human skills and the cunning of the beasts. Anyone would see all that. Who else would see the perfect pawn? No one. Nor would anyone else be able to control such an elemental force.

Fox signaled him forward, and Jones pushed himself across the stony soil and prickly growth in noisy imitation of a snake. He ignored Fox's pained gestures demanding silence. Fox would have to learn that leaders weren't expected to perform like creatures of the field. For an exciting moment, Jones' mind flowed with lush images of retribution.

He was close enough to the crest to look over now, if he stretched. Savoring what was to come, he resisted the impulse, pushing himself the last scratchy inches to his first view of what awaited him so that it would be free of any distraction.

Fox's scouting report had been very descriptive, so Jones expected no surprises. What was important was to see it properly, to absorb the scope of it. It must come to him in a burst, all at once, to fill him with the power of its potential.

Eyes closed, he felt the earth slope away under his palms and splayed fingers. He rested his chin on the back of his hands. Looked into the future. Looked at the engine sent to carry him in glory into the new world.

The nomads covered the immense floor of the valley between crenellated mountains. The camps were separated, sometimes by a mile or more. The campfires were just flickering to life in the purple-gray dusk. Great, high-wheeled wagons loomed like stolid beasts in the crepuscular softness. The tents were domes, with saucerlike caps above the smoke holes in the roofs. Some, with cookfires burning inside, glowed like coals studded into the flat valley floor. The haze from so many fires combined to create a shimmer across the landscape. Its wavering translucence added to the impact of the scene, giving it a mystic, transient air. Jones imagined blinking, then opening his eyes to discover everything gone.

The notion was a delicious fright. He shivered. Fox clamped a restraining hand on his shoulder. It was a gross liberty, and for one blind, raging instant, Jones thought of his rattlesnakes, the thick bodies compressed in S-curved anticipation, measuring . . .

He composed a placating smile.

With the disappearance of the sun, the darkness was pierced by fires below and stars above. Jones found it awe-inspiring, an omen, a battle for dominance between sky and earth.

Torch-bearing nomad security patrols began riding in. Fox sneered. With his mouth practically touching Jones' ear, he said, "They destroy the night eye. Worse, they tell everyone where they are. My warriors would follow, like wolves trail a lamb to the flock. These people are fools."

Before Jones could comment, Fox gestured for silence. It took a while before Jones heard the approaching horses. Fox held up five fingers twice, pointing toward the sound. Jones hurriedly indicated retreat. Fox shook his head in a negative.

Riding in two loose columns, the patrol passed within fifteen yards of the men hidden on the ridge. They paused directly below to light their torches, giving Jones ample time to study them. The leader was a tall, swarthy man with a mane of hair bound in a club that trailed almost to his waist. Two of his patrol affected the same style, while four were shaved completely bald. The latter all wore hats, which they'd taken off, now that the sun was no problem. Jones noted that two of the bald ones showed the scars of old wounds; one in particular made him reach to touch his own injury.

All wore long-sleeved cloth shirts. Trousers were cloth, with tie-on leather covers in front to protect against brush. Footwear was boots, but where some reached almost to the knee, others barely reached the ankle. Every man carried the same weaponry. Most obvious was a lance. Jones estimated it at about eight feet in length. The sharp end was a barbless iron cap; the butt was leather-wrapped. A brass tubular fitting on each saddle at the rider's right rear provided a holder. With the butt inserted in the tube, the point rode to the rear, angled at such a degree that no rider closing from behind would impale himself. In addition, the men carried bows and arrows. When the leader drew his sword from its copper-bound leather scabbard to point toward the camp while giving orders, Jones saw it was relatively short, almost exactly as long as the man's arm from wrist to armpit, with a thick, massive blade.

Remembering the Dog warriors who'd harried him and Altanar southward out of Ola, Jones wondered how the two forces would match up in combat. These people rode bulkier horses and their weapons indicated a different philosophy. The Dogs relied more on speed and elusiveness. This was heavy cavalry. Their bows and arrows were long, designed to be launched from a distance. That would disorganize the opponent. Then the charge with lances. Finally, the cleaverlike swords, battering as well as hacking.

While Jones analyzed and measured, the unsuspecting patrol got their torches burning satisfactorily, then descended the mountainside at a fast walk.

Once inside the camp, the torches split off, each seeming to drift among the tents like an errant spark, glimmering out when the individual rider arrived home.

For some time the camps bustled with activity. Faint sounds drifted up to the watchers. Music. Laughter, on one occasion loud and rollicking. Horses whinnying, cattle bellowing. Incongruously, a rooster.

The camp quieted slowly, so that silence simply slipped over it.

Then, shuddering across the valley, came the low mourning of horns. Jones inhaled audibly.

Fox had reported the night horns, as well as the deep, rolling chant that flowed from each camp even as the brazen echoes continued to call. He had failed to convey the stunning effect.

Recovering his composure, Jones said, "The chant of the moonless night. I've never heard the ceremony so magnificently done."

165

While he spoke, fires leapt to life in the approximate center of each camp. Dimly, they could see the firemen, the ones who would keep the flames alive through the darkness. Jones went on, "What a pleasure it'll be to perform all the rites among such a throng, among people dressed in richness."

Fox was defensive. "We do all the rites now, just as you instruct."

"Of course you do." Jones patted his arm, placating. "But see how much more impressive it is down there? Hundreds—thousands—of people, all obeying the same commands?"

"What matter how many believe, if a thing is the truth? Are we less good Moondancers because we are few? Or poor?"

Jones sighed, letting silence convey his irritation.

Both men shifted, suddenly aware how long they'd been in one position.

The other noises began shortly after that. Far to the east, a wolf howled. Haunting, chilling, an answer rose from the south. Down in the valley, close to the now-invisible tents, a coyote yammered. Several others joined his song, touching off barking challenges from the camp dogs. Moments later, a dog snarled, then yelped. Immediately, it was screaming, and the sounds of animals fighting erupted. The screams ended sharply. Humans shouted. Mocking coyote yowls answered.

Silence filled the valley once more.

Jones slid back off the crest, indicating Fox should come with him. When they could stand with no danger that their heads might be silhouetted, Jones looped his hand under Fox's belt in the back. In trail, he let the more nature-wise warrior lead to their previously established campsite.

The walk took nearly twice as long in the dark as it had in daylight, even with Fox leading. Still, when they reached the narrow cleft between a pair of downed trees, they settled down by mutual understanding, too intrigued by what they'd seen to simply fall asleep.

Jones started the conversation as Fox built a tiny fire in a hole. "Don't misjudge their scouts and the torches," he said. "They're not fools, Fox. Fools don't roam and conquer as we hear they have. What you saw is confidence. They've scouted this land. They know they're being watched. They're telling the watchers that they don't care if anyone knows where they are. 'Attack, if you dare,' they're saying."

"I'd attack. The Mountain People are like the tiger. Step on our territory prepared to die."

166

"True," Jones agreed equably. "And when men choose to, they hunt the tiger down and kill it, not because they're stronger or better hunters, but because there are too many of them for the tiger."

Fox's voice from the darkness carried the image of wounded pride. "Then why have you had me and my men endanger ourselves by observing them? If they're too strong for us, why do we approach them?"

Jones poked in the firepit long enough for a fresh-cut green stick to ignite. The faint light sharpened his features to acute angles. After grinding out the flame, he rose. Pointing at his companion with the smoldering wand, he said, "We shall defeat them, then command them. You are my weapon. Strike their patrols. Strike those who search for you. Creep into their camps, strike at their sleeping hundreds. Kill, and kill again. This leader, this Katallon, must understand that he follows false prophets. You bring him confusion and irritation. I will bring him relief, and then I shall show him conquest beyond his imaginings. We shall create."

"Create? Something to impress Katallon? After we've killed his people?"

Throwing back his head, Jones laughed. The metallic ring of it made his companion shift nervously. When Jones resumed speaking, his voice rasped. "Exactly that. Be with me, serve me with all your heart and skill, and I will give you Katallon's warriors to command. *Believe.*" He thrust his face within inches of Fox's. Sweat-dampened skin gleamed red as fresh blood in the coalglow. When Fox stared back into the probing eyes fixed on his, the embers were reflected there, burning at him from deep, deep in Jones' skull.

Fox stood, trembling. "I do believe. I obey. Moonpriest. Reborn to rule above all other men."

A son. The man responded like a true son. Jones' throat tightened with emotion.

Moonpriest, Fox called him. Moonpriest. Religion personified. Certainly.

CHAPTER 29

The column moved warily, horses and men combined into one immense, sinuous beast that slipped through the dry forest. Flankers searched the ridges paralleling the valley's swift-flowing stream, while a point force of twenty men led the way. Another group of twenty rode rearguard. Teams of two riders each scoured the ground between the flankers and the main body, following an erratic course that took them from one potential hiding place to another.

Approximately a mile from where the lead riders carefully picked their way through the trees, the valley bent to the north at a sharp angle. The earth had broken there, twisted by a spasm beyond imagining in a time lost to man's memory or present learning. A stream leapt into space at that break, creating a waterfall that cloaked the granite wall in swirling, lacelike folds. The midmorning sun struck at the sheeting flow, transformed it into exuberant silver. The delicacy of shimmering rainbows contradicted the tumult of falling water and the wind it stirred up.

High above the canyon, Jones stood motionless beside a tree and watched the advance. From behind him, on slightly higher ground, Fox said, "It's as you suspected. The man's leading them to our camp."

Jones nodded easily. "I didn't suspect. I knew. No protector has the skills to avoid trackers. As soon as he deserted, I knew he'd be captured and tell all he knew." He changed the subject. "The commander of that column is quite good. You were right to advise against an ambush in the valley."

"We've taught them caution."

"You're phenomenal people. Three dead in three weeks of raids. And Katallon's patrols only got the body of one of them. They must think your men are ghosts."

"I hope so. But I think we should leave now. The column should be working itself into an attack position shortly before dark."

It was a short walk to the reverse side of the ridge and their horses. On the way, they passed the other men assigned to observe the column. Some were former protectors, some were Fox's Mountain warriors. Despite his earlier remark, Jones was im-

168

pressed by the improvement in the field skills of the protectors. Nevertheless, there was something about them that made it obvious that they were fugitives. Fox's people had the eerie ability to suddenly appear in one's vision, and the worst thing about them was that they were invariably watching. They were simply, suddenly there. They made Jones very nervous, made him think of the tiger that he and the other crèche survivors saw on their first day leaving the cave. He had known fear—yes, even terror—in a world of poison gas, nuclear weapons, and terrorism. In this world he'd looked *into* death the moment his eyes met those of that animal. It still made his breath come in sharp, almost painful bursts to realize that another life-form saw him as nothing more than food.

The experience continued to color his perception. Other men judged as men. Moonpriest must evaluate from a different, higher, viewpoint.

That was how he dealt with these, his nucleus.

The Mountain warriors were deadly, but only men. Dirty men, at that. At least they bathed now. Jones shuddered at the memory of their sanitary habits before he could convince them that washing wouldn't make them more vulnerable to the unseens of other tribes. There were so many things like that—rituals and prayers with no known origin, customs that served no apparent purpose, but which had acquired the authority of tradition. The Mountain People they'd met on their southward journey weren't nearly as fierce as Fox's tribe. Why was that? And why did they have a sacred fire, and Fox's branch didn't?

Those questions, and others, kept his mind occupied during the ride to the campsite on the plateau behind the waterfall. By the time they arrived, the sun was halfway between its highest point and the tops of the higher mountains to the west. As Jones dismounted, rubbing the inside of thighs that never seemed to adjust to horseback, one of the protectors hurried up, sliding from the saddle, hitting the ground at a trot. His horse ambled a few paces farther. The rider approached Jones, reporting. "The scouts are almost up to the plateau, very excited, talking a lot. Our patrol leader's afraid they'll attack as soon as they see the camp."

The danger of an undisciplined charge by the advance elements of the column was very real. If it happened, it would cause problems. Even followers as thoroughly cowed as his would be affected by the deaths of their women and children.

So far, his judgments had been perfect. The plan would work.

All his plans were perfect. The signs were unarguable, inescapable.

Which didn't mean that details should be ignored. Jones told the rider, "Go back to your leader. Tell him to follow my instructions." To Fox, he said, "Go, assure that everything's in order."

The camp appeared normal. Children played. Warriors around a fire sharpened weapons. A group of women skinned and butchered a wildcow. Slabs of meat were passed to women at a small table. They rubbed them with handfuls of salt, then layered them with more salt in a large stoneware jar.

The steady clash of metal on metal drew Jones' eyes. A man was raising a bowl by pounding a sheet of copper on a rounded tree stump. A bed of coals glowed dully next to the worker, and as Jones watched, the man took the roughly rounded form and worked it down into the coals. With a pair of tongs, he moved it around until he was satisfied, then settled back to wait for it to heat properly.

Jones knew that the heat treatment restored the ductility of the copper. Without that annealing it became brittle, and instead of forming a smooth curve under the hammering, it shattered.

The Mountains' version differed. They said that because the metal was born of fire, it took life from fire; the coldness of the hammer could kill it.

Jones sighed and turned away. Suddenly, the sight of the conical little tents depressed him. Barbaric, cramped, smelly leather painted with symbols of superstition. He squatted and waddled through the ground-level entry of his own tent. Rising inside, his head nearly touching the crown where the poles met, he slumped back to his knees. He considered falling over on the bed, then rejected the idea. A cloth bag full of rough herbs and pine tips. Wonderfully scented, but a couch for a man destined to lead all men to salvation?

To the side, the rattlesnakes watched him from their individual rectangular baskets of woven willow. Patient eyes, sharp as obsidian chips, watched his every move. Supple forked tongues darted. Only Moonpriest could thrust his arms into those baskets and extract them entwined in living death.

To what purpose? To awe less than two hundred and fifty savage men, women and children who seriously believed that flutes made of human bones were superior to wood? To command the obedience of a squad of unemployed torturers?

He sprawled on the bed, let the aromatics settle on him. He surrendered to his mind, let it take him where it would.

The nomad column would be destroyed. But how was that to help him? Surely he wasn't expected to spend the rest of his life skulking through the forest, a jackleg priest spreading Moondance gospel while hiding from Katallon or someone like him?

He'd prefer to irritate the snakes, then put his head in the basket.

He pictured them striking. It would hurt. Oh, yes; terribly. He'd groan. And pull back. But he'd persevere. The wounds turn purple-black. Jones' eyes bulge. A fang penetrates one . . .

A fitting end. A death to refute whatever unknown power gave him dominion over those creatures in the first place.

Engulfed in melancholy, he crawled to the exit hole and gazed out at the camp again. A boy yelled angrily and goats bleated; a woman called for her daughter to come start the cookfire. The woman was packing a large jar, fine enough to be called porcelain, into a carrying case of woven branches. Thin supports encircled the jar, protecting it and preventing spills.

On the edge of the camp, a man ran his fingers lightly over a hoop drum. The bass whisper floated through the trees. Beside him, a younger man with a long, round piece of copper hammered one end to a point. Forcing the smaller end through a hole bored in a steel plate, he grabbed the protruding bit with pincers and pulled the whole length through. When he was done, he had a longer, thinner piece. He coiled the length around his wrist.

That, thought Jones, summed up their highest ambitions. They knew nothing. None of them. What use could they be in helping a man like him reach his destiny?

Acid tears filled his eyes.

And then he saw it all, every detail.

He laughed, the joy erupting in bellows, in lung-stretching howls, in an ecstatic paean.

When he stopped, heaving for breath, the silence of the camp filtered through the leather tent walls, pressed against him. A tremulous voice finally lifted in wavering song. It was a Moondance hymn, asking for protection from madness.

Fixing a fatherly smile, he moved outside. It was nearly dusk. Far to the east, Fox and the bulk of his watchers were just coming into sight on their return to camp. Beyond Fox, about an hour's fast walk, was where the climb from the valley ended and the plateau began. Jones felt the hating eyes of the nomad scouts burning across the distance.

The woman who'd been singing looked away. He walked to her, took her by the shoulder. "Look at me." She turned her head painfully, forced herself to meet his gaze. Gently, Jones said, "I understand your fear. Don't try to understand me or what I do. I am not of your understanding. Trust me. Obey. And I will deliver you to a world beyond your dreams." He continued to stare directly into her eyes until she wavered. Her eyelids fluttered. When he asked her if she believed in him, she was barely able to mutter "Yes," and when he released her, she staggered away as if drugged.

Jones shouted, letting joy propel his voice. "Everybody! Somebody! Find Altanar. I want my fool. Bring him to me. This evening Altanar entertains us all."

Outstretching his arms, Jones turned slowly, extending blessings to all. "Be calm, my people," he said to the gathering group. "Tonight we begin our march to glory."

CHAPTER 30

Fox tightened his grip on the thick branch supporting him before stretching his torso out into the night. The ground was invisible, but he remembered only too clearly how far below it was.

He inhaled deeply, slowly, casting for any helpful eddy of the wind.

The warmer air of the valley rose, bringing with it the story of the day's activity. He smelled the crushed pine needles of the trail, the gritty dust kicked up by hooves, the rankness of horse droppings and urine. Running through all of that was the salty, bitter scent of men anticipating action; frightened, excited, men. On a hunt they had a similar smell, but less pronounced. Unless, of course, they pursued a wounded prairie bear, or a tiger; it was the prospect of injury that honed the odor to its finest edge.

Lastly, almost apologetically, a final aroma. Softer, out of place, there was the tight, crackling-clean smell of the scrubbed air that passed through the waterfall's mists. It had no importance for him, and he shook his head irritably to clear it.

It had been a long time since the nomad warriors silently poured up and over the lip of the plateau. The final scout reports revealed their plan of attack. Two groups of about forty men each had started working their way forward and to the flanks of the camp shortly after dark. They carried no bows or torches, but had swords. It was obvious their primary task was to assure no one escaped past them.

That left considerably more than one hundred men to stage the frontal assault on the village. The scouts reported the main element was in two lines, perhaps fifty paces apart. Only the men of the second line carried torches.

To Fox's right, a coyote yipped a short chorus. A moment later a deer barked somewhere off to the left.

Congratulating his enemy on excellent imitations, Fox settled against the branch, concentrating.

This was the most elaborate ambush he'd ever planned. It had to be flawless. The thought dried his mouth. Everything had to be flawless for Moonpriest. Nothing was as frightening as that thin, wounded man. He saw into people.

Church missionaries spoke of the tortures of the Land Under. Jones had tasted those pains. Fox saw to it, himself.

Jones died.

Moonpriest came in his place.

Fox shivered.

When a fake owl hooted, the first rank of nomads was directly under him. In near-perfect silence, they checked their alignment. Fox permitted himself a grin of pride. His own examination of the ground suggested that this was the correct distance for the assault unit to gather itself before making its final move into the village.

Unable to see them, impressed by their wordless discipline, Fox sniffed deeply again, curious to see if he could learn more.

Greased weapons. Greased leather. A tinge of wax; bowstrings. Something else. Sharp. Familiar. Completely out of place. He was still searching his memory when the long line of nomads stepped out. The advance began on the left, each man fractionally behind his companion on that side, so their movement was a soft sigh through the forest.

Small flames illuminated a few tents. Cookfires smoldered their last in the outdoor firepits.

Fox reached up, located the line that ran from himself to the village. As soon as he yanked it, a baby squalled. The advancing line paused. Fox pictured the enemy as a flash flood moving down a dry creekbed, momentarily checked, concentrating force.

To the left, a man screamed, a cry like a cougar. It was picked up by the whole line, and suddenly they were all charging into the village.

The illuminated tents were the first to burst into flame as the nomads cut the support lines. They also drove their swords through the walls, searching sleeping victims.

173

In the surprisingly bright glare, Fox was impressed by the methodical attack. Nothing was left to chance. The second wave hurtled in behind the first, some flinging torches at downed tents as they joined in the hacking and slashing. Almost absently, Fox noted the increased power of the earlier, unidentified smell.

By that time, the attackers were increasingly aware of arrow casualties. Simultaneously, it became apparent that no sleepy defenders were rushing out of the tents to be cut down, nor were there cries of agony and fear rising from the flames. In fact, the only dying screams were coming from nomads.

Several of their number, more alert than others, noted that the arrows had a plunging angle. They looked up into the trees. The Mountain warriors, discovered, shouted war cries, continuing to rain death from their perches.

At that point, Fox dropped the line coiled on the branch beside him and slid to the ground. All through the forest other Mountain warriors were doing the same thing. They would operate in two-man teams, keeping to the darkness, their enemies silhouetted against the light of the burning tents. As for the nomads, the dark cover of the forest appeared to be safety.

The error of that conclusion was quickly announced by the cries of the first to retreat in that direction and die.

Fox operated alone. His kills were his, shared with no one. Moving in a crouch, he seemed to float from tree to tree. The first nomad to come his way was a youth, probably no more than sixteen. An arrow protruded from his shoulder. His eyes were so wide with shock they appeared to glow. Fox pressed against a tree, became part of it. When the boy was abreast, he whipped out his ma in a horizontal arc. The decapitated body continued to run for two more steps before dropping.

Stunned, disorganized, the nomads wanted only to reach the valley, their horses, and escape. Night vision destroyed by the fires, courage sapped by surprise, most simply ran, each man his own savior.

Fox moved among them, reaping a murderous harvest. He lost count of the number to fall at his feet, remembering only those who managed any sort of defense. The battle at hand was practically over when he came across the three men together. Two supported one in the middle, although Fox quickly noted that the wounded one still carried his weapon. The trio moved with deliberate speed, unpanicked.

They were too composed to allow caution. He would have to

174

depend on speed and surprise to overwhelm them. Leaping forward, he shrieked his battle cry.

The two outside men leapt to the side, leaving the supposedly wounded man standing alone, clearly unhurt. He parried Fox's ma and sent a counterstroke whistling through the air an instant after Fox leapt out of range. He cursed himself. These were practiced, skilled fighters, not rattled runners. Their ruse nearly worked. He backed up, wondering if he should break away, let them make their escape.

But he couldn't. The blood fever was in him, and even as he watched them spread out and advance, making it ever more difficult for him to defend himself, he welcomed the hot, throbbing excitement of a true fight.

He said, "Know me. I am Fox Eleven, Manhunter of the Mountain People."

The nomad in the middle said, "We are People of the Long Sky. My name is Ban of Blue. My friends are Habab of Green and Dalicor of Blue."

Fox said, "I will remember. Your people will know from me that you died well."

"I think not," Ban said, feinting a thrust, then striking backhanded. Fox deflected the blade easily, kicking from a low crouch at the man named Dalicor, who rushed while the first clash still rang. The foot stopped Dalicor in his tracks. Pivoting on the other foot, Fox spun completely around, hacked at the back of Dalicor's neck, and leapt away to resume his defensive posture while a wild sword stroke by Habab slammed harmlessly into the tree protecting Fox's side. Stepping back, Fox calmly reached around the trunk and stabbed him.

The next thing Fox knew, he was stumbling, falling sideways. He never saw Ban's thrown metal water carrier, never actually felt it strike his temple. He was only aware of disorientation. Instinctively, he dropped low, keeping the ma raised in front of him. Twice Ban struck heavily, only to have the blows deflected. Nevertheless, the second effort glanced off to strike the top of Fox's forearm. Biting to bone, the edge turned, lifting meat like a man filleting a fish.

Fox's ma dropped to the ground. He fell backward.

Ban lunged at his unprotected stomach. Fox heard the man's straining grunt as he drove his weapon down and forward with his entire weight and strength. Fox tried to scream, but his throat was frozen.

175

Ban came so hard he fell forward, dropping onto Fox. Living fire seemed to roar through Fox's entire body.

Yet he lived.

Ban rolled off him. Fox struggled to move. There was a sword sticking out of his thigh. A figure wavered into view. It said, "Be still. You'll make the wound worse."

"Altanar?"

"Quiet! I didn't kill this nomad just to have you get me killed. You know what Jones would do to me if he learned I even touched a weapon." Altanar was on his knees, poking at the edges of Fox's wound. Then he bent the leg at the knee, lifted it. In spite of himself, Fox groaned. Hissing angrily, Altanar said, "Show some strength. I have to pull the sword free. It's going to hurt. I've heard your friends, the Dogs, have a way of denying pain. You know it?"

"Witchcraft. Mountain warriors accept pain. You insult."

Altanar responded with a giggle that lifted the hair on Fox's neck. "I know about pain. And insult. Oh, yes."

The shock of the extraction bolted through Fox's mind like a great light, brought him a mental clarity that frightened him. It took a few deep breaths before he could speak. "Why were you looking for me?"

Clinical, Altanar said, "There's lots of blood here, but no spurts. Not heavy enough for a vein, either. The arm's no worse. You'll heal easily."

"Answer me."

Altanar rocked back on his heels. In the light of the dying fires, the lines of his thoughtful frown were like scars. Fox was barely aware of the aftersounds of combat around them as Altanar answered musingly. "I thought tonight would be a good time to kill you. But when I saw this one here about to stick you, I couldn't let it happen." Roughly, he whipped off Fox's belt and made a tourniquet around the wounded leg. As he worked, he said, "I know something you're just beginning to suspect. We're living in the tiger's mouth. Together. There may be a time when we can help each other hold it open."

Fox felt he could literally smell the madness on Altanar. He said, "Perhaps you saved my life. I'll save yours. I won't tell Moonpriest of this conversation. And if I ever find you behind me, I'll kill you. Stand where I can see you, and we may both serve the tiger so well that it only fattens on others. You understand?"

"Perfectly." Altanar put a hand on each end of the sword scabbard he was using as a lever for the tourniquet. He giggled once again as he wrenched it around with all his might.

CHAPTER 31

By the light of the dying fires, the Mountain people rushed to abandon the camp. While the adults packed belongings on horses and treated their wounded, children prowled through the fallen, looting. Jones marveled at the merriment when they came across a particularly well-made weapon. Jewelry and exceptional clothing occasioned lesser excitement. He made a mental note to have Fox assign an adult to supervise, in future. In the world he intended to create, the young were a special project. It wouldn't do to have some vindictive, wounded fool injure one of them. Not only that, there was no way of telling what the little wretches stole.

When the salvagers discovered a still-living nomad, they called for adult help. Older women were assigned the task of examining those victims. Jones had directed that the wounded deemed likely to survive were moved to a central location, bound, and watched. If the women decided a man had no chance of recovery, they dispatched him.

The women assigned to the task complained vigorously. Even now, long after Jones' adamant refusal to change his orders, one of them confronted him as he strolled through the wreckage. She said, "Why do you do this to us? How are we to avenge our hurts if we're not allowed to make these ones suffer?"

Jones turned a stiff smile her way. He said, "We lost two dead. Six are wounded. Five of them will recover completely. More than a hundred of our enemies died. Many of those who escaped are bound to die. We have over seventy new horses and much loot. Isn't that enough of a victory?"

The old woman spat. "Victory. Defeat. We lose sons and husbands and fathers, no matter. It's our way to spend our grief on any prisoners we take. It's dangerous to change the old ways."

"Any other time. I promise. The prisoners have value to me. Treat them as I say."

"You make our women bandage enemy wounded. The nomads will think us weak."

Jones bent to her. "You think me weak?"

She stepped back hastily. "Not me." She made a vague gesture over her shoulder with one hand while reaching for the moon pendant at her breast with the other. "The others. I . . . we thought . . ."

Jones left her sputtering. At the rough pine bough shelter protecting the camp's wounded, he found Fox lying on his back, in between the two other warriors too badly injured to continue normal activity. The smell of the fresh-cut pine struggled to mask an almost visible fog of herbs, sweat, and stale breath. Jones acknowledged Fox's companions before speaking to him. "Will you be able to ride on a litter?"

"What choice?" Fox rose up on his elbows, wincing. "I understand you've forbidden the women their amusement with the prisoners. It's being said you even have them treating their wounds."

Dropping back flat, Fox glared, waiting. A muscle twitched in his jaw. Jones let the silence drag out before continuing. "I told you, 'Serve me with all your heart and skill, and I will give you Katallon's warriors to command.' "

Fox's nod was quick enough, but Jones saw the undercurrent of suspicion. Poor Fox hid so little. Jones said, "We haven't the force to conquer outright, so we must take control some other way. You and your warriors hurt Katallon badly this night. He must respect that. Now we spare those we've captured. He'll be pleased to get them back. When he learns I wish to speak of peace, he'll be curious. He'll want to see us."

Fox laughed harshly. "Once you're out in the open, he'll have you cut down like a wildcow calf."

"Me?" Jones drew himself erect. His face flamed, his words grated. "It is not time for me to rejoin my mother, the moon. I will leave the earth for my home when she calls. No man will choose my time. I am Moonpriest."

Fox scrambled to apologize. Keeping his injured leg straight, he crabbed forward on his elbows. The wounded men beside him murmured fear at Jones' glowering rage. Fox, with his head twisted awkwardly so he could look up into Jones' features, reached for his hand. "I wasn't thinking. Moonpriest, I know. It was I who saw you die and return. I saw. I believe."

Jones squeezed the hand clutching his own. "It's good that you worry about me. I've already told you I will die. Not until my mission here is accomplished, however. Power is coming to me, power you'll never understand. Now, tell me what happened to you."

178

Fox gestured with his bandaged arm, pointed at his leg. "Some fought well," he said dryly.

After a perfunctory smile, Jones said, "At least we took prisoners. We need information. We're lucky enough to have the son of a minor chief. Varnalal of Red, he calls himself. His tribe is the Long Sky. How long before you're ready to travel?"

"As soon as the pyre for the dead is burning."

"Then we go." Jones walked to the burning site, where he ordered a Mountain warrior to fetch him a prisoner able to ride. When he returned with the man on an unsaddled horse, Jones was standing before the blazing symbolic mountain.

"This is the man I asked for?" Jones' question snapped the warrior erect. He answered quickly. "His shoulder's broken. He has a wounded leg. I've lashed him to his saddle so he can't fall off."

"Will he live to reach Katallon?"

"I think so. If an animal doesn't take him."

Jones interrupted. "Send two, then. Three. Just be certain Katallon gets my message." He grabbed the horse's reins, pulled it closer, then clutched the prisoner's knee. Knuckles popped aloud under the pressure of his grip, and the drooping prisoner gagged and jerked upright. He stared down at Jones, who said, "Tell Katallon and his war leaders their wounded are here, bandaged, waiting for help. I give all the captives their lives, as a sign of my desire for peace. Soon, I will send Varnalal to Katallon's camp to make arrangements for talks. Tell him"—Jones paused, squeezing the knee again, forcing a moan from the prisoner—"tell him I have fought him enough. I will bring him power and glory to gladden his heart and burn his enemies. I wish to be his friend."

He released man and animal, stepping back. He raised an arm and pointed east, posing regally in the light of the pyre. Its roaring collapse at that moment was approval, he was sure.

The prisoner's head pivoted from the flames to Jones' face, as if seeking something rational to focus on. He made a low sound in his chest, jerking the horse around with his good arm. Bent low in the saddle, clearly anticipating the first arrow in his back, the first shout of cruel laughter from his joking tormentors, he flogged the animal into the night.

Jones pursed his lips, shook his head sadly. "Send two more. That fool will probably run right off the edge of the plateau. See the others have the same message. Be quick. I wouldn't be surprised if Katallon's not already mounting another raiding party. We won't trap the next one so easily."

Jones supervised Altanar's loading of his belongings on a pair of packhorses. He wondered if anyone from Ola would recognize the former king now. Probably not, he decided; the man was a tribute to systematic degradation.

Dressed in foul rags, without shoes, wearing a floppy wool hat several sizes too large, Altanar dashed about madly, trying to obey the blizzard of instructions from Jones and the bent, lame old man who was Jones' personal servant. Every order from one of that pair drew an almost instant counter-order from the other. Nothing was done to satisfaction. Or fast enough. The personal servant cuffed and cursed his decrepit victim with an unabashed glee.

When his few possessions were securely lashed to the horses, Jones signaled the young warrior who was acting as camp leader while Fox recovered. A series of bird-like whistles started the march.

The prisoner Varnalal was more than Jones hoped. Young, chagrined by his capture, but unafraid, he talked freely of life in Katallon's camp.

"We are nine tribes," he said, "with people from five or six others. We are the strongest, the People of the Long Sky. Beyond our lands is nothing, only the home of the sun and forests where the slaves live."

"Slaves? If they're slaves, they live with someone else, surely?"

Varnalal shook his head. "Uncaptured slaves live there."

Jones smiled. "A person isn't a slave until someone else owns him. Or her."

"We own them. We just never catch all of them."

"Ahh, I see. They wait for you to come, and then give themselves to you?"

"No. They fight. Not honestly, though. They live in their forests, where it's hard for real people to ride. Like . . ." The young man's eyes went to the Mountain warriors riding near them, and then he looked to Jones again with a touch of fear.

And defiance. Jones savored that. Here was a man ripe with possibilities. Young. Strong. Born to authority.

A subject to be considered.

There would be need of influential people in Katallon's camp.

Jones pursued the slave issue. He said, "You speak of the slaves as though they were part of your past. Why?"

"Because they are." In the darkness, Varnalal's teeth gleamed in a brief smile. "We left our lands twelve years ago. I barely remember that place. That was when Katallon came among us. Windband was only two tribes, then—his own, the Grasslanders, and the Ironmakers, from farther north. Our people fought for four years. Then a plague came, and many people of all three tribes died. Our new chief talked with Katallon, and it was decided that all of our people would run from the plague and find another place to live. When other tribes attacked us, we all fought them together. Since then, we move toward the afternoon sun, toward a land our legends say rests against a sea that reaches beyond anything men know."

Jones said, "What do your legends call this land?"

"Katallon says it's the land of milk and honey."

The phrase startled Jones. He pulled up his horse so sharply the animal whickered and danced. Varnalal stopped with less flurry. "Have you heard it called that, too?" he asked innocently.

"As a matter of fact." Jones chuckled, then. "What would you say if I told you I've seen that ocean? Bathed in it?"

"Truly?" Varnalal made no attempt to hide how impressed he was. "All of us, everyone in Windband, dreams of that. Is it really salty? Can you drink it? Is it really too big to see across? My people say it must be like our country, the Long Sky, where a man can ride all day and still be in sight. Is it so?"

"You'll see for yourself."

Varnalal was quiet for a long moment. He said, "A man such as yourself shouldn't make such promises. Such a thing is known only to our mother, the moon."

"Then it is known to me." Jones rolled the words up from his chest, let them fill the night. "Believe in me. If I tell you it will be so, it will be. You must learn, all must learn, that I am Moonpriest. I tell you now; I will see you taste the Great Ocean. Hear and believe."

Varnalal stared wide-eyed into the empty blackness long after it had swallowed Jones from view, long after the sound of Jones' individual hoofbeats were lost among those of the column.

A voice from ground level growled up at the young man. He looked down where Fox grimaced at him from a dragger. Fox said, "You're asking yourself if Moonpriest is what he claims to be. I tell you he is, but my words are worthless to you. He's made us believe. He'll make you believe."

"Maybe. And maybe he has the head sickness."

"Wait. You'll see."

Thoughtfully, Varnalal said, "In Katallon's camp are women

181

who call themselves Healers. They used to call themselves Church. Our Moondance priests and priestesses turned their minds. We've got Earthsingers, from far north of my own lands; they heal people, too. They know the spirits—secrets of weather and seasons—things like that. They're all going to be very angry to hear this stranger name himself Moonpriest and claim to be more powerful than they are. They'll challenge him."

Fox's smile colored his voice. "That'll be interesting."

"If Jones is destroyed, Katallon will punish his followers."

"No one will punish us. Moonpriest is a holy one. Moon's own son."

"You don't fear?"

"Of course. Always. But I have to know. Don't you?"

Silhouetted against the pinpoint lights of the stars, Varnalal straightened in the saddle. His chin rose, throwing his head back. "Windband already knows. We have Moondance and we have Katallon. We go wherever we choose, and we conquer. This Jones is very strange. I think he's mad. And perhaps all of you with him are as mad as he is."

Fox's laughter came as a series of sibilant, gusting noises, like a breeze through rain-washed leaves. "All leaders are mad, Varnalal. But you will follow Moonpriest."

CHAPTER 32

"Tomorrow night," Altanar said, and Fox looked up quizzically from the pile of furs where he rested outside his lean-to. Altanar indicated the near-dark sky and elaborated. "Moonpriest said he'd contact Katallon, and Varnalal's getting ready to leave tomorrow night."

"You call him Moonpriest, like us. I never thought I'd see you believe."

"Oh, I believe," Altanar said, with a lopsided smile. "I'm not sure we believe exactly the same things, but I do believe."

"You swear on your life that he is Moonpriest?"

"I do."

Not entirely satisfied, but unsure how to pursue the matter farther, Fox grew thoughtful. He shifted his position, grunting when it was necessary to lever himself on the elbow of the wounded arm. The thigh seemed to be less trouble. He said, "You squirm around in the truth the way a snake wiggles through the grass."

"You'd never trust anyone not Mountain-born."

"Never. Moonpriest. That's all."

"What about Katallon's men? He expects you to lead them."

"It'll be their responsibility to trust me."

Altanar bent the conversation in a different direction. "I suppose I'll be the one to watch your back, then. For a man who's seen so much combat, you've learned little about caution. That reminds me of something else: You should be careful who you compare to snakes. What if Moonpriest heard? You've forgotten his pets?"

Fox shuddered. "No one forgets them." He glanced around. After a moment's hesitation, he went on, "It wasn't the snakes. I made one of my men examine it." When Altanar stared mute incomprehension, Fox snapped at him. "The horse. You remember he had us bring him the rabbit, and then the pig? And then the horse?"

"Oh, the animals. Certainly I remember. He didn't let the snakes kill them?"

"Don't you listen? I told you it wasn't the snakes. On the right side of the mountains we know what a rattlesnake kill looks like."

Frowning heavily, Altanar squatted to bring himself closer to Fox. He was careful to stay at the corner of the lean-to, assuring no one approached without being observed. He said, "He's been up in that small canyon since we withdrew beyond Katallon's patrols. He won't let me in there. What's he doing?"

"Who knows? He took the smith and his son, and our best woodworker. No one's seen any of them since we got here. Moonpriest only comes out himself to eat and order more firewood. And beeswax. Beeswax! He'll get us all killed. Men cutting wood make noise. And the smith, hammering."

"Varnalal says he's mad."

Bristling, Fox said, "I know. Varnalal best learn to mind his tongue. Someone might cut it out and put it in his pocket."

His memory flashed to his own conversation with Varnalal. He'd said far too much. Moonpriest was a child of a goddess; he knew everything. But if that was so, why did he allow his firmest believer to entertain such painful doubts? Fox agonized over it, not understanding himself. When he spoke of Jones to another man, he questioned. When he faced Moonpriest, he adored.

"What do you think killed the animals?" Altanar asked.

"I haven't seen them. Lightning weapons?"

"No noise. Where are the bodies?"

Gesturing, Fox said, "Moonpriest said to dump them down in the valley. Didn't you hear the wolves after them?"

Altanar heard little of what was obvious to the Mountain People. It irritated him, and he ignored the question. "I'll see what I can learn. Maybe there's something left of the horse."

Pulling Altanar close before he could rise, Fox whispered, "The men say the animals were cut up in pieces. Even the horse."

Altanar suddenly focused on something in the distance. Fox twisted to see, uselessly, with his vision blocked by the hide wall behind him. When he turned back, Altanar was scuttling swiftly through the trees. Fox settled back to wait, knowing Moonpriest was coming, wondering what he wanted.

It had taken five days of almost nonstop travel before the small group of Mountain People and their new companions, the protectors, were beyond range of Katallon's patrols. Persistent ambushes, set every night on their back trail, had finally discouraged the warriors of the Windband. The result among the people of the camp was a sense of uneasy truce.

Contrary to their nervousness, Jones, on his infrequent appearances among them, brimmed with confidence. Now, standing in front of Fox, he positively beamed. He wore a butter-soft doeskin jacket that had practically become his uniform. It was a pullover design, with lacing at the throat so it could be drawn tight. The design of the necklace pendant centered on his chest was a rayed moon of hammered silver. His headdress was a strip of cloth, tie-dyed to simulate rattlesnake markings, intricately wound around his head. A pair of rattles dangled in the back. At his every step or movement, they rustled dry suggestion. He said, "Tomorrow Varnalal goes home to prepare the way for my visit with Katallon. When he returns to tell us we have guarantees of safety, I'll leave immediately."

Fox interrupted. "I go with you."

"No. I need you to watch—"

"I go with you." Fox repeated himself, and Jones stared in disbelief. Fox was pale, his lips a smudge against his drawn features. He went on. "I'm the one who tortured you. I didn't know who you were . . . are. Now I do. How can you deny me the opportunity to be by your side, especially in time of danger?"

"I want to leave in seven days. Can you ride by then?"

"I will," Fox said, left hand massaging the swollen right arm. Coolly, Jones peeled back the poultices on both wounds. He poked at each, watching Fox's expression dispassionately. Fox's eyes flashed, but he didn't wince, nor did he complain.

When Jones was finished, Fox said, "You may trust this Katallon, Moonpriest, but I don't. Varnalal's a good man, and no liar, but he's from the Windband. How do we know Katallon won't lie to us?"

"He will. He'll tell us it's safe to come talk to him, but he means to kill us."

Fox blinked foolishly, mouth working. When he finally found words, they came in a strained, insulted pitch. "It's not respectful to ask me to die like a sheep led to the knife. If you order it, I'll ride into the Windband camp and strike until they kill me. This other thing . . ." He spat. "You speak of slaughter."

Jones exploded in a bubbling belly laugh. When it had passed, he bent down to clasp Fox's shoulder. His features tightened, as swiftly grim as they had been amused. Slitted eyes fixed on Fox's. "We'll be tested. We will not die. Not if you do exactly as I say. Obey me, and live."

"Always, Moonpriest. In everything." Once again, Fox's mind leapt to the damning conversation with Varnalal. He turned his betraying eyes away from Moonpriest's wisdom.

Jones rose, saying, "Loyalty is never forgotten. Your rewards will outrace your dreams." He spread his arms to embrace the entire camp. "Kings will serve me. Princes will fight to serve you. Their women will rush to your protection. As long as you obey."

Fox licked his lips. He turned his face back to Moonpriest. It was safe. What he felt in his heart, what he knew to be in his expression, was more eloquent than words could ever be.

Varnalal returned to the camp of the Mountain People on the heels of a slashing spring storm.

The camp was situated at the end of a long, crooked lake which nestled brightly in a large hollow. The surrounding meadow was still pocked with isolated heaps of snow where shade held off the sun. As Jones and Fox rode to meet the returning Windband warrior, they passed some boys pouring grain into leather nose bags for the horses. The animals were enclosed in a pen of stakes and boughs to hold off predators. There was some natural fodder about, but nature never intended to support so much stock in that restricted area. The grain sacks were nearly empty, and the horses were bony.

Varnalal's approach paralleled the small creek that drained the lake. The white flag that had gotten him safely past the Mountain outposts was carelessly slung across his horse's rump. When he waved greeting, his easy smile was a gleaming bar of white in the shade of his broadbrimmed hat.

Jones halted on dry ground a few paces from the creek's boggy beginnings. Varnalal closed quickly, although his horse was clearly exhausted. The man greeted the pair almost as if returning to visit friends. He said, "Katallon sends you his greetings. He's willing to forgive you for attacking us, because you're Moondance believers. He wants compensation for those who died, though."

Jones said, "He knows we had casualties, too?"

Varnalal glanced away. "It wouldn't be wise to bring that up. I had to tell him you've only lost six men to us." He diverted the conversation. "Fox. You look completely recovered."

"Not completely. I—"

"Gossip later." Jones' displeasure crackled. "What else did he tell you to tell me?"

"That he wants to make you welcome, and he's pleased that you offer to bring your power to the Windband. I'm to guide all of you to him."

"All?" Jones' eyebrows leaped.

Varnalal nodded eagerly. "Katallon says he knows how hungry and weary you must be. Because you offer to make peace and join him, he offers you his hospitality. While you discuss how you can best work together, the Windband will feed your people."

"Well." Jones smiled at Fox. "I told you Katallon would respect our strength, didn't I? You see how right I was?" He faced Varnalal again. "You're tired. Your horse is about to collapse. Go get some food, some rest. We'll talk afterward."

With his message delivered and accepted so positively, Varnalal's tiredness asserted itself. His eyelids drooped, and his shoulders sagged. "I can talk now, if you want," he said, clearly hoping it wasn't necessary. Jones waved him off with more compliments. Meanwhile, he indicated Fox should stay where he was.

Once Varnalal was out of earshot, Jones turned his horse so he was facing Fox again. A smile still creased his face, but at the sight of it, Fox braced himself.

Jones said. "Fools. Both of them. Varnalal comes like the lulling hand of sleep, all smiles and stupid innocence. '. . . he offers you his hospitality.' Katallon, the gracious opponent. Varnalal I can forgive. Katallon's insult is beyond mercy. I ask you, if you were a conqueror and I offered to come to your camp and make you stronger than ever, wouldn't you even ask how I meant to do that? And why didn't Katallon give me some idea of what he means by 'compensation' for those we killed? How do we bargain if I don't know his terms? And not once did he call me Moonpriest. Not once."

Tentatively, Fox asked, "Do we attack him?"

Jones laughed harshly. "In a way. We'll go back with Varnalal, all right. We'll bring our own bargains, however." He slapped his reins across his horse's shoulders, heeling it forward simultaneously. Startled, the animal bolted several steps before he could get it back under control. He galloped off toward the draw that sheltered his tent and entourage, shouting over his shoulder that they would make further plans at first light in the morning.

Fox watched the display of incompetent horsemanship attentively, then rode back to his lean-to. Dismounting, he limped inside, where he sat down and stirred the coals of his cookfire, rekindling a small blaze. When he had a pot of water boiling, he dumped in a handful of dried material. Shortly, the small shelter filled with the scent of chicken and herbs. His movements were the patterns of habit, his attention obviously elsewhere.

Scraping the last drops from the sides of the bowl with a finger, he licked it clean, then made his way to the lake and washed the bowl. That done, he doused his face, wrinkling his nose at the cold, as well as at Jones' pointless insistence on cleanliness.

Flopping onto his furs outside, he lay on his back. Above, the blinding bright sun was filtered by pine boughs, broken into erratic shafts and blotches. That was what his life had become, he thought: everything shifting, hiding, and then reappearing.

Plans behind plans. Katallon. Jones. Altanar. Possibly even Varnalal. What a man saw them do might have nothing to do with what they wanted.

Moonpriest had a right to be sly. Even deceptive. He was building a world, a holy one.

But he wasn't tribe. Fox Eleven was responsible for these Mountain People. Souls and lives. Moonpriest could ask for both, but was he doing it with the proper sense of tribe?

Why did he yearn to worship, even as he questioned?

Why did he, who knew Jones was Moonpriest, hope that if Katallon killed them all, he'd live long enough to see Jones die first?

CHAPTER 33

Through the smoke of Altanar's cookfire, Jones watched the group assemble. He squatted on his haunches, holding a piece of bread clenched in a cleft stick over the flames. Altanar stood off in the distance, anxious, afraid to take his eyes from the master who ignored him completely.

Jones' mind scurried from subject to subject like a mouse in spilled grain. The interminable discussions of the preparations still rang in his ears. At least he'd persuaded Fox that more than ten men as escort was useless. Katallon expected to ambush their entire group. He would emplace a crushing force. If they were to reach the Windband, they must employ guile, not strength.

He idly stroked the thick cloth bags slung across his breast under his blouse, feeling the coiled muscularity packed there. The snakes were comfortable, up against his warmth on one side and the heat of the fire on the other. Each was digesting a small pullet he'd fed them a few days ago. Just about the time they reached Katallon's side they'd hunger again, acquire a fine edge of aggression. Amazing creatures. So lovely, so repellent. So innocent, so lethal.

Jones munched his toast absently. Katallon would be impressed by the snakes. They would never be conclusive, however. Jones half turned to his left, examined the wicker carrying box holding the porcelain jar.

Everyone was aware that the jar was important. Altanar said—the fool heard more than anyone realized—that Fox made it clear that anyone responsible for harm to any of the equipment would live long enough to regret the accident in a proper manner. It was ironic: they knew their lives depended on protecting the loads, yet none would ever understand what they guarded.

Sadly, they could never properly appreciate the beauty of things such as the jar, either. How the woman had managed to salvage it in the first place, much less protect it from breakage, was beyond imagining. As fine a piece of porcelain as one could ask, Jones was sure it was less than a quarter of an inch thick, executed with an almost-machinelike precision. He'd measured it against his foot, and decided it was eighteen inches in diameter and about twenty-two inches deep. The top fit snugly, with barely enough room to move in its well.

As lovely as the porcelain was, he was even more proud of the rest of the equipment, all his own design. Unconsciously, he stuck out his lower lip, glaring into the dancing flames. The smith and woodworker who'd done the actual work knew the penalty for ever discussing what they'd seen. Nevertheless, they'd remember. In time, they'd be tempted to tell. That was the way. Small, weak people never actually struck the finishing blow at the strong. Invariably, however, they betrayed the chink in the armor.

Patience, he chided himself. Remember the snakes. Only strike when necessary, only strike to kill.

The first direct rays of the sun brushed the rising curtain of smoke in front of Jones into a lustrous haze. Almost obscured on the other side of it, a figure approached on foot. The limp identified Fox. Jones extended his left arm out and back. Altanar leapt to place a mug of hot herb tea in the hand. Jones saluted Fox with the drink. "Care for some?"

Fox shook his head. "The camp's mounted, Moonpriest."

"Packhorses ready?"

"According to plan."

Jones tilted his head, peered at Fox like a bird inspecting a leaf. "You say 'plan' as if it tastes bad. Explain."

"I don't question it." Fox's gaze seemed unable to leave the swelling where the sacks held the snakes.

Jones said, "Don't lie. It's not necessary, and it offends. What's the problem?"

Resolution overrode the reluctance in Fox's features. "Our men have Katallon's patrols frightened almost to ineffectiveness. Varnalal is angry. He says more than he should. Nomad warriors were claiming to be ill. Horses were going 'lame.' We can raid Katallon until he comes to you for terms. Why go to him at all? You endanger yourself."

Jones sighed. "You can't see, can you? Katallon must think I'm his willing servant. He must trust me completely. And you. How else can we isolate him? I don't want his tent; I need the loyalty, the faith, of all his people. If I destroy Katallon, I'm merely a usurper. I must make his people destroy him and raise me to his place. And you will help me."

"As you will, Moonpriest. We believe."

"I know. Go get everyone moving."

Jones squatted by the fire again and busied himself toasting another slice of bread. He chuckled quietly as he watched the rough texture brown nicely. Fox was an amusing creature, actually. Sooner or later, once he'd tasted real power, he'd begin to count swords. And scheme. Well, it would have to be borne. Fox would be used, meanwhile. After all, that's what they were all for.

Jones shouted at Altanar. "Get on your horse! Bring me mine. Are you asleep again?"

"No, Moonpriest! Never. See, I hurry." Amazing, Jones thought; even the voice was changed. The high-pitched arrogance was now shrill supplication, every syllable a hopeless plea for kindness. It grated on Jones' hearing, and he grabbed the unlit end of a burning brand and flung it. The running Altanar howled, although the stick missed him by a good ten feet.

They were riding eastward, slowly descending from the higher elevations. It was the third day. Fox was remarking that it was time for the midday meal, when a scout came to report Katallon's trap.

He was a young warrior, already a scarred veteran. His eyes were so wide the pupils looked adrift against the whites. A mix of weariness, pride, and incipient battle fever gleamed on his face. "Many men, in a standard two-leg ambush. Twenty Sage scouted the attack leg. Three hundred men hide behind the ridge that parallels our route. Elk Ten says the blocking element astride the trail is at least another one hundred and fifty. I myself scouted to the north of our route. Fifty more men wait."

Fox was tense, but controlled. "Exact location. Plan."

The young man's features fell. He was being tested, and concern intruded on his earlier enthusiasm. "They're where you expected them to be, just this side of the last small range of hills between us and the flat valley where Windband camps. The ambush is about one day's slow ride from that camp; at our normal pace, we'll hit the blocking element in about half a day. From the high ground, the nomads'll see our column's point soon. When we hit the blocking element, most of the attack leg will charge down on us from the ridge. Some of them are undoubtedly assigned to swing behind us to prevent escape. The element to the north must be expected to stop us if we try to get away in that direction."

"Good." Fox turned to Jones. "As expected, Moonpriest. Katallon thinks he has us. Again." His lips curled in a proud smile.

Twitching, twisting fingers worked Jones' reins, rolled them into loops, then let them fall free. The scout attributed everything to Fox's foresight. Of course Fox anticipated Katallon's ambush, where it would be, how it would function, and so on. He and Katallon were one and the same: simpleminded killers. Tactics. Games for children. He snapped at the warrior. "How do we know you weren't seen, followed back here? And why haven't you bathed?"

Fox answered for the younger man. "He'll wash now, Moonpriest. He wanted us to know as quickly as possible."

The scout's expression pleaded. "We'd never lead an enemy to your camp. We'd rather die. Anyhow, the Windband people are soldiers. They don't know the wild ways, as we do."

Jones was somewhat mollified, but couldn't resist a jab. "I hope they're not as good as the Dog People. Especially Gan Moondark, and his friend, the one called Clas na Bale."

Beside him, Fox visibly flinched, then his face became an expressionless mask. "I'll meet them both again. They'll die."

The bitterness of the response brought Jones up short. He tried to smooth over the situation. "I know they will, Fox; I know. All I ask is that you save the Church witch, Sylah, for me. She owes me entertainment."

The scout was ready to flee. Assuming his most placating tones, Jones said, "Your skill and bravery are why Fox chose you as a scout. Still, I worry about my followers. Wouldn't I be failing my responsibilities if I didn't ask such questions of you?"

The youngster beamed. "I understand, Moonpriest. I swear on my life, the Windband warriors don't even know we observed them. Four of us watch them still."

"You do well. Now go. And remember—cleanliness."

At Fox's hand signal, the warrior bit back whatever he'd been about to say and left at a gallop.

Jones grimaced as he rode beside Fox through the dust stirred up by the man's departure. A glance showed his companion wasn't even aware of the thick cloud. Jones sighed, wondering how the tribe survived before, when it never bothered to clean clothes, and hardly ever washed their own skin. They accepted the occasional War Healer from Church, but steadfastly rejected any of the Healers who dealt with disease. The Mountains had a brutally efficient answer of their own. The old women who treated the ill did so under the harshest duress. Since they were widows without exceptional skills and past childbearing, they were not merely expendable, but essentially useless, in the eyes of the tribe. If the patients lived or died, if the caregivers lived or died, all was decided in a sickhouse far beyond the boundaries of their fortified villages. When a person went down with a sickness, the family sent the victim to stay with the women of the sickhouse, sang the death songs, mourned, and that was the end of it. When someone survived, there was celebration. Normal life resumed.

Moondance hymns now replaced the old songs. Jones composed them. His experience as a minister had given him a certain knowledge of music theory, and he was pleasantly surprised to discover the Mountains had a flair for harmony. He was truly sorry they'd had no time to stage a proper song for the casualties of the battle with Windband. He resolved that they should be included when next there was a cremation. They would all lift their voices as one to speed the lost ones to the Land Beyond.

Again, Jones laughed aloud. Engrossed in his thoughts, he failed to notice Fox's sidelong glance. If he had, he would have explained happily that he was anticipating composing further hymns, celebrating his own powers. Glancing over his shoulder, he saw the men escorting his pack animals.

It was going to be such fun to see their reactions when they discovered what they were handling.

Fox said, "Moonpriest, I see you have much on your mind, but I have to ask: Are you satisfied with the plan as it is? Do you want to make any changes?"

"No. The plan is perfect. Change nothing." The question shattered Jones' good humor. He glared. Fox rode off without another word.

Long, black spires of shadow slowly reached out from the western crests. The column continued on, away from the lowering sun, silently regretting the gradual loss of its comforting warmth on their backs. To the north, the wavering cries of a wolfpack broke across the gathering dusk. Southward, a second pack answered in an echoing tumble of sound.

Fox ordered a stop and supervised the setting up of camp, riding among the tents, shouting orders. Small drums began to beat, quickly joined by the twang of metal stringed harps and the caroling of flutes. Fires sprang to life. The smell of cooking eddied through the rapidly erected shelters.

Jones watched his servant and Altanar squabbling their way through the erection of his own quarters for a while. Tiring of that, he decided to ride through the camp alone. The scout who'd reported the ambush plans approached. When Jones stopped, the man said, "Fox says to tell you that nomad scouts watch. From the peak to the north, from the next ridge west, from the bluff off to the south. Five men, each place. The ambushers sleep in position."

Jones rode away without answering. All was as it should be. Warriors looked up from whatever they were doing when he passed. They nodded; most smiled. Children waved to him. He noticed how closely the mothers watched, saw their hooded expressions.

The women.

His mind burned, throbbed with the fluttering roar of the steel-maker's gluttonous flames.

The women. Helpless. Property. Watching. They reached their ignorant hands to the heads of their worthless brats and watched him. Savage, warning eyes that followed, followed, followed.

Trying to see inside him. Inside Moonpriest.

Like Sylah. Wanting to touch his brain, wanting to own his every thought, every secret. She did that to him. Witch. Foul witch.

Rage surged in him.

The women. He was risking their children. They watched.

Rage collapsed.

Moonpriest knew fear.

CHAPTER 34

Jones shivered in the darkness. He moved to find a comfortable position, and although he was sure he was silent, one of Fox's men turned to him. By the cold light of a gibbous moon, Jones saw the man raise a finger to his painted face to signal silence.

The fleshy hole in Jones' skull warmed. Admonished by a whelp. The boy was a fool. A liar. Jones couldn't even hear his own movement; how could anyone else? It was an arrogance, a false—

A hand touched Jones' shoulder. The scream that had lurked in his throat since they rode out of the camp tried to force its way free. He contained it by lunging to stuff his forearm in his mouth.

Fox tightened his grip on the shoulder, pulled gently to indicate Jones should follow. Shifting the snake-carrying bag onto his back, Jones dropped to his stomach, following Fox's example. The reptiles were quick to register their disapproval. Jones felt them squirm; one actually made a halfhearted buzz.

Inching forward, Fox and Jones made their way through the trees until they were looking directly into the camp of the Windband scouts. As their own reconnaissance had reported, there were five men. Three slept, while two observed the fires of the Mountain camp in the southwestern distance. One of the men sleeping snored quietly. Jones estimated he was two body lengths away from the trio, and perhaps twice that far away from the other two. The ones awake talked to each other, muffled male voices in easy conversation. Between the sleepers and the men on watch, coals in a cookpit glowed dully.

Far away, an owl sent his questioning call rippling across his hunting territory.

Two Mountain warriors rose behind the murmuring nomads, like hunting cats, unseen, unsuspected. In perfect unison, they struck with their mas. A dizzying wave of sheer ecstasy threatened to overwhelm Jones as the moonlight turned the blades into whispering silver petals. The heads sprang from the bodies and crashed into the brush. As if in afterthought, great sprays of blood blew up from the necks. Only then did the bodies topple.

Other Mountain warriors were on the sleeping trio. Mas rose against the shining curve of the moon, stabbed.

Then the attackers were invisible again, disappeared into darkness.

Jones was staring at the dead men, amazed at the terrible difference between the earlier warmly human comradeship and the stillness that held the place now, when Fox spoke. "The way's clear, Moonpriest." The words were breathy, soft. A predator's sound. Fox in his element.

Jones shivered again, cursing the cold under his breath. The eyes of the Mountain women came back.

Fox pointed into the darkness. "Windband's learned some lessons. No fires tonight." He jerked his chin at the watcher's camp. "These fools didn't learn. But on the ridge over there, and in that valley, their friends wait for my people to ride into their trap tomorrow morning."

Swallowing first, Jones said, "Bring the bodies."

Fox asked, "What bodies? None of us . . ."

"The Windband men. On their own horses."

Jones could almost hear Fox's disbelief. When he eventually responded, it was with resignation. "We'll be delayed. We'll have to pad the horses' hooves, as we have ours."

"Then hurry," Jones said.

Despite the delay, the small group made excellent progress through the rest of the night. When the first spears of light were rising from behind the eastern mountains, Fox signaled the column to a halt. Before them, the valley sloped away to south and east, revealing the panorama of Katallon's camps. Smoke rose from fires. Early risers meandered through the hodgepodge of randomly positioned tents. Herds of horses and cattle stirred, lowing or whickering greetings to the new day, shaking and rolling in the dirt. Cockcrow rose from every quarter. A great uproar arose among some chickens. Movement caught Jones' eye. He looked to see a coyote with its catch in its mouth streaking away from the domed tents. Feathers drifted in the air behind the thief. Long after he was safely into the scrubby sage, the hysterical cackle of surviving hens continued.

Jones said, "Lift the white flag. We'll move in slowly." The long pole with its square of white cloth rose. When Jones turned to the front again, there were several people in the nearest camp staring in their direction. As the group commenced its advance, those people began to run. In seconds, their cries of alarm reached the riders. Soon horns and drums sounded, calling out all of Windband. Jones' column of twos closed against each other. He swiveled to look back at them, and his heart swelled at the bright determination on their faces. At least two were beaming, anticipating life or death with equal joy.

Jones committed those faces to memory.

Fox said, "The large tent with the six wagons drawn up behind it is Katallon's. It looks black now, but when the sun's brighter you'll see how red it actually is. They say the cloth is dyed in blood. The wagons are for his wives and children. He never sleeps with the same wife two nights in a row."

It was old news. Jones understood that Fox was talking to control his own nerves. Jones let him go on. The part about the sleeping arrangements was especially interesting. Some might believe it had to do with domestic harmony. Jones was certain it indicated currents of power and hostility in the camp. The thought helped him remain calm in the face of the growing number of Windband warriors mounting horses and racing toward them. They'd been merely noisy, at first. Then one unleashed a war cry. In the next instant, the morning air seethed with shrieks and screams.

Fox snapped orders at his men. They formed a tight circle, enclosing Jones, the packhorses, and the shrouded bodies of the Windband warriors. The white flag remained high.

It was Jones who excited the most interest. With his turban and a large Moondance disk held above his head, he was exotic. Rising in his stirrups, he turned slowly, displaying the disk for all. He sought direct eye contact with as many of the encircling Windband as he could, staring haughtily, challenging. Where his

195

vision struck, there was silence until it passed on. Then there was a low hum of confusion.

The crowd continued to grow as late arrivals from other campsites poured in.

A man with flowing silver hair, riding a pure white horse, approached at the head of a loose group of riders. He wore a Moondance disk on his chest a good ten inches across. His followers wore smaller disks. Jones was surprised to see similar examples on the foreheads of the horses. The crowd parted before the latest arrivals as water breaks from the prow of a boat.

Jones locked eyes with the leader. The man was old, spare, his face weathered into crags and valleys that mirrored the dry, harsh terrain around them. His clothing was a dark, brooding blue, under a hide cloak. The latter was as pliant as cream, flowing from the bejeweled gold fastener at the man's neck, over his shoulders, and across his mount's haunches. He rode through the encircling Mountains and reined in just before the animal collided with Jones' horse.

The man said, "I am the Windband Moondance priest. You are the ones who killed them, the ones who killed others of our people."

Jones remained silent.

The priest spat on the ground. "You kill our men, then come among us with the bodies? You think to hide behind the white flag?"

Again, Jones refused to answer. The priest's color rose, as did his voice. "You will burn with them!"

The mob around Jones' tight circle exploded in cries of anticipation. It took all of Jones' will to maintain the calm eye contact that was their sole hope of survival. Fox growled orders at his men.

The priest raised a long arm, pointed at Jones, then moved the hand so the gesture included the entire party. He waved the other hand in a circle over his head.

The crowd howled. Swords appeared.

Sweat ran down Jones' sides. Still erect in his stirrups, he dared not sit down, yet his knees grew weaker with every heartbeat. Already they trembled almost uncontrollably. Behind him, he heard a warrior praying. To Moonpriest.

Jones swung the disk in his extended hand. The glimmer of smile that flicked across the austerity of the other priest reeked of scorn and triumph.

Above the tumult, the blast of a horn demanded attention. Everyone quieted once again, turning toward the disturbance. Jones had only to look at the man approaching to know it was Katallon himself. If that hadn't told him, the behavior of the crowd would have; where they parted for the Moondance priest, they crowded around Katallon, vying to move with him. Only the presence of a party of four mounted frontrunners allowed the gaily dressed figure to proceed uninterrupted.

In open-throated scarlet jacket and yellow trousers, Katallon wore a beige high-crowned hat with a wide, curled brim. For one mad instant, all Jones could think of was the picture of a Mexican vaquero in one of his childhood history books. The moment passed at the first clear sight of Katallon's features. There was grim anger there, which Jones was prepared for. More than that, however, there was a charisma that reached across the space between them.

Jones lowered himself back to his saddle. Instinct told him that one addressed Katallon of the Windband in a posture of respect.

The frontrunners cleared the crowd so Katallon could take a place next to the priest.

Jones cleared his throat. He said, "I salute Katallon. I come to surrender to him. I offer to join our forces with yours."

"You know me?"

"By sight, no. By awareness. You are Katallon."

"What if I told you I am his War Chief, come to approve Wippard's determination to have you cut to pieces?"

"I would call that a lie."

A collective sigh went up from the crowd. From the corner of his eye, Jones saw swords raised again.

Katallon said, "You're not bold, you're foolish. You have the bodies of my warriors on those horses. Our horses. You must know my warriors are slaughtering your people by now. You think to bargain some sort of escape for yourself and these murderers? You expect me to accept your coward's surrender?"

Fox's chin rose. His eyes flashed.

Jones said, "There will be no slaughter, Katallon. Before light, our warriors stampeded the horses of your men. The rest of our people had long since retreated to the mountains. No one rode into the trap. Your warriors are walking back to your camp now. Some will have recaptured mounts, I'm sure. You can expect them fairly soon."

Katallon's face darkened. He said, "You die today, false priest. If you're lying to me, it'll be a very painful death."

"I do not lie. I will not die today, nor on any day of any man's

197

choosing. It is not time. Although I am only a man, as all other men, I tell you it is not time for me to rejoin my mother."

"You know that, do you?" Katallon grinned. "We'll see."

The priest named Wippard leaned forward. "Your mother may not want you to come home, fool, but we'll send you to her tonight, when the mother of us all shines her face on us. I promise you you'll beg both mothers to let you come home, wherever that is."

Not deigning to look at Wippard, Jones spoke to Katallon. "I do not come to one as mighty as Katallon to offer something as unimportant as my own small following. Nor do I come to beg for an opportunity to run from you. We want peace and union with Windband." He paused, turning slowly from Katallon to survey the crowd. He raised his voice. "I come to Katallon to offer the power of the moon. I do so under the orders of my one mother, the moon. She sends me."

"Blasphemer!" Wippard spurred his horse forward. Katallon grabbed the priest's reins and was nearly pulled out of the saddle. A frontrunner forced his mount between Wippard and Jones. Order was restored quickly, Katallon pushing his hat off his head to dangle down his back by the chin strap. The agitated rumble of the crowd had no effect on him at all.

"Your warriors have embarrassed our best," he said. "You've outguessed every trap we've set for you. Now you speak of the power of the moon. If you can show me what you mean, if you can share this power with my War Chief and his chiefs, I may let you live. But if you ever again say you are the child of the moon, I can't answer for what our priests will do to you."

"I will share everything I have with Katallon. I will not deny my heritage. If this Wippard one thinks he is more to my mother than I, then let him defy her. Tonight, when she visits us in her most glorious, test us. See if he, or his priests, can surpass the power she gives me."

"A test? Between priests?" Katallon laughed hugely. "Who could resist that?" The crowd, on cue, laughed with him. He shouted, "Prepare the pyre for our warriors. Treat these warriors as true men of the sword. Tonight this braggart priest and our Wippard will contest. You will all judge. If the stranger is this much less than what he claims to be"—he held up thumb and forefinger, practically touching—"then he'll entertain us further. And so will every man with him." He dropped back into the saddle, returning his attention to Jones. "Come with me, whoever you are. What do you call yourself?"

198

Jones saw cunning, as well as the charisma. And there was the tiniest flare of uncertainty, the fear-spark of a man confronted by something he isn't entirely sure of.

"Moonpriest," Jones said. "I am Moonpriest."

CHAPTER 35

Fox glowered at the mob surrounding the Mountain group. His people sat in an oblong, with a small fire of wildcow chips in the center. Each man watched out for the safety of the backs of the companions across from him. They all pretended to ignore the hostile stares and occasional insult.

The only time they broke the security of their formation was to check the condition of the packhorses still burdened with Jones' equipment. The animals were all tied to a picket line, and hobbled as a further precaution.

To his men, Fox said, "If these Windband dog droppings are treating us the way they treat all 'true men of the sword,' I have to wonder how they treat the untrue."

"If Moonpriest doesn't perform some very convincing magic, we'll learn," one answered easily. He might have been commenting on the weather.

Fox grunted, then. "I wish Moonpriest hadn't made us wash off our death paint. It's not right I should go to the moon mother with my face undecorated. And my arm's still weak where I was cut. If they come for us, crowd close to my right side."

"How long do you think we'll last?"

"Not as long as we will if they take us alive."

One of the other warriors said, "How long until sundown?"

Another answered. "You don't mean sundown. You mean moonrise. You're afraid Moonpriest'll fail."

The accused one dropped his head, drew aimless marks in the dirt. The firm believer dismissed him with a sneer and turned to Fox. "Has Moonpriest talked to you about the new power his mother gave him? How'll he beat this Windband priest?"

"He's never told anyone how he controls the snakes, has he? He only let me see him come back from the dead because he needed a witness. He'll show everyone when it's time."

"I hope," the man beside him whispered.

Fox spun to confront him. Barely audible, he said. "Enough. If

Moonpriest fails, it's because he's called home to his mother. Not even he can know everything. If that's the way, it's our honor to go with him."

Fox turned his attention back to the crowd. Once he thought he saw Varnalal, but couldn't be sure. He didn't blame the man for not coming close. It wasn't a consolation to be associated with Jones' destiny.

The guards had insisted Jones dismount to follow Katallon and Wippard. Four men were assigned to escort him. He took the time to face each one, meeting their eyes with his own stare. One by one, he rejected their intimidation. When they finally boxed him in and moved off, Jones reveled in their edgy glances.

The snakes in their carrying bags moved incessantly, somehow warned that the world outside their warm, soft sanctuary had radically changed. When they merely hungered, their movements were abrupt, nervous. This was different. Slowly, powerfully, they flowed across Jones' chest. He was glad his flowing shirt hid the activity, but he mentally enjoyed their stretching, vicariously shared their strength.

Looming ahead, Katallon's tent demanded Jones' attention. The woolen cloth was, as Fox said, a venous purple-red. Wind ripples gave it the look of a beating heart. Its lines were leather, held taut by friction toggles. The outside poles were taller than a mounted man, each capped with a spearhead. There was no other ornamentation, no pennants, no insignia.

Jones' warrior escort stopped at a small awning projecting over the entry.

Jones entered alone. Dozens of candles arranged on triangular stanchions provided light, as did flaps in the ceiling. Only a few of the latter were open at this time of the morning, due to the lingering chill. Sun shot through those facing east. Candle smoke writhed in the beams.

Tapestry drop cloths featuring hunting scenes created a large room. Against the far wall a throne stood on a raised platform. Katallon indicated a slit in the drop to Jones' right. Wippard was already disappearing through it with the ease of familiarity. Before Jones could move to obey Katallon, a hitherto-unobserved guard stepped away from the wall by the front entry. He reached for Jones' chest, and Jones warded him off. The man's sword was out immediately.

Katallon shouted, "No! Don't kill him," then asked, "what are you carrying under there?"

Jones said, "Spirit creatures. Animals sent to me to symbolize my being."

Wippard's furious face reappeared in the exit slit. "Animals? Moondance has no spirit creatures."

"I speak for me," Jones interrupted coldly. "My powers are mine alone."

Turning to Katallon, Wippard said, "I won't be in the same room with this fraud and his stinking shirt full of manure."

"Sit in the next room and listen through the wall, if it suits you better," Katallon said. He watched Jones carefully. "You say these things symbolize your being? We know people who call them-selves People of the Bear, or Tiger—many things. Is that what you mean?"

"In a way. It's my intention to show you."

"This is the power you claim to have from your mother?" Katallon's smile threatened.

Jones managed nonchalance. "The smaller part of it."

Katallon gestured for Jones to follow Wippard through the slit, bringing up the rear himself.

The second room was obviously a place for more-select gather-ings. There were chairs, made of wooden frames with leather seats and backs. Small cushions on the floor beside each allowed the user to arrange his own comfortable padding. Wippard was al-ready in place. His choice was no accident, Jones saw. Katallon obviously used the largest chair. Wippard's was on the east side, which meant the sun was to his back. While Jones watched, Wippard used a long pole to lift a flap above his head. Soon the angle of the sun would throw a beam directly on the chair facing west. It would be uncomfortable, distracting.

Katallon said, "You've caused me trouble. Now you've chal-lenged our priesthood. None of it was wise or necessary."

"I wish we could have come together under better circumstan-ces."

"You could have ridden in with your people and joined Windband."

"What other people have you so welcomed?"

"What's important is that you've killed many of my men. My people demand compensation."

"And we demand consideration. We know you intend to con-tinue west. We are between you and the sea. You crush all in your way, absorb those who surrender. We had to make you understand that we have no wish to be crushed, so we surrender on our terms."

201

"Terms? Demands? You sit in my tent, surrounded by my thousands, and you use these words? To me?" Despite the fury before him, Jones' heart soared. Any ordinary man could be angered. An extraordinary man could command an inter-tribal nomad horde. What seized Jones was the raw ambition, the ferocious implacability that emanated from Katallon. Any defeat was temporary for this one. As long as he lived, his energy would be concentrated on the next battle. And the next. All conquest was opportunity for further conquest.

Jones hoped the racing of his heart wasn't evident in his voice. "I understand you, Katallon. I know what you want. You've heard stories of the Great Ocean, of the ease of the climate beyond the mountains. You want to rule there. I can make it possible."

Wippard scoffed. "Liar. Katallon needs more warriors, more food and water. He needs more knowledge of the mountain passes and the lands beyond, he needs . . ."

Katallon glared, and Wippard abandoned his recital of Windband's weaknesses. Lamely, he continued, "We need the guidance of Moondance. Only through belief can we fulfill our lives and souls."

Jones bent forward. "Was your father chief of your tribe, Katallon?"

Startled, Katallon stared, then burst out laughing. "You mean to serve a high-born leader? Not here, Priest. I never knew a father. My mother died of my birth. I was raised by her sister, and she made me her slave. I learned to take what I want in order to live. I'm no chosen leader. I lead because I choose."

Jones knitted his fingers together, placed the hands on top of the snakes. Their predatory singlemindedness seeped through the cloth and into him. "You came into the world naked and alone. You rose above those who appeared dominant. So I say to you, do not scorn me because I appear weak and useless. You can kill me as easily as your aunt could have killed you. My loss to you would be great."

Katallon turned away, clapping his hands. A woman hurried into the room. She was dressed in a tan skirt that swept the ground, with a darker blouse. She stopped just inside the slit in the tent. Katallon said, "Meat. Beer. Bread." At a flick of his hand, she was gone.

Facing Jones again, Katallon studied him, unspeaking. For some while, Jones stared back, then looked away. Wippard smiled, enjoying Jones' discomfiture. Jones fixed his eyes on a point far beyond the tent roof, concentrating on what he must do that night.

The more he envisioned it, the more assured he became.

The food came on a table borne by two slaves. Each had a thin steel band around his neck and both wrists. Loops riveted to the bands obviously served as tethering rings. The men were naked to the waist. When they turned to leave, Jones saw one's back was disfigured by the lumpy, slick welts of flogging scars. Jones' hand stole to his turban. He envisioned his own offended, humiliated flesh. Sylah's patrician features swam in his mind's eye.

Katallon was watching; he nodded at the departing slave. "Discipline's strict in Windband," he said, then picked up the carving knife and sawed off a slab of meat. It ran red with rich juices and its heady redolence struck Jones so hard it made him unsteady. He snatched up the knife before Wippard could reach for it, cut a slice, then placed it on bread, as he saw Katallon do. The beer was in individual tankards, the foam on top like tan cream. Jones forgot all his problems for the moment.

Katallon was draining the last of his drink when a bell chimed from the first room. Katallon responded with a shouted order. A guard stepped in. He said, "Part of the ambushers—about twenty, who caught horses—have returned. The War Chief comes."

Katallon clapped once more to have the meal cleared. After a quick glance at Jones and Wippard, he settled back in his chair, waiting.

The man who stormed into the inner room looked less like a War Chief than anyone Jones could imagine. He was considerably under five and a half feet tall, and nearly as big around. The small head sat on the massive, stumpy body like a cruel joke. Not even the warning inherent in the numerous scars crisscrossing its shaved expanse, or the menace in the wild, remaining eye, could detract from the illusion that the entire creature was made of left-over parts. Then Jones' more-analytical view took hold. The man's arms, though short, were hugely muscled. Thighs like kegs led to bulging calves, all supported on small feet and comparatively delicate ankles. Sweat stains on his leather shirt showed where body armor had rested. Jones imagined him tearing it off, throwing it aside on his way to this meeting.

The one eye searched, settled on Jones. Without warning, the chief drew his fighting axe from its scabbard and attacked.

Jones' stunned brain comprehended the curved blade as descending on him with the syrupy slowness of something from a mad dream.

Overeager, the chief stumbled. A look of exasperated disbelief flashed across the coarse features. He struggled for balance, tried to adjust the suddenly awry aim of the axe. The effort spun him further off center. He staggered, twisted, ended up directly facing Jones. His weapon swished past Jones' ear, struck the heavy back support post of the chair.

The sound was melodic, the clean thud of wood, and then the faint ring of metal, like a distant bell. Even as Jones felt his bladder empty, he registered the tones, knowing they'd be with him as long as he lived, as would the stinking panting of the chief, the red, wet open mouth as he strained to free the blade.

Jones looked down to discover the snakes. He didn't remember reaching for them, yet they were out, his hands grasping their middles.

The chief saw them an instant later. His eye bulged. When he screamed, saliva splattered Jones.

The furiously rattling snakes struck him simultaneously. Then again. And again. They struck his straining, ridged throat, his face, his chest. Poison pumped into him. One struck his arm at the inside of the elbow as he belatedly threw himself backward, releasing the axe handle.

On the pounded earth floor of the tent, the chief rolled and screamed, kicking, flailing his arms as if still attacked. Katallon and Wippard were stupefied, as were the guards who tumbled into the room, the late arrivals jarring aside the earlier ones, all bunching into knots of disbelief at the entryways.

The chief rolled to a sitting position. A waxy, blue-white sheen palled his flesh. Eerily, the fading, dying eye sought Jones, fixed on his face yet again. Unable to move, Jones sat and stared back, the squirming, rattling snakes coiled round his extended arms.

The chief's focus changed. He strained toward Jones. From that close, it was clear he was trying to regain his axe. Behind his back, Katallon and Wippard watched, transfixed.

Recovering quickly, Jones crammed the snakes back into their sacks. With his right hand, he lifted the moon disk on its chain and held it out toward the chief. Rolling the words from deep in his chest, he said, "I forgive. Like me, you shall rise from the dead when my time next comes, and you shall join me in life eternal beside my mother the moon."

Mouth working, features contorted, the chief strained toward Jones, reached for his weapon. The hand pawed at Jones' knee. Jones bent forward, wedged his hand under the man's chin. He was gratefully surprised to discover just how much strength and coordination the man had lost; it was like restraining a heavy infant. Jones said, "Come to me, my son. I comfort. Believe in me, and go, prepared to rise again at my call. I, who am Moonpriest, say this to you."

The chief dropped in convulsions at his feet. They all watched as he shook the last of his life away.

Jones leaned back in his seat. He ignored the clamminess where he'd voided himself. Maintaining the projection quality of his speech, he directed it at Katallon. "The moon dies to be reborn. Thus was I. The snake sheds its skin and lives renewed. Thus was I. The snake is but a symbol, however. There is more within me, a power you cannot imagine. It makes the venom of snakes as dew on the grass. I offer it to you. Harm my people, harm me, and you lose that power forever. In its place, you will bear the curse of Moonpriest to your burning, down to the seventh generation."

Slowly, deliberately, he turned his gaze on Wippard. "You would test Moonpriest, in your arrogance. So you shall. So you shall."

CHAPTER 36

"Hurry, you fools," Jones snapped.

Fox blanched. It troubled him deeply to see Jones so nervous. He'd never been like this since his rebirth. Unceasingly, he paced the ground inside the roped-off area where the confrontation with Wippard was to take place.

The bodies of the dead Windband warriors rested on top of their pyre, at the back of the square. A large chair outside the rope faced the device Fox and his men worked on. Fourteen smaller chairs flanked it. Katallon, Wippard, and the other dignitaries from the tribes of Windband would watch the test from there.

The huge crowd already waiting outside the rope barrier added to Fox's discomfort. The only other time he'd seen that many people gathered was at what his people simply called the Battle. That was when Gan Moondark crushed Ola.

Adding to the problems, Jones' strange device had only been seen by himself, the smith, and the woodworker. Construction was slow, clumsy. The crowd saw the confusion. They jeered raucously and speculated on the death Wippard would order for the entire group, once he'd exposed the fraudulent priest.

Nevertheless, the work went on.

The base of the device was a squat knee-high table. Down the length of the tabletop, off center toward the back, ran a large wooden frame. It held a thin sheet of wildcow leather a full five feet square. Both sides were illustrated with four vertical columns of seven squares. On the far left, the squares were each bisected by a diagonal line ranging from the lower left corner to the upper right. The top, or dominant, triangle was painted white, the lower triangle black. In the next column the squares were all white, separated by black lines. The third section was an inverted version of the first; the diagonal ran from top left to lower right, and black was dominant over white. The final column was all black squares, divided by white lines.

Above each painted column was a metal representation of the proper moon phase. They were fashioned with metal tails, which fit into holes in the frame.

While they attached the frame to its end braces, Fox noted that the leather was impregnated with beeswax. It reminded him of the way his people boiled leather in oil to create the shell of the body armor they called a barmal.

There was something vaguely disturbing about the odd looking creation taking shape. Fox easily recognized the symbolism of twenty-eight squares arranged to illustrate the lunar cycle. The moon disks his men were presently unpacking clearly had religious significance. But what was all the talk of power, of a gift from the moon mother? Fox caught himself chewing the inside of his lip. It infuriated him to realize he was succumbing to nervousness, and his anger turned to Jones.

Moonpriest. He'd promised many people many things.

Fox looked to the east. Peaks in silhouette presaged moonrise. Moonpriest's power revealed? Or a cold, pitiless light to guide them all to the Land Beyond?

The russet middle of each moon disk was about three feet across, made of sturdy ceramic material. There was a large hole in each center and deep indentations at the outer rim. Then there were the long, slightly ridged pieces of highly polished copper, tapered from a blunt, fat end to a small, rounded end. Jones supervised as the warriors fit the metal pieces into the outer indentations, where they were held in place by copper pins inserted into holes provided for the purpose. Extending about six inches past the rim, the fatter ends of the metal pieces created the effect of a red-rayed harvest moon.

A disk went on each side of the waxed screen. Two warriors fitted the disk center holes over axles at the apex of triangular stanchions. Locked in place, the disks rotated smoothly.

The waxed hide between them completely hid one disk from the other, and the disks almost totally obscured the paintings.

Fox could see no sense to it.

A small steel rod attached to each stanchion. There was a small brush of fine copper wires at the farthest ends of the rod, where they could whisk the copper rays. Fox noted that the brushes on the front disk touched upper left and lower right. The brushes on the back touched opposite top and bottom points.

Why?

Each axle had a small pulley on it, with a looped leather belt that ran to larger wheels a few feet away. The big wheels were fixed to a thick beam that ran under the table. The wheels had handles for turning. There was a seat at each end of the beam. Obviously, men were expected to sit in the seats and turn the wheels, which then turned the smaller one and rotated the disk.

Again, why?

Continuing activity drew Fox's attention. Two large wooden posts were sunk through holes cut in the wood of the tabletop and wedged securely in place. The poles extended about an inch below the tabletop and flanked the framed leather barrier. The woodworker had endowed them with beautifully carved rattlesnakes. A pair entwined each post in high relief. One of them reached the top, just short of the decorative knob there, its head turned to glare balefully out at any spectators. The second stopped halfway up, holding a thing in its mouth that Fox could only call a pair of copper combs. The teeth of each comb faced the teeth of the other, parallel to the ground. They were so close to touching the metal rays of the moon disks that Fox stood on tiptoe to look directly down and assure there was no contact.

A wedge between beam and table tightened the belt to the smaller wheel.

Jones ordered the system tested.

Both disks spun properly between the combs. The little copper brushes made a soft whisper. An ominous mumble came up from the axles.

There was another noise. A sinister, crackling hiss. Jones saw Fox's troubled puzzlement and smiled. The expression bothered Fox as much as the strange sound.

Jones himself attached a copper rod to each pair of combs with pins. The rod fed horizontally into a hole bored in each post. A few inches below that, a short chain of copper links exited a similar hole. Jones clipped a length of identical chain to the post chain. It reached down to coil on the tabletop.

Warriors unwrapped an awkward, heavy construction. Fox grimaced at the sight of it, finally understanding why Jones had stripped the camp of every scrap of copper they owned. This last piece looked like stair steps, but, only as thick as a knife blade, and unbraced, that was impossible. It was far too clumsy for a shield.

The crowd jeered. Fox's face warmed.

Jones laid down several thicknesses of waxed hide on top of the small table. The top lip of the copper thing, reaching from the front edge of the altar almost to the moon disk, rested on the hides. Long wooden pins passed through holes in both copper and leather padding, fastening all to the tabletop. The center portion hung down to the ground. The lower piece extended out as a kneeling platform, resting on the earth.

Jones attached a copper wire to the right hand pair of combs. There was a hole in the corner of the metal slab on the table, and the wire was strung to that, looped through it several times, then tied off.

Once more Jones signaled the wheels to be turned. The rumble seemed even throatier to Fox. The wet sizzle sounded again.

He was surprised to discover he was sweating. Heavily. It was reasonable to be confused by something as secret and new as Jones' device. Why did it make him . . . ? He surrendered to the word: *Afraid*.

One of the warriors spoke to Jones. "Moonpriest, we're ready."

Fox jerked himself away from the lure of the thing in front of him. Men pulled back the hide covering the last packhorse's burden. They exposed the willow basket Otter Five's wife used to carry the jar that was her proudest possession. As one warrior lifted the jar free, another took two highly polished copper pots from a basket on the opposite side of the horse. Jones had the larger metal pot placed on the tabletop's copper plate. The porcelain jar went into that, and the smaller copper pot inside that. The pots were about a finger's length shorter than the jar, and they fit so close, inner and outer, they literally sleeved it.

Fox could only shake his head at what the smith had accomplished. The pots were seamlessly joined, the bottoms perfectly flat.

An apron of white cloth, tacked to the edge of the tabletop, flanked the copper steps. It draped to the earth. Fox admired that touch; it gave the entire object a more solid, stable appearance.

From the piled baggage, Jones produced a thin copper club with a large flat disk at one end. Moving closer, Fox saw it was actually a cast figurine. An elongated man stood on the circular base, arms pressed to his sides, legs rigid, fists clenched. The body's posture suggested agony.

The face defined it.

White quartz eyes bulged horribly, lines made canyons across the features. The mouth gaped wide, baring bone teeth in an unending, unheard scream.

The figurine stood in the inner copper pot. The tortured head and hunched shoulders extended above the top.

War horns groaned. The first silvered edge of the moon crested the distant peaks. Katallon and his party made their way to the chairs.

In the pregnant hush, Fox heard the silence of the crouched leopard. He knew that this was the highest moment he would ever see. This was not face to face with an enemy, steel against steel. This was looking into the eyes of fate.

Of faith.

Jones watched Katallon's arrival with euphoric confidence. Never had he felt more alive, more aware of every nuance of his body. It was as if each limb, each joint, each hair, sang of accomplishment.

He was destined to bring truth to these people. And then more. Conquests of love. All people, captured in righteousness.

Wippard addressed the crowd. "Katallon gives this blasphemous priest opportunity to defend himself. You will choose his death. You will be given his followers, as partial compensation for the deaths of our warriors. When we destroy his tribe, the survivors will be shared among you."

"Kill him now! He killed our War Chief!" The demand lifted from far back in the crowd. More voices agreed.

Katallon frowned, staring straight ahead. Jones raised his arms for silence. The gesture only aggravated the situation.

Katallon stood. Windband held its collective breath. Katallon said, "Today my War Chief shamed me in my tent. He bared his weapon. He attacked this one. No man has ever stood against the War Chief. This one killed him."

Sullen fury moaned like a storm wind. Katallon needed only a gesture to silence it. "Most of you have heard that spirit animals killed the War Chief. This is true. Rattlesnakes. At this one's wish, they struck. He has claimed even greater powers. He offers them to Windband. We test."

With Katallon reseated, Wippard signaled one of his priests forward. The man proved to be a skilled juggler. He kept four balls in the air while performing acrobatic contortions. Jones noted wryly that the balls were painted to suggest phases of the moon. Then the priest made a large silver moon disk disappear and reappear with appropriate religious commentary aimed at Jones, who disdained the entire performance.

The second magician-priest was more of a challenge. He placed a moon disk in a box. It disappeared from that one, to reappear in another. Next, he ostensibly produced an egg from the air. Moving to a small basket, he unfolded a bolt of cloth perhaps four feet long and a foot wide. He arranged the material to pad the inside of the basket, long ends hanging free outside. The egg was nested on the cloth, and a volunteer folded the loose ends over it. At the priest's instruction, he drove his fist down on top of it.

The crowd hushed. Jones realized they were seeing this trick for the first time. Wippard was determined to outperform his opponent.

Snatching up the cloth, the priest opened it to reveal it free of blemish. Then he picked up the basket, turned it upside down, and dumped out a live, squawking chicken. It fluttered and ran crazily around the cleared area until it found its way past the grim darkness of the waiting pyre. The crowd erupted into laughter.

Wippard spoke while the young priest hurried off. "Who else but Windband priests could create a grown bird from an egg? This cheat claims greater powers than we have. Let him be judged."

The answering roar staggered Jones' small group. Some of them reached for weapons. All looked to Jones.

Proudly, he stepped in front of Katallon. "Insulting tricks. Entertainment for children. He disgraces Moondance." He glared down at the seated priest. "Chickens?" The word dripped contempt.

Turning back to Katallon, he said, "Can the mothers and wives of the five dead warriors be brought here? Can someone bring me the liquid Windband uses to start fires?"

Katallon ordered a man to see to both requests.

Jones signaled his Mountain warriors. Two trotted to the device's seats. Facing Katallon again, Jones drew himself erect, pitched his voice to its resonant best. "Does Wippard dare test himself against me? He says I must be judged. That is right. I must be worthy of Katallon, I must be worthy of Windband. I must be worthy of Moondance. Is there one to disagree?"

Silence. Captivated silence. Jones went on. "I challenge Wippard to touch the power of my mother. First, you will see it spare me, the son, and then one of you, an innocent."

This time there was audible eagerness.

Jones went to the device. Standing at the left side of it, he said, "This is my altar." Bracing by holding the decorative knob, he spun the massive front disk, rubbing the copper rays with a cloth as it rotated. He repeated that routine at the rearward disk. His lips moved in continuous silent prayer.

Back at the front of the altar, he brought out a ceramic flute from an inside pocket of his cloak. He used it to lift the copper chain into the inner copper pot. That done, he faced the moon, playing a short, mournful melody. When he stopped, the two warriors started turning the wheels.

The spinning disks rolled a deep, self-satisfied mumble. The hissing noise grew to a menacing crackle.

Jones walked to the baggage once more, returning with a piece of copper shaped in a crescent. It attached by a sleeve to the end of his flute. After waving it at the crowd, he place one end of the crescent on the altar's copper top. Slowly, he rotated the upper end of the crescent ever closer to the figurine in the inner pot.

Suddenly, explosively, a fat, blue spark fired across the intervening space.

The entire throng recoiled. Women screamed. The sound of blades drawing free of scabbards was like rain.

It took Katallon himself to restore quiet.

When Jones presented himself in front of Katallon again, the man who'd been sent for the women had two younger ones, probably wives, and one who was clearly a mother. Jones went to the elder, dangling his silver Moondance symbol. Her face was a wrinkled mass of hatred. "Your noises don't frighten me. You killed my son. I hope Wippard skins you alive." She spat on him.

Jones closed his eyes. He shivered. When he was sure he was back in control, he looked. The spittle was a frothy mess running down his shirt. "Your son will be beside me forever. He's forgiven me, because he understands that I give him eternal life in the moon, with my mother. As I will give you, when your life in this world is ended. As mine will end one day." He pointed, saying, "Come with me. I must bless you at the altar."

The woman snarled up at him. "Don't touch me! I'll kill you myself."

"Go," Katallon said. "Wait for him." To Jones, he said, "If the old woman is harmed, I give you to Wippard. You understand?"

The woman stood in front of the altar, frightened eyes darting in all directions. Jones had her kneel on the lower copper step. He repeated his cleaning of the disks.

After the wheels had turned awhile, he asked, "Mother, do you see anything in the jar?"

She stiffened, but looked inside. "No."

Jones held the flute toward the moon. "I tell you I have called power from my mother, the moon, into it."

The woman paled.

Jones ordered the men on the wheels to stop work.

Kneeling beside the woman, he faced the altar at a three-quarter angle, assuring the maximum number an unobstructed view. Slowly, deliberately, he reached for the figurine. "I ask your blessing, Mother," he intoned. "I prove my faith. I pray to you to prove your love."

He clutched the figurine, lifted it out of the container. Nothing happened.

The crowd jeered, shouted curses, threats. Unperturbed, Jones replaced the figurine.

Once again, he went to the altar, cleaning, praying. The wheels spun. When they stopped, he returned to the shivering, weeping old woman. He took her wrist, forced her hand toward the figurine. When she twisted to peer pleadingly at Katallon, he said, "Do what the priest says."

Jones let go of her. Tenderly, she put her fingers on the metal head. Gaining confidence, she clutched it, lifted, brandished it.

"Nothing!" Bursting with bravado, the old woman shouted. "There's no magic! I hate him, and it didn't do anything to me. He has no power. We'll put him in the Land Under tonight."

Frowning, trembling, Jones repeated his earlier demonstration with the crescent moon attached to the flute. There was no reaction.

Even Katallon had trouble settling the crowd. Wippard and his priests howled laughter. The animal smell of a mob sullied the night.

Jones composed his features. He retrieved his figurine from where the old woman had dropped it. Distractedly, he wiped more of her spit off it, then replaced it in the pot. Yet again, he performed his ritual. The men turning the wheels streamed sweat. The whites of their eyes showed prominently.

Facing Windband, Jones spoke. His voice was uncertain, his

gestures excessive. "The metal man is the Man Who Is Death. He strikes the false, the evil, those I will not bless. See. And believe." He pointed at Wippard. "I blessed the woman. She has done what I have done, and lives. I challenge you to do the same, but I cannot bless you. You have dirtied Moondance. Repent, Wippard. Repent, agree to serve me, and my mother will spare you."

Wippard stood confidently. A breeze ruffled his long, silver hair. When he reached Jones, he scoffed. "You think to frighten me with this failed toy? You think I don't know you made the first fire by burning clear-clean? We of Windband Moondance knew the uses of fear and clever hands generations ago. You disappoint."

Boldly, Wippard strode to the altar. Jones had to rush to catch up.

Burlesquing obedience to Jones' demand that he kneel before the altar, Wippard mimed fear of the rumbling disks. Looking into the container, he recoiled in mock horror. The crowd cheered lustily. Playing to them, he posed dramatically, preparing to reach.

"Stop!" Jones held out supplicating hands. "Don't touch it. Please, fellow priest, don't shame me. Let me and my friends leave this place without your blood on our consciences. Take my life, if you must. Please, free my friends. But above all, do not touch the Man."

Softly, Wippard said, "Save your tears. You'll need them later." He grabbed.

A ravenous blue spark leaped to check the oncoming hand. A shattering crack split the night.

Wippard convulsed backward, tumbling to earth as if his bones were melted. A tiny wisp of smoke curled from a seared finger.

The huge sigh of amazement raced through the crowd, and then it fell as silent as death.

Calmly, Jones walked to a gaping Katallon. When the guards moved to confront him, he waved them away with his flute. Pitching his voice to the crowd, he said, "I am Moonpriest. I am sent to Windband and Katallon. Hear me. See. And believe."

CHAPTER 37

Sylah shaded her eyes against the afternoon sun. Beside her, Conway slouched in his saddle.

"I don't like it," Sylah said, continuing to examine the distance. "There aren't any people."

Conway said, "It's five houses, Sylah. There's livestock everywhere, so there're people. If it'll make you feel better, I'll send the dogs ahead and we can wait here until they look the place over."

It was what she wanted to do. The cluster of houses was a mile away, though, and by the time the dogs got there, sniffed about, and returned, they could cover the distance themselves. Perhaps she was being overly cautious. She mentally corrected herself; she knew she was worrying too much.

She couldn't help it. The inexplicable death of the man who murdered the Tender and kidnapped Dodoy nagged her constantly. The white arrow indicated it was a second protector who killed the first. Why would one renegade do anything to assist her in conflict with another?

Indecision and unanswerable questions had become wounds that drained her. No matter how insignificant the development, before she could act, she found herself wondering what Clas might do. When she did manage to do something, there was a sense of him peering over her shoulder. The presence was always benign and caring, but she couldn't rid herself of the feeling that she was constantly being graded.

Even that was preferable to the dreams of the Harvester. There were times that one supplanted Clas' image in the lonely, aching reaches of the night. The Harvester sneered. Beckoning, taunting, she coaxed Sylah onward, into a future that whirled with visions of doors that turned into laughing, mocking mouths, of Church symbols that transformed into hating faces.

Occasionally Sylah woke, cold, and the silence of the forest joined that discomfort, seeped through to blood and bone. Then she wondered if her mind might be failing.

Occasionally that concern struck in full daylight. As now.

Conway was right, of course: The people who lived in the houses could very well be off on a communal hunt, or fishing. Raiders would surely have torched the buildings, slaughtered the stock.

Conway said, "When we're about halfway there, we'll send the dogs ahead. That way we get a warning, if we need one, and we don't lose so much time."

She agreed. Time was becoming important. They'd already lost so much she was concerned about being delayed through spring and into summer. The tales of heat and dryness surrounding Church Home made it important they reach there in milder weather. She'd lost count of the number of times they'd retraced miles of useless path. In addition, it seemed every stream was at flood. Every trail had blowdown trees, or rock slides, or misleading forks that died away to worthless rabbit tracks.

Every morning now, when she faced the rising sun, she completed her required ritual. Then, however, she spoke words of her own. Church taught that informal prayer lacked the force of ordained routine. A tiny piece of her mind had always rejected that, and now, consumed by doubts, she found solace in the effort. Sometimes, after having addressed a problem, she was embarrassed to realize how tartly she'd expressed herself. One wasn't supposed to scold the One in All. Each time she survived such an experience without permanent injury or other evidence of supernatural disfavor, she felt a bit closer to that unseen listener.

Conway sent his dogs ahead. Mikka was back quickly. The grizzled female sat off the trail, facing Conway. When he stopped his horse, she looked over her shoulder then back to him. He praised her before turning to Sylah. "They've found something. Tell Tate I've gone on ahead." Right hand holding the wipe ready, he signaled Mikka, following her.

When the dog slowed to a stalk, Conway dismounted. For a while he ran from cover to cover, then crawled the last yards to where Karda lay on the ground behind a tree at the edge of a small potato patch. The translucent verdancy of the sprawling new growth looked tentative and delicate against the harder green of surrounding weeds. Lying prone, Conway examined the village.

The houses were of logs, chinked with mud and moss. Identical in size and shape, each had a stone chimney poked through the crest of its shingled roof. There were five windows—two in front, one at each side, and one in back—and one door. Hides across the windows admitted some light, and Conway noticed that several were missing, apparently to provide ventilation on this soft spring day. All the plank shutters were pulled back, secured by leather loops.

And no human stirred.

Each house had a three-sided, roofed animal shelter and identical corncribs on pilings. Pig noises rose over the rails of a stout pen in the middle distance, and a goat bleated from some undiscovered location. Cattle lay about, placidly chewing cuds. Despite a growing sense of concern, Conway couldn't help noticing the size of the animals. Karda was easily as tall as the nearby bull, although nothing like as heavy. Black, heavily muscled, the sturdy animal sniffed the wind blowing from Conway's hiding place. It got to its feet, and rolled white-rimmed eyes and tossed a wicked pair of horns. A hen wandered out of the nearest house. A scatter of chicks followed, cheeping constant wonder at unending discoveries.

When Conway made as if to crawl past Karda, the dog swung his muzzle around to look off to the right. He seemed to be indicating an interest in a clump of scrub alder.

Behind him, Conway heard the others approaching. "Watch," he ordered the dogs.

Keeping flat, Conway hurriedly backed away until he was sure the forest shielded him. When he got to his feet, it was just in time to wave the others to a halt. He reported, suggesting he and Tate take the dogs and approach through the forest.

Sylah objected. "Church has no need of stealth. If there are people hiding from us, it's out of fear. Lanta and I will ride in and let them know we're Church."

Tate said, "Too risky. It's only ten days ago we found the dead Tender. What if we promise we won't attack anyone who doesn't attack us; fair enough?"

Lanta said, "Conway and Tate must've dealt with many similar situations in their travels."

Sylah thought she saw something suspiciously like guilt in the look the two strangers exchanged, but when Conway's eyes met hers, his expression was perfectly bland. Tate dismounted and warned Dodoy to stay close to the priestesses. He nodded.

Sylah was impressed by the way Conway and Tate moved off through the forest. They'd gained confidence.

She smiled to herself. Beside Clas, they were clumsy.

The humor faded. The image of Clas wouldn't go away. His expression, his eyes, yearned. It took every fiber of her will, the employment of every technique of mind control, to dispel the frighteningly inappropriate emptiness straining to overwhelm her.

Conway and Tate pressed ahead. As one took a covered firing position, the other advanced a few yards beyond. Karda and Mikka were farthest ahead. Tanno and Oshu assured no threat infiltrated from behind.

When the point dogs came trotting back through the forest, Conway and Tate jacked rounds into the chambers of the wipes, spread out, and went forward quietly. The dogs moved out ahead and to the flanks.

Their behavior puzzled Conway. They were too relaxed. He had the strange sensation that they were enjoying a new game.

He looked down at his hands. The skin across the backs shone from being stretched tight. He flexed his fingers to restore circulation.

Ahead, a baby cried. The sound was cut off. Conway gestured his dogs closer and saw Tate do the same from the corner of his eye. Pressed against a substantial tree, he shouted around it. "People from the village! We're travelers—two Sisters of Church, a man, a woman, and a boy. We want to buy food."

Small rustling noises broke the forest's silence. Tate cupped her hands to her mouth. A shout stopped her. "Go away!" Shrill fear robbed the voice of definition.

"We mean no harm," Tate said. "We need fresh supplies. We hunger. We'll pay."

"Leave us alone. You'll bring them back."

Conway and Tate exchanged looks. "Them?" she said softly to Conway, then louder, "We're coming. Peacefully."

Feet drummed off through the forest. The same voice said, "Leave us alone, so I can tell them we never saw you. Go away. Please?"

Tate answered. "Don't do anything silly, all right? No trouble."

Without the dogs, Conway and Tate quite likely would have walked past the boy's well camouflaged den. He was backed into a small hollow in an old maple trunk, with grass and bushes piled in front. The dogs grinned at him through the cover. Four heavy tails thrashed in greeting. The boy raised a broken sword, the stubby blade ground to a lopsided point, the cutting edges nicked. Nevertheless, he extended it through his makeshift screen steadily, his small, bright eyes unwavering. His expression was a rending blend of exhaustion, fear, and determination.

Conway squatted to speak solemnly. "The dogs are trying their best to say they like you."

The boy spared him a glance. "They won't bite me?" Conway shook his head. The boy turned a questioning look on Tate. She said, "Word of honor." The boy thought it over. "What about the rest of us?"

"Your parents? Call them in. All we want is to buy some supplies."

The boy blinked, but a moment later, he bent around to shout into the forest. "It's not the raiders. Or Kossiars. Come back."

Tate gave him her name, asking, "Who're you? How old are you?"

"Tarabel," the boy said, tapping his forehead with two fingers. "I'm twelve." He blinked again, swallowed loudly. "There aren't any parents."

Noise interrupted. Conway and Tate turned to see children filing out of the forest; seven, including an infant. None appeared to be as old as Tarabel. The girls were dressed in crude smocks, the boys in leather trousers and homespun shirts. Some wore raccoon-skin capes that hung past the knees. Innocent faces watched Conway and Tate, full of confusion. And accusation.

Tate's voice was uncertain. "No adults?"

"Some of us had time to hide. Aunt Minlee went with us. Now she . . . Everybody else . . ." He looked away. "Raiders came. Looking for you."

"Us? Who's looking for us?" Tate asked. A little blond girl reached up and took her hand, inspecting it solemnly. Tate started at the touch. She smiled absently at the child and returned her attention to Tarabel, who said, "The raiders. The ones who . . . who took away the others." He looked to the other children, then sent silent appeal to the adults.

Tate understood. "Come on, back to the village. We need to get food into you all. Washing wouldn't hurt, either."

The little blond girl smiled, gripping Tate's hand purposefully. Tate smiled back at her, welcoming this time. Tapping her forehead with two fingers as Tarabel had, the girl said, "My name's Nandameer. Who're you? What happened to all your skin?"

"I'm Tate. And I'm this color because I'm magic. Come on, I'll tell you all about it."

They turned to go as Conway reached for Tarabel. The boy shrank back. Smiling assurance, Conway said, "Hey, I won't hurt you. Come on."

Tarabel said, "I'll do it myself." The last word was practically a grunt. He levered himself forward with his elbows, pushing against the tree. His knees buckled. He pitched forward on his face.

Tate gasped. "Oh, no, Matt. Look at his leg."

The right thigh stretched the material of the trousers. A foul smell rose from wetness on the back of the boy's leg. Conway scooped him up, ignoring the pathetic, dropped sword. "Karda," he said, "get Sylah. Go."

Karda hurtled off through the trees. Conway hurried after him, Tarabel in his arms.

Nandameer brushed blond bangs out of the way. "Tarabel's going to be dead," she said. Tate was dumbstruck. She stared at the tiny child and shook her head, gently at first, then almost violently.

"Yes he is," Nandameer insisted. "Just like the others. He thinks we don't know, but we do. Everybody got dead. Now the bad men'll come back. We'll get dead, too. Tarabel says sometimes it hurts. Please, Tate, when they do it to me, will you make it not hurt?"

CHAPTER 38

Conway sat in the doorway of one of the houses and marveled as the children wrestled rags free from between jaws that could have taken the tugging arms off at the shoulder. Other children pulled on abused ears or wrapped themselves around legs. And all the while, Karda and Mikka rolled their eyes toward their master, tongues lolling foolishly.

"Killers. Terror of the battlefield." He snorted scornfully, reaching down to extricate Karda's tail from a toddler. As long as the child merely considered it an aid to walking, Conway foresaw no problem. Now, however, it was about to be tested for edibility.

Karda wagged the tail. Toddler sprawled backward, sat down hard. He scrambled back onto his feet with animal-like quickness. He poised, tense, searching in all directions. The reaction lasted but a moment. Then he was laughing and after the tail again.

The vignette bared the dark underside of the surface gaiety. Conway's heart clenched like a fist at the memory of other times, other children. Dead for centuries now, they also had acquired the identical habit of suddenly checking around them with too-old, too-fearful eyes.

Blond Nandameer lobbed a stick for Mikka. The dog who'd been too proud to perform for her master leaped to snatch it out of the air. The child's squeal of delight almost drowned out Tarabel's tormented cry. Conway looked to the house where the three women were inside with the boy.

Lanta came out, gestured him over. Calling the dogs, he left the children chorusing complaints. Lanta extended him a goatskin waterbag. "Fill this, please. Hurry."

He ran for the village stream.

The water was crystal clear. Small fish and water striders scattered when he plunged the container to the bottom of a handmade rock-rimmed pool. Downstream, watercress mounded the creek bank and shallows with emerald. Conway jiggled the sack impatiently to force air out the open neck.

On the far side of the pool, something out of place plucked at his vision. Through the tangled growth, he identified a tiny house structure, perhaps the size of a man's torso, open at the front. A shrine—knocked down and kicked aside. Three stream-polished

219

agates set into an eave suggested Church. The broken figure inside was a crudely made Sister in typical black robe. The wooden neck was splintered where the head had been snapped off. One arm was missing.

Back inside the house, he poured water from the goatskin into a pot hung on a swingarm at the fireplace. Lanta added cotton rags. He commented that she was ripping up a perfectly good blouse. She shook her head. "There's no one to wear it." Then, "We'll need many bandages. We have to open the wound. Dirt creatures have invaded."

Conway moved to the boy's bed. It was a rude rectangular frame, the suspension a netting of leather straps. The mattress rustled when Tarabel turned his head to look up. "They want to make me sleep. We're the only men here, and even me and Dodoy are just boys. When the raiders come back, you'll need help."

Off in a dark corner, Dodoy stirred. Conway told Tarabel, "You have to get well enough to travel. Let the Healers help."

"I can't."

"You've already been brave enough, Tarabel."

"I wasn't brave. I told Aunt Minlee we should stay hidden. She wanted to go look for the adults. I couldn't let her go alone. We found—everybody. The raiders caught us. They said she had to tell when you came here and how long you stayed. They wouldn't believe you never did. She died."

Tarabel licked his lips. The dry tongue seemed to scrape. His eyes wandered, and his voice took on a dreamlike tone. "The man holding me wasn't careful. I bit him. I ran. They shot me with an arrow. When they couldn't find me, they laughed. Said I'd burn in the Land Under, 'cause I helped the false Church. What's that mean? Is that why they kill us?"

Sylah appeared at Conway's elbow. "Church heals, Tarabel. Please, let us heal you."

Tarabel's eyelids slid downward. His breathing leveled off. Conway turned a smile to Sylah, but the boy picked that moment to jerk and come fully alert. Seeing the young eyes brighten, then start to lose their luster nearly undid Conway. It was like watching a fire burn itself out. Tarabel said, "You'll wake me if they come?"

"I promise."

Tarabel raised his head, frowning at the effort. "I'll do what you say," he said. The calculated gruffness in the childish voice made Conway's throat close painfully.

Sylah extended a potion in a wooden cup. It passed under Conway's nose. Dark brown, it had a greasy cast on the surface and a dank, organic smell. Conway's mind flashed to deep shade, where furtive insects rustled under decaying leaves and the soil was forever damp.

Lanta came to dab at Tarabel's lips and brow with a damp cloth. The boy sighed into heavy slumber. Conway asked her, "What did you give him?"

"The easing mushrooms. Very strong. Dangerous."

"Dangerous?"

"We only use it when there's no choice."

"He's that bad?"

Lanta looked away. Conway reached to give her a reassuring pat on the shoulder. Her swift recoil startled him. He excused himself to put more wood on the fire.

Sylah returned to the bedside with her healer's kit. Lanta replaced the large pot on the fire, adding more strips of cotton homespun to the boiling water. When she stirred the cloth, Conway saw the small knives at the bottom. Looking up from that unpleasantness, he caught Lanta putting in a saw blade.

She colored. For a moment, he thought she was leaning toward him, but dismissed the idea. She said, "If it's necessary to save the life, we'll sacrifice the leg. Surely you do the same in your land?"

He nodded.

She prepared a pad of clean cloth on clean straw under the boy's wounded leg. Sylah took a large obsidian rock from her bag. A sharp blow with the back of her shortknife dislodged a thin leaf-shaped piece of stone. To Tate and Conway, she said, "Will you help us?"

"What do we do?" Tate spoke for both.

"Gather the children outside. When we start the Prayer for Protection Against Unseens, I want them to join."

"Leave that to me." Tate gestured to Dodoy. He hurried to follow.

Sylah and Lanta washed. Then Sylah offered up the razor-edged obsidian in both hands, chanting the prayer. Lanta joined her.

Tate knelt just outside the door. She strained to hear, repeating Sylah's words a half beat behind. Sweating with effort, her unexpected aura of mingled spiritualism and hard-edged concentration surprised Conway. He would have sworn he'd seen all of Tate's manifestations, and here was a woman he never suspected.

The rising volume of Sylah's chant distracted him. Outside, the children's bright voices rose and fell in innocent awe and hope under Tate's direction.

Sylah's precise strokes exposed corruption. Evil stench billowed through the room. Lanta shoved rags at Conway to wipe with as she worked free the stub of arrow shaft and its steel head. Tossed into the fire, it sizzled and sputtered nastily. Tate heard it, and made the children chant louder.

Sylah curtly demanded a knife that lay glowing in the coals. She pressed it to blood vessels. More stinking and sizzling followed, but the bleeding subsided.

Tarabel paled. A pulse at his temple throbbed, then suddenly faded to mere vibration.

Lanta's hands darted into her bag, reappeared with a smaller one of soft leather. Unwrapping the drawstring closure, she took out a pottery tube with wooden plugs at each end. Holding it vertical, she unplugged one end, keeping it carefully upright. Reaching back in the bag, she drew out a small box, sealed with wax. Stripping off the cover, she opened it to produce a short stick with one end leather wrapped. It was a snug fit for the original tube. The other article in the box was a wooden plug that exactly fit the open end of the tube. A hollow feather quill protruded from its center. Conway stifled an amazed exclamation. The device was for injections.

Bending to the boy, Lanta jabbed the quill through an exposed artery wall. She pushed the plunger. Liquid, already in the tube, rushed into Tarabel's bloodstream. Color replenished his cheeks. The thready pulse strengthened.

Bandaging and final cleanup were over quickly, with everything flammable burned. When the three of them stepped outside, Tate waited with the children. The priestesses explained patiently that Tarabel needed quiet. Tate led them off to play. Sylah excused herself.

Alone, Conway asked Lanta about the injection. He called the tool a needle. She corrected him; it was called a hipe. The contents were surm. "I can tell you this surm is made of a plant called foxglove. All surms are Church secrets. I don't always believe keeping such secrets is right, but it helps Church keep her position. Without that, she loses her ability to influence men. You understand?"

"Completely," he said. "And now I'm going to take my dogs and scout the area. I'll be back by midmorning tomorrow, at the latest."

"Stop." The word was out before she realized it.

He was already halfway through the door. He turned, more amused than obedient.

"Is it really necessary? Can't you just send the dogs? What if you find the raiders? Or they see you? It's not safe." She heard herself chattering and bit off further questions. Her face was warm, and she turned back to Tarabel, needlessly cleaning.

When she looked at Conway again his good humor was gone. Her heart lurched at his narrowed eyes, sullen mouth. He said, "I appreciate your concern, Priestess. I'm not one of your super-warriors, but I'm not completely incompetent." He spun out the door.

Why? she asked herself. Why can't he understand? Am I witched, that everything I do or speak must come backward? He touches me, and I flinch, because the wanting for that touch is so strong it frightens me. And he hates me for it, doesn't understand anything.

If I can look inside my heart and admit a love that I didn't want—don't want—why can't he see what that heart tries to tell him every time I look his way.

I know the others look at me and see. Yet he, of all, is blind. *Will he never see me?*

CHAPTER 39

Listen to the music of the ride, Conway told himself. The high, soft friction of leather on leather, the jingle of metal, the regularity of the horse's easy breathing, underscored the steady plod of hoof-beats. Rather than that, however, he heard Lanta's concern. In the flowing movements of branches, he saw the grace of her worried gestures.

He was as good as he needed to be. Regardless of what any of them thought.

Shadows stretched long when he came across the juncture of his trail and another. A sharp whistle brought the dogs running, and together they all explored the new find for a while. It led south, then angled off to the east, opposite the direction Sylah wanted them to take.

He retraced his steps to the junction and proceeded on the other fork. He went only a hundred yards or so before the appearance of a small stream convinced him to rest awhile before returning to the village. Uphill, just visible from the trail, a tiny waterfall splattered down a rock outcrop.

After bringing in the dogs, he led Stormracer a short distance beyond the waterfall. Settling against a huge old fir, he complimented his choice. A gap in the trees exposed a sweeping view. Thin, wisping clouds drifted toward him from the west. In the valley, a small river crashed across jagged rocks before entering onto a wider, slower stretch. Massive spring-run salmon prowled the quiet depths like dark ghosts. Cobbled banks kept the forest and a belt of pale green brush at a distance. Gray bleached driftwood, including some logs as thick as a tall man, littered the rough surface.

Conway looped the feedbag strap over Stormracer's ears and fed him a measure of grain. For himself and the dogs there was dried venison. They gulped their share greedily, catching the tossed strips with a noise almost as loud as handclapping.

They watched Conway's more-leisurely meal hopefully. Only when he licked his fingers and showed them his hands were empty did they give up. Karda heaved himself onto his feet long enough to reach Conway's side, then collapsed, pressing against his master. Mikka was content to lie on her stomach, chin on fore-paws, facing him.

The animals warned him, all three suddenly alert, testing the wind. Then he heard it. A poignant low trumpeting. There seemed to be no point of origin.

Chickadees continued to skip and whir and flutter in the branches above. The trees sighed on, unaffected.

By disappearing, the sound emphasized everything remaining.

And then it came again, from down by the river. The tone lacked the basso thrum of a warhorn, but had a similar urgency. It made him think of the murdered Tender, and the women waiting back at the village with the children.

The raiders said they'd be back.

Karda and Mikka faced north moments before he, too, heard the hoofbeats racing toward them. Conway ordered the dogs to silence.

The rider thundered by so swiftly only small details registered. A war mask, the laces undone so that the flaps weren't closed across his face. Cropped black beard. Leather jacket; vertical metal bars. Narrow scarflike banner flapping behind him in the wind of his passage.

Something familiar. Something Conway knew he should be able to identify. He pounded his fist against a tree trunk and cursed himself. There was something there, something important.

The hoofbeats receded in the distance.

He mounted and hurried to the trail junction, relieved to establish that the stranger had traveled the secondary trail, not the one leading back to the village. He was sure there was a connection between the rider and the lowing horn. Cautiously, he returned to the viewpoint.

A running figure broke out of the wavelike sway of the wind-blown brush belt that marked the transition from rocky river beach to forest. Conway thought he saw a limp, but the range made it impossible to be sure. A glint of light beside the figure proved to be an arrow. It flashed by to plunge harmlessly into the river.

The man made his way to a huge weathered log that was stranded on the beach just below the rapids. Perpendicular to the flow, its tangled web of roots was almost in the water. The man sheltered behind them. Conway silently cheered the clever tactic. Reasonably shielded from arrows, he could only be approached on foot; even someone on the log itself would have trouble getting to him.

Twelve pursuers appeared. Arrows from the brush indicated more hidden there. Running, dodging, losing arrows at their quarry, the attackers closed inexorably.

One of the defender's arrows struck home. Then another. The horn sounded again. Moments later, a man on horseback forged through the scrub growth. Conway recognized the rider who'd thundered past his hiding place. A sword glittered at the end of his gesticulating arm.

The men on foot rushed forward. One dropped, the victim of a last arrow before they swept around the end of the log. Back against his gnarled wall, the lone defender made a ferocious stand. Distance silenced shouts, the clash of blade on blade, yet in Conway's imagination those things rose triumphantly, then crashed to moans. Two attackers stumbled away, doubled over. Another fell, writhing. A pair went backward into the river to be carried downstream. Their peaceful, heedless drift contrasted cruelly with the frantic action that cost them their lives.

And then the lone man was down. A knot of men pummeled him mercilessly. A signal from the rider stopped that. He gestured with the sword. Yanked upright, the prisoner walked with the slack legs of semiconsciousness. Nevertheless, one man held each of his arms while a third kept a swordpoint at his back. They marched him to the horseman. Everyone was motionless until a soldier stepped forward and drove a fist into the prisoner's face. The victim's head snapped back. He slumped, then straightened.

Ordering the dogs to follow, Conway hurried away. None of it was his concern. He'd given his word to support Sylah's quest. Getting involved would jeopardize it.

He thought he heard a scream.

He galloped back. The prisoner was on the ground. A man was pouring river water over him. The others lounged about, watching. The horseman leaned over, prodded the fallen man with the point of his sword. Conway jerked in sympathy. The reflex became a grab for the sniper rifle.

Sliding the case out of the sealskin wrap, he worked with unwarranted certainty. The weapon fitted itself to his hands, lifted to his shoulder as if of its own volition. On foot, he braced against a tree.

The captive was covered with blood. Two men now held him spread-eagled and erect against the tree trunk.

Conway placed the sight's dot on the horseman. Captured in the magnifying scope, details leapt to clarity. And there was the thing he'd tried so hard to identify. The proud pennant snaking down the rider's back. Black and white vertical stripes. The identifying colors of Jalail, a kingdom now become one of Gan Moondark's Three Territories.

One of the rogue nobles who fled, who still supported the deposed Altanar.

Conway scanned the other attackers. Several carried white arrows, white-feathered. Protectors.

The dot tracked back to the horseman as if self-willed. A strange, floating sensation filled Conway. Blood pounded in his temples; his arms grew heavy with swelling, arrogant strength. It wasn't the same as at the river. That was fight or die. This was vengeance, justification, proof of worth. It was emotional turbulence, dark, and frightening.

The report of the weapon had the majesty of distant thunder. In truth, he realized dimly, if the weapon hadn't recoiled, he might not have recognized the noise for what it was.

For a sickening moment, Conway thought he'd missed. His intended victim jerked violently, both arms rising, so he appeared to point both hands at the man against the log. Conway thought he saw a haze around the horseman's head. The western sun could have been responsible for the reddish cast of it.

The horseman's collapse came simultaneously with the first roaring echoes. The body, still erect, hands clenched against dying, tipped sideways. Gaining speed, it slipped farther, pitched down onto the rocks.

The rest of the men scattered. One stepped toward the prisoner, sword raised. Conway snapped off a shot, not quick enough to stop the blow. The prisoner dodged, was struck, but still managed to break for the river.

Conway hammered his targets, watched them sprawl like squashed insects. The warm wood stock was an erotic caress on his cheek. The perfect curve of the butt wedded itself to his shoulder. The weapon was alive to his touch, his thoughts, responding, demanding.

Every settling of his eye called a man's fate, every movement of his finger on the trigger was death.

He screamed his own name, told all of creation of his power. And then there was nothing to shoot.

Eight bodies and some discarded weapons littered the beach.

On the near shore, the former captive hauled himself out of the water. He disappeared into the trees.

Riding to the riverbank, Conway followed the dogs to where the man lay. His wounds were massive. New gashes cut across old scars in several places. The man watched Conway with eyes swelling shut. There was a brooding calmness about him. Not resignation. Controlled, Conway thought. The man was studying him with all the intensity he could manage. Even while being bandaged, his eyes followed Conway's every move.

Suddenly, as if it were an act of will, the man was unconscious. Conway loaded the limp form on Stormracer.

Darkness had long since fallen when Tate and her dogs intercepted Conway outside the village. On the way to the house where Sylah and Lanta slept, he explained the presence of the unconscious man lashed behind him. At the sound of voices, the two Church women were awake. While Conway once again told his story, Sylah and Lanta rushed to throw on robes. They came outside as he finished untying the unconscious stranger. The four of them carried him indoors.

As she examined her patient, Sylah asked Conway to describe the horseman. When he was done, she nodded shortly. "You did well," she said. There was quality to the words that warned of memories too harsh to be shared.

The injuries were dangerous, she said, but unlikely to kill the young warrior. Kneeling beside him, she excused Tate and Conway from the prayer. Lanta joined her in treating the wounds.

Sylah studied her patient. Muscular, he gave an impression of solidity even in his present condition. Calluses revealed hours of bow-and-arrow practice. The palms were oddly soft. She looked his hands over more carefully, and decided from the callus pattern and sun coloration he must normally wear fingerless gloves. Curious. His hair, washed and brushed out, glowed like raven wings in the light of the small candles. Sewing the last open wound,

Sylah was surprised to see how much stronger his pulse had become. A blue vein in his neck pumped in perfect rhythm with her gleaming needle of walrus ivory.

Brushing her own hair back, Sylah sought Conway. He sat on the floor across the room, back to the wall. She said, "Did he tell you why the band was after him?"

Conway shook his head. "Hasn't spoken yet."

"We should leave tomorrow. The renegades are desperate men, marked for punishment by the true Church. Their only hope of survival is to eliminate us and claim protection from the false one."

"Go. Now." Forced past the stranger's mangled lips, the resulting mispronunciation added its own sinister overtones.

Sylah and Lanta bent over him. He snored gently at them.

Rising, Sylah was thoughtful. "Should we risk bringing him with us?"

Conway heaved himself to his feet. "Draggers."

Tate nodded. "Right. We can walk. One horse for him, one for Tarabel. The smaller children can ride, too."

"Let's do it that way." Sylah turned away, closing off the conversation. More than that, she hid a smile of satisfaction. They were making sacrifices now, making decisions that brought them together. If anything could eliminate the residual divisions created by Dodoy's capture, cooperation would. To herself, she said, "Thank you, Abbess, my friend, my teacher. Your lessons never fail. Whenever your foolish student remembers. 'Adversity is to character as heat is to steel.' "

She made her way back to her blankets, was pulling them up around her chin, when she felt the stare.

Dodoy's round, probing eyes watched. Tired, irritable, she matched his look. He smiled, baring his small, gleaming teeth. Whispering, sharing his malice with her alone, he said, "They always make you do what they want. You think it's your idea. You just get used. Always did. Always will."

Shocked, furious, she rose on an elbow to respond. Dodoy's features went blankly innocent. He twisted away, turned his back to her. For a moment, she panted with frustration. Whatever she said, he'd simply deny. She'd look like a fool.

Jangling, screeching, she heard his voice echo in her mind. ". . . just get used. Always did. Always will."

The burning behind her eyes was fatigue. Malevolent, evil child; senseless words. Harmless.

228

CHAPTER 40

Morning dawned sluggishly, snared in thick tendrils of mist that webbed the trees and buildings. Sylah felt her way outdoors. Pressed against the rough lumber of the house, she hugged herself, clutching her robe. The chill damp dictated she go inside and put on something warmer. She was too anxious to see Tate's return from nightwatch.

Fog and the moist ground muffled the approaching hooves. Tate's ghosting appearance gave her a start. Likewise, Tate, seeing unexpected movement, brought the wipe to bear with catlike quickness.

Sylah broke the silence. "You've had a long night. Are you able to travel?"

Slinging the wipe over her shoulder, Tate dismounted. Red lines mapped the whites of her eyes. Words formed as if moving the lips taxed her. "No options, Sylah. I heard that horn Conway talked about. Just before first light. It won't take anyone long to figure out where we are."

"Come inside while I fix you some tea."

"This poor horse is as wet and tired as I am. He needs feeding. I'll be along."

Sylah was mock angry. "Care for the horse first. You're just like my husband."

"Proud to hear it. He's the one who taught me." Tate winked. Her quiet laugh was rough, but for a moment her face was alive, the way Sylah liked to remember it.

Entering the house, Sylah thought, Everyone's at the edge of exhaustion. We need to rebuild strength. But there's even more need to run.

She looked at the wounded man on the floor. If the jouncing of the horse was too much for him, there was nothing to be done. He had a warrior's chance.

The children were a different matter. She glanced over to the dark corner where Lanta lay beside the sleeping group. Like puppies, wadded in an untidy, heartbreakingly sweet heap. Her gaze fell on Dodoy. He's one of them, she told herself; he didn't create himself. A hard world bred hard children.

Lanta opened her eyes. She rose instantly with swift grace. "Something's wrong?"

"No, everything's all right." The children mumbled and muttered, burrowing closer, resisting the new day. Sylah turned her attention to them. Each one woke soft-featured, the uncertain definitions of youth muzzy with sleep. With full consciousness, however, alert eyes swept the room. Bodies tensed. Muscles in the little faces pulled flesh into tight wariness.

Inexpressible anger hummed in Sylah's blood. She had trouble dismissing it.

In preparation for leaving, Sylah and Lanta had searched out extra clothing for their charges. It ranged along the wall now in neat stacks. Both adults remarked on the lack of decorative work. Girls' smocks had narrow handwoven bands of material decorating cuffs, collars, and skirt hems. The only color in the male outfit was the belt. They, too, were woven, and the design—arrowhead, circle, square, lightning, or diamond—identified the family.

Every child now had one of the raccoon fur capes. They were made with leather inner straps to hold them to the shoulders. The front could be closed with small toggles and rawhide loops. Slits provided armholes, and the inner surface was waxed, providing waterproof cover. In addition, there were pouches inside for food or other articles.

Sylah turned away from her inspection, hiding a frown. She'd been a fool.

Now the uniformity of the coarsely woven material leapt at her, as did the cut of the clothes. The shirts were two pieces, a front and a back, joined down the sides. The same was true of the sleeves. The tailoring of the trousers was as basic as the structure would allow, with no flies or pockets.

Household utensils were almost entirely of wood, bone, and horn. In examining the cooking area, Sylah found several obsidian and flint blades, but only one of steel. It was worn down to a sliver. There was one copper pot.

People normally found a way to trade, no matter how poor they were. This group obviously avoided all contact with others. They knew how to make two kinds of cloth, the shirting and the colored bands. If there was any further technical ability, it was well hidden.

Only desperation could create such determined self-isolation.

When fully clothed, the children stood in two chattering rows. In their capes, they reminded Sylah of small, eager animals. Leading them off to the stream with Lanta, she couldn't remember the last time she felt so lighthearted and simply gay.

The children were well schooled in ceremony. All but the very youngest solemnly stripped off capes, bent to wash, then faced where the sun would have been, were it not for the mist. The icy creek water put blazing color in their cheeks, and when Sylah and Lanta finished the ritual prayer with three signs, the children responded with their own variation. They used an open hand, palm out, to touch each shoulder, then forehead, and finally stomach. It was an awkward technique. Sylah asked why it was done that way.

Nandameer answered. "To show everyone our hands are empty. We don't have weapons, we don't have anything to steal."

The priestesses looked at each other, then Sylah asked, "Does everyone who comes here want to fight or rob, dear?"

"Yes." The blue eyes couldn't believe Sylah's ignorance.

Lanta said, "We don't. We only want to help you."

A wiry, long-jawed boy spoke up. "You're stealing us," he said.

Sylah recoiled. "You? Steal?" She almost choked on the words.

"They always said someone would. Didn't say Church, though. Can we stay with you? You don't hit us. Not yet, anyhow."

Dodoy laughed from the edge of the group. They turned to look at him. From his hand-span height advantage, he sneered down at them. "They don't keep slaves. They'll take you to Church and get rid of you."

Before either woman could correct him, one of the children said, "Where's Church?" It was exactly what Dodoy was waiting for. He laughed shrilly. "They don't know."

Sylah said, "Go to Tate. Now. Not another word. Get *out*."

Still grinning, Dodoy ran off. When Sylah looked back to the children, several were near tears. Lanta moved among them, stroking heads, soothing.

"You're coming with us only because we think the bad men who hurt Tarabel are coming back," Sylah said. "Anyhow, you couldn't live here alone. What if a bear came? Or a tiger? Dodoy's right about us wanting to take you to Church. Because we want you to have a place to live, not to get rid of you. And we don't steal. We especially don't steal children."

The priestesses led the children back to the houses. Conway and Tate were loading the packhorses. Tarabel and the warrior lay on draggers. Tarabel seemed to be staging the rapid recovery of youth. The warrior also appeared much better. He never spoke, however.

Nor did anyone else, once Conway opened the stock pens and the group was on the move. Finally, Lanta could stand it no

231

longer. She approached Sylah. "I've been watching Conway," she said. "He seems almost too calm. Distracted."

Sylah said. "Post-battle problems are as different as the men involved. You know what the Apocalypse Testament says: 'The Healer must address the mind before all else, for it is man's mind that creates and suffers the most dangerous injuries. A man may kill his enemy and suffer no injury, only to have his own mind rear up and strike him down.' The Iris Abbess put it more pungently: 'Think of a warrior as a nail, my dear; pure iron, straight and strong, and the only purpose his head will ever serve is to stop a hammer. More, once bent, a nail's worse than useless.' I laughed then. The Abbess didn't. In time, I learned why."

Pensively, Lanta said, "Do you think one of us should talk to him, see what's troubling him?"

"I wish I could, but I really think I should be tending to Tarabel and the stranger. Would you . . . ?" She left the request hanging.

"If you think it's a good idea. I'm not a War Healer."

"I don't think it'll make a difference," Sylah said, turning away to hide her expression.

For her part, Lanta was too nervous to examine any expressions but Conway's. It took her some time to address him. She spoke his name from directly behind him, and he gave a small, startled hitch at the first sound. She stumbled on. "You're very quiet. Are you well?"

"I'm fine." He smiled slowly. "Just thinking."

Emboldened by his friendliness, she pressed ahead. "I thought you might be. You've been—thoughtful—since the incident at the river."

"I suppose I have."

"It must have been awful."

"Not so bad." She saw his jaw tense. A pulse below his ear leaped erratically. He lied. Couldn't he understand why she was there?

She said, "You did the right thing. Still, it was unpleasant."

"Not so bad. Excuse me, would you? I have to check on the dragger bindings."

A point of ice formed in her throat. No one, not even those who openly feared her, had ever rejected her with such disdain. She stopped, watching him pretend to inspect the dragger.

The cold thing melted. In its place came furious heat.

Walking point, Tate stiffened at the sight of Oshu loping back down the trail. Stepping aside into cover, the hound faced the way

232

she'd come, then dropped flat, hackles raised. Tate ran back to the others at a fast trot. "Someone coming," she said.

Lanta hurried the children into the forest shadows. Sylah led off the horses dragging Tarabel and the warrior. Conway ran to a position behind a tree uphill with his dogs. Tate took the left, whistling for her own animals. They appeared a few moments later, watching behind. Going directly to Tate, they sheltered a few yards away, behind a downed tree. The huge trunk was a nursery; as it decomposed into soil on the bottom, other trees grew from the top of its length. The dogs peered from between fencepost-like saplings.

The man who walked toward them was short, compact. He wore a tight jacket and trousers of mottled dark brown homespun and a leather hat. The latter was more of a skull cap, leaving the ears uncovered, but with a flap hanging down the back of the neck. He carried a very short, very thick, recurved bow. There was a sense of immense power about the weapon, and a look at the forearms poking out of the shortsleeved jacket confirmed the owner's great strength. There was a jagged scar under his chin, as if someone had literally cut his throat.

He rolled when he walked, and although he carried a white cloth in his raised right hand, he appeared far more relaxed than the situation warranted. Stopping, he lifted his chin, scenting the air. Bright, quick eyes searched the forest ahead of him. He seemed to simply drift off the trail and disappear.

Conway glared toward Tate and pointed. Tate responded with a head shake, trying to tell him she couldn't see the man anymore, either.

Suddenly the white flag was in the middle of the trail, dangling from a long stick emerging from behind a tree.

Loudly, Tate said, "We're travelers, making no trouble. We'll defend ourselves, though."

A deep voice answered, "We know who you are."

At the word "we," Tate and Conway nervously peered into the flanking trees.

Tate said, "Let us pass."

"Not with the children."

"You're slavers?"

There was a dull silence. Shock tinged the answer. "*You're* slavers. Those are Smalls children. Our tribe."

Tate exposed half her body from behind her tree. "That's a lie. They were abandoned."

"Not abandoned. Victims. You're stealing them."

There was disbelief and irritation in Tate's voice. "You prove you're Smalls, and we'll turn them over to you."

"That's who we are," a child shouted, unleashing a chorus of agreement.

Sylah decided it was time to take charge of the situation. With the children trailing her under Lanta's supervision, she walked forward, hands raised over her head to join forefingers and thumbs in the peace signal. "Come speak to us. Our only interest in the children is their welfare."

The response was silence. Then the stocky man was on the trail. Able to see him for the first time, a boy shouted. "Bizal! It's Bizal!" In spite of Lanta's attempts to quiet them, the children buzzed excitement.

Stroking his throat, the man smiled. His eyes remained on Sylah. "The scar does it, Priestess. Not many know my face. It takes some getting used to, having people know you by your throat."

"I know you, Bizal." She introduced herself and the group, explaining their circumstances, then, "These children are under Church protection."

Bizal nodded, then swept his arms wide. "I've twenty men around you. I saw what magic your weapons do. No matter. We'll take the children, if we must." In his intensity, he took a step forward, raising a clenched fist. He was either completely unaware of the swift tension of the dogs or brave enough to ignore them. "Smalls have ever been victims of all; Kossiars, slavers, raiders from the mountains, River People. Everyone considers us animals. No more. We fight now."

Coldly, Sylah said, "That had the sound of a threat. I will know your plans for these children."

Bristling, but calmer, Bizal said. "Protection. One day they'll fight, too."

Conway said, "Sounds like Gan."

Surprisingly, Bizal nodded. "A Peddler told us some stories of the Moondark one. I'm not so ambitious, but not so different. My people will be free."

Sylah said, "Take the children then. When I reach Church Home, shall I tell them you need Healers?"

"Yes. But only strong ones. We have to move often." A slash of bitter smile touched his features.

Softly, Tate asked, "Are you sure you don't want us to take the children to Church Home? They'd be safe there."

"They'll be safe nowhere." Bizal glanced in her direction, seemed almost apologetic. "There are many more raiders than your

234

man killed. They say Church itself wants the Rose Priestess dead. Kos hunts you. I don't think you will ever see Church Home."

"Very encouraging. Thank you." It was Conway, sardonic, stepping away from his hiding place with his dogs.

Bizal faced that way. "I can only speak the truth."

"You could help."

"No. We're too weak. We can't properly defend ourselves yet. My people's needs come first."

Conway stopped beside Sylah. Tate moved to join them.

Bizal went on. "The raiders left, west. They'll recover, come after you. We've seen no Kossiar patrols for several days."

Conway persisted. "Can't you scout ahead for us? We're not asking you to fight."

Bizal frowned. "Priestess, I wish you luck on your quest."

Conway scoffed. "You and the twenty invisible men surrounding us."

For the first time, Bizal truly smiled. The change was radical. In that instant, he was younger, more appealing. He said, "Smalls have some skills. We're learning more. And every man enjoys a brag from time to time. Your dogs know we're here, but not even they're sure exactly where, because the wind's from one direction."

He raised a whistle on a lanyard to his mouth. It trilled twice, then one longer blast. Answers came singly, quick single bursts, first from one direction, then another. Piling on top of each other in such rapid sequence from all points of the compass, they had a sinister, disorienting quality. Sylah tried to count them; by the fourth—or fifth—she was too confused to continue.

Conway faced Bizal. "My compliments."

Tate grinned and winked. "Me, too. But I'll bet there's only nineteen."

Bizal laughed, flushed with pride.

Sylah led the good-byes. Tate knelt to hug Nandameer. They ended by wiping tears from each other's face. Tarabel, groggy, afraid, watched Sylah anxiously until she bent over him and kissed his forehead. "You're going to be well. Keep the wound clean. Grow strong. Bizal's going to need you."

At his grin, Sylah's eyes turned suspiciously bright. She left quickly.

Moving down the trail, she reflected that the boy's look was what she treasured above anything in her work. She created hope. Joy. Suddenly, she heard the voice of the Iris Abbess, remembered something from one of their late night conversations. The older woman had said, "One of the things about the Door that we rarely hear is the happiness it's supposed to hide. Almost everything the Teachers promised concerned power. There was that other side, however. Imagine, a force to make people happy. I wonder what they meant by that."

Much later that afternoon, Sylah rode ahead to be with Tate. The other woman studied her so long Sylah grew a bit uncomfortable. Finally, Tate spoke in a tight, self-conscious voice. "You made Tarabel happy. That's what I want for Dodoy. You all think all I want is to have him lead me to other black people. I do. But I want to see him smile like Tarabel. I want to see him when someone he trusts tells him everything's going to be all right."

Ahead, Conway was hurrying back to them.

Tate tensed, bent forward in the saddle. Very softly she said, "I want that for Dodoy. And me. Just once. Even if it's a lie."

CHAPTER 41

"There's a horseman up there," Conway said, jerking a thumb southward. "Armored. Military. Under a white flag. There're other troops, but they're staying clear, keeping under cover. They're all mounted, all armored. I counted twelve before I left."

Sylah nodded, looking where Conway indicated. It was Lanta who asked, "Did they see you? Can we get around them?"

"They've got the whole valley outposted, so I doubt we can avoid them. He knows we're coming, or he wouldn't be sitting there with his white flag. I might as well go see what he wants."

The quest was at its most dangerous point yet.

Sylah couldn't say exactly how she knew that—and she smiled inwardly at her assumption of Lanta's talents—but there was no question in her mind that what she did before this day's sunset would determine if her mission continued or ended. Looking up at Conway, she said, "Please, will you take the others and leave me alone for a while? I need privacy."

Conway frowned. "This isn't going to take long, is it? I don't want to ride up on this man in the dark, and I don't want his men coming for us in the night either."

Reaching, she touched his fingertips with hers. "A little while is all I need."

He shrugged and left.

Confusion crowded her thoughts, bullied her attempts to concentrate. The words of the chant came slowly, caught on hooks and thorns of tension. She immersed herself in the soothing, mind-claiming sounds. Slowly, reluctantly, stresses fell away. Controlled body rhythms dispelled the irregular beat born of worry.

Her place of calm came into her inner vision, a place of giant trees, where a liquid-gold shaft of sunlight shimmered down to the earth. She stood in the center of that glory.

There was a voice. *All your life, you followed.*

That was so. The Sylah who acted, but dared not speak. She of deference, of carefully phrased advice.

You are the seeker. Who will lead?

She was woman, her role predestined.

Support. Refuge. Companion.

Follower.

Woman.

The word howled confusion through her mind, nearly shocked her out of the trance. The chant was sanctuary. The words hummed anxiously, then softly. They calmed her once again.

Behind that renewed silence there was a sound like the breath of trees, or the sibilance of stream waters. Another voice. The Iris Abbess'. No clear words, but enfolding serenity. Guidance.

Memories. Long, hushed conversations in the confidence of the Abbess' rooms, when dawn so often came as a shock, with the entire night gone like an hour.

So many lessons. Inspiration.

War Healer. What men broke, she repaired. What men tore, she mended.

Suddenly the answer was there, so simple, so clear.

So dangerous.

What must be borne, grasp. Reeds bend to any wind, yet it is the reed that confronts land, confronts water. And creates its own place.

Woman creates.

Deep within her, something stirred. Not entirely pleasant, not entirely disquieting. There seemed to be a presence. In the midst of an increasingly dizzying confusion, she remembered Tate's admonition: "You don't know how to quit."

That was true. Too true.

Sylah can no longer follow. Sylah leads.

The voice again, each word a whiplash.

Leaving the trance always touched her with a thrill of alarm. There was the fear that full consciousness might elude her, leave her suspended in the half state of inwardness. Light and sound beckoned her as the surface beckons the submerged swimmer. This time there was instant awakening. She was suddenly, triumphantly, looking at her friends, resting under the trees. She rose, walked to them.

"We go forward," she said.

The squeal of leather drew the attention of all to the wounded warrior, where he was propping himself on one elbow on the dragger. While they goggled, he said, "Kossiars. Don't trust them." Sweat beaded on his forehead, but his eyes were clear. "I'll be able to fight in a few days. Avoid the Kossiars, and we can handle the ones who attacked me."

Tate said, "You weren't doing all that well when Conway found you."

The man watched Conway. "No one trusts Kossiars. They'll make prisoners of you."

"And not you?" Sylah inquired mildly.

"Only until I heal. Not long."

"You're my patient, and I am Church. No one will harm you."

He colored. "Nalatan Sohna fears no harm." To Conway, he said, "Give me a sword. Leave me now."

Sylah held out a languid hand, a good three body lengths from the man's reach. "Come here for it."

Nalatan strained at the lashing. Conway half rose, clearly intending to help. Sylah's sharp hiss sat him down again. The struggle went on for what seemed an interminable time. Blood began to seep from under some of Nalatan's bandages. Tate turned beseeching eyes on Sylah, and was ignored.

Nalatan fell back against the dragger straps. "Water." Defeat ached in the word. Conway hurried to him. Nalatan glared at Sylah while he drank from the canteen, handing it back with abrupt thanks.

Sylah met his cold anger firmly. "You've studied the secrets of self-healing, Nalatan. But I know if you can travel, fight, survive alone." He opened his mouth, and she was on her feet, an imperious gesture demanding silence. "No! I have more to do than contend with your pride."

To the others, she said, "Conway and I ride in front, side by side. Lanta follows with Nalatan. Donnacee, take rear guard with Dodoy. Keep your dogs far back, in case we're being followed."

When Sylah moved away, Tate looked to Conway and rolled her eyes. He smiled, shaking his right hand as if the fingers burned. He said, "Is this Rose Priestess Sylah, or Our Lady of the Iron Fist?"

Laughing, Tate said, "Lady's got her back up. From here on it's going to be, 'Heels together, feet at a forty-five degree angle, and when I say *Eyes right*, I want to hear eyeballs *click*.'"

"Right at home, aren't you?"

Tate smirked. "Semper fi, chump. Try to keep up."

The sinking sun broke under the covering clouds just as the group left the forest. The trail cut directly across a brush-pocked meadow. In the middle of it stood a riderless horse, hipshot, relaxed. It raised its head, whickering a greeting. Sylah's horse responded. Stormracer flattened his ears and stuck his neck out. Conway twitched the reins and whistled in his dogs.

A man stepped out from behind a clump of brush. The soft light of the late sun turned hard where it struck his metal torso armor and helmet. He raised a white flag, waved, then settled back against the horse to wait for them.

Sylah almost smiled at his carefully posed arrogance. He wore his horsetail-decorated helmet tilted back on his head. His leather shirt was open to expose glinting chain mail. Worn bands on leather trousers indicated where some sort of shin and thigh guards could be attached. She halted a horse-length away from him. Conway was just off her left side, a bit behind. From the corner of her eye, she saw him signal the dogs to cover in the brush.

The soldier saw it, too. He said, "No one's going to trouble you. I'm here to offer help." His speech pattern was slow, with a lilting rise and fall. A soft accent contributed to the melodic effect.

Sylah's training unmasked the deceptiveness of his language. The wary blue eyes were too wide, the square young jaw too set. And, although the right hand so casually hooked over his belt was well clear of his sword, his posture clearly indicated a tense readiness to make a sideways move. To the right, she reckoned.

Conway ignored the proceedings, scanning the area.

Sylah said, "Kos welcomes no strangers."

His poise wavered when he was addressed by the woman, rather than the sole healthy adult male in the group. Shifting his attention back and forth between them, he didn't notice Tate until she was almost directly behind Sylah. His eyes bulged and his mouth dropped open. He was considerably less self-assured when he spoke again, even though the words were clearly rote. "The Chair has known of your coming for many moons, Rose Priestess Sylah. My patrol is one of many sent to watch for you, to invite you to Kos. The Chair expects you."

Sylah felt no surprise. The Harvester had passed through Kos. The only surprise would fall out of whatever mischief that one had left behind. Sylah drew herself erect. "I have my own plans. This Chair means nothing to me. Nevertheless, we would camp with you this night." She introduced the rest of the group. On finishing, she asked pointedly, "Are you given a name?"

Coloring, he said, "My apologies. My name is Gatro. My rank is Lance. I command a troop of fifteen mounted warmen. Again, I invite you to accompany me to the safety of Harbor, where the Chair would speak with you."

"And again, I must refuse."

"Perhaps I can convince you." He raised a hand over his head and dropped it back to his side. Three men rode out of the brush. Two were Kossiars. The one in the middle was bound, hands behind his back. On closer view, he was much the worse for wear.

The trio stopped a few yards from Sylah. The Kossiars saluted by touching a fist to their lips. The battered man glared hatred. And fear.

Gatro gestured far too casually. "We caught two like this. They say their band numbered over fifty. We can't believe them entirely, however; not only are these people murderers, rapists, and thieves, they're liars. They say you killed one of their leaders and some others with thunder and lightning. Scum. Can't even admit being beaten in a fair fight."

Sylah looked to Conway, and he responded for her. "I killed them. With thunder and lightning."

Gatro sighed. "As you say. I warn you, though, everyone knows the Chair doesn't approve of magic tricks. But we have serious business to settle. You won't come with me to the friendship of the Chair?"

Tiny signals beckoned Sylah. Dilated pupils. The aggressive rise of his chin. More revealing than either of those, however, was the quick, almost imperceptible forward tilt of his body. Expectation.

Gatro had set a trap. She was sure of it. But where was it? How did it work?

Peripheral vision provided a possible answer. The captured raider was also trying to hide increased tension. And the warmen watched him. Not their leader, not herself.

Physical clues were telling her the raiders were free to attack them if she refused his offer. The Chair could say it offered help, even protection, to the one seeking the Door. It could deny complicity or responsibility if that seeker should die.

What must be borne, grasp.

"I've changed my mind. I accept your offer."

Gatro was pleased. For a single, thudding heartbeat Sylah

feared she'd misread him, then it dawned on her that he'd set two traps. She'd fallen into the minor one. Braced for his next statement, she eased closer to Conway.

"As our guests, we'll accept it as an act of friendliness when you entrust your weapons to us," Gatro said. Before either Sylah or Conway could respond, Tate did. "We're not that friendly, Lance, and never will be. We'll keep our weapons. You keep your distance."

Sylah was ready for any reaction but the one she got. Gatro stared, awed. His mouth worked spasmodically before he managed to speak. "Are you painted? Is it your custom?"

"It's my skin, boot, and that's the last I want to hear from you about it. Did your Chair tell you to keep us sitting here forever? We've got a wounded man. Take us to camp."

Gatro's salute was halfway to his chin before he caught himself. Lamely, he turned the movement into a sort of wave. He put on a stern face and spoke to Sylah. "I'm permitted to use force to take your weapons if I suspect any—unpleasantness."

Conway said, "I give you my word, we mean only to use them to protect ourselves. And anyone who's our friend."

"Protect?" Gatro's jaw muscles bunched. He rose in the stirrups, pulling a short, straight horn of brass from his belt. Putting it to his lips, he blew a short call, three rising notes. Lingering echoes accompanied the rush of his men from their hiding places in the brush. They made a brave arrival, sliding to a stop, horses rearing. Falling into three groups of five, with a senior man in front, they lined up facing their Lance.

Proudly, the young leader said, "We are the ones who protect. We do it without tricks."

Conway said, "We have no tricks. We have weapons."

"Thunder and lightning?" Gatro sneered.

Shaking his head, Conway said, "It's not important right now. We want to be friendly. Can we work together?"

The almost-singsong speech grew even softer. "We will." To Sylah, he said, "Priestess, will you follow me, please? Our camp is just over there."

Sylah was pleased to see that the Kossiars scrupulously left her group alone. She had no doubt a watch was posted somewhere off in the forest, but it was done with discretion.

Nalatan did, however, call to them from the darkness as the last flames of their campfire were dying. Except for the sleeping Dodoy, they joined him where he lay on the dragger that was now his cot. He spoke with startling strength and assurance. "Rose

Priestess, what do you know of the warrior-monk brotherhoods that guard Church Home?"

"Only that they exist. And are brave men."

"You should know more. We volunteer. We leave home. The brotherhood becomes family. Our fortified villages are self-supporting training grounds. Church's enemies are our quarry."

"What of wives. Children?"

"Brotherhoods differ. Some villages are family places. Some are all male; wives remain in their birth-village, raise their children there."

Conway interjected. "What about your brotherhood?"

Nalatan's face twisted almost imperceptibly. He answered calmly enough. "We have a family village, but we also have an all-male place of study. Part of the year we live—lived—there." His suddenly harsh tone and flare of intensity shocked his listeners. When he went on, it was obvious he was exercising an iron control. "A year ago, a priestess calling herself Harvester came to the master of my brotherhood. She told of your quest and said you would be cast out for it. My master said it was the bravest thing he ever heard; shorn of Church's life protection, a woman dared challenge all. The Harvester demanded we stop you. He refused."

Sylah said, "A year ago? We . . ."

"The Harvester said Church Home has expected you for many years. A person she called the Seer of Seers told her you were coming. She called you by name. She also called you the Flower, who will be brought to glory by the white and the black, by all-powerful magic." He closed his eyes for a moment, went on. "Two weeks after my master refused her, our well was poisoned. Of our sixty-four, ten live. As he died, my master tasked me to assure the Flower's success. Then he told me I must make a place in glory for our brotherhood, make all people for all time sing songs of the warriors we were. Only then can I die."

Conway smiled down at him. "Then I'm especially glad I came along when I did, Nalatan."

The wounded man grimaced. "I swore to my master I would see the Flower reach her goal. To mark us as supreme among warriors, I swore to my master to kill the white magic. You, Conway. My rescuer. Can you hear the One In All laughing at his joke?"

BOOK II

THE PATH
OF CONFUSION

CHAPTER 42

"I swear I smell saltwater." Tate's manner dared argument.

Conway laughed, poking at the remains of the evening cookfire. "You're probably right. West wind. Gatro said we'll see Harbor from high ground tomorrow."

"If the weather's right." Tate affected a shiver. "Where's spring?"

"I was wondering about that myself. Remember the vidisk in the crèche? It said they had years with cool summers, a nuclear winter thing. Could that start a cycle? Climatic changes? Pendulum swings?"

"I try not to think about any of that. Everything I see reminds me we killed a world."

Conway made a confused gesture. "Months of riding to cover distances we used to drive in hours. Interstate highways, mined for rebar steel."

"Everything we ever built is evil, dangerous, or raw material. Humbling. How many miles do you think we traveled today?"

"About average. Twenty, maybe a little more. We'd have made better time on the whole trip if it weren't for me going sick those times. Whatever I picked up in that blackberry patch, it won't let go."

"Careful. Sylah said never admit it's illness. As long as she has the Kossiars convinced we're stopping 'cause she needs rest, we're all right." Tate fell silent again, then, "Do you get impatient, Matt? Discouraged?" She rose. The unexpected swiftness of the move cut off Conway's words. She bent forward aggressively, firelight dancing against taut features. "Tell me the truth. This is about as long a conversation as we've had since we joined up with Gatro's warmen and your buddy Nalatan."

"I've been working hard with the dogs. Stormracer. Nalatan."

Tate affected a fist-on-hips pose and burlesque dialect. "You've been uncommunicative and preoccupied. I'm the onliest mama you got. Best you talk to me, boy."

She earned a wan smile. "I'm scared, Donnacee. I don't know who I am."

"Come *on*, Matt; this is not a world where we play barroom psychology games." When he looked up from the fire, she saw his hurt. Immediately, her hand went to his cheek in apology. "Oh, Matt. I'm so sorry."

"It's all right. It's just that, that day you fought the Skan captain, I thought I'd come to terms with myself and this world. Even though I still think that's true, some of the responses are all wrong."

Tate withdrew her hand. "If I ask you what that means, will you tell me?"

"I'll try. I'm a transportation expert, right? I mean, look at me. I sat at a desk and punched buttons. Sacks of cement, off to Boise. Tons of mushrooms, Miami-bound. Now I'm stuck here. All I can do is fight. Okay. So if I fight for the right cause, I can make a difference. Make a contribution. Does this make sense so far?"

Very thoughtfully, Tate said, "I'm listening."

"I've got a gut feeling Sylah's Door's going to help people. Being part of that's important to me. I can't be like Gan or Clas, but I can use our weapons, and that makes me a man who can contribute. I'm proud of that. But I blew it."

"Blew it? Blew what?"

"Me. My reference." He paused, and a pained smile touched his face. "The kids used to say to someone who was confused, 'You got no ref, man.' Kids' slang, but I thought it was perceptive. And here I am. No ref."

"I still don't know what you're talking about."

"The day I saved Nalatan I had to kill one raider. Two, maybe. I killed every one I could get in my sights, Donnacee. I did it because I liked it."

"Nonsense. There's a difference between the heat of battle and liking killing."

"I bushwhacked them."

"I don't have any easy answers for you. One thing, though; you're no crazed killer." She talked over his attempted response. "I believe what you said happened. Once. Those were very bad people. Just the fact that it worries you shows you're rational."

"What if that sort of thing becomes normal to me?"

246

Throwing up her hands, Tate said, "Then worry. Eat yourself up. Don't ask me or any of the others to give up on you that easily."

"You don't cut much slack, do you?"

"All that's necessary."

He came around the fire to hang an arm across her shoulders. She pretended to ignore him. He said, "I haven't been good company, have I?"

She sniffed.

"I should have tried to talk things out."

"You bet. Friends let their friends help them."

"It's not always that easy. I'm glad you're there, though." His grin turned teasing. "You don't think Nalatan'll mind if I take up some of your time?"

"That's supposed to mean something?"

"Tell me you haven't noticed how he hangs around you."

She stepped away. "We've been riding together for a month. .How could we not spend some time together? Unless we shut everyone out, like some people I could name."

Conway pretended to ponder. "He's not bad looking, once you get past the scars. You ever notice him washing up before his prayers in the morning? That cut on his back, on the right? Curves like the old interstate, where it left D.C. Kind of jogs."

She swatted his arm. "He got that from slavers. He was just a kid. He was fighting one, and a second one came up from behind." She stopped, squinting dangerously. "You rat. You're laughing at me."

"Of course. You two make a great couple."

"I don't have time for that."

"You've got to get interested in someone someday."

Shaking her head, she hugged herself. "Maybe after I get Dodoy to his people, find my own people—maybe then."

They chatted a while longer about carefully chosen, inconsequential things. Tate realized she'd made little effort to engage Conway in any small talk while he was being so withdrawn; the silence wasn't all his fault. It made her sad and angry. Preoccupied by her own concerns, she'd allowed a friend to suffer. Perhaps she couldn't have helped. At least he'd have known someone cared.

Alone.

The word was a touch of ice.

When Conway called to his dogs and excused himself to go on

247

nightwatch, she broke out of her introspection long enough to acknowledge him. Her train of thought drew her back irresistibly.

No one understood. Loneliness was separation from friends, loved ones. That hurt, fiery pain.

Aloneness was being *not us*, a dull grinding at the edge of consciousness, an ache that never left. Alone was a world without touching.

Of course she was surrounded by friends. Dodoy would be lost without her, and who could be closer than Sylah? Lanta was a darling. And Nalatan was a fine traveling companion. Reticent, though. He answered questions without apparent hesitation, and still there was a sense of holding back.

Conway was right about one thing: Nalatan was very much aware of her. A most-unsoldierly warmth flowed through her body, roamed self-willed and mischievous. For a moment it frightened her. Probing, prying, it made her think of an enemy, determined to test her defenses. She smiled into the darkness, entertained by the fantasy.

Intriguing was a better word for Nalatan. Just as she appreciated his ability to keep part of himself in shadow, he was most likely drawn by her own refusal to discuss herself in any detail. Of course, in her case, the less she said, the fewer lies she had to keep track of.

And there was the matter of the oath to kill Conway.

Men. Fools, all. Especially Conway and Nalatan. Polite. More than polite. Friendly. Still and all, they watched each other. It was Sylah and Lanta who pointed it out. Nalatan watched Conway's eyes or his hands. As soon as Nalatan got close enough for swordwork, Conway's chin dropped. His shoulders hunched forward almost imperceptibly. And he hooked his right thumb over his belt, the hand then in contact with his pistol.

"Just like dumb old dogs," she muttered aloud, jamming a stick down among the last flickering flames and red-glowing coals.

"What have the dogs done?" Nalatan's soft question startled Tate. A squeak of surprise popped out before she could stop it. Forearms and the back of her neck prickled. Oshu and Tanno were completely at ease. They'd obviously watched Nalatan approach while her mind wandered.

"Sneaking up on me isn't a good idea. What if the dog hadn't recognized you?"

"I came from upwind, to alert them. You were very deep in thought." He spoke slowly, as always. Tate had the feeling that he reviewed sentences before actually speaking. His voice came from his chest, so heavy that a sort of rumble trailed it. Tate thought back to how ragged he'd sounded when he was injured. That rich voice was the last thing to recover, as if he needed it least.

Nalatan squatted on his heels across the fire from her. The fitful light painted a warm glow on his leather vest. Tate's attention went directly to the neatly sewn repairs. The stains surrounding weapon penetrations were more apparent in the firelight than in the brightness of day.

Dark, unfathomable eyes gleamed at her from beneath heavy, tapering brows that ranged a broad forehead. He had thick, glossy black hair, cropped in a helmet shape that tapered down the back of his neck and left his ears uncovered.

Tate busied herself rearranging coals.

Silently, he extended some dried meat. She refused with a curt shake of the head. Deliberately, he twisted off two pieces. Handing them over, he indicated the dogs. Tate accepted them. For a moment she considered complimenting him on his awareness that only she should feed the animals.

When he finally spoke, he repeated her last words. "You said I should call out, 'next time.' I'm not banished, then?"

"Of course not." She winced inwardly. Too snippy.

"I waited until Conway left. Sylah and Lanta are talking to Gatro. He's telling them about the sacred grounds of Harbor." The last was sarcastic, but before Tate could remark on it, he continued. "I wanted to speak to you alone."

"About what?"

"Survival."

"Then talk to all of us."

He blinked at her sharpness, then pressed on. "Have you noticed that Gatro avoids contact with the local people?"

"Yes. He says it's by order of the Chair."

"He spoke the truth. A Kossiar can be executed for exchanging good mornings with a Peddler. Did you notice the slaves?"

"I certainly did, and if anyone—"

"Stop." Nalatan's voice was as quiet as ever, but authority swelled in it. "You noticed most wear leg chains."

"I saw some with chains from wrist to a chain belt *and* leg chains. Who are you to stop me criticizing something like that?"

"One who means to keep your head on your shoulders. Listen. Kos survives on the backs of slaves. Rumors of revolt are rising like spring flowers."

"Good. How do I help?"

Sighing heavily, Nalatan ignored the question. "When we get to

Harbor, we'll be required to live on Trader Island. It's a rotten place, lawless. Sooner or later, we'll be approached to help some poor, abused slave escape."

Tate spat on the fire, triggering a nasty hiss and a writhing, red-tinted sprig of steam. "Anything I can do to help a slave, I'm going to do it."

"The Kossiars will send such people to trap us."

"How do you know what they'll do?"

"I know. Will you help me? I've seen you react to the field slaves we've passed. The others care about them. You hurt with them. You can only help them by helping me."

"Why me? If I'm the one most affected, why put me up front? Why not someone more tough-minded?"

"You won't be able to hide your feelings. The false slaves will seek you out. Do nothing, say nothing to indicate suspicion. Point them out to me. If they're true, I'll find out."

"Aren't you going to warn the others?"

"Yes. They may not confide in me. I have to be sure you will."

"You don't trust them?"

A broad, bright smile illuminated his face. Tate was so taken by the instantaneous switch from forbidding conspirator to a inviting presence that she was totally unprepared for his answer. "I trust them completely. It's you I want for a partner."

CHAPTER 43

Copper plodded through the fog with an air of resignation. The horse seemed to be signaling Sylah that he had no idea where this trail led, couldn't see far enough to gauge its dangers, and was therefore resigning all responsibility in the matter.

Sylah felt it was a reasonable attitude.

Huge trees crowded the wagon-wide trail. Vaguely threatening branches arched overhead. Leaves captured the thick fog and concentrated it into fat drops, so that the rough shuffle of the mounted column was underscored by the irregular splat of falling water. To add to the otherworldliness, the tree trunks were greenish beige. Bark peeled like diseased skin, and had an oily pungency.

Eucalyptus oil was an important part of Sylah's healing arsenal. Plowing through dismal fog, hemmed in by scabrous, shedding trunks, she wondered how she could ever have considered the scent pleasant.

The trail exited onto one of the meadows Sylah had grown to anticipate. Out in the open, with the growth almost exactly as tall as Copper's belly, the penetrating smell of eucalyptus blew away. In its stead, Sylah luxuriated in the mixed aromas of shrubs, weeds, and especially the grass.

Her mind brushed aside the present, carried her back to the prairie of the Dog People, where she met Clas.

There was no smell like wet grass, and at no time was it as full of delicate promise as in the morning. The smell accumulated potency during the day, until a rain at dusk brought out an aroma so robust it fell to the earth, oozing down slopes and into draws and hollows, filling them like syrup.

On this strange and different hillside, that familiar morning tang filled Sylah with a rending mix of sadness and determination. The suggestive powers of new growth strengthened her resolve even as haunting reminiscence made her ache to abandon everything and return to Clas.

There was no turning back. The long ride south had settled that. Her decision to accept the complete role as leader had grown stronger daily. She was at ease with it. She was also aware that for her entire group, the trip had been a time of introspection, of inner searching and growing awareness. Flicking an impertinent drop of condensation from the end of her nose, she smiled to herself at the image of Nalatan's dogged efforts to avoid being caught observing Tate. The plain fact was that the man couldn't keep his eyes off her. Another fact was Tate's disinterest.

Sylah reconsidered. That observation wasn't as accurate this morning as it had been yesterday. Tate looked at Nalatan differently. With increased . . . what? Attention?

It wasn't wise to make assumptions about Tate. Her completely one-sided devotion to Dodoy obligated serious reservations.

As for Conway, he seemed a bit more convivial at the morning meal. Even the dogs were frisky. What inner problem had he solved?

Nothing that brought him closer to Lanta. Sylah glanced to her right, where Lanta rode with her hood pulled forward, bobbing along in self-constructed solitude. Fog was the perfect environment for her, a metaphor for cloaked mystery. Such a painful irony, Sylah thought, wishing she could console her friend. Lanta's fate was to receive secrets she dreaded, yet she was helpless to open the mind of a man she loved. Somehow, in the tragicomedy of man–woman relationships, those two had found a way to demolish a perfectly reasonable friendship that wanted to grow to something more significant. Sylah was sure it had something to do with Conway's attempts to be a warrior. Beyond that, she was uncertain.

Conway sought out Nalatan. That, too, was a weird situation. Once Nalatan announced his oath to kill Conway, they became confidants. And what did they speak of? Fighting. Nalatan, as if assuring himself the worthiest possible opponent, talked endlessly to a rapt Conway about thrusts and parries and feints until Sylah wanted to scream. Similarly, Conway allowed Nalatan to ride Stormracer. Sylah couldn't believe her eyes. Nor could Stormracer. Nalatan grabbed a great deal of air that day, and ate what he called "enough dirt for a farm." Even now, Stormracer only suffered his presence.

Almost silently, Tate's mount brought her abreast of Sylah. The women exchanged silent, almost conspiratorial smiles, riding beside each other companionably. Sylah found herself thinking of Tate—her loyalty, her value to the quest—and considered how very fortunate she was to have such a friend. Impulsively, she turned to the black woman.

"I've been thinking about you, Donnacee. Do you know why?"

Tate burlesqued angry defensiveness. "If it has anything to do with the burned stew last night, it wasn't my turn to cook. Don't blame me."

Sylah laughed easily. "Far more important than that. I've been thinking that you may be the only woman I know who'll understand exactly why I'm so pleased I decided to come to Kos."

Patiently, Tate said nothing, waiting. Sylah went on. "Only this morning it came to me. Suddenly, I understand my own decision. I've accepted—sought, actually—the quest for the Door for a long time. Now I know there's more. It sounds very self-important, but I don't mean it to. What I've realized is that I'm at the center of something far, far grander than I ever imagined. The world calls to me from the other side of the Door, Donnacee."

"Why am I supposed to understand all that? It's your quest, not mine."

"Because you're a warrior, as well as a woman. You understand struggle and control. Dominance. Yes, that's the word, the thing you seek. To dominate. Not for gain, but to assure a stable, comfortable place around yourself."

Uncomfortably, Tate shifted in her saddle. She attempted to make light of the remarks. "I've got enough trouble controlling

252

this horse. I like the idea of being comfortable, but I don't want to dominate to do it."

Too intent on her own argument to realize the depth of Tate's discomfort, Sylah gestured blithely. "We can argue about the exact words, but I think my analysis is right. We have our goals. Nothing's going to stop us. If the world doesn't fit us, we'll cut it to our size."

Full of dreams of the future, of expectation, Sylah failed to notice when Tate fell off the pace and Lanta moved to take her place.

The fog broke. One moment it blotted out the world. Then it became a mere haze. A few more yards uphill, and it was wisps that muted colors, so faint one had to squint to actually focus on it. And then it was gone, and an early morning sun as glorious as song poured full, warming light on them. Without thinking, Sylah executed a three-sign. Beside her, Lanta did the same, then threw back her hood to stare.

They were on the military crest of a mountain, the point where downhill vision to the valley is essentially unobscured. Behind them, the fog billowed and tumbled in a white sea. Before was a panorama of staggering beauty. A huge bay spread inland. The far shore at the narrow entry was a sheer cliff rising from a tumble of surf-lashed rocks. The near side was fogbound, so that only the vaguest suggestion of that bluff was apparent.

The enclosed bay crawled inland spectacularly. The serpentine coastline defined innumerable inlets and creek mouths.

On the far shore, a tangled forest clothed the hills down to the water's edge. Raw wounds, earthquake scars, blotched the greenery in some places, and there were patches of white rock, as well. An island basked in the sun. From Sylah's position down to the gray-green enclosed waters, the land was a patchwork of trees and grassland.

At water's edge, however, an unwalled city rested in one of the larger coves. Fishing boats crowded the harbor docks. More boats dotted the water, some anchored, others with sails bellied and white wakes purling. The city's gleaming, graceful repose made Sylah think of a jeweled breastplate.

Separated from everything else on its own small promontory, a stone fort dominated the settlement. The neck of land was crossed by three distinct walls that ran from water to water. Farther out the peninsula, backing up the three barricades, was a moat that fronted a high stone wall, creating an artificial island.

A large building inside the walls was the castle of Kos' ruler,

253

the Chair. Gatro had spoken of its roof of blue tiles. Bold, bright as jay feathers, they gleamed pride.

Stepped back from the walls, it towered above them. It was composed of three main parts. A wide east-west arm connected two narrower north-south arms at the center. Sylah thought it looked like the letter H.

She dismissed the thought instantly. To say such a thing out loud could be interpreted as helping someone learn to read.

Returning to her examination, Sylah determined the opening on the northern side of the blue-roofed building was a courtyard. There was a rectangular pond on the opposite side of the castle, just inside the southern wall of the fort.

Lanta's gasp snapped Sylah out of her contemplation.

Westward, at the entrance to the bay, the wind had suddenly unveiled a looming incongruity. As if shrugging itself free of the fog, there appeared a structure of such mammoth, unimaginable proportions that Sylah knew instantly she was looking at a renowned work of the giants.

The Gate.

Legend explained that the huge, monolithic gray pillar on the north side of the gap was a post. It was emplaced by the giants so they could suspend a gate that spanned the bay's exit to the sea. The south face of the post was rough and disfigured. The legend said that's where the hinges were fitted. Trees grew at its base, and tufts of plant life sprouted randomly from cracks and faults in the once-smooth surface. Seabirds, bright as snowflakes in the sun, circled about it. White streaks, bold against the weathered gray mass, revealed favored perching sites.

A low moan brought Sylah around to look behind.

Tate stared out at the scene, features filled with a pain so great it made Sylah's knees weak. Grief poured unending from Tate's mouth, as if the sound lived, needed no breath to lift it. Coming to stand beside her, Conway was grim and pale.

CHAPTER 44

"Remember, don't attempt to speak to anyone," Gatro said. The young Lance's face was stern, the singsong vocal pattern more pronounced. "Don't show interest in anything you see."

Nervous irritability fairly crackled around Tate, as it had since the stop at the viewpoint far above them. "You expect us to ride with our eyes closed?"

Nalatan answered for Gatro. "He means we shouldn't stare."

Gatro nodded, frowning. "The Chair welcomes you above all guests, but I have the authority to blindfold you."

"I've got your authority." Tate exploded. Tanno and Oshu went into wide-stanced threat display. Gatro's hand dropped to his sword. In the distance, his warmen stirred. From the corner of her eye, Tate saw Conway casually grip his wipe.

Sylah urged Copper forward between Tate and Gatro. Facing Tate, she said, "Donnacee, whatever's upset you, either bring it out in the open, or put it aside."

Tate relaxed slowly. Peering around Sylah, she said, "Sorry, Lance."

Gatro smiled eager acceptance. "You know I'll be rewarded for bringing you to the Chair. Only the wealthiest traders ever meet him, and they never visit inside the castle. I want everything right."

Tate smiled, a bit tighter than normal. "Leave it to me. I'll see to it you get medals as big as manhole covers."

More baffled than reassured, Gatro signaled his men into motion. He led the group the last few yards along their narrow road, then turned left onto a thoroughfare wide enough for two wagons. They descended toward the town, passing fields of vegetables, wheat, corn, and pasture land heavy with cattle and sheep.

Tate drifted back to wait for Conway and Nalatan. When they reached her, she asked Nalatan if he'd mind letting her ride alone with Conway for a while. The warrior agreed readily, but Conway was almost certain he saw something like hurt in the other man's expression as he turned away. He was about to make a teasing remark until he saw how distraught Tate was. Conway decided it wasn't a good time to try being funny.

For a while, Tate said nothing. Conway studied the increasing number and variety of buildings they passed. One was a pottery factory, U-shaped, with a two-story base and arms of one floor. Three brick kilns studded the flat ground enclosed within the arms. Rippling heat waves rose from each. Stacks of finished ware ranged against the walls, gleaming bright blues and greens, rich browns and rust.

Suddenly, Tate blurted, "San Francisco, Matt! Such a beautiful place. How could they? Millions of people, skyscrapers, museums."

"Shut up." Conway grabbed her upper arm, shook her. She set-

255

tled back in the saddle, breathing heavily. He spoke quickly, but softly. "It's no different here than it was around Seattle. You weren't like this up there."

"Family." She gulped air. "My aunt and uncle lived out toward the county line. Over there." She gestured without looking. "Imagine the firestorms, the erosion. Earthquake. Remember how everyone worried about 'the big one'? How many 'big ones' have they had in the past five centuries, Matt? Does anyone care?" Her breath was quick, biting lunges again.

"Easy. Easy. Don't do this to yourself."

She nodded. "I'm all right. I keep wanting to slip off the edge, but I won't. I wonder if anything ever changes. Seems to me everyone we meet here has a full seabag: greed, lust, hatred, plain dirty-dog meanness. Just like the good old days."

"Honor, pride, selflessness. Even love, Donnacee."

She shot him a hard, searching look. Conway continued, "I feel the same as you, you know. Still, I won't tell you the challenge of this life isn't stimulating. I won't lie about that."

"Wouldn't work if you did. I see how hard you're working to fit into this mess. We two do seem to be more interested in the excitement than our friends back up north."

"I think we'll see plenty of that here." He nodded at the squad trailing behind.

"Security-conscious, that's all. They've got no reason to worry about us."

"You know that. I know it. The locals aren't all that convinced."

Their conversation had brought them to the city's streets. In unspoken accord they closed on the rest of the group.

The intense curiosity of the city dwellers became a palpable pressure. The riders crowded into each other. The war-horses responded irritably, nipping at the others, shouldering, maneuvering room for themselves. The great dogs padded alongside nervously, gazes shifting from the hooves of the horses to the humanity lining their route.

Unlike Ola's geometric street plan, Harbor sprawled. Streets and alleys followed land contours. Or some long-dead cow's whim. Homes and business buildings were built of every material imaginable: brick, chunks of concrete, stone, wood, tile. Most had windows, crazy quilts of salvaged pieces. Clear glass was obviously most desirable. Next, anything transparent. The poorer examples were made of very small pieces of translucent stuff. Wooden planking was clearly the prestige building material.

Conway remarked to Tate that much construction suggested ship-building, with tarred seams and outer boards pegged to the frame.

The group came to a road that paralleled the water. Large stones covered the downhill side, where driftwood and debris marked the reach of the tide. Following the waterfront, the group headed directly for the fort on its commanding peninsula. Gatro, almost unstrung at the prospect of entering those walls, repeated, "The blue tiles mark the castle. All the rest is considered the fort."

Sylah turned to Lanta when they were still a good hundred yards from the turnoff to the fort. She said, "How quiet the people are. They don't seem hostile; they simply watch."

Lanta asked, "Did you see the work crew we passed?"

"No." Sylah looked surprised. "Where?"

"In one of the alleys. They ran as we came abreast. The adult chased them. He had a staff, with a curved handle at the top. He beat them with it."

"You said adult. The workers were children?"

Lanta nodded. She didn't look well. "No older than Dodoy. Carrying brooms and baskets. All in smocks, long-haired. I don't know if they were boys, girls, or both."

"Don't say anything to the others. Not yet."

A high, steep-graded berm across the base of the peninsula was the fort's first line of defense. Sharpened stakes studded its front slope. It dropped vertically on the seaward side. No cavalry would pass that wall, except by the road the group now rode through the gap. Sylah noticed a gate of massive planks to her left; it was on rollers, for ease of operation. Beyond the berm, the ground for approximately fifty yards was graded flat, unblemished by any hollow or knoll to provide cover. Carpeted with wild flowers, it would have been a beautiful meadow, were it not so obviously a killing ground for defenders shooting down from the second berm. It had a sloped reverse side. Again, the only way past that obstacle was through a gate. Another fifty yards beyond, the peninsula narrowed drastically. An attacker faced the moat. Ten yards across, the bottom greenly visible perhaps six feet below, it heaved gently under the influence of the open sea at its ends. The sturdy drawbridge crossing it drummed under the hooves of the horses. Sylah looked down to see a school of fish slash past, a silver constellation that gleamed startling brightness and disappeared.

The fort's wall reached upward at least twenty feet, a daunting face of stone. It was marked by archers' window slits at eye level, with more about fifteen feet up. A crenellated top provided more defensive positions. Projecting towers enabled other archers to fire parallel to the wall in mutual support. Where the wall reached the sea on either flank, it turned, disappeared. Sylah remembered looking down at it from the hillside, remembered how the sea licked at the other three walls, as a child licks at a piece of ice in its hand.

Tate echoed her thoughts. "I'd hate to have to crack this nut," she said, craning to look up at the wall before entering the tunnel-like passage leading off the drawbridge. The entry's twin doors were hinged at the top, with lines and pulleys to swing them up to the ceiling.

In the echoing darkness, Sylah said, "I'm not sure it could be done."

Tate disagreed. "No place is impregnable. The important thing to remember about any defense is that it breaks easier from the inside."

The remark was cynical enough to surprise Sylah, and before she was prepared to respond, they exited into a dazzle of sunshine. It was another killing ground, a large square surfaced with stone and chunks of concrete. Stone buildings surrounded it. Tate pointed out to Sylah that the few windows were too narrow for a man to get through. She added, "I don't believe anyone's ever attacked this place, Sylah. Look at the walls. No burn stains. There's a shingle roof over there so old it's rotting. They've been safe behind these walls a long time."

Gatro led them toward another wide gate. The smell of stone and bricks baking under a hot sun drew Sylah back to Ola instantly. She didn't want to think of that place. The present and the future were all she dared dwell on. Forcing herself out of reverie, she sought things that were different. This was a fort, after all, and not a city. Unlike Ola, this stone smell wasn't greasy with garbage and unwashed humanity.

Despite the reassuring cleanliness, Sylah was uneasy in her mind. She felt watched, as if held in an invisible net. The sensation was so strong it was like the touch of sea-wind, the wet cold that cuts through clothing and settles in the bones.

Breaking out of the dim passage through the wall into the sun was a blessing.

A few yards farther stood yet another wall, this one more decorative than protective. Barely taller than the knot of men clustered in front of its wooden doors, its stone was carved in replica of a stormy sea. Sharks with polished silver teeth ranged below cresting waves.

The waxed wooden doors behind the men were ajar. Flowers and blooming shrubs beckoned from the courtyard there. Sylah yearned to be among them.

She had time for one quick glance at the castle. The thing that struck her most were the walkways connecting the three stories. They were disturbingly delicate rope bridges, flung across the space between the arms in airy, graceful openness. She hoped she'd never have to cross one.

Sylah fastened her attention on the waiting men. Their footgear was a sort of half boot, but leg wrappings reached the knee. Those bands appeared to be about two inches wide, and alive with color, as were their full, flowing blouses. The shirting itself was white, embroidered with a fantastic array of designs, symbols, and patterns. Trousers, also of cloth, were black, tucked inside the leg wrappings. Every man wore two swords, one on each hip. They were short, slender weapons, with large handguards.

All nine men were of average build and height. Each wore a mustache; none had a beard. One stepped forward. He spoke to Sylah, pointedly ignoring her companions.

"Rose Priestess. Most welcome of guests. On behalf of the Chair, I welcome you to Kos. All men will forever envy you, as all are envied who see the wonders of our lands. You are honored above all. You and your friends will sleep in the castle. My master, the Chair, has said it. This has never happened before."

No one smiled.

Sylah looked up, beyond the shark-carved wall. Far away, high on the gap-toothed rampart of the fort's eastern wall, the Harvester looked down at her.

CHAPTER 45

Conway's impression of the castle's interior was of smoking darkness.

Despite the brightness of the day, a fire roared in the immense fireplace across the room from the front entrance. The man standing next to it provided scale; Conway estimated one could roast a cow on the spit.

The flat ceiling was no more than seven feet high. Light came from two sources. Primary were the narrow archers' slits that dropped vertically from near the ceiling to about chest high. There were wooden stands at each one, and wooden shutters, cunningly operated by foot levers. An archer could loose his arrow, and slam the portal shut against spear thrust or return fire. Ventilation slits admitted paler light just under the ceiling.

The combination of low ceiling, dim light, and the thick stone pillars bulked under rough wooden crossbeams generated an oppressive atmosphere.

Still, as Conway's eyes adjusted, he saw the walls were thickly hung with bright pennants and banners. Some were ripped and torn, tattered remnants of former bright glory. Trophies, he decided. The residue of conquest.

The official who'd greeted them outside accompanied them. He wore an odd-shaped metal thing around his neck on a white cord. Lifting it to his mouth, the man demonstrated that it was a whistle. It warbled from one high note up to one higher yet, then slid back down past the original pitch. Beside Conway, Tate made a strangling noise.

"A bosun's pipe," she managed to whisper in Conway's ear.

"A what?"

She spelled the word *boatswain*, then pronounced it again: *bosun.* "The bosun's a sailor's sailor, the man who knows lines, rigging, ship's procedure, all that swabby stuff. That whistle was the thing they used to get attention before an announcement—like 'All hands heave out! Reveille!' That kind of thing."

Before either could say more, the man was turning to them. Conway and Tate separated like children caught talking in class. The man said, "My title is Bos. The fort, including all hands who man her, is my responsibility." Emphasizing his words, the seven men from the steps came inside to join him, as did several other people who'd obviously been waiting just outside the doors of the main room. They formed two lines behind Bos. There was a minimum of confusion, indicating that this was a routine.

Bos went on. "All officials are drawn from two groups of what you would call nobles. The inland Kossiars are administered by a Board. Here, in Harbor, the highborn are called Crew. Staff here use the ancient Crew titles. I won't introduce you to everyone. There are a few you should know, however. This is Guns. He oversees the fighting forces of Kos. The next man is Stores. His responsibility is to advise the Chair on matters of supplies and the administrative needs of Kos. This is Emmay. He supervises law and order. These others are staff, the people who run the fort for Chair."

He stopped, expectant, and Sylah introduced her companions.

Her manner was strained, and her friends exchanged troubled glances. Nevertheless, when Sylah finished, Tate could contain herself no longer. She said, "You actually have guns?"

The man of that title frowned, puzzled. "Have? I *am* Guns. That's not my name, of course. We abandon names when we take the grade."

Tate nodded, mute. She seemed dazed.

Bos said, "The Chair has had a stateroom prepared for you. He assumed you'd want to stay together, so it's one large room, with folding wood and hide partitions."

Sylah thanked him, and he dismissed his staff. Sylah's group followed him outside to walk the length of the courtyard. It featured a large formal garden. The centerpiece was a towering mound of white rhododendrons. The southern end of the yard featured a fountain, which fronted a tall pole that rose above the walls of the building. Rungs led to a circular shelter almost at the top.

Tate nudged Conway. "Listen, what's hurting Sylah? What got to her?"

"I give up. One minute she was fine, the next she wasn't. She must have seen something the rest of us missed."

Behind them, Dodoy said, "She did. She looked up at the roof, outside, when the man with the funny name was talking. Something scared her. Why do all these people talk funny? Their voices go up, down, up, down. It's a stupid way to talk."

Ignoring his question, Tate said, "What did she see? What was up there?"

"I don't know. She looked, not me."

Conway gritted his teeth. Lengthening his stride, he pulled away from Tate and the boy.

They were almost to the end of the courtyard by then, proceeding on a brick walk under overhanging wooden balconies extended from the two stories above them. Conway remarked on the ropewalk connections between the arms of the buildings. Unanimously, they expressed the hope of avoiding them. Tate reached down to pat Oshu and Tanno. "Gut check, puppies," she said. "We may have found something you can't handle. Momma's not that sure of herself, if you want the truth." The attempted humor was brittle. The responding laughter was polite.

At the juncture of the eastern arm and the north-south arm of the castle, Bos stopped, gesturing at a door's heavy planks. "The Chair instructs me to see that you're comfortable, and to invite you to his presence when you've refreshed yourself. If you'll eat with him, that will be in about two inches."

Sylah was reaching for the door handle and stopped. "Inches?"

"Yes. Inches. Of time?" Bos could have been talking to a child.

"I don't understand."

"*Inches.* On the timetube."

Sylah shook her head.

Bos raised his eyebrows. He collected himself, but contempt tainted his words. "A timetube is a water container with a hole in it. As the water drips out, the water level tells the time. A day is twenty-four inches. Everyone has one."

"Not us." Conway signaled the dogs to stay as he took a half step forward. "We're too independent to jump just because someone loses his water. I suppose we'll have to be polite, though, so you'll supply us with one of your toys, won't you?"

"It's my duty." Bos' tone made it clear what he thought of his duty. Reaching past Sylah's stilled hand, he opened the door. A quick blast on the bosun's pipe caught the group by surprise. The children in the stateroom had obviously been waiting for it.

Ranging in age from about sixteen to no more than twelve, they straightened to frozen-faced attention. The tallest, a boy on the right end of the lineup, said, "We're your hands, Rose Priestess. What instructions?"

Turning to Bos, Sylah's voice lowered to a dangerous growl. "What are these children doing here?"

Bos said, "They're slaves. Servants."

Rigidly erect, Sylah examined the children. "Fourteen of you."

Confusion crushed the boy's confident mien. Eyes darting from Sylah to Bos, he stammered. "Two for each of you. Except the boy. Four for the stateroom. Is something wrong?"

"Not with you. Where do you sleep?"

"Five here. Outside. On the walkway. Five in the barracks. We'll take turns."

"Go back to your barracks. All of you."

Stricken, the boy turned to Bos. "What have we done?"

Sylah interrupted him again, her voice so taut it threatened to crack. "Do as I say." Struggling, she found a softer, gentler manner. "You've done nothing wrong. You'll not be punished. But you must go."

Again, the boy sought Bos. The man nodded. His lip curled in a sneer. The children literally ran, sandals slapping the brick walkway.

262

With them gone, Sylah faced Bos. Blue eyes glacial, she said, "You will not assign slaves to us."

Bos smiled, waved a hand. "If that's what you wish."

Sylah leaned forward, seething. "Would I say something I didn't mean? You think my orders are mere whims? I said nothing of wishes. I told you what I will have."

For a moment, Bos stared in disbelief. His face paled. Equally quickly, it flamed with ugly, growing blotches that melded into a furious whole. "Indeed I heard, Rose Priestess. I have your instructions. You'll eat with the Chair?"

"We will. Please send us a timetube."

"It's my duty." The door thumped solidly behind him.

"Whoo-ee!" Tate broke the silence with her low exclamation. "That was some show."

Lifting a shaking hand to her brow, Sylah steadied herself against a heavy oak chair. Lanta was beside her instantly, sliding a shoulder under the raised arm. A moment later Sylah stood solidly alone. Without preamble, she said, "The Harvester is here. I saw her. On the roof, just before we entered this place."

Tate glanced at Dodoy, who seemed not to have heard. Nalatan said, "You told me she went back to Church Home?" making it a question. Lanta said nothing; her hand went to her bosom, then dropped away. Conway took the wipe from his shoulder. "I think we all owe the Harvester something."

Sylah gestured sharply. "She's Church. You mustn't harm her."

Conway put the weapon down on the table beside the oak chair. "She's tried to kill three of us. Does she have to succeed before you admit we have an obligation to return the favor?"

Sylah reached out to stroke the cold steel barrel of the wipe, trailing her fingers down its length with an almost sensual deliberation. Without looking up from the weapon, she said, "I think she's terribly, despicably wrong. I can't use her methods."

Conway said, "If you lose to her because you lack the will to use whatever methods are necessary, what purpose is your 'goodness' then? If you won't fight to win, why fight?"

"Can you answer for me, then, my friend?"

"Will I fight to the death for your cause? I think so. No man answers that question until the moment comes. I don't want to be a martyr. But I won't be a victim. The decision about when one becomes the other is mine."

"Fair enough. Tate? Nalatan?"

Tate shrugged. "What he said: Me, too."

Nalatan bared his teeth in a cold smile. The picked-over quality

263

of his words suggested a secret amusement. "My master said I must help you discover the secret of the Door. I swore an oath. If I fail you, life, not death, would be punishment."

Sylah turned from the wipe, put her hand on Lanta's shoulder. "I won't ask you. Church has her own demands on you. Promise me this: Whatever happens, you'll protect yourself."

"Only if I can do it without injuring you."

Sylah embraced her.

A moment later the group was chattering and exploring the stateroom, pulling out the folding partitions, poking at beds, moving furniture.

All but Lanta. Overlooked, withdrawn, she stepped behind one of the partitions.

The level of trust Sylah afforded her was almost too much to bear. *Church has her own demands on you.* The phrase wouldn't stop pounding in her ears. She closed her eyes, squinting so hard the muscles in her forehead were like steel across the bone. Between her breasts, the True Stone was a living firebrand.

CHAPTER 46

Bos appeared as the timetube dripped away the last bit of water signaling the hour. When Dodoy complained mightily about being left behind with the dogs, he sent the boy a look of sheer hatred. As for the dogs, they gravitated to a corner as far from Dodoy as possible. Mournful dark eyes watched the adults leave.

Bos led the group to the third floor of the central arm of the castle. Lanta attempted to make conversation, asking about the age of the fort.

"Several generations," Bos answered brusquely, then, looking at her innocent curiosity, grew expansive. "There are two siahs honored in Kos. You have this word, *Siah?*"

Lanta nodded. "A founder, or a first leader. It's interchangeable, because the legends are so old they get confused sometimes."

"Not in Kos. Our history is pure. The first siah came to the coast people. His name was Skipper. He was born of the sea when she was impregnated by the east wind. When Skipper came to Kos, the people lived in ignorance. He showed them how to build, how to use the sea. Generations passed. The people of Skipper multiplied. They explored the land to the east, where they found the people of the farms. The name of their siah is lost. He formed the first Board, showed the inlanders how to irrigate, taught them about animals. Together, the two peoples united to create Kos, build Harbor, and elect the Chair."

"Elect?"

Bos hesitated in his recitation. When he continued, there was a touch of forced enthusiasm in his tone. "For several generations, the Chair was elected. Pressures from enemies, drought, plague—many things demanded firmer, steady leadership."

Conway interjected. "An overriding need for stability and continuity?"

Bos stopped in midstep, startled. He spun to face Conway. "Exactly. Stability and continuity. Our first permanent Chair's words. How do you know our history?"

Dryly, Conway said, "I don't. The notion seemed to have a familiar tone, that's all. One hears so many things."

Unsure how to react to Conway's words and manner, Bos chose to deal with Lanta. "Under the hereditary Chairs, Kos has prospered as no other land. Our ships reach south beyond the land of the savage Hents. Our warmen range north to the banks of the Mother River, south to the shores of the Long Sea, and east beyond the Enemy Mountains. We are the most favored of people. Our land is sacred."

Sylah asked quietly, "Why is this Chair so eager to deal with me, who has nothing with which to bargain?"

A vein leapt into view at the side of Bos' neck. He acted as if he hadn't heard, leading them the last few steps onto the top floor.

As one, they stopped abruptly. They were at the end of the central, or east-west, arm of the castle. A passageway extended its entire length. The south side, on their left, was covered with dozens of pairs of open shark's jaws. They stretched away in silent, menacing ovals, completely covering the wall. Soft light poured in the six doors on the balcony side of the hall, to the right. The serrated triangular teeth sparkled suggestively.

Armed warmen stood beside each of the balcony doors. There were only three doors on the left side of the hall, each flanked by a pair of warmen.

Bos led the way down the long hall. At the first door on the south side, he stopped, holding up a hand for quiet. "You will ask the Chair for safe passage. It's a formality, and he will grant it, of course. It means you're allowed to stay in Kos."

"What happens if he changes his mind?" Tate asked.

"Then you have to leave." Bos enjoyed saying it.

Conway said, "And the Harvester?"

Turning away to hide any change of expression, Bos gestured them through the door. Inside, they turned right. The room, like the hall, stretched the full length of the castle. At the western end, too far away to distinguish features, a figure sat in a chair.

Tate made a low, humming sound of amazement, and Conway whispered, "Whoa." Sylah and Lanta stared in silence.

Behind the low dais, light blasted through a rectangular window perhaps three times as wide as its height. Fragments of glass ranging in size from bits no bigger than an eye to slabs the size of serving trays were randomly leaded in place within a formal grid. Irregularly shaped, the multicolored shards vibrated with the hues of an exploded rainbow. As Bos herded them forward, the group watched how flaws and subtleties in thickness caused shifts in the color. There was clear glass chemically stained to purple-blue opalescence that changed intensity at every movement of the observer. Conway and Tate knew it had to have been buried for centuries.

There was no furniture in the room. Two fireplaces flanked the window, their stone construction jutting out to complete a massive frame for the throne. Coals glowed on the grates. It occurred to Sylah that the man on the chair sat in a well-warmed nook; in front of him was a cold, damp, sea-smelling emptiness. Bos' soft-soled boots scuffed on the polished wood floor. Sylah's party all wore boots. Their steps echoed with almost martial precision from the walls.

On arriving in front of the dais, everyone stepped onto a thick mat of braided cording. The Chair looked down on his audience from an advantage of perhaps three feet.

Clean-shaven, dark-haired, dressed in shimmering green matching blouse and trousers, he watched the group advance impassively. Full-lipped, high cheekboned, square-jawed, he was around thirty years old. Sylah had expected a graybeard. This man exuded vitality.

His posture troubled her. Apparently relaxed, he practically sprawled in the seat, an elbow on its arm, his fist under his chin. The other arm dangled lazily, and his legs stretched out in front of him, ankles crossed. He wore a faint, reassuring smile.

The impression was a ruse.

Sylah's training emphasized observation and analysis. More than that, however, the sisters continually emphasized what they called "the knowing." They never completely explained it, even admitting that some seemed to have the ability more than others.

Sylah felt the knowing as she listened to Bos' ongoing introductions.

The Chair measured. He weighed. The dark eyes flicked, and Sylah knew that in a moment he'd examined the lightning weapons as closely as most people could in minutes of lifting and turning. The eyes shifted again, and her costume had been inventoried, evaluated. As had her entire being. She suddenly felt exposed, vulnerable, as if that quick vision stripped her naked. Then the eyes were gone to Lanta. A pang of anger swept Sylah; after practically undressing her, the man dismissed her.

Bos was saying, ". . . intercepted by Lance Gatro, who extended the Chair's invitation."

Flustered, Sylah realized Bos was finished. She quickly asked for safe passage. The Chair granted it with a wave of the hand, adding, "As much as I admire your courage in your quest, Rose Priestess, I admire more your ability to surround yourself with loyal supporters. These friends, by their presence alone, tell me more of you than all the tales and rumors."

The earth-dark eyes held hers. She said, "My quest breeds enemies, as well. I saw the Harvester."

He smiled. It was less than pleasant. "It's not important. You're in no danger from her in Kos."

Sylah tossed her head. "I have no fear of her."

"Of course you do. The only reason she hasn't had you killed, as she tried to have the Matt Conway one killed, is because you have knowledge she doesn't. It's her aim to cheat you out of your prize. You fear her as you fear nothing else."

Forcing herself to stay focused on him, despite the cold image of the Harvester at the edge of her thoughts, Sylah said, "I respect her—capabilities—but I don't fear her."

The Chair swept them all with a warning look. "Odeel won't harm anyone. Nor will she be harmed. If one of you does, all die. No questions, no appeals, no mercy. Is it heard?"

Sylah said, "None of us would risk the others."

"Of course." The Chair rang a small bell. A door at the end of the dais swung open. The Harvester stepped through, hooded, flashing a welcoming smile at the Chair that turned venomous when she directed it at Sylah and her group. She directed her attention to Conway and Nalatan. "I'm told I have you two to thank for Sylah's arrival here. I'll find a proper way to make you aware of that error."

"Not on Kos land," Conway said. "And if I ever see you outside its boundaries, you won't make me aware of anything."

Nalatan made a three-sign, then said, "You know my oath. Keep out of my way, Harvester."

She swept off her hood. In the diffused light filtering through the multicolored window the silver hair took on the patina of an ancient helmet. Eyes blazing, she said, "Your master put himself in my way by refusing to cooperate. You saw what happened to him."

"Enough, Odeel." The Chair's order was hardly louder than ordinary conversation, but it carried unquestionable authority. Nalatan trembled violently under the strain of containing himself. Conway noticed Bos' hands stealing to the handles of his twin swords. The doors leading to the hall were suddenly filled by the warmen guards. Ignoring all of it, attention fixed on the Harvester, the Chair said, "Harvester, you and the Rose Priestess are both here because the search for the Door has split Church. I mean to decide how I can best serve Church and Kos by observing you while you shelter in my lands. Don't force me to base my judgments on petty feuds."

Sylah said, "My search takes me to the land of Church Home. Every day, every hour, I lose here means more danger to us from the summer heat of the Dry. Even the nomads may interfere with our goals."

"Good points. The last one's better than you realize." He gestured at Bos, who hurried into the hall. A moment later, two warmen half carried a bound man through the nearest door. His face was hidden, hanging down. The part of his forehead that could be seen was swollen, discolored. He wore a shredded singlet and torn trousers. More bruises marred the exposed flesh, and one ugly cut ran across his shoulder.

Sylah said, "I must tend to him. He's infected."

The Chair said, "His treatment's been arranged. This is a nomad, from the Long Sky People. He says all of you will reject Church and accept the silver disk of Moondance or be exterminated."

The man raised his head. The face was a bloody, shattered mask. Barely intelligible, he said, "We come. S'ren'er or die."

"Nervy," the Chair said, gesturing. The warmen hustled their prisoner out.

To Sylah, the Chair continued. "He was a scout. The rest escaped. They're elusive. His group was exploring a route from the Enemy Mountains to Harbor, following the Duckhunter's River. Other raiders have struck our farm communities even farther south. They tap here, tap there, looking for weakness. I can feel them building up behind the mountains like a summer storm. Ride toward Church Home, and you stand an excellent chance of stumbling into them. But that's enough serious talk. I invited you to eat, and I've neglected my responsibilities as host."

When he rose from his seat, it was obvious he was tall. Only when he was on the floor beside them did his true height register. Conway and Nalatan, both a shade over six feet, came to his chin. When he moved, it was with a supple, assured grace. Leading the way, he took them into the west wing and a sumptuous dining room.

Dozens of people were already seated at the benches of massive trestle tables. Helping Sylah to a place, the Chair explained, "These are mostly staff; Crew, as Bos explained. Some are visiting Crew or Board. Your presence brought them. Excuse the clumsy dining arrangements. One of my ancestors was killed after a particularly festive dinner by a cousin armed with a chair. No one will ever lift this furniture and bring it down on someone's head."

The Harvester was directly across the table from her. The Chair leaned toward the other woman, their conversation too low to follow.

Too friendly, thought Sylah, and consciously arranged a serene expression. What made the scene particularly galling was the way the Harvester postured and preened. It bordered on obscene. The woman was old enough to be his mother, and she positively simpered for him.

Beside Sylah, Tate said, "Are you going to eat?"

A steaming bowl of soup seemed to have materialized in front of her. Sylah tingled with embarrassment. She told herself the spectacle of the Harvester literally trying to seduce their host was enough to distract anyone.

The soup, in its porcelain bowl, was a savory combination of mussels and cream, with a gloss of onion. Servants in bright yellow sped silently from point to point. As the sun faded, they lit copper lanterns mounted on the stone walls. A salad arrived, crisp and fresh. Bread came in large, round loaves, to be broken in chunks. The main course was a huge beef haunch, carved at an adjoining table, served steaming hot on more porcelain, which had a strength its delicate appearance belied.

Under the obsequious, near-invisibility of the servants hurrying about their duties, there was a sense of furtiveness. Sylah thought of the expression "hidden in plain view," feeling she was seeing something and still not aware. A shiver of discovery flittered across Sylah's skin as she realized that every aspect of her group was under intense scrutiny by the slaves. No gesture was too small to go unseen. After a while, Sylah noted that all deferred to one woman. It was done with such clandestine grace that Sylah almost missed it. The rest of the yellow-clad crew came and went around her in the manner of bees treating the queen in a hive.

The Chair finally broke off his conversation with the Harvester and turned to Sylah, asking her to comment on her travels. As he did, the dominant servant presented Sylah with a plate. The inside of her wrist slid across Sylah's shoulder with the touch of a leaf. Later, removing a glass, her fingers brushed the back of Sylah's hand, a contact no heavier than a sigh.

Later, Sylah left the dining room with the Chair, leaving the seething Harvester to follow. She absently put a hand to her throat. The drawstring of her cowl was missing.

CHAPTER 47

The south wall of the castle was breached by a pair of triangular portals, widest at the bottom. They were only a few feet across at the base and approximately ten feet high. Leading into the castle from the bay, they ended at a square pool, a docking place for small boats. Presently, there were six vessels crowding it. Four were single hulls with folding masts. Two were balancebars, the outriggers raised, the masts unstepped. Secured for the night, they tugged at their mooring lines nervously and muttered frustration, eager to slip free and dance with the waves.

Outside the fortress wall, which was separated from open water by a narrow ledge of native rock, a heavy chop drove in from the sea. The play of the dark water showered silvery spray in unending lacework against night's ebony. The rush of wind and water paralleled the peninsula's face, so that each wave sheared against the land as it went. The resultant hissing crash burrowed into one's consciousness.

Lanta, immersed in the pounding, liquid roar, stood outside the wall, a few yards from the boat portals. Silent, unmoving, she could have been an irregularity in the stone surface behind her.

Matt Conway had been seated beside her at dinner. He spoke to her occasionally. Conversational crumbs, thrown to her the way he'd feed birds.

She wished she had the strength to hate him.

Part of her treasured those crumbs. Part of her wanted to spit on them, and on him for his condescension.

She clenched her fists, insisted to herself that she did hate him. Because she loved him.

Admission was a physical shock. She reached for the stabilizing solidity of the wall. Cold and damp had penetrated cloth and flesh while she was preoccupied, and now her joints rebelled with pain at the long-delayed movement. Throat muscles contracted, released a small cry of hurt. Crushed by the incessant roar of surf, the sound went unheard even by her.

She turned to leave.

A figure loomed over her, black against black, practically touching her. This time she heard her full-throated scream. Even as she did, she knew her puny effort would never be heard by anyone else.

The figure bent down, forced her to the wall. "Priestess, it's me—the Chair. I came out to talk." His deep rumble successfully challenged the sea's tumult. Surprisingly gentle, he took her arm and guided her back toward the boat portals. They walked through them on the wooden catwalk she'd discovered for herself.

There must have been a guard watching the portal who reported her. Lanta made a mental note to pass that along to the others.

Taking a seat on the bow of one of the small boats, the Chair gestured for Lanta to join him. She chose a different boat; it was close enough for conversation, yet afforded her distance from this strange, large man.

He said, "I'm not exactly sure where you fit into this puzzle that's been delivered to my land, Priestess. Will you speak plainly with me?"

"Will you believe me if I say yes?" It was said before she took time to think. The effrontery startled her.

The Chair threw back his head and laughed. At the sound, Lanta noticed movement around them. Warmen, discretely distant, guarding from the darker corners. It amused her. What sort of protection could this giant need?

"No, Priestess," he said, "I wouldn't believe you. I've learned to believe no answers completely. Fairly said, that includes my own. The difference between me and everyone else is that I change my mind. The others are all liars." He laughed at his own joke, enjoying himself. "Now that we understand each other, why are you accompanying Sylah?"

"Because I'm her friend."

271

"Odeel says it's because you expect Sylah to make you the Seer of Seers."

Lanta forced calmness into her words. "The Harvester's wrong."

"Nevertheless, if Sylah's successful, she'll treat you properly. As a friend."

"She'll treat me as a friend. No more, no less. And what of you? Why involve yourself in our pursuit of a thing that may not even exist? A thing that's already split Church, a thing the Harvester has tried to kill for?"

She felt the change in the atmosphere even before she heard the faint squeal of stressed cordage when he shifted his weight and caused the small boat to lean harder into its lashing. He said, "Tread carefully. You're on treacherous ground now. Unless your gift . . . ?"

"I have Seen nothing. My powers are exclusive to Church, not used for personal benefit."

"These are facts, known to all. My responsibility is to learn the truth."

"Facts *are* truth."

The Chair's laughter was quiet. "Not even numbers are always true. We all use facts to suit ourselves. We all lie. Except me. As I said, I change my mind."

Lanta said, "Sylah's only concern is Church. If you help her, you have no guarantees of anything, except the Harvester's hatred."

There was a pause, and she knew he was thinking out his next statement. It came as a surprise. "My ancestors were largely responsible for the Purge. Kos was very important to the Teachers, who were highly regarded by my ancestors. Yet they killed the Teachers. I have tasted power, little Priestess, so I understand why men do such things. Fear or greed. The Teachers had something my ancestors wanted, and either couldn't get, or couldn't control. I want it. If I must, I'll share it. Until I find a way to own it."

"You're saying you'd take it from Sylah, if you could."

"For power, everyone steals. However, I can offer Sylah protection against the Harvester and her allies."

The True Stone seemed to tremble between Lanta's breasts. She filled with a swift, ridiculous fear that it was glowing, would reveal her crime to this man, of all people. She hunched forward, fighting to keep her hands and eyes away from the evidence. "Why tell me all this? Why not go directly to Sylah?"

"Oh, I will. But a friend is never a loss, as they say. You'll tell her what I've said. I expect she'll tell you whatever I say to her. I've seen how close you two are. Still, I want you to hear my words directly from me. You understand?"

"Will you offer her this alliance you mentioned?"

"Not right away. And I hope you won't, either. Let's see if the idea will come to her, shall we? But if you feel you have to mention it, by all means do; it's not a secret."

"I hold no secrets from Sylah." A surge through the boat portals made the small pool heave. It excited the moored boats, set them to yanking on their restraints. Lanta wished she could shout at them to stop their sarcastic squeals.

The Chair said, "I had such a friend. Once. Never again." He rose, bulking darkly. In the background, the warmen stirred. "If you ever remember anything I say to you, let it be this: Such a friend is the most precious thing in life. Guard that friendship against everything." In the melodic speech of the Kos people, the last word resonated like a lament.

And then he was swallowed by the night. His escort moved to follow, their swift, obscure shadows more suggestion than reality. Alone again, Lanta begrudged the destruction of her mood.

The thought was shoved aside by the sudden realization that she'd seen a similar reaction in Sylah at the dinner table. The Chair had drawn her, as well.

It was a shocking concept, all the more disturbing in that Sylah herself was undoubtedly unaware of the man's effect on her. Lanta chewed her lower lip, thoughtful, remembering. She closed her eyes, recreating every minute alteration in Sylah's features during the meal. What she recollected was both relieving and disturbing. Lanta was sure the attraction was purely political.

That, of course, spoke well of Sylah's personal qualities. The question was, what did it portend in the matter of Sylah's ambitions?

Lanta hated the question. Sylah was a friend, and one didn't suspect a friend's ambitions.

The sheer power of the Chair's attention forced one to look inside. Lanta shook her head, dislodging that unpleasantness. Conjecture about friends was bad practice. Introspection was even more painful.

It was one thing to stand at the edge of the sea and be romantic and sad and abstractly envision a violent end to problems and troubles. It was something else again to confront stark reality. The Chair forced her to contemplate the enormity of her dishonesty. She'd come to terms long ago with her rejection of Violet's instructions to betray Sylah. It troubled her that she hadn't had the courage to do it when she'd been approached. Still, she'd made a choice based on right and wrong.

The True Stone was different.

She wanted it.

That irregular little purple rock, with its peculiar flaw, *was* Violet. To hold it meant to grasp the heart of the family that chose her, raised her, was all she'd ever known. Every night, curled up in her blanket, she clasped the stone as if holding it was her lifeline back from the soft death of sleep. She pressed its one smooth surface against her warm flesh, the gold chain woven through her fingers. Lying quietly, her heart swelled with dreams of the Priestesses who'd preceded her, how they healed, guided, consoled. And Lanta, the Chosen who had no one of her own, now possessed them all, because she had the True Stone. Lanta, the Seer, feared by everyone, was transformed to the beloved of everyone.

There were other dreams. An embarrassing number were about Matt Conway. She remembered only that he was central, and that strange delights lingered in her body when dawn interrupted.

She wondered if her life was to be all dreams, all Seeing.

Lanta rose from her seat on the bow of the small boat and made her way back into the fort. Gleaming sconces held lamps that illuminated the austere stone hallways. Wrought of gleaming brass, the holders represented sharks. They balanced on their tails, holding chains in mouths studded with silver teeth. The lamps dangled from the chains. Soft, wavering light created regular islands down the passages. The oil they burned was scented with herbs; Lanta recognized thyme, bay, the prickly dustiness of sage. She raised her chin, breathing deeply, soothed. Her pace slowed.

At the end of the long hall, where the hollow behind the projecting stairway to the next floor created a dark hide, Lanta thought she saw a movement. She continued her advance, telling herself tiredness was stretching her imagination.

Then she saw it again. Lurking.

Behind her was emptiness, all the doors firmly closed. Normally there were warmen everywhere. Now there was no one.

Could that be intentional?

If she ran forward, she could be on the stairs and halfway up before whoever waited in the darkness would realize they'd been discovered.

She took another step. One more. Gathered herself, tensed.

"Lanta."

"What? What? Who?" Inane, idiot words. They tumbled out of

her. She knew who: Conway. Her face burned. Why did he do this to her? Why did he make it impossible for her to be anything but a stumbling, choking *fool*? "Hello?" She croaked, and wanted to bite off her tongue.

"I've been waiting for you," he said. "There's something I've got to talk about, and you're the one I want to talk to. Please, have you got a little time?"

"Of course." She managed it.

He had waited for her. For *her*.

CHAPTER 48

Conway took Lanta's arm and led her outside to the central courtyard. Her mind soared with that meaningless touch. She was completely aware she was being silly, and was powerless to dismiss a flood of idyllic images.

Neither spoke until they were walking a path through rose bushes that came to Lanta's shoulder. In the darkness the yellow and white varieties had a soft luminosity that Lanta's overworked imagination transformed into gentle, smiling ghost faces. The picture sent a delicious fright singing along her spine even as she delighted in their beauty. Perfumed air embraced her, and she thought of the contrast between those tender, invisible eddies and the crushing surf that mumbled in the background.

Conway said, "Something's been troubling me. It could cause Sylah a lot of trouble. With the quest, you know? I mean, two people getting involved."

Words were hot in Lanta's mouth, but when she answered, her tone was tentative. Still, she wanted to be encouraging. "Sylah understands that sort of thing. After all, it was during her own escape from the Dog rebels and the Mountain People that she fell in love with Clas."

"I never thought of that." He stopped, causing her to turn so that she was facing him. "When I tell her, I'll remember to mention it. If I have to bring it up at all. Sylah sees just about everything."

"I think she'd have said something to me, if she'd noticed." Lanta wanted to scream at him to be direct. She couldn't tolerate much more oblique chatter.

Conway said, "On the other hand, I may be wrong. I mean, Nalatan's never said anything, not in words."

Lanta's heart banged once, a throb that took her breath away, so that when she repeated the name, "Nalatan?" it was an ugly, rasping sound.

"He's getting pretty interested in Tate. She claims she doesn't have time for him. I don't believe it. Sometimes people are sort of afraid to say what they really feel, you know? What bothers me most is Dodoy's probable reaction."

Lanta felt lightheaded. She seemed to float around this suddenly bizarre scene. Words came automatically, but they had a slurred sound. "Yes. In his way, Dodoy loves her."

Conway went on. "I don't want to see anyone hurt. I have to be careful, you see?"

It was almost unbearable, Lanta thought. What had started out so precious, so dear, was now low comedy.

"What's wrong? Are you all right?" Conway had her by the shoulders. He looked worried, almost afraid. "You look almost ready to cry. Or laugh, maybe." His grip loosened, and he pulled back slowly.

Lanta straightened weak knees. His hands fell away. She said, "Nothing, nothing. I'm fine now." She turned to walk toward the door. Conway followed, and Lanta went on, "If you get involved, you'll be seen as a meddler, no matter how it turns out." She laughed, and was instantly sorry. Each pealing note ripped like a claw.

They fell into a mutual silence. Her smaller steps and lighter boots tapped out a staccato counterpoint to the heavy crack of his heels.

She wanted to see him die. She wanted to see him battered and broken, so she could hold him, heal him, nurse him back to health and back to her. She wanted to hit him. To throw her arms around him with a wantonness that made her blush. She wished she could escape this place, these people, and never see them again.

Karda and Mikka were already on their feet, great tails flailing at the sight of their master. Karda barked once. Echoes raced up and down the long hall. Conway went to them, a hand for each huge head, tousling the fur, tugging the ears. Ecstatic, the hounds pushed and shoved against him, sent him staggering.

When he turned to Lanta, some trick of the oil lamp softened his features, cast his eyes into a strange, secretive shadow. There was something inexpressibly sad about him. Watching the dogs' antics, he said, "I envy these brutes. We say they're less intelligent than we are. Don't you feel it's more like an innocence? We puzzle and pose. We talk, but we don't listen. We look, but we don't see. These two are what they are. No questions. No recriminations. Just loyalty. Love. I think they have that; love." He paused. "Don't you?"

She tossed her head, rejecting pointless discussion. "I never thought about it. They really are just animals."

"Aren't we all?" he said, and laughed. Lanta was dismayed to discover that his amusement seemed to have the same nasty sharpness as her own.

He turned away, signaling the dogs to follow. "I suppose you're right. I get too close to the problem. Thanks for your help. Sleep well. I'm going to take these two out for some exercise."

She called, "Good night," and he half turned, saluting.

Outside the castle, Conway headed for the flank of the closest defensive berm. Torches atop the wall threw a faint light. The crest of the berm was silhouetted, and Conway realized there were torches beyond it. When he reached the point where the land dropped precipitously into the bay's waters, he turned to climb up to the berm's crest. The back slope was an easy grade. A trench on top allowed warmen to defend the landward side with no more than their heads exposed. The torches, set at the base of the berm, served a dual function: they prevented surreptitious approach, and any attempt to extinguish them would warn the defenders of impending attack.

Without speaking directly to the warmen, Conway shouted at the dogs to make sure his presence and purpose were known. He jogged for a while with the team, then released them to chase each other.

In the pale illumination of the torches, they stretched out, reveling in their freedom and strength. Growling ferociously, Karda launched himself after the fleeing Mikka. More agile, she waited until he was abreast and poised to deliver the shoulder blow that would send her tumbling. Then she swerved, leaving him nothing but air. Dodging, cutting, reversing herself, she led him back and forth in front of the wall, turning the meadow into their playground. Finally, however, Karda caught her. Conway held his breath as Mikka went hurtling sideways. She fell with an audible thump and accompanying grunt. Legs flailed as she tumbled, but when she came upright, it was to charge recklessly. She surprised Karda, rocked him back on his haunches. He rose on his hind legs, holding her off with forepaws. She did the same. Roaring at each other, snapping great jaws, they towered far taller than Conway. Then they were back on all fours, leaping, feinting, exuberant as puppies.

Behind Conway Nalatan said, "If I traveled north to where these Dog People live, would they part with one of those?"

"They told us they'd never given any to anyone before."

Nalatan was thoughtful. "The first time they make a gift of such animals, and one recipient is a woman. She's a very different person."

Dryly, Conway said, "You could say that."

Oblivious, Nalatan plunged on. "I don't mean the obvious differences—the strange weapons you two use, or her color, or her attachment to that Dodoy. You both reek of secrets. That doesn't bother me. There's something else, though: I don't think you yourselves are aware of what makes you the way you are."

Conway laughed softly. "That's complicated, my friend."

"Oh, I know how self-important I sound. But you both walk in a different sort of light than the rest of us. I can almost touch it, but I can't name it."

Conway was becoming very uncomfortable. "Look, let's talk about something else. How long do you think we're going to be here?"

Nalatan spat into the darkness. "Kos invented lying. They've been perfecting it since. The Chair won't let us leave until he has a reason to do so."

"What reason does he have to detain us?"

"Discontent among the slaves, coupled with trouble with the nomads. With most freeborn Kossiar males already full-time army, they could barely handle the situation; now they've got the nomads pressing them from the east. The Chair's looking for allies."

"Why get mixed up in this Church thing? Church has no armies."

"There are more believers than you think. The Empty Lands support quite a few settlements of Smalls. They keep to themselves, but they grow stronger every moon. Even the Hents respect Church. If the Chair controls Church, he controls all believers and cloaks himself in a faith to recruit others."

Conway mulled that over, then, "If I were the Chair, I'd be more interested in Gan and Clas na Bale. Who else is going to keep these nomads from attacking Church Home?"

"The brotherhoods will defend it."

"How many men is that?"

"Perhaps three hundred." At Conway's obvious disappointment, Nalatan went on. "Remember, defending Church is our life. Every mountain, every rock, every blade of grass is our ally. The nomads have tested us before. So have the Hents. We've even had 'visits' from Kos."

"You think the Chair wants to keep us here because he believes we're spies?"

"My advice for the rest of you is, trust no one here."

"Trust?" Conway's mind flew back to the earlier conversation with Lanta. "I can't even understand my friends."

"You had a disagreement with Tate?"

"I was trying to discuss something with Lanta. She blistered me. For no reason."

"She's a gentle woman. You must have said something."

Biting back a retort, Conway whistled in the dogs. They came slowly, happily tired, and threw themselves down at his feet. Only then did he answer Nalatan. "Actually, I was asking her advice. I guess I expected her to be a little pleased to know how much I respect her opinions."

"Advice about what?"

"Nothing important."

"Well, there it is, then. She expects to be confided in, not condescended to. Women are like that. They know they're not as intelligent as we are, so they try to make up for it by being clever. They can be surprisingly observant."

Again, Conway was silent for a long time, contemplating the collision between this man and the fiery Tate. He sighed, then said, "You're in for some exciting experiences, my friend."

"More riddles." Nalatan grumped under his breath, reaching down to twist Mikka's ears. She panted and wagged her tail.

Conway said, "I'm off to bed. You?"

Nalatan straightened. "I'm staying outside awhile. There are things I want to think out."

"If one of the things is named Donnacee, you better start thinking from the very beginning. That's *my* advice to *you*."

Nalatan watched his friend approach the yawning, black maw of the castle door. Faint light from behind two archers' ports directly above the drawbridge created the image of slitted eyes. Someone moved a torch or lantern behind them. They gleamed brightly for a moment, as if Conway's movement had attracted the hungry attention of a slumbering beast. The entryway appeared to inhale the man and his dogs.

* * *

The Harvester moved away from the narrow window. Her eyes flashed in the light of the lantern in the Chair's hand. "Mindless dolts. They know nothing."

The Chair said, "Don't lie to me, Odeel. I watched you. You were intrigued."

"I compliment you on your observation. The deceased Seer of Seers was of Violet. Shortly after her lamented death, that abbey dispatched an emissary to contact some unknown person. I know she traveled north. It's my belief she contacted Sylah and arranged an alliance with her."

"This person made an alliance with a visionary and her rabble of three? Plus the boy; I forgot him." The Chair was sarcastically dubious.

The Harvester responded tartly. "I say she did, and it was her one prudent move. Fool that she was, the emissary took something of priceless importance as an identification token. I need that article. I *will* have it. Should Kossiars apprehend the emissary or discover her talisman, either must be handed over to me. I intend to be the new Sister Mother, and the talisman will help me consolidate my authority. As Sister Mother, I will intercede with the nomads and Moondance. Church Home is impregnable. Wouldn't it be worth an alliance to know that such a fortress was always available to you?"

"If I were sure of that . . ." The Chair's tone suggested more than his words.

"We could arrange a treaty. Secret, of course, for our mutual protection. I'd even be willing to include some words concerning Church's efforts to maintain good order among Kos' slave population."

The Chair pulled back. One eye tightened to a squint. "Mind yourself, Harvester. I would be disappointed to learn that you've been spying on us."

"There are no spies in Kos. Everyone knows that. The power of speech exists, however, as does the ability to hear and see. One looks and listens. There's restlessness out there. Everywhere."

"You've been misinformed."

"As you say. Things do get twisted. However, consider how eagerly the slaves would respond to Church if something dreadful—rumors of plague, for instance—came to Kos. Wouldn't it be natural for the Chair to assure that only tractable workers received treatment?"

Still fuming, the Chair answered stiffly. "My concerns are for real problems, not conjecture. The nomads are foremost. The

280

power of the Door may be the answer to them. I care nothing for your struggle with Sylah, but I care very much that I share in any discoveries that can benefit Kos. I must place all the pieces of the puzzle before I commit myself to any faction."

The Harvester made ready to leave. "I hope you have no 'place' in mind for me, Chair. I must control Sylah or any discoveries she makes. She is a sickness within Church's body. Disease is always burned. The Apocalypse Testament decrees it. Plan for her whatever you will. Make no place for me in your puzzle. I will not fit it."

"Too late." She checked her departure, spun to face him. His smile promised danger. "As perceptive as only you can be, Harvester, you should have noticed that your place is already determined. Here, beside me."

She made light of the statement, waggled a finger at him, and smiled. The gesture could have been playful. Or a dismissal.

She would have held the gesture and swallowed the smile, had she waited for his final words.

"Now hear this: You will remain in Kos so long as I feel it necessary. You will never again in your life be out of sight of me or my agents. Ever."

CHAPTER 49

As Conway and Tate walked across the courtyard the following morning, the Chair approached them. Bos and a pair of warmen shifted about nervously where the Chair positioned them out of earshot.

After exchanging greetings, the Chair said, "Would it be improper for me to ask why you both place such confidence in the success of Sylah's quest?" The characteristic rise and fall of the Kossiar speech pattern couldn't hide his intense curiosity.

Tate said, "We promised to help her. Win or lose."

"I assumed you were bound by tribal or religious formality. Are you simply friends, then?"

Conway said, "We think that's a good reason."

The Chair put up a defensive hand, smiling past it. "Please, no misunderstandings. My appreciation of friendship tends to be objective. I sacrificed such luxuries to take the Chair many years ago. And speaking of friends . . ." He indicated behind them. Tate and Conway turned to see Nalatan coming. Tate was impressed by the way the warrior smiled greeting for herself and Conway, then, without visibly altering that expression, managed to convey cold neutrality to the taller Chair.

Tate was suddenly aware how very alone and threatened Nalatan truly was. Sylah's decision to travel to Kos was a leap into danger for all of them, but for Nalatan it was outright exposure. Her glance went to Nalatan's hand, resting on the outsize handguard of the Kossiar sword he carried in lieu of his lost gear. She looked away quickly, not wanting to think of him drawing it.

The Chair said to Nalatan, "You dislike me. Why?"

Visibly surprised by the directness, Nalatan hesitated. His color rose. "Many reasons. When the people who trade come to the borders of Kos, they must trade on Kos' terms, or do without. My brotherhood has sent men to the Enemy Mountains to recruit fighters to defend Church Home, as is our rightful mission, and Kossiars have attacked us. Kos has never assisted us in our battles. Many travelers have entered Kos and failed to come out. Yet Kos admits no searchers, offers no explanations."

"Everything you say is true. We expect to profit from trade. Is that wrong? Do you allow anyone to recruit on the lands claimed by Church Home? If two groups of nomads squabble, do you rush to help whichever one asks? Do you allow my warmen to search your lands for those we believe have fled our customs or justice?"

"Kos ends at the crest of the Enemy Mountains. As for Kossiar custom, we know something of that."

"Territorial rights are something your leaders and I could discuss. I've requested such talks."

"You forgot to mention the slaves." Nalatan spoke as if pronouncing sentence.

It was the Chair's turn to color. Still, his manner was unruffled. "Our economy is our concern. As for the treatment of our slaves, most live better here than they did in their homelands."

Before Nalatan could respond, Tate interrupted. "However you defend slavery, we hate it."

"Many say hatred springs from ignorance."

Tate couldn't pretend dispassion any longer. "I'm ignorant about a lot of things, not about slavery. I'd die first. Take as many with me as I could."

The Chair smiled. "No one's going to enslave you here. You have my word. Anyhow, slaves only work. You're clearly a fighter, even though you're just as clearly a woman. Our women don't fight, and our warmen aren't slaves. You see, we wouldn't

282

know what to do with you. Whatever you did in Kos, you'd be free, I assure you. And very wealthy."

Tate was shocked by the clumsiness of the approach. Then she reconsidered. There was nothing haphazard about this man. He'd been direct with Nalatan because he was sure Nalatan would react best to that. The Chair was well aware that she and Conway placed friendship above wealth. Nevertheless, she was almost certain he'd made an offer. She decided to press. "We go where Sylah leads. Even if we could live where slavery's tolerated, there's nothing for us here."

"Still, it may happen that we can collaborate in some way."

Nalatan said, "My brotherhood forbids." He sent a surly glance at Tate.

The Chair said, "The brotherhoods provide dispensation for necessary acts that benefit the brotherhood and Church."

Shocked, Nalatan gaped. "You know our rules?"

"Kos has existed longer than the three brotherhoods. We're familiar with you." The Chair faced Tate again. "We'll talk again some time."

He walked away. Nalatan broke the heavy silence left behind. "It almost sounded like you were interested in his promises of wealth, Donnacee."

"I wondered what he'd offer, what he wanted. He's crafty. You see what he did? Dangled the bait, got me to bite at it, then left me to wonder about it. That's a bad man."

Nalatan continued to sulk. "He's a Kossiar."

Conway said, "Why do you hate him so intensely? It's almost a personal thing."

Uncomfortable, Nalatan tried to wave the question away. Conway and Tate refused to let him. Finally, he said, "Everything I've heard is rumors. Escaped slaves aren't likely to speak kindly of their owners."

"*Say* something," Tate demanded. "No more hints."

"Sacrifices. Battle sacrifices. Sacrifices to the sea. They kill slaves."

Conway said, "How can that be? Sylah said they supported Church, and Church doesn't allow that."

"It's custom. Old religion. That's what I've been told."

Tate heard them, but as from a distance. She looked around her. The hearty plants, the glowing flowers, all had seemed so lovely only moments before. Now they were repellent. A sense of decadence oozed through the carefully tended lushness. Impressive stone walls had become confining, oppressive. Even the spray of the fountain was changed, from the sound of laughter to the rattle of drear, chilling rain. A world that had smelled of danger, of exotic intrigue, was now a loathsome prison.

Sylah's voice broke her concentration. Tate hadn't heard her approach. "Bos says the Chair wants all of us to attend a ceremony. At the Gate."

"Why?" Tate's question was a snarl, left over from her earlier depression. Taken aback, Sylah could only stare.

Lanta, standing beside Sylah, answered in her stead. "Bos said it would help us understand Kos. That's all we know. What's wrong?"

Conway nudged Nalatan, and he repeated the tale of human sacrifice. Sylah shook her head vigorously. "You said it was all rumors. We'll ask the Chair; if it's true, he'll admit it."

Tate said, "We know they keep slaves. The field workers we saw on our way here weren't happy. The kids they assigned to us were scared witless. I believe Nalatan."

Sylah took Tate's hands. "No one feels more strongly about slavery than I do. Confronting the Chair won't help. Are we strong enough to overthrow him?" Reactions ranged from Conway's open amusement to Lanta's blank rejection of the question. Sylah continued, "Then we do as Church has always done. We work for betterment. We work quietly, constantly, with the weapon of truth. Agreed?"

Assent was grudging, but unanimous. They walked to their quarters, where Dodoy waited impatiently. The dogs greeted Tate and Conway joyously, eager to be out and moving.

At the nearby stable, the war-horses were almost as demonstrative as the dogs, kicking up their heels, tossing their heads. It was an impressive group that trotted out the door of the castle. Conway and Tate, weapons gleaming in the sun, flanked Sylah. The shining horses knew they were on display. They stepped high, snorting pride and power. The dogs, more purposeful, padded along outboard of their masters. Nalatan rode directly behind Sylah. Lanta trailed a bit behind and to the right, with Dodoy. Bos and a squad of warmen met them at the landward berm, trotting ahead to lead the way.

Passing through town, Tate was intrigued by the inhabitants. Many poured out of the buildings, obviously curious, but there was no animation in them. They stood silent, heads swiveling like mechanical things as the riders passed.

On the road leading west from the town, Bos bent inland at a fork. They followed a circuitous route to a slope overlooking the concrete fragment called the Gate. Due south of the viewpoint, huge sand dunes rose over what had once been the western limits of San Francisco. The sun, having passed its highest point, painted the western faces of the mounds a soft gold that accentuated the dark shadows on the inland sides.

They were much closer to the Gate itself now, only a hundred yards away. Details were clearer. Tate drew Conway aside. She pointed surreptitiously. "The landform's changed. There was a span, a small bridge over a draw, leading to the bridge pier. Now it's all filled in level with where the old highway used to be. Could these people do that?"

"Earthquake's my guess. They may have smoothed things out a bit, but they didn't build it. As you say, there's no sign of the old approach road, but the one that runs from the pier back into the brush and woods is impressive."

"Slave labor." Tate spat the words.

People crowded onto a ridge east of the Chair, clambering up onto the flattened promontory in quiet order. Their viewpoint was slightly lower than the top of the Gate, about fifty yards away; a narrow, deep gully separated them from it. Looking down at their arrival, Tate was reminded of herded livestock.

A man appeared from within the wooded area penetrated by the road that ended at the Gate. From face-shielding silver helmet to boots, he dazzled with mirror-polished metal plates sewn to blood-red skintight clothing. He proceeded to the very edge of the concrete, looking out over the narrow seaway. Opening a small bag in his left hand, he took out a silver chain, perhaps six feet long. There was a rectangular golden object at one end. Slowly, the man swung the chain and its attachment in a circle.

Lanta was the first to comment. "What's that noise? I don't like it." She hunched forward on her horse.

Conway said, "A bull-roarer. The wind makes the end piece vibrate. Simple."

Sylah glared fury at Bos. "A god-call. Shame! Church forbids. The Apocalypse Testament commands: 'That which pretends to speak to gods other than the One in All shall be destroyed. So also shall be destroyed those who commune with idols, false gods, false prophets, and all blasphemy.' That man can be cast out."

Bos was pointedly unconcerned. "The Chair exercises the voice of our fathers. The people like the old beliefs. Church has forgiven the Chair for generations, because the Chair unfailingly supports Church."

The hollow boom of the god-call swelled louder now, rising and falling.

Sylah's knuckles were bone white where she gripped the reins.

Tate, intent on Sylah and the near-hypnotic howl of the god-call, failed to notice the massive object approaching from the Chair's rear until it was almost in place. She was so startled she spoke without thinking. "A catapult!"

Bos corrected her, his expression suddenly shrewd. "Wallkiller. When Skipper's people were uniting the land, they used wallkillers. Now we tolerate no walls in Kos, and so there is only this one. What name did you call it?"

Trapped by her outburst, Tate looked to Conway for help. He made his question a demand. "What's a weapon doing here? You said this was a religious ceremony."

After a lingering suspicious look for Tate, Bos turned to Conway. "All will be clear. Watch." He indicated people filing through the brush that had hidden the Chair and the wallkiller. They followed the machine, which was propelled by men leaning into a long pole projecting from the rear of its carriage. The whole issue rolled on wheels as tall as a man.

The Chair continued to whirl the god-call. The squeal and groan of the wallkiller's progress joined with it to create eerie, discordant song.

The small crowd following the wallkiller crew was as gaudy as butterflies. Color leapt from rich, flowing robes and cloaks. Nevertheless, there was a subdued, hesitant manner in their progression. They made their way around the now-halted machine, forming into a loose knot between it and the bright circle of the god-call.

Bos chose that moment to indicate that Sylah's group should move down the slope, closing the distance between themselves and the Chair. They stopped about twenty-five yards away.

Conway pressed close to Tate. "What's going on?"

"Trebuchet, I think."

Conway goggled, mute, and Tate realized how confusing her answer must have been. She smiled apology. "Trebuchet. If I remember right, that's what they called the catapult that worked with weight on the end of the throwing arm. Simple stuff. What I can't figure out is why it's cocked. See that guy in the rear, with the maul? All he has to do is knock out that pin on the trigger and *whoosh*. The big rock up front drops, the long arm goes up, and there goes your missile. Only we don't have one."

The roar of the god-call subsided. The blur of the chain slowed.

Tate looked away, out toward the bay. While they'd been preoccupied, a veritable fleet of boats had materialized. Most were balancebars. There were several variant designs, including some large trimarans. Singlehulls added to the mix. One of the latter was the largest vessel by far. It featured a double bank of oars. All gave it plenty of sea room. A long, narrow pennant of blue, bisected lengthwise by a serpentine yellow line, snapped from a staff at the stern.

The Chair put the god-call back in its carrying bag. Holding it in both hands, he extended it toward a member of the crowd, who stepped forward to receive it.

Sylah's exclamation incorporated pain, disbelief, shame. One hand jerked to cover the round "O" of her mouth. The other pointed in accusation.

The Harvester took the small bag. She blended back into the group, her black figure overwhelmed in the surround of bright colors.

A second group approached the wallkiller's rear. Eight warmen—four in front, four in back—carried a box slung from two long poles on their shoulders.

Conway said, "An offering of some kind, I'll bet."

Tate nodded. "These people just now following the warmen must be the ones who donated it. They look like poor farmers; it's probably their crops that'll zoom out to sea."

The fancifully dressed gathering took a position to the right of the wallkiller. The eight carriers put down their load.

The newcomers Tate thought were farmers cowered. There were women as well as men, and children ranging from babes in arms to youngsters nearly grown. Males stood with heads bowed, so they looked out at the world through their eyebrows. Hands were clasped, fingers interlocked, tucked up against the stomach.

At the approach of the Chair, the shabbier group shrank in on itself.

Tate glanced away, down to the water. There were dozens of boats now. Slicing back and forth, they scarred the surface with white, curling wakes. The warming sun embraced the taut, multicolored sails. Even the dark waters seemed caught up in the excitement of the boats, rebounding sunbeams skyward in a myriad diamond lights.

The Chair's rolling voice reached up the hillside to the group, bringing Tate back to the more immediate scene. Distance and wind made the words indistinguishable. The tone was so formalized there was no suggestion of emotion. Nevertheless, the scruffy audience behind the wallkiller cringed as if whipped.

Bos spurred his horse into a full circle, so he faced Sylah's group. The squad of warmen circled behind him. They, too, turned their backs on the ceremony. The development made Tate edgy. She checked the sling of the wipe. From the corner of her eye she caught Conway doing the same thing. Faint metallic scraping behind her suggested Nalatan might be loosening his sword.

Clearing his throat, Bos said, "Today you voiced disapproval of slavery, and the Chair assured you that we are fair and just. These slaves at the wallkiller all belonged to one man. One of them killed the owner and his entire family, as well as two house slaves who threatened to reveal their plot. The Chair, in his mercy, is sparing their lives. Children will remain with their mothers."

"And fathers?" Sylah inquired softly.

"To be sold away. Such men are bad examples. Other fathers will be found."

The implications stunned Tate. Conway gripped her bicep, hard. "Hang on," he said, keeping his eyes on Bos. "I have a feeling this is going to get a lot worse, and there's nothing you can do about it. *Nothing.*"

Activity below drew their attention. The carriers took the lid from the box. Reaching inside. They lifted out something roughly round, covered in bright red cloth. It was a clumsy load. The carriers had trouble placing it in the wallkiller's netted missile basket. Their task done, all but one retreated to join the other warmen.

The man with the maul stepped up to the trigger device.

The Chair gestured at the warman still beside the basket, who responded by tugging at the red cloth. He whipped it away and flourished it like a banner.

The thing in the basket was a man, trussed so compactly the only thing that moved was his head. A gag of coarse rope split his face in a manic grin. Wild, terrified eyes spoke more truth. He tried to speak. The gag turned his terrified words to mad gabble.

"The poisoner," Bos said.

The sound of horns and shouting rose from the milling boats. Shark fins, dozens of them, ripped the water.

The Chair raised a hand, held it poised.

Tate said, "Don't do this. Don't. Don't."

Conway squeezed her arm.

The Chair dropped his hand. The prisoner wailed. The warman with the maul swung once. The trigger released. The massive

288

boulder plummeted, flinging up the long arm. The weight struck its stops with a horrendous crash. The arm hurled its burden.

A terrible silence fell across the watchers. The wind, unnoticed before, sighed through the grasses and shrubs of the hillside.

Then, keen as a knife, the scream slid back down the arc described by the hurtling man. The wind played with it.

The bundle soared out over the tossing waters. And fell. And fell.

A great noise of distant celebration greeted the strike and pluming splash of the body.

Past clenched teeth, Tate told Conway, "You can let go of my arm. I won't do anything. But I'll see him dead. I'll spit on his body, if it's the last thing I do."

Sylah turned to her. The normally beautiful countenance was fearsome in its flinty control. "Patience. And memory. Never forget, never hurry."

Sylah looked back at the Chair. He was walking back from the lip of the site. Stopping, he removed the silver helmet, the armor. Next he stripped off the boots and leggings, to stand dressed entirely in scarlet. His face was painted to match. Behind her, Sylah heard Tate's sharp intake of breath, her hoarse, awed comment. "Flayed. Like he was skinned alive."

Nalatan sneered. "Just another Kossiar lie. Red's their mourning color."

As if he'd heard, the Chair turned to look upward. His eyes found Sylah's. Blinking away that attempt at connection, she couldn't avoid his expression. It pulled her across the distance. Try as she might, she saw no hatred in him, no faintest sign of triumph. If it was a ruined face, it was a ruined nobility. If it was a cold face, it was frozen by inescapable fate. Whatever he'd been required to do, humanity stirred behind his fixed features.

But was she seeing warning? Pain? Plea?

Sylah heeled Copper, spun him roughly away from the haunting, demanding features. Her hands juggled the reins. Fear washed through her, wave after wave, crashing against her reason.

Not fear of the office of the Chair, nor of the man who held that office.

She feared the woman who could look at that man and see what might have been.

CHAPTER 50

The blue green bay glowed in the sun of a soft afternoon. The flashing waters bore their burden of sleek sailboats with sparkling amusement. The scene contradicted the dour attitude of Sylah's group.

Bos and his warmen forged a clear path for them through the returning spectators. Leaning close to Sylah, Lanta said, "Remember how the crowds cheered when Altanar's protectors whipped someone in Ola? I expected the same bloodthirsty, mindless excitement here. These people cheered at the execution, but there's something like worry among them, and yet the executed man just murdered a whole family. I don't understand."

Sylah raised her chin. "I'm going to have some answers." Copper leapt ahead at her urging, quickly overtaking a family walking beside the road. "Hello!" she said to the surprised people. "May I ask a question?"

Leaping as if stung, the father clutched his wife to him with one arm. With the other hand he reached to pull a small boy against him. Simultaneously, both parents yelled at the other three children. Like obedient chicks, two girls and another boy sprinted to get behind the parents. Wide eyes stared up at Sylah.

Before Sylah could speak again, Bos and the squad were around her and the family. The father babbled at the warmen. "No one spoke to her. We called the children. No one said a word to her. Not one." The melodic Kossiar speech made his protest a whine of fear.

Bos let the family watch his hand lovingly progress up the scabbard of his sword to rest on the hilt. He said, "I know what was said. And what wasn't. Be glad I was close." A movement of his head sent the family hurrying away. A boy in a green blouse lagged, filling his eyes with Sylah. The mother reached back for his collar and yanked him along.

Sylah said, "You won't keep your people isolated forever."

"Yes we will. We have everything we need. We trade for whatever else we want. We use you un—you foreigners. When it suits us." He spurred his horse into a fast trot, signaling his troops to follow.

When the escort had resumed its lead position, Tate said, "Everyone else noticed the little mistake?"

Lanta said, "He started to call us un-something."

Nalatan answered Lanta; he looked at Tate. "The word they use for the rest of us is *unpeople*."

By then, the group was passing through Harbor to the sound of horse hooves clopping on the packed-earth street. Mournful music brought the riders' heads up, seeking. Bos signaled the escort. The rear warmen closed up, while the lead element dropped back. With Sylah's group more tightly enclosed, they moved forward at a quicker pace.

The singing voices multiplied, coming from all around. Tate looked to Sylah. She spoke in awe. "Harmony. Where are they?"

Conway overheard. "They're everywhere. Women's voices. And children. It's lovely. Heartbreaking."

A voice rose in harsh anger from a building beside them. The whistle and slash of a whip cut across the minor-key melody. Defiant, the scream of pain that followed struck a perfect blend with the tightly bound voices of the invisible chorus. Stark, pure, it hung in the air.

The whip cracked again. The note crumbled. Throughout the town, the song staggered, faded away.

Karda howled.

Conway reined to a stop, glaring at the warmen, daring them. Twice the hound sent his own song across the silence of the town. With a look at his master, the dog appeared to signal his satisfaction.

The rest of the ride back to the fort was carried out in thoughtful silence.

With the horses stabled and the dogs unhappily confined to the communal sleeping room, the group wandered into the courtyard. A sharp line of shade cut across the enclosed area, irresistibly shaving away the day. While the adults continued to speculate about departure, Dodoy found himself a playmate. Smaller and younger, the other boy was amusing himself with a top. In minutes, Dodoy learned how to wrap the string and hurl the top to make it spin. Their laughter was ironic background to the adults' conversation.

Sylah said, "The Harvester debased Church as well as herself in order to gain the Chair's favor. I intend to tell him we'll leave the day after tomorrow."

Tate said, "Why not in the morning? The sooner the better, Sylah."

Nalatan said, "Supplies. No one's going to sell us anything until we're clear of Kos. And I need a good smith; I'm sick of this clumsy sword. I may need more than two days."

"I want out of here." A muscle twitched in Tate's jaw. "You can make do with your sword."

Stubbornly, Nalatan shook his head. "Without the right equipment, I may not do so well in my next fight. I stay here until my needs are met."

"We'll miss you." Tate sent him a flashing look of dismissal, then turned her back.

Before anyone could respond, Bos' strange whistle shrilled. Dodoy spotted him on the third-floor balcony and pointed, shouting. When the piping notes trailed off, Bos shouted down. "Hear this! The Chair requires his guests lay up to flagplot. The Chair requires his guests lay up to flagplot." He disappeared through the door behind him.

Sylah blinked, round-eyed. "What's he mean? 'Lay up'? 'Flagplot'?"

With a nervous look for Conway, Tate said, "I think I know what he means. I think we're supposed to go up to that room where we were yesterday."

Sylah nodded. "What strange words. What etiquette allows a host to 'require' anything of his 'guests'?"

Conway grinned at Tate. " 'Curiouser and curiouser,' " he muttered, as Tate signaled Dodoy to hurry. To Conway, she said, "You recognized the old Navy jargon? Flagplot was where the admiral ran things, and only swabbies talked about laying up, laying aft, and all that stuff. Whoever this Skipper was, he made a mark. Must have been a good man."

Conway affected shock. "Coming from a Marine, that's akin to sainthood. Saint Skipper. That'll ring bells at Church Home."

Tate jabbed him in the ribs and was rewarded with an anguished yelp. She was still smug when they caught up to the others.

Standing spread-legged against the trembling intensity of the multicolored shards, the Chair was still garbed in tight scarlet. He appeared to hover, flamelike.

Conway noted Bos, Gatro, and a squad of warmen at the far end of the room.

Slaves placed seats in a semicircle facing the raised dais. Each one, before leaving, paused in front of the Chair, pulling open his jacket and baring his chest before hurrying to the door. Once

292

there, each faced the Chair again, dropped to all fours, and inched backward. Only when out did they stand and trot off.

The group waited in rigid silence until the last footsteps slapped down the hall.

Dodoy shattered the air of smothered outrage with a loud giggle. Pointing at the emptied door, he said, "That was funny. What if someone was standing outside there with a spear pointed at their bottoms? Why'd they do like that?"

Patiently, the Chair answered, "A slave bares his chest to show his life belongs to me. They fall to the floor when they leave to show thanks because I let them live."

Dodoy frowned. "I was a slave. I didn't like it."

"Not being free is terrible."

"Do you have many slaves? Are you going to make us slaves?"

The Chair's laughter was deep, pleasant. "Never. Nor will anyone else as long as I can prevent it. You're my guests." He sobered then, turning to the adults. "Today you approached some of my people, a family. Gatro warned you long ago; if they'd spoken to you, my warmen would have been forced to report it. My duty is to order the execution of any who speak to you. None of us want that."

Sylah said, "You executed a man today."

"A poisoner who slaughtered a family? He deserved to die."

"Did he deserve to be a slave?"

Beads of sweat lifted on the Chair's forehead. Leftover traces of the red face paint caught in them, shining pink, like the residue of washed blood. Rasping, he said, "Fate decrees who is free and who is not. Not even your little Seer knows all tomorrows. The man wasn't executed for struggling to be free. He was punished for murdering innocents."

"And if he'd only murdered his owner, and not the others?"

Shaking, fists clenched, the Chair battled with himself. Bunched muscles strained against the red-glowing cloth. He closed his eyes, raised his head slowly, teeth clenched.

It was an image of violent death, and Sylah leaned forward, wanting to rush to him. Lanta held her arm, but she, too, was bent forward, prepared to help.

The Chair bellowed, a sound that was half shout, half scream. It tumbled over itself in hammering echoes. Bos, Gatro, and the warmen ran forward.

When the Chair quieted, he dropped his chin almost to his chest, glaring out at the group from beneath brows locked in a black, exhausted frown. A gesture sent his men back where they'd come from. The Chair's rough breathing scraped across bleak silence. Painfully, he turned his head to focus on each of them, a wooden, nonhuman motion. He returned to Sylah.

"You." He said it as disbelief, as accusation.

And as something more.

So soft the sound, Sylah wondered if she'd truly heard a word, or if that penetrating look forced her to know it existed.

Inappropriately, she had a sudden memory of repairing a broken skull, lifting shattered bone and torn membrane to reveal the pulsing, living brain.

The vision melted as the Chair said, "I can't excuse my people from their laws or me from my duty. In order to protect all of us, I've decided the Church women will stay here in the castle. You'll be restricted as Church is traditionally restricted." He straightened as he spoke, color and control returning to normal. "The others will go to Trader Island. The Priestesses may visit back and forth, but must never leave the island or the fort."

Conway shrugged the wipe free of his shoulder, letting it drop to waiting hands. With the muzzle pointed up at the juncture of the Chair's throat and jaw, he said, "We won't be prisoners."

Tate and Nalatan whirled to face the onrushing Bos and the warmen guards. The wipe clattered menace as Tate jacked a round into the chamber and slipped the safety. Nalatan's bare sword swayed from side to side.

"Stop!" Sylah reached to depress Conway's weapon. For a long moment he resisted, eyes locked on the Chair's. The sound of the advancing guards slowed, stopped. Conway let Sylah push the weapon down.

Sylah said, "We came to Kos to build a friendship. I saw the Harvester prostitute Church by participating in your pagan ceremony. Next, because of my innocent, if foolish, impulse, you seek to divide us, make us prisoners. Let us go. If you don't, I won't overrule my friends. We'll fight for our freedom."

The Chair whirled, presenting his back, unprotected. He took the two steps to his throne and sat down. When he raised his face to look at them all again, he was unspeakably weary. Where his voice had been like rending metal before, now it was sere, a broken branch wearing itself away against stone. "Even the child speaks of freedom as if it had substance, as if it were a matter of color, for instance, as she's black and we're white." Intent on his point, he failed to notice Tate's dangerous tensing. He went on, addressing Sylah. "The man executed today wasn't alone; other slaves died, as well. Not so ceremoniously, but they're just as

294

dead. If I'm not harsh, if I fail to stop what's happening, we'll have revolt, blood beyond measure. I must restore balance and order to gradually eliminate all slave ownership. If I move too hastily, I destroy our entire society. The Empty Lands to the north are lush, ripe for settlement. But the colonization must be done in an orderly manner. I need time."

Sylah nodded. "You've said nothing about treating us as prisoners."

"Not prisoners. Restricted. It's our way, applicable to all un—strangers. Also, the Enemy Mountains have become a refuge for many escaped slaves. They have no fear of Church's mortality edict, no fear of dying. I can't afford a sufficient escort to assure your safety."

"None of that's your concern. I seek the Door. We will go where that search takes us."

"You." Once more, the single word, so gently soft, so arrow-sure into the deepest center of her being.

"Bos!" The chair barked the name. "Send the others out. You go to the far wall. There's no danger."

When the foot-dragging departure was complete, the Chair said, "Will you send your friends away? I have something to say to you. Alone."

"Forget it." Conway raised the muzzle of the wipe. The Chair watched Sylah. A muscle jerked at his jawline, but his eyes never wavered.

Sylah touched Conway's arm. She raised her voice, that the others would hear. "Please. I trust him."

Once her friends were at the opposite end of the room, the Chair stepped down from the dais. He still towered over Sylah. He said, "You claw my pride like a she-leopard, and I feel only admiration for you. Can't you understand that my reasons for trying to keep you here are more than political?" At her attempted protest, he held up a peremptory hand, continuing. "There's a far more vital reason for you to stay. For just a while longer."

Warily, Sylah waited.

The Chair inclined almost imperceptibly closer. "I must show you." He raised his head to nod at Bos, then turned away from her. For some reason, Sylah saw the Chair's return to the throne as a retreat.

At the sound of footsteps, Sylah half turned. Bos led a quartet of young women through the central door of the long room. The woman immediately behind him wore a full-sleeved flowing one-piece gown. The pattern was of green triangles on a white back-

295

ground, the widest figures at the bottom, rising in decreasing sizes to mere points at the neckline. The effect, when she walked, was of shimmering ice and water. Her hair was piled high on her head.

She was beautiful. And very pregnant.

The women behind her wore similar dress, but theirs lacked the length of train.

Facing the Chair once more, Sylah raised her eyebrows in silent question.

The Chair said, "My wife, Yasmaleeya. As you can see, she's expecting. Very soon. There are difficulties." By that time, the woman was beside Sylah. After a sidelong glance and tentative smile for Sylah, Yasmaleeya looked up to her husband. Slowly, awkwardly, she sank to her knees, bent forward to place her palms on the floor. Grunting and puffing, she leaned to touch her forehead between her hands. Sylah moved to help, but a warning hiss from Bos stopped her. Yasmaleeya completed her supplication and rose, red-faced. A sheen of perspiration coated her forehead and upper lip.

After nodding absently to his wife, the Chair spoke to Sylah. "The Harvester tells me you have secrets to maintain woman and child. My wife requires you. She was selected to bear my son and heir, as was her sister before her. The sister died in childbirth. The child died, as well. Fortunately, it was a girl."

Overriding the Chair's wanton disregard for innocent lives lost, Sylah's mind seized on what was being required of her. Midwifery was part of her learning, but there were no secrets. What was known to one Healer was shared by all. It was a primary law of Church. This was the Harvester's hand, subtly accusing a sister of magic. That alone was deadly. But this was worse. Now the Chair would blame no one but Sylah if the delivery was a failure; he'd believe magic failed, not Church.

The Harvester had stripped her enemy's armor.

Sylah mentally phrased protest, then reconsidered. Denial would be seen as evasion, and gain nothing. A glance at the girl reaffirmed Sylah's first impression; Yasmaleeya was healthy. Sturdy, in fact. Now, however, she stood with hands clasped on her swollen stomach, huge blue eyes fastened on her husband with a worshipful awe that made Sylah's skin crawl.

Sylah heard the words again: *What must be borne, grasp.*

"I have no secrets. I have knowledge and caring. Yasmaleeya will be my patient and I will be her friend. Her child, male *or* female, will receive every care."

The Chair bent forward. "Bos, tell her our custom." He continued to stare into Sylah's eyes as Bos' insinuating voice came from behind. "The bearer of the Chair's son is chosen by the Crew. If the bearer fails to produce a male child, a second bearer will be selected. Children must be correct in all regards. Two incorrect children will be considered grounds for beaching the Chair."

" 'Incorrect'? 'Beaching'? What are these words?" Sylah demanded.

Bos said, "Incorrect means what it says, Priestess. Bring me an acceptable child. Pray to the One in All that you do, and that this bearer lives."

When Sylah rounded on the Chair, he was gone. Seeking Bos, she spun again. He was waiting, grinning. "Mighty Priestess, whose 'orders' are no whim. This woman has no chance. Her child will never breathe. You'll personally learn about beaching." Pushing his way past the other three women, he left, sneering, waving jauntily at Sylah's friends.

Sylah lifted Yasmaleeya's chin and looked into the teary blue eyes. The girl said, "He should have told you about the witch-wife."

Sylah said, "A non-Church midwife? You have one? I can talk to her?"

Yasmaleeya turned away, looked skyward, gusted a whistling, exaggerated sigh. "She and her family were poisoned. You saw the slave who did it executed." Suddenly Yasmaleeya turned, clutched Sylah's shoulders. "Everyone says my baby's cursed. The Harvester says you have magic."

Sylah tried to deny this blasphemy, to ask the myriad questions demanding answers. Forestalling her, Yasmaleeya fell into Sylah's arms, sobbing aloud. "The witch-wife said I'll die, Priestess. I don't want to die, I don't want my child to die. If you don't save us, you'll die, too."

CHAPTER 51

Standing on the dock, soothing the horses, Conway, Tate, and Nalatan exchanged speculative stares with the idlers watching from the landward end. The handlers of the cargo boat that landed them on the island were already casting off mooring lines. Among themselves, the three adult passengers easily agreed that the boat's crew were the shabbiest Kossiars they'd ever seen. Even so, the boatmen openly scorned the inhabitants of the island. The attitude couldn't completely hide the taint of fear.

Dodoy crowded against Tate's back, peering around her nervously. She kept a hand on his head. To her two companions, she said, "Talk about jumping to conclusions," and when they turned to her for explanation, she jerked her chin at the men ashore. "All morning I was feeling sorry for Sylah and Lanta, but look at this mess of cutthroat slugs we've got to deal with."

Nalatan said, "My master once told me that for every honest ship that comes here, ten others are pirates. The worst are the Skan."

Tate said, "We know the Skan. We didn't get along."

Dodoy said, "I want to go back to the castle. These are bad men. They'll steal me. I'm afraid."

Tate squatted beside him. "Stay close to one of us all the time, you hear? No one's going to bother you."

"Let's go," Conway said. "I'm tired of being entertainment. I'm hungry, too."

Tate laughed. "I thought the ride on the cargo boat ruined your appetite forever."

"Don't be cute." Conway made a sour face and started off the dock. The adults each led a riding horse and a packhorse. Dodoy led Sylah's Copper. The dogs trooped along beside their masters.

The loungers watched them come, exchanging comments, pointing. Tate was an item. Conway started to drop back to be closer, then noticed Nalatan already beside her. Conway smothered a smile at the contrast between Tate's affected nonchalance and Nalatan's almost eager truculence.

Taking the initiative, Conway spoke to the men. "We need a place to stay, where we can stable our horses." The man he addressed sat on a large keg, his back against a stack of baled wildcow hides. He wore full, homespun wool trousers, gathered at the ankle, and a quilted shirt. The shirt had been bright once. Now it was faded and torn. Like his companions, he wore a small copper hand dangling from a greasy neckband. His most striking item of adornment was a leather belt about four inches wide that ran diagonally from left shoulder to right hip. The buckle was a massive brass square. Two brass and leather scabbards above it held bone-handled knives. If the blades actually filled the scabbards, Conway decided, they'd qualify as short swords.

With slow deliberation, the man turned away to inspect Tate. "Heard about her. Which one of you she belong to?"

Tate said, "Don't let your mouth overload your head, fool. I'm in no mood to put up with trash." She edged even with Conway. Her pistol was in her hand, muzzle down.

The man turned red. Still seated, he straightened, threatening. "Woman, remember your place."

The explosion of the pistol sent men falling all over each other and gulls shrieking for the sky. Tate's round blasted into the wooden keg between the man's knees. Full of liquid, unable to confine the kinetic energy of the bullet, the keg did the only thing it could do: blew up. The force dissipated sideways and downward was of no consequence, except to send staves skipping about that knocked over the stacked bales of hides. That energy which fled upward hammered the keg's lid against the seated man's posterior. Suddenly aloft, arms awhirl in simulated flight, he described a short, blunt arc, ending with his face burrowed into the rough gravel. Tate's pistol remained fixed on the man while he scrambled to his feet. Whatever menace he'd originally projected was now hopelessly shattered by his behavior—dancing wildly, with both hands clasped to his hindquarters—and the tiny bits of gravel protruding from his face. Having to spit out additional small stones and debris further dented his prestige. Sputtering violently, he backed away until several of his friends recovered their wits and rushed to take his arms and lead him off.

Obviously impressed by the pistol, the other men were far from cowed. One said, "That was woman's stupidity. You made enemies. None of us'll forget."

"See that you don't," Tate said. The pistol centered on the man's middle. He stepped backward.

Swinging into the saddle, calling his dogs to position, Conway said to Nalatan, "The road parallels the shoreline. I think I saw signs of a community on the west end. I say we go right."

"As good a choice as any," Nalatan said. Tate agreed with a nod. Boosting Dodoy into his saddle, she ordered Tanno and Oshu to guard his flanks. Slowly, reluctantly, they left her to take position.

The dock loungers watched them go without comment.

Wagon wheel ruts created a high-crowned gash of a road a few yards inland from the dock, where it split into east and west routes. Each fork disappeared into heavy forest.

Out of hearing of the dock group, Conway turned to Tate. "That was some pretty strong overacting back there."

"Not all acting. I'm sick of hearing women—meaning me—put down all the time. I don't like some thick-witted toad assuming I 'belong' to someone. And I've got a feeling we ought to impress a few folks. The word about Mr. Hospitality back there'll get around. It'll get back to the Chair, too. I want him to know we can bite, if we have to."

Nalatan said, "I've been curious about the lightning weapons. Very impressive. Noisy, though. How do you get the thunder inside something so small?"

"It's a long story." Tate waved a languid hand. For Conway, she rolled her eyes. Leaning toward him, she whispered, "You realize that's the first time I've ever fired that damn thing? I wasn't even sure it'd work."

Nalatan saw the aside, even if he couldn't hear it. He was beginning to look offended. Looking over Tate's head at him, Conway smiled broadly. "Isn't she wonderful? Always thinking, this girl." The cloying sweetness of it stuck to his tongue.

Moments later, all three adults voiced surprise at the sudden appearance of triangular, head-high buildings among the trees. Bales, baskets, crates, and sacks filled them. Armed guards in pairs patrolled the lanes between the shingled sides. Other guards, armed with bows and arrows, manned boxes high in the trees.

Tate said, "Can you believe all this stuff? Look, that sack; it's leaking. I'll bet that's salt. And there—furs! And sulfur." She sniffed. Her eyes widened. "I smell oranges. Oranges. And almonds; that's got to be almonds."

Nalatan was more composed. "Everything anyone makes, from Nion and your own north country to the lands south of the Hents and east to the nomads, Kos trades. Any ship that wishes to trade with Kos must come to this island."

"How do you know all this?" Tate asked. "Do your people do business with Kos?" They were passing the last of the warehouses.

"Never. There are trading posts in the Enemy Mountains, but we don't deal with them. What we know of Kos we learned from people fleeing the place."

"Slaves?"

"And some freemen." Nalatan looked a bit uncomfortable, but continued. "Most were Moondance converts. I didn't want to say anything to Sylah and Lanta, but Moondance steadily gains popularity here, especially to the east. Many small landholders and artisans feel the big merchants and farmers of Kos fatten at their expense. Moondance promises that all will share all things. Desperate men believe desperate solutions."

They rode on in silence for a short while, and then, after a sharp bend in the route, the forest ended. A large flock of sheep cropped a meadow extending before them. The crowned road arrowed directly at a cluster of buildings. All shapes and sizes, they seemed to have been slapped together without measurements, and in a terrible hurry. Windows were rough rectangles, with translucent hide tacked over them. One door slatted in the breeze, hanging drunkenly from its single remaining hinge. Chimneys seemed to have a universal urge to either escape from the sides of buildings or topple over onto the slap-shingled roofs. Litter, ground into a homogenized, noisome mass, almost filled the ruts gouged by wagon wheels.

There was no sign of human life.

A dog barked. Another, farther away, answered.

The war dogs perked up, cocking, twisting heads to locate this latest interesting development.

The group advanced on the eerily silent settlement. As they reached the first buildings, they heard the noise, an excited rumbling. It seemed to come from the forest on the right of the houses. Tate jerked her thumb at one place as they passed. Ceramic bottles on strings hung from a horizontal bar extending over the doorway. A smell of sour beer drifted out at the riders. Wincing, Tate noticed the windows on the second floor. "That's got to be the inn," she said, and groaned, holding her nose. "We'll be better off camping."

Conway said. "Is that noise voices? We ought to check it out."

Riding toward the sound, Conway sensed a strange passion in it. He noticed Tate edge closer to Dodoy. The boy, too, was tense, but he avoided Tate's approach. Without appearing to, Dodoy slowed his horse, drifting backward at the same rate as Tate, so the distance never closed. Meanwhile, his small, narrow head was turning this way, then that, the way the dogs had twisted as they tried to locate the barking. Conway had the feeling Dodoy was *reading* the sound, as though it told him things the rest of them couldn't know.

A few minutes more, and they were looking at the source of the noise. A hillside sloping to the sea provided a rough amphitheater. Nearly a hundred men in a wild variety of costume sat among the trees at the forest's edge, intent on two men dueling on the beach. One man leaned on a narrow, dark shield, its butt end buried in the sand. In his left hand, he held a long, slim sword. A gory slash across the left side of his face had cost him the vision in that eye. The good one was dull, fading, but it held fast on the other man, who circled toward the blind side.

The second man wore a small, round shield strapped to each of

301

his arms. His left hand, encased in a basket hilt, grasped a short stabbing knife. The right swung a vicious little axe on a chain. It whirled constantly, darting toward the wounded man, then away, coming from one direction, then another.

The injured man dodged the axe. He used his sword to parry the stabbing knife.

The injured man sagged. Once, twice, the axe seemed certain to end his weary struggle. Each time he avoided it by the smallest of measurements. Then he fell. On his knees, he clutched the shield with both hands, the sword falling sideways in a grasp gone limp. The axe sizzled a song of triumph at the end of its chain, dove at the exposed bowed head. At the last instant, the wounded man slumped backward, which pulled his head behind the shield. The axe dug harmlessly into the sand. The chain went momentarily slack. It jerked clumsily when pulled back into the air.

That was when the wounded man lurched upright and threw the handful of sand into his opponent's eyes. Before anyone quite realized what was happening, the long, slim sword was past the bright stabbing knife, between the twin shields, and into the pit of the axeman's stomach. The dark, narrow shield—suddenly firmly gripped—erupted from the sand. It drove into the axeman's chin, sending him into a knock-kneed, staggering retreat. The sword pulled free, dripping red. The one-eyed man lunged forward. Again, the sword was in his enemy, and then, horribly, extending from the man's back.

The wicked little axe hit the limit of its chain. Nerveless fingers failed to check it. Sparkling, spinning, it fled up the beach, falling unnoticed to the sand.

Yanking the long sword free, its owner poised to strike again.

The stunned silence of the audience broke in a rising mumble of surprise.

The axeman dropped his arms to his sides, stared confusedly at the insignificant-appearing puncture marks just under his rib cage.

The swordsman was already knee-deep in the cleansing sea before the dying axe-wielder swayed one last time and dropped on his back.

The victor never saw. He was too busy sluicing his wounds.

A single voice cheered. Others joined in. The whole audience rose and ran to the beach, some to inspect the dead man, others to congratulate the winner. They milled in happy, sated confusion until someone spotted the riders at the top of the hill. A shouted exclamation, and the crowd was still, looking up. Finally someone challenged.

"Who are you, and what right have you to be here?"

"We were sent here," Conway answered. "The Chair ordered it."

"Sailors." The tone made it clear the definition wasn't a compliment. A man with a grizzled beard stepped free of the crowd. He wore a leather apron that covered him from the top of his chest down past his knees, and a floppy, round leather hat with the general shape of a soggy pancake. "You're not allowed to linger on landward side. You know the rules. What's the matter with the one in the middle? Are you burned?"

Tate made a growling sound, and Conway reached to grab her wrist as she shrugged the wipe off her shoulder. She twisted free, glaring at Conway, then answered the man herself. "No burns, old man. This is me, the way I am."

Nodding satisfaction, the man spoke as he advanced toward them. The crowd followed. "We've heard of you. The Black Lightning. White Thunder. Both of you guards to the Flower, the Priestess Church fears. You'd be Nalatan, the warrior monk. And the brat's the one stole from the Skan by the Black Lightning."

"Dodoy's not stolen. I fought for him. And won." The bearded man was directly in front now, and Tate leaned forward on her mount to glare down her nose at him. Her dogs edged forward to stand just by the horse's forelegs, the order to guard Dodoy secondary to the perceived threat to Tate.

The beard moved. The man might have been smiling. "Witchcraft. No woman outfights a Skan sea fighter. Witchwork. Doesn't count. Not fair."

"It was fair." Tate bristled all the more.

The man was amusedly disbelieving. He shook his head. "Don't care. No liking for Skan here. Feed them all to the crabs, suit us fine. Bad people."

Tate's teeth ground audibly. She edged her horse forward and slapped her sword. At its rattle, the dogs growled eagerly. The bearded man's eyes darted to them, then back to Tate. She said, "I stuck that fat pig. There was no magic."

"We heard your sword fell into the sea. You were dead. The sea woke you, put your sword back in your hand. You rose up in the air, stabbed him. Everybody saw." Suddenly, he stopped. He tilted his head to the side, looked at Tate from the corner of his eyes. "Thought I heard a noise a while ago. Fight was just started. You two? Lightning weapons?"

"About a dozen of your people met us at the dock. One of them insulted."

"What'd he look like?"

Tate described him. At the mention of the copper hand, the man interrupted. "He dead?"

"No."

The man shook his head, spat. "Too bad. Not us. Sailors." He half turned to the crowd, pointed at a man. "You heard, Ellum. Take twenty-five men. Get the sailors back to their side of the island." Facing Tate again, he tapped his chest with a forefinger. "Name's Helstar. Smith to the island."

Conway elected to use the Dog People's formal greeting style he'd learned from Gan and Clas. "I know you, Helstar. I'm Matt Conway." Tate followed Conway's example. Nalatan had his own mannerism. He bent his torso and straightened instantly, a swift bow. Then he said, "We meet as friends. My name is Nalatan, of the First Star brotherhood, and I am no man's servant."

While Tate and Conway stared, surprised, at this heretofore-unobserved formality from Nalatan, Helstar said, "Come. Fight's over. We'll eat and drink."

Falling in behind Helstar, Conway said, "We never saw you do an introduction like that before. Where'd that come from? And what's a First Star? You never said a word to me about that. You're beginning to irritate me, you and your secrets."

Nalatan chuckled. "What other secrets are *you* hiding? Anyhow, the greeting's our way. There was never a need to use it, or the name of my brotherhood, until now. That's not important. What's puzzling me is this crowd. If they're not sailors, who are they?"

Conway snorted. "We'll find out soon enough." He reined up, dropped back to allow Tate and Nalatan to ride side by side. He looked over his shoulder, wanting a better look at the crowd. A movement just at the edge of his vision piqued his curiosity. By the time he turned completely around to look over the other shoulder, Dodoy was fumbling at his saddlebag. Far off the path, outside the limit of the crowd, the boy was stuffing away the vicious little chain axe.

CHAPTER 52

Tate was right.

The ramshackle building that smelled like a dirty tavern was exactly that. On the inside, the stink took on stomach-churning proportions. That was why she and her friends sat behind the building, elbows parked on a thick-timbered trestle table, drinking surprisingly good beer. Slabs cut from a warm loaf of fresh bread filled a wooden platter. For a spread, they had a tub of pale, creamy butter, set in a larger tub of cold spring water.

A large crowd, including the shy women who'd remained hidden until allowed out of their houses, surrounded the table at a respectful distance, content to watch these amazing strangers eat and drink with one of their own. Children dashed about, shouting, fighting, doing their best to attract attention. Dodoy watched them with polished disdain.

Helstar tapped Conway's forearm. "I asked if they told you anything about the island," Helstar said.

Conway said, "Only that it was a place where all strangers to Kos live. Where are you from?"

Instead of answering, Helstar played to the crowd, turning around, winking, mugging. Everyone laughed uproariously. Helstar swung his arm in a gesture of inclusion. "All of us are Kossiars. Criminals. Some counterfeiters, a few pirates. Not many pirates live to reach here. A few murderers. Loan defaulters. Some assaulters—have to make a habit of that to be sent to the island. Mostly thieves, though. Ordinary."

"The only strangers are the sailors, then? This is really a prison island?"

"Not exactly. Traders and their gangs, over to south and west. They live there. Kossiars live here. We do business with the unpeople. Me, a smith. Him, standing there, a tanner. A leatherworker. There's another. Women cook, sew, weave. Over there's a carpenter. So on."

Tate asked, "Criminals from Kos can work here, is that it?"

Helstar straightened, lifted his chin and a mug of beer, simultaneously. "The best criminals. We like a person, they're welcome. Got to have a trade. Good character. Can't have just anyone. Families. Little children. Have to think of them."

Softly, Nalatan said, "You refuse some?"

"Of course. Bad people. Ones who steal from friends, beat up all their neighbors, kill someone without a good reason. Low characters. We turn them down. Off they go."

"Off?" Tate repeated.

"Off the wallkiller. Off to the slave list. Chair sells most. If we choose them, they live here. Better'n slavery. Better'n the wallkiller. Whooo!" He drew an arc in the air with his fist, ham-

305

mered the tabletop, bounced the utensils. The crowd howled merriment.

"The supplies we passed belong to the Traders?" Conway asked.

"Exactly. Six traders. Each one has a hawn. You know that word?"

Conway shook his head. Helstar went on. "Hawn's like a Lance. Sees that what the Trader wants done gets done. Toughest men around. Hawns control the gangs."

Tate said, "Who are the gangs?"

Helstar grimaced. "Each Trader has a gang. Twenty men. No more. Protects his house, his goods. Killers, all. Worse'n sailors."

"Uh-oh." Tate's comment expressed the concern immediately visible in the faces of her male companions.

Helstar caught it, as well. His short laugh was bitter. "Fight you saw? Gang man, him with the axe. Wanted Luro's woman. Luro's the one that won. One of us." Suddenly confiding, Helstar leaned across the table. "Lots of coin here. More trade stuff than the Chair could use. Those lightning weapons? You and us workers? Burn the gangs, take the goods, get the sailors to join up with us. Up the coast, river port. Free and easy. Lots of Smalls. Don't show themselves much, but they're there. Slaves. Good living."

Tate said, "We'll think about it. You sure have some good ideas."

Helstar downed his beer in one long swallow, slammed the mug down on the table. "Why I'm here. Thief. Think big. Even robbed Crew."

Nalatan asked, "How many Crew are there?"

"Don't know. Maybe a hundred."

"They run Kos?"

"Right. Warmen all belong to the Chair, but all warmen got families living where Crew people own the land. Balance. Everybody afraid of everybody else."

Conway said, "We're going to have to meet these Traders. What'll happen if the Chair finds us living with you, instead of them?"

The entire crowd exploded into wild laughter, Helstar right along with them. "They didn't tell you nothing, did they?" Helstar's question fought through amusement. "Lambs to wolves. No outsider lives with Traders. Don't trust no one to step inside fancy homes, much less to stay. Sailors won't have you, 'less you want to pirate. Even so, if they try to take you off island, and patrol catches them—zip, right up to the wallkiller, all of you. Big

306

day. Celebration. Stay with us? Look around. Everyone here already counting your money, pricing you for the slavers. 'Less you join us, help us."

Tate smiled sweetly. "And if we do say we'll help you, how do we know we can trust you? How can we be sure someone won't try to rob us and sell us?"

Huge blue eyes round with affront, Helstar leaned away from the table. He tapped his chest with a forefinger again. "Word. Swear to it. Friends don't rob friends. Don't sell them, either."

Conway unfolded himself from the table bench, getting to his feet. "I think we'll camp by ourselves while we figure things out."

Helstar agreed heartily. As the others rose, he moved close to whisper. The words seemed to whiffle through the beard. "Choose camp careful. Sailors'll be angry about embarrassing them. Might come in dark."

Tate brushed past him. "Way ahead of you." She stroked her horse's muzzle, fed him a slice of the bread. "Have you ever seen what was left of a man after a Dog war-horse finished with him?" She swept up into the saddle, pulled the horse into a rearing, pawing demonstration. The cleared area around her expanded rapidly. Helstar threw his arms over his head, dodging backward. When her horse was back on all fours, calming down, Tate said, "Talk about that to your sailors and Traders and gangs and everyone else on this rotten rock."

Helstar assured her the message would be sent. Nalatan put an arm across his shoulders. Helstar froze at the touch. Smiling, Nalatan said, "You said you're a smith. I'll go back to your forge with you. There are some things I need. You can make them for me."

Helstar managed a lip-licking smile. "How'll you find your friends? Best go with them, come tomorrow."

"I'll have plenty of daylight to search." Leaving Helstar for Tate, he grabbed onto her reins and said, "Watch your back trail. Someone will try to follow you. I'll track you later."

She frowned down at him. "You're crazy. Leave you here alone? Forget it. Come with us."

"Helstar's a leader. I'll keep him too busy to follow with his friends. I'll be safe enough. Don't worry."

"I don't like it."

"It's best. Go."

"Don't tell me what to do."

Color swept across Nalatan's face, a flash of emotion that failed to change his expression. Steadily, he said, "*Please* go. If they see you're concerned, it'll make them bold. Can't you understand?"

Tate pulled her reins free. "You aggravating . . . *man.* You can't let it go, can you?" She snapped the startled horse's head around, immediately patting his neck, muttering apologies. Her look at Nalatan made it clear who was to blame.

Gathering up the lead ropes on the packhorses, Conway winked at Nalatan and fell in behind Tate. Dodoy raced to be beside her.

Both Conway and Tate had improved their fieldcraft considerably since leaving Ola. Automatically, they sought a place that afforded observation of all approaches while providing cover in case of attack. They avoided several locations close to the water; the view was superb, but the sound of the sea could easily screen approaching raiders. In the end, they settled for a brushy copse on a slight rise. The intermingled young manzanita trees and cypress indicated an overgrown burn. There was plenty of thick, entangled scrub to break up a mounted assault, but a little work with a sword created good sighting paths for the wipes. Deep in the cover, Tate and Conway slung two tents. Then, while Tate dug a firepit, Conway took his dogs and busied himself setting snares for rabbits.

He returned from the seaward side to find Nalatan making his way up the hill from the direction of the inland village. Trotting, Conway was able to intercept him.

Leading Nalatan into the camp, Conway asked about the village. Nalatan shook his head, as if saddened. "Fools, all of them. Liars and thieves. A pack of them followed me out of the village. Six men, crashing about in the brush, thinking they were being sly."

They were at the campsite by then, and Nalatan's last words brought Tate to her feet. Holding clenched fists against her stomach, chin jutting, she shook with anger. "You want them to come after us, so you can have another glorious fight. We've got a child with us, a helpless child. It's bad enough you'd risk our lives without considering our feelings, but you've endangered a boy who depends on us. If those cutthroats come for us tonight, I'll never forgive you."

Muscles jerked in Nalatan's throat, bunched in his jaw. Speaking very slowly, he said, "No one will come."

"You can't say that. You don't know. You said they followed you."

"They won't come. Helstar won't let anyone murder me until he has the coin I agreed to pay for weapons and armor."

Tate's anger seemed to be shading off into guilt, and Conway stepped into the breach. "Helstar's making something for you?"

Nalatan was eager to change the subject. "Yes. A proper sword, and knives. I bought a link shirt, too. He's a surprisingly good smith." He opened his outer blouse to reveal a chain-mail vest over a quilted undershirt.

"Well, it's not as bad as I thought," Tate said. Conway faked a coughing spell, working his way behind a tent. Watching Tate try to apologize without actually sounding apologetic was almost overwhelming. Leaving them to work out the finer points of their argument, he hiked over the hill and down to the water's edge.

This beach was small rocks, none larger than a fist, and dark sand. Something silvery caught the edge of his peripheral vision. When he looked directly, he saw nothing. It happened again. Then again. His head swiveled like a wind vane, and although he knew something was going on, he couldn't identify it. His temper was fraying badly when at last he looked straight down, and a tiny jet of water leapt from a hole in the wet sand. As soon as he'd seen one, he saw dozens; little spurts popped up like reverse rain.

"Clams." He said it aloud, his mouth already watering, savoring the salt-and-iodine tang of fresh seafood. Dropping to his knees, he clawed at one of the holes. Cold, insistent seawater filled his excavation as fast as he dug, so he found himself working by touch. Every rock was a clam until he worked it free and could look at it; then he tossed it aside. Finally there was the rock that actually *was* a clam. A fat one, bigger than the palm of his hand. He whooped, and widened his prospect hole.

It took hardly any time to dredge up twenty, most of them a good three inches across. Using his shirt as a sack, he rinsed his catch and headed home.

The sun was lowering when he reached the crest of their hill. The first star of the night was shining in the east. The flame colors of the clouds overhead were burning out, leaving a soft and gray ashen drift from horizon to horizon.

Looking north, Conway saw the green and gold hills losing shape and color, surrendering to night's advance. The enormity of the world he'd fallen into suddenly seemed more than he could sustain. It was alien, savage. He felt the logical, trained part of his mind trying to reason with him, trying to make him realize he was outmatched. His intelligence wanted him to admit that he was too intelligent to keep fighting a losing battle.

He thought of rescuing Nalatan. A good man. Conway spoke into the gathering darkness. "If it wasn't for me, he'd have died

309

there. If a man saves a good man, even just one, doesn't that mean he lived for a purpose?"

Reluctantly, he remembered the crumpled bodies, the remains of his killing spree with the sniper rifle.

That had been wanton. Evil.

"They were evil men. Nalatan's a good man." He was writhing inside. "I won't do anything like that again. Hysteric. That's what it was: hysteria. I made a mistake."

He turned his face to the sky, as if to search out an answer among the barely visible forms of rolling clouds. No voice came, no magical answer.

So he supplied his own. "I'll be a man who makes a difference. I can do that. I'm here, in this world, in this time, to do that. I'll make mistakes—not as bad as the last one—but I'll contribute good things. I can do that."

He hefted his burden, took a deep breath, and struck out for camp again. He imagined the looks of pleasure he'd receive from Tate and Nalatan when they saw what he was bringing them.

Tate, his closest friend. She loved Nalatan. It might take her a while to discover it, but it'd come to her.

Nalatan, the friend, well met. In love with Tate.

For a moment, Conway felt satisfied with himself, felt placed in his niche. Secure. At ease.

Friends.

Until he killed Nalatan. Or died defending himself.

Sad. Why think about something so dreary, so far in the future?

Pushing a branch aside, he heard a sound. It brought him up short. More puzzled than apprehensive, he wondered what it could have been.

Birds called. Far away, a seal barked.

The sound came again, just as he started to resume his progress. Faint. A piercing, keening note. It was in his head; his ears were ringing. His heart hammered. It was the sickness, claiming him. Swirling, burning colors blinded him. Sagging against a tree, he watched them coalesce into surreal imagery.

He imagined the duel with Nalatan, recoiled at the bite of a blade, exulted at the sight of other flesh, welling blood.

He yearned for that test.

The pictures faded. Reality fell on him, heavy with questions.

Violence had never been part of him before. Or was he so much like his own culture, a breaker of worlds? Or had he become typical of this one, a savage who killed as a substitute for logic?

310

Listlessly, he made his way to the campsite. Dropping the clams at Tate's feet, he shambled off to the tent he shared with Nalatan. To their worried inquiries, he replied that the walking and digging had tired him.

They woke him to the aroma of cooking. Tate explained how she'd added the chopped clams and some smoked bacon to a dried corn soup mix. The steam rising from the wooden bowls was too stimulating to permit depression. Between the stew, dandelion root tea, and the uncomplicated affection of his friends, Conway dismissed his worries. He ate, laughed, joined with Tate in learning a song Nalatan called a fire song. It had to do with man lighting his way, and was very sad and very comradely. The dogs crowded against their masters, relaxed. The horses whickered softly. Dodoy slept soundly, curled in a tight, warm ball.

The fire was cold when Tate and Nalatan went to their respective tents. Conway and his dogs took first watch.

CHAPTER 53

The sentry position provided a three-quarter view of the approaches to the camp. Conway faced generally east, in the direction of the village. To the west, the crown of the hill blocked the sea's mutter. Anyone who came from that direction stood a good chance of being silhouetted and discovered as they topped the higher ground. Further, there was brush downhill from the crest to act as an obstacle.

Nalatan materialized beside Conway. Somehow, the warrior monk had gotten through the thick brush on Conway's flank in complete silence. Shaken, Conway scolded. "That wasn't very smart." The querulous tenor of his voice irritated him further. Deliberately pitching it lower, he added, "You're lucky the dogs are out scouting. What if you'd startled them?"

Nalatan said, "I waited until you sent them out. I'm not taking any chances with those devils."

"Just with me." It was another ill-tempered remark, unpleasantly spoken. Conway wished he could pull it back.

Moving closer, Nalatan was sympathetic. "Something's troubling you. It's not just what happened here."

"Nothing's troubling me."

"You're not feeling well. Sylah and Lanta couldn't hide you

from me the way they kept you out of sight of Gatro's warmen. Lanta told me you fought with a boar, and something happened to you. She wouldn't tell me more."

Conway rounded to face Nalatan. "Look, I've seen you fall asleep and wake up any time you want. You came out here early because you've got something to say. If you think I'm sick, say so."

"We have techniques that free the mind to help the body. I could show you. It would help you with this thing that makes you weak."

Conway noted the care with which Nalatan avoided words such as *sick* or *ill*. He was certain it was the one thing Nalatan genuinely feared, and his solution was to talk around the problem. It was an immense concession, and a tribute to his friendship. Conway was further ashamed of his earlier manner. He said, "We can talk about that any time. Why don't you tell me what's really on your mind?"

In the darkness, Conway felt, more than heard, Nalatan's uncomfortable shifting about. "Why is she always angry at me? I try to please her. She knows—she must know—I'll defend her as long as I can move. I told her if I ever married I'd leave the brotherhood. That was just conversation, understand. I was very subtle about it. Why does she reject me? How do I offend her?" In any other circumstance, the plaintiveness would be laughable.

Conway was too concerned by the recurrence of his lightheadedness to be entertained. When he touched his forehead, his hand came away glossed with sweat. He had to pretend normalcy. "In the first place, you treat her like a woman."

"Of course. That's what she is. Don't make fun of me."

"Just listen. Don't talk. Donnacee's not like any woman you ever saw. From your point of view, she's more like a man."

Nalatan bristled. "You insult her. I don't think I like this conversation any more."

"What conversation? You keep interrupting. Donnacee's a warrior, the same as you. She's got a mission, the same as you. I think the reason she's a little rough on you is because she's attracted to you."

"You did it again."

"Did what?"

"You said she's more like a man. Then you said she doesn't want to be attracted to a man. She's not one of those man-women. I'd know."

"Yeah, sure," Conway muttered, then, before Nalatan could re-

312

spond, "Look, she doesn't want to be distracted, and you're distracting her. It irritates her."

"That's very helpful. The more she likes me, the angrier she becomes, so the more she hates me. Thank you. A man could live a long time and not find a friend like you. If he was lucky."

A hot wave of nausea caught Conway in the middle of a soft chuckle, ending it in a quick gasp. Nalatan heard the contradictory sounds, and reached a hand to Conway's shoulder just as the dogs eased through the brush. Karda ignored the warrior to nudge Conway with his nose. Whining softly, the dog backed away, then moved a few short steps to the east and faced in that direction. Mikka joined him, pointing the same way. Their mutual growling was almost inaudible.

"Someone's coming. From the direction of the village. It looks like Helstar decided he'd rather have the coin without the work." Conway forced the words through sick pressure rising in his throat.

"I'll wake Tate and ask her to join you," Nalatan was already on his feet, crouched. "Then I'll scout south. They may be trying to surround us."

"Take her with you. Her dogs'll be a help."

Nalatan's smile was a flash of white. "If Helstar's out there, it means he broke his promise to me. Tate's a warrior, as you say, but I don't want her to see what happens to him."

With Nalatan's departure, Conway felt his strength ebb faster than ever. Moving forward to join Karda and Mikka made him breathe heavily. He reminded himself to keep his mouth closed, to inhale and exhale slowly, steadily. The ringing in his ears returned. Where it had been an irritation before, now it was a hazard. Some sounds it distorted; he couldn't be sure it didn't completely obscure others.

On order, the dogs advanced toward whatever had alerted them. Conway was sure it was human. There were differences in their warning behaviors. Larger animals brought on a stiff-legged, coiled-spring movement, as though the dogs consciously prepared for battle. When asked to search out game, they grew eager, boisterous. Confronting humans brought on wary determination. Conway believed the latter grew out of a true understanding of which quarry was most dangerous.

Positioning himself between the dogs, Conway let them support some of his weight. He flicked off the wipe's safety. It took two tries, his sweaty thumb slipping off the knurled metal the first time. The quiet snick seemed thunderous.

Again, the dogs warned him. Utterly silent, they pressed against his thighs, effectively stopping him. There was a small bush to his right. He sidled to it, pushing Mikka along sideways. He squatted beside the growth; the advantage of his uphill position would be compromised if anyone saw the team outlined against the stars. The bush broke up the form that said "man" to hostile eyes, while the prone dogs were virtually invisible.

There were people below him. He had no idea how many. Panic speared his guts at the thought that Nalatan and Tate might already have been eliminated. The notion passed quickly. He couldn't believe anyone could so overwhelm that pair, as well as Tate's war dogs, so quickly that no warning would reach him.

Even so, he determined to open fire on the people below him at the first sure sighting.

Under Conway's hand, Karda's rough coat bristled as the dog's skin tightened. Biting ammonia scent rose from the animal. It picked at Conway's nostrils, made his own skin crawl, touched off another terrifying swirl of dizziness.

He gagged.

And then they were coming. So many figures yelled and charged out of the nearby brush he had the frightening image of the whole hillside rushing at him. He responded with the boop. It's hollow, full-throated launch was followed almost immediately by the cutting crack of the bursting round. He would have sworn the red-orange of the explosion still lingered in the air when the first screams scarred the night. He only had time for one more boop round. The attackers were fewer by then, and he blasted at them with the wipe, not troubling to aim. Honed steel gleamed in his weapon's flash.

Released, the dogs were devastating. Cloaked in darkness, so close and so fast the attackers had only an impression of their presence before they struck, the huge hounds crashed into the nearest men. Conway heard the roaring ferocity. Shrieks of terror mingled with cries of pain.

Leaping sideways, Conway drew his sword. As he expected, his enemies continued to attack the now-unoccupied bush. Conway's first sword stroke eliminated a man. Slashing, stabbing, Conway retreated. Adversaries seemed to materialize. He blocked blows, struck back. Called for Nalatan. Unable to see the dogs, Conway still knew exactly what they were doing. Karda was trained to select the victim, charging in. Mikka drove at whatever opening the male created. If they failed to kill, they savaged. Leaping away to avoid any counterstroke or support from another man, they ran. And turned to select another target.

Cries told Conway they were being effective. Yet the mob pressed ahead.

Lightning exploded in Conway's stomach. He dropped the wipe, fell to his knees, pitched forward as nausea emptied him. A blade whistled through the air where his head had been. Sheer terror whipped him up off his fists. He drew his sword, literally fell forward in a lunge. A man tumbled away, calling out for help. Karda responded. The plea disappeared under horrible crushing, tearing noises.

"We've got him!" The yell came from up the hill.

There were more. Charging from behind.

Tate's voice came to him. "Matt! We're here. We're with you." Her wipe's hard crack hurt his ears.

Another wipe man struck at Conway, who warded it off with his sword. The blade sang as it flew out of his hand, a weird, off-key song of defeat. Falling sideways, too weak to resist any longer, Conway felt the peace of night's cool earth hurrying to ease his pain.

The grass was soft. Sweet.

He clawed fingers into the roots, holding to all the life he could find. A sudden, blinding dazzle told him his fight was over.

The soil dribbled away from his senseless grasp.

CHAPTER 54

Tate stood looking down at the still, pale features of her closest friend. Firelight swirling across his features created a cruel semblance of animation. Blurring tears added to the confusion of her vision, so that several times she thought he moved. Each time, she'd bent forward, speaking his name in hope. The great dogs lying next to him watched with trusting, begging eyes. They'd allowed her to treat their wounds, but their mute loyalty kept them bound to Conway's side.

There were other men present. Gathered in a semicircle, they stood well outside the firelight, as silent and brooding as the trees of the grove. Black clothes blended with the shroud of night.

Beside Tate, Nalatan forced cheerfulness. "His breathing's steadier. The blood beats stronger at neck and wrist, too."

When Tate failed to respond, Nalatan tried another tack. "Did you see the honor he gained? Not just with the lightning weapons: blade at blade, he killed two. Two more will never fight again. The dogs—I knew they were ferocious, but you have to see what they can do—they slew four more. All together, lightning weapons, sword, and dogs, eleven men went to the Land Beyond to tell them of our Matt Conway. A great warrior, Donnacee Tate. A man to bring pride to you and all your people."

Without taking her gaze from the man at her feet, Tate said, "I don't care about any of that. I want my friend to sit up and talk to me." When she turned to Nalatan, she looked out from a face gone ugly with worry. Returning her attention to Conway, Tate was oblivious to Nalatan's offended hurt. As he left, his lips moved in muttered lament: "How can you not know what I'd do to hear you say half as much of me?"

Dodoy crept forward as Nalatan stalked away. The small, bony figure appeared awkward, but he made no sound as he came. Once beside Tate, he leaned against her. Automatically, she reached to put an arm around the thin shoulders. Watching Conway, Dodoy said, "If those men came sooner, they'd have saved him."

"They didn't know we'd be attacked. They came as fast as they could."

"Who are they?"

"I don't know. Nalatan heard them coming and challenged them. By the time they got everything settled, Matt was almost killed."

"Nalatan made a big mistake."

"He did the right thing, I think. Everything was confused."

"We should go back to that castle. We were safe there. Comfortable. It's cold out here. I don't like it. Those men scare me."

"They helped us save Matt, honey. Maybe even saved all of us."

Conway twitched, his hands and fingers jerking in small, tight movements. His eyelids trembled. He mumbled gibberish. Suddenly, he was completely coherent. The words were soft, confiding, shaped for a child's ears. "It's the way the wings curve, sweetheart. The air going across the top goes faster, see?" He smiled, a ghastly parody of devotion. "When you're a big girl, we'll go for a ride in a sailplane. You'll fly like all the other pretty birds. Would you like that?"

Tate was horrified. Should she answer? Quiet him? For a moment, the problem appeared solved. Conway sagged. Then, without warning, he thrashed upright to a sitting position, screaming warning. "Bacteria! The tester says it was a bacteria warhead! Clear the area, get to decon! *Hurry!*"

Tate wrestled with him, tried to force him down. He threw her aside, amazingly strong. Then he collapsed.

Wiping away cottony spittle clinging to Conway's lips, Tate kept her voice calm. "Dodoy, get me some water in that bowl over there, please."

The boy was back quickly. Putting down the bowl, he extended the other hand. It clutched a wad of leaves. "I know this plant," he said. "The sailors used it. They put it in a pipe and ate the smoke, like this." He mimicked drawing through pursed lips, then held his breath, finally exhaling in a thin hiss.

Tate squinted suspicion, took the leaves. She sniffed at them. "That's marijuana," she said, hardly believing it. "Where'd you get this?"

Troubled by her tone, he was evasive. "Over there. It won't hurt him, if he uses it just once." He glanced around, and when he met her gaze again, his expression was slyly confident. "The sailors ate the smoke and said they felt good. I saw how hard you and the others worked to keep Gatro and his warmen from learning that Matt Conway's sick. If these new people find out he's not just hurt . . ." He let the sentence die.

When Tate spun around, Dodoy was almost quick enough to hide a malevolent grin. She saw only part of it, and quickly convinced herself it was a nervous grimace. Still, she decided, it wouldn't hurt to warn the boy. "He's not the only one who'll suffer. They'd shun all of us, maybe kill us. There's nothing funny about it."

Stung, Dodoy returned to the darkness.

Lacking a pipe, Tate used another bowl to hold a coal from the fire, then dropped the leaves over it. Acrid smoke curled out of the small pile. Lifting Conway's head, she gently blew the tendrils toward him, and was rewarded to see it bend to his shallow inhalations. After a while, he seemed to sleep a bit more easily.

Nalatan, having stopped to watch Tate talk to Dodoy and minister to Conway, now made his way to the men. A sturdy figure with a thick black beard stepped forward. He asked Nalatan, "Is he dying? Now he's in the firelight and we can see, his wounds appear very light." The man pushed his face closer to Nalatan's. "He's not sick, is he?"

"He's well. Controlling the lightning strains him sometimes."

The bearded man struggled with uncertainty. Finally, he asked, "You told the woman who we are?"

Nalatan shook his head. "There's been no chance. You say you know them?"

"Back in Ola. How come you're with them?"

"I'm sworn to help the Flower find the Door."

"Rose Priestess Sylah," the man interrupted. "I know her, too. And little Lanta. I have to talk to Tate." He moved to pass Nalatan. The warrior monk shifted to block him. The bearded man stiffened, then smiled reassurance. "Would we have come to warn you about these raiders, or help you, if we weren't friends?"

The sincerity was unmistakable, but Nalatan was compelled to point out the flawed logic. "You got here too late to warn us of anything. Conway practically destroyed the attack before we chased them off. If you're willing to test Tate's temper right now, I won't stop you, because you say you're an old friend. I'll be behind you, though. I mean no offense, but you're not *my* old friend. Do we understand each other?"

Laughing softly and moving past Nalatan, the man said, "We do." He was still smiling when he stopped across the fire from Tate. The flame picked bright spots on his beard. He said, "I know you, Donnacee Tate."

Tate's head tilted to the side, as if she'd heard something far away. Uncertainly, her gaze pulled away from Conway. Seeing the newcomer, she exclaimed wordlessly, her hands flew to her breast. "Wal? *Wal*. Here? How? Why?" She rushed around the fire to hug him.

Nalatan was trying to look stoic and failing badly when she pulled Wal to him. "Look who it is, Nalatan," she said, holding up Wal's hand as if it would help the monk place this stranger. "We helped Wal and Gan Moondark overthrow King Altanar." To Wal, she said, "What're you doing here? How'd you know we were here? I had no idea it was you who came tonight."

"We were coming to warn you that sailors were coming for you."

"Not the villagers?"

Wal waved as if aggravated by flies. "The attack was set up by the sailors. Pirates, to be accurate. Villagers may have joined in; I don't know. You can't trust any of them. It takes four men to say hello in this place—two to talk and two to watch their backs. Anyhow, the Trader I deal with said you'd be coming here today, and told us to be prepared to help."

The three of them sat down. Tate positioned herself so she could see any movement by Conway. To Wal, she said, "Poor Sylah. She must feel really awful about all of this. Have you seen her, talked to her?"

"No chance of that. But I do know that if you hadn't accepted Gatro's offer, you were headed directly into nomad patrols. The Kossiar warmen report skirmishes with them every day. And the renegades from Ola had permission from the Chair to take you, if they could. The Harvester had already sent a Messenger to Church Home saying you'd rejected the Chair's hospitality and offer of escorted passage."

"At least now they know she's a liar."

Wal laughed, a sharp, hacking sound. "As soon as she saw you, she sent another Messenger to explain that she'd been misinformed. She doesn't get caught out that easily."

Tate brushed some damp hair back from Conway's forehead. She said, "How's a sailor come by so much information?"

"Borbor, my Trader, is one of my tribe. A For, from the Whale Coast. All the Traders have spies." He spat into the fire. It made a short-lived black spot on the glowing coals, hissing and crackling. "Ola was cruel, Tate; worse than here, I think. Altanar hurt people because he enjoyed seeing them suffer. There's plenty of hurt and misery here, too. But Kos is evil. There's no truth at all in this place."

Again, the threesome fell silent. Wal broke it with a transparent attempt at enthusiasm. "That's enough of that. You're in good hands now. Dawn'll break soon, and we'll get our friend Conway back to the Trader's, where we can heal his wounds. He must have been hit in the head, don't you think?"

Tate heard the suspicion, knew that Wal was probing to see if Conway was sick. She barely avoided a telltale glance at Nalatan. She said, "There's a bad bruise behind his ear."

Wal visibly relaxed. "I've been hit there. I walked around for days listening to music no one else could hear. He'll be all right. She'll take good care of him."

Tate straightened. "The Chair sent the others over here? Where are they?"

"I'm not talking about Sylah and Lanta. I'm talking about my cousin, Tee. She's out to sea on a fishing boat, but she'll be back soon."

"She's here?" Tate tried to muffle the dismay that surfaced in spite of herself.

"That's right, the one he fell in love with, the one who ran away from him. She still can't believe that after what Altanar and his protectors did to her, any man would want her. Foolish. Female stuff. No matter. He's here, she's here. They'll work it out between them. Just when you think something's too complicated to ever make sense, something happens, and it's all perfectly simple."

In her mind, Tate saw Conway, Tee, and Lanta, whirling like dust motes in a sunbeam. "Simple." It sounded as if she were cursing. "Oh, my friend Wal, I would give my *teeth* to tell you about simple."

Nalatan's sudden coughing fit interrupted. Before she could continue, he pointed out that morning wasn't far off, and the day would require clear heads. Wal agreed.

Tate remained with Conway while the others drew away to sleep or mount watch. Dabbing at her friend's superficial wounds with a damp cloth, she whispered to him. "So what're we going to do about poor Lanta, buddy? As soon as you see this old flame, you're going to catch fire all over again, aren't you? And won't that warm things up?"

Morning brushed the island with rags of fog. Sleepily, rubbing bloodshot eyes, Tate tucked in loose edges of the tent fly that protected Conway from the damp cold. He lay motionless on the rough stretcher Wal's men had fashioned from saplings and the other tent fly.

Downhill, the heavy chunk of an axe echoed from a grove where Wal's crew prepared the ceremonial pyre for the men who'd died the previous night.

Tate's gaze went to Karda and Mikka. She'd been horrified the night before to discover them licking off bloodstains. Not their own blood. She'd scrubbed them with an almost-compulsive vigor. Now when she looked at them, she could have sworn they looked back in a different manner. Something new, something *knowing*, glinted in the dark, deep eyes. Reason told her it was imagination. Nevertheless, a quick thrill skittered across her shoulders. The dogs broke off the unintended staring match with the slow dignity of accommodation. They still wagged tails when she stroked the massive heads.

She decided Oshu and Tanno still had an immature look, an innocence she suddenly treasured. When the time came for them to respond, as it had come for Karda and Mikka, they'd do exactly the same things. It was more than training. It was breeding. "In the blood." Nasty phrase.

Nalatan was saying, "The pyre's burning well. We've done our duty. It's time to leave. Possibly past time."

His tone warned her. "Past time for what?" she asked.

For answer, he pointed. Men carrying bows skulked on the next hill. Once they realized Nalatan had spotted them, they dodged into the cover of some brush. "Sailors," he scoffed.

Wal came up in time to overhear. His smile was tight. "You won't talk like that if they ever catch you at sea, monk. That's where we fight our way."

Tate snapped at both of them. "We've got a si— wounded man here. Argue about how brave you are after we get him taken care of."

Both men winced. Wal bawled for litter bearers.

The balancebar was held in place offshore by a stern anchor and a pair of mooring lines running from two widely separated trees to the bow. Tate reluctantly relinquished her horse to Nalatan. Her dogs plunged into the water with every sign of disgust, following her as she waded out to the harness lift dangling from the cargo boom. The water was calm, but cold. Almost waist-deep for Tate, it rose up the dogs' sides. They stood in it, rocking with the slap of each small wave, their expressive faces dripping equal amounts of saltwater and accusation. First Oshu, then Tanno, were swiftly plucked from the sea and deposited on the deck. Mikka and Karda followed the men carrying Conway, but when another sailor attempted to help Tate harness Mikka, the frightened dog made him understand his error. Tate took over the task of preparing the sling, and Mikka, legs pumping furiously, was hoisted aboard.

Karda refused to leave Conway's side. When Tate reached for him, he braced, hackles up, teeth bared.

"All right, big fella," Tate said, dropping the rig. It drifted back toward the boat. Still using the same placating tone, she said, "Hook up Conway's stretcher. Get him aboard. *Move it!* If this dog figures out what's going on, you're going to have to swim for your lives."

As soon as the cargo line went taut, Karda understood. With a noise that was roar and whine, he bolted past Tate, breasting the water in lunges. The last one lifted him within a hand's breadth of the dangling stretcher. His teeth clashed on empty air, and he tumbled backward, submerging ignominiously. Surfacing, he attacked the hull, biting, pawing, howling and barking distractedly.

Tate forced her way to his side, calling his name. For a few moments, the tumult continued as he ignored her. Then he backed away from the boat. He watched her. She could almost feel his confusion, his fear and anger. When she extended a hand, he growled. Then whined.

"I know, I know," she said, moving forward slowly. A trailing hand snagged the harness. "I tricked you, you poor, dumb brute. People are like that, Karda; they do what they just *know* is best for you. C'mon, let me put this rig on you. A quick ride, and presto, you're with the boss again. Trust me? Please?"

Karda watched her hands secure the lashings. When she signaled the crew, they dropped a rope ladder over the side. A man said, "We bring him on after you're aboard. Not before."

Karda stood shivering, resigned. When they lifted him, he didn't even look down. His eyes remained fixed on the point where he'd seen Conway disappear. When the form on the stretcher came into view, the dog struggled as if he'd fly to him. Once aboard, he continued to tremble while Tate released him. Free, he trotted to Conway. One confirming sniff, a lick of the still features, and he flopped beside the man.

Calling from the shore, Nalatan said, "We should all learn from him. That's a true heart." He brandished the reins of their horses. "These three aren't much different. Copper wants nothing to do with me, and the war-horses are furious. It's going to be an interesting ride to the Trader's place."

Wading to the boat, Wal turned to Nalatan, saying, "All three men I'm leaving with you know the island. Keep to the coastal trail. As soon as I drop Tate and Conway, I'll come back to look for you."

Two of Nalatan's companions cast off the mooring lines. Astern, four more men hauled on the stern anchor, pulling the boat seaward. Working with a darting activity that suggested chaos, but which Tate saw was actually smooth teamwork, the anchor was heaved aboard, the mooring lines were coiled and stored, and sails were raised. She was startled to see how soon they were speeding away, leaving a creamy turmoil of wake.

Peering over the rail, she felt something cold touch her hand, and she jerked it away. Looking down, she stared into Karda's glowing eyes. He licked her hand, wagged his tail. Squatting, she took his ears in her hands, gently turning his head from side to side. She had to look up at him. "Apology accepted," she said aloud. Her voice caught. She glared around, in case anyone heard. Reassured, she added, "Nalatan was right, you big, ugly, ol' sweetheart."

Pulling back gently, Karda disengaged himself. With her hands

322

off his ears, he stepped forward and, before she could dodge, licked the side of her face from jaw to hairline. Giggling, she pushed him back. He retreated to Conway's litter, thudding to the deck across from Mikka with what appeared to be great satisfaction.

An unexpected wave jarred the boat. Tate looked forward, where Dodoy huddled out of the wind in the shelter of the bow. She called to him. He turned at his name. A slab of green water peeled up over the gunwale. It collapsed on Dodoy, drenching him. Leaping to his feet, he glared at Tate. She scrambled to reach him. Confused, her dogs struggled to their feet, getting in her way. When she shoved them aside, the pitching of the boat sent them stumbling and sprawling.

Dodoy dodged past her, running toward the stern, darting between crew members and rigging with the adroitness of experience. He turned once, to gesture angrily for her to keep away.

Tate returned to her former position. When Tanno and Oshu came to lie beside her, she was too preoccupied to notice.

CHAPTER 55

It was two days before Conway was completely conscious. Lanta arrived at the Trader's compound within hours of Wal's docking. From that moment on, she was at his side. Fortunately, there were no repetitions of his dangerous ramblings.

Lanta was the first thing he saw when he woke. He smiled recognition. Spooning broth into him brought color to his cheeks. When he slept again, his features were calm, his hands stilled.

Lanta fell asleep sitting on the floor beside him, head pillowed on his arm. She dropped off while tears of relief still jeweled her cheek.

When he woke again, he tried to extricate his arm without waking her. Drowsily, she clutched it, mumbling sleepily until she suddenly realized where she was. Embarrassed, she rose in ungainly fluster, feet catching on the hem of her robe, hair flying, hands in all directions. When she straightened, red-faced, he was laughing. It was weak, but it was laughter. Words formed slowly. "How'd I get here? Where are we?"

She poured him fresh water, answering while she held the mug to his lips. "I came in one of the Chair's oared boats. You came in Wal's balancebar." She smiled at his delayed amazement. "That's right, the same Wal. From Ola. He trades pelts, jade, ivory. He's talking about selling wool and yarn here, then carrying back cotton."

He said, "Tate. Nalatan. The dogs. Stormracer."

"All fine. All here at the Trader's." He drank more while she told him what she'd learned. She ended by saying, "You're in the Trader's healing house. Maybe today I'll explore a bit. Tate says the Trader's quarters are very big, very nice."

"It's more than nice, it's luxurious." Conway and Lanta both looked to where Tate leaned against the doorjamb, her dogs forming an imposing foreground. She'd spent time reestablishing her appearance. A yellow blouse complimented a softly glowing leather vest. What appeared to be a skirt was actually very full woolen trousers. The pattern was revealed as an abstract design of horse heads, beige on brown, when she whirled away from her pose, making the material flare. Her new midcalf boots were black, highly polished. Her hair, tied back in a braid, glowed from washing and brushing.

From the foot of Conway's bed, Karda wagged his tail in welcome. Mikka came over for a quick pat, then returned to her watchful position.

Lanta clapped. "You look wonderful. Exciting clothes. I'd forgotten how beautiful you can be. Oh, that sounded awful. I meant, on the trip, the same marching clothes all the time—"

She might have spent the rest of the day stammering, but Tate interrupted. "I know what I looked like out there. Another of the beasts, and that's a fact." She walked to Conway, planted a kiss on his forehead, then straightened to smile down at him.

He made a face. "A peck on the forehead? That's it? You my sister or something?"

Looking to Lanta, Tate rolled her eyes in mock exasperation, then, posing, "You get stronger, I'll come back and give you one of those on the lips. I do you one of my Late Night Specials while you're in this shape, you are *dead*. All that soup Lanta's been ladling into you comes steaming out your ears in one big hiss. Good-bye Conway." Then, taking his hand in hers, she grew serious. "Lanta and I haven't spoken to anyone but a couple of servants since we got here. Nalatan came back overland, with the horses and gear, you know? As soon as he got here, he talked Wal into going back to that Helstar's village with him. The Trader's out to sea with the other Traders. Word is, there's a Nion boat headed this way, and they're all trying to be the first to do business with it."

Conway asked, "No gang here?"

"Mercenaries. Bunch of cutthroats. Wal says they're loyal. Sure. We slept both nights with the dogs inside. With the wipe beside me." She turned a soft, fond smile on Lanta. "I slept. This one's hardly closed her eyes. You owe her, man. No one ever got care like that." Then, mercurial as ever, Tate was bubbling again. "You've got to *see* this house. Paneling, neat furniture, a couple of baths. Even a hot tub. Made me think of all the things they used to say about this area when there was a Marin County, remember?"

"When?" Lanta's question brought both Tate and Conway back to their present reality. Conway spoke first. "Just an expression. When do Nalatan and Wal get back?"

Lanta answered, "Tonight, they said."

Conway elbowed himself onto his side. Both women hurried to him. He waved them off. "I can do this." It came through clenched teeth. Sitting upright seemed to strengthen him. He gestured for his trousers. "Out," he said. "I'm well enough to want some privacy, please."

Tate sniffed. "Our pleasure, believe me. We'll be outside, where there's interesting stuff to look at."

Shocked, Lanta let herself be led out by the elbow. Her feelings dithered between hilarity and fear. What Tate said was funny, especially the way it made Conway's face turn to vinegar. Nevertheless, she'd seen women beaten for neglecting to use the proper speech form when answering a question. No woman talked to men the way Tate did. Except Tate. She did it all the time. And most of them seemed to like it. Or accept it, anyway.

It was all so strange.

Tate was saying, "What have you learned about Yasmaleeya? Is there anything wrong with her?"

Lanta winced. "She has a cold. Or did, when I left. We can't tell much while she's fighting unseens. We can only wait. She's hard to work with. A spoiled brat."

"What's the Chair doing? And our good friend, Bos?"

"I don't know. I saw them talking in the courtyard with the Harvester, but that's all."

"There's a lovely trio," Tate said, finally letting go of Lanta's arm. They stepped out onto a stone-paved deck. In the distance, the bay gleamed blue. A solitary boat skimmed across the dazzling surface, too far away for any wake to catch the eye. Closer at hand, waves silvered the coastline. Trees had been felled to create a view. Flowering shrubs grew among the vine-camouflaged stumps. Butterflies tripped erratic paths from blossom to blossom, ridiculously haphazard beside the whizzing efficiency of honeybees.

Tate picked up the conversation again. "If I were in Yasmaleeya's place, I think I'd be very careful."

"I'm sure she is. She really wants the baby."

Tate sent her a quizzical look that melted to affection. "You're a sweetheart. You really are. You look at Yasmaleeya and you see a woman who wants her child and is taking care of herself accordingly. I look at her and see another piece in the power game. That Harvester witch is using her to try to hurt Sylah. And you."

White-faced, Lanta pulled back. "Never say that. If you call anyone in Church 'witch,' you can be burned. Using that word is never funny."

"Setting fire to people you don't like isn't exactly kissy-kissy, is it? But I'll remember. The point is, if you and Sylah bring this off, and Yasmaleeya delivers a healthy baby, the Harvester's going to look bad." She shook her head, confirming her own opinion. "Our Odeel's got some mean little secret."

"I'm afraid I had the same bad thought." Looking up, Lanta laughed at Tate's burlesque shock, then pretended irritation.

Tate said, "You could do that trance thing; look off into the future. I know, I know: Forbidden. But maybe just a tiny peek?"

As Lanta's amusement faded, Tate made a face. "I knew it. Why do I always get stuck with nice people?"

"Pooh. You're as nice as anyone. You're teasing me. Again."

"Me? Seriousness is my life." Tate paused, looking past Lanta, then continued. "And here comes Mr. Serious Privacy, all washed, shaved, and dressed up like a big boy."

Conway threw a sloppy salute. "Everything works, but it all hurts. Whoever got my clothes washed, thanks. And where'd you get that costume you're wearing, Donnacee?"

"One of the servants got it for me. I gave him some coin. There's a town, called Rathole. Creates an image, doesn't it? It's where the sailors buy and sell and do all the fun things sailors do. I was thinking of going in this afternoon."

"Alone?" Conway almost yelped the word. "Are you crazy?"

Tate brandished the pipe. "Who's going to mess with me?"

"Who's going to watch your back?"

Lanta chimed in. "I heard you embarrassed one of the sailors, back on the dock. They'll be even angrier after losing so many in the fight with Matt."

Conway pursued the new subject. "Sailors? Not villagers?"

"Mostly sailors," Tate said. "There were only two villagers in the ones you dropped."

Conway said, "I was running away. Two men caught up. Somebody shouted. From the top of the hill. I remember falling."

Tate explained about Wal and Nalatan, continuing, "You and the dogs took out eleven raiders. Nalatan thinks you're acceptable. He actually said that: acceptable. His idea of high praise. How you doing?"

He looked at his bandages. "It didn't hurt. I couldn't think. Just noise. Moving." He shivered briefly, then all the shock, the lingering stress, surfaced in one word. "Eleven?"

Lanta said, "A brave fight, Matt Conway. It will be remembered."

"Yes. I'm sure."

Tate moved closer to Lanta. "Lanta got here almost as soon as you did. They signal from here to an observation post near Harbor with a mirror. The signal's relayed in. In bad weather or darkness they use lanterns."

He smiled wanly, and Tate continued. "What bothers me is, she gets a couple of hours' sleep, and she looks good as new. Pretty as ever. It's enough to make an ordinary woman weep."

Lanta stole a glance at Conway. He was watching her, his smile a bit broader now. He liked looking at her. It was in his face, the way he touched with his eyes. But *why* did he look? Was it speculation? Affection? The last word rolled back and forth across her mind. She thought of waking beside him, warm with the touch and smell of him.

What had Tate said about spying into the future? "Just a tiny peek."

She wished desperately that she could help him. He didn't know what he wanted. Nothing could be more dangerous.

What if she did help? How could it be evil to try to save a man's life? And who would know? The Seeing didn't always come. Could it be a sin to try, if nothing came?

No one would know.

Tate was demanding to be heard. "Boats! It's got to be the Traders, coming into port."

With a servant guide, they rode to the Trader's beach. Sitting on the horses at the forest's edge, Conway idly asked the young man who'd led them if he, too, was a For.

"I'm a Kossiar, assigned to the Trader Borbor." The youngster drew himself proudly erect. "Borbor's the first For we ever had. Did you know Wal's his cousin? And the other—"

Tate kneed her horse sideways, nearly spilling the man. "Sorry. Spooky animal. Probably thirsty. Tell me, how come a free Kossiar works here? I thought the island was only for aliens and criminals."

"Every Trader's required to have three Kossiar house workers. We work for three years, staggered so that one man leaves and a new man joins every year. The Traders pay well. We watch them for the Chair, so we work for Kos, too." The earnest face turned smug.

Conway said, "That's a lot of responsibility."

"We report everything. Bos says to suspect everyone, 'cause everyone envies Kos."

Amused, knowing glances slipped back and forth among the mounted trio, literally passing over the head of their naive spy. In the silence that followed, Tate decided he wasn't so much naive as supremely confident. In the man's mind, Bos was correct. Kos controlled every aspect of local life; it was natural to assume an observable fact was universal.

Tate's mind flashed back to the oddly distant manner of the people of Harbor. She remembered the surly stares of the slaves in the fields. You see less than you think, my spy friend, she thought.

The six Trader boats swept down on the island. Four were monohulls, one a trimaran, and one a balancebar. Far behind, just edging past Harbor's peninsula, a much larger vessel made its way. Conway said, "The big one must be the Nion. Did you ever see anything as colorful as these boats?"

Admiringly, Tate said, "They do appreciate color." To their guide, she shouted, "Which is Borbor?"

"The one leading," he shouted back.

Twin-masted, with a small jib forward, Borbor's balancebar drove hard for the anchor buoys bobbing offshore. Her sails were striped in forward-pointing vees of alternating blood red and daffodil yellow. The hull was also red. She flung herself across the blue of the sea and the silver chop of the waves with the mad gaiety of flame.

The monohull closest behind was black; her sails were red and white in vertical stripes that diminished in width, bottom to top. The other monohulls favored white woodwork; their sails exploded with color, one in slanted stripes of blue, green, and black.

Another featured concentric circles of orange and blue, while the next blazed in randomly mixed vertical stripes of every hue. The trimaran's sail of black was adorned with the image of a leaping orange tiger.

Caught up in the brilliant display and the excitement of the race, the threesome cheered for Borbor as if they knew him.

In preparation for the Trader's return, a smaller balancebar was carried out into the water by a group of men, two of whom leapt aboard as crew. The carriers hurried back to join another group in setting up a table. Hampers of food and drink were emptied, the contents arranged simultaneously with the raising of a covering fly of almost-transparent gauzelike cloth. The rich smells of hot meats, of vegetables, of cheeses and fresh bread mingled with the tang of saltwater and the spice of sun-struck wild plants. Workers shouted orders, jokes.

Dismounting, Conway walked toward the water. Lanta followed. Tate hurried to catch up. She watched nervously as two people clambered over the side of the moored large balancebar and into the smaller one. One of the figures was bulky, slow moving. The second was small, quick. Tate knew it was Tee; her heart sank. Turning from the festive, bustling activity, she tried to think what to do.

Animated, Conway seemed practically over any effects of his relapse. He leaned toward Lanta, almost touching, laughing and talking. Her eyes devoured him, her smile a sun of love.

In the speeding balancebar, Tee sat with her back to the shore.

Tate said, "They're preparing a welcoming here. We shouldn't intrude."

The guide overheard. "It's for you. I thought you knew. Borbor wants to meet you."

"We should've been told." Tate practically snarled at the man. "Why didn't you say something? We're not properly dressed. Stay here. Tell your master we'll be back later."

Shocked, the house servant backed up a few steps, then turned and hurried away.

Equally appalled, Conway and Lanta were motionless. Conway broke the silence. "That was pretty rough, Tate."

Her defense was lame in her own hearing. "He was supposed to let us know." When she turned back, her friends were walking inland. Knowing she was only postponing the inevitable meeting, knowing what it would do to Lanta, Tate followed, hoping her friends wouldn't turn. When she caught up and Lanta sent her a puzzled, sympathetic smile, Tate felt it as a burn.

The small balancebar skidded up onto the beach while Conway and Lanta were still short of the forest and the waiting horses.

The larger figure leapt out of the vessel, onto the sand. Offering up a hand, he helped the second passenger. Both were dressed in black leather blouse and trousers. The smaller person had multi-colored trim at wrists and ankles, with a wider vertical strip centered on the blouse, where large white shell buttons blinked in the sun.

Conway and Lanta turned back to the sea, reins in hand.

Tee looked directly at Conway. She stopped in her tracks, unbelieving.

Conway's eyes met hers. To himself, he said, "It's you. I've found you." His step forward was uncertain.

Bustling, full of cheer, the heavy man in black advanced at a trot. "Welcome! Welcome! I'm Borbor. It's a pleasure to greet you." He grabbed Conway's unresponsive hand, pumping it. Shouting back to Tee, he said, "What do you think of my surprise? Now you know why I pulled you off that fishing boat. Here's your friends, Conway and Tate, come all the way from Ola. He needed a couple of days to heal. Good as new, now. Look at you: too surprised to talk. I never thought to see the day."

Unnoticed by anyone but Tate, Lanta inched away until she felt far enough removed to turn and make her escape. Leading her horse, she walked with head down, her step a dead, listless shuffle. Tate tried to force herself to catch up to her friend. Cowardly feet refused, rooted in embarrassment. Lanta stopped, looked back at Tate through tears.

"You knew. You let me hope. Why hurt me so, Donnacee?" A strange, fiery light touched her eyes, and was gone. She seemed to draw in on herself, as if concentrating a fierce energy. "We all take our amusement where we find it, don't we? I should have thought of that. And we all take our turn laughing. Perhaps you'll think of that."

When Tate opened her mouth, extending a hand, the diminutive figure drew back sharply, making a tight, hissing sound like a tormented cat. Tate checked, her protest intimidated.

Lanta hung her head once again, resumed her shuffling retreat. Tate thought she looked old, old beyond all joy.

CHAPTER 56

Sitting across the table from Tee, Conway feasted. His eyes danced. He talked loudly, incessantly.

Tee's steady smile was a matter of proper muscles performing. She listened with that distraction that marks the person who has something desperately important to say, and no idea how to say it.

Occasionally her glance slid away to Tate, sitting beside Conway. The look was harried.

For a while, Tate pretended to be unaware. Burdened with the weight of Lanta's hurt, torn by her accusation—as unwarranted as she knew it to be—Tate wanted nothing to do with Tee. She knew Tee wasn't responsible for Conway's infatuation, nor had she meant to hurt Lanta. Regardless, growing resentment battered at Tate's rationality.

Interrupting Conway's ceaseless chatter, Tee addressed Tate. "I've wanted to ask you: what's your impression of Kos?"

Tate said, "We never should have come here. Conway told you what happened to Sylah."

"You could leave. The Chair would let you."

Tate made no effort to hide her offense. "We're Sylah's friends. We leave when she does."

"I hoped that's what you'd say." Tee's smile was genuinely warm. "But you haven't told me your impressions."

"We met one of your Kossiar house servants," Tate said pointedly.

"Then you should know the other two. That's one, carving the wildcow meat. The third is by the beer keg, where they get their best information. The information we want them to have."

Tate nodded. "Everyone else can be trusted?"

"Completely."

"All right, then. Kos stinks. Anyplace that tolerates slavery's evil. I don't think people should trade with them." Warming to her subject, Tate leaned halfway across the table, gesturing with her shortknife. "Something else; Kossiars are all weird. Everyone acts like they're looking for a hole to hide in."

"What makes you say that?"

Conway didn't want the pleasure of his moment interfered with.

He pushed into the conversation. "Tate's talking about the reaction we saw after an execution. That's not a fair judgment."

Tee ignored him. Tate went on. "He's right. It's a feeling. I think they expect a slave revolt."

Conway said, "Come on, this is all too serious. I want some more of that meat. And some beer. Come with me, Tee." He was around the end of the table, at her side pulling her elbow. Rising without argument, she continued to watch Tate until it was necessary for her to turn away. When she did, it was with renewed concentration on Conway. A casual observer would have smiled at the way the attractive, lithe young woman paid attention to her obviously doting escort. Tate, unfortunately, could only brood over radically changed interest.

Tate left the table, wandering toward the long serving bench. If she'd ever seen a better case of unrequited love, she thought, she couldn't remember it. Tate reflected that what little she knew of Tee didn't square with the image of a woman who entertained herself by tormenting a man. Especially a man in love. After all, she told herself, they all knew Tee's courage. Tee had been a toy for Altanar's protectors in Ola, and exacted revenge by helping lead the resistance that brought them down.

No one could question Tee's cunning, either.

Tate wondered if Tee's toughness had twisted into the egocentricity that had no qualms about manipulating others.

A great shout rose at one end of the gathering. Pulled from her considerations, Tate realized the yelling was being taken up by everyone.

Nalatan and Wal rode toward the beach party. Across the crowd, Nalatan saw Tate immediately. He waved. Each of his arms sported a sheathed knife strapped to it at the bicep. Uncovered, his chain mail gleamed. When he swung out of the saddle, he drew a new sword, swinging it in a wild, singing circle of light. In his left hand, he held a peculiar metal rod that was about as thick as a man's finger, and approximately four feet long. There was a conical metal fitting riveted to it at the center. The cone's maximum diameter was perhaps twice a hand-span; the point was elongated, sharp. The attachment was obviously designed to protect one's grip on the metal rod, as well as deflect opposing blades. More, the point provided another thrusting weapon. Each end of the rod was a metal ball the size of a small apple.

The men roared approval as a grinning Nalatan executed a series of flashing cuts, thrusts, and blocks. He leapt, spun, tumbled, always defended by the rod, always seeking, slashing with the long, curved blade.

Witless, war-oriented savagery, Tate told herself. Masculine foolishness.

One of the watchers flourished a large round object over his head. Translucent hide, drawn taut over a deep hoop, glowed in the sun. Holding the drum by its crossbrace, the man ran swift, sure fingers across its surface. Enlivened, the drum sang. Surprisingly deep notes boomed from its center. Tangy bites of sound rapped out from its edges. Cutting across the voices of the watching men, it silenced them, demanded they listen.

All but Nalatan. As the performer, he commanded. One foot stamped the ground. The sword blade clashed against the iron rod, sending out a cadence. The drummer pushed to the inner edge of the circle surrounding Nalatan, took up the beat. Around that steadiness, the fingers drew rhythmic arcs, angles of embellishment.

Nalatan responded with increased vigor.

The men took up a wordless chant. Deep, primeval, it rumbled mystery.

Nalatan moved faster. The circle of spectators tightened, forced Tate closer to him. His eyes were blank, features taut in concentration. He breathed in rough gusts.

A strange, humming sort of tension welled in Tate, drew flesh tight across muscles that ached to move. She refused that urging, battled the woman inside her she couldn't acknowledge, a woman who filled her with a fear she wanted to embrace. Her blood felt thick. Hot. A sheen of perspiration tingled on her skin. She was part of his dance, an accomplice in his every sensation. And fantasy.

Again, she told herself that this was all wrong. She rubbed wet palms on her thighs.

The sword and rod darted and whispered in complex curves. Through that glitter, his eyes sought hers. For the briefest of moments, there was contact. A sensation of unrestrained joy seized the muscles at the small of her back in an icy fist.

Everyone *else* saw Nalatan's war dance; Tate knew he danced for her.

She saw raw, animal strength channeled into grace and controlled power. She saw a mind capable of restraint freed to concede its passion. The dance was an expression of totality.

Entranced into the fabric Nalatan wove before her, Tate soared. Tightness gripped her throat. She realized with a sudden, frightening vulnerability that were it not for that constriction, she would long since have shouted at him.

To encourage him to greater effort, out of admiration and involvement? To make him stop, out of fear of what his dance said of risk and mortality?

Silence held the crowd still for a good three heartbeats when Nalatan finished. Then, like one of the bay's waves crashing on rock, they cheered. Several men ran to him, half dragging, half pushing him to the table. Dripping sweat, flushed with effort and excitement, he rose on tiptoe to see past them, searching for Tate once again. Finding her, he lifted the sword high, waved at her. His eyes held hers fractionally longer than before, and she believed she read them, told herself there was hope and question and fire there.

Reaching the table and its food, he said something to the group, then stepped away. Stripping off the chain mail and the padded, quilted jacket under it, he put it on the ground, then added his arms. He trotted to the water and plunged in. When he finished bathing, a man met him with a large bunch of greenery. Nalatan brushed the moisture off with it, then headed back toward the table.

He grinned at Tate. She nodded, waved back, reminding herself to control her smile. It had to be friendly. Not a bit more.

Conway touched her shoulder and Tate squealed surprise. She rounded on him. He grinned down at her. She said, "You startled me," and wanted to bite her tongue.

"I noticed. He's something, isn't he?"

"Exhibitionist. Is that the gear Helstar made?"

Conway shrugged. "Ask him. He's coming over here."

As Tate turned, she noticed Tee beside Conway. Her expression was contemplative. Once more, Tate had the feeling the other woman was weighing things, factoring everything about both Conway and Nalatan. Tate wondered if she'd been so examined herself.

Nalatan was wolfing a slab of bread piled with meat. His color was still high, and his skin gleamed. Tate braced herself for when he came close, and was pleasantly relieved to discover he had a clean, athletic scent. Overlaying maleness was the sea, and a mix of mint and thyme, obviously the leaves he'd used to rub down.

"I should apologize for behaving like that," he said. "It just feels good to be carrying my own kind of weapons again. That Kossiar sword's as clumsy as it is ugly."

Tate said, "Helstar made all that stuff this soon?"

Nalatan smiled. "He already had the knives; it was just a matter of having someone fit the scabbards to the leather bands. A couple of apprentices made the rod and hand shield. He had a blade similar to our style, so he didn't need much time to finish it."

Tee stepped forward. "Exactly where do you live? What's your tribe like?"

Nalatan swallowed a bite before answering. "No tribe. I was born to one, of course, but I took the monk's staff in my sixth summer. The brotherhoods live in the mountains, not far from the villages that supply most of the monks. We serve no master. We live only to protect Church."

"Why help Sylah, then? Your brotherhood's taken sides in Church's split?"

Nalatan explained his present situation. Conway added, "For us, the important thing is to get Sylah out of here in good condition. The Door's become our mission as much as hers."

Tee looked from one to the other of them with a pent-up energy in her manner that warned of challenge. "I, too, do Church's work here." She smiled crookedly. "Church isn't exactly aware of it."

Conway struck his forehead with his palm. "I knew there was more to this Borbor and his tight little compound. It's the slaves, isn't it? Just like Ola. You're working with the slaves."

Unsmiling, Tee said, "That's very observant, but if something warned you, it's probably warned the Chair's agents, too. I'd best tell Wal and Borbor."

Conway grabbed her arm before she could leave. "I didn't see anything. I know you. I guessed. What've you done?"

"We've rescued six slaves. Wal took them to the Whale Coast. And he brought back a hundred swords." She waved an arm, encompassing east and south. "The swords are out there now, ready to cut down slavers and slave owners. Wal has room for twenty escapees this time, inside false bulkheads in his boat."

Tate said, "I'm proud of you. What you're doing is wonderful."

Tee's smile was tight. "It's good you think so. I'm asking you to help us."

CHAPTER 57

It was a week after Lanta's return from Trader Island when Sylah faced the Chair defiantly. "You task me with your wife,

335

your unborn child, but won't let me go beyond the walls of this fort? What contradiction is this?"

The Chair looked uncomfortable. "One of my primary responsibilities is to protect the people of Kos from . . . from . . ."

"Contamination. That's what you're trying to say." Sylah spat the words. Her arm-flinging gesture almost struck Lanta, beside her. "Are we so dirty? Ill? Does the sight of us cause pain?"

"The opposite." The gray day behind the Chair muted the multicolored window. His yellow blouse and green trousers had the look of a spring morning suffering a chill rain. The heavy cedar smell of the paneling, normally soothing, seemed rank.

"Yasmaleeya needs to see her mother, her sisters, her home. I can protect her body. You're responsible for her mind. If you fail her, she's lost already. We'll suffer for it, but you'll know the fault is yours."

"I am the Chair!" He was on his feet, hand on the jeweled hilt of the dagger at his waist. For several deep, heavy breaths, he leaned forward. Lanta touched a shoulder against Sylah's arm. Sylah told herself to be firm; if she was to save Yasmaleeya and so save the search for the Door she had to have information. Yasmaleeya's family had to supply it.

The Chair said, "I could have you tortured."

"I am Church."

He laughed unpleasantly. "At least half of Church would sing thanks. How do I know Priestess Lanta hasn't already Seen that Yasmaleeya dies? You could be looking for a way to escape."

"You insult. Abandon my friends? Say it, and spare me any further need to deal with you."

Lanta said, "Your accusation of me is wrong. Your accusation of Sylah is unforgivable. Yasmaleeya deserves Sylah. You don't." The shoulder touching Sylah vibrated.

Befuddled rather than angry, the Chair watched Lanta declaim. His look slowly changed to wry acceptance. He sat down, slumping, shaking his head. Addressing Sylah, he waved weakly in Lanta's direction. "Do you know what I would give to have someone feel such loyalty for me? Or to experience the loyalty and affection you hold for your friends?" His expression shifted. The faint smile broadened, but it turned bitter. "I did well; using your sense of loyalty to assure Yasmaleeya of your attention is effective."

"It's our duty. We won't fail her."

He elbowed himself upright. "I won't fail her either. Bos will make arrangements for an escort." He addressed Lanta. "You said 'your Yasmaleeya' when speaking of her. She belongs to me, of course. She's only the bearer, however. There's no romantic attachment. There are rumors enough within these walls; let's have none on that subject."

"I understand." Lanta backed away with Sylah.

Outside, the two dark robes rustled and whispered past the gaping shark jaws. Sylah was unaware of their silent menace. Her thoughts were on Yasmaleeya.

The girl was as healthy as a mule. Not much brighter, unfortunately. And every bit as stubborn. Still and all, her naive sweetness could be touching. Since recovering from her cold, Yasmaleeya's childlike homesickness daily improved on an already magnificent capacity for inactivity, food, and liquids.

Sylah found her patient lounging in a hammock in the courtyard. Looking up at Sylah, she extended a porcelain cup, the movement painfully slow. Red-rimmed eyes blinked rapidly. "Strawberry rhubarb?" Yasmaleeya sighed the invitation. Sylah shook her head. The cup sagged, spilled. Yasmaleeya said, "I'm so tired. You're sure you won't have some? Very good for the blood. See how red?"

Sylah shuddered. Church continually fought against such assumptions. Of course strawberry and rhubarb were good for the blood. So were onions and apples. They were all good for health in general. Color had nothing to do with it. Sylah's thoughts flew back to the Chair and the Harvester participating—*sharing*—in pagan ritual. Small wonder Yasmaleeya and those around her believed in "like benefits like."

It was time for Yasmaleeya's walk. Another battle, Sylah thought. She closed her eyes, preparing herself. When she opened them, they were drawn to the far side of the courtyard. Cloud shadow raced across the inner wall. Idly, she watched it. Light bathed one of the high balconies. Her eye caught the silver glimmer of the Harvester's hair as she turned to go inside.

The Chair was on his throne. The Harvester walked the length of the room with her firm, self-assured stride. Inside a flowing sleeve, she picked at a loose thread, rolling it between her fingers.

Stopping at the dais, she nodded greeting. It was far short of the effusiveness normally afforded the Chair. The faintest suggestion of a frown touched his brow.

The Harvester said, "She's in the courtyard with the bearer. We can speak."

337

"Everything went as we planned. As you predicted, to be fair. You know Sylah remarkably well."

"I know what she needs, what she wants to see and hear. The work is yours."

He laughed easily. "Pleasant work. She's quite beautiful. It's a shame to waste her."

The Harvester's patrician features hardened, the thin lips drooped at the corners. "We are agreed to a plan."

"Did I suggest a change? You're an invaluable ally, but it's not pleasing to question my every comment. Or interpret what I say. Have I deceived you in any way?"

"No. You've been scrupulously honest. I'm concerned, though. I worry that you may be enjoying your games too much. Sylah's no fool. The antislavery plot is very real, very dangerous."

His look was pitying. "Dear Harvester. Look at me; product of generations of plots, coups, intrigues, rebellions. My ancestors rode earthquakes and tidal waves to supremacy because we're as ruthless as nature. Our power helped Church to her highest glories. We crushed her when it suited us. You suggest this raving Priestess and her noisy followers are a great, terrible danger. Consider, please. Two make noise; they kill some scum of no consequence. One is a monk, a brave, stupid warrior, who helps the first two, and whose greatest ambition is to die with glory. One's a woman who pretends to see the future, and refuses to do so. The leader of this fearsome band has a vision of a secret that died generations ago. If she's simply a misguided fanatic, she's a lovely one, and it'll entertain me to sample whatever amusement she can provide. Men use women. Church uses belief. The Chair uses you all."

Dryly, the Harvester said, "Thus Kos prospers."

"Exactly." Raw malice made the Harvester yearn to look away. He said, "You babble of truth and moral determination and integrity. In the name of Church, you condemn your own. In the name of honesty, you betray. This Sylah is no more than a drink of cold water for my thirst. I will have her, this Flower of your Church. I will have the killing magic possessed by her companions. You're so proud of seeing and reading all our human gestures. Hear this: from birth, I was taught to hide within myself. Expressions? Reactions? You see what the Chair wants you to see. As a child, I was beaten for crying when hurt, or hungry, or afraid. Even for showing pleasure. To me, your incontrovertible signals are merely techniques."

Shining pearls of sweat traced the paled curve of the Harvester's upper lip. "I pride myself on reading people. You've deceived me. It's a frightening realization."

"Honesty is your protection. Our agreement was made in good faith; Kos and Church will be as one. Let Sylah know you as her indomitable enemy. Already she thinks of me as one who can be made to understand, even to help."

"And Yasmaleeya? How does blaming Sylah for her death force Sylah closer to you?"

The Chair's rugged, square face was disingenuous. "Everything can be turned to advantage, if one will only think. Yasmaleeya is mindless. To my chagrin, it took me several days to discover that. Certain attractions clouded my thinking. The Chair's son must have an intelligent bearer, so when you said the midwife expected Yasmaleeya to die in childbirth, I determined to use the fact. When Yasmaleeya dies, those who would see me beached will reveal themselves. Bos will see to it that Sylah is named a witch; the blame will be hers. My enemies will stand exposed to me, and Sylah will be driven to me for protection. Along with her friends. We'll have their complete confidence and cooperation. Now, isn't that better than having some clumsy torturer slice little snippets of information off them?"

"Yasmaleeya and the child may survive."

"Your determination to underestimate me is becoming very irritating. If childbirth doesn't finish the useless bitch, other arrangements are in place. Nevertheless, you said childbirth would kill her. It better."

The force of his sudden, growing anger was like a fist against the Harvester's chest. She took a half step backward.

Instantly, her face flamed, warmth flowing down her throat, under the high collar of her robe. She deliberately reclaimed the lost ground. "Rumor says sailors nearly captured one of the lightning weapons. Perhaps we're preoccupied with Sylah."

"Sylah and all her forces will come to us. My methods are subtle, but they'll produce the best results."

The Harvester put a hand on the edge of the dais. "Subtle? Your lust screams aloud. You risk the loss of people and weapons capable of defeating armies because you want her body. She isn't worth our goals."

The Chair swept upright to step forward. He dropped dramatically to his knees and put his face close to the Harvester's. "I will have whatever I want. *Obey!*"

Blotches of color swirled across his contorted features. For one terrifying instant the Harvester's imagination pictured ferocious evil boiling under the flesh. White-hot rage mocked his bragging claim of control over all his responses. Madness choked the air around him with a thick, soured-milk stink.

Thoroughly frightened, the Harvester wasted no time on good-byes. She backed away quickly, awkwardly, turning to dash for the door to the hallway. Out there was safety. The gleaming, hungry ovals of the shark maws were symbols, nothing more.

CHAPTER 58

Yasmaleeya extended a lazy arm beyond the sedan chair to flick open her folding fan. Bits of glass set into the tips of the wooden blades caught sunbeams, tossed the light. Wan, eyes closed, she reclined in the roofed, ornate chair, carried by eight sturdy slaves. The men wore sweat-stained coarse shirts and loin-cloths; more sweat dripped from their noses, squished in their crude sandals. Lounging, shaded, laved by the soft air of her passage, Yasmaleeya's flowing chiffonlike layers remained clean and fresh.

Sylah and Lanta rode horses alongside. When Yasmaleeya unleashed a sigh and let the fan drop to her breast, Sylah rolled her eyes and grimaced. Lanta turned away to giggle.

Sylah wasn't terribly surprised that the drama of Yasmaleeya's decline coincided with the slaves' turning off the road. At the end of a graveled approach sat a large sprawling house. Flowers, shrubs, and shade trees crowded spacious grounds inside a rail fence. Between the fence and the road, cattle kept the meadow cropped. From the roof and several windows, servants cried welcome and sympathy. Heroically, Yasmaleeya waved. The strain exhausted her. The hand flowed back to her breast. Her eyes closed. Her head lolled.

The wailing from the house doubled in volume.

Through clenched teeth, Lanta muttered, "You don't suppose we're going to have to put up with a whole family as silly as her, do you?"

Sylah didn't reply. Her worried look was answer enough.

Passing through the gate, they were met by an older woman dressed in a gleaming blue robe of simple elegance that reached to her feet. Smiling a welcome at the two Priestesses, she reached to take a fold of flesh at Yasmaleeya's upper arm between her thumb and the first joint of her index finger. Still smiling, she pinched like a demon. Yasmaleeya was instantly rejuvenated. Immense belly notwithstanding, she vaulted out of the sedan chair with a shrieking agility that left Sylah and Lanta slackjawed. The poor slaves, unexpectedly relieved of their load, practically skipped several steps before staggering to a halt.

Yasmaleeya hopped about, rubbing her injury and shouting indignation. Smiling benignly, the older woman stalked her, fingers poised like a pudgy little crab claw. Yasmaleeya squalled and retreated.

Sylah tore her eyes from the blue-clad woman's implacable advance. To Lanta, she said, "What in the name of holiness have we stumbled into?"

Amazingly, the older woman heard her over Yasmaleeya's yowling. Abandoning her prey, she turned her smile on Sylah. "You're the Sylah one. You're the Seer, Lanta. I recognize a certain inevitability about Yasmaleeya being serviced by a War Healer. I'm her mother. My name's Jeslaya."

Sylah said, "I know you, Jeslaya. I'm Sylah, Rose Priestess of the Iris Abbey. This is my companion, Lanta, Violet Priestess of the Violet Abbey."

Jeslaya frowned, "Of course you know me. I just told you who I am. How could you not know me? Are all unpeople so foolish? I've never met one."

Sylah ignored the questions. "The Chair asked us to help Yasmaleeya because he fears for her. Is there a history of difficult births in your family?"

Jeslaya shook her head. "Difficult, yes, but not until Yasmaleeya's sister has one of us been lost to childbirth. You knew the baby died, too?"

Lanta leaned forward. "We know. Why did it happen?"

Jeslaya's features collapsed. Grief scarred them, was quickly chased away by the return of determined control. Still, her hands wadded the soft cotton of her dress at her sides. "My daughter was healthy. As strong as Yasmaleeya, just as pretty. She was solid-minded, too, not full of sighs and songs, like this one. She had an easy pregnancy, Priestess, but the last weeks the baby grew. So fast. The midwife tried everything."

Yasmaleeya took a few tentative steps toward her mother. "I'm lots stronger than my sister." She faced Sylah and Lanta. "My sister was always the favorite. Now I'm the bearer, and they're all jealous. My baby's going to be the next Chair, and I'm going to be the most important woman of Kos." She rounded on Jeslaya.

"You always loved her best. All of you." Then, without any warning, she fell into Jeslaya's arms, begging forgiveness, blaming pregnancy for unsettling her mind.

Gazing over her daughter's shoulder as she absently patted a back shaking with sobs, Jeslaya raised her eyebrows in an expression of fond surrender. "She's my child. I love her."

"I love you, too!" It was more blubber than declaration. Yasmaleeya stepped back, hands on the shorter woman's shoulders. Holding back more tears, she said, "I'm fine, Mother, I really am. Sylah says I eat too much and there's too much water, but that's just because she's unpeople, never treated a Kossiar before. I need my strength. Everything's going to be all right. I haven't gained all that much weight. See?" She spun around. The stomach lagged, caught up. Momentum carried it several degrees before it swung back to a jiggling halt. Yasmaleeya smiled as if it were all an acrobatic accomplishment.

Sylah controlled herself. To Jeslaya, she said, "What was the sister's name?"

Jeslaya's chin rose. Emotions cut the expressive features into confused disarray. "Family mustn't speak the name of a woman who died in childbirth. Family is shamed. Children are women's purpose, and women mustn't fail their mission. Isn't it the same among unpeople?"

The sense of the last question was hope, a plea that pulled Sylah to the older woman's side. She linked arms with her. "Not exactly the same, but little better. Where we live, however, change is coming. Slowly. We grow stronger."

Yasmaleeya interrupted. "Woman's place and duty is to live to serve."

Jeslaya sneered. "She's so proud of her new position she doesn't care what happens to the rest of us. Ever since Bos selected her to bear that monstrous fool's get, she's been so female-proper it makes you sick."

Moving to place herself between the house and her mother, Yasmaleeya looked genuinely ill. "Stop! What if a servant heard you? Or worse, a slave? Even I couldn't help you."

Nervously, Jeslaya fell back on bravado. "If anyone asks, I meant 'big' when I called him a monster. He'd be happy about that."

Lanta said, "What of your husband, Jeslaya? And your father? Large men?"

"Large men, large boy babies. We scream, they boast. Family tradition."

"Mo-*ther!*"

They all ignored Yasmaleeya's plaint. Lanta said, "I must ask: you're sure there weren't other deaths? Perhaps close relatives?"

Jeslaya made a three-sign. "Never. We've been very fortunate. That's why Bos chose my daughters, you know; the big babies thing. It's important that the Chair's son be grand and impressive." She glared at Yasmaleeya, daring a response.

In an uncharacteristic show of intelligence, the daughter pretended to have discovered a hangnail. A moment later, she shouted at the house for a slave to bring water, amending that to fruit juice. "Raisins, too. Lots."

Jaw set, anger steeling her expression, Jeslaya said, "Many believe Yasmaleeya's midwife and her family were poisoned because she brought bad news to the Chair. They believe an innocent slave was blamed for it."

"Why would she be killed?" Lanta's high-pitched question reflected her shock.

"The Chair is not to be disappointed. All Kos knows that."

The group fell silent as a young woman in a shapeless yellow smock ran from the house with a tray holding a pitcher, four mugs, and a large bowl of raisins. When the woman put her burden down and left, they all settled to the ground beside it. Yasmaleeya grabbed the raisins. Pouring grape juice, Jeslaya went on, "I tried to make Yasmaleeya understand when Bos' men started asking questions. Being the bearer is no honor. Having a large child is a dangerous thing."

"*My* son will lead all of Kos to ever greater glory."

Jeslaya looked at her daughter as if she'd just discovered this exotic creature on her grass. Slowly turning to Sylah, she said, "The best midwife in Harbor. Probably in Kos." Suddenly, her eyes were wet, glistening. "Why couldn't she save my little girl? They say the other Church woman, the tall one with the silver hair, talked to the midwife. Now the Church one says my Yasmaleeya will die, too. They say you have magic. More than that Harvester? More than the midwife?" The older woman, her dignity all but shattered, tore her gaze from Sylah. She lunged forward and grabbed her daughter's wrists. "Listen to me. If the midwife said anything to you, or if the Harvester did, tell these women. They're trying to save your life."

Gently, but determinedly, Yasmaleeya disengaged a hand, then used it to pop a handful of raisins through an arch, superior smile. Talking, chewing, she said, "The old woman was a fraud. I happen to know that my Chair was going to send her far away, in-

343

land, because she didn't save my sister. It was just bad luck that slave poisoned them all. He was a rebel and a thief. If the Chair had the midwife killed, why would he kill her whole family? Do you believe every rumor you hear?"

Jeslaya's voice admitted defeat. "You're too foolish to be afraid. It's unimaginable."

Yasmaleeya laughed merrily. "I'm smart enough to make the Chair think I'm afraid. He'll be all the more grateful when his son's born strong and healthy."

Sylah and Lanta exchanged glances. "Have you ever spoken to the Harvester about the midwife?" Sylah asked Yasmaleeya.

"No. They talked together. All huddled and secretive. Like you and Lanta do sometimes."

Sylah stilled Lanta's angry twitching with a warning look that gradually turned thoughtful as she watched Yasmaleeya simultaneously squirm about in search of a comfortable position and pour the last of the grape juice into her mug. The raisins were gone.

Abruptly, Sylah rose. "Get up, Yasmaleeya. We're going to examine you."

"What, again? You did that just four or five days ago."

"Five. And we're doing it again. Now." To Jeslaya, Sylah said, "Is there a room where we'll have privacy?"

"Of course. Come." Regaining her composure, the older woman moved with swift grace, clearly pleased by Sylah's sudden decisiveness. "You've thought of something. Anyone would see that. I'm glad you're trying. Someone has to; Yasmaleeya certainly won't. How could I have raised such a vain stonebrain?" She stopped, pulled Sylah to her side so she could whisper. "She's not witched, is she? Like my other poor girl?"

Sylah said, "Church won't accept witches. I believe they're just talk."

Jeslaya blanched and made a quick three-sign. "You just don't know what to look for, because you think Church is the only truth. Church didn't save my other girl."

"Church is trying very hard to save this one. And if we find any witch interfering, Church will tend to her, as well."

Sylah regretted saying it as soon as the words were formed. The image of the Harvester, her harsh features split in a triumphant laugh, filled her mind.

It took all of Sylah's will to dispel it.

By then they were entering the house. The architecture was unlike anything Sylah had ever seen. Massive wooden posts supported equally heavy crosstimbers. The latter, with square

344

surfaces, provided the base for roofstruts. There were no load-bearing interior walls, although where wings branched off, those corners were double-posted. Examining the interior, she remembered that the exterior was a sheath of lightweight boards; so were the inner walls, although the latter were polished. When she asked about it, Jeslaya told her, "Terrible stuff if there's a fire, but much safer when we have an earthquake. The support posts move alarmingly, but they don't often fall."

They entered a small room with its own fireplace and a window much like the Chair's. Unfinished sewing projects lay on the table at the room's center, and two cabinets overflowed with cloth, thread, and sewing paraphernalia.

A protesting Yasmaleeya was soon stripped and on the table. She continued to complain while Sylah and Lanta poked and prodded. All that was as nothing, however, when Sylah asked for a brass basin, and demanded that Yasmaleeya urinate in it. Only Jeslaya's powers of persuasion and sacred oaths got the matter accomplished.

Sylah signaled Jeslaya they were finished, and indicated the door with a covert nod. Jeslaya hurried her daughter off with promises of mint-and-honey tea while the latter was still rearranging clothing.

Peering outside, assuring they were unheard, Sylah said, "Your observations?"

Lanta was grim. "Just as Jeslaya said: the child grows faster as each day of its due time approaches. Also, the uterine fluid's excessive. I'm a poor Healer."

"You're an excellent Healer. We're dealing with something very unusual, very insidious. And you've described almost all of the symptoms. The Iris Abbess talked about a similar case. Sweet sickness."

"But Jeslaya's a good mother. If there was sweet sickness in the family, she'd watch her children like a hawk."

Sylah nodded. "That was the terrible thing about the other incident. All the trouble came during pregnancy. Only afterward, discussing it, did anyone guess. The mother and child were both lost, so no one's ever been absolutely certain."

"You're saying that even if we're right about the sweet sickness, the other woman may have died of something else. And so might Yasmaleeya's sister. And so might Yasmaleeya." Lanta stared at the basin, transfixed.

Taking a deep breath, Sylah exhaled in a rush. "We'll worry about that next. First . . ." She let the sentence trail away. Gripping the edge of the table with one hand, she closed her eyes. Quickly, as if to complete the task before her mind could grasp what she was doing, she dipped her fingers in the fluid and tasted.

Outside, a gull squalled ribald amusement.

Lanta offered a drying cloth. Sylah chewed on it, scraped at her mouth, tongue, teeth. Next she grabbed at a proffered mug of water, rinsing, spitting out the window. She poured more water over her hands, drank more, scrubbed and spit. After a final deep breath and a shiver, Sylah spoke. A bit too forcefully, Lanta thought. She kept the observation to herself; Sylah appeared to be in no mood for constructive criticism.

"It's there. The sweet sickness. No mistake." Sylah said, and made a three-sign.

"You're sure?"

Sylah's eyes flashed. She jerked a thumb at the basin. "You doubt? Taste."

Blushing, Lanta shook her head. "What do we do?"

"Risk. I feel the Harvester's hand in this. She wouldn't hesitate to arrange the midwife's murder." She paused, laughed bitterly. "There was a time when I couldn't have imagined that, much less said it so easily. Anyhow, with the midwife dead, she could easily convince the Chair that I should treat Yasmaleeya. If I lose the girl, I eliminate myself from the Harvester's game."

Lanta squirmed nervously. "How could she arrange a murder? She can't leave the fort. I think the Chair's involved."

Sylah thought back to their first dinner, remembered the slave woman who was the center of so much deference by her fellow servants. Musing, she said, "Somehow, Odeel's made Church her weapon here in Kos. There are spies here. I'm sure there are those who do as she orders."

"Then we have to tell the Chair right away."

"We'd only be accused of failing. Our friends would suffer."

Lanta inhaled until she thought her lungs would burst. Her emotions spun inside her, filling her with apprehension. Sylah refused to see how far her delusions about the Chair had carried her. Rueful awareness shot through Lanta, obscured everything momentarily: She was, after all, the authority on infatuation.

Nevertheless, someone had to speak.

Lanta said, "The Chair is capable of his own deviousness, his own murders. Odeel is wicked; no one argues that. You mustn't make excuses for the Chair, Sylah. Your view has become confused. This talk of the Chair as ally; do you mean Church's ally? Or yours? Remember what you set out to accomplish. It had nothing to do with alliances. Your will isn't your destiny. Your will is the way *to* your destiny."

Sylah gestured distractedly. She dismissed Lanta's words. "You—all of you—only see the surface. You don't understand him. He's been a great asset to Church. He'll be a greater one in the future. I know. Our only real enemy is Odeel. To thwart her, we must save the mother and child before it grows too large. It's our only chance."

Lanta backed away. "I know what you're thinking. You want to bring the baby early. What if we make a mistake?"

"You have what we need in your bag? The blackness?"

"I have it. I've never used it. Must we? I fear, Sylah. We could kill her."

"The Iris Abbess always said she believed sweet sickness swelled the child until the birth passage was impossible. If we force out the child early, we may save them both. If we wait, we certainly lose them both." She reached to grasp Lanta's shoulders, forced the smaller woman to stand erect. "We'll fight, Lanta. We must. Not like the men, though. We do it to save life, to create life. Our battle is the proudest of all. Savor it—the excitement, dread, hope. We've been dared. We accept. We *live.*"

CHAPTER 59

Conway harangued Tate and Nalatan enthusiastically, oblivious to their worry. He paced the small room like something caged. New clothes reflected his identification with Tee's For people. Black leather vest over black cotton shirt, black full trousers, black boots. He was saying, "The slaves we're freeing are some of Kos' best artisans. Their loss is a serious blow to Kos. They're a tremendous asset for us. I mean for the For, for the economy of the Three Territories."

Nalatan was less sanguine. "The loss of twenty slaves will irritate more than harm. Getting them all together, much less safely to sea, is going to be very difficult."

Irrepressible, Conway jabbed a finger at them. "Tee says they're all alerted. They can go in minutes."

Skeptical still, Nalatan said, "Twenty slaves holding the same secret. You have ten times twenty chances of being betrayed. These men live under the lash. Or worse. For some a day without pain is a luxury, a dream. Many men break for much smaller reasons."

"These men would rather die than live as slaves. They've got enough character to take a chance."

A hint seemed to taint the words. To one as sensitive as Nalatan it was a shout. Flushing, he was on his feet instantly. He shrugged through Tate's restraining touch. Only when she called his name did he stop. She tensed at the wounded pride in his face, but disguised her alarm. A gentling hand on his shoulder assured he stayed in place. Conway, pacing again, saw nothing.

Tate spoke to him. "We haven't heard from Sylah or Lanta for almost half a moon. What happens to them if this operation of yours comes apart? What if you're identified as part of it?"

"Sure, there's some danger of that. But we're freeing slaves."

Tate shook her head. "You're going to bring down repression like hailstones. It won't work. And we're not here to free slaves, Matt; we're here because we agreed to help Sylah. Don't you think you should at least let her know about this?"

Enthusiasm drained from Conway's manner. His shoulders slumped. "I guess that means you two aren't interested in helping."

Tate's anger flared. "You know how I feel about slavery, Matt. But we promised Sylah."

"And you've got your own project. You forgot to include that."

Tate recoiled. "Everything I've done has been for our goal. What I do for me is on my own time."

Dismissing her argument entirely, Conway left. He turned right down the hall. Fat candles burned in a pair of sconces, the farthest illuminating another door. Carefree shadows skated along the polished wood walls and floor. Entering the next room, his manner brightened. Seated at a long table, flanked by candelabras bearing a thicket of burning tapers, Tee sat facing him across a table sawn from a single massive log. Wal was with her, his back to Conway. Seeing Tee's shift of attention, the For sea captain looked over his shoulder. He waved greeting.

Rounding the table, Conway sat beside Tee. He broke his news dejectedly. "They won't help."

Frustration and anger cut across Tee's features, left a dark frown. "I expected better of them."

"And I told you they have reasons to keep out of it. I couldn't bring myself to tell them what you told me—if you don't fight slavery, you condone it. I agree, but I just couldn't say it to them."

Wal stood up. The dark man's expression was blank. "You're a good man. I welcome your help; never doubt it. But I think you're both mistaken here." He nodded a good-night and left.

For some time, neither of the couple moved. Finally, Conway slumped forward, forearms pressed to the table, fists clenched. "Everyone wants to tell me how to help. I give my dogs more freedom."

Tee got up, slid in behind him, massaged his shoulders. Conway continued, "The Door's Sylah's search, Tee. Her goal. I have to be something on my own. I want to share my dreams and my goals with you. Only you."

Tee stepped back. "We talked about that a long time ago."

Leaning back against the chair, he reached blindly for her hands. She pulled them behind her, retreated another half step. Her face was pained, confused.

Conway put his own hands back on the table. He said, "Don't you believe that if one person wants something, he can make that something come true for someone else, as well?"

Tee sighed. "You speak generalities. I'm talking about us. About me. I'll stay as I am forever."

"This is how it started for us," he said. He stared, heavy-lidded, at the fine grain of the table. His voice dropped to a husky rumble. "Remember? We were in my room in Altanar's castle. My back to you, your hands on my shoulders, rubbing away uncertainty. Fear. You knew I needed you. You wanted me then, Tee; I know you did. I think you still do. I'll always need you. Want you."

"I needed you, too," she said. Unlike the aggressive cast of his lowered pitch, her own softer tones were reticent. Sadness touched her voice as she continued. "You made me know I was a person, not a thing. All my life, I'll remember. But how can you ask me to live with you, knowing those things may *not* happen again?"

Swiftly, smoothly, he rose and turned, taking her in his arms before she could get away. She stiffened, cold as steel against him. Too excited to notice her reaction, he said, "That kind of spark never goes out, Tee. We can find it. I'll be so good to you, you'll have to love me. We'll have a lifetime of good moments."

His hands slid down her back. They came to rest just at the rise of her buttocks, the fingers splaying, pressing. She raised her hands to his chest, pushed her way out of his embrace. She was pale, her eyes round. She begged. "Don't do this. I'm not who you think I am, not the woman you want me to be."

"You can be. You made me more than I was. Let me help you."

She took a jerky, awkward backward step, shook her head in a vehement deniàl. The movement excited the candle flames; they swayed and cowered.

Tee ran for the door. When she turned, she said, "Wal called you a good man. He missed the mark. There never was a finer one, Matt Conway. Whatever else I am, I'm not blind."

Conway stared at the empty doorway for a long time, as if the power of his yearning would fill it with her body, her voice, the aroma of her, one more time. After a while, he straightened, rubbing his eyes. He licked the ball of his thumb and the tip of his index finger. Contemplatively, he snuffed out the candles, one by one. Occasionally he wet the fingers again. His lips moved as he worked. By the dim light of the last, hesitant flame, he smiled. "She loves me," he said.

The tiny hiss of the wick could have been the sibilance of an affirmative yes.

Or derision.

Nalatan hadn't spoken for so long Tate wondered if he'd fallen asleep. His breathing was slow and steady. She turned her head enough to examine him in the final touches of fading day. He'd rid himself of his armor and weapons, except for the sword that seemed to be as necessary as footwear. His shoulder nearly touched hers where they shared the backrest of a gnarled oak. Relaxed hands lay folded in his lap. She smiled softly, a touch of self-mockery in the expression; she'd been examining his profile, thinking of it as rich with character. Then it occurred to her she'd never considered a broken nose a mark of particularly high distinction.

Her mind did contrary things when it settled on Nalatan.

He said, "Did you hear it, too?"

"What? Hear what?"

"The seal. Barking. You were so quiet, I thought you were listening. Did you fall asleep?"

"No. I thought you were."

He chuckled. "I was thinking."

"Want to talk about it?"

"Some of it. I was feeling sorry for Conway. And me. He's facing a lot of trouble."

"Tee?"

His features were almost a silhouette in the steadily falling light. He nodded. "If we could keep him away from her, maybe he'd come to realize she doesn't love him. You'd be surprised how many of us think we've found the true love of our lives, and

350

then, because we can't be with her, we have time to think things through and change our mind."

The whole thing was as distasteful as anything he'd ever told her. Tate said, "What's this 'us'? Did you change your mind on some poor girl that believed in you?"

"Never. There was one. We agreed we should walk different paths. But it wasn't me who changed."

"Right." Tate's dry sarcasm made Nalatan squirm a bit. His jacket scraped on the rough tree bark. The smell of oak and leather whipped Tate's mind back through the centuries. She was sitting in the officers' club, drinking a chilled Chardonnay. There was a man across the table. She'd been unable to keep her eyes off his hands, imagining them discovering her, herself discovering them.

Nalatan's accusatory tones snapped her back to the present. ". . . left plenty of men dangling," he said.

Scrambling in her mind, she vaguely remembered what he'd been saying. "Me, lead a man on? You bet. Only fair. They're always trying to take advantage of a girl."

He made a choking sound, and she came erect, turning to hit his shoulder. "You saying I did something wrong?"

Pretending to cower, he laughed aloud. "I'd never say so. I value my life."

She settled back. "Don't ever forget it, either."

The comfortable silence drew around them again. Tate was watching the stars come to life when Nalatan spoke again. He was subdued. "You make me laugh. Not like anything that's ever come into my life before. That's the main reason I feel sorry for Matt Conway. There's no laughter, Donnacee. He thinks he loves Tee, and she thinks she can't love anyone. Lanta's afraid to confess her love to him. He knows fire, but he doesn't know warmth. I wonder if he'll ever learn the difference."

Uncomfortable with the weight of the conversation, Tate tried to deflect it. "This is strange ground for a monk, a warrior."

Nalatan was unperturbed. He rose easily, unhurried. Extending a hand to Tate, he said. "Walk with me. I need to move."

"Need to?" She took his hand, careful to keep her question light.

He nodded, a shadow against the stars. "In my brotherhood, we're taught to in-study. That means we sit and think. I always fall asleep. My master beat me until he realized my spirit needed movement in order to focus."

"I can't imagine anyone beating you. And surviving."

Softly, Nalatan said, "I love him. And he loves me. That's why he beat me."

Tate snorted. "That's dumb. You don't hurt people you love."

"If you deny Dodoy something, it hurts him. Do you do it from love, or malice?"

"He's a child. It's not the same. You're twisting things."

"You deny a child because you know things that he cannot. Shouldn't you do as much for an adult who's ignorant?"

Exasperated, Tate stopped, forcing Nalatan to turn to face her. "If I try to do something you know will get me hurt, would you beat me to make me stop?"

"Beat you? No. But if I loved you, I'd do anything to save you. Why ask? Do you plan something foolish?"

He seemed closer, and yet Tate wasn't aware that he'd taken a step. A disturbing warmth swept through her, exploring. The weight of his dark presence seemed to feed it. He said, "We're having at least two discussions, Donnacee. Both of us are saying too much, too little, and, quite possibly, nothing about what's really on our minds."

Turning him, she linked her arm through his to show him she had no fear of physical contact or any apprehension that the conversation had gotten out of hand. Donnacee Tate controlled herself, and she controlled what went on around her. Donnacee Tate had dated the smoothest, the most determined. She could afford to be as comradely as she chose. It was important to assure his feelings weren't hurt. She said, "We're just hearing each other out."

"As you say. Sometimes I'm more aggressive than I should be." He paused, then laughed at some inner thought, before adding, "We might never have met otherwise."

"I don't understand."

"My original plan was to follow you, protecting from a distance, until Sylah found the Door. Then I'd challenge Conway and kill him."

The unequivocal certainty lifted the hair on the back of Tate's neck. It also irritated. "If you're so good, how come he had to save your bacon, that day by the river?"

"Bacon? Pig meat? Yours is an amazingly crude dialect. They captured me because I was rash. They were preparing an attack on you. I thought I could kill a few of them and escape in the darkness. I was half right; my horse took a sword thrust and the escape part didn't happen. I killed more than I expected, though. Had to. Couldn't outrun them."

"Ridiculous." Tate breathed the word. "You think you're some kind of one-man army?"

He stopped, turned to her. "Since my ninth summer, I've been trained to kill. Not fight, Donnacee. You're a fighter. So is Conway and Sylah and Lanta. I admire you all. But I kill. You understand the difference? People play games to win. Make war to win. Gamble to win. I'm sworn to protect Church, and I kill those who threaten her. I'm allowed to defend a victim, protect someone weak, attack evil. If I choose to. If I believe it benefits Church, I have no option. My life, my skills, are born, live, die in my oath to Church."

"Church trains you?"

"My master. We of my brotherhood are his weapons. Conway's a noble man to agree to fight me. Because he saved me, he could cancel the challenge."

Shocked, Tate reached for his arm. "He knows that?"

"Of course. He needs the answer, though. And I can't break my oath."

"What if you win?"

"Oh, I'll win. He won't use the lightning weapons."

"He saved your life. You're *friends*. 'He won't use the lightning weapons.' How could you live with that, with killing a friend, just to make a stupid point?"

"I'm not sure I could. I've come to like him very much. When it's over, I'll probably shave my head and ride to attack the Moondance nomads."

"You're crazy."

"I understand why you say so. I've considered letting him win. I'm not ready to die, but I've had to consider it. It makes a man look into his heart, try to precisely define things such as honor and integrity. Conway's greatest fear isn't dying, it's living unsatisfactorily. If you save him from me, he'll be ashamed. You'll force him to seek death, and such men always do regrettable things."

"You've got all the answers, haven't you?"

Nalatan's murmured answer contrasted with her stridency. "Would it help if I told you I'm sorry I ever made the vow?"

"I'll stop you. Somehow."

"Can you stop Conway? He welcomes the contest. In his heart, he knows he'll lose. In a moment of mindless vanity and pain, I vowed to kill a stranger. Can't you, his tribeswoman, make him release me?"

"Maybe. Maybe." Hope was a small break in Tate's despair. "Tee could convince him night's day."

"She'll have to be very clever. But you're right. A man in love will do things."

A hard, callused hand lifted her chin. Instinctive reaction almost jerked her head back, but something checked the movement.

The woman who was always in control abandoned Tate.

It was as if his touch emptied her of everything save awareness of him. He said nothing. The wind herded wisps of mist through the trees, and leaves sighed at the passing. His face was almost in contact with hers; she felt its warmth, inhaled the humid masculinity of him. The other hand loomed at the edge of her vision, pale, descending, drifting closer. It touched her temple. He stroked her brow, then deliberately traced the arch of each eyebrow. The fingertips were rough; their touch was moth soft. They read her cheekbones, lips, the jaw line to her ear.

It *was* the memorization of a blind man, knowing each feature as a tactile message.

She told herself to move, to stop this.

Noiseless as a cat, he was suddenly gone. Bewitched by the suddenness, the completeness of it, one of her hands flew to her face as if to catch his. The other reached out, vainly.

He was so far away she could barely make him out in the starshine.

"I . . ." She swallowed, tried again. "I want to go back now."

"Yes." Hard, rough. Like his hands. As gentle, as tender.

Arm in arm, unspeaking, they walked toward Borbor's house. His step was unerring, confident despite the darkness. She moved to the pressure of his arm, letting him lead as if they danced.

Her head ached for coherence, for a return to a past whose simplicity lay shattered, along with her clearest dreams.

One touch. A shrill, scornful voice taunted her. One touch, and you're nothing but another empty, yearning vessel. Look at yourself. Weakling. Quitter. *Woman.*

She straightened her shoulders, lifted her head. Woman, for sure, she told herself. Problems, dreams, and all. Proud of it. And no quit to it.

Time to be honest, girl, she went on.

She cut her eyes his way.

He meant to kill Conway. She had to stop that.

Whatever happened, Nalatan had to live.

The ease of that transition sickened her, freed the nasty, name-

354

calling voice once more. It chattered guilt. She bit the inside of her lip until tears welled, and finally broke free of the nagging.

The guilt remained, a sticky, foul taint that clung to her every thought.

It made no difference.

She wanted Nalatan to live. She wanted him beside her.

She wanted him.

CHAPTER 60

Lanta stepped ashore on Trader Island wishing the ground would open up and swallow her.

It was vital that her friends know of developments in Harbor, but she dreaded facing them. The argument with Sylah about which of them should make the trip was unpleasant. Yasmaleeya's tantrum demanding that "the assistant Healer" go was the deciding factor. One more humiliation.

Sylah's a War Healer, Lanta thought, picking her way across squiggling lines of tide-strewn seaweed. I should be the one to attend to a pregnancy.

A dead fish gaped up at her, the eye sockets pillaged by the rapacious gulls.

She hated gulls. Snowy white, gracefully carving lovely patterns against a background of sea or sky, they screamed and fought and fouled constantly. Like life: a swift-winged facade of beauty, hiding cruelty and filth.

Behind her, the crew leapt over the side of the boat, heaving it up onto the beach.

At the house, Borbor himself welcomed her. Apologizing, he explained that her friends had all gone into Rathole with Tee and Wal. He added that Wal wanted to hire extra crewmen, and it was the only place to do it.

Borbor asked Lanta to wait at the house with him, but she refused, telling him how little time the Chair allowed her. Accepting the situation, Borbor sent for a horse and escort.

Lanta's hand stole to the True Stone at her breast. She thanked Borbor for his concern.

After an uneventful ride, the man in charge of Lanta's four-man group halted at the edge of the collection of huts that constituted Rathole. "We can't take you any farther, Priestess," he said.

"Trader's rules. A gang's only allowed a certain number of men in town at one time, and our quota's met. We'll watch from here. If anyone makes trouble before you reach the tavern, we'll ride them down. The Traders can argue the legal points after. Go ahead on in. Just act like you own the place."

The sound of him drawing a sword as she left wasn't reassuring. She felt eyes from every window, every doorway. There were so many horses tied to the hitching rail outside the tavern, she had to secure hers several yards from the sagging, leather-hinged door. That done, she moved as fast as dignity allowed, almost bursting into the noisy room.

It was dark. After the light of day, she found herself unable to recognize anyone. A coarse, heavy hand fell on her shoulder. An arm draped across her neck. She was drawn tight against the side of a stinking torso. Her head barely reached midpoint on the dimly perceived chest beside her. "Save me, Priestess." The breath carrying the voice stank worse than the body. The smell oozed through her hair, the sensation raising bumps on her flesh. She tried to slip away. The grip pinned her effortlessly. The voice went on. "I'm a bad man. I need someone to be nice to me, so I can learn how to be good again. Come upstairs; help me."

Leaning into him, she gained a lessening of the pressure on her shoulder. It gave her room to twist and spin away. The man was quick. Both hands reached for her. Lanta was even quicker. She had the shortknife out and pointed as he closed on her. Without either of them realizing exactly what was happening, he impaled his hand on the blade.

Pulling up short, he jerked the hand back. Disbelief made his face comical for the length of time it took him to study the wound and comprehend how all the bleeding had come to pass. Anger followed like a slow, inexorable tide. He roared and lunged. She dodged him easily, going under his reach. By then, however, the byplay was the center of attention for everyone. Hands grabbed her as she tried to escape, spun her around. They shook her, like a rag before a bull, mocking him. The man licked his lips and came forward grinning.

Nalatan and Tee broke through the wall of shouting faces. Nalatan's sword was bared, aimed at the man.

Tee said, "Sober up, Malor. The woman's Church and a friend of mine."

Malor put his hand on his sword hilt. "The bitch cut me. Get out of my way. No one cuts me." He hauled at the weapon.

Lanta would have sworn the words were still in her ears when the tip of Nalatan's sword disappeared between the teeth of Malor's open mouth. The shaggy head snapped back, lanky hair splaying out like wet mop strands. The sword froze. Nalatan said, "You act like a man who wants to die. You have three heartbeats left. Yes or no."

Gagging noises boiled out around the steel between Malor's teeth. His eyes rolled. Nalatan stepped back. Wiping saliva off the end of the weapon on Malor's trousers, he examined the blade distastefully before sheathing it. With exaggerated seriousness, he said, "You had me fooled, Malor. I thought you were ready for the next world. I almost made an unfortunate mistake."

Nalatan turned to where Tee was holding Lanta. "Are you all right?"

Conway repeated the question, hurrying up, full of concern. Lanta looked past him as she nodded. Tate stood halfway up the stairs leading to the second floor, back against the wall. She held her wipe leveled at the crowd. Dodoy cowered behind her.

Lanta smiled a greeting, thinking how cleverly Tate had chosen her position. She dominated the entire room from where she stood. As much as Lanta admired Tate's skill, she wondered about the culture that could produce her.

Conway blocked Lanta's view, moving to lead her outside. It broke her train of thought, pulled her attention back to him. She looked into his eyes. Such a beautiful, dark blue, so alive.

Why couldn't he have come to help her, instead of Nalatan?

Tee put an arm around her, saying, "Come outside, Lanta. Wal can finish our business by himself. This is no place for you."

Now that her eyes were adjusted to the dim light, Lanta was shocked to discover other women present. Ragged, dirty, they stood apart from the surround of men, still intent on herself and her friends. Glancing up, she saw there were others on the upstairs balcony. As she watched, a naked man opened a narrow door behind one of the women. Growling something unintelligible, he grabbed her and pulled her back in with him. The woman's eyes never left Lanta's.

Lanta remembered watching a wolf spider's funnel web one lazy afternoon. A cricket bumbled past the dark, silent entry. Lightning quick, the spider was on it. The cricket died almost resignedly, as if fate was so natural it was unremarkable. The hopeless acceptance of the woman on the balcony was no different.

Out on the dusty street, Tate joined them. Dodoy still clung to her leg. When Lanta looked up at her, Tate grinned. "Lovely crowd, but a bit informal."

Lanta had to laugh. When she did, she felt knotted muscles unwind. As soon as Tate had dispatched Dodoy out of earshot, it took little time for Lanta to give a very abbreviated summary of events at Harbor. She made no mention of the sweet sickness or the proposed induced birth. Tate promised to relay the information to Conway and Nalatan. Her only question was to ask if Lanta believed the Chair truly intended to release them if Sylah saved Yasmaleeya and the child.

Lanta hedged. "Sylah believes him. She says the Harvester is our major danger."

Tee said, "Sylah's mistaken. The Chair's as bad as Altanar. Only the slaves are willing to resist any longer. Most of them still remember freedom. The people of Kos never tasted it; they fear it. Now they fear the slaves, as well."

"Moondance," Lanta said. "As much as I agree with the slaves struggling to be free, I can't approve of Moondance. It's evil."

Calmly, Tee agreed, then, "We don't care, though. If Church is concerned, then you better get some people involved who'll provide leadership and support. Moondance is, and the slaves are flocking to their recruiters."

Lanta, flustered and embarrassed, stammered. "Could I work with you now? With the slaves, I mean? I'm a Healer. I'd be very valuable, if there's any trouble."

Tee's smile barely missed being patronizing. "If there's trouble, we'll need a War Healer. It's too early for rebellion. For now, we're moving out healthy, skilled men whose loss hurts Kos most."

Tate interjected. "No women?"

Tee glowered. "Not because I don't want to. Female slaves aren't allowed to learn complex tasks here. They even call the work they do 'slavehand.' Can you imagine how tiresome it can be to warp a loom to weave that fine material they call moonlight? It can pull your eyes out of your head. Well, that's slavehand. A male slave supervises her, a male slave does the weaving. The loss of a woman slave in Kos is an inconvenience." She nodded at the tavern. "And even the slaves pity the women who work in there."

"At least they made a choice. A rotten one, but their own," Tate said.

Tee looked at her pityingly. "They were sent here. They're Kossiars. Barren. Every year or so, the Chair sends out warmen to round them up. They're shipped out here, where they can earn coin and inform on their customers. Everyone knows they're

358

spies, just like the servants who work for the Traders. Drunken sailors and gang members either forget that, or never care."

Quietly, Lanta asked, "Can't a man love a woman without having children?"

"Not in Kos." Tee's smile was vicious. "No babies, no husband. The best thing that can happen to a woman slave here is to be owned by the husband of a barren woman. If the owner loves his wife. Say a slave gets impregnated by her owner. The owner's wife wants to claim the child as her own. See how wondrously that increases the slave's status? The truly lucky ones even live out their lives with the family and watch the child grow up. She has to be wise enough to never show any affection that might be seen as parental, of course."

Tate said, "There's no end, is there?"

Lanta rounded on her. "There *must* be. We must see to it." To Tee, she said, "I have to help."

Tee looked to Tate, an eyebrow raised, her head cocked. It was a silent challenge, understood by all three women. The pause stretched into a contest. Tate spoke. "My allegiance is to Sylah. For now. When this Door thing is cleared up, things'll be different."

Softly, chiding, Tee said, "Conway feels he can do both."

Tate lost her temper. "If you gave a solitary rip what Conway feels, you wouldn't use him like a tool. Don't you dare tell me what Conway feels. You're not a well-respected authority on his feelings."

Tee colored. Still mild, her voice was edged. "I'd use the One in All, if I knew how, and never a thought for His feelings. Nor any apologies." Turning to Lanta, she asked, "Would you walk with me? We should have a talk."

Torn, Lanta didn't know what to do. Tate continued to fume. Tee, icily controlled, waited patiently. Lanta merely wanted harmony. She struggled for the words to soothe this wound.

Tate decided the issue. "I'm taking Dodoy back to Borbor's house. Whatever you decide, Lanta, I'll support you any way I can. Understand; I'm Sylah's trooper."

"Fair enough."

Tee led Lanta down the rutted street past the last house, where she turned off to sit on a downed log. She patted a space beside her. Lanta settled there. Tee said, "We may be the two most different women in Kos. Maybe in the world."

"Why is that important?"

"Because we love the same man."

Lanta rose swiftly, too startled to hide her reaction. Tee laughed quietly. "Why should we dance, Lanta? You've heard all about me. Men; when they're happy, they bawl their secrets like bull calves. When they despair, they cry to everyone who'll listen. And all the time they brag about their iron-willed silence. Faw!" She stood to face Lanta, putting her hands on the smaller woman's shoulders. She forced her to look up and meet her gaze. "I want Matt Conway more than breath. But I fear, Lanta. Am I too broken to heal? I may destroy him. So I dare you. Fight me for him, force me to be the best I can. Maybe I can find the woman I wanted to be once." For a moment she was lost to a time and place only she could see. Then she was back at Lanta, fiercer than ever. "If you win his heart, I quit him. I give him to you. Love him for both of us. Give him the joy we both wish him."

Lanta gripped Tee's blouse at the collar, twisted it in her fist. "Who are you—*what* is he—that you make him a possession? I take my happiness in what you lose? How dare you?"

"Pride? I confess my heart to you, and you spout shallow, witless pride? Stop it! He's no present. He thinks he loves me. Poor fool, he can't see that he loves you, too, or that you love him. I'm offering you a *fight*."

It was so candid Lanta released her, turned away from the righteous anger. Tee spoke again, cajoling. "Join with me, Lanta. Help me. Conway needs to know he's more than the man who controls the lightning weapons. His future is grander than that; his wife must be grand. Between us we'll help him find himself. And one of us."

"You want him to help you smuggle slaves out of Kos. If he's caught, all of us die. The quest for the Door is defeated."

Tee pushed on Lanta's shoulders, gently increasing the pressure until Lanta was seated on the log again. Tee knelt in front of her. "The Door is Sylah's dream, Lanta. Maybe it's there, maybe it's not. Matt Conway's very real. So are you. So am I. Three people, each able to help complete the other. If Sylah's Door exists, can its discovery do that for any of us? If it doesn't exist, will you be able to live with that failure, knowing you sacrificed the full life that Conway—or you, or I—might enjoy because you were afraid to let him grow? If the Chair catches us freeing Kossiar slaves, of course we'll die. If I must die, then I'll die now, young, beside a man I love, rather than old and alone, cold and unfulfilled."

By the time Tee finished, Lanta was nodding rapt agreement.

CHAPTER 61

Sylah watched in dismay as Lanta approached across the courtyard with Dodoy in tow. The boy appeared quite pleased, smiling, inspecting everything around him with an air of happy return. Lanta, spying Sylah at the second-floor window, made a face and cocked her head almost imperceptibly toward Dodoy. Sylah's nod was equally circumspect. She left her vantage and walked downstairs.

They met in the covered walkway on the ground floor. Dodoy amused himself terrorizing the fish in the ornamental pond. Lanta said, "Tate begged me to take him off the island. Too much bad influence."

"Yes, those sailors and the gangs. And the exiled Kossiar criminals. Dodoy could corrupt all of them."

After quiet laughter, Lanta summarized her trip. She detailed Conway's involvement with Tee, and Tee's evaluation of Moondance inroads among the slaves. She ended by saying, "Tee feels that a revolt will succeed, if they plan well. The slaves intend to create a nation of their own in the Empty Lands. The Smalls there aren't friendly, but they're not hostile, either."

Sylah didn't respond immediately. Lanta knew she was analyzing. It had become automatic with this new Sylah.

Thinking about the change in her friend, Lanta was surprised to realize how extensive it was. The other Sylah never forgot to pay close attention to what was going on around her. That woman always moved after careful consideration, then with determination. This woman was different. Consideration had been superseded by calculation. The new Sylah planned alternative routes based on possible obstacles and resistance. She led. She sought counsel, but her conclusions were her own. Her orders no longer carried the feminine tone of deferral, or even suggested she was hoping for consensus.

Sylah said, "A slave revolt, even if they only succeed in fleeing and don't destroy Kos physically, will undermine the nation. A colony of escaped slaves near her northern border will be a serious threat for at least two generations, perhaps longer. Further, Church can't tolerate a Moondance outpost on this side of the Enemy Mountains. We must oppose the slavers of Kos and the unbelievers of the slave nation. The ethical considerations are exactly balanced by the practical ones: We need the slave uprising to eliminate slaveholding in Kos while we need the strength of Kos to prevent the spread of Moondance."

Lanta had waited patiently to make her suggestion. "Tee slips over to the mainland almost every night. She'll let me go along with her, I know she will. I can treat the ill, talk to the slaves, make them see the advantages of Church's truth over Moondance superstition. You don't need me for Yasmaleeya; she doesn't even want me."

Sylah objected. "We can at least claim no knowledge of Conway's involvement because he's on Trader Island. You're different."

"I think we have to help the slaves. Can we ignore an opportunity to free people, to defeat Moondance?"

Seeing Sylah's difficulty, Lanta pressed her case. "We didn't have to come to Kos, Sylah. There was a choice. I think you made the right one. Don't you think it's possible we were meant to come here? What if this is a test? What if we're being asked to compare our beliefs with our personal goals?"

Sylah wanted to cry for her, and at the same time, she wanted to strike out at her. How could she be so blind? Love was luring Lanta into all the devious passages of self-delusion.

Deep in her own heart, Sylah cringed at the tiny flame of doubt so easily fueled by Lanta's argument. Had the power of Church directed her to take the path to Kos? *The dream voice that insisted she discover the Door had been strangely quiescent. Was that a sign?*

Could she think of herself as a true representative of Church if she avoided helping the oppressed, especially when non-Church people such as Tee and Conway were willing to take the risk? If she failed to confront the Harvester's efforts to benefit by Church's schism, was it to pursue a higher goal, or self-interest?

"Help if you can," Sylah said, turning her back to her friend. "Please be careful. If any of you are hurt, I'll never forgive myself."

"I knew you'd understand." Lanta bubbled gratitude and enthusiasm.

The irony of Lanta's phrase brought a wry smile. Sylah knew she could do nothing to stop her. Love rejected orders, ignored pleading.

Another voice penetrated her concern, turned her head. The Chair was a few yards away, watching her with a quizzical smile.

When she greeted him, the smile broadened. "You didn't even hear me. You think too deeply, Sylah; you'll get a bad reputation."

"Being accused of thinking doesn't frighten me," she said tartly. "I use my head the best I can."

He walked to her, took her arm, and linked it through his own. "You use it very well, for thought as well as attractiveness. I'll hate to see you take it away."

It was the rankest sort of flattery. Still, it did no harm. "I've no intention of losing it. Which brings us to Yasmaleeya, I think. She's doing very well. Lanta and I are quite confident she'll deliver a healthy baby."

Ignoring Sylah's attempts to direct the conversation, the Chair peered over her head. "I seem to have distressed your small friend." Sylah turned to see Lanta practically scurrying away. The Chair went on, "She sees me as cruel and rapacious, as does everyone else. Almost everyone. How did a Priestess, a War Healer, learn that the first cost of power is the loss of normal human contact?"

Sylah bridled at what she first perceived to be even worse fulsome flattery. The rebuke she intended, however, wilted. There was a plea in his manner. She finally said, "I've seen those who hold power suffer for it, and make others suffer with it. I know the power of holding a life in my hands and the fear that my power may not be enough to save it. But no woman will ever completely sympathize with you. Try being a woman for one day. One hour. Learn what pain it is to be utterly without power even over yourself."

Clutching at his heart, reeling in burlesque agony from her verbal thrust, he forced her to smile at his antics. Once she did, he sobered, saying, "I won't lie to you. Oh, I would, but you'd see through it. You see, I'll never relinquish my authority. I fought very hard to be what I am, because I'm the best man for the position. Still, I never realized how hard it is to think of everyone, with no chance to think of any *one*." He paused to draw a weary hand across his eyes. "Did that make any sense?"

Sylah's mind wanted to slide away, to examine her own conscience on matters of power. The Door. Loneliness. She willed concentration on the Chair's words. "You probably made more sense to me than yourself. I can feel sorry for you; you dare not feel sorry for yourself."

"Exactly." He drove an enthusiastic fist into a palm. He looked around suspiciously, started to speak, changed his mind. With the single word "Come," he led the way to the small boat basin inside the south wall. Once there, he sat Sylah just forward of the mast of a small balancebar, then untied the mooring lines and cast off. A small paddle moved them through the tunnellike exit to the sea, the raised balancebar just clearing overhead.

As soon as he had room, the Chair lowered the bar. Lithe, sure-footed, he worked the length of the hull. Despite his size, he moved without rocking the boat. On one occasion he actually anticipated a larger-than-usual wave. His weight leaning outboard damped the swell to almost unnoticeable proportions.

The day was perfect for a trip, crystal clear, with the chilling edge of a light breeze offset by the warming sun. As soon as he hoisted the sail, it bellied full and content, like a milk-fed cat. They set off across the bay smoothly. From aft at the tiller, the Chair called Sylah closer.

As soon as she was settled, he pointed toward shore. When she looked, two larger boats were leaving the peninsula near Trader Island. One was a balancebar, the other a singlehull. The latter was under sail, but a picket fence of raised oars showed she could make way without wind. The Chair said, "My guardians. Good men. Prepared to die for me. They have no idea how I hate them."

"How can you? They love you."

"They love the Chair. Not me." He shook his head, frowned. "I don't hate them. I hate what they do, hate what I am. The most powerful man in Kos. Probably the most powerful man anywhere. Trapped."

Sylah laughed. For a moment something dark and deadly spoiled his features. It passed, and he said, "I understand what you must feel at such a statement. Nevertheless, I'm an image, not a man. Everything I do, every move I make, is either determined by tradition and protocol, or else requires a decision that affects the life of every person in the nation. There is no *me*."

"Yet you wanted the position. Still do."

"I killed for it." At her shocked recoil, he gave a crackling, bitter laugh. "When the Chair dies, our tradition allows his firstborn son to assume that rank. However, any brother may challenge. Each man is allowed a club and a knife, exact matches. Any son of a Crew member of the same birth year may also challenge. You understand? My brother can challenge me, regardless of our age difference, but only a Crew member of my birth year is allowed that privilege."

"Your brother challenged you?"

"My father had four sons. I was the youngest."

Sylah's hands felt cold, weak. "You challenged them?"

364

"Three brothers. And two Crew members."

Memories crowded out the sound of wind thudding in the sail, of the balancebar hissing across the surface. Sylah remembered flames and swords and blood. Dimly, she saw a family without faces, without remembered words or laughter.

Yet here was a man who murdered three of his brothers. For power.

He avoided looking at her, concentrating on his course. He said, "Now you understand the choice of Yasmaleeya, in any case. My son must grow large, as well as wise, in order to rule. Like me, he'll be shown what ruling means, even know reading, writing. Numbers."

"Killing." Sylah couldn't stop herself.

Whiplike, his words slashed at her. "Clas na Bale. Are your husband's hands so free of blood?"

Sylah was too shocked to retort. She gaped. The Chair's ferocity melted. Once again, he looked to his course, eyes fixed on the distance. He seemed to sag. "My father's dying instructions to me were to become the Chair in his place. 'Our people need you,' he told me. 'The Crew is a nest of inbred schemers and plotters. None of them will be true to you, so you must be forever true to yourself, expect no honesty in return. Or gratitude or kindness or honor. You must save Kos, disregarding all else.' So I cut down my brothers. So I will have a fine, strapping son from this pregnancy."

By then, he was almost whispering, his voice a part of the sibilant press of sea against hull. "I want very much for you to understand. You embody all the things I dare not dream of; you're warm, thoughtful. You have friends who respect your leadership, yet they love you beyond that. We are both leaders. We both have our mission. I have the power to crush all of you to dust, to scrub all knowledge of you from the world. But you are more than I can ever be. I wish we could be friends."

Suddenly, it was all clear to Sylah. He did care about his unborn child. In his own way, he cared about Yasmaleeya. A man schooled to reject his own humanity would naturally refuse to admit concern for anyone else's. He revealed his flaw, however, by acknowledging his wish for a friend. Beneath the layers of repression, the man inside him struggled for freedom, for expression. For caring.

How well she understood a life bent to the will and necessity of others. She dealt with it with her wiles and meticulous maneuvers. He responded by ruling with an iron grip, knowing his own strength was his prison.

Such a man could be persuaded, could be made to lead his people in the right direction. Moral argument might not persuade him to be moral, but simple practicality would. It would free the real man before her, replace this carved image with a person.

She said, "I'm your friend now."

He jerked back as if slapped, eyes wide with alarm. "No. You must never say a thing like that. I've already endangered you by bringing you out here like this, alone with me. When we get back, you must tell everyone I did it in order to bargain with you for Church Priestesses to raise my son. You will say that I don't trust the Harvester, that I want care for the boy, and I suspect she'll try to acquire him. Nothing else passed between us, Sylah, remember that. My fort is the most dangerous place you've ever seen, as my father warned me. You and your friends are helpless here. My spies see and hear everything, and they report to me faithfully. The One in All only knows how unfaithfully they also report to someone else. Trust no one. Believe no one. Protect yourself at every turn. If you would truly be my friend, deny that friendship at every opportunity."

He broke off the conversation at that point, simultaneously changing course, sending the balancebar into a heeling, drumming turn that lifted the bar high in the air. Water curled away from the bow in ribbons of silver. The Chair made no comment when Sylah turned around and made her way forward. She settled down facing the bow, back against the mast. The life of the boat, the marriage of wind, water, and wood became part of her. Muscles relaxed. The warmth of sun touched her, filled her with a carefree lethargy.

The Chair had enumerated their similarities and differences brilliantly. That, too, was a clear sign of human feeling. Of caring. She smiled inwardly as she burrowed into the coziness of her robe. He'd overlooked the one thing that, above all, marked them as similar.

Loneliness.

Strange: a man who wished for a friend, yet one who rejected friendship out of concern for someone who offered it. So contradictory. So revealing.

Emotional isolation did that, twisted a person's conception of everything, everyone. It hurt, as well. There was a quality to that sort of hurt that could even shut out the nearest and dearest of friends. The loneliness she shared with the Chair was bred of making decisions.

Who understood such loneliness better than the survivor, the Chosen, the one who'd been forced to become Rose Priestess Sylah, the Flower of Church?

CHAPTER 62

Dodoy cocked his head to the side, wondering what had Lanta so excited. Mousy little Lanta, he thought, watching her scamper across the courtyard to the quarters, tiny and timid. With Conway gone, she was even gloomier than usual.

That made no sense whatever. The two of them seemed to always find a way to get close to each other, but then they ended up stomping off in opposite directions. Adults were stupid.

He thought of the woman the Skan captain lived with. A witch, certainly. The Skan only beat him to make him obey. The woman enjoyed hurting him. Flinching unconsciously, Dodoy remembered biting his fist to keep silent while she laid a belt across his legs. She liked to hear him cry. When she saw him smothering his own weeping, she nearly bit his finger off. He could still hear her, see his own blood spraying from her fat, wet lips. "You like biting better than being whipped? Answer me!" The belt had cracked again, and this time he screamed. He never knew if it was the screaming or simple weariness that stopped her.

What he did know was that women had a deeper, meaner nature than men. They hid it well, but he'd seen. He knew.

Which made it all the more confusing to see men chasing women as though their lives would end if they didn't catch one. Dodoy had long since made up his mind he'd have nothing to do with them.

Except to return the many favors granted him by the Skan captain's belt-wielding woman.

He shivered. Afternoon's lengthening shadows cloaked the courtyard. A sudden chill pierced to the bone.

He followed Lanta to the quarters. Bending and twisting, he was able to peer through the slit of the not-quite-closed door. Lanta was busy at something.

Wisping smoke from the brazier that warmed the room convinced him he should go in.

Lanta fluttered like a quail. It took her a moment to find her voice. "You startled me. You've been told to knock."

"I forgot." A teapot on a grill stuttered softly above the coals in the brazier. An empty cup waited on the table beside it. Lanta's medical bag lay open beside her bedroll. Dodoy pointed at it. "Going back to the island?"

Her eyes widened. "Who told you?"

"No one. Yasmaleeya doesn't like you, so you're not going there. Where else would you go? The other boy says they'll kill us if we try to meet anyone outside the castle."

"What other boy?"

"The one I play with. He lives here with his mother and father. We're the only two children here. He does what I tell him, or I won't play with him. He's a fool."

"The only other child?"

"See, you never noticed. You don't care. It's all your fault, too. Sylah's, anyway."

Lanta stopped packing to look at him. "Explain that, please."

"The Chair made them send the slave children away, 'cause Sylah said she didn't want them around. No Crew children live here, except the boy; he says his family's not safe outside the fort. Some Crew people and some inlanders wanted to kill the Chair, and the boy's father informed on them."

"Poor child. He must be very lonely. He needs a friend."

"I'm nice to him because he tells me things. The adults talk where he can hear. He's little, so they think he's worthless." Dodoy glanced obliquely at Lanta from under lowered eyelids, trying to appraise the effect of his words.

She said, "A friend is the most precious thing there is."

Dodoy was certain he saw a change in her color. It gave him an idea. "Are you going back to the island to be with your friend Conway?"

That startled her. And something else. Dodoy couldn't be sure what it was before she spoke again. "Yes. And my other friends. Tate and Nalatan. And Wal and Tee."

"Tee? She's no friend of yours."

"Don't say that!"

Delighted, Dodoy saw real anger. He pretended sympathy. "All she wants to do is free slaves."

Lanta calmed immediately, actually smiled. "Oh. Well, that's a good thing. You know that."

Of course he knew that. She must think he was stupid. He thought hard; when he said Tee wasn't Lanta's friend, Lanta got angry. Then, when he said why he thought she wasn't a friend, Lanta didn't care any more. So what upset her?

Conway. Dodoy cursed himself for not seeing it sooner. Conway chased Tee the way men chase women and Tee didn't care. Lanta wanted to be near Conway and Conway didn't care. There was opportunity in that. "I think Tee likes Conway a lot."

Lanta's color flamed. She rummaged busily in her medicine bag. "He's a fine man."

"He talks to her all the time, over on the island."

Lanta straightened slowly. Dodoy thought she looked more like a mouse than ever. A sick mouse. She looked straight ahead. "They're together a lot?"

"Almost all the time."

"What do they talk about?"

"All kinds of things." Dodoy's mind raced. A mistake could warn her off. She'd be furious. Worse, the fun would end. He said, "A lot about Ola. I think they want to go back there."

"I wish I'd never left."

Dodoy said, "I'm sorry," and she whirled to glare suspicion. He gave her his most innocent stare. "You're nice. Not always yelling at me, telling me what to do. It's too bad you didn't use your Seeing when we were in Ola. You'd have known all this, and you could have stayed there."

Her lower lip trembled. "I can never do that, Dodoy. The Seeing belongs to Church. It's a terrible sin for a Seer to use the gift for anything except Church work."

She was very sad now.

Dodoy remembered the bloody lips of the captain's woman, remembered how his finger swelled. For a week he cried, slept in snatches because of the pain of that infected mess. He said, "How do you know the other Seers don't use it? You're so nice; you believe anything."

"They wouldn't. It's wrong."

"Who'd know?" Dodoy gestured grandly. Curls of smoke swirled from the brazier. "If I leave and you close the door, who'll know what you're doing? The other Seers can close a door. I think they use the Seeing. Not to help themselves, 'cause the One in All watches everyone, like you keep telling me. But doesn't the One in All say we're supposed to help others, any way we can?"

Her sidelong smile was far sharper than he expected, and for a sinking moment he was afraid he'd said too much. Her words relaxed him, however. "Dodoy talking about scripture? Am I present at a miracle?"

He resolved to keep away from that subject. "I don't know anything about Church. I'm just a child, a freed salve. But if Conway's going to get in trouble, won't that make it harder for Sylah to keep looking for the Door? And if she doesn't find it, won't the Harvester be the most important one in Church?"

Lanta made a three-sign. "Go away, Dodoy. Now." She faced the window. Reaching in his pocket, Dodoy pulled out the remaining wad of leaves Tate called marijuana. All the sailors had assured him it was worth a lot of coin in the castle, because marijuana was forbidden off the island. He crumbled a third of the mass into the teapot, adding an extra dash of herbs.

As soon as he'd done it, he grew nervous. What if something happened to her? The sailors said it didn't hurt to smoke the leaves, or eat them in food, but no one said anything about brewing them. What if she died? All he had to do was bump the pot, knock it over. No one would know. He reached for it.

Lanta turned. His heart pinched shut. He withdrew his hand, took a backward step. She reached for the pot, smiling, held it over her cup. "Did you want some, Dodoy?"

He shook his head, too frightened to speak. She filled the cup, sipped it. Wrinkling her nose, she held the cup out, examined it. "Strong. The soil must be very different here." She moved the cup in a circle, sending the liquid swirling up the walls of the container. Steam silvered the air above it. Testing again, she tilted her head and drained it.

Dodoy groaned without meaning to. Lanta looked at him quizzically. "Are you all right? There's a little tea left in the pot, if you feel unsteady."

"No!" He heard the volume, and repeated himself. "No. I'm fine. I want to sleep. Please?" He backed away, watching her carefully. She seemed healthy.

In short order, he had the hide partition around his sleeping place, bedroll spread out. Fully clothed, he crawled under the covers, pulled them over his head so his breath would warm the tiny cave. Enclosed in dark comfort, he listened intently for signs of trouble. He reminded himself that if she collapsed, he must empty the contents of the teapot down the hole in the latrine room. He'd shout for help afterward. In a while, he poked his head out. Candle light bathed his cubicle in a soft glow. On the other side of the partition, Lanta hummed. The song was uneven, rising and falling in volume.

Lanta was intrigued by the way her eyes seemed to be focusing independently, pulling things close, then projecting them out beyond reach. In fact, nothing seemed to be coordinating. Odd.

Stress, she decided, and told herself there was no reason for it. Why should she worry about Conway? The Door? Sylah? Silly Sylah.

That was funny. Silly Sylah. Nothing was ever that funny. Ever. Laughter bubbled up from her stomach. She clamped her lips closed; it squirted out her nose. Silly Sylah. The words splashed in her head. They blurred, became even more liquid, turned to water-music nonsense.

Like sobs. And tears. Wet on her cheeks. Where had they come from? Why was she curled up in a corner? Life was so confused, so sad; the world should cry with her.

Stress. The Abbess said mental stress could kill.

Lanta pulled herself upright. She didn't want to die.

The trance.

There was something wrong. The trance would reestablish control.

The proper words wouldn't come. Eyes closed, willing herself to calm repose, she felt her body rebel. Her mind scorned her, raged along at its own erratic pace. She strained to envision her place of repose, the small Church sanctuary with its cool, unassailable walls of stone. Horribly, massively, the chiseled boulders rolled inward, hung insanely over her, suspended in impossible positions.

A voice—her own?—calling for Matt.

And then, riding a lightning bolt of fear, the gift.

The curse.

Dodoy, spying through the hole in the hide partition, choked back a shout. He'd seen many fall the way she did, tumbling like wet cloth, then beating the ground with their heels. All stopped breathing. Died.

Lanta lived. Eyes wide. Stone-bright. They looked at him, in him, prying. Opening him up.

Backing, he reached the door. He squeezed the handle, hard. Told himself to think. If he went for help, they'd ask questions. They'd find out he was spying. They'd find the marijuana.

He flung open the door and ran. She'd live or die. An accident. He meant no harm. Really. Wanted to help.

If he didn't tell, no one could know.

In the darkness, he burrowed under the overhang of the rhododendrons. For a long moment, he was sure he'd been seen. There was a sense of eyes on him. Watching. Waiting. He risked inching to the edge of the shrouding leaves, peered out. There was no one.

The feeling went on. He felt *thoughts*.

Pity.

It pitied him.

Dodoy bit the scarred finger until pain flushed everything else from his mind.

This seeing was unlike anything Lanta had ever known.

Scenes. So real she felt them.

Buildings like cliffs, like shining mountains. They burned, fell. A sun gone mad, come to earth in fury, dissolved them with light.

Another scene.

Different buildings, similar, not as tall. Lanta knows they're dwelling places for the slaves who served the giants. She knows she's seeing a godkill, without knowing how she knows. Slaves, strangely costumed, come out of the buildings. They look to the sky, afraid. One doubles over, gagging, falls down. Screams in convulsions. Another starts to run and falls exactly like the first. More people—unimaginable numbers of them, as if each building housed an entire tribe—rush from the dwellings. They claw at themselves, collapse. They litter the ground, but in this place, the ground is one unbelievable gray rock, utterly flat, like a stone river with stone banks.

Another scene.

An indescribable object hanging in the air above a landscape torn and burned. Smoke rises everywhere. Soot-raddled skies absorb the sun, turn midday dusky. The noisy, chuffing thing moves, suspended from a shimmering disk. Lanta sees faces peering from inside it.

Conway.

Then, blankness. Next, the words come, written in fire across darkness. For the first time in her life, Lanta welcomes them, because they blot out the mind-breaking images.

What the Door shields will not remain possessed, nor will its power be controlled.

Lanta cried out in her mind, the words echoing plaintively. "Me! What of me?"

Lanta prostitutes her gift. That one will be punished. See more, then. The Conway one comes to hate the Lanta one, and Church. Yet will the Lanta one give him his future, and in the giving, lose the one meant for her.

She struggled to hold the trance, begged forgiveness. Black silence answered. Waking, pulling herself upright, she stumbled to the window in a daze, assuring herself that the walls were real, that the stars weren't blotted by the evil smut of the world she saw in her visions.

Stiff-fingered, she unrolled her bedding, pulled the quilted blankets tight around her.

The Seeing. It was exactly as the Apocalypse Testament described. Giants, with unimaginable powers, crushing the arrogant slaves.

She shivered, despite all her coverings.

The men who organized the destruction of the Teachers claimed the Teachers brought the same arrogance, and endangered all mankind.

The Door. *"What it shields will not remain possessed."*

Conway. *". . . comes to hate the Lanta one."*

CHAPTER 63

Lanta leapt ashore from the bow of the small singlehull. She skipped lightly through the frothing tumble of a retreating wave, and barely turned around before the Kossiar sailor was rapidly rowing himself back out to sea. When the water was deep enough, he dropped his centerboard. That done, he spat over the side and made for the point offshore where he'd anchor, fishing, and wait her call.

When Lanta faced landward again, Tee was approaching. "What brings you back, Lanta? Conway?"

"I've come to work with all of you, to carry the word of Church to the slaves."

Tee took Lanta's arm and set out toward Borbor's house. "Conway and Tate are collecting supplies. Nalatan's with some of Wal's men over on the mainland, preparing the last waiting place for the escapers. There's a godkill up the coast; slaves mined it until an earthquake caused it to flood. Some shafts are still accessible. We hide the escapers in there. No Kossiar'll step foot in a godkill tunnel."

"You've never moved so many before."

Tee stopped abruptly. "Have you heard anything over at the castle?"

Lanta wished she could tell her of the previous night's trance, of the message about Matt Conway. She wished she could tell anyone. "Everyone exchanges rumors: increased patrol actions, repressions. They don't include us, but Yasmaleeya hears everything, and repeats it."

"The escapers have started moving. Twelve out of the twenty are already hidden at the godkill. The others are being smuggled from one safe place to the next. Patrols are tearing up the countryside looking for them. Why isn't the Chair going wild?"

"No one speaks of anything they think may disturb him. I think the Crew just doesn't care that much. Twenty slaves, even twenty trained slaves, is no crippling blow to Kos."

Tee was still dubious, but the answer mollified her a bit. She said, "Perhaps it's all happening too fast for the Kossiars to react properly. I hope so. The slaves leave the godkill the first night there's no moon. We're hiding them in hidden compartments on Wal's boat. As soon as the Kossiar border guards pass it, they're away." Suddenly animated, Tee smiled broadly. "Two of the slaves are from way over near the mountains. They've heard stories of some new Moondance siah in the east. They also say Katallon's nomads get bolder every day, raiding farms and villages. They even tried to storm a town. The only thing that saved the Kossiars was a mirror signal that brought a Kossiar military garrison. On a rainy night, the nomads might have succeeded."

"I don't understand."

"Between Harbor and the Enemy Mountains, the Kossiars have a system of mirrors, mounted on towers. The towers are very tall, made of stone or timber, windowless, easily defended and manned constantly. Usually, each one can be seen by two others. The mirrors catch the sunlight, send it on. The warmen signal with lanterns or fires at night. They say a signal from the Enemy Mountains can be seen in Harbor in less than two inches. The flaw is bad weather; it blinds them."

They were nearly to the door of the house when Lanta said, "If there were signals to the Chair about the slaves, can anyone working with you read the messages? Has anyone noticed if the patrols have been more active than usual since your slaves began moving toward Harbor?"

"We'd know if the Chair suspected anything. We have people watching his boats and warmen. We're in control."

Lanta bristled inwardly at Tee's condescending manner, but decided not to confront it. More disturbing than the condescension was Tee's abrupt change from nervousness to complacency. That was a stress reaction. Lanta shuddered; she knew the effect of

374

stress. She wondered if the center of Tee's concern was the same as her own.

Tee showed Lanta to a different part of Borbor's house. The trader had built an open-air extension high on the south side. The view was spectacular. To the west rose the infamous Gate with the tumbled headland directly across the channel. Directly south of the house was the huge godkill. The oak-studded hills and lush meadows disguised most of the ancient destruction there, but an occasional glint of concrete bore silent testimony to the wrath of the giants who destroyed that world. Gazing at it, Lanta's mind twisted with the image of Conway looking out at unimaginable havoc. A sense of connection, of linkage, plucked at her thoughts, but trailed away in confusion.

Tee said, "I'm going to tell Conway you shouldn't be allowed to go over to the mainland." She kept her gaze locked on the far shore.

Shocked, Lanta faced her. "You mustn't. You can't."

Taking a seat in a chair of smoothly bent bamboo, Tee gestured for Lanta to do the same. The Priestess refused with an angry shake of her head. Tee went on. "When I suggested Church send someone to counteract Moondance, I was thinking of someone practiced in clandestine missionary work. I admire you, but you want to trust everyone."

"You trust, or you'd deal with no one."

"We're very careful. None are approached until we're certain they prefer death to slavery. They'll never inform."

Lanta sat down, perched on the edge of the chair. "You're not as sure of your people as you pretend, or you wouldn't be asking me if I've heard anything at the fort. My duty, my life, is to bring the word of Church to all. Anyhow, you know the law: the Chair is required to destroy anyone who harms me."

Harshly, Tee cut her off. "Church is split. Three things keep the Chair from throwing all of you in his dungeons and naming the next Sister Mother himself. First, the mindless Yasmaleeya and her child. Second, the possibility that Sylah and the Door are fated to come together and change Church. Last, something called the True Stone. Your sect, Violet, is key to the Harvester's plan to command Church. I'm told that this True Stone is some sort of talisman; no one controls Violet without it, and no one can find it. Foolishness. How powerful can Church be, how honest, if a little rock determines who rules?" Tee broke off, suddenly leaning forward. Her hand reached out for Lanta, fell short. "I didn't mean to be so hard. You've gone white as clouds. My mouth gets away sometimes."

Lanta shook her head, using the time to compose her thoughts. "What you said is true. I don't trust the Chair. We can only hope he'll let us go after we bring him a healthy child and wife. He must. Sylah can't find the Door, otherwise."

Tee grew thoughtful. "He's playing his own game. He must think the Harvester can get the True Stone. But why hold you? As you say, Sylah can't find the Door here. And why burden you with that idiot, Yasmaleeya? It puts you at risk, and supposedly no one's in more danger than he, if the child and mother aren't perfect. If he thought Yasmaleeya and the baby were a real danger to him, he'd have them both killed."

"No." Lanta's stomach threatened.

Tee laughed. "You still believe there's some good in everyone. The Chair means to rule Kos and share control of Church and whatever power the Door hides from the world. Your life is less to him than a drop of water. My life's of smaller importance yet. I don't want you risking it with preaching. After the slaves rebel, you can talk to any of them. For now, no."

"You have no right to stop me. If all your arguments are true, my life is nearly over. I have the obligation to spend that time in Church's work."

"I don't need rights. You can't go if Conway and Wal won't take you, and I mean to see they won't."

Lanta flung herself out of the chair, stalked to the rail at the edge of the view deck. Turning her back on the bay, she pointed at Tee. "It's Conway. You don't want me alone with him."

Tee's hands clenched over the ends of the chair arms. A fiery red stain worked along her cheekbones, flared to cover her whole face. Far below the deck, a bird called incessantly, the measured notes marking the thick silence between the two women.

Lanta's mind flew to her surrender to temptation. . . . *the Conway one comes to hate* . . . Her resolve buckled. She forced herself erect. "I don't know how to fight you, Tee. I don't even want to."

When Tee didn't answer, Lanta accepted the silence as the end of the conversation. She whirled and ran down the stairs, clutching the rail, blinded by tears. There was no way for her to know that Tee had been coming to her, hands outstretched, beseeching.

CHAPTER 64

Lanta was in no condition to hail her boat and return to Harbor right away.

She found her way to the healing house where she'd nursed Conway. It was a good place, shaded, quiet, and isolated. Brushing off the room's single chair, she sat down. Idly, she drew small triangles in the dust on the leather straps of the bed. When she leaned on one of the bands, it tightened against its retaining slot in the wooden frame and squealed discreet complaint. The sound brought a wan smile. The noise was much lustier when the injured Conway used to turn over and pressure the whole network into simultaneous clamor. Still, it reminded her of the way he'd been, sick and wounded. Needing.

He was hers, then. She made him well.

And now she had to accept losing him.

She never really had him. She called him hers, treasured him against her breast and dreamed of bright days of laughter and warm nights that soared to fire and exhilaration.

The broken man needed her. The healed one wanted Tee.

At the sound of something hard striking the wooden steps leading into the building, she clutched her shortknife and faced the danger. Karda took one more claw-clacking step on the wooden floor and stopped at the open door, half in, half out. Mikka's brown head appeared beside him, shoved past Karda. Less reserved the brown female made her way into the room; even so, she stopped just out of Lanta's reach.

Conway didn't see Lanta until he was inside. He stopped as if caught by the end of a tether, even made a grunting exclamation. Lanta laughed, and he joined her, then said, "What're you doing here? I thought you were a permanent resident over in the Chair's stone pile."

"Supplies." The lie came easily. "I remembered some things from here that we may need for Yasmaleeya."

"Me, too. There shouldn't be any need for bandages and salves for the escapers, but it won't hurt to have the stuff aboard."

Suddenly, she couldn't rid herself of the image of him inside that unimaginable flying thing hanging from its shining disk. In that instant, she realized he was fleeing. Death and destruction as far as the eye could see, and he was fleeing. Yet she felt no sense of cowardice. Resignation. Desperation. Yes, he felt those things. Fear, too, but not the mind-rotting cowardice that sends men screaming from danger.

All of it was impossible. Still, she *knew* he'd seen horrors too great to be borne. Despite that—because of it?—there was yearning in him, a need for something far different from escape.

What could he be seeking?

Why must he come to hate her?

". . . worry too much," Conway was saying. "You and Sylah talk a lot about freedom, but you're not willing to fight for it the way Tee does. Not even Tate is. She would have once; she did for Dodoy." Suspicion sharpened his features. "Did you ever talk to Tate about helping us, helping Tee? You never did get along with her. I saw the way you looked at her in that tavern. She gets along with most of those people, so you think she belongs there, is that it?"

Lanta was indignant. The heat of it swelled uncontrollably.

How much insult, how much rejection was she expected to absorb? First her own Violet tasked her to inform on another Priestess; a rejection of her integrity. Then Yasmaleeya, choosing a War Healer as her midwife; a rejection of her competency. And all along, him, Matt Conway, hinting at his interest in her, only to reject her. Worse, he was making up reasons to accuse her of creating the rejection. It was insufferable, and he was heartless to hurt so. Without character.

"You offend. I like Tee very much. She helped me, tried to stop that man in the tavern. We're friends."

He sneered. "You haven't wasted ten words on her since we got here. She doesn't need you, anyhow. She fights her own battles."

"She was certainly willing to speak up for me. So was Nalatan. He's the one who faced the crowd, put a stop to what they were doing to me. I'm grateful to both of them. But where were you? You didn't say a word."

"I was outside. If I'd been there, I'd have done something."

Lanta saw the apology that swiftly turned to defiance, the fleeting hurt that tightened the corners of his eyes. She was glad. He'd hurt her, struck out at her falsely. Conversely, she was sorry. Her sense of being wronged triumphed. Like a fighter moving against a weakened opponent, she struck again, hating her words as they came. "Nalatan didn't hesitate. He acted. So did Tate. Tee was grand. How can you find the words to say I'd plot against them, refuse Tee? The only reason I came here today was to talk to her

378

about working with her, bringing Church to the slaves she's trying to free."

Stung by Lanta's criticism and unexpectedly spirited defense, Conway seized on the latter remark. "See? You lied. You're not after supplies. What lies did you tell Tee? How Church can save her if she'll convert slaves instead of freeing them? Or isn't she pure enough for you, after the protectors used her? Talk about people not being there. Where were you all those years? I'll tell you something else, too. Forget what happened to her. In spite of it, she's a woman, not a frozen, frightened little saint. More woman than you'll ever be."

Pressure surged in Lanta's skull. Constraint, respect, consideration—all those things disappeared from her thinking. She was so eager to hurt she almost salivated as the bitter, scorched, delicious words slipped off her tongue.

"I came here hoping to bring the word of Church to the slaves, but that's impossible. I see that now. You all preach freedom, but you're too important to be concerned with faith and moral matters. The Apocalypse Testament tells us, 'No soul can be saved by the Healer's knife. Any body can be forced. The mind must be persuaded.' You save bodies. You ignore souls."

"That's a backhanded swipe at Tee. I want to know exactly what you and Sylah are planning, you and that stud that calls himself the Chair." He gestured the increasingly nervous dogs outside, snapped a command at them to guard. He closed the door behind them, faced Lanta once more. "You pretend to be so kind, so loving. You led me on. You know you did. And I believed . . . almost believed you. What an unscrupulous liar you are."

Lanta rose. It was exactly the word she wanted to hear. "I lied to you about why I came here. I confess it. When will you confess your lies, Matt Conway? You forget; I am a Seer. I know things of you, and I know you have not spoken the truth to me. I know of the strange deaths in your land, of the destruction. You fled. Just as you found it inconvenient to help me. You fled."

He grabbed her shoulders, the fingers like teeth. "You used that—that *thing* you have on *me*? What did you see?" Fear chased after contempt in his voice.

"Let go of me!" She twisted in his grip, pushed against his chest with her hands. When she saw how little effect her strength had on him, she looked up from her hands to the wildness in his eyes. What should have frightened her had the reverse effect. He'd broken her heart. Now he threatened to break her bones.

Fury screamed through her whole body. She kicked, struck, struggled. Uselessly.

His voice husked in his chest. "Tell me what you saw. Our weapons; you learned about our weapons, how to make them work, how much ammunition we have. That's what you saw, isn't it?"

"No! I saw you, the real you, the one who came late when real danger threatened me in that stinking tavern you like so much. I saw you escaping. While others died."

His eyes rolled back until there was only glowing, empty white. Frothy spittle appeared on his lip. Still, his hold never weakened. As awareness flowed back into him, Lanta knew she was looking into madness.

Grasping, tearing hands reached for her, twisted the collar of her robe, tore it. Her mind balked, refused to accept what was happening. Even as terror melted her strength, part of her watched, stupefied, as tendons in his neck bowed outward, whiplike muscles in his wrists strained and bulged. His breath stank of acid.

She drove a knee into his groin. Shock pulled his features in on themselves. His grip relaxed enough for her to pull free. She staggered back against a wall, holding her robe together, shielding herself where his rough hands abraded her skin. Worse than physical hurt was the agony of feeling her life and dreams collapse within her.

Conway overcame his pain, straightened to full height. Iron gray, dispassionate, he advanced with a cold determination that froze Lanta's spirit.

She surrendered.

"Do what you will." She released the robe, uncaring that its diagonal rip exposed the top half of her breasts. He hesitated. Animallike, he cocked his head at her voice. Lanta felt a strange, contradictory sense of triumph as she continued to speak. "I can't match your strength. Nor can you control your weakness. I accused you of cowardice. You're no coward, Matt Conway. There's a demon in you, a thing of confusion. It twists everything you see and do. You mean to rape me. You'll blame me for it, tell yourself you do it because you hate me. Liar. *Liar.* You love me. As I loved you. Once. The man I see here isn't the man I could have loved. You take by force what I would share with that man. Tell your demon it wins nothing. I spit on it. I reject its victory. You're too weak to acknowledge your true soul. I'm too strong to acknowledge the evil that infects you. I pity you."

Conway blinked. Red rage paled. Eyes seemed to sink deep into his skull. "You pity . . . ? You dare say that to me? One who knows you for what you are, who despises you?" Slowly, clumsily, as though responding to ill-heard commands, rather than the will of a functioning mind, Conway raised his hands and advanced the last steps separating them.

Lanta looked into the dead, vacant face. Her hands instinctively went to her throat, encountered something small. Smooth and rough, at the same time.

The True Stone.

The True Stone would save her. She clutched it, willed her mind deep, deep inside that purple brilliance. The rhythm of the chant whispered through her body, rose to a thunder that swept away the feeling, thinking person that was Lanta. In her place was a woman the real Lanta could weep for, a fool who hoped for love.

Consciousness abandoned her.

Conway was completely unprepared for the full pressure of her slight weight. Convulsively, his hands closed on her throat, exactly as he intended, but with the totally conflicting purpose of saving her from falling. Shaking violently, he held her, blunt thumbs pressed heavily into the soft hollow of flesh at the base of her throat. Curved fingers were an anvil of muscle, braced against the back of her neck. A moment's pressure . . .

An indigo vein pulsed at her temple. The slow, almost imperceptible movement took so long between beats he unconsciously held his breath, fearing her death. When the vein moved again, his eyes narrowed. His shaking returned.

"More deceit. There's no end to it. I can't believe it." He shook her. The closed eyes fluttered open, sightless, uninvolved. For an instant they were wide, staring into his.

Conway remembered battle dead, men with eyes that looked past this world.

"You're doing this on purpose." He spoke aloud again, unaware of his own voice, sharp-edged, grating like broken glass. "You're trying to frighten me. You're hiding, the way you always do. I won't put up with it. I won't. You lie. You make me believe . . . think . . . Then you change. Hide from me." He moved toward the bed. Dragging boots whispered slyly across the rough floor. Lanta was light in his hands. Her body, between his straddling legs, flowed easily with his every move. He lifted her, put her on the bed. Leather straps squealed, a sound of distant laughter, maliciously scandalized. Conway reached for the gaping tear in Lanta's robe, took a section in each hand.

"It's all your fault. Used me. All of us. Deserve whatever happens." Knuckles cracked as he clenched his hands on the material. He swayed drunkenly. Words slurred, clung together. "How I hate you. Your fault, all of it. Destroyed me. Destroyed. I should . . . kill you. Should. Hate you."

He sagged, dropped the ripped material. Tenderly, he folded it back together, covered Lanta's bared flesh. One hand drifted up to brush aside disheveled hair.

Stumbling to the door, he yanked it partially open, then paused.

Outside, Karda frantically threw himself at the barrier. A dark, snuffling nose thrust through the narrow gap.

Ignoring the dog, Conway looked back at the silent, limp form on the bed. His lined, strained face contorted into bunched fury. "You cheated me again, didn't you? You knew exactly what would happen. You're so clever, so bright. You thought I wouldn't see through it all, didn't you? Well, I did. I know. I'm not fooled. You hate us. Trick us all. And I hate you. You'll see. I hate you."

The slam of the door was a hammer blow. Lanta didn't stir.

The soft, sorrowing notes of the dove known as the mourner sought her out. Gently, kindly, the call insisted she rouse herself.

She was lying on her side. White sheeting, bundled and wrinkled, took her thoughts back to Snowfather Mountain, the winter-white crests of the Enemy Mountains.

The Chosen Lanta loved to look at those mountains. In her imaginings a tall, handsome warrior came riding for her from there one day. He would see Priestess Lanta, and fall completely in love. They would cherish each other.

The Chosen was gone. A grown woman was in her place. A Priestess, who had loved a man who hated her. Who raped her.

She was fully clothed.

In the few seconds that she'd been regaining consciousness, her only thought was that she'd been raped. With expanding awareness, she suddenly realized that hadn't happened. Her throat hurt. She was stiff and sore. Taking off the torn robe, she examined her underclothes, her body.

He'd reached for her. Meant to choke her. She'd seen the insensate lust in his face. The rage. Then he left her. Without . . . the other.

A flame of joy burst in her, forced hot tears of happiness to well in her eyes. As quickly as that emotion came, however, it dashed to pieces on the realization that he'd simply changed his goals. Rather than shame her by rape, he humiliated her by discarding her.

Despise. He said he despised her.

One didn't trouble with something despicable, didn't even use it. One didn't soil one's self.

Unsteadily, she got to her feet. The sun was low. She'd been unconscious most of the afternoon.

The world didn't know what happened to her. Didn't care. She must continue to live. Pretend she didn't care, either.

Hurriedly, she gathered up the torn robe, forced herself to be calm. The damage wasn't as bad as she feared. There were needles and thread in the hospital supplies. The shining needle, the mending stitches, had a healing effect.

She was able to think of tomorrow.

No tomorrow would ever be the same.

Revenge. The word slithered across her thoughts, skittered in and out of dark corners of her mind.

She dismissed it. Revenge was what had happened to her.

She replaced the True Stone around her neck, then slipped the protection of the robe over it and herself. The heavy cloth hid everything, the stone and her bruises.

Her smile was raw with self-contempt. Not everything could be hidden by cloth.

If she waited until dusk, no one would notice the stitching in the heavy material.

Another secret. Lucky Lanta! So many things only she knew.

CHAPTER 65

Night closed on the fort as Lanta's boat approached its rock-shielded shore. In the crepuscular light, the small waves broke there with an almost luminous froth. The mass of the walls loomed darkly. Directly overhead, straggling gulls flew swiftly to their rest. The sleek forms sped into view from nothingness, only to fade again. Sometimes a faint cry drifted down to the boat. Unlike the usual gull stridency, these were anxious, plaintive notes.

The Harvester stood at one of the fort's crenellations overlooking the sea, watching Lanta's approach. Beside her, the slave woman who directed the Chair's dining room crew hung back, carefully out of sight. The Harvester chided her lightly. "You needn't be so cautious. No one could see you. Anyhow, in that frightful yellow robe, you're just another slave."

Protesting, the woman said, "Not a slave. Your holy oath. 'Learn when and how the slaves are to leave,' you said. I did that. Church Home, you said; I'm to go with you to Church Home. You promised." A hand, shapeless in the darkness, clutched at the Harvester's voluminous sleeve.

The Harvester pulled her arm away, pretending it was to hug herself. "How cold it gets when the sun's hidden." Then, soothing, "I remember my promise, never fear. You've served me faithfully. Your rewards will be rich."

"When do we leave?"

"Just as soon as the Chair allows." The yellow-robed woman recoiled, and the Harvester continued hurriedly. "What you've learned gives me bargaining power. The Chair will agree to anything I ask in exchange for your information. He'll reward us. I'm forbidden to accept, of course, so everything will fall to you. You deserve it, too. You've worked hard."

"Thank you. Thank you, Harvester." The woman bobbed in repeated bows.

The Harvester resisted the urge to grab her by the throat. Peering over the wall's edge at Lanta's boat, just disappearing into the tunnellike entry below her, she spoke almost casually. "This cousin of yours; he can learn exactly when the slaves are to go aboard the ship?"

"I never said that!" The voice rose in alarm. "He said there were to be twenty of them, that they were to gather at the old godkill digging. He'll get a day's warning before the last ones arrive, so he can meet and guide them. I never said he knew when the boat would come for them."

Turning away from the sea, the Harvester was solicitous. "Now, now; there's no need for concern. I'm so anxious to gain your freedom for you that I overspoke myself."

"You must be more careful, Harvester. One wrong word in this place, and the sharks under the Gate fatten on me."

The thought of advice from the slave nearly pushed the Harvester out of control. She mentally tallied the things that could reveal out mind to an observer—heartbeat, breath, facial expression, posture—and assured herself all was correct. Yet she knew the Chair would have seen. Dilating pupils. A hand tremor. Something.

Grudgingly, she conceded that the slave had a point. Trying to rush could be disastrous. Arranging things to suit one's purposes was only the minor part of success. The major accomplishment lay in the ability to seize the unexpected, the unarranged, and twist it to advantage.

The Harvester permitted herself a small sigh of regret. Arranging was her personal weakness. So much more entertaining. One had the pleasure of watching the players squirm uselessly.

Sylah. Her turn was coming.

There was a proper example of planning. The fool was trapped like a mouse in a barrel. True, there were numerous escape holes, but the dirty little beast had no way of knowing there was a trap at each one.

The slave retreated from the Harvester's smile. The Harvester said, "It's dark now. I want you to try the Seeing again."

Shaking her head, the slave backed another step. "It was very difficult for me to come back the last time. My head hurt for days."

"I wasn't with you then. You'll be safe with me. Now, hurry. Get the soulseeker you stole from the Rose Priestess Sylah and your other things. Meet me in the healing house."

Cringing, the slave gesticulated frantically. "Not there, Harvester. Death spirits hold that place. Maybe, when I leave for the Seeing, they catch me, keep me. I fear." She paused. Renewed vigor in her voice said she felt she was delivering her strongest argument. "Healing house is Church. I'm not Church. Seeing is forbidden, except for Church, by Church. All know."

"You'll be working for Church." Draping an arm across the slave's shoulder, the Harvester eased her along the battlewalk. "Did you know the Seer of Seers went to the Land Beyond? That was why I traveled all the way to the kingdom of Ola. Lanta is a Seer." At the slave's abrupt stop, the Harvester pulled her closer, continuing to push forward and talk at the same time. "Oh, yes. Hers is weakening, though. Perhaps because she's near one who's stronger. You, my friend. Could it be? Am I beside the new Seer of Seers, even now? Dare we think of it?"

"No, no, no." The declaration dwindled to silence under the force of awe rapidly transforming itself into speculation.

"Perhaps you're right. Perhaps I ask too much of you." The Harvester laughed easily.

"The Harvester is too wise for such a mistake. And kind. How much you risk, for one such as I. I feel the power growing already."

"Excellent!" The Harvester gave the slave a gentle shove in the direction of the slave quarters. "I'll await you impatiently." She watched the woman hurry off into the darkness.

The Harvester's lonely wait in the dark healing house was an ordeal. She kept hearing the woman's words: "Death spirits hold that place," and it took concentrated will to avoid hearing other voices in the sighs and whispers of the night wind that caressed the walls. She busied herself draping blankets over the shuttered windows. When the hunched-over figure of the slave scuttled into the small room just west of the boat basin, the Harvester couldn't get the thought of rats out of her mind.

For several breaths, both women stood utterly still, the slave peering back the way she'd come, the Harvester, squinting past a lifted blanket corner. Satisfied they were unobserved, the Harvester closed the door.

In the ensuing pitch-darkness, the Harvester heard her companion's rustling, shuffling movements. The sudden glow of a coal was a relief. The squatting slave blew it to flame, then touched the fire to a candle. With that, the Harvester saw the small leather bag, its surface marked with symbols. The Harvester recognized a stylized bull's head, a flying bird, and an eye. The latter seemed to glare at her, and she made a quick three-sign behind her back.

The bag held a small drum. The frame, over which was stretched a single head, was scarcely bigger around than a man's hat, with a depth of about one finger joint. It was crossbraced for additional strength. That, and the thick lacing binding, suggested a very taut playing surface.

The slave passed the drumhead over the candle flame, mumbling to herself as she did. Two rows of three silver bells dangled from opposite sides of the form. As the drum moved over the flame, their arrhythmic sibilance was barely audible. Still, the sound plucked at the Harvester. It made her think of the wind's chilling sighs, and made her feel she'd forgotten something very important, but couldn't remember what it was. Occasionally the slave drew the drum away from the fire. When she did, she rubbed it up and down her arms, across her thighs, all over her torso. Eyes closed, head thrown back, she tapped the instrument. The erratic, single notes were high, penetrating. The tone rose as the heat affected the hide.

The slave reached in the bag and drew out the drawstring of Sylah's hood. That, too, was passed over the candle. Satisfied, the slave took it in her teeth at the center, the ends hanging down, vinelike.

Then she began to play. Sound burst out as fingers fluttered like wings. Then stopped. A single beat followed. From there, the slave built her pattern. The heel of the hand struck a solid, throbbing note; the blurring fingers surrounded it with a thicket of smaller, higher tones.

It took a while for the Harvester to discover that her heart was perfectly blended with the single beat. Taken aback, she resisted, altered her rhythm, controlled herself.

The seductive tingling of the bells, the pattering insistence of the embellishing music, coaxed the Harvester. Like a superior, amused adult talking to a child, the slave's drum beguiled her away from solid reality and into altered perception.

The slave chanted. Her deepened voice remained hushed, heavy with urgency.

There was fear, as well. Hackles rose on the Harvester's neck. Her forearms tingled.

The little drum quickened.

Again, the Harvester noted her heart adjusting to that pace. The drum demanded—took—her full involvement.

The chanting stopped in midsyllable, replaced by grunts and coughing, barking noises. The drawstring, soaked with saliva, fell from the slave's gasping mouth like foul drool. Her eyes flew open, staring, fixed on a point only she could comprehend. The drum dropped from limp hands, rolled to a stop a few feet away. The silver ringing of the bells sounded like a distant, failing warning.

A hoarse, rasping voice the Harvester had never heard said, "Love brought to dread will earn the True Stone for the Harvester. Church shall sing of Odeel through eternity." The slave's lips pulled tight and thin, forming a macabre upside-down smile.

The Harvester said, "Thank you. Thank you. But what of Sylah? She dies here? I'm rid of her?"

Gibberish spouted from the slave's mouth. In her own voice. After choking on several false starts, the slave managed to say, "Help me. Give me steps, to come back. My drum. Steps. Please."

The Harvester scrambled to the drum, pounded it. The high tone came out as a whining vibrato. "Tell me of Sylah," she demanded.

"Help me." The slave swayed.

"Tell me. Tell me Sylah dies here in Kos."

The slave gagged, coughed violently. She shook her head. "When back, tell. Help."

Furious, the Harvester drove the heel of her hand against the hide, pecked with her fingers. The delicate tracery of the earlier

387

music was replaced by awkward clattering. The slave jerked and thrashed. Her arms suddenly flew out, first clutching at the air, then spearing forward as if to catch herself. "Falling." Long, drawn out, the word echoed somberly. The slave jerked, rapidly, grimacing with pain. "They see me. Please, quick. Steps. Good steps, for home. *They come.*"

"Sylah! Tell me!" In her anxiety and frustration, the Harvester let the drum fall silent. There was only the laughter of the bells.

The slave tried to scream, her face a frozen mask of horror. The only sound she made was a reptilian hiss.

Suddenly frightened, the Harvester beat the drum as hard and as fast as she could. For a moment, the slave seemed to recover. Her hands went to her throat. She struggled to escape an invisible assailant.

The Harvester ran with sweat. She bent forward to examine the slave. Stilled, the other woman's eyes were vacant, lifted in a perpetual stare that penetrated ceiling, clouds, the sky itself. A trail of saliva trickled down her jaw, dripped unnoticed onto the yellow robe. Her fingers writhed together, meshing and disengaging, forming an endlessly remade braid.

"Stay, then, wherever you are." Sneering, the Harvester dropped the drum into the slave's lap. "Nothing but lies and bragging. I ask about Sylah and you tell me of my own glory. As if I didn't already know. Impertinent bitch." She rose slowly, waving a last, precautionary hand before the other's fixed eyes. Stepping out onto the walk, she drew up the hood of her robe. Inhaling, the Harvester poised, then screamed. The echoes were still tumbling over themselves within the stone confines when she shouted, "Guards! *Guards!* I've caught a witch. Hurry!"

CHAPTER 66

The pounding of running feet approaching froze Sylah and Lanta in the midst of their preparations for dinner. Sylah, clad only in the short-sleeved linen bodice and half skirt of her inner garments, grabbed her robe from the bed and shrugged her way into it as a fist struck the door. A male voice shouted, "Open. The Chair commands."

Sylah glanced to the corner where Lanta huddled in the wooden tub the Chair had ordered built to Sylah's instructions. Normally quite modest, Lanta seemed excessively shy this evening, Sylah thought. Not only had she insisted on moving the tub to the darkest corner of the room, she'd arranged two chairs and hung clothing to provide as much of a screen as possible.

When the fist thundered a second time, Sylah moved swiftly to yank the door open. Because the door moved away from him, the warman missed hitting it with the edge of his hand; instead, he caught it a glancing blow with his knuckles. His expression of irritable officiousness disappeared under a wave of surprised pain. Before he could recover, Sylah had pushed him backward into the midst of the other warmen clustered behind him. She stepped outside to confront him, and slammed the door behind her. Stiffly erect, fists clenched at her sides, she raged. "You beat our door like some beast threatening trembling girls? You offend. State your business. Then go, while I'm still prepared to overlook your uncultured rudeness."

Gulping audibly, the warman regained a measure of composure. "The Chair orders—"

"Orders?"

"Ah-h-h, no. Not exactly." Someone in the squad tried to smother a choking fit. The warman in front of Sylah twitched like an angry cat. When he spoke again, his voice had a new edge. Still, he was carefully deferential. "The Chair requests you come to examine a witch."

Sylah's fury evaporated. "What? Where?"

"In the healing house. The Harvester caught her."

"We'll be right there." When Sylah turned, Lanta was already opening the door, both medical bags in hand. "Is it Yasmaleeya? Has she started?"

Sylah grabbed her bag, pulled Lanta into a hurried walk beside her, explaining as they went. The warmen had no further details.

The first thing Sylah saw as she was ushered past the guard at the door of the healing house was the gaze of the yellow-clad slave squatting by the guttering candle. The blank look, fixed on the entryway, stopped her with the force of a blow. Unliving. It was the only word Sylah could think of to describe the eyes. They were fixed, yet Sylah felt them watching. Not in this world. Elsewhere. The woman lived, but somewhere her body couldn't reach. What did she watch there?

Church taught that an eyeball was no more revealing than an exposed kidney, and to assume otherwise was not only blasphemous, but poor observation technique. Nevertheless, it was to those eyes Sylah was drawn. Ignoring the Chair and the Harvester, who hovered at the edge of the solitary candle's light, she forced herself forward. Raising the candle, she passed it across the slave's face. The pupils dilated and contracted properly, but held to their upward search.

Sylah bent forward to replace the candle. Straightening, her face mere inches from the slave's face, she was shocked into a muffled cry of alarm. The pupils continued to react as if exposed to light changes. When the Chair and the Harvester leaned closer, Sylah gestured them back with a preoccupied imperiousness. Signaling Lanta to her, Sylah wordlessly pointed at the phenomenon. Exchanging glances, both shrugged helplessly.

Inexplicably dizzy, Sylah dropped to her knees. Her mind swam, formed a picture of the accused witch hurrying, bent forward, elbows pressed to her sides. No longer dressed in her required yellow, the woman wore a loose, flowing costume of crimson blouse and trousers. She walked a featureless landscape that reached to an unbroken horizon in all directions. Overhead, thick clouds raced on a wind that provided no breeze on the ground. Shadows dappled the scene, so the woman was in shade one moment, sun the next. There were small marks on her clothing, tiny symbols unknown to Sylah, red on crimson, almost invisible. The woman frequently brushed at them, as if to rid herself of them.

The Chair's hand on her shoulder pulled Sylah back to her own world. He was beside her on one knee, worried features almost touching hers. She managed a weak smile for him. He returned it, clearly relieved as Sylah resumed studying the slave.

Sylah and Lanta labored a full inch to elicit response from the woman. When herbs and shouts failed to cause so much as a blink, Sylah tried pinches and slaps. She stopped quickly, sickened. It was like abusing an infant. Worse, she was dogged by an image of the woman in her red raiment, endlessly trapped on that barren plain, suddenly afflicted by hurts that gave no warning and had no cause.

The Harvester was of sterner stuff than the two Healers. Pulling a slim, bejeweled shortknife from her sleeve, she stabbed the tip into the slave's thigh. Blood welled thickly, staining the yellow robe. Sylah and Lanta recoiled in stunned disbelief. Even the warmen muttered. The Harvester yanked the blade free with a curt, "Bandage that," to Sylah. To the frowning Chair, the Harvester said, "She's not faking. Too bad. We'll never know why she was practicing her dark craft. What do you know of her?"

The Chair shook his head. "She's been with the staff for ten, twelve years. Quiet. Devoted to Church. Or so I thought." He cut his eyes at Bos, who flinched appropriately. The Chair spoke to the Harvester again. "How did you come to find her?"

"I told the guards. I heard the drumming. I thought it was just someone practicing until I detected its sinister nature. I rushed in and confronted her. She cried out, 'I'm free. All slaves shall be freed.' And then she was like this."

"She said that, did she?" The Chair was grim, thoughtful. " 'Shall be freed.' Interesting. You're sure there was nothing else?"

"Certain. She just seemed to leave her body. Look at her. Like corn husks, dried out and empty."

The Chair straightened. "There's one punishment for witches. Beaching."

The Harvester said, "Church thanks you for your cooperation. As senior Church woman, I declare Rose Priestess Sylah and Violet Priestess Lanta official witnesses."

Bos answered, "You shall watch, Harvester. The law requires."

"What law?" The Harvester bristled. "I answer to no law but Church."

The Chair said, "He quotes Church law. As agreed to by my ancestors and your predecessors who lived among us. Witch death is witnessed and confirmed by all Church in the fort." He paused, then, "If I must . . ." Sylah saw the way his gaze swung her way, almost reached her. He checked, visibly controlled himself. After another minute hesitation, he snapped orders at Bos. "Announce the ceremony throughout Harbor. Send mirror signals to all towers within a six-inch ride of the city. There will be maximum attendance. Maximum. Establish a proper time. It must be after sundown, two nights from now. Questions?"

"None."

"Execute."

Bos spun on his heel. Sylah recognized members of Crew as they filed out after him.

On the Chair's order, warmen seized the unresisting slave, raising her to her feet. She continued to stare into space. Sylah reached to put a hand on the Chair's arm, ignoring the warning clash of warman swords being drawn. The Chair put an end to that action with a look.

Sylah said, "Give her to us, Lanta and me. She may recover. We have no proof she's a witch. Even if she is, you can see her mind is gone. What more punishment can you inflict?"

The Harvester stormed at her from behind. "How can you say

there's no proof? You see the evil drum. Witchsign scribbled all over her bag. Could this be more of your defiance of Church? You defend one of your own, is that it?"

A low murmur rose from the warmen and those spectators who had gathered at the doorway. A frown touched the Chair's brow. Sylah said, "Odeel, you risk your soul. You know I'm no witch. Your accusation is profane. You endanger yourself, not me."

Coolly, the Harvester answered, "I'm the one who caught the creature in her unholy rites. I frightened her into the condition you see before you."

The Chair said, "Rose Priestess, I entrusted Yasmaleeya to you because I understood your magic was Church, and therefore good. What's been said here is very disturbing." He reached to rub his temples with both hands. It appeared a gesture of weariness, but Sylah caught the almost-imperceptible change in his expression, saw the plea that touched his features.

She understood instantly, naturally. He was asking her to provide an argument he could support.

Why, when he was so clearly revealing his deeper feelings, was she so coldly afraid? Why should the clandestine revelation of his desire to be a compassionate conspirator frighten her more than the public figure of tyrant?

She broke free of the quandary, addressed the Harvester. "I practice no magic, no witch work."

The Harvester spoke to the Chair. "I've been told otherwise. Her companion is a Seer. Church acknowledges Seeing is magic."

The warmen holding the slave unobtrusively relaxed their grips and eased away from the woman.

The Chair's look at the Harvester was unpleasant. He went on questioning Sylah. "Why do you want this woman, if not to protect her?"

Earnestly, Sylah said, "What if we can wake her, and she can explain?"

"Of course she'll explain," the Harvester scoffed. "She'll have some story about being surprised while she was amusing herself. Simple lies. Witches know questions before they can be asked, so they have the proper answers. They blind ordinary people, so they can conduct their foul business unseen. Only Church officials have the training to apprehend them. Anyone who associates with a witch does so only to learn their evil ways. I suspect Sylah has designs on the child within the bearer."

The Chair told Sylah, "You must answer."

Deliberately, Sylah straightened. The act pulled her back from the Chair, forced the warmen behind her into hasty retreat. With her left hand, she reached to flip the long black hair cascading down her back. Her sleeve fell, revealing a startlingly white arm encircled by the massive gold bracelet given her by the Iris Abbess. Metal and carved amethysts seemed charged with light from the candle. "I would help this woman as I would help anyone because, even if she is a witch, I'm confident the One in All will protect me from harm. If Odeel is so crafty a witch catcher, why is it she ate food served by this woman, as we all did? Tell me, Chair, who recommended me as Healer to Yasmaleeya?" She smiled sweetly at the Harvester.

The Chair picked up the small drum and its case, examining the symbols. Without raising his eyes, he said, "Your faith is an inspiration, Rose Priestess. Nevertheless, I believe the Harvester's judgment of witchcraft is correct. She'll be chained to the criminal's post in front of the warmen barracks in Harbor for all to see. You men take her there. She's not to be harmed, you understand? She'll live to be beached, or you'll all take her place. Go."

The warmen carried the woman away. She gave no sign of being aware of them.

After a few moments, the Chair followed. He motioned the Harvester along in front of him. At the door, he turned. His eyes sought Sylah's. Once again, there was pleading in his expression. Sorrow.

Instinctively, Sylah's reached to console, to reassure. It was an abortive movement, less than a gesture, and then he was gone.

CHAPTER 67

Torches flared against the night in a precise semicircular line, starting and ending at water's edge. People gathered along the curve. Several paces from the deepest arc of the torches, across open beach, the sea caught the light on a glistening susurrus of small waves. The darkly patient water mocked the excited mumble of hushed conversation rising from the crowd.

Beaching was an execution. It took no feat of perception to determine that. Sylah ached with the fear that this one was not only unnecessary, but false.

Death penalties, as such, held no horror for her, not even when they were carried out in the name of Church. Church held that the struggle against evil could afford leniency, but not lack of resolve.

Sylah couldn't rid herself of the suspicion that this spectacle had far less to do with witchcraft than with power. The Chair was the one who passed sentence, but the Harvester accused. Sylah knew no reason why the Harvester would want the woman dead. Nevertheless, she was certain the slave had gotten caught up in the Harvester's treachery.

No one would tell Sylah the details of this ceremony. Even now, following Bos' warmen through the crowd and toward the eagerly beckoning torches, she had no idea what was to transpire.

Beside her, Lanta tripped along with short, brisk steps. Her chin was up, shoulders back. Only one who knew her would spy the too-wide eyes, the pale edging of the lips. Even so, Sylah hoped her own outward appearance was equally official.

The Harvester, behind them, was simply irritated by this inconvenience. Sylah knew the woman was familiar with this event, as she'd known all about the wallkiller. She'd made no effort to prepare her sisters for whatever awaited them.

Breaking free of the crowd, forging out onto open beach on the seaward side of the torches, Sylah recoiled as the knot of warmen near the water's edge parted to reveal their prisoner.

The slave's full, flowing costume of blouse and trousers was blood-red.

Almost exactly as Sylah had envisioned in the healing house. Imagined?

The warmen leading the Church witnesses showed them where to wait, then moved off to the side. The Chair strode past the three women, telling them to follow. No more than three paces from the prisoner, he indicated they should stop. Instead of his official mourning garb, he wore a long-sleeved shirt and trousers of somber gray and white. The white was a cleverly sewn elongated round that started at his knees and rose to his throat.

Shark. Sylah recognized the pattern.

The woman's behavior was unchanged. She acknowledged nothing, still intent on her own unknown vision. She was bound, hands behind her back. Chains bound her ankles.

The Chair stepped to the side. A warman hastily ignited a separate prepositioned torch as the Chair uncoiled the familiar bull-roarer from its case. Without preamble, he sent it into action, whirling, sending out its call. A moan lifted from the crowd behind Sylah. It took a few beats for her to realize it was a chant, calling on the sea to cleanse the people of evil.

Sylah and Lanta made three-signs.

As the bull-roarer swept to slower circles and silence, excitement eddied from the crowd. Hundreds of feet shuffled. Bodies rubbed together; cloth scuffed across cloth. The accumulated noise prickled Sylah's neck, made her think of a snuffling, hungry beast testing the air. Even the Harvester was affected, muttering, "Get on with it." She was careful to assure the Chair couldn't hear, nor would she meet the eyes of Sylah or Lanta.

At the Chair's signal, two of the warmen grasped the prisoner, one on each side. Their grip took her just above the elbow with one hand, while the other went in her armpit. They strained to lift her vertically. For the first time, Sylah saw the chain that had been hidden behind the woman, attached to the leg bindings. The individual links were enormous, thick as an arm. Six made a length equal to a tall man.

Thunderous, the single stroke of a drum pulsed in from the night-black sea, its source hidden, its voice shivering through every living thing in its range. It sounded again, then again. Sidestepping in time with the beat, the warmen carried the prisoner toward the water's edge.

Four slaves bearing long poles sprinted past the Church witnesses. Lighting torches at the end of each shaft, they placed them in prepared holes that formed a square. The new light revealed a small circle of stone blocks about the diameter of a man's reach. The blocks were ankle high.

Warmen carried the accused witch to the ring. The four torchbearer slaves ran to lift the chain, pushing it into the circle. It disappeared with a sharp clatter. The slaves raced for the anonymity of the crowd. Lanta exclaimed wordlessly, then, "It's a *hole*."

Behind her, the Harvester laughed. "How very observant. Now do you understand the significance of the chain?"

Unsure, Lanta remained silent. The Harvester clearly enjoyed enlightening her. "The chain's an anchor. The drum marked the turn of the tide. In a little while, the sea will reach the stone circle. Soon after that, it'll be lapping at our feet."

Lanta pointed. "Her head barely clears the top of the circle. They're drowning her."

The Harvester said, "Kos kills no witches. The sea does that work."

Far to the flanks, the crowd surged forward, carrying the torches with them. Warmen controlled the movement, allowing them only so far. The Harvester continued explaining. "See how the warmen turn the witch toward the oncoming water? Now, watch how the worthy folk of Kos rush out into it. From there they can watch the prisoner's face as she sees death creep toward her."

Inexorably, the waves advanced. With a cruelty that seemed human, it launched probes at the wall. Trickles seeped between the blocks. Gradually, torturously, it reached the top of the circle. A sheen of water flowed over the edge, began the work of filling the pit.

Lanta pulled up her hood. Sylah put an arm around her. "Pray for the walls to collapse," she said. "At least that would end it more quickly for her."

The Harvester's hand flashed out, disappeared inside Lanta's hood. Twisting, she pulled the small Priestess upright, a clawlike hand entwined in her hair. Her eyes darted from Lanta to Sylah, daring them to object. Voice rasping with repressed fury, she railed at them. "Thinking like that is why I'll destroy both of you. You can never stand against me. You're weak, and you're ignorant. That hole is permanent, constructed of stone so it can't collapse. You simply can't comprehend the strength needed to confront the real world. That pit, this execution, is *normal*. You see it's like every day of your life, and simper and smile and twitter and pretend things will get better. They won't. And the death of one witch will never even be noted in the final story of the battle for Church."

Sylah calmly reached to disengage the Harvester's hand where she still clutched Lanta. "I'm noting it, Odeel. That woman's a helpless nobody. You defile everything Church stands for. You'll answer for her. You'll answer for all your sins. By this, I swear." Too quickly for the Harvester to do more than squeal and flail ineffectively, Sylah's flicking hand touched the Harvester's forehead, her breast, both her shoulders.

"No!" The Harvester paled, stepped back. "Forbidden! You . . . You . . ."

Sylah's words turned harsh. Her speech pattern melded with the insistent thunder of the invisible, threatening drum. "I put the mark on you. I mark you evil, and I will destroy you or give my life in the effort. The One in All will decide who is true."

For a long breath, the Harvester was rigid with disbelief. Finally, clumsily, she managed one step backward. Her eyes remained fixed on Sylah's. Another step failed, and she staggered. The attempt to avoid falling seemed to break a spell. She whirled away, stumbling toward the crowd, then dropped to her knees, violently ill.

The crowd howled laughter.

At the Chair's angry gesture, Bos and two warmen rushed to raise her. She was still retching as they disappeared into the mob.

"I think I'm going to be sick, too." Lanta moaned, sagging against Sylah. She rearranged her hood to hide from the sight of the prisoner, now standing in water to her chin.

Sylah put an arm around Lanta, kept her upright. She twitched her head in the direction of the crowd. "Don't let *them* see you weaken."

Lanta moaned again. "I can't stand it. First the island, now the—" She stopped abruptly, appalled by the enormity of her slip.

"Do what you must," Sylah ordered, too distraught to fully comprehend Lanta's speech. "Stare at the Chair. Make him feel your disgust."

Impossibly, the woman in the water moved. With unimaginable determination, she forced her body around. She was suddenly returned to awareness, distorted with wrath. "You! Mighty Chair!" Straining to keep her mouth above the reaching water, she continued to shout. "Enjoy my death, as I have enjoyed watching yours. I am innocent. I have been betrayed, as I have seen you betrayed." A wave slapped her face. She choked, sank up to her eyebrows. Her hair fanned and flowed outward. Bubbles jeweled the delicate netting. Screaming, she forced her face up, spitting and coughing. "I am destroyed. Hear this: *You* are destroyed. Destroyed!"

Shrieking laughter ravaged the thick pause between drumbeats. At the sound of the next stroke, the sea claimed its due. The woman's triumphant derision strangled.

CHAPTER 68

The day following the execution, Lanta collapsed.

Thoroughly frightened, she planted her hands flat on the table, not trusting her grip. At Yasmaleeya's yip of concern, she had the presence of mind to push herself back, so she wouldn't sprawl on top of the mounded abdomen that suddenly seemed to loom like a snowdrift in front of her eyes.

That was when she realized her knees were giving way. The fear was already gone, and she accepted her steady descent with equanimity.

Time distorted in her mind. She felt capable of dwelling at length on anything as she slid toward unconsciousness. She thought how sleep had refused her after the beaching of the slave. Memories of Conway's attack, of the drowning woman, of Sylah's unimaginable, unmentionable marking of the Harvester, were companions in her torment.

Sylah had dared the world.

For a woman to even hint at a knowledge of the religious significance of the cross could call down the wrath of all males. All knew the legend of one who had been murdered on a cross by other men, one who had been mourned since. Women who referred, however obliquely, to that mistake could die for it. Many had.

For a Church woman to put that mark on another was a blood declaration. Lanta had never seen it done. In fact, she'd heard of the act only a few times in secret, whispered girl talk among her Chosen abbey mates.

Girl talk. Lanta winced. The innocence of that time was shame and mockery now. Since that afternoon on the island, her most difficult task had been keeping the secret from Sylah. Lanta was proud of how she'd deluded her friend.

Then came Yasmaleeya's daily examination.

The girl was as big as a cow. She had been lush, voluptuous. The woman on the examining table was encased in fat.

That morning Sylah looked across Yasmaleeya at Lanta. There was a sly cast to her expression that sent a vibration of apprehension swarming across Lanta's skin. Sylah said, "This baby will come sometime between twenty-four and thirty-six inches."

That simple statement was the blow that claimed Lanta's consciousness.

Where the pink-white nudity of Yasmaleeya's body met the cotton sheet, there was a hollow, just behind her buttocks. Lanta was sweltering, and all that whiteness suggested snow, soft and inviting. A person could sleep in a place like that.

A person would be secure. Safe from love that could be stolen and trampled. Safe from any more nights rank with the stink of death-sweat from packed, panting watchers. Safe from friends declaring blood feud. And childbirth medicines that threatened not only the life of mother and child, but whoever administered it.

Oblivion called, and Lanta welcomed it.

Sylah was in motion before Lanta sagged out of sight behind Yasmaleeya. Pawing hurriedly in her medicine bag, she found a small, blue ceramic bottle. She pulled the plug as she raced around the table. Yasmaleeya floundered and squealed. Sylah ignored her.

Ammonia fumes jolted Lanta back to a consciousness she clearly didn't want. Before she was fully out of her faint, she was demanding to be left alone. Sylah soothed her as quickly as she could, then turned her attention back to Yasmaleeya, who stood beside the examining table, pulling on clothes and complaining of lack of respect. Harried almost beyond endurance, Sylah leaned against the comforting solidity of the stone wall and closed her eyes. She felt her courage wavering, heard herself whispering, *It's too much, my Clas. I'm so alone. Why did I ever leave you?*

Sibilant, the secret voice that lurked in her mind whispered reply. *Sylah seeks the Door. Too much has been risked. Too much has been suffered. Sylah must continue.*

Bitterly, Sylah retorted, *All have goals I can only suspect, yet I dare not think about it, lest I fall prey to unending doubt. Let the quest go to one stronger. I need rest. Peace.*

Sylah. Persevere but a while longer. The Flower must bloom fully. What must be borne, grasp.

The fingernail-on-slate of Yasmaleeya's self-pity scraped across the silence. "I don't believe my baby's coming so soon. It's too early. You're just trying to frighten me. I want to go home. I want my mother. You treat me worse than a slave, you have no sympathy."

"Then go." Sylah pointed at the door. "Your mother should be aware of how her daughter behaves."

Sylah expected instant retreat. Instead, she got higher-pitched indignation. "You see? You don't even listen to me. I told you earlier, I can't leave the fort. I can't even leave the castle."

"What? Why not?"

"Why should I tell you again? You won't listen."

Embarrassment at having ignored something of potential significance stifled Sylah's urge to shout. Pouting, Yasmaleeya primped in a polished silver mirror. Sylah said, "My attention is entirely yours. Why are you restricted?"

"Well, why do you think? Because he's worried about me. I told him his son kicked as hard as a horse and tossed and turned all the time, and the Chair was very upset. He asked all kinds of questions about my treatment." Here she sent an arch glance at both Healers, then went on. "I told him I was keeping up my strength, in spite of all your foolish exercises that just make me tired and sticky-sweaty, and I told him I'm old enough to eat what I want. He laughed. He said Healers don't know everything, and

I was behaving exactly the way he wanted. He likes me." Fluffing her hair, studying the effect in the mirror, she went on, "That's a secret. I'm not supposed to tell you everything he says. If you tell, I'll say Lanta used the Seeing to find out, and you'll be punished. So there. No more silly walks. And if I want honeycakes or sweet wine, I'll have all I want."

Sylah hung her head. "I can only defer to the wishes and wisdom of the Chair. You are the bearer. It would be wrong for me to interfere."

Still seated on the floor, back to the wall, Lanta goggled openly. Yasmaleeya fired a suspicious glare at Sylah, but when she detected no sign of ridicule, she tossed her head and flounced out the door.

Half choking, Lanta clambered upright. "How could you do that?"

"We must hurry." Sylah's manner stopped Lanta in midspeech. "The other night, when that poor slave was caught, the Chair repeated words the Harvester claimed the woman had said. Remember—'shall be made free'? He stressed 'made.' Last night the same woman predicted his destruction. Now we have Yasmaleeya confined within these walls, and for reasons only our Yasmaleeya could believe. Something's going to happen, Lanta. I think the Chair means to bring in the leadership of the slave population, in order to control them."

Lanta cocked her head to the side, birdlike. Still pale from her faint, her eyes seemed extraordinarily bright. "You speak of controlling slaves. I would have said repression, myself. You would, too, once."

Sylah's hand flew to her cheek, as if to hide the sudden color there. She stammered. "What are you saying?"

"I'm asking you to look at this Chair. He's as cruel as Altanar, a tyrant, a torturer and a murderer."

"He has to be harsh. He doesn't enjoy what he has to do. He wishes he could be more merciful."

"Really? Who told you? Him? Have we seen one mote of this sweet mercy? Perhaps he'll repress this possible slave unrest by overwhelming them with gifts."

" 'Sarcasm cloaks bad argument.' Please remember that I acknowledged his possible heavyhandedness with the slaves. If my choice of words offends, I withdraw them. May we return to the matter of Yasmaleeya, please?"

A muscle quivered in Lanta's jaw. She answered quietly. "Of course. I gather you mean to bring the child."

"It's unavoidable. You felt it, saw Yasmaleeya's weight gain."

"Yes, and I heard her say the Chair contradicts our instructions by saying he approves of her stuffing herself. Why won't he support us?"

"You heard her; he cares for her. I believe it. He's like all men. The only way he can express himself is through excess."

Wryly, Lanta said, "Perhaps I misjudged him. Perhaps he thinks mercy's a weakness. Like indulging a spoiled brat."

Relief sparkled in Sylah's laughter. "There, you see? We imagine men to be complicated, but they're really very simple. If you can imagine a thirsty bull smelling sweet water, you understand all there is to know about a man and his capacity for deep thought."

Chagrined, startled, Sylah watched an inexplicable fury storm across her friend's features at the harmless remark. Lanta appeared on the verge of some explosive outburst. The two of them stood frozen, Sylah knowing that Lanta was fighting a terrible energy inside her. Sylah dared not move for fear of causing that force to break free. Finally, stiff-legged, back arched like an angry cat, Lanta walked toward the door. Passing Sylah, she said, "They're not complicated. But their thoughts go beyond thirst. Or kindness. You'll excuse me now. I feel weak again. I'll be back in an inch."

Exiting, Lanta clutched the doorway, gathering balance, mental and physical. Now was the time to confront Sylah directly; she must see the Chair in his true image, even if it took the destruction of friendship.

How could Sylah not see him for what he was? Sylah, so perceptive, so intuitive—and totally blind to everything but what she *wanted* to see.

But was the Seer any better? The question was a knife in Lanta's heart. She'd tried to make Sylah understand, to see. For what? It was wasted breath and earned her nothing but dismissal. Who was she, a victim, too ashamed to confess her victimization, to warn anyone about misjudging a man? Instead of speaking to Sylah, she covered her face with her hands and fled, overwhelmed, determined to outdistance memory as well as conscience.

Sylah watched Lanta go. Clues had swirled from her in a welter as confusing as the fall of autumn leaves. One needed no skill to see her anger, nor was it a feat to perceive that the real subject of her commentary was Conway. The more Sylah thought about it, the more annoyed she became. Lanta must have confronted him on her last trip to the island. Perhaps she saw Conway and Tee together.

Lanta needed some straight talk. She had to learn that Conway was entitled to his own life. Petty jealousy could turn into a searing obsession, Sylah knew, and that could cripple the quest as surely as the Chair.

Sylah took a doehide bag from her medical kit. Inside it was a mirror of polished copper. Arranging her collar and brushing stray hair into place, she told herself Lanta was reacting without logic. That was to be expected in a matter of romance, but it was unforgivable in matters of survival. Because she'd been hurt by Conway's reunion with Tee, she assumed all men were thoughtless. Even cruel.

Sometimes the world demanded brute strength, and a man had no choice.

Clas na Bale was a strong man. Forceful.

For a second, she remembered that he was also a ferocious warrior, a man who took trophies.

Even Clas did wrong things. Yet she loved him. Longed for him, yearned to see him, hear him, feel the amazing gentleness of his strength.

Shaking her head, she rid herself of the burgeoning fantasies, forced her thoughts back to Lanta's problems.

A thinking person learned to reach the root of truth. Control eliminated delusions about such frailties as physical attraction. It enabled a person to rise above things like loneliness. One who was Church-trained had no need to worry about even those unidentifiable fears that loitered in the farthest reaches of the mind, back where instinct and sensation share chaos.

That was why Sylah could deal with a man like the Chair and Lanta couldn't. Poor Lanta. A little more experience would show her the way to contend with a minor problem like Conway's misplaced affections.

The Chair must be approached again. There were questions that had to be answered, unknown schemes that had to be discovered and unlocked. More than anything, he was needed. If the Harvester was to be denied control of Church, he could be pivotal.

Lanta was right about him, however; he was cruel.

No. Harsh.

Sylah wished Lanta understood the difference, understood that he was a man. In any guise other than the Chair, he'd be respected, admired, sought as a friend. His harshness was the behavior of the Chair, not the man. Anyone denied normal human contact and companionship would be as he was.

Giving her robe one last adjustment, Sylah corrected her posture and strode into the hall and on her way to the throne room. Under her breath, she said, *"What must be borne, grasp."*

The phrase buoyed her. She felt good. Capable of anything.

CHAPTER 69

All day the fort hummed with activity. Mounted warmen patrolled the landward end of the fort's peninsula, allowing no unauthorized entrance or exit. The mirror signal overlooking the fort wall blinked continuously. Normally manned by a team of two Messengers, today there were four.

There were the other Messengers, as well. Sylah remembered Gan Moondark's dislike for Messengers, how he described them as carrion birds, uncannily aware of potential trouble. She wrinkled her nose. Messengers certainly didn't come in somber colors. Indolent, gaudy, they lounged about. For amusement, they rode their fine horses back and forth past the guards, flaunting their exemption from ordinary restrictions. It occurred to Sylah there were considerably more Messengers than just a few days ago. The memory of Gan's attitude returned. It sat uncomfortably. She looked away.

The bay, normally speckled with fishing boats and other traffic, was practically vacant. Harbor huddled against the hills at its back, the streets nearly deserted, the docks unpopulated even by the children who usually handlined for small fish. Wisping smokes from cookfires seemed anxious to dissipate before they were noticed.

Sylah worried about her friends on Trader Island.

Night fell before the Chair was free to see her. As the sun dipped behind the mountains between the fort and the Great Ocean, a pair of warmen knocked on the door to Sylah's quarters. One was clearly agitated. The second was smug. It was the latter who spoke. "The Chair requests you join him, Rose Priestess."

Bearing down on "requests," he allowed himself a smirk before turning to march away. The twitching of the nervous one increased dramatically when Sylah remained in place. He cut his eyes at his retreating partner, than gestured for Sylah to hurry. His beseeching look fled a bare moment before the first one looked back. Sylah was surprised that he remained amused, then was further angered when she recognized his affected tolerance as a bully's condescension.

Skin tightened at the back of Sylah's neck. "I'm not accustomed to mockery, Kossiar."

Kos' melodic speech added an undercurrent of taunt to the man's smiling answer. "Right, Priestess. Me and Doro here aren't 'customed to slavehand errands, but 'cause you're too tender to talk to 'em, we get their duty. For now."

The one called Doro appeared ready to come undone. "That's enough, Heldring." It was more plea than command.

Heldring's features twisted, all the false humor blown away. "You make me sick, Doro. This unperson is a witch-lover; you understand that? What the Chair wants with her is his business. I say we kill all witches."

"You'll get us both flogged."

Heldring grinned at Doro, then at Sylah. "I've heard their Church babble. She has to forgive. It's not nice to get people hurt. Anyhow, unpeople got no feelings, no rights. This is Kos, and we don't want no Church and no witch-lovers. If the Chair wants me whipped for saying so, every warman alive, except maybe you, will back me up."

Helplessly, Doro looked to Sylah. He swallowed audibly. "We better hurry, Priestess. The Chair don't like to wait."

They passed down the hall with its yawning shark maws, past the throne room. There was a door at the end of the passageway; Sylah knew the stairs behind it led to the castle roof. Bos was waiting at the door with a pair of warmen. He said, "I oppose your private meeting with the Chair. I'm forbidden to disturb you. I'll be here, though. Any indication of unusual activity, and I'm coming in, orders or no."

Haughtily, Sylah asked, "With only four warmen? Are you safe behind such a tiny army?"

Heldring stepped forward belligerently. "Careful, woman. Church don't mean that much here."

Bos' slap cracked on Heldring's jaw like a whip. Heldring spun disjointedly, clattered off the door and to the floor in a jumble. Sylah automatically moved to help the downed man. Seeing her come toward him, Heldring snarled and pushed himself away. Roughly, Bos shouldered Sylah aside. He was standing over Heldring, poised to strike again when the door flew open. The

Chair took in the scene with a flat, dangerous expression. "Explain." He bit off the word.

"My fault," Heldring said, picking himself up. "I was moving to knock for the Priestess and tripped over Bos' foot. I'm sorry. Clumsy."

Indignantly, Sylah pointed at Bos. While she spluttered angrily, Bos spoke. His hot, angry stare never left Sylah's eyes. "The warmen are tense, Chair. Heldring was distracted. They don't like you being alone with one who protects witches."

Turning away, the Chair extended a hand to Sylah. "Come in. Dinner will be served as soon as we're ready. Are you hungry?"

Sylah tried to tell him the truth about the episode at his door. He shook his head wearily. "Let it go," he said, almost whispering. Holding her hand, he pushed the door shut behind them and led her up the stairs. Sylah felt the hostility of the men outside suddenly cease, as if he'd shut out a cold, wet wind.

With her hand still in his, the Chair showed her onto the roof. At the corner of the flat expanse, the crenellated wall shielded twin candles illuminating a small oval table. When they reached it, Sylah noted porcelain plates on delicately embroidered linen. Both were the finest she'd ever seen.

Sylah turned to find a slave approaching from a kitchen tent erected in another corner. The man carried an ornate ceramic container of white with a design of pale blue flying cranes. Sylah watched him pour, fascinated. She only noticed the thin-walled delicacy of the tubular winecups when hers was already full. Catching the glow of the candles, the still, golden wine was a perfectly set gemstone.

Another slave brought a tray of shrimp artfully circled around a dish of red sauce. The Chair picked up a tail. It had been carefully severed from the head, peeled, then replaced so the creature appeared whole. Dipping the tail in the sauce, the Chair urged Sylah to do the same. "Hot," he said, raising his eyebrows.

The cold shrimp was perfectly done, tender and sweet. The sauce was wonderfully fierce. Sylah loved it, and said so. The Chair managed a faint grin. It warmed her to see his tension fade.

More slaves hurried in with food. The Chair relaxed further as they ate and drank. He spoke of his youth, of his love of the forests and meadows of his country. Constant training denied him frequent access. "Trainers," he said, making the word a curse. "Each convinced he was the one who'd go down in history as the man who perfected the boy who grew up to be the Chair. Escape from that place was a step into a world that tormented me because

I knew I could never enjoy it. I had everything but life. While he lived, my father saw I was well supplied with girls. Soft, perfumed packages of delight, raised to believe I did them honor. The staff and Crew treated them like queens for the time they spent with me. They received lavish gifts, too. I had the Crew continue the practice for a while after I ascended to the Chair. I was young, filled with self-importance and simple lust. And great stamina, fortunately. I reveled, I tell you. Then one morning I woke up with a girl beside me, and I had no recollection of her. I couldn't remember anything specific, you understand? My recollection wasn't of her, but a dimly visualized accumulation of facial features, breasts, thighs, scents, textures; it all ran together in a catalog of mindless, heartless pleasures. It frightened me. I shook like a coward. I bent over her, desperate for a memory I could identify as human contact. She was snoring. A line of drool ran from the corner of her mouth, across her shoulder and onto the sheet."

He grimaced self-annoyance, then raised his cup, emptied it. Immediately, a slave removed both cups and replaced them with smaller ones of translucent porcelain. They were no bigger around than a large man's thumb, and about the same depth. The Chair took the new bottle from the slave to pour himself. A bright yellow stream gurgled free. The glossy black jug was a flat-bottomed cone. The Chair said, "We like to finish a dinner with what we call sunwine. The name isn't just for the color, but for the way it captures the sense of a lazy, warm afternoon. I think you'll like it. It's very sweet."

Sylah touched the cup to her lips. The aroma was sprightly with berries, flowers, grass. The taste was even more complex. Honey, primarily. She thought she savored thyme. Fruit, certainly; oranges, blackberries. She raised her cup in salute. "It's all you said. And more. We have nothing like it in my country, but if I ever come back to Kos, I'll bring some of our best in appreciation."

He winced. Sylah lowered her cup. "I said something wrong?"

Massaging his temples with his free hand, he gestured with the other, sending swirls of wine slopping onto his fingers. The viscous liquid clung to him, gleaming in the flicker of the low-burning candles. In a moment, he sighed and straightened in his chair, carelessly wiping the wet hand with the hanging edge of the delicate tablecloth. "No one may offer food or drink to the Chair. It could be seen as a bribe, and the Chair must be seen as above all temptation. Why do you think the Crew was willing to keep me so abundantly supplied with women? A sated man doesn't lust

406

after what belongs to someone else. That's the theory, anyhow. One my grandfather never understood, I gather. Another story. For another time."

He drained his cup. Turning it upside down on the table, he rose, walking to the wall. Arms folded across his chest, he stared into the night. The breeze from the bay had strengthened; it ruffled his hair.

Sylah felt he looked incredibly sad. Not vulnerable. He wouldn't look vulnerable as long as his heart beat. Instead, he seemed a perfect image of loneliness. She ached to make him aware that someone understood.

She corrected herself. She didn't understand, nor could she possibly condone. What she wanted to say was she knew it wasn't his fault. "They make us," she heard herself say. It startled her.

"How do you mean?"

She walked to stand beside him at the wall. The stars were very bright. The breeze felt wonderful. The white roses were dots of softness far below, the rhododendron a stationary puff of cloud. In the distance, a black sea caught the gleam of the last quarter of the moon in a silver bar. So high, when her hair moved to the breath of the wind, it was like flying. Her words came from thoughts she normally dared not express to herself, much less to this man who held such terrible, terrifying power. She felt she was exposing herself, making herself far too susceptible to that power, yet he must learn that someone could be trusted, was willing to trust him. "They mold us like clay, make us what they need. They say it's our duty. For me, it was Church, Healing, and now my quest. For you, it was ruling Kos, keeping the alliance with the Board, defending your lands. Maybe we'd have done those things if they'd left us alone, but they didn't. They make us, and say it's for the good of all."

"Do I hear a touch of rebellion?"

"Never." At his crooked, questioning smile, she went on. "I love Church. Still, I know what she's done to me. With one breath, I glory in the search for the Door. The next, I curse it. But under everything, my love for Church is forever."

"Forever, dark-haired Priestess, Healer of warriors? Forever is longer than I care to think about." He faced her. It was a disturbing proximity, and Sylah leaned away against the wall. He made no move to close the distance. Contemplative, he went on. "If we're made by others, do I go to the Land Under for cruelly ordering that witch beached? What of my trainers? They made me. They're already in the Land Above. Does someone up there tap them on the shoulder and say, 'Look what your boy's done down there. Naughty on you. Off to the downside?' "

Acting out his joke, he leapt up into one of the crenels in the wall. Hanging on with one hand, he leaned out into space, pretending to jump.

Afraid, amused, Sylah grabbed his arm. "You'll kill yourself, you great fool." She dragged him back. At the last moment, he caught his heel, almost sprawling. She caught him. Staggering in a clumsy dance, they held onto each other, laughing, her hands on his forearms while his rested on her shoulders.

Suddenly, he wasn't laughing anymore. He looked into her eyes, forcing her to meet a steady, insistent gaze. His hands tightened, so slow the increased pressure was almost imperceptible, yet, by the time he spoke, it was almost painful. "I could believe you're a witch. Many warned me of you, even before the incident with that slave. Odeel was only the latest." Ignoring her shaken protests, he let go of her shoulders, took both her hands in his. "You dominate my thoughts. You confront me, even argue with me in front of my subjects, and I find I like you all the more for it. You break the generations-old customs of my people and I approve. Worst of all, you make me happy. Everyone must please the Chair. No one must make him happy. No one. You do it without effort. Tell me I'm not witched."

Sylah flinched inwardly when she realized the warmth had fled from his hands on hers. She squeezed them. "I know what it is to be in constant conflict with everything they say is proper. It was that way when I lived in the Iris Abbey. My Abbess saved my life, my mind. If I've helped you, you should thank her."

"If she were alive, I would treat her very badly. I'd tell her that such wisdom can never be allowed to rest, and I'd demand she become Sister Mother."

Sylah chuckled. "My Abbess was the most demand-resistant person ever born."

The Chair looked rueful. "You needn't tell me. I know her child." Something happened to his features. He released Sylah, turned his back, walked to the wall. "Go. Leave me now. I have work to do, and it's late."

"Not without hearing what troubles you."

He turned. The face that sought friendship only moments before was stiff with anger. The pale flutter of dying candles made the eyes fiery, erratic. "The Chair surmounts his own problems. Most assuredly no unperson is capable of helping the Chair." He stopped, stricken. His hands rose, fell to hang at his sides. "I'm sorry. I wanted to hurt you, make you leave. I can't maintain the pretense. But you must leave."

"Why?"

"Why? Because you're everything denied me. You'll be free to go as soon as the slave problem's under control. I'll be here as long as I live. I have all this, and it's hollow, rotten. You've seen all the activity here today? The inlanders, the farmers, are speaking of talking to the slaves to forestall an uprising. How do I make them understand that we must maintain unified control until the time's right for all to free their slaves? You see yourself as alone, struggling for goals you don't fully understand. Look at one who can never *not* be alone, yet never know friendship."

Sylah said, "I offered to be your friend. I do so again."

Swiftly, he moved forward and took her in his arms. He kissed her with a passion that stunned her, swept like surf over the shocked objections clamoring in her head. She forced herself to think of Clas, her husband, of his trust in her. Of her love for him.

Her body betrayed her. Pinpoints of heat touched where only Clas had started such fire. Her mind rejected his image, yet swung wildly to memories of what he did, how he did it. She ached with sensation, with a yearning she knew was forbidden.

His lips left hers. Almost dazed, she put her hands on his chest to push away as he reached for her breast. His touch was a whiplash. She thrust him away with all her might.

Fury distorted his features. He bellowed. *"No!"* He shouted, repeating it, louder. Sylah covered her ears. He swept her aside. By the time she recovered her balance, his footsteps were thundering down the stairs. She turned, and saw what he'd seen.

In Harbor, three separate fires sent pillars of flame into the sky. As she watched, another leapt to life.

CHAPTER 70

Dodoy said, "You couldn't find me in a hundred years."

"Could so." The other boy was named Fraylan, and he was a head shorter than Dodoy. Fraylan watched Dodoy with the quick eyes of a worshipper confronted by a particularly capricious god.

Dodoy walked away. Fraylan hurried after. Confident the smaller boy would be immediately behind him, Dodoy spoke without turning. "All right, then, I'll hide. You have to find me before the timetube falls this far"—he held up two fingers to demonstrate—"or I get to hit you on the arm as hard as I want."

Fraylan stiffened; even gods must be challenged. "No fair. We don't have a timetube. Anyhow, you took longer than that to find me, before. I should get to hit you."

"I changed the rules because you'll never find me. We don't need a timetube. I can tell the time, 'cause I'm good at that."

"You always say that. You think you're good at everything."

"I'm better than you." Dodoy spoke with the supreme authority of at least an extra year's life experience. "Are we going to play, or do I leave you here in the courtyard?"

"Don't go. I'll play."

"I don't know. You always argue about everything." Dodoy pretended to consider the matter. While Fraylan begged him to stay, Dodoy examined the courtyard carefully for the best place to hide. It occurred to him that there was no reason to stay in the courtyard. From up on the second-floor balcony, he could watch Fraylan chase himself in circles while time ran out. Dodoy pictured the look on Fraylan's face when he popped up, pretending he'd been hiding all along. Then he'd hit the little fool. He told Fraylan, "You stand over there with your face to the wall. When I holler, you take two more breaths, then come look for me. No peeking, understand? Everybody hates cheaters."

The smaller boy nodded.

Dodoy raced for the far end of the court. Standing on the back side of the rhododendron, he shouted, "Now!" then ran to the door.

Dodoy stepped onto the second floor and ground his teeth. Every door leading to a balcony was closed. Irritation overcame his fear of discovery. He hurried to the first one, tried the handle. It opened easily. He knocked, ready to claim an innocent mistake and back away. No one responded, so he pushed in far enough to peer around. There was a narrow bed for daytime reclining or hot-weather sleeping, as well as a small table and some light chairs. Closing the door behind him, Dodoy crouched and scrambled to the railing.

He laughed silently at Fraylan, speeding about in useless search. It had been a long time since Dodoy thought about his cockroaches in their box, but that was just how Fraylan looked. Only better. Cockroaches didn't have faces to look scared, and Fraylan was really worried.

It was so entertaining, Dodoy's first warning was a muffled voice on the other side of the door. The handle turned. The years of living among the Skan served Dodoy well. Unhesitatingly, he flung himself under the bed. With a presence of mind born of painful experience, he reached to steady the sway of the draped spread that reached almost to the floor. Then he silently eased back until he pressed against the wall where the length of the bed contacted it.

The voice, no longer muffled by a closed door, froze his heart.

The Harvester said, "We can talk here. There's no one in the courtyard but that demented child. What can he be looking for? And the other balconies are too far away for unwanted ears."

"Such secretiveness." The Chair was amused and scornful, at the same time. "Unless you know the whereabouts of the murdering slaves who set fire to the homes of their masters and escaped my warmen last night, I don't think you need be so cautious."

"I can tell you why I think the fires were set. And more."

There was a long pause, and Dodoy twitched at the menace in the Chair's impatient, "Well?"

"The fires were planned as a distraction. I predict more."

"Nonsense. The miserable scum discovered our preparations to crush them and lashed out."

"Your torturers haven't gotten one admission. Every slave you've rounded up swears no knowledge of the fires."

The Chair barked harsh laughter. "Would you admit to angering me?"

"Instantly, if subjected to the pain they're suffering."

"Dodoy! Come out! I'm tired of looking for you." Fraylan's thin piping drifted up from the courtyard.

Outside his hiding place, Dodoy heard the Harvester and the Chair shuffling about. He saw the hem of a black robe trimmed with blue and green swirl past the foot of the lounge on the way to the wall. The Harvester said, "So that's it; he's hunting for that orphan rat that travels with Sylah."

"Come on, Dodoy. You're not even here. Where'd you go?"

Dodoy heard a tiny, high-pitched noise and choked at the realization he was whimpering. He bit his lip.

More footsteps. Heavy and assured. "Boy! Leave the courtyard." The Chair's orders echoed.

"I have to find him!" It was a wail of childish woe, heedless of ranks and titles.

Dodoy hoped the Chair would order a warman to kill him.

Surprisingly, the Chair laughed. His voice was stern, nevertheless. "No arguments, young Fraylan. Go home. Now."

There was silence then, another reason for Dodoy to be afraid; the adults, so close, must hear his heart pounding.

The Harvester's robe swept past the edge of the bed again, and she resumed the conversation. "I treated Fraylan's mother for a cut finger. The boy talked incessantly of this Dodoy." She chuckled softly. "I'd be delighted to have such a one in my service. If I had two like him to watch him."

The Chair was brusque. "Enough. The slaves. If you know something, let me hear it."

"Very well." Without warning, the Harvester sat on the bed. Her weight forced a bow in the leather-strap suspension, almost touching Dodoy. He jammed himself against the wall, trying not to breathe. He almost missed her next words. "The escaped slaves you were seeking before these fires started are hidden at a godkill dig. The plan is to smuggle them out by boat. My assumption is that the last of them arrived last night, and the fires were set to see your reaction. Everyone's aware you plan some sort of massive disciplinary move against the slaves because of the rash of escapes and the rumors of rebellion. The smugglers have to know where your patrols search and where roadblocks are emplaced."

"Well reasoned. Tomorrow night begins a moonless period. That For, Wal, is scheduled to ship out the next day. He requested a departure inspection for that morning. Tell me where you got your information."

"Church has its mysteries and its secrets. It was ever so."

The toes of the Chair's boots poked under the edge of the bed. Dodoy barely had time to start at the sight before the bulge in the straps descended, dangerously close. Simultaneously, he heard a disturbing gurgling sound directly above him. Then the bed inched away from the wall. Almost imperceptibly, but definitely, his hiding place was being pulled off him.

The Chair's voice was almost sad. "Why do you provoke me? We're going to rule together, remember? Church's missionaries, Kos' warmen. Undermine and overcome. Never presume to speak to me again of secrets. Are we united in this?"

More gurgling. And choking.

Apparently the noises satisfied the Chair. The lump in the bed returned to normal. The Chair's feet moved away. The bed stopped moving. Dodoy inhaled, relieving starved lungs.

Choking sounds continued for a moment longer, then the Harvester, suddenly hoarse, spoke. "The slave I said was a witch knew the guide who takes the escapers to the godkill. The slave

412

had a kind of Seeing. She was trying to help me—help us—learn more. Something went wrong."

"I suspected as much. There was a black ropelike thing on the floor beside her. It was a Church article, wasn't it? A soulseeker, for Seeing a particular person. Sylah."

"Her hood cord. The slave stole it from Sylah's robe at her first meal here."

"If you'd confided your plans in me, instead of lying, your slave Seer might still be alive, and none of this would be happening."

"How was I supposed to know she'd go mad?"

"You're supposed to know two things, Odeel. Know how to control your Church. Know that we have a partnership, and I'm in charge of it. I've promised you Church and I've promised you Sylah when I'm done with her, but be warned: try to deceive me or obstruct me once more, and I'll denounce you to Sylah and Church."

The Harvester's voice trembled, but she mustered a touch of defiance. "Sylah's doomed. I told you. Yasmaleeya and her child are going to die. You said yourself Sylah would be blamed."

"Things change. A prudent man changes with them. Sylah's merely another woman to me, Church prattle notwithstanding. Her friends are another matter. They love her, and White Thunder and Black Lightning control immense power. Nalatan's worth ten of my best warmen. None of her group will ever transfer loyalty to me. Worse, they're all simpleminded enough to try to avenge her death. It was already on my mind to be rid of them, and this slave thing may answer."

The Chair's voice changed. Dodoy pictured him deep in thought. "They stay with Borbor, who houses Wal, who wants permission to leave Kos. If I can find the slaves, I'll set a trap. An ambush. I'm not ready to challenge those lightning weapons directly. Not yet. There has to be a weakness, a way to separate them. I have to think."

Leather squealed as the Harvester changed her position. "Think of treating me with more respect. I'm the one who's uncovered the important information here. You see I'm not without resources. I insist on the respect I'm due."

Dodoy heard the hollow bravado, as he'd heard his own bluster. He hated her for reminding him. She moved again, mashing the mattress, flooding his hiding place with an exhalation of warm, musty, straw-tainted air.

413

The cockroaches. It smelled like that where the cockroaches hid.

Casually, the Chair said, "I know how Church disciplines those who connive with profane Seers." His footsteps moved away, toward the door. The hinges sighed. The Chair spoke again, in a cruel tone Dodoy knew too well. "Or I may simply cut your throat." The door closed.

Dodoy had no idea how long he waited under the bed after the Harvester finally made her way off the balcony. He was still shaking. He checked the hall before leaving, forced himself to walk away with nonchalance. Once in the quarters he shared with Sylah and Lanta, he threw himself facedown on the bed.

He thought of the Harvester, glad she was in such trouble. Soon, though, he was more curious about how she'd wriggle out of her problems. He was sure she would.

He rolled over and sat up when the Priestesses came in. One look, and they remarked on his color, his nervousness. Lanta asked what was wrong. Sylah asked what had happened. Dodoy noted the difference. He answered Lanta, telling her that the slave-smuggling plot was exposed. When he added that the Harvester suspected the time of the escape attempt, he thought the small woman was going to be ill. She turned to Sylah. "We have to warn them."

Sylah paced the room, brow furrowed. When she spoke, there was a quality to her voice that reminded Dodoy of the Chair. It made him angry in a way he couldn't explain. Sylah said, "It's time for Yasmaleeya to deliver her child," and when Lanta tried to say something, Sylah cut her off with a significant look. Dodoy noted that, as well. Sylah continued, "There's going to be a great deal of excitement. It's going to bring the child. I'm sure you understand."

Lanta nodded, although Dodoy wasn't sure she really did understand, from the dazed look of her. Then she said, "How can we warn the others? The Chair's sure to learn exactly where the slaves are being kept."

"The danger goes beyond that," Sylah said, still pacing. "He wants more than the slaves recaptured. He wants whoever's behind the effort to free them. Now he knows it's someone on Trader Island. He'll attack." She stopped in front of Dodoy. "You've been gone all afternoon. What else did you hear?"

"He said he was going to be the Harvester's partner, and she could have Church."

"What? You're sure? That's exactly what he said?"

414

It was what Dodoy expected. Disbelief. Always the same. She never liked him.

They were both very frightened. The only one with the strength to help him was Tate. Getting her off that island and close to him was important. That, and making sure stupid Sylah knew only what he wanted her to know. "The Harvester said you'd be blamed if anything happened to Yasmaleeya and her baby. Then the Chair said things change. He said everyone loves you, but he wants the lightning weapons." That was enough for her. It would make Tate come for him, too, and then they could run away. That was a necessity. And if Sylah didn't want to believe the Chair meant to get rid of her, then she could find out for herself.

Sylah was flushed. She said, "That's not the same as saying the Harvester will have Church. Not at all."

Lanta said, "That's not important. We have to escape from here. Warn the others."

"No." Sylah shook her head, mouth drawn down. "I've got to deliver that child, healthy, with a healthy mother. Church can use them, and I have to save him for the Chair and for Church. We have to get you to Trader Island, though. Is there a slave we can bribe? We need someone who can sail a boat."

"I can," Dodoy said.

The women stared, openmouthed. He snapped at them. "I was the captain's slave. Who do you think he sent on errands in the small boat? I know everything about sailing. Anyhow, where would we get a boat?"

Sylah put a hand on his shoulder, not gently. "You're going to steal one."

CHAPTER 71

Lanta and Dodoy crouched in the darkened healing house, seeking the guard they knew must be present. The boat basin was deathly still, without even the occasional slap of a wave. The shapes of the boats were indistinct, black on black.

The couple whispered agitatedly, Lanta certain she'd heard a cough. Dodoy was equally sure the Chair's planned action against the slaves had stripped all warmen from the fort, save those manning the berms on the landward side.

For once, the boy had been completely cooperative. He even

learned that the reduced guard force contained no watch reliefs for the night; the warmen on post would remain until sunrise.

Both Dodoy and Lanta also knew there was sure to be a defensive gate of some kind to close off the exit tunnel to the bay. If it was secured, escape was probably impossible.

Cramping limbs demanded they move. Clumsily, they crept out, keeping together by touch. At the basin's edge, Dodoy disengaged himself from Lanta, leaving her alone. When his shadowy figure materialized silently beside her and his hand returned to hers, icy cold, it nearly broke her composure. He put his mouth to her ear. He smelled of seawater. "There's two gates, one at each end of the tunnel. I fit between the bars. Come."

The control was a large spoked wheel that raised the triangular gates. Lanta berated herself for never having noticed them. Embarrassment over her lack of observation further eroded her confidence.

Dodoy was whispering again. "You open the gates. I'll take a boat out, tie it up, and come back. You walk out then. I'll lower the gates and squeeze out."

She grabbed him, pulled him back. "Why don't I take the boat out and wait for you? It'll be quicker."

He pulled away roughly. "If you do something stupid, I'll be outside where I can get away, that's why. Let go of me."

Lanta had to let go or wrestle. A few moments later, she heard the soft noises of disturbed water. She turned the wheel to allow Dodoy and his stolen boat out. Fortunately, the apparatus was well greased. Nevertheless, water dripped from the emerging iron bars, the splash sounding to Lanta like a river's flood. When Dodoy bumped the boat against the side of the exit channel, she was sure the walls must collapse from the force of the collision.

Before she realized it, her dripping companion had them out on the open water. She wanted to shout, to sing. Until Dodoy raised the sail. The hoist squealed. The boom groaned. The sound of the rushing water was thunder, the white sail was a beacon.

The thought that they had to go all the way to Trader Island made Lanta's stomach turn. Then she considered they had to come back, do this all over again. She leaned over the side. For a while she was too preoccupied to be afraid.

Landfall on Trader Island was an anticlimax. Dodoy drove the small boat crunching onto the beach with authority. Lanta hopped ashore dry-shod. They were securing a line to a tree when Borbor's gang arrived. By torchlight, they greeted the new arrivals with suspicion.

Ushered into the Trader's great hall, Lanta and Dodoy were greeted with warm surprise. Tate, Conway, Tee, and Wal were there. Nalatan was with Borbor at a traders' meeting. Once the gang men were gone, and Tate had assured that none of the Kossiar servant-spies were about, the group took seats in front of the yawning fireplace. Lanta explained her mission.

Conway's appearance nearly destroyed her. She couldn't bear to meet his eyes, but her first view of him clawed at her heart.

She remembered the mindless, animal look of the man who'd hurt her as nothing ever had. Consuming hatred coiled across his face now, the same way tongues of flame whirled and twisted around the wicks of the oil lamps dangling from the brass chandelier.

Hate for her, hate for himself.

It suddenly occurred to Lanta that she was no longer ashamed. She'd been shamed; she had no reason to be ashamed. Conway did. And was. Which was why he was angry.

Why, then, if she knew all those things, did his pain hurt her almost as much as her own?

Tate came to her, put a hand on her shoulder. "Are you all right? Is something else wrong?"

Dodoy's smug superiority saved her. "She fed the fish all the way over here. The sea's no place for a woman."

Conway strode to the fireplace, put his hands on the marble slab mantel and stared into the cold, black maw. The others waited for him. He spun on his heel, pointing at Lanta. "Prove it," he said. He looked flushed, feverish.

Blinking, Lanta was struck dumb. Tate spoke for her. "Prove what? That the operation's been blown?"

"I heard the Chair. I heard the Harvester. I was there." Dodoy's voice rang with indignation.

Conway ignored him. He walked to Tee's side. "If anyone knew where the slaves are hidden, they'd have moved on them already. The Chair knows Wal's the only one who's requested customs inspection." He bent to Tee, spoke to her from the side of his mouth, his eyes locked on Lanta's. "You told Lanta about Moondance's successful recruiting among the slaves. Then Lanta came back because Sylah wanted her to counteract Moondance's progress. What did you tell her, Tee?"

"I said I'd recommend against it to all of you. That doesn't mean she's lying."

"Yes it does. They both are. What did Sylah promise you,

Dodoy? Or did you make this up because you want to be with Tate and this was the only way you could get here?"

Red-faced, Dodoy shouted denial. "I'm not lying. You don't like me. I heard the Chair. I don't care what you believe."

Tee said, "Lanta, I know you'd never lie to us. But the last group of men arrived last night. If a patrol had even come close to the hiding place, a scout would've seen them and given us an alarm."

"They're here? Were they guided in by anyone who guided the others?"

Conway said, "Of course. The guide's one of *us*." The accented last word was spiteful.

Pleading, Lanta said, "Can't you see? The slave who was beached knew the guide. Torturers will be questioning everyone that poor woman knew. They could already know who he is. He'll tell them. He won't be able to resist."

Deeply troubled, Tate said, "Maybe you ought to listen to Dodoy, Matt. This is sounding really bad."

Conway brushed her counsel aside. "The boy wants to be with you. That's all he cares about. As for you, Lanta, what you said just now isn't what you said before. You told us the accused witch said where the slaves were to be hidden, and that they were to be loaded on a boat. Now you tell us she got the story from the guide himself. You said that *after* I let you know the guide was the same man in every case. Tee, she's making it up as she goes along."

Wal said, "You're saying too much, Conway. Let it go. None of it matters, anyhow. We don't dare put those men on my boat now. The inspectors will tear it apart. They'll find the hidden compartments."

"Let them." Tee's brow was wrinkled in concentration. "Wake your men. Cut doors into those compartments tonight. The customs people won't be here until morning; when they look, they'll see nothing but honest spaces, packed with goods. You'll leave on schedule, then slip back into the bay after dark. We'll meet you with the slaves in small boats, transfer them over, and you'll be away."

Everyone spoke at once in spirited argument.

Lanta's voice rose above all. She stood, hands outstretched, tears in her eyes. "Save yourselves. Make Wal's ship safe. Pray the slaves haven't been found. As cruel as it sounds, you can't try to rescue them. Not tonight. If they survive until tomorrow night, you can assume the guide died without revealing their location. Even then, attempting to help them will be terribly dangerous. The Chair may leave them in place as bait to trap you."

Conway said, "You're determined to frighten Tee away from her mission, aren't you? It kills you to see her accomplishing something you and your broken-down, oh-so-pure Church can't do, doesn't it? You're quick enough to give up on the slaves, too. They might already be Moondance, so let them die, right? Admit it, all of this is jealousy, personal and Church, just to spite Tee."

Wal rose slowly, a prairie bear's towering on hind legs to better examine some irritating disturbance. "I spoke to you about your manners once, Matt Conway. I'm wondering if your fists are half as active as your mouth." He was unbuckling his sword belt as he spoke.

Lanta put a hand on Wal's arm. "He doesn't mean it. It's all right."

Tee held Conway's shoulder. It checked him, but couldn't erase his expression. Lanta ached to ask him to at least be fair. If she'd goaded him and embarrassed him, could that justify what he'd done, what he was doing? She conceded she was too weak to forget, but she was willing to forgive. She was trying to save his life, the life of the woman he'd rejected her for. What can possibly be left for me to do? she wanted to ask. She was the one wronged, the one hurt. Must she be hated, as well?

Wal was gentle, apologetic. "It's best you go back, Priestess. This island's going to be very dangerous in a little while. For that matter, Sylah's going to need a courageous friend beside her."

Dodoy leapt to his feet. "I'm staying with Tate. There's no one in the castle who can protect me. They'll make me a slave again."

Tate came to him, took his face between her hands. She was very firm. "You'll go with Lanta. You'll do exactly as she and Sylah tell you. I'm staying here with Nalatan. As soon as this trouble's over, you can come back. I'll be waiting. Don't argue. I love you, child, but I swear I'll tie you up like a chicken for market and carry you to the boat, if I have to. You understand?"

Dodoy knew he was beaten. He headed for the door. "You coming?" he called back to Lanta, not slowing.

She made quick good-byes and hurried after him.

The path to the water's edge was far more difficult in the dark. Lanta stumbled frequently, to Dodoy's muttered disgust. During one of his longer complaints—the words indistinguishable, the tone all too clear—he stopped abruptly, with a short exclamation of surprise. They were on nearly level ground by then, and Lanta assumed he'd stepped out onto the beach. A moment later, she was on open ground herself. Against the starlit sea, Dodoy seemed to loom, as though he'd grown several inches.

The arm that snaked out of the darkness to close against her throat struck with swift silence. Her attempt to scream died against choking pressure. Her struggles were completely ineffective. She was lifted, her feet dangling. Clawing fingers sought her captor's eyes. Too quick for her, he buried his face into the back of her head. Desperate, feeling consciousness drain away, she scratched at flesh. A male voice exclaimed angrily. A jerk of the arm around her throat nearly broke her neck, but it also changed the arm's position. She forced out a gasping cry.

Then the pressure was back, and she was sinking.

From out of the night came a voice. Mocking. Nalatan. "Careful, careful. You'll never get answers out of her if you kill her. And think what the Chair will do to you then."

CHAPTER 72

Pain.

It throbbed through Lanta's skull, sent out vibrations that shivered along muscles and nerves throughout her body.

Motion.

Swaying, rising and falling, irregular and unpredictable.

A deep voice intruded. "She stirs. I think she's coming around."

Other sounds slipped into her awareness. Water. Wind.

Without moving, Lanta slowly opened her eyes to peek out from the depth of her hood. She was semireclining, her back wedged into the bow of a small boat. A figure astern held the tiller. Closer, between the mast and the gunwale, someone faced her. The person was large, heavily bearded.

Lanta read the stars. The boat was moving west. There was no way for her to tell if they'd passed the fort. So slowly it made her skin twitch with impatience, she pulled her left arm across her body. The black sleeve against the black robe was invisible. She slipped her right hand into the sleeve, clutched her shortknife.

The chant filled her mind. Little by little, it compressed the fear, forced it farther and farther from her consciousness until she could ignore it.

She drew the knife from its sheath. Struck.

The bearded man grunted, a bass rumble of pained surprise. She pulled the blade back. Struck again. The man caught her forearm in one hand, grabbed her wrist with the other. He said, "Don't do that. That *hurts*."

She'd stabbed him. He was indignant.

It was too funny to bear. Hysterical laughter bubbled out of her. Tears drowned the amusement.

The strong hands took the knife. Then, unbelievably, she was inside an embrace, cradled, comforted. Deep, soothing sounds rolled in the massive chest of the man holding her. The beard tickled her ear where her hood had fallen back. She felt safe.

She decided that meant she'd gone crazy, but she didn't care.

Dodoy said, "I told you she had more tricks than a fox. You didn't believe me. Nobody believes me."

Lanta lifted her head, looked aft. "Dodoy? You're here?"

Scornfully, Dodoy answered. "Keep your voice down. Where else would I be? You heard what Tate said."

Straightening, she pushed herself away from the man. He made no effort to hold her. Neither did he make an effort to give back her shortknife. Lanta said, "Who? What? Where?" and bit her lower lip to stop the babble.

The man said, "I'm glad you feel better, Priestess. Please go back to the front of the boat. There are things I must tell you. In confidence."

"You almost killed me."

Dodoy's muffled laughter was like a cruel whisper. "He and Nalatan saved us. "Don't you know anything?"

"A man choked me. Nalatan said the Chair wanted me alive."

Gently, but with irresistible firmness, the man forced Lanta back to the bow. Leaning close, he whispered, "Nalatan caught the spy-servants trying to steal you and the boy. They'll trouble no one again."

Lanta swallowed, trying not to think about the significance of the last remark. She said, "You were there?"

"With Nalatan. Name's Helstar. Smith to Trader Island. Me and Nalatan heard your scuffle with the Kossiars on our way to warn the Tee one. The slaves are discovered."

Lanta straightened. "I warned them. The Chair knows everything."

"Chair doesn't know the slave revolt starts tonight. Why I'm with you and the boy. Show the Flower to Safety."

"I know who you are. My companions on the island spoke of you. You're not their friend."

Helstar's quiet chuckle had the sound of release. He said nothing for a time, and then, as if to confound Lanta completely, he continued in an entirely changed speech pattern. The voice was the same. Nothing else was. "There are things I am ordered to tell you. That's the other reason why I'm here."

Lanta's failure to answer was as much a matter of shock as caution. Helstar read it as the latter. "It pains me to be suspected, but I understand."

"Pain." Lanta blurted the word. "Your wound. I stabbed you."

Helstar extended the shortknife. As Lanta took it, he said, "A little thing like you isn't likely to drive a blade through a mail shirt made by Helstar the smith. The point pricked me enough to sting."

"Oh. Well. You said you have something to tell me?"

"Much. Listen well. We've little time. There are those who think you possess the True Stone or know its location. You will keep whatever you know to yourself. Trust no one. Those who instruct me direct me to tell you to use whatever knowledge you have to see that Church survives. For now, however, serve the Flower."

When he paused for breath, Lanta practically spat hushed, strained words at him. "You dare speak to me of what I know? Don't know? Must say? Can't say? I serve Sylah because she is my friend, because I believe in what she does. You have nothing to say of Church. Leave me."

"Priestess, listen. Church has eyes and ears beyond your dreams. I am but one who helps. I've delivered my message. You will do as the One in All moves you to choose. My other mission is to guide you and Sylah away from the fort."

Something about Helstar's resolute dignity made Lanta pause. If he was telling the truth about the Kossiar spy-servants, he'd probably saved her life. Now he claimed to be sent to save Sylah's, as well.

By whom?

The best liars were the ones who told the biggest lies. "Why do you say the slave revolt starts tonight?"

"All Kos knows the Chair means to repress all hope. The slaves are convinced they must rise while the nomads threaten. They hope the nomads will help them."

"Will they?"

Helstar's voice slowed to worried thoughtfulness. "They say the new siah among the nomads owns lightning stronger than the weapons of your friends. They say he is the moon's own child. He enslaves all. Moondance is his lash, his chains. The slaves ignore that. You cannot make a man who's drowning at the dark bottom of a well fear the heat and thirst of the sun."

"Can the nomads overthrow the Chair?"

"Who knows?" There was a pause, a sound that could have been a chuckle. "I'm told you're a Seer."

She smiled in spite of herself. "There are things I'm not allowed to discover."

Dodoy's warning hiss was like an icy spray. Helstar and Lanta tensed. The boy scrambled forward from his tiller, catlike, to drop the sail. Instantly, the boat lost way. In the absence of the cloth's soft drum, the adults heard what had frightened Dodoy. Voices, many of them, mumbling indistinctly. Dodoy flattened himself on the gunwale, scanning toward shore. A moment later he pointed. Lanta and Helstar got as low in the boat as they could.

Four large Kossiar balancebars stood out in silhouette against the starry night. Ghostly pale sails drove them east, plowing white, curling waves. A horse whickered. A rough voice followed. Helstar's single word was a warning whisper. "Warmen." The trio drifted until they were sure the vessels were out of hearing. Dodoy hoisted the sail slowly, listening.

They were only under way a short while before Helstar touched Lanta's wrist. "The wall. There. I join the boy now. Be silent. Whatever happens, remember; the Flower must leave here immediately."

"You said you'd guide us to safety."

"I hope so, little one. If I fail you, forgive me. But run first, you understand?"

Cautiously, Helstar and Dodoy eased down the sail. Stroking the sea with muffled oars, they inched into the small channel leading to the entry tunnel.

Lanta was certain the pounding of her heart would bring a challenge.

Dodoy slipped into the water without a splash. Lanta watched him paddle to the iron-barred gate and wriggle through. An eternity later, the gate shuddered, swung up and open. Dodoy returned, clambering aboard. As the boat entered the tunnel, Lanta cowered in the angle of the bow. There was a light burning in a room high above the boat basin. She was sure its beams sought them.

When she looked aft, Helstar was gone.

Dodoy guided the boat into the basin, going to the same ring. He slipped past Lanta to tie it up. That done, he darted away like

423

some small, furtive animal. By the time Lanta was out of the boat, the inner gate was easing into place.

Helstar was nowhere to be seen.

Her search was interrupted by Dodoy's sharp cry.

In the dim light from above, Lanta saw the warman standing by the gate wheel. For a moment, she thought he'd frightened Dodoy away. Then she realized the man held the boy under his arm. The thin, bony figure hung brokenly.

Lanta turned to run. A second warman was waiting for her, sword drawn, teeth bared. Lanta drew herself erect. "Put away that weapon. I am Church. No one dares strike me."

The sword held true. "No more. The Harvester said."

The warman carrying Dodoy joined them. He gave the boy a shake. "He won't give me another scare."

His partner made a snorting noise. "You're lucky they came back."

"It was the only chance I had. They were already out of the gate when I woke up. If I'd called in an alarm, everyone'd know I was asleep. Anyhow, I told you this one'd never leave the other Priestess. Two fingers on one hand, they are."

"Lucky," the other said, turning to push Lanta toward the castle.

They stopped at the door leading into the castle. The overhang of a roof created a pocket of pitch darkness. Lanta's guard fumbled at the door handle. She turned to find Helstar doing something behind Dodoy's captor. The bearded smith appeared to be casting a spell. He raised his hands over his head, then crossed them at the wrist. He held short sticks in each hand. Flipping both hands forward, he kept the wrists crossed.

The man carrying Dodoy dropped him to raise his hands. Before they reached his throat, blood jetted from a gaping wound under his chin.

Lanta stumbled aside as the warman at the door turned. He had his sword raised in defense even as he spun to face whatever waited for him.

The move saved his life. Helstar's sword glanced off the warman's blade with a sparking clash. The warman kicked him in the groin. Helstar doubled over with pain. Stepping inside an overconfident raised sword, he managed a weak hack at the warman's left arm.

Unfazed, the warman poised his foot again. Helstar crouched, protecting himself, ready to grab.

The move was a feint. Tricked, looking the wrong way, Helstar barely glimpsed the descending sword. Diving forward, he tried to close. The handle of the Kossiar's weapon struck him across the back of the skull. There was a finality to the sound. Head first, Helstar went down, huddled on the ground without moving.

The warman stood panting, one hand covering a bleeding bicep. The sword remained pointed at Helstar's back. Lanta prayed the battle madness would fade before the Kossiar gave the blade that one last thrust.

Something sliced the darkness, something that glimmered like a small silver bat. The warman glanced up, only had time to register sick disbelief before shining steel struck him just above the eye. The shock of the blow snapped his head back. He said, "I thought you . . ." very clearly, then dropped his sword. It landed on Helstar, sliding off onto the paved walk with a quiet clink. The warman, with the metal thing jutting from his head, looked at the fallen weapon as if it were the most important thing in the world. He collapsed and died with the same earnest intensity still on his face.

Dodoy trotted forward to jerk the little chain axe from his victim. Lanta was already running to the boat basin, soaking one of the voluminous sleeves in the cold water. Hurrying back, she bathed the smith's face and wrists. He recovered consciousness almost immediately. It took a bit longer before he was steady enough to walk. Once ready, he looked to Dodoy. "You do that? With that thing?" He indicated the chain axe with his chin.

Dodoy nodded. Lanta thought he looked a little less pleased with himself than she expected.

Helstar bent to the first warman, picked up the two small clubs. For the first time, Lanta saw the wire connecting the two of them. Helstar saw her expression and hurriedly jammed the weapon in his pocket, mumbling, "Sorry."

Helstar and Dodoy dragged the bodies to the basin. Working quickly, they loaded the pair in a balancebar, then shoved it down the tunnel to the sea. As they raised the sail, sending the vessel off with its grisly cargo, Helstar tapped Dodoy's shoulder, pointing. Just off Trader Island, lights were coming on aboard Kossiar boats. They ran back to Lanta.

She led the way into the castle.

CHAPTER 73

Stormracer's hooves on the wooden ramp between boat and shore sounded like rolling thunder in the utter stillness of the night. Conway sighed relief when the animal was finally on quiet earth.

Nerves. They accentuated every sound, gave movement to every tree and bush in the crowding forest around him.

He fell in behind Tee and the three men from Borbor's gang. Saddles squeaked. Hooves shuffled. The regular, damp breathing of the horses weighted the night with a pleasant thickness. It blended with the smooth scent of leather, the tang of bruised plant life, and the acrid bite of salt marsh. Karda was a silent presence. Conway strained to see Mikka, bringing up the rear of the column.

Everything was going well.

Conway's jaws tightened at the thought of Lanta trying to undermine the antislavery effort. More Church hypocrisy. First the Harvester tried to kill him, and now Lanta was striking at him through his need for Tee.

He couldn't deny he'd given Lanta cause to be vindictive. It was as much her fault as his, though. He tried to be friendly.

He shook his head. The truth was, he tried to be more than friendly with Lanta. She never cared, not at all. It was too bad he never realized she was only leading him on, teasing him. Didn't even respect him. A man took only so much, and then he . . .

It wasn't as if he'd set out to hurt her. She was the one playing foolish games.

Tee saved his life, gave him purpose.

Lanta was a sham. Pretty—all right, beautiful—but there was nothing there. Distant. That was it. If she'd just talked to him. There must have been something she could have said.

He almost bumped into Tee. They were off the narrow trail through the heavy forest, and she'd dropped back to wait for him.

The godkill was a large expanse of high ground surrounded by extensive marshes, with the bay to the south. Tee stood at the intersection of the trail from the stream bank and a broader wagon track. Long ago, slave miners used the wider, rutted road to haul their discoveries to barges that plied the stream. Years of disuse rendered the road an overgrown swath. Fire, as well as browsing deer and goats, kept it stunted to waist-high scrub.

Tee said, "Borbor's gang men are scouting to the left, back to where the larger road meets the stream. We'll wait here for them, then all go ahead to the hiding place."

"You should have let me do the scouting." Petulance marred Conway's objection, and it made him all the more irritable. "With the dogs and Stormracer, I can do the job faster and better."

"The lightning weapons are our strength. If there's anyone lying in ambush, I need you for the counterforce."

It made good sense. Still, Conway rankled. "If you're so afraid we'll be trapped, why are we here? I thought we decided there was no danger."

"You said there was no danger. You don't trust Lanta. I do." She paused, then "We have to talk about that. There are things you should know about her."

The reflective, almost sad quality of her tone intrigued him. When he tried to question her further, she hissed him to silence.

The trio of gang men were moving rapidly when they returned. Nervousness sang in the leader's whisper like a fine wire in the wind. "The guide's safe signal's not in place."

The safe signal was a simple thing. The old wagon road ended at the remains of a dock. The guide's instructions were to pretend to fish the streams that meandered through the marshes. If he saw no warmen in the vicinity he left a long sapling stuck in mud next to a piling.

A cold snake of doubt wrapped around Conway's throat. They had to succeed. Had to. He said, "It probably fell over. We'll move quickly."

The leader of Borbor's men said, "There was no safe signal. We get out. Wal told us the little Violet Priestess warned this might happen."

"She's a liar." Conway ignored the sharp intake of breath from the men. "You can't desert now."

"We agreed to rules, and one of the rules is a safe signal from the guide. You agreed, too."

Tee said, "You all stay here. I'll go for the escapers."

The gang man said, "It's too dangerous. You feared a trap, or you wouldn't have brought the White Thunder. Now you've got proof of it."

Conway could barely see the man's pointing finger, but the accusatory pressure of it was palpable. Reacting, he struck it aside.

427

In an instant, there was a rasp of metal on metal as all three men sought to draw weapons.

The dogs growled heavily. Conway swung the wipe to bear, slipped the safety.

Tee's hand stayed him. The three gang men each took a step backward.

Conway said, "You men don't understand. This is more than freeing some slaves. Lanta's an agent of power. She hates Tee. And me. She wants us to fail because Church suspects the escapers might be Moondance."

Once more, Tee said, "You three stay here. Conway and I go ahead. If you hear sounds of trouble, get back to the boat, warn the others on the island. Understood?"

The gang men muttered assent.

Mounting the horses, Tee and Conway rode slowly through the scrub. They'd covered about a hundred yards when Conway signaled a halt. The horses remained calm while the dogs scouted ahead, which Conway interpreted as further proof that all was well. When the dogs returned and took up position to resume the march, he flashed a triumphant grin at Tee. He was disappointed when she merely resumed progress.

Another five hundred yards or so brought them to a point where they could see the shanty that covered the godkill mine entrance.

The dogs inspected the area. Off toward the bay, a marsh bird cried continuously. Its call was a high, wavering note that broke, then descended. Conway silently cursed its unnerving lament.

Suddenly the bird squawked alarm and took flight in a welter of splashing and rustling reeds.

The dogs returned. Both seemed confused. They circled, heading back the way they'd come, growling softly. Karda came to Conway, rising on his hind legs, his forepaws on Conway's thigh. He nudged Conway with his muzzle. Conway rubbed the animal's neck to soothe him.

Tee leaned to Conway from the opposite side. "Something's very wrong. Stay here. I'm going to the shaft and call the men out."

Since he could see her at all times, Conway offered no objection. Putting the dogs in the down position, he locked and loaded both the wipe and boop. He checked his pistol. Lastly, he moved his sword in its scabbard.

Tee set her horse toward the building at a fast walk. It surprised Conway, and then he realized there was little use for great stealth.

The dogs' indicated no sure presence of strangers; their confusion was disconcerting, but they'd have left no doubt if other humans were present.

Tee galloped back. Her eyes shown white in the darkness. She clutched at his arm. "They didn't answer. The mine. It smells. Awful. I heard something. Scratching. Squealing. Rats, I think."

A distant scream wounded the night, freezing Tee and Conway. Shouting followed, alarmed anger, fear. "The boat," Tee said, "they're attacking the boat."

As if proving her point, the ruddy glow of fire smeared the sky. Sparks and brands lifted above the shielding forest between the couple and their lost escape.

A pounding gallop announced the approach of the gang members. Barely allowing time for them to stop, Conway said, "We go east, to the high ground on the other side of the swamp. We'll steal a boat and get back to the island."

No one answered. Conway knew it was because no one had any more hope for the prospect than he did. They all assumed Kossiar warships were already cruising off the marshes like sharks, waiting for anything foolish enough to venture into deeper waters.

Nevertheless, the dwindling tumult spoke eloquently of events at the burning boat. It was a matter of very little time before the men who'd fired it came looking for its passengers.

The group raced across the scrub at the mine site. Once on the other side, however, the thick forest began again. Slowing, closing on each other, the five pressed ahead. Conway took the point, with Tee immediately behind. The dogs disappeared forward. Suddenly, however, both dogs were back. They were agitated, crowding close to Stormracer. The horse, ever mindful of his legs, skipped about irritably, ignoring Conway's soothing pats on his withers.

Huddling close, the others listened as Conway said, "The dogs found someone ahead. We've got to cut north, away from the bay."

The gang leader disagreed. "There's a town that way, with a warman barracks. We'll be riding right into their swords."

Tee said, "The warmen are probably spread out, looking for us. Hunting slaves."

"They'll be thick as cornstalks to the north. Whatever's east of us is just a screen."

To Conway, Tee said, "He may be right."

Conway asked her, "What do you know of the marshes? Can we get through?"

Tee said, "Possibly. There's one place where it's narrowest. I think I can find it."

"You can bet the warmen know where it is," the gang man said. His short laugh had an acid bite. "They're probably sitting on it."

"Not much choice," Conway said. "Which way, Tee?"

"Bear right. We'll be looking for a ridge paralleling the coast. It's almost like a wall."

They'd covered very little distance before they heard the enemy behind them. Shrill whistles called back and forth. Torches flared. Conway cursed the trees that turned the light into erratic flickering. They'd deflect his rounds. Worse, his muzzle blast would signal exactly where he was. The pursuit didn't need stealth. On the contrary, they relied on the noise to panic the prey fleeing them.

Luck relented for the first time that night, bringing the group to the ridge quickly. Conway noted how abruptly it rose, how nearly uniform its height and width. For a moment he allowed himself to wonder what lay under the earth and trees. Something man-made, he was certain. How foolishly and how wondrously his long-dead people built and destroyed.

The group he was with was about to be destroyed.

Lanta warned them. She begged Tee to stay on the island.

Tee might have. If he hadn't encouraged her to ignore the warning.

Could Lanta have known the site was an ambush? Would loyalty to Church prevent her revealing that knowledge?

The clarity of his perception dazzled Conway. He felt himself sway, the force of awareness almost a physical blow.

Lanta knew. Unable to expose herself by speaking all the details, but she knew.

Whistling its malevolent death-song, an arrow sped overhead from behind, the music ending in a solid thud against a tree.

Conway called to Tee. "They're flanking us to our right."

The five picked up their pace, not willing to gallop headlong and risk running into a tree in the dark. Even so, a shout of pain announced an injury to one of the gang men. There was a scuffling pause, and then they were on their way again. The leader pulled abreast of Conway. "Lorgan's shoulder's broke. He won't be worth much in a fight. We'll give you the best we've got. Good luck."

There was no time for more talk. Commands erupted directly in front of them. Conway heeled Stormracer ahead. When he reached her, Tee had her sword out, head down, bent forward behind her mount's head. Conway whistled the dogs close. One-handing the wipe, he urged Stormracer into a run as they broke clear of trees and into pre-marsh scrub growth.

The interlaced saplings and small trees were as much help as hazard. In constant danger of being swept from the saddle, the riders were also partially protected from arrows. Most went harmlessly overhead. One actually struck Conway; slowed by the brush, it bounced harmlessly off his leather jacket. If he hadn't seen it, he would have thought it was merely another swat by a branch.

The Kossiar warmen were waiting for them at the edge of the marsh. Salinity eliminated everything but the hardiest of land plants there. All were squat, tough little things that barely came to the fetlocks of the horses, and they stretched for a good fifteen yards.

For the fleeing riders, it was the equivalent of dashing across a lawn.

A warman rose in front of Conway. A blast from the wipe spun him backward into the reeds. In answer to a hail of arrows from both flanks, Conway popped a boop round in each direction. Cries of pain and fright followed the satisfying *crump* of each round. The dogs bored straight ahead. Following them, Conway glanced back to check on the gang men. There were only two. As he watched, one rose in his saddle, straining upward. The second went over backward off his horse. The panicked animal bucked and kicked wildly.

The reeds closed behind Conway. Ahead, Tee's mount lunged on. Stormracer drove without urging. The dogs quickly discovered it was easier to follow the horse than struggle along beside him. Arrows continued to plunge down, a vicious, killing rain.

Conway lost track of time and distance. Conserving ammunition, he fired only two more boop rounds behind, blindly attempting to arc them so they'd fall on any pursuit. The effort seemed to work. Despite the splashing, rattling racket of their retreat, he was sure the sounds of pursuit were dying out. Nevertheless, when he turned once to see how the other man in their reduced group fared, his heart sank to find no one behind him.

When they at last broke free of the clinging muck and growth of the marsh, the horses staggered weakly onto meadowland. Conway caught up to Tee, who was literally weaving back and

431

forth in her saddle. Without turning to look back, she asked, "The others? Are they hurt?"

"They didn't make it. I'm sorry, Tee. Are you all right? You sound strange."

She ignored him, raising a slow, weary hand to point seaward. "Look at the lights out there. The Chair's boats. Looking for Wal, hoping he'll come after us. More headed for Trader Island, probably." She leaned against him heavily. "I made a mess of it all, didn't I?"

Conway put an arm around her. "Don't talk like that. We'll get out of this. Look! Over there. A fire. And there, another one! What's going on?"

Tee pulled herself upright. Conway noted she used a hand on the pommel, as if she lacked strength in her torso. Still, there was excitement in her voice. "It's started, Matt. The slaves are rebelling. It wasn't for nothing. I didn't fail. Not entirely."

"Don't talk about failure. You made them realize they have to fight to be free. The way you fought, Tee, they'll win, too. The way you won."

Conway looked toward Trader Island. He shouted surprise. "Harbor's burning, Tee. Look, the island's a perfect silhouette. The whole town must be blazing. Signal lights blinking, too; everywhere you look."

She moved to turn, dipped, almost fell. Clutching at him with her right hand, she said, "Take the reins, please. Turn the horse for me. I want to see."

Backing Stormracer, Conway brought both animals around. As he finished the maneuver, fires blossomed to the north. A bell rang hysterical alarm, and a drum boomed urgent call. Conway said, "That must be the barracks town the gang spoke of. That's why they're not chasing us. They're trying to save the town and whatever else is under attack."

Tee barely gave the new fires a glance. Her attention was riveted on the fiery sky beyond Trader Island. "It's the end. A beginning for some, an end for some. The wheel never stops." She took his hand from the reins, pressed it between her own. Lifting it, her eyes on his, she kissed it, held it to her cheek. In the starlight, in the faint glow of ever-more fires, her eyes glittered abnormally. She leaned so heavily against the hand she held, Conway had to brace his elbow against his ribs. Head bowed, she said, "I wanted to love you, Matt Conway. I wanted to be your wife, bear your children. Did you know you made me dream? Of fireplaces, of meals that made you fat and lazy, of long walks where neither of

432

us said a word to the other and we were both too happy to notice? Did you know I could dream like that? I didn't."

"We're going to be all right." Conway reached to tilt her chin up so he could look into her eyes. "We'll ride for Church Home, meet the others there. It's all going to be fine."

Tee twisted in the saddle. She coughed, a huge spasm. He almost lost her when she slumped. He reached around her neck with his left hand, clutched her near shoulder with his right.

She gasped when his left hand struck the arrow in her shoulder and pushed it sideways.

Conway echoed her when he realized what the blood-slick thing under his hand was. Two-thirds of it were driven vertically into her body. For several crashing heartbeats, he couldn't move. When he could, he gripped her horse's reins again, led it off. "We'll find help," he said. "There's got to be a farmhouse or something nearby. You can rest. I'll get a boat. I'll go for . . . for . . . Sylah. I'll go for Sylah."

"Slower, Matt, please. It hurts to bounce so. There's no reason to hurry. It's my arrow, the one sent for me. I don't mind, really. But find me a place to rest, please. It hurts, and I'm too tired." She made an effort to straighten. "I have to tell you. Lanta. Me and Lanta."

She coughed again, and Conway said, "I don't want to hear about her. Not now. Never. This is all her fault. It's all her fault."

Tee shook her head, too seized by choking to answer. She gestured that she wanted down. Hurriedly, he guided the animals to a stone outcropping. In a moment he had her on the ground, propped to look seaward. Left and right, fires pockmarked the dark. The Kossiar boats sped for Harbor.

After a lip-moistening touch of water from Conway's canteen, Tee closed her eyes. Afraid to speak, he knelt beside her, holding her hand, feeling it weak and cold.

Tee said, "I could never be what either of us wanted. I was never what you saw, never what I hoped to be. But I made a difference. I can say that, can't I?"

"Tee, don't talk like that. I'm going to get you through this."

She smiled up at him. "You won't see the most obvious things. Exasperating man." She coughed. "Two dreamers. Different dreams. Wrong dreams. Listen. Lanta. Good woman. Told her. Fight. You. She happy now."

"Don't do this. Tee, I love you. Don't leave me. I'm begging you."

Softly, wearily, she sagged against the rock. Conway carefully

433

avoided looking at the obscenity projecting from her shoulder, concentrated on the serenity in her features.

Swiftly, terribly, a grimace tore apart her repose, twisted her face mercilessly. She gave a soft cry, tried to rise, lifted her hands to him. He clutched at them as if he could pull her back from the thing that was claiming her. She opened her eyes, gazed her entire soul into his. "Oh, Matt, why does everything have to hurt so much? Why wasn't I the one? I love you. I . . . Kiss me. Hold me. Tight. Please."

He covered her last word with his mouth.

CHAPTER 74

Sylah looked up in confusion as her door flew open and Lanta ushered in her soaking-wet companions. At the sight of the lumbering Helstar, Sylah pointed, and in almost desperate appeal said, "What?"

Helstar's teeth gleamed through the dripping beard. "It's kind of you to ask, Rose Priestess, but I'd rather 'who' than 'what.' I'm Helstar. A smith." The shrewd eyes were watchful then, and the smile was fixed. A quick change, and subtle. Warning stirred in Sylah's mind. This was no muscular bully, as the clothes, rough voice, and general bearing trumpeted. Behind the coarse facade prowled complex cunning.

Lanta and Dodoy disappeared behind partitions to change. Throughout Lanta's narration of her evening's events, Sylah watched Helstar study her with the same intensity she was applying to him. It made her think of being stalked by a tiger. A benevolent tiger, perhaps, but a predatory animal that made itself part of its background all too easily. A leap of intuition called to mind the Harvester. She had no idea what triggered it, but in that instant, her interest in Helstar took on a far deeper urgency.

Lanta reappeared from behind a partition, wearing dry clothes. She was saying, "I tried to explain to Tee and Conway about the escaped slaves. If they go after them, they'll be taking a great risk."

Dodoy came out as she finished. "The Conway one wouldn't believe her. He's stupid."

With a consoling look for Lanta, Helstar said, "I wouldn't tell you before, Priestess. I ordered the boy to keep quiet, too. When

Nalatan and I finished with the Kossiar spy-servants, he went to the house to report. Tee and Conway were already gone after the escapers. She insisted. They took three gang men and five extra horses on a cargo boat big enough to carry everyone. The Kossiar boats carrying warmen up the coast are probably to block any seaward escape. Still, your friends have a chance."

"What can we do?" Sylah asked.

Melancholy deadened Helstar's voice. "It has nothing to do with you, Priestess. Nalatan and I learned some very hard news tonight. The slave leadership's betrayed. In desperation, the revolt will start immediately. They cannot win. The vengeance of the Chair will be demonic." He paused. His knuckles whitened, cracked ominously in the silence. "The uprising may interfere with the plans to trap your friends. There'll be fires, widespread attacks on slave owners and their property. Panic will consume Kos as flame consumes straw. Which brings me to my purpose here."

"I wondered about that," Sylah said, and Helstar acknowledged her irony with a wryly apologetic smile. She went on, "If it's anything to do with the castle slaves, you're too late. All but a few girls, personal slaves, were moved out, chained."

Helstar nodded briefly. He turned to Dodoy. "Guard the door. I'll be checking to see if you're eavesdropping."

Dodoy threw out his narrow chest. "You can't tell me what to do."

Helstar's thick, gnarled hand reached out. Dodoy backed up a step, although the man was a full body-length away. Before Helstar spoke, bravado crumbled to sulk. Dodoy hurried to obey.

With the door closed, Helstar beckoned the women to the farthest end of the room. He said, "Since the first siahs, even before the Teachers, certain men have worked for Church."

Sylah snapped upright. "Nonsense. Church is womankind. Church heals what men damage. It is the way."

"There is more than one path, more than one servant on every path. Not all smiths are Church's men. Once it was hereditary. That system failed. As it did with our brothers, the Peddlers."

Lanta gasped surprise, clapped a hand to her mouth.

"Yes, small Priestess, smiths and peddlers. What the Seer of Seers cannot discover, we seek to learn for her. Not even the Harvester knows of us. Once more, each of you is chosen."

"It can't be," Sylah said. She shook her head, physically reinforcing the need to deny. Helstar's revelations were rocking the very foundation of her beliefs.

435

Helstar was adamant. "Perhaps, Rose Priestess Sylah, you recall your old traveling companion, the Bilsten one? Of a matter of some dead roses on a door in the house of a Baron Jalail? You were fleeing then, and needed to be warned. My hand is to help you now. Your danger is greater than ever."

Speechless, Sylah gawked. Helstar said, "I am instructed to tell you what I have said, and no more, save this: You will continue the search for the Door. My mission is to help you. Your friends have already escaped Trader Island."

"I can't leave."

Lanta paled.

Coloring above his beard, Helstar said, "It's nothing to me if you believe what I've told you. If you must have it, I swear by the story of the cross denied women that it's all true. You are the Flower, and you must be saved. We must go."

"Yasmaleeya." Sylah fluttered uncharacteristically, aimless starts and retreats. "She's already in labor. Started four inches ago. I just came here for equipment."

Helstar spit out words. "Your responsibility is to Church, not to the pampered pet of the monster who sired her child."

The language brought Sylah up short. She glared. "Pampered. You'd say so. She'll deliver her child tonight."

"So early? The gossip said later."

Risking a quick look at Lanta, Sylah answered. "It's assured." She saw Helstar's canny change of expression, the instant understanding that a secret had been expressed. He said, "Well. The Flower is truly a rose—thorns and all. Do what you must. Understand, we have few hours of darkness. If this child comes late, it brings us into a sunshine that must kill us as surely as it burns off the fog. How can I help?"

Instead of answering, Sylah picked up her saddlebags, indicating Lanta should do the same. At the door, she called softly to Dodoy, who swaggered out of the darkness. "I didn't listen," he said, and Sylah cut him off with a snap of the fingers. "Get your things. We're not coming back here."

Holding to dark corners, slinking from shadow to shadow, the foursome made their way to Yasmaleeya's second-story apartments.

They saw no warmen on guard. Knocking on Yasmaleeya's door, Sylah identified herself. A frightened girl in slave yellow admitted them, sliding back against the wall. Yasmaleeya sprawled prone on a large bed, dressed in a voluminous robe of pale blue. The spread under her was an underwater scene, fishes

436

and dolphins in rainbow colors embroidered on a sea green background. Without turning her head toward the door, Yasmaleeya berated the slave for her sluggishness, switching over to complaints of Sylah's absence.

Sylah said, "You should have sent the girl for me. What progress?"

"You're the Healer," Yasmaleeya said. "You should have known ... Ow! See? A pain! They're coming faster now. Harder, too. Who's that old man? Go away, you. I'm having the Chair's son. You're not allowed here. I'll have you flogged. Get *out*."

Sylah pulled Lanta to the side. "Light the fire. Put on the water for boiling the cloths. Prepare many. I swear she's gotten bigger since yesterday. There's going to be blood. And trouble."

She left Lanta, went to Helstar. "I have two missions for you. First, find one of the Messengers hanging about here in the castle. Tell him he must ride to Clas na Bale of the Dog People. Tell Clas I am going to Church Home because of the revolt in Kos. Clas should send warriors to meet me there."

Helstar's smile was hard. "Assuming I can reach a Messenger and talk to him without a guard taking my head, how do I pay for his services?"

"Clas na Bale is my husband. He'll pay very well for news of me."

"Your faith in husbands and Messengers is an inspiration to us all, Priestess. I'll try. What other wonders would you ask of me?"

"Take Dodoy with you. Find the castle winery."

"Wine?" Helstar blinked.

"Listen." Sylah's order crackled. "Open the vats. You'll find crystals on the sides. Get all you can. It's important. When you've done that, hide in the room next to this one. Most of the interior guard and the Crew are off after slaves, but someone may come if she starts screaming."

"If?" Helstar tugged his beard. His eyes nervously flicked to Yasmaleeya and away, then back again. "She'll shout down these walls. Can you save her? Or the child?"

"Not if you keep babbling. Can your man-soft knees carry you away? Good." Helstar swallowed a retort. He clamped a hand on Dodoy's shoulder and stalked out.

Yasmaleeya groaned and panted constantly by the time Sylah reached Lanta. The fire in the tripod brazier already licked the sides of a copper cauldron, and the first wisps of steam slicked across the surface of the water in it. To the slave girl, Sylah said, "You're released. Go to the barracks."

Yasmaleeya elbowed her upper body off the bed and rolled partially onto her side. A pendulous breast slid free of the robe's covering. Uncaring, Yasmaleeya went on. "I want her here."

Sylah tried to reason. "She'll only be in the way, Yasmaleeya. Let her go."

Petulance and craftiness fought to dominate Yasmaleeya's already pain-honed features. "You think I'm a complete fool. You think I haven't heard the stories, that you're a witch, that you have magic to save me from something that's wrong with my baby? I know he's big, and now he's coming early, but there's nothing wrong with him. Or me. That's why that old Harvester wouldn't help me. She's afraid. At least you've been nice, even if it is only because you like my husband. See? I see more than you think."

Her speech was punctuated by grimaces and short grunts, reaction to her contractions. She took a deep breath before continuing. The vindictive tone softened, acquired a musing sadness. "I heard the other thing, too. That he doesn't like me, doesn't want this child. Mother says he's evil. She says you're a good person, but an idiot like all Church women. She hates the Chair. She says if there's something wrong with me or the baby, you're the one he'll blame, you and your friends." She groaned, long and loud, reaching for Sylah's hand, grinding the knuckles with unexpected strength. "All I wanted was to live well. That doesn't make me a bad person. But I'm afraid, Sylah. There's too much I don't understand. I want to live. I want to raise my baby. I don't care if it's a girl. Just make it be healthy, please? Promise me, Sylah. Promise."

Sylah smiled gently. "I promise. Now you've got to let me go. I have to examine you, prepare our equipment."

Disengaging herself, Sylah moved away. Not as easily dismissed were Yasmaleeya's frightened revelations. Sylah remembered the night on the roof, the heat of the Chair's presence. She felt the irresolution of her body, the unacknowledgable yearning.

Guilt swept her.

The rumors were malicious. Nothing happened that night. Or any other time. If the rumors were untrue about her friendship with the Chair, they were equally untrue about his reputation. People didn't understand. He was alone. Unsupported. Why couldn't anyone see that he was authoritative, not maliciously cruel?

No man could want to raise his children in a world that despised and feared the father.

It was in her grasp to make them all understand, prove to them

438

that he was a good man in his heart. A healthy child, a loving mother; those would be the beacons to reveal his true self.

He'd be her friend. Church's friend. Rose Priestess Sylah would bring him to his rightful place.

It was a proud feeling.

CHAPTER 75

Moving to Lanta, Sylah spoke quietly, "I think it's time. I'll examine her as soon as we've got everything ready."

Practically on cue, Yasmaleeya scrambled to a kneeling position on the bed. Her features tightened. Sharp cries pressed out between thinned lips. "Can't you make it stop hurting? It goes on forever."

Murmuring assurances, Sylah worked Yasmaleeya free of the flowing blue robe and got her to lie down, covered with a cotton sheet. Lanta dropped folded linen cloths into the boiling water. With a roll of twine and a trio of chairs, she made a drying rack on three sides of the brazier.

Sylah caught Yasmaleeya's sudden inhalation, saw her face grow frenzied. She stopped the incipient scream automatically, stuffing a clean cloth in Yasmaleeya's opening mouth. Leaning over the startled woman, Sylah said, "This is the child of the strongest man in Kos. Don't force me to tell him you were weak. Such a beginning for the boy would be a dreadful omen. Bring him bravely, quietly. In time, he'll sing your praises for it. So will the world." Removing the makeshift gag, backing away, Sylah spoke quietly to Lanta. "There are still some guards here. We can't have her yelling and bringing them down on us. The poppy sleep. Quickly."

Rummaging in Sylah's bag, Lanta asked, "Are you sure, Sylah? You had her eat the blackness, the purge?"

"Yes. Inches ago. I used the flour to make cakes. They were sweet, so she was happy to get them. Of course." Despite the scornful tone of the last words, her glance at the figure on the bed was agonized. "I've never used it before, didn't even have time to build up the dose slowly. I fear, Lanta."

Wrapping her arms around Sylah, Lanta said, "She, or the child, or both, were going to die if you did nothing. I heard what she said about the Chair, and who'd be blamed. We're going to save her. And the child."

Freeing herself, smiling gratitude and renewal, Sylah said, "I'll use a very small taste of the poppy sleep." As she took a clay bottle from her bag and poured the dosage into a cup, she went on. "I'm so afraid for her I entirely forgot how you excel in the healing music. Help me, Lanta. We need you."

"Of course."

Sylah returned to the bedside. "Yasmaleeya, we're going to help you relax now. You have to work with us."

Yasmaleeya gave a muffled noise. Her head bobbed.

Sylah proffered the cup. "Drink. It soothes." Yasmaleeya gaped like a nestling, swallowing eagerly. Sylah spoke of peace, of repose. She bound Yasmaleeya's mind to her own with an iron concentration that belied the deceptive, liquid murmur of her words. Slowly, visibly, Yasmaleeya calmed.

Almost unnoticed, Lanta hummed as she went about her work. The song rose sweetly. It could have been a lullaby. It was, in fact, a birthing hymn.

Taking a glossy piece of obsidian from her bag, Lanta rapped it smartly with a piece of steel, flaking off a leaf-shaped shard with an edge so fine it diffracted the candlelight. Sparkling rainbow colors imbued the nearly invisible sharpness with living eagerness.

Other instruments came from the bag. A large forceps with brutal steel jaws. A leather sack of things that scraped and clattered with metallic menace. Sylah inspected them out of Yasmaleeya's sight: an auger, sinuous curves and glinting point; huge scissors; lastly, reluctantly, a blunt-nosed hook. The tools of extremity, the weapons of defeat, to sacrifice the child when there was no hope for it, and little more for the mother.

Sylah bagged them, couldn't bear looking at them.

In a corner, the slave girl cowered. Her face shone with her horror of the instruments.

Sylah sent a smile at the slave. She hoped the gesture wasn't a lie.

The larger bag produced a needle. Threaded with fine cotton, it went into the boiling water. A pouch held puffball spores to staunch blood.

Lastly, Lanta extracted a small brass round. About the diameter of a dinner plate, it was made of concentric rings of different thickness. Seamlessly joined, they formed a shallow dome. A braided cord knotted through a hole at the edge provided a handle.

The striker was a silver-handled, leather-headed mallet. The silver was deeply carved with stylized, rayed suns. Generations of handling had burnished it to flowing smoothness, its darker depths accentuating the higher surfaces. Lanta used it with delicacy. Haunting, brazen melody suffused the room.

The rhythm was that of a healthy heart.

Major, minor. Statement, confirmation.

Yasmaleeya, already touched by the poppy sleep, embraced the song. Where there had been stress, now there was effort. She was still a woman in the pangs of birthing her first child, but she was consoled. Befriended.

Sylah poured alcohol over her hands, fanned them dry. Her lips moved in a silent prayer. Lanta accompanied her, maintaining the compelling drumming music. Sylah explained to Yasmaleeya that she had to determine how the baby was moving. Yasmaleeya nodded and directed her attention to the ceiling.

To Lanta, Sylah said. "The cervix is up. Soft. Wet glove leather. Yes, there's the bag of waters. Very firm. We've a good passage." Sylah wiped her hand with a clean cloth that she then threw into a corner, away from her patient. "Wonderful, Yasmaleeya. We need only a tiny bit more clearance. Half the length of a fingernail, no more. You're perfect."

Yasmaleeya continued to watch overhead, enduring. The steady, seductive pulse of the music held her. Despite her contractions, her head moved, ever so minutely, in time with the metallic singing of the little gong.

A little later, without warning, radical change washed across her expression. From being lost within her situation, she was transformed to a picture of excited hopefulness. She threw out a hand, clasped Sylah's, gestured for Lanta to come close. "I have to push," she said. "I feel him. My son. He *comes*. *Pushing.* Ooh!" The bag of waters broke with an astonishing gush, splattering almost to the wall. The slave girl yipped surprise and scrambled for a cloth to clean up.

A thick, sour-sweet aroma filled the room. Lanta ceased drumming, smiled down at Yasmaleeya. "That smell. Exciting. It's fertility, birth itself." She wrinkled her nose. "If it weren't for being connected with babies, I think it'd be awful. But it is babies. And it's wonderful."

"Yes. Oh, yes." Yasmaleeya's glad agreement was little more than grunting as her child began his struggle. Sylah and Lanta exchanged conspiratorial, pleased smiles before Sylah moved to visually examine the patient. Again, she reported to Lanta, this time excitedly. "There's the head. With hair. Blond. You've got a blond baby, Yasmaleeya. Push. Push hard, so we can see all of it. We all want to hold it."

"I am pushing. Believe me. I am." It was said in good humor. Her whole being was focused on delivering her child. Sodden with sweat, lying on a bed soaked with amniotic fluid, denying pain, she glowed with accomplishment and purpose.

Sylah wiped Yasmaleeya's face with a clean cloth. "You're doing fine. I'm proud of you. Proud of your son."

Yasmaleeya's head snapped around. "You're sure it's a boy? How do you know?"

"I'm hoping. Just like you."

Groaning, gritting her teeth, Yasmaleeya forced words. "He'll be strong. Powerful. A ruler. You'll see."

Time dragged. Yasmaleeya's long hair became lank, stringy. The anticipation in her face turned to confusion, then worry. Her muffled cries grew sharper, louder.

Lanta resumed her percussive music. Sylah continually reassured the straining, weakening Yasmaleeya. Both Priestesses exchanged increasingly worried looks.

Sylah straightened determinedly. She arched eyebrows meaningfully for Lanta. Her voice remained bright, however. "Yasmaleeya, this is a very big baby. If I massage around his head, I think we can hurry things up a bit."

"Do it." It was curt, discouragement leavened with apprehension.

The head was in good position, facing toward the mother's back, bowed to the chest, so that all Sylah could see was the little blond cowlick. Yasmaleeya, who'd continued to grunt and strain, seemed to gather herself. The child's head receded a fraction. Yasmaleeya pushed, hard. She gave a cry more of determination than of pain.

The baby's head came free. Magically, it was fully visible. Sylah shouted, "His head's here! Your baby's coming. Push, Yasmaleeya. Now!"

The panting, groaning woman tried.

Caught in flesh that could yield no further, the baby's face grew congested. Sylah shivered with fear of the situation building before her.

The flesh just beyond the child's head was stretched drum-tight, already slightly torn. Sylah's kneading had no effect. Extending her hand to Lanta for the obsidian blade, she told Yasmaleeya, "This may hurt a bit."

442

Bitterly, Yasmaleeya answered, "Everything hurts. Get this over with."

The black shimmer of stone slid across the taut skin. For an instant its course was but a delicate red trace the length of Sylah's first thumb joint. It was a shocking understatement from such a dangerous-looking tool. And then the wound blossomed open and blood flowed busily.

The child still refused to exit. The image of the ugly forceps picked at Sylah's mind.

With every pulse of her body, Yasmaleeya was closer to being killed by the innocent, obdurate size of her baby. In horrible balance, she was equally closer to killing it because she couldn't deliver it.

A tinge of blue—deadly, malevolent—palled the child.

Sylah's expression warned Lanta. Moving rapidly, keeping her tone conversational, Sylah said, "We're going to have to give him a bit more room. Lanta, help me move our girl to the end of the bed. Buttocks right on the edge."

Lanta joined Sylah's inspection when Yasmaleeya was in place. The baby's head was now turned to the side. Lanta whispered, tension roughening her voice. "The color! Obstruction. The cord must be pinched. I'm going to check."

"Yes." Sylah frowned, unmoving.

Working her hand past the baby's head, Lanta explored carefully. She withdrew quickly, whispered again. "Shoulder's jammed against the pubic bone. Cord's caught. You're the strongest. Pull. *Pull.*"

Sylah was ashen. Dark lines etched outward from the corners of sunken eyes. A muscle danced at her jaw. "I fear. The old ones say pulling destroys something in the shoulder. It can kill."

With a harshness that sent Sylah recoiling in shock, Lanta said, "Damn your fear. You claim to be a good Healer, you pretend to be a leader. While you whine and weep, those who depend on you die."

Astonished, hurt eyes still on Lanta, Sylah reached blindly for the baby's head. On touching it, she was vitalized. She grasped with both hands and pulled.

Lanta moved to stand beside Yasmaleeya. She carried the brass round and its striker. The rhythm now was urgent, an intricacy that spoke of two hearts, not one. The larger struggled, urged. The smaller one fought. Grim, Lanta drove a music of strength, of battle. Of love. Fierce, unyielding love.

Yasmaleeya's head tossed left and right. The only sounds that passed her clamped lips were a low moan and the grinding of teeth.

Sobbing, Sylah knelt on the floor and forced herself to exert ever more force against the soft, helpless infant. She pulled down, hard, biting her lip to smother anguish.

And found herself holding a boy.

His head was mashed into a near cone shape, but it was whole. His nose looked like something that should have been attached to a wrestler, but it worked. His color was cold, awful, but improved with every heartbeat. His hair was sparse, wispy. He was wet and sticky and smelly and downright repulsive and Sylah shouted and wept for joy at the wondrous, transcendent beauty of him.

Yasmaleeya's gusting sigh resounded. Lanta's music stopped with a triumphant clash.

For a moment, Sylah looked away to gaze at the new mother, who lay still, eyes closed, taking in air in a huge, slow inhalation. Opening her eyes wide, she raised her hands slowly. "My baby. My son. I want him."

Sylah filled with pride for her. For all her faults, Yasmaleeya had performed flawlessly in her greatest test.

"Let me clean him off," she said, laughing. "Just a moment, I promise."

Turning her attention back to the baby, Sylah thought she saw a weakness, a looseness in his left arm. That was what the old ones said to look for; a palsy in the injured shoulder. From that could come a withered limb. Or death.

Sylah watched carefully while she and Lanta cleaned him and tied off the ends of the umbilical cord. When she checked the boy's limbs, she delayed the left arm to last. Pulling the right arm straight, she was surprised by its strength, delighted to see how the wrinkle-faced, red man-to-be jerked it back, fist clenched.

The left arm was weak, almost flaccid. The fist was merely a curl of the fingers.

Lanta cut the cord. Sylah raised the boy in the air. Without waiting for any stimulation, he arched his back, beat a clenched fist against the air, and yowled his dissatisfaction with a world that welcomed a stranger with such consummate rudeness.

Yasmaleeya smiled, reaching for him. As soon as he was in her arms, she was in her own private world, pain and worry simply put aside.

"It never fails," Lanta was saying, features aglow in the sharing of the moment. "No matter how difficult the birth, they get that look when they see and hold the baby. Triumph and an amazement of love. I adore it."

Sylah managed a brief answering laugh. The boy's shoulder preyed on her mind. She asked Lanta to tend to Yasmaleeya's incision, offering the excuse that she was exhausted, her hand unsteady. In truth, she wanted to study the child further. Ignoring Yasmaleeya's muffled cries as she endured Lanta's stitches, Sylah tested the child's arm again. There was no movement, but, as she remembered, stillness alone wasn't decisive. She wanted to scream at her lack of sure knowledge, her ignorance.

Lanta gestured Sylah to her. Stepping away from Yasmaleeya, she whispered. "I'm finished. There's heavy bleeding, though. Internal. It's bad."

After watching for a bit, Sylah said, "Perhaps it'll stop when the placenta comes. Let's see." Examining Yasmaleeya, she nodded satisfaction. "Good recovery. Uterus is already hard, a little larger than my fists. I'll tug just a . . . There we are." The placenta came with a large blood clot. Both women watched with dark frowns as more blood continued to issue.

Lanta said, "There's a technique. You squeeze the uterus. If the laceration's there, sometimes it'll stop the bleeding. It hurts. A lot."

"It has to be tried."

Yasmaleeya was too preoccupied with her baby to be concerned when Sylah warned her that she had to be hurt again. Sylah almost smiled, thinking of the effect her child was having on this most unlikely of doting mothers.

Sylah bent to yet another onerous task. Lanta offered Yasmaleeya a linen cloth to bite on.

Yasmaleeya jerked with the pain. The smothered yell had a distant, lost sound.

The bleeding continued. For the first time since the actual delivery, Yasmaleeya wavered. She continued to clutch the child, but her features sagged. She struggled to keep her eyes open. The pressures of the birthing weighted the lids, and they slowly closed.

Sylah said, "She'll be all right. The bleeding will stop soon." Lanta agreed heartily.

Each avoided the other's eyes.

Together, they hurriedly cleaned up, replacing the ruined bedding, tying everything tightly in two bundles. For a moment they stood uncertainly. Normally, the material would be ceremonially burned immediately. By unspoken agreement, they shoved the bundles into a corner, made a three-sign, and ignored them.

Satisfied with the room's condition, Sylah passed a small ceramic vial of ammonia under Yasmaleeya's nose. Her eyes flew wide, but they lacked genuine awareness. Pupils still fluctuating uncertainly in the aftereffects of poppy sleep and stress, Yasmaleeya found a smile. Despite her ordeal, despite her seemingly infinite capacity for self-interest and self-delusion, the new mother cradled her baby and bent to gaze at him with a love and pride that knew no distinctions of place, time, or culture.

A sound pulled at Sylah and Lanta. They whirled, and there in the corner wept the forgotten slave girl. Both Priestesses hurried to her. The girl cowered until she was assured she wasn't going to be beaten, then she said, "The baby. He fought so hard. He earned his life. And the way my mistress looked at him. I never thought she could be so sweet." She stopped, choked by renewed apprehension.

Lanta patted her hand. "We understand. We'll be leaving very soon. Can we depend on you to help care for him?"

"Oh, yes. Like he was my own." A darkness touched her. She looked away. "Or until I get free, and have my own. I'll have no child that's property to anyone." Emboldened by their sympathetic silence, she brightened again. "He'll be a good boy. Did you see how big he is?"

"We noticed," Sylah said dryly, turning back to Yasmaleeya. To Lanta, she added, "He's also hard as a little rock. There's good material in that one. You did well to shame me into working for him. I'm indebted to you."

Lanta blushed. "I didn't know what else to do. Can you forgive me?"

"I bless you. Between you and what this young woman just said, you brought my mind back from misguided directions. But it was you who told me I wasn't alone." Sylah reached for her friend's hands. They were standing so when the door to the hallway smashed open and Bos stormed in with three warmen behind him.

446

CHAPTER 76

"Kill them all." Bos drew his sword.

"Stop!" Sylah's imperious command froze the warmen with their weapons half-exposed. Bos managed a clumsy step, then he too held his place.

Sylah's left hand was raised, palm out. Eyes like blue ice fixed on Bos. "This is the bearer of the Chair's son."

Bos returned his sword to the scabbard. His men shifted confusedly. Then Bos applauded. Slowly, mockingly. His grin redoubled Sylah's fear, robbed her knees of strength.

Bos was casual, as though this were an ordinary chat. "I've known the Chair all my life, and still he amazes me. There's massacre out there tonight. My country is stabbed in the back by slaves. Murdering scum. And my leader tears me from the hunt. He says to me, 'Get back to the castle. If the Priestess can bring the child during this confusion, she will. The uprising started with a witch, it'll end with one. Kill her. Rid me of that cow Yasmaleeya and her brat.' You see, Priestess, he wastes nothing. He'll name you as the partner of the witch the Harvester exposed. The people of Kos will hear that you killed the bearer and the heir as part of the slave revolt." Hardening, he spoke over his shoulder to his men. "Come."

Yasmaleeya's scream acted as a signal.

Bos drew his sword. Sylah stumbled backward, Lanta beside her, hands outstretched in a hopeless defense.

The unhurried deadliness of the warmen's advance was more unnerving than yells.

None of them saw or heard Helstar step through the shattered door. Before the warmen knew he was in the room, one was falling, his helmet and head split. A second turned at the sounds and had his throat slashed.

Bos and the remaining man would not die so easily.

Attacking immediately, they hammered at Helstar. Swords clashed, sparks flew. The smith, surprisingly adept, was nevertheless forced on the defense. With few opportunities to strike at his enemies, he was doomed to a fight with only one possible end.

Dodoy pushed open the door from the adjoining room and leapt into the melee, swinging the chain axe over his head. Sylah and

Lanta crouched by the bedside, protecting Yasmaleeya and the child with their bodies.

The shining axe darted at Bos' unprotected back. It struck with a satisfying thump. And fell to the floor. Dodoy lacked the power to whip the small weapon through the chain mail under Bos' shirt; like Lanta's knife thrust at Helstar, it cut without doing damage.

Bos planted a foot on the axe head. Reaching down, he yanked on the chain. Dodoy shrieked as the links pulled through his grip. He continued to yell, staring at his ripped fingers, a cry that escalated wildly when he looked to see Bos over him, sword poised.

Dodoy rolled into a screeching ball, waiting.

Bos kicked him aside, wild eyes fixed on Yasmaleeya and her child. The sword remained ready.

A flash of yellow flew across the room, bowled headlong into Bos' left side. As he staggered sideways, he lashed out. His sword slit the soft, white underside of the girl's arm from wrist to elbow. She gasped and clutched at the upper limit of the wound. Thick, red jets pulsed between her fingers.

Sylah leapt at Bos as the stricken, dying girl attacked yet again. Her functional, bloody hand clawed at Bos' eyes. It was only a distraction, but it saved Sylah's life for the moment. Instead of Bos' blade striking Sylah's skull, it was the handle. The blow sent Sylah tumbling into the slave girl. Both fell to the floor.

Lanta spread herself across Yasmaleeya and the baby. Biting her lip, face screwed into a tight mask of dread, she turned away from Bos, away from the dripping, rising sword.

"Don't do it, Bos." Helstar, sword wavering unsteadily, walked with careful, pained steps across the room toward Bos' back. A wound ran from his eye to his chin, and he held his left elbow clamped against another cut on his ribs. The third warman writhed on the floor behind him. Helstar repeated himself, almost pleading.

Both hands clasped on the handle of the raised sword, Bos didn't move. "Whoever you are, I am Bos, second only to the Chair. I carry out his order. I can make you rich. If you're a slave, I declare you free. If you kill me, where will you go? The Chair will find you. When he does, you'll envy those who died here."

"We only want to escape."

Yasmaleeya thrashed to free herself of Lanta, who hung on determinedly, still refusing to look at Bos. Yasmaleeya shouted. "You lie! My husband loves me. He'll love me more when he sees his son. You're afraid you'll be displaced." She twisted painfully, craned to see Sylah, who was clawing her way upright at the wall. The slave girl lay white and still at her feet. Sylah turned unsteadily when Yasmaleeya called her name. "Sylah. He's lying. I was wrong when I told you those things. I was in pain, and I wanted you to hurt, too. Stay with me. I need you."

Sylah tried to think. Her head throbbed. Her legs wanted to buckle. She found Lanta. "What should I do? The Chair could be saved. I know he could. And what of Yasmaleeya? The bleeding. I shouldn't leave her." She had to break off, lean against the wall to gather strength.

The unexpected response provided Bos a way out. "Perhaps you're right, Priestess. If you save the life of the bearer, the Chair may see the error of his ways. He may even—"

The argument ended in a hoarse shout. When Sylah's eyes focused, Bos was collapsing backward. Helstar was in a near squat, spread-legged, sword in both hands, the blade just coming to rest after a full-swinging horizontal swipe. Bos landed flat on his back. He tried to push himself upright, sword slashing at the bed.

Yasmaleeya screamed, clutching Lanta to her. "The baby!" she shouted. "He's trying to kill my baby!"

Bos half turned, aimed a thrust at Helstar, forcing him to parry. Quick as a cat, Bos turned again, thrusting at the women and the child on the bed.

Helstar brought his sword down on Bos' shoulder. The sword seemed to leap free of his suddenly limp hand. It clattered across the floor. Bos fell back. His left hand grabbed at his wounded shoulder. He seemed oblivious to his hamstrung knees, the result of Helstar's first blow.

Sylah rushed to him. Examining the wounds, she spoke to Helstar. "You shouldn't have done that. We were close to an understanding. Now it's all ruined."

"Get away!" Bos shoved her hard enough to knock her backward from her kneeling position. She hit the floor hard, forcing a cry of pain. Helstar took a step forward, sword raised once again. Bos' crooked smile stopped him. Then Bos said, "How'd you know? A blink of the eye, Beard, and I'd have spitted the three of them to the bed. How'd you know?"

"The wrists. You tightened up the wrists. The only thing was to take out your legs. Should I finish it?"

As the battle flame faded from Bos' features, pain rushed in to take its place. He swallowed hard.

Sylah got to her knees, crawled the few feet to Bos' side. "I can stop the bleeding. I can save your life."

"Not my legs. Nor my honor. I failed the Chair." A thing that

449

might have been a smile twisted his face. "I'm dying. As you will. And that fat fool and her child. Mine's the easiest departure of all. I'll be laughing at you from the Land Beyond."

"Hit him." Dodoy's shrillness jarred them all. "Stick him, Helstar. Make him stop talking."

Bos' eyes rolled up and he toppled. Helstar ignored the boy.

Lanta rolled off Yasmaleeya. She and Sylah leaned on each other.

"If we hurry, we have a chance," Helstar said.

Yasmaleeya lifted her free hand. Her baby still nestled in the crook of the other arm. "Take the child. Save him."

The Priestesses protested in a flurry of denial. Yasmaleeya, in her most objectionable, superior voice, shouted them down. "The bearer is not denied. Liars. I saw your faces when you spoke of my bleeding. That's what I feel, isn't it? My insides dying?" Diamond-bright tears shuddered at the rim of eyes that refused to acknowledge them. "This dead pig was sent to guarantee I die. With my son. Can you hear nothing? At least save my child."

Sylah's mouth worked. No words came. Her head still ached from Bos' blow; her mind reeled with the acceptance of how idiotically she'd allowed the Chair to violate her trust. Now this.

Rising on an elbow, Yasmaleeya said, "I do not ask. I charge you. You helped me bring him into the world. You alone can save his life. Take him." Falling back, she raised the child, extended him. Her tears burst forth. Shorn of pretense to throne and power, they were suddenly nothing but the grief of a mother.

Sylah bundled the baby to her. She kissed Yasmaleeya's cheek. "I've never known a braver woman."

"Nor I such an infuriating fool. Now hurry."

The word fool stung Sylah. She looked guiltily to Lanta, and saw a forgiveness and understanding there that was almost too greathearted to accept. Sylah rushed for the doorway.

A shout interrupted her. Turning, she stretched to peer past the others to see what Yasmaleeya wanted.

"His name is Jessak." Yasmaleeya spoke firmly. She pronounced the name as if a *d* preceded the *j*, and with a harshness that grated against the normally melodic Kossiar dialect. The accented second syllable gave the name the sound of a slashing whip and the striking crack at the end of the blow. Yasmaleeya continued, "Jessak, child of Yasmaleeya, daughter of the house of Vang. He must rule. His name is Jessak."

Turning away, Sylah found herself alone. Lanta peeked around the broken doorframe gesturing for her.

Helstar waited with Lanta in the hall, literally shifting from foot to foot. His color was gone, his eyes in a constant, jittering movement that always found its way back to Yasmaleeya's room. He muttered inside the brushy beard; when Sylah came abreast of him, she heard, "Terrible, terrible."

He led the way past flickering sconces, bloodstained sword in one hand, baggage in the other. Beside him, Dodoy strained under the weight of a large leather hamper. Under it, the chain clutched in a bleeding hand, dangled his fierce little axe. Sylah and Lanta carried the remainder of their possessions.

Suddenly, eerily, shrill laughter ranged the stone passage, echoing from before, behind, all around. It stopped the fleeing group, held them as if in a giant grasp.

Sylah broke the silence. "Yasmaleeya." It was a shocked whisper.

Helstar started to look back, but caught himself. Eyes doggedly front, his fingers twitched, and Sylah was sure he'd executed a covert three-sign of some kind. Then he said, "The sound of revenge. I knew. I knew. Hurry," and they were moving again.

The laughter pursued.

CHAPTER 77

Sylah's group raced out of the building and toward the boats in the basin.

Although few men remained on guard in the fort, the fugitives were seen. The men manning the signal tower, unable to determine the exact nature of the disturbance, lit the torches that indicated a major attack. As Helstar slashed the mooring line on a balancebar, he said, "Everyone knows certain signals. I never expected to see that one. Dodoy, Lanta—raise those gates quickly."

Sylah stepped into the narrow hull as Dodoy and Lanta returned. Throwing equipment aboard, pushing, pulling, they helped Helstar get the boat through the passage. Torches were bobbing into the basin area as Helstar raised the mast. Lanta and Helstar gripped the sail halyard, poised. At Dodoy's command, the cloth lifted rapidly, bellied, pulled eagerly at the vessel. A freshening breeze sent the boat surging ahead.

Harbor flamed. The glow was a red, shifting wall scrawled with smears of thick, greasy smoke and meteoric flits of burning debris.

Jessak cried. Sylah was forced to ignore the flames in an attempt to quiet him.

More torches appeared on the crest of the wall. Some burst out of the tunnel, their light seeming to erupt from the overall glow they created within its depths. Arrows hissed past the balancebar. One, then another, tore through the cloth of the sail with hollow pops. Sylah moved forward, got the mast between herself and the archers, her body a protective curve around the small body clutched to her breast. Lanta wedged herself beside Sylah. Helstar pointed out Dodoy's course, then turned to shield both women. Flat on his back, protected by the gunwales, Dodoy steered by the stars.

The deadly whistle of the arrows stopped. Helstar spoke in a low growl. "All eyes alert. The bay will be full of Kossiar boats trying to catch anyone who escaped Trader Island."

Everyone automatically turned to look at the island. A bright light flared, and Lanta said, "Look, a signal. From Borbor, I'm sure. That's where his house is."

Helstar peered out, bent forward. Sylah did the same. Simultaneously, both said, "Fire."

Sylah's question was hoarse. "Did you send a Messenger to my husband?"

"I spoke to one. I was as convincing as I could be. I can't swear he'll do it."

Dodoy threw the balancebar into a heeling, sail-rattling turn. His passengers grabbed wildly for handholds, exclaiming shock. "Hang on," he said, coldly unsympathetic. "We've got to get away from that before we're silhouetted."

Sylah said, "Why aren't we steering for the bay entrance?"

"Have you looked west?" Helstar asked. Sylah twisted to see, and inhaled sharply. Torches mottled the blackness where Kossiar boats cruised back and forth across the bay's entrance. Farther out, tiny lights flickered where more vessels searched. The roar of the great shark horn droned barbarous invitation.

Sylah asked, "If we can't get out of the bay, where can we go?"

"Duckhunter's River," Helstar said, gesturing, and Dodoy bent the course around to almost due east. "We join Wal and the others. You'll head upstream on his boat. The Kossiars are thinner on the land to the east; they're heavily outnumbered by the farm slaves. I expect most of the slaves will try to escape north, toward the Empty Lands."

452

"They won't try to join the nomads?"

"Some will." He suddenly crouched, broke off with a sibilant hiss, then whispered, "Everyone down. No one make a sound."

Obediently, all bent lower inside the narrow hull. Sylah pulled Jessak's bundling cloth up over his head and turned him so his face was pressed to her. The effort was in vain. He howled his hunger.

"Quiet him." Helstar growled urgency.

Sylah dropped forward. Jessak was on the deck on his back. She arched over him, her clothes and his robe all tenting him and his cries.

A voice lifted in discovery. "I heard something. Over that way, between us and Trader Island. Come about, see if we can spot them against the burning buildings. Bring your boat closer to ours. Wave your lantern; where are you?"

A bright eye of light swung in broad arcs, then stopped. It was too far away to reveal them, but it made Sylah feel helpless. She cowered lower. The next thing she knew, the sail fell on her with a slippery, breathy sound, and Helstar was whispering hoarse orders at Dodoy. Sylah pulled the edge of the sail clear of her head just in time to see the pair lowering the mast.

Jessak continued to cry.

Again, the voice called to a companion. "I heard something, I tell you. I still hear it." There was a pause, then an angry rejoinder. "Who cares if you don't? Something's out there." Another pause, longer, then, "Don't be a fool. Would you try to slip past that many boats? The clever ones'll see the bay's blocked and go south. It's the clever ones'll have the most loot."

Helstar groaned. Settling beside Sylah, he said, "Amateur pirates. Opportunists. They'll kill first, then search the bodies and boats. If they see us, I'm going straight for them. Move, Dodoy: I'm taking the tiller." Then, pleading with Sylah, "Can't you quiet the child?"

"Kill it," Dodoy's whisper rasped. "If it brings those people, we'll all die. Drop it in the water."

Sylah ignored him. Wrapping Jessak tighter, she told Helstar, "I'll give him a finger to suck on. It may help."

"Pray it does. Lanta, Dodoy: paddle. Lean on the gunwale, get your hands in the water. *Silently.*"

For a while, there was no further sound from the other boats. The lantern disappeared. In the thick darkness the distant fires, the mournful bellow of the shark horn, the lights tossing on the ships

453

at the bay mouth—all seemed irrelevant, unimportant. The next shout underscored that.

"I see the boat! There! Come this way. I'm hooking on. Come quick!"

Helstar's sword scraped out of the scabbard. Dodoy whimpered. Still and all, he had the chain axe in hand.

Jessak's squalling faded away to fitful snuffling, sucking noises. The little head burrowed hard into Sylah's unrewarding breast. She patted his back, made soft, soothing sounds in his ear. Then, inexplicably, an eerie calm descended on Sylah. She had the irrational feeling that *she* was the one protected.

A solid *thump*, wood against wood, was followed by wild cries bursting out of the darkness. Sylah and the others peered toward the racket. Torches flared, frighteningly close. Helstar's heavy "Down!" kept them flattened, eyes even with the gunwales.

Three boats wallowed in the small chop, a smaller one grappled and flanked by two larger ones. All three caromed off each other with cracks and thuds. Confused voices, high with excitement, punctuated the arrythmic battering. Sails slatted. Shadowy figures leaped and scrambled aboard the middle boat.

A yell of revulsion and fear cut the night. The boats continued to slam each other. Then a man said, "Warmen. They're both dead. What's that?"

His question ended on a rising note of fear. Another voice sounded. "Shark! Another. Two. Look, they're everywhere!"

The raiders held a half-dozen flaring torches high. Ruddy light painted the heaving sea all around them, and in that glow, tall fins sliced the water at every point. The persistence had an ominous sense of something more than brute predation.

A massive fin, far taller than any other, slid gracefully into the ring of light. The silence of dread fell across the·men. The shark quartered, ever closer to them.

A cracking voice screamed to cut the grappling lines, get under way. An arrow plunged into the water beside the black, glistening fin. It made a comical *poop* sound as it struck. An instant later, it popped back to the surface, feathers first, bobbing uselessly.

Disdainfully, the great fin submerged.

The boat still connected to the derelict balancebar lurched upward. The mast snapped back and forth like a reed in the wind. Men screamed. One, standing in the bow, somersaulted gracefully, shrieking, out into the waiting blackness. Agile beyond belief, he barely touched the water before his hand flailed upward, caught the gunwale, flipped him back aboard.

Where he'd been, the water boiled savagely. Whirlpools told of a huge, devouring presence.

Boats heeled in desperate tack, reaching for every inch of speed. Streaming sparks from their torches, both boats beat for land. A lone voice continued to shout incoherent terror.

Helstar barked orders. "Help me get the mast up, then everyone to the back. I want this bow high." In moments the sail was up and they were spearing through the chop. He kept glancing behind.

CHAPTER 78

Sylah knew when they were into the delta of the Duckhunter by the change of air. From the sea's mouth-cleansing, copper-bright taste, they'd sailed into the thick, fecund breath of tidal wetlands. The smell reminded her of the pungent amniotic fluid; there was the same contradictory mix of unpleasant stink and exciting, fertile renewal. She pushed the cloth away from Jessak's tiny, sleeping face.

Helstar's concern continued unabated. "Dawn." Frowning, he inclined his chin to the east.

Sylah reached to pat his knee. "We're in time, then." Dour, he made no answer. Sylah smiled. "What better occasion for Lanta and me to greet the sun? I'll include a prayer for your safety, my friend."

She was turning away when he said, "Please do. I'll be grateful. And ask for yourself."

His tone brought her head around. He pretended to be intent on the increasingly visible brushy riverbanks.

Sylah and Lanta performed the ritual washing as best they could, dipping their hands in the sluggish river. The crisp, cold waters of the Inland Sea and the streams of the Dog country loomed in Sylah's mind like the stuff of dreams.

Only by dint of some careful bending and twisting were the two women able to face the sunrise without the sail blocking the way. Helstar, seeing the problem, changed course. He muttered complaint the whole time and snorted satisfaction when they were done.

Then Sylah announced that she intended to baptize Jessak.

Helstar sat bolt upright, his concern for ambush completely dismissed. "Not here." He stopped, chewing on his beard. Inexplicably, he dabbed a hand in the water, tasted it. Some of his agitation faded.

Sylah said, "The boy must be named. How would he be known in the Land Beyond, Helstar? It's a terrible thought, but we must face it; the world is dangerous for him."

Helstar's laugh was cruel, out of place. Still, all he said was, "Be thankful the sea's diluted by fresh water. Do what Church requires. It can't be helped."

A crude, foreboding benison, Sylah thought angrily. The child had no faults, couldn't be blamed for his father. And at the end, his mother displayed character few could match.

Premonition touched Sylah, a chill hand on her cheek.

Yasmaleeya was dead.

His mother would never see Jessak grown, supple and strong. The Chair would.

The revelation came and went, startling as a falling star.

Sylah held Jessak while Lanta did the honors. A wet finger touched forehead, the outer corner of each eye, then chin. In chorus, the women intoned, "May the One in All grant a mind that creates a life of truth and virtue. May the One in All grant eyes that seek the right and the good in everyone. May the One in All grant a voice that praises Him and ever speaks with honor."

Helstar added his amen. Once more, Sylah caught the flutter of fingers; she was more sure than ever it was his three-sign. He offered no comment, she asked no questions.

Day pressed down on the small balancebar. With every moment of increased light, the small party felt more vulnerable. Thick reeds bending in the breeze suggested attacking boats about to break from cover. Every bend in the course was a potential shield for ambushers. Birds cried greeting to the day; Sylah and the others squirmed anxiously, imagining warmen signalling assault.

They were in a veritable sea of reeds when the sun was first bright enough to cast shadows. The river was wide, slow. Smaller streams, blind byways, presented themselves in ever-changing variety, yet there was a sameness to the place that bred apprehension. Sylah, biting her lip to avoid making critical comment, was sure they'd passed one particular break in the crowding growth at least twice. Possibly three times.

Refuting her, a slowly curving bend revealed an island ahead. Trees crowned it, in some places reaching to the very edge of the river. Helstar drew the sail as taut as he could, put the balancebar into a sizzling tack that sent spray spinning off into the wind.

Hanging, swaying branches loomed closer and closer. Sylah turned questioningly to Helstar. He said, "Everyone down. Flat."

The boat plunged into the green curtain. Sylah saw no more, her face pushed hard against the stinking, gritty wooden hull. They stopped with a battering crash. It was all Sylah could do to protect Jessak. He awoke with a furious bawl that ended so abruptly and completely Sylah feared he was injured. Examining him quickly, she found no damage. His eyes remained screwed tightly shut.

Sitting up, Sylah found herself staring at neat planks of seasoned wood, artfully joined, caulked with wool and tar. Craning her neck, she looked up, into the black eyes and grinning, dark features of Donnacee Tate.

"We were beginning to worry about you," Tate said. She pointed at the torn leaves and snapped twigs drooping behind the balancebar. "Great entrance."

Sylah had to laugh. She marveled at this strange, lovable friend, who seemed to have an absolute need to make light of everything. Lanta giggled, and even Dodoy smiled. For his part, Helstar shook his head in disbelief.

Nalatan appeared beside Tate. "Wal says we have to go. Come aboard." Emphasizing Nalatan's haste, Wal's voice ordered lines cast off, oars readied to pole the craft free of her hiding place. The deck thudded with running feet.

Lanta and Dodoy climbed nimbly over the larger boat's rail. Helstar handed Sylah up. The open cargo well yawned in front of her, only a couple of steps removed from the narrow walkway that paralleled the gunwales. The rowing benches were neatly stowed against the hull, restricting the passage as little as possible. It took a moment for her to realize she was looking at Copper down there, as well as other mounts and packhorses. Forward, crowding into the vee of the bow, Oshu and Tanno wagged tails in greeting.

The thought of those brave animals facing the Dry made Sylah's stomach roll. Spring was nearly lost already. Summer in the Dry was said to be as close to the Land Under as the world had to offer.

When she turned back to the balancebar, Helstar was already reseated at the tiller. He smiled up into her surprised expression. "The Empty Lands will be needing a smith." He winked, shoving the balancebar away from the larger hull.

Sylah quickly handed Jessak to Lanta, just as Tate returned. Ignoring Tate's walleyed "Where'd you get *that*?" Sylah turned back to Helstar, protesting. "The Kossiar warmen will suspect you helped us. The slaves don't know you're a friend. It's too dangerous, Helstar. Come with us. We need you. Church needs you."

A sheen of annoyance glossed his features. It passed quickly. Signaling her close, assuring no one overheard, he said, "The name of Jessak is a curse. Men say he conspired with the darkness, that he held dominion over sea creatures."

Sylah interrupted. "Superstition. You, of all people."

"Legend says he never chose the shark as guardian for Kos; the shark chose him. They say the dead rose for him. I'm Church, Priestess, and I'll die for her, if need be, singing hymns in her name. But I saw the king of all sharks come when the babe was threatened. I saw a boat carrying two dead men intercede for him. I was *there*." Looking past her, he bit off further words.

A young sailor approached Sylah. Rushing, Helstar whispered, "There's more. No time. Treat him well, Flower." The last was entreaty, then the frown marring Helstar's brow melted away to a guileless smile for the sailor, who now stood close by, coiling a braided leather halyard. When Helstar spoke again, his voice was louder, harsher. Sylah was confronted by the smith of Trader Island. His look was sidelong, calculating. Broad shoulders arced forward in an aggressive curve, and his head bowed, bearlike. "Smith's always needed. Goes where the business is. Anyhow, if I can't depend on my own armor and weapons, would I dare sell them? Don't worry about Helstar. Never doubt he's your friend."

"I can never thank you enough."

Waving, Helstar backed away. "The crystals you wanted are in the leather hamper. With a few bottles of the Chair's best wine. A going-away present." The cloak of branches and leaves trailed across him in lingering touch, just as Sylah's eyes sought to hold him. A moment later there was only a faint flutter of leaves to show he'd ever existed.

Tate put a hand on Sylah's shoulder, bringing her around to face the new situation. The boat lurched and pressed into the upstream edge of the overhanging cover. They spoke of the night's developments. Lanta had already described events at the fort. Tate, ill at ease, told of the disappearance of Conway and Tee. Lanta said nothing, her eyes cast down, her shoulders slumped. Tate was as tactful as possible. Her optimism for their safety was too loud, too certain. Until her voice broke dramatically.

Embracing, Tate and Lanta consoled each other.

The boat was out into the current then. All hands managed to be busy, found a way to keep clear of the grief. Lanta straightened first. Her chin jutted, and she knuckled away tears as if she meant to crush their very memory. "He *will* be all right. I won't believe anything else. I won't." She turned to Sylah. "The Apocalypse Testament: 'Faith, and only faith, can conquer the past, can create a future. Plans without faith are speculation. Faith without constancy is gambling.' I believe. Matt Conway will live."

Gently, consoling, Sylah said, "I hope he will, too, Lanta. He's friend to all of us. Nevertheless, what you quoted refers to a belief in the One in All, not help for one who's concerned about another. Please be realistic. I couldn't bear to see you hurt anymore."

"Faith is faith. Mine can accommodate the small as easily as the great. I believe Matt Conway has a place in your quest. I won't believe he's to die before his mission is fulfilled." Lanta struggled with the speech, voice strained.

Tate put an arm around Lanta's shoulders. "Class. Just hearing you makes me feel better. You stay close to me; I need that sort of help." Looking across Lanta's head, Tate grinned at Sylah. "You wouldn't know about all-day preachin' and dinner on the ground, or the solid sweet heart of good gospel. I only went once, actually, with my daddy. But that's my kind of faith. Lanta and me, we're primitives. We'll get that hardhead Conway through this. You watch."

It was so unabashedly supportive Sylah's throat blocked for a moment. "Thank you. Both of you." She made a clucking noise at Lanta, pretended to scold. "That's twice in less than half a timetube you've put my feet on the right path. I'll be in your debt forever."

"We walk it together. Sister." Then, with a hug for Tate, Lanta added, "Sisters."

Nalatan stood at a distance, watching unobtrusively until Sylah looked up and he caught her eye. She waved him over. He, too, tried to apologize for not stopping Tee and Conway. Sylah stopped him. "I know you all did everything possible. They did what they believed was right."

Nalatan thanked her, then pointed into the distance. He asked the women, "Have you noticed the smoke? There? And back that way?" He went on. "The uprising. We can expect ambush any time. Wal and his men can take us no farther upstream than the first major godkill. From there, they go north on land. We go east. Once we reach the sunrise slope of the Enemy Mountains, I suggest we camp over until fall. There's good water, plenty of game. We'll need rest, as well. We don't want the burden of facing the summer Dry."

Sylah said, "Kossiar patrols are looking for us?"

He smiled crookedly. It wasn't an expression Sylah thought she could learn to like. "You have the Chair's firstborn son in your arms. You'll be accused of murdering his wife and of siding with the slaves that are butchering their owners. The slaves are riddled with Moondance preachers who'll spread the word you're a Church witch. Anyone who can lift steel is looking for us."

"Are you saying we can't make it?" Tate demanded.

Nalatan's laughter was harder to bear than his smile. "We'll make it. If we're cunning. Ruthless. Lucky. We need all those things. But we have one unfailing advantage."

"Yes?" Sylah was impatient.

"Humankind." Nalatan lazily indicated the rising pillars of smoke. "This killing is in the name of freedom, but as soon as it stops, the real struggle will begin again, the one for power. However many slaves break free, they'll soon be at each other's throats, fighting to see who's in charge. Everyone's so dependably determined to kill each other, they may overlook us. Or weaken each other, making it easier for me and Tate to kill them. It leaves a loyal protector of Church bad choices of what to pray for."

Sylah spun away, offended and furious. Lanta blushed, embarrassed by such flirting with blasphemy; she busied herself fussing with Jessak's wrappings. As a result, only Tate saw the way Nalatan's head swung up and east, yearning, as though he already saw the sanctuary of the cool mountains.

The anger that she felt on hearing him so bluntly condemn Sylah smoldered, but the sight of his suffering pulled at her. She ached to reach out, to touch him.

And defeated herself.

The unnamed, unknown thing in her that denied him rose up yet again. Her hands remained at her sides, her words locked tight in her heart. She knew she was behaving foolishly, even destructively, and was helpless. She felt possessed, controlled by forces that laughed at her even as they whipped her into obedience.

Tate made her way to the side of the ship. Leaning out over the side, she watched the swirling, shifting surface roll and tumble in infinite pattern.

The problems and dangers of the forthcoming trek to Church Home refused to come into focus in her mind. Shamefully, she was unable to concentrate on Conway and Tee.

Nalatan. Why couldn't she respond to him when she so desperately wanted to?

This new view inside him was disturbing. He was deeper, more complex than she imagined. What did she really know of him? Was her subconscious warning her?

That wasn't the problem. She told herself she might as well be honest. She was terrified of loving him, terrified of losing him. Donnacee Tate was her own worst enemy.

CHAPTER 79

Two prone nomad warriors watched the lone rider following the narrow game trail through the tight ranks of slim lodgepole pines.

The distant figure drifted in and out of sight, slumped in the saddle, paying no heed to his mount's course. As for the animal, it shuffled wearily, hind hoofs dragging, forefeet barely clearing the ground. It kicked a fallen pine cone at nearly every step, sending the prickly things skittering into the manzanita undergrowth like so many excited rats.

The larger of the watchers, dressed in dark brown homespun shirt and trousers, asked, "Should we kill him?"

The smaller man, not much more than a boy, shot him a surprised look. He was dressed like his partner, but iridescent rooster tailfeathers dangled from the long hair on the back of his head. When he turned, jewel colors darted across their smooth blackness. He said, "Yes. He may have something in the saddlebags. I claim the horse."

"You don't just claim. Not you, not Lolal. Not on me."

A third man, older, appeared from behind a cluster of boulders. Unlike his companions, he sported a thick leather vest, beaded bands at biceps and wrists, and leather shorts. Laced boots reached high enough to cover his legs, except for the exposed knee joint. He bent to a crouch, ran to the brushy patch where his companions hid. Looking at the rider across the prone bodies, he said, "That's sure no Peddler; no pack animals. Dressed too plain for a snot-nosed pretty-pretty Messenger." He was thoughtfully silent for a while, then, "This is our last day on patrol, so we'll take him alive. If he's an escaped slave or a Kossiar warman, we'll take him back with us. Moonpriest wants information."

"And fun." The smallest of the trio grinned over his shoulder.

The older man frowned. "Moonpriest says torturing isn't just entertainment or experience for the youngsters any more. We draw strength from the prisoners. The braver they are, the longer it takes them to die, the stronger we grow."

Chuckling, the small one returned his attention to the rider. "Nobody's going to get strong off that one. He's half dead already. See how his head wobbles? He's sound asleep."

"We'll be careful anyway." The older man, keeping low, scuttled back to his original hiding place, where three saddled horses and a packhorse were reined to saplings. The others joined him. He said, "Get ahead of him. Let him get good and close, then show yourselves. Put an arrow in him if he tries to run."

The tallest warrior swung aboard a roan. Looking down at the high-booted man, he said, "I don't need you telling me how to do things, Lolal. Being leader of a scout team means you can say where we go and when we go and who takes what watch. That's it."

Without looking up from where he was checking the edge on a thick, stubby sword, Lolal said, "Do what I told you."

The younger men rode off, exchanging smirks. Lolal put away the weapon and glanced after them. His thin frown was more puzzled than angry. Once the others were out of sight and hearing, he got on a pinto saddle horse. Cautiously, he edged the mount forward until he could peer between two boulders. The rider coming up the mountain had made the progress Lolal expected, and he found himself in position to watch.

He wished he could name whatever was making him so edgy. They were ten days' ride south of the scout camp. Main camp was another seven days north. Seventeen days of scouting, and no sign of people, except for a straggling family of used-up slaves. On foot, if anyone'd ever believe that.

A hand drifted to the soft leather sack at his side, fondled the cushioned hardness of Kossiar coin. There was a kind of humor to the whole thing, he thought; a slave father bargaining to save his family with money stolen from the master he'd killed.

Complications came when you settled in one place and tied your life to dirt. People like that were just things, no different from their own cornstalks. Never even offered to fight.

Harsh squawking broke Lolal's reminiscence. He glanced around, told himself no horseman belonged up here where the bold black and white jays were at home. Tight little trails kept a man squashed between trees close as hairs on a bear's butt. Well, today would see them on the sunrise slope and headed downhill.

Lolal returned his attention to the trail below. The lone rider gave no sign of hearing the jay's noise.

That was exactly the sort of thing that made a man nervous, Lolal thought angrily. Normal people looked around when a jay sounded alarm. It wasn't right not to. Lolal spat. Nothing about these mountains was right. Too quiet. Too empty. Too peaceful.

A man started *waiting* for something to go wrong. Like it had to happen.

Checking the packhorse's lead, he got under way. Swinging wide, he intersected the winding game trail. Iron-shod horse tracks nearly obliterated smaller, sharp-edged deer prints. Lolal studied the former. A healthy animal. Tired. A large notch in the left fore shoe. Coming across fresh, steaming droppings, Lolal reined up in surprise. Corn. Not much, but any at all was remarkable. How'd a man grain his horse way up here in this high country without a pack animal to carry it?

One thing after another.

Many who thought they knew Matt Conway would have failed to recognize the man who silently watched as the rider of the pinto slipped out of the forest and onto the trail ahead.

It was more than Conway's different clothes. True, the padded undershirt under the chain mail bulked his figure considerably. Long leaves of armor protecting his thighs gave them the appearance of excessive mass, as well. The raw line of a three-inch scar that started just outside the flare of his right nostril and slashed horizontally along the cheekbone was quite thin. If anything, it should have added a certain dash to his features.

This man's face brought to mind the eager, locked features of a stalking leopard.

The intensity of hunting cats frightens humans; they attribute it to implacable ferocity. Humans misjudge the animals. In Conway's case, the assumption harbored wisdom.

His chain mail had a patch in the center of the chest where the linked rings were clumsily hammered back into approximate flatness. The work surrounded a jagged hole where the wipe flechette had ripped loose four rings. What that amount of energized metal had done as it traveled through the warman who was wearing the chain mail at the time was as impressive as it was messy. Several links in the back of the shirt were stressed, warped, but remained unbroken.

Conway had hunted down a second warman to acquire an unruined padded undershirt. As an afterthought, Conway took that man's armored skirt, as well. He retained his old sword, the one from Ola. Additionally, he wore the original knife he carried out of the crèche. It rode in a scabbard at his left bicep, a style copied from Nalatan.

Constantly scanning the forest, Conway absently drew the knife. He stroked his thumb across the edge rhythmically, counted to fifteen.

Fifteen days since Tee was killed. Betrayed.

Matt Conway was the blade that would avenge her.

The rider ahead slowed. Conway took cover off the trail. Stormracer picked his way carefully through the undergrowth, well aware that stealth was necessary.

Conway worried that the dogs had been seen.

The leather-clad man shouted something. Conway couldn't catch the words, but the voice pitched upward, questioning.

More shouting answered from farther up the mountain. Then there were hoofbeats, running, and a yell of alarm from the man Conway followed. Moments later, a riderless mount thundered past Conway.

A nudge sent Stormracer moving quickly through the trees. Conway drew the wipe. Muting the clatter of working parts, he eased a round into the wipe chamber and thumbed off the safety.

Conway spotted the ambush site from a distance. A tumble of rocks uphill overlooked the wide swath scoured by an avalanche some years past. Reclaiming growth was generally only chest-high, affording an unusually long view for this country. By moving farther downhill, Conway was able to cross the avalanche path below the line of vision of the two riders heading downhill to meet the leather-clad third man. Conway moved swiftly, picking his way along the back side of the rock formation, then dismounting to scramble up to a vantage point only a few yards from the trio.

The two men had triggered the ambush far too early. All three stared at an object on the ground. One was afoot. He was tall, dressed in brown homespun. He poked at the thing with his bow. The other two remained mounted. The one in leather fumed.

"Otraz, I told you to give him a chance to surrender. You shot without warning. You ambushed *corn*."

The mounted one, wearing rooster feathers, looked sick. He said, "It looked like a man, Lolal. It's even got a face. With a nose."

Almost absently, Lolal lashed out with the back of his hand. The smaller man reeled in his saddle. When he straightened, he aimed an arrow, drawn to the head. Trembling at the strain of holding the bow poised, he breathed in tight, rasping gulps.

"I doubt you could hit me." Only Lolal's lips moved. "That dummy full of corn didn't come up this trail by itself. Someone's following it. Get back down the trail. Find him."

Otraz, still on foot, said, "Kill him, Nar. No man hits one of us."

Lolal remained unflustered. "Put that thing down. The man who tricked you could be watching us already."

"Nar, he's trying to frighten you, like some milk-mouthed boy. Are you going to let him do it?"

Nar pulled the arrow to full draw again. Lolal ignored him. "That's it, Otraz. When we get back, I settle with you. Out beyond the tents. Or you can whine for the scout group leader, if you'd rather. Up to you. Nar, stop fooling around before someone jumps on all of us."

Conway almost missed Otraz's treacherous stroke. The tall man moved forward, as if to mount, then looked down the trail. He jerked fully erect, pointed. Like Lolal, Conway looked to see the cause of alarm. Otraz's movement stopped him. A quick step put the tall man uphill of Lolal. With his left hand, Otraz lifted the skirt of Lolal's jacket. The knife in Otraz's right hand glittered up and into the exposed side. Conway had time to think of a shining dragonfly's wing cutting the sunlight before Lolal twisted away. His shocked agony echoed through the trees. Yanking the reins, he spurred his horse. Startled, it reared. Lolal tumbled off its rump. Something cracked, loud. After some sharp spasms, the man was still. The only sound was the nervous stamping of the horse that threw him.

Disbelief tightened Nar's voice to a boyish tremolo. "You killed him. What if someone's coming? What'll we do?"

Otraz blustered, unnaturally loud. His face was red. "Whoever sent this ahead is way back, or we'd have heard by now. Help me move Lolal. We'll be ready when they get here."

Nar continued to stare at the sprawled figure. "You killed him. You move him. I'll get the dummy."

Scornfully, Otraz said, "No, you didn't kill him. Barely brave enough to kill that slave's old woman, weren't you? Give me a hand, boy."

Nar turned red, then white. He raised his bow, drew the arrow.

Otraz backed up a step. "All right, I got excited. You get the dummy. I'll get Lolal. But hurry up."

Nar turned to put away his weapon, and Otraz was on him instantly. The knife flashed again as Otraz hauled the smaller man out of the saddle. Nar struggled to break free. Otraz struck and

465

struck long after Nar was still. One last, vindictive slash cut the smaller man's throat. Nar dropped on his face. The rooster feathers fluttered gaily in the sunshine.

Otraz wiped the blade clean on Nar's leg and replaced it in its sheath.

A tremendous racket broke out back down the trail. Otraz leapt into his saddle. He hesitated, making tentative moves toward the packhorse, just now trotting into view. More loud roaring decided Otraz. He spurred his horse away.

Moments later, Conway's dogs appeared. They came hurriedly, looking back, heads and tails down. A bear appeared at the edge of the brush, rose on her hind legs, and squalled threats. Her cubs crept up to watch in silent awe.

Conway assured the crestfallen dogs no harm was done. The bear, in apparent agreement, dropped to all fours and huffed her offspring back into the trees.

Two nomad horses thrashed and crashed about in the brush, snagged by dragging reins. Conway got them and the packhorse under control. Ignoring the bodies, he tied off the dummy's punctured shirt, then scooped up the spilled corn and repacked it. Half smiling, he discarded the smashed round basket that had been the figure's head. Slinging the bundle across one of the nomad horses, he was preparing to lead them to Stormracer when a sound checked him.

Lolal was watching.

Conway leapt. "I thought you were dead."

Lolal winced. "Not yet. You saw? Otraz? Nar?" He fought for the words, but delivered them with surprising clarity.

"Otraz ran. The boy's dead."

"Moonpriest says we die for him, we go to the moon, wait for him there. Hope so. Want to see Otraz again." He closed his eyes, then, "You not Kossiar."

Conway started to tell him he was nothing, a man alone.

Dreamily, Lolal opened his eyes. He managed a half smile. "Con Way. White Thunder. They said you lived."

"Who said that?"

Lolal ignored him. "Dummy. Decoy. You behind. Smart. Moonpriest said."

"We heard there was a new siah."

"*The* Siah. Make us strong. Many peoples. Moondance siah. Knew you. Other life. Told us. You go. North. He forgive. Be one us. Kill. Kill all."

"Knew me?" Conway sat down beside the man. There were

466

only two men alive who knew him in an "other life." "Jones? His name is Jones?"

"Moonpriest." It was a rasping exhalation.

"He has a scar. Big. Over his ear."

"Tur-ban."

Conway said, "It's him."

Lolal sighed. His muscles loosened. Ropey tendons in his neck relaxed, his cheeks drooped. Slowly, gently, he smiled. A wonder of happiness flooded the cruel, hard features. "Moondance conquers. Live forever."

It was a long time before Conway moved again, so long that his knees cracked angrily when he rose. Even so, he finished the conversation with his dead companion. "I've already lived forever, you fool, and I'm sick of it. North's as good a direction as any. As long as it's away from Church."

CHAPTER 80

Conway sat with his back to the cliff wall and watched the broken line of dismounted nomad warriors advance up the hill. Dust billowed softly in their wake, smoking up from the sun-mottled floor of the thick forest. Below them, a mountain stream crashed through a narrow gorge in a jumble of ever-changing greens spangled with silver and diamonds. Where the water shattered into spray, miniature rainbows dazzled and collapsed almost before the eye registered them.

The men themselves—Conway counted twenty—added color of their own. Dressed for war, they flaunted bright headbands, multicolored shields, garishly painted faces. Some wore monstrous masks designed to protect the wearer from the weapons of any opponent not terrified into fleeing.

Working a round into the boop, Conway couldn't help admiring the savage beauty of the scene. The sheen of exposed arrowheads and bared swords, plus knowing he was the quarry, added immediacy.

When the line was about a hundred yards distant, Conway rose. He raised both hands in a sun sign, thumbs and forefingers joined at the tip, fingers splayed. After he was sure all had seen him, he cupped his hands to his mouth to shout, "I come in peace! To meet Moonpriest."

One man ran downhill toward the party's tethered horses. Riding one, leading two, he returned. Only then did Conway realize the nomad search line was gone. Of the twenty men he'd counted earlier, only three were still visible, including the man bringing the horses. The trio mounted, made sun signs, and advanced at a walk.

Conway whistled to the dogs to remain hidden, then called Stormracer to him. If the nomad wanted to speak from horseback, Conway wasn't going to be afoot. The pinto packhorse, firmly hobbled, made a halfhearted effort to follow Stormracer, then stopped, hipshot, resigned to being left.

Watching the advancing warriors, Conway's mind flew back to western movies, films that were antique long before he was born. This was a cowboy flick gone mad. The lone rider watched the war party coming to parley; with that, all similarity ended. One of this war party wore a hammered brass breastplate, golden in the sun. Another carried a curved sword that looked like something from the even-more-ancient *Arabian Nights*. The center man, leader of the trio, wore a black and white spotted skunk hat and leather body armor. He also sported elaborately beaded leather forearm covers that extended from wrist to elbow. Polished steel bands ribbed their length. A painted eye glared in the middle of his forehead.

The leader stopped a few feet in front of Conway. "Who are you? What are you doing on the Windband's land?"

"I come to see Moonpriest. I am Matt Conway."

The two subordinates rose in their stirrups, exclaiming wordlessly. The leader's eyes widened. Conway went on, "I circled your camp last night, then came up here to wait for you. I knew you'd find my tracks and follow. What are your names?"

"They call me Copper Shirt. The man on my right is Watches Clouds. The other is Stonethrower. We are Buffalo Eaters. Moonpriest says you have turned against him."

"I'm his friend."

"Moonpriest has no friends. Moonpriest is holy."

Conway gave a minute shrug. "Whatever makes you comfortable. Take me to him."

Watches Clouds spurred his horse forward, leaned over to speak in Copper Shirt's ear. The leader spoke to Conway. "Moonpriest has said that if the White Thunder or the Black Lightning will come, he will talk. You must give us your weapons."

Smiling crookedly, Conway said, "I can't do that."

"You must." Copper Shirt's hand dropped to the handle of his sword.

Conway aimed the wipe at the nomad's chest. He said, "Are you so ready to die?"

Copper Shirt looked from the black hole of the muzzle to Conway's eyes. "No."

Conway was shocked by the equanimity of the answer. Copper Shirt clearly believed Conway could and would kill him. The man simply accepted dying as inevitable, natural, no more than light or darkness. Given that power over death, a man was free to dismiss it.

Conway remembered how Lolal died praising Moondance, sure of going to a better place to await reunion with his master. Copper Shirt believed. So must hundreds of Windband warriors.

Something stirred in the back of Conway's consciousness, a swirl of reaction too tentative for him to grasp. It could have been respect. Or revulsion. Envy. *Hope?*

Copper Shirt said, "No one has to die over the weapons. Now. Moonpriest will decide. Another thing must be talked about. You come from the south. Three of our scouts are late returning from there. Did you see them?"

Conway said, "The Otraz one killed Lolal and Nar. He left them."

Copper Shirt looked Conway in the eye, not challenging, but clearly warning. "I see Lolal's horse. I wondered how you got it. You say Otraz lives?"

"Yes."

Copper Shirt nodded. "Otraz is a Salt. Bad people." He smiled suddenly. "We'll see him again, I think." Conway thought he detected something covert in Copper Shirt's manner, as if there was a joke being played on the stranger. It was very irritating.

The silver whistle's silent signal brought Karda and Mikka in a sprint. Skidding to a stop, they stood looking at Copper Shirt. It was an impressive entry, and Conway bared a knowing smile of his own at the way Copper Shirt's knuckles whitened on the reins.

Moonpriest stood on the lowest copper step of the moon altar. His white robe was actually several layers of diaphanous material. Webbed with a random silver thread that caught the blazing sun, it glowed when the breeze made it stir and billow. The white turban featured a polished silver moon disk centered in front.

Katallon had carefully formed the mass of people in a semicircle that flanked and backed their siah. Fox and a group of his

469

Mountain warriors patrolled to hold back any overenthusiastic spectators. It was an easy task; the Mountains, despite being the smallest tribal group making up Windband, were universally deferred to. They brought Moonpriest to Katallon's Windband. They helped Moonpriest build the whirling, shining altar that snapped lives away in a flash of blue fire. They also fought exceedingly well.

Windband's people were drawn up in quartermoon configuration on a flat plain in the foothills of the Enemy Mountains. Behind the crowd, the heart-colored tent of Katallon dominated the haphazard scatter of smaller shelters. Moonpriest's tent was subordinate to Katallon's massively symbolic construction. Nevertheless, the eye sought the white material.

Conway first glimpsed that snowy brilliance on the descent from the mountains. His first thought was *pure*. He imagined whispers of cool shade and mysteries of things seen and not understood, of things believed and yet unseen.

When Conway looked away, it pulled him back. A prickling nervousness made him squirm in his saddle.

Another word sprang to his mind. *Seductive*.

Now Conway had arrived on a slight rise within a quarter-mile of the camp's edges. In the farther distance, other camps scattered separately along the wide valley's green grasslands.

Boys flanked Conway's escorting Buffalo Eater scouts. When the youngsters got too close, a warrior would chase after them, using his lance as a club, belaboring his victim about the head and shoulders. Bloodied, half-dazed, the wounded fled to rejoin their less-foolhardy comrades and brag of their exploit.

As the escorting Buffalo Eaters reached the horns of the formation, they halted and remained in place. The patrolling Mountains joined them. The high-spirited boys and their eye-rolling, excited mounts raced all the way around the crowd to watch events from the back side. Soon Conway was advancing alone. When he was ten yards from Moonpriest, an unseen signal initiated a ceremonial greeting. The entire mass of people hummed. High, low, middle notes flowed together. The curvature of the formation focused the sound at the point where Conway, Stormracer, the dogs, and Moonpriest stood alone. Conway's insides tightened under the pressure of so much life-force channeled directly at him.

Stormracer pranced, ears back, angry and frightened. Karda and Mikka stood with legs braced, heads swaying in confused search for a source of danger. They settled on Moonpriest. Staring, lips trembling with repressed snarls, they challenged him to move.

Moonpriest ignored them, beaming a smile of welcoming pleasure at Conway.

The chorus faded to silence.

Karda and Mikka threw back their heads and howled. Proud, powerful, the voices swelled to the distant hills and echoed. Moonpriest bent backward, away from the raised muzzles.

Like the people, the animals stopped without warning or flourish. They seemed to expect praise, and Conway lavished it on them, telling them what fine singers they were, and how wonderfully they'd greeted their host.

Irritation washed across Moonpriest's face. Still, he greeted Conway affably. "It's been quite a while, old friend. I've missed you."

Conway said, "Thank you for the welcome. It's good to see you again. You look well."

"Getting by, Matt; getting by. One does what one can. These are my people. My scouts told you I'm their siah? I'm a god."

Plain, ordinary tone notwithstanding, madness cloaked this strange, altered man so palpably that Conway had the sensation that if he reached to touch him, his hand would mire in gelatinous, clinging ooze.

More than that, Conway knew he was being tested. His mind went back to his impression of the white tent. This was a dangerous place. The thought exhilarated him. "You've found yourself here, haven't you?"

"*Was* found. My mother claimed me, her lost child. Epiphany, Conway. Not as ordinary humans understand it, or abuse the word, but in the true ecclesiological sense. I am the twice-born."

Formally, Conway bowed his head, but not so far that his vision was obscured. "I rejoice for my old friend. For the new siah."

Moonpriest beamed, but the smile dropped away like a snuffed light. He lowered his gaze to stare at the ground. "It's not all joy. I need a friend. Someone who can understand my burdens, someone to appreciate my mind as well as my holiness. I'm loved, Conway. Loved, but unknown. Can you comprehend that?"

Picking words carefully, Conway said, "I think I can imagine it. Even though all these people are wise enough to recognize you for what you are, they're still primitive. Compared to you."

"Exactly. My human guise makes me as mortal and vulnerable as any of these, but even as an ordinary human, I'm a man of infinitely more attainment. I understand completely a myriad things these poor savages can't even imagine. And I have goals. The

471

most farsighted of my followers can't think beyond the next bloodletting. They're a fantastic weapon, but unsophisticated. A club. I need a sword, a rapier. No, neither of those." He stepped away from the altar and its wheel. Hands behind his back, he paced, talking at a furious rate, as if he'd forgotten everything around him. "A blade of flame. That's what I need, what I *will* have. A scourge, to cleanse the land, that Moondance may grow, become what it—and I—must be. To flourish is not enough for Moondance. Moondance conquers."

Doubtfully, Conway said, "Conquers whom? Understand, the Kossiars expect you, now that the slaves have made so much trouble. The uprising is devastating the country, but the Kossiar army is still very effective."

Moonpriest stopped pacing. His sideways smile at Conway was secretive. "Why do you ask who I'll attack?" He barked a laugh, pointed at Conway's suddenly concerned expression. "You see how my mind must work? How I must examine everything, to discern deeper meanings, unexpected agendas? But I trust you. At the base of all my problems is Gan Moondark. I'll deal with him when the time comes. Kos teeters on the brink of dissolution. The Three Territories are dynamic, eager for change and progress. I must control that. Such energy is only rightfully engaged in my service."

It was an unsettling thought. Conway was careful to keep his voice neutral. "You march north?"

"South." Moonpriest's grin was an almost-childlike glee at Conway's continuing surprise. "Church. Earthly thrones are of no concern to me, Matt Conway, except as they contribute to my mission to bring humankind to my mother, the moon. Your mortal time has no meaning for me, land has no boundaries that affect me. My sphere is eternity, my dominion universal. Church is false, a whore to lead minds away from their true mother. And me. I must eliminate the slightest memory of those carrion-picking, black ravens." Moving backward, seeming to float in the silver and white aura of his robe, he raised his hands and face to the sky. "Moondance conquers!" The crowd immediately turned it into a chant. "Moondance con-quers! Moondance con-quers!"

While the chant hammered on, Moonpriest lowered his arms. He extended his hands, and Conway knew he was to take them in his own, signal his loyalty.

Moonpriest stood on the copper plate.

"*. . . controls the lightning . . .*"

The remembered words blasted through Conway's consciousness, stripped it of everything but terrifying understanding of the altar.

Copper darts on the ceramic wheel's surface. Arms with brushes to touch that metal. Wires. Connections.

Lightning.

Moonpriest. On insulated copper. Hands extended. Smiling.

Conway's mind exploded into fragments of thought. The offered grip might kill him. Arguments for living or dying raged.

Tee was dead. Because Church wanted no more Moondance converts. Church betrayed the slave uprising.

Lanta.

Treachery.

Moonpriest waited. Tonight was the first night of the full moon. Conway wondered if he was welcome friend or sacrifice.

Moondance. War on Church. Vengeance.

Conway dismounted, took the few steps to Moonpriest with a feeling of risk that neared ecstasy. Stepping inside the welcoming hands, he embraced Moonpriest.

And was embraced. Unhurt.

Life thrilled in Conway's veins, hot as molten gold. He lived. In the grasp of death, Matt Conway lived.

Windband heard his grating laughter over the pumping beat of their chant. They looked at each other and nodded knowingly.

CHAPTER 81

When Conway first heard the noise, a rustling no louder than stiff cloth dragged across gravel, he dismissed it and continued shaving.

He sat in an oak-framed chair with a tooled wildcow back and seat. The design was a stylized buffalo, surprisingly sophisticated. Originally, it gave Conway pause. He wondered if he'd misjudged Windband's culture. In the end, he decided it was loot. The wooden chest facing him surely was. All the joints were fine dovetails, the fit of drawers in the case mere thin slits. Presently, its polished brass decorative trim and hardware glowed softly in the light of a four-candle candelabra on its top. Next to that candelabra, his steel mirror leaned on his holstered pistol. The chest also featured a fold-down shelf with a hole for its own brass basin. Hot water sent tendrils of raspberry-scented steam coiling up and around Conway's face. He rinsed lather from the blade of his combat knife, sending the steam wisps into a dancing frenzy.

As he raised the blade again, the noise was repeated.

Louder.

He turned in the chair, looking over each shoulder. The light of the candles fell short of the cloth walls, giving the room a cavernous feel. Conway called out. There was no answer. If anything, the silence deepened.

Wetting the blade, Conway resumed shaving.

The next time the noise came he was prepared. He flipped backward in the chair, tumbling until his feet were under him. Rising to a crouch, he scrambled toward the wall on his left, the knife thrust ahead.

A figure leapt upright from behind the room's frame-and-webbing bed. Unidentifiable in the darkness, it shrank from the knife, keening a muted terror that begged for secrecy as much as for life.

Conway grabbed it, slapped the flat of the blade against the neck. "Who are you?"

"Your friend. Your friend. The only one you have in this place, Matt Conway. A man who's been wronged and would spare you his sad experience."

Conway dragged the unresisting figure into the light. The man kept his face half-shielded, an instinctive creature of the dark. Conway gaped. "Altanar." It was spoken certainly, but with wonder. "I heard you and Jones ... Moonpriest ..."

Altanar interrupted, winking, leering. "Ahhh, very clever. Clever. You learn quickly. But not perfectly, and even the smallest mistake can bring you to the Man Who Is Death. The name Jones is forgotten. The name never was. Cannot be used."

Lowering the knife, Conway asked. "He denies being one of us? The travelers who came to Harbundai and Ola?"

Altanar gestured at the single chair, made it a gracious offering. Conway sat, waiting for an answer. The former tyrant, now dressed in plain cotton pullover vest and baggy trousers that reached only to midcalf, drew himself to full height. His head rose, chin out, and the shadow of the former King of Ola was resurrected for the moment. "He's not so crude as to deny. He 'suggests' it not be discussed. Only his life now is important. Following his rebirth." Altanar pronounced the last word as if it were a joke. Conway noticed that no amusement touched the ragged man's face, nevertheless. He also noticed Altanar's minute pause while he scrutinized his listener. The whole situation was intended to trick Conway into revealing a disbelief or disrespect for Moonpriest.

. Conway wondered if Altanar had any notion exactly how much his clumsiness revealed.

"Tell me of this rebirth," Conway said, and Altanar leaned forward conspiratorially.

"You see? You do need a friend. Did you know that Fox insists you should be killed? Katallon, on the other hand, wants to keep you alive. He wants to torture your secrets out of you, make you show his nomads how to make lightning weapons, how to use them. *Then*, he says, Fox can kill you."

Wryly, and mostly to himself, Conway said, "Timing is everything." Then, "Has Moonpriest ever told this Fox why he wants me alive? Or Katallon? Exactly who is Fox? And how come you're so close to Jo—Moonpriest? Frankly, you don't look like a close companion to a new siah."

Conway was interested to note that Altanar could still react to a slight. The way he quickly covered the response was the telling fact. Altanar wasn't changed, Conway realized, but had learned to keep his feelings wrapped. That was when Conway first saw the round scars on the backs of Altanar's hands. Burn scars. And the man's toes, peering out in the front of his sandals, grew in all directions. Broken. Never treated. Conway looked away.

Altanar was saying, "Move very carefully. You cannot survive here without a major ally. I'm too weak to be anyone's ally, too despised to have a friend. Even the slaves that escape Kos are treated better. If they can fight, if they embrace Moondance, they're free men. I can only turn to you, Matt Conway. We were enemies once, so I know you well for a man of courage and honor. I throw myself on your mercy. Befriend me, and I swear to work for you day and night. All I ask in return is your effort to make my life a little less painful. You're right to think I'm no adviser to Moonpriest. He loathes me. I'm a trophy. My downfall glorifies his eminence. To him, I'm dirt. But like dirt, I cling." A hand fluttered forward, tentative and erratic as a moth. It touched Conway's sleeve, retreated in confusion. "I seek no revenge. Suffering has made me contemplative, satisfied with the simplest of pleasures. It would be false friendship indeed for me to entangle you in Windband's intrigues. In this place, a friend protects a friend. I would gladly give my life for such a one."

"They've treated you very badly."

"It's not as bad as it was. No more actual torture. Beatings.

Blows. Constant contempt. Sometimes I think dying is a way out. But I never forget Church's aversion to suicide."

Conway interrupted. "Church's rules and wants don't interest me."

"Of course, of course. Officious. Yes, far too officious. Still, I'm not ready to die."

"Nor am I, and I remember you for what you were. As you say, though, I can use a friend. For now, tell me how this Moonpriest thing came about."

Squatting on the pounded-earth floor, Altanar rocked back on his heels. Eyes fixed on Conway with almost hypnotic intensity, he recounted the escape from the Three Territories that culminated in his servitude and the alliance of Fox Eleven, Katallon, and the new Moonpriest. When Conway questioned him about the altar, Altanar's concentration almost broke. Clearly frightened to the depths of his soul, he described its origin, ceremony, and effect on its victims in horrified detail.

Conway continued to listen, but his mind wandered, enumerating the "contributions" the people of his time had visited on this world. Back in Ola, Leclerc had improved lifting cranes, adding safety and efficiency to construction. He'd also built the first coke ovens. Everyone rejoiced. Better defensive walls, better swords. Another boon was the reinvention of black powder. Lots of cultural uplift there. Now Moonpriest was enslaving Windband through the magic of an electrical generator.

Conway was unaware of the wolfish, bitter smile he showed Altanar. The latter misinterpreted it. Pitching forward, rising angrily, he said, "You doubt me? You've never seen the altar, never seen the look of a man when the Man Who Is Death burns his life away. Don't mock what you cannot understand."

Pointing at the wipe, Conway said, "I know something of controlling lightning. Do you think I don't realize that's why Moonpriest hoped Tate and I would join him? You insult."

"Forgive me. I'm overly sensitive. Overly. Abuse does that to a man; he begins to see offense in every gesture."

"Nervousness can have the same effect. I spoke too quickly. Tell me, what other miracles has Moonpriest performed?"

Altanar was shocked. "Others? None. Why should he? He's risen from the dead. I was there, saw it. So did Fox. He has animal spirits that do his bidding. He brings the light of the moon to strike his enemies and unbelievers. What other miracles could be wanted?"

"Is it moonlight that kills, or is it lightning?"

"Both. Moonpriest explained to us. When the moon spreads her light over all the world, it's soft and benevolent. When she concentrates it in one place, then it's lightning, and it kills."

"I see. But even with all his power, Moonpriest doesn't rule Windband. You mentioned intrigues. Who plots against whom?"

"No one plots. Yet. But everyone thinks. Fox trains a scout-strike force. All the men are his own Mountain warriors or Buffalo Eaters. Everyone knows they're his personal troops, fanatically loyal to Moonpriest. Katallon hates them. Hates Fox. But he needs them to increase Windband. Katallon suspects Moonpriest wants to rule in his place, but Katallon fears to offend Moonpriest. The people are uncertain. Moonpriest is a god, but Katallon's a leader. Most worship Moonpriest, yet many still believe the affairs of men belong to men alone. A living god among ordinary people is a dangerous thing. Beware of him. He holds the power of life and death, with no conscience or punishment in this world or the next."

"Speaking of careful, tell me how you got in here. This tent's amazing, full of hallways and rooms; it goes on forever. There's a guard everywhere you look. How do you get past them?"

Altanar was suddenly shrunken, as if he collapsed inwardly. He cowered, and yet his whole being suggested defiant malice. Edging back into the darkness, he said, "Altanar is harmless, knows how to be amusing when he's caught. Most of the time, he's unseen. Altanar knows how to move in the dark. When even the moon is blinded. Blinded. Then Altanar is unseen, unrevealed. Could you want a better friend?"

With that, the coiled little man blended into the blackness. When Conway walked after him, Altanar was already behind the bed once again. "Wait." Altanar's word was a command. Surprised, Conway checked. Then, angry with himself and Altanar, he strode forward purposefully. He yanked the bed aside.

The cloth wall scraped across the dirt. It was a repeat of the earlier sound, the one that announced Altanar's unsuspected arrival. Now it laughed softly in the wake of Altanar's equally effective escape. Conway dropped to his knees, lifted the cloth to peer under it. The adjacent room was empty. There was no telltale sway of cloth wall to suggest Altanar's route.

CHAPTER 82

The dining hall of Katallon's tent-castle was a scarlet chamber large enough to seat forty people at its long, single table.

Conway found himself unable to appreciate the multicolored shields and trophies that festooned the walls. The dominant hue reminded him of the Chair's red mourning clothes. It did little for his appetite.

It was a reaction the new Conway considered a character flaw. Remembering the Chair unleashed a torrent of sensation—loss, anger, sadness. Those were positives. Whatever nurtured the constant flame of hatred in his heart was good.

Anything that exposed remnants of sensitivity in the new Conway was bad.

The Chair was merely one of those who had much to answer for to the new Conway. Nothing would be allowed to interfere with pursuit. Time was of no matter, nor was means. In the end would be revenge. The old Conway survived being hunted across Kos. That Conway metamorphosed, became someone else. At first, he struggled to stay alive and mourned Tee's death. By the time he duped the ambush near the crest of the Enemy Mountains, he was the hunter, no longer the hunted. Every breath the new man drew was in the name of Tee's murder.

Conway fixed his gaze on the red walls, thought of the Chair's hypocritical remorse. He forced himself to drain his wine mug without flinching.

Discipline. Commitment.

To Conway's right, just beyond Moonpriest, was Katallon. His bulk was accentuated by the broad beaded stripes running across his leather vest. Gold bracelets dangled from the wrists he planted on the table, gold rings gleamed on every finger. He leaned forward over the wooden slab that passed for a plate in his tent. It was an openly aggressive posture, aimed at Conway. "I'm told your lightning weapon strikes men dead farther away than most men can see. That's hard to believe. Have I heard the truth?"

Conway patted the wipe hanging from the back of his chair. "This one won't reach so far, but it has other advantages."

Moonpriest was troubled. When he moved in his chair the sil-

478

ver threads of his white robe bent sinuously in the candleglow. "Where's the other one?"

"Tate has it. If she lives."

"It could be lost? In the Chair's hands?" Moonpriest twisted around, the better to face Conway. "A rifle like that could destroy a hundred men."

Conway said, "First, you need ammunition. Second, you have to know how to operate it. You have to understand solar energy, computer chips, electronics. I don't think our present contemporaries are geared for that. Do you?"

Across from them, Fox raised a hand, frowning. The expression matched his somber leather garb. Obsidian ear bobs on silver wires were his only decorative concession. He said, "You use unknown words. Speak so we can understand."

Soberly, Conway continued. "Controlling the lightning is a powerful gift. Moonpriest and I share secret words, just as we share the ability to control. His powers are much greater. I'm simply a man with a weapon. Moonpriest is holy. No one is as he is."

Katallon's expression belied the enthusiasm he put into his toast. "Raise your wine to Moonpriest, bringer of victory."

Approval murmured as men in various costumes lifted mugs in unison. Katallon continued. "The Black Lightning stole this special weapon from you?"

"When we were betrayed, I was away from Trader Island. The weapon was in her care. If she died, the secret of the lightning weapons died with her." Never before had Conway allowed himself to think of Tate as dead. Nor could he now. Not really. It was a consideration. Not even a possibility. The same was true of all of them. Even Lanta. Her. The guilty one.

Moonpriest said, "Whether the Black Lightning lives is unimportant. We have the White Thunder. Soon, all weapons everywhere will belong to Windband, and the glory of Moondance."

Katallon rose. His wine mug, refilled, sloshed when he raised it over his head. Katallon laughed hugely at the splash, threw the mug the length of the table, snatched up the wine jar itself. Hoisting that, he spoke. "Tomorrow we send patrols to sweep the sundown side of the Enemy Mountains clear of Kossiars."

Conway embraced the surge of primitive excitement. He exulted in the rankness thrown off by forty savages sweating with bloodlust.

His breath jammed in his chest. His heart pounded.

Suddenly he pitched forward, almost went facedown on the table. Jerking erect, he was shocked to see he'd been pressing his spoon against the table so hard it was snapped off at the bowl.

Katallon understood. He roared approving laughter, then went on. "When the Kossiar coyotes are driven clear of the mountains, when we've looted their homes and taken their women and children, we move against Church Home. They say her fortress is invincible. Women's talk. We'll grind the walls and the highnosed bitches behind them into the dust. The treasures of all history will be yours."

The gathering erupted in war cries. The cloth wall behind Katallon drew open like a stage curtain. Slaves streamed out, bearing wooden platters. Conway recognized the pork, beef, game. Whole chickens. A turkey. More slaves brought round loaves of bread and butter. Steamed vegetables were delivered in copper cauldrons. Salt came in deep bowls, pepper—in the form of ground, dried chilies—in smaller bowls. A last condiment came in jars with wooden, holed stoppers. Conway sniffed at one and twitched it away from his nose. Moonpriest was watching, laughing. "Peppers in vinegar," he said. "Especially good on the tougher meat. Try it."

Conway shook his head. "I just want to eat the meat, not the fire that cooked it."

Fox heard the conversation. Draining his wine, he pulled the stopper from the vinegar and poured the fiery liquid in the empty mug. Whole peppers splashed merrily, the wet-shining crimson like tiny flames. Fox raised it in a silent toast, filled his mouth, swallowed. Chewing the remaining peppers, he winked at Conway.

Conway said, "You must be made of iron."

Fox chuckled, slapped his chest. "Mountain babies suckle this stuff when their mothers can't nurse."

Everyone laughed and hooted.

Conway lost track of the number of mugs of wine he emptied, the number of times he speared another slab of meat. The flash of knives was constant, as each man sank his teeth in the meat and sawed off that mouthful with his knife. Bones littered the floor. Conway was surprised at how quickly the vegetables disappeared, and staggered by the amount of salt that went on them. He thought back to the taboos and cautions of his diet before he entered the crèche, before he woke in this insane, savage world. A pounding sadness swamped him with despair. Clutching the table, he gulped more wine.

The trouble passed.

The sharp eye of Moonpriest registered the moment. The white-clad figure came closer, hovered, cloudlike. "Is something wrong, Matt?"

Conway shook his head, wondered at its unsteadiness. It took a moment for him to realize it was his entire body. His eyes wouldn't focus. Awareness that he was within a few swallows of being falling-down drunk almost shocked him back to sobriety.

He cursed himself, still keeping a fixed smile in place. Fox watched, eyes as bright and hot as his namesake's. Katallon was bull-like, massive, contemplative. A trickle of wine, like blood, ran down the left side of his chin.

Fox said, "He drinks too much. Not a man to lead my warriors."

"Windband warriors," Katallon said. Even drunk, Conway caught the poisonous glare Katallon sent Fox. Looking at Conway, Fox failed to see it.

Moonpriest said, "It's my wish he lead."

Conway struggled upright. Both hands flat on the table, he leaned into the hostility and scorn. "Make you a bet. Me, the dogs, Stormracer. Even wi'out the lightning, kill any three warr'ors you pick."

The words burbled off his thickened tongue. Conway grinned, too clever for them. He saw. Meanness sticking out of Fox and Katallon like spikes on cactus. They were baiting him. Why? Jones—whoops, watch that—Moonpriest looked nervous as a declawed cat. Conway said, "Not now. Drunk. Tomorrow afternoon. Gonna hurt in mornin'." He remembered to keep grinning foolishly.

Suddenly he was afraid. He admitted to himself his judgment was adrift in an alcoholic fog. He was sure of one thing only. He had to get away from this situation. Rising unsteadily, he said, "Too much to drink. Foolish. Go now."

Katallon glared. "The evening's just started. You offend."

Conway gestured helpless apology. "Leave, offend. Stay, talk too much, offend more."

Fox said, "The Otraz one says you killed Nar and Lolal."

Once again, shock cleared Conway's brain for a moment. The hostility of Katallon and Fox was explained. No one had ever mentioned Otraz before. Now Conway knew why. He also knew why Katallon and Fox were pleased to have him drunk. Conway said, "Otraz lies. I saw."

Moonpriest smirked. "I will test Conway. Loyalty is such an

481

absolute necessity, and such an uncertain thing. It's our new friend's word against Otraz's."

Katallon nodded. "Otraz is a good man."

Forcing himself erect, Conway said, "No. Lolal was a good man. Otraz stabbed him. And Nar. I take any Moonpriest test. Glad to."

Fox said, "That's fair, Katallon," and got another furious look for his effort. This time Fox saw it. He met it with an even stare. It was Fox who turned away, but even in his fuddled state, Conway was sure Fox's deference was a function of necessity. He had the feeling that when Fox decided to confront Katallon, there'd be no hesitation.

Sluggishly, Conway's mind plodded back to his own situation. If Moonpriest was in charge of the test, all was well.

Snapping his fingers, Katallon ordered a pair of slaves to help the wobbling Conway to his room.

Once in his own quarters, Conway put the wipe beside his bed and waved off the slaves. Settling heavily in his chair, he looked at himself in the mirror. "Fool," he muttered.

"At least you recognize the fact." The voice was dry, penetrating.

Conway jerked around in the chair, searching. This time Altanar was in plain view, smiling. "I thought better of you. Still, you escaped without insulting anyone."

"Drunk. Le' my guard down. Not worthy. Failed her." Conway hung his head. Tears of remorse burned his eyes.

"Her?" Quickened interest raised Altanar's tone.

From maudlin sadness, Conway leapt directly to angry defensiveness. "Not your business. Get out."

"Very well. I only wanted to help."

"Sorry. Sorry." Conway put his hands to his temples. "What want? My friend."

Dubiously, Altanar said, "Nothing. Not now. Perhaps not ever."

When Conway looked again, he wasn't sure Altanar had ever been there.

Still, when Conway collapsed on his bed, he only pretended to sleep. After faking a few snores, he rolled over, listening. Rising to a sitting position, he managed to stand. Fighting for balance at each step, he walked into the hall, where he practically fell forward from one support post to the next. Each post had a fat candle in a holder, and his impact sent mysterious, weird shadows up and down the passageway. He staggered outside with a great sigh of accomplishment.

Karda and Mikka crashed at the end of their restraining chains as if sheer delight could snap the links. Conway sat down clumsily to free the threaded bolts securing the collars. It seemed to take forever. The impatient dogs sandwiched him between them. Finishing at last, he led them into the tent.

Just outside his room, the dogs warned him of another human presence. Softly, Conway said, "Altanar?"

A strange voice said, "No. Not Altanar," and metal scraped against metal. Instantly, Conway ordered the dogs forward. The voice cried out, hushed, "Don't let them bite! Please."

"Step out here where I can see you. Who are you?" Conway held a post, straining to overcome the alcohol in his system.

A slave stepped forward, his status clear by the one-piece smock covering his body and the small-linked chain around his neck. He carried a tray with a pair of metal objects on it. As he moved, they slid, explaining the noise Conway mistook for a sword coming from its scabbard. The man was terribly scarred, a wound that ran from next to his right eye diagonally across his face. It sliced his nose, so it had healed with a twist. The welt drew the skin taut above the man's lip, leaving him with a permanent snarl.

The slave said, "You'll need this in the morning. There's tea in the pot. This metal thing covers a metal plate. There's bread and honey under it. You want me to leave it in the room?"

Conway nodded. The man darted inside. Conway followed, made his way to the bed and sat down wearily. From the door, the slave said, "I'm called Man Burning, of the Black Bear People. That's north of Buffalo Eater country. Windband raided a Buffalo Eater camp while I was there. Bad luck." He stepped closer, warily watching the dogs. When Conway looked up, Man Burning peered deep into his eyes. "Don't you remember me?"

"No. Don't know Black Bear country. Never been." The puckered scar was only inches away. Conway's blurring vision made it seem to move.

Man Burning went to the door. "I helped you when you left the dining room. Best you remember me. Man Burning. I belong to Katallon. He'd give me to you, if you ask. I can be helpful."

"Ever'body wants help poor Matt." Conway surrendered, fell back onto the bed.

Man Burning stepped forward, cocked his head to the side with a hand beside his ear. "I couldn't hear you."

Conway was already unconscious. Under the watchful approval of the dogs, the slave backed out. He was smiling.

CHAPTER 83

Morning was devastation. Conway's head throbbed, each expansion an explosion, each collapse a landslide. His stomach preferred up-and-down antics, leaping vertically to claw the back of his throat, only to plunge into a sodden mass behind his navel. His tongue felt like a composted corncob; it tasted worse.

The water left by Man Burning beckoned. Conway poured the mug full. The stream's purity, the look of diamond-cold relief, had his mouth working in unconscious anticipation. Closing on the mug with both hands, he raised it to his lips.

He drank greedily, refilled the mug, drained it again.

Karda nudged his elbow like a battering ram. Conway put an arm around the rough-coated neck, stretched with the other hand to twist Mikka's ears. She groaned happily. When Conway rose, he noticed her attention to the mug. He winced. "You're thirsty. I'll get you water."

Pulling on trousers he didn't remember taking off, Conway stepped out into the hallway. Man Burning was just coming around the corner. He smiled at Conway's appearance, but said nothing.

Conway said, "Where can I get a large basin or bowl of some kind? And water for my dogs."

"I'll take care of it. Do you need anything?"

Conway shook his head, stepped back inside his room, and went to the wooden chest. He lifted the metal cover resting on its tray. Rich, yeasty bread fumes wafted up, sent his stomach into acrobatic expressions of rejection. Conway turned away, gulped. Hunger drove him back. This time it was the honey that tried to finish him. Whatever flower the bees visited, it had punch. "I'm starving," he said, not caring that he was talking to himself or that he sounded like Dodoy on a bad day.

A bite of bread and honey went down hard, but it stayed. The next one was easier. Conway threw some bread chunks to the dogs. By the time Man Burning returned, the food was gone.

Conway greeted the man with a sheepish smile. "I think I'm going to live."

Man Burning's expression went flat. Avoiding meeting Conway's eyes, the slave chided, "You remember nothing of last night? The camp talks of nothing but the trial." He put the water down. The dogs looked at it anxiously, then turned to Conway. At his signal, they drank noisily.

Conway said, "There was something said about a trial. Something about Otraz."

"And you. Most say you killed Lolal and Nar."

"I told them Otraz did it. Exactly what's this trial like?"

"The people would prefer you fight Otraz. Katallon and Fox say you'll be tested by Moonpriest."

Conway put on a judicious look. "Moonpriest has no favorites."

The slave made no effort to hide his surprise. "I'd fight ten like Otraz before I'd be tested by Moonpriest. Many suspect Otraz. They say Moonpriest will favor you because you both control lightning."

The dogs rose in unison, facing the door, alert. A moment later a voice from outside called, "Conway. Matt Conway. Are you there?"

Fox's voice was unmistakable. Conway ordered the dogs to a far corner, then admitted the Mountain chief. On seeing Man Burning, Fox stopped instantly. Conway turned to see the slave on his knees, head bowed as if in prayer. Fox looked up at Conway. The difference in height was unremarkable, perhaps three inches, but it clearly irritated Fox, who said, "Come outside with me. There are ears in all these tents. And stink." He looked down at the unmoving Man Burning.

Gesturing at the wooden chest, Conway said, "I haven't washed up."

"Not necessary. Moonpriest ordered baths built. There's a special one. You'll be using it. I'll show you where it is. In fact, I'll join you. I haven't bathed today." He paused, then proudly said, "I do it because Moonpriest says it's good. All Mountain People wash clothes now. Wash hands, faces. Bathe almost every day. Not so much sickness."

Conway remembered Sylah's lament that preaching cleanliness to the Mountain People was like preaching softness to rocks.

Conway turned to pick up his wipe. When he faced the door again, Fox was standing over Man Burning. The slave's eyes fixed on Fox's moccasins. Fox said, "Have you heard anything that was spoken?"

"No."

"Remember that. The name of Matt Conway and my name must never come from your foul mouth. If you ever speak of us I'll reopen that ugly scar and peel your face. You understand?"

485

"Yes."

Bending to the man, Fox whispered in his ear, obscenely sibilant. "So leave, slave. Should I spur you with a sword?" Man Burning broke forward onto all fours, rising to his feet as he drove out the door. His bare feet thudded away on the carpeted hall floor.

"That wasn't necessary." Conway stroked the trigger guard of the wipe.

Fox strode out the door. Over his shoulder, he said, "Moonpriest told me how you and the others feel about slaves. If you had to deal with them, you'd know better. Keep them in fear, or they'll turn on you."

More resigned than angry, Conway said, "That's how the Kossiars felt. The ones who're still alive probably still do."

With the dogs padding along behind, the men strolled into the main camp. A dazzling early morning sun angled light through the tents, silvering the rising smoke of cooking fires, charging the colors of banners and shields festooning the tents. Chickens clucked and crowed unendingly. Horses whickered and whinnied. At the edges of the camp, jingling bells tracked the departure of herds of goats, sheep, horses, cattle, and long-necked, vaguely concerned llamas. Small boys in charge shouted back and forth. Craftsmen were setting up shop: leatherworkers, woodworkers, a cooper, two barbers, a potter, a smith. One block of tents belonged to an extended family of feltmakers, rope spinners, heavy cloth weavers, and tent-construction experts. Fox spoke darkly of how the group almost completely controlled tent manufacture within Windband.

Fox proudly pointed out shops where dried and pickled products beckoned. Later in the season, Fox assured Conway, the shelves would bow under the weight of fresh fruit and vegetables.

Stopping at the north end of Katallon's camp, Fox indicated a dove-gray tent on the bank of a stream. It was shaded within a grove of thick-trunked pines. "The bath tent. Most of the men you saw at Katallon's feast are allowed to use it. There are other tents for other people. Each camp has a similar arrangement."

"I understand the Dog People have something like that."

Eyes straight ahead, Fox said, "You served the Gan Moondark one. I'm sworn to kill him and his whole family. If you're his friend still, you're my enemy."

The man was deadly serious, but the entire situation was so bizarre Conway had to laugh. To his surprise, Fox joined him. Conway said, "Did you bring me out here to challenge me?"

Fox continued to laugh. He shook his head. "We have other things to concern us. I want you to ride with my men."

"You want the lightning weapon."

"We may grow to understand each other. I'm Moonpriest's right arm. I protect him. Against everyone. I expect you to help me."

Without further conversation, Fox led off for the tent. Conway kept up, with effort. Not that Fox was trying to be impressive. He simply moved, swiftly. Conway noted that without conscious thought, the Mountain warrior avoided things that would make noise underfoot. Conway had watched a leopard on a hunt. The cat moved the same way, feet placing themselves as if possessed of their own vision.

Walking through the pines around the bath tent, Conway's knees suddenly turned soft, uncontrollable. He reached out to steady himself, frightened. Not once while he was fleeing the Kossiars had his strange sickness troubled him. Now, there was no hope of disguising or denying it. Windband would kill him for bringing sickness.

Even as all that flashed across his mind, sadness twisted inside him. He heard the voices of childhood friends, dead for centuries. They laughed and shouted through his memory. Old, old songs, melodies he hadn't thought about since waking in the crèche, thundered in his ears. He visualized a store. Ice cream. *Sugar Bob's.* A gathering place when he was just a boy. Guys in letter jackets. Girls in bright clothes that flaunted. Laughter. Some forced, some faked, but most of all there was a gorgeous, ringing *carelessness.*

Vanilla.

Where did he get the smell of vanilla?

Conway surreptitiously dabbed at burning eyes.

His hand smelled of vanilla.

Fox chuckled. "The wine strikes again, eh? That's why I drink our good beer most of the time. Easier on a man."

Ignoring him, Conway sniffed at his hand. Leaning against the tree, he smelled it. Faintly, almost delicately, it gave off a tinge of vanilla. Enough to trigger a ferocious nostalgia.

Conway said, "Yes. The wine. My stomach."

"We'll cook it out of you," Fox said.

A little later Conway stood naked under a stream of water. There were no stalls in the room, but each bather had his own pull-cord that opened a door in an overhead trough. There was one temperature: frigid. Next, Fox showed Conway into a room

487

with a large shallow pool. Conway sped toward the sight of steam rising. "For soaking," Fox explained, following an already-settled Conway. "Wash in the shower, soak in the pool. Good for old joints, old scars."

Conway saw why Fox could appreciate the latter. He carried the marks of combat from his forehead down to one across the instep of his left foot.

The translucent gray cloth overhead carried a pattern of pale green leaves. The hard sun, passing through the material, was softened to a benign glow. Conway was reminded of Ola, where so many days had the same cloaked quality. About the time Conway thought he might dissolve with sheer relaxation, Fox climbed out, saying, "Now we get kneaded, like bread."

The third room of the tent featured cots, waist-high, sturdy. Conway turned from inspecting them and discovered two young women standing at the far door. Expressionless, they were unmoving, silent. Conway scrambled to hide his nudity, ignoring Fox's bellowing laughter. When he could, Fox said, "They're blind. Knew they'd startle you."

"Blind?"

"As stone. Only use blind slaves in here."

Fox flopped on a cot, snapped his fingers, called a name. The summoned girl moved to him quickly. She carried a basket. Conway noted jars. He assumed they held creams and salves. She had small cloths, as well. He moved to a cot several feet from Fox. Closing his eyes, he refused to acknowledge that the second girl was beside him, going about her business.

Fox droned about the need for a particularly swift, light cavalry to clear the western slopes of the Enemy Mountains. He spoke of the number of arrows each man should carry, the requirements for food, water, fresh horses. Conway listened, responded on cue with monosyllables. In time, Fox wearied of his own voice and stopped.

Shortly after that, the girl's voice brushed Conway's hearing. For a moment, he wasn't sure she'd spoken, and he raised his head. She pushed it back down. "Please." She was begging. "Can I talk to you?"

Her hand was on the back of his head. He nodded. She went on. "You're the Matt Conway one? The White Thunder?"

He nodded again. A little confidence lightened the girl's voice. "You were with the Flower. When you saved the children. The Smalls."

Surprised, Conway twisted to face her. Her hand stilled his

488

question before he could speak. Conway risked a look at Fox. The warrior dozed. Conway patted the hand of his own attendant. She continued, "I am—was—a Small. All know what you did for us."

"Nomads captured you?"

"Yes." Her head lifted slightly, as though the shuttered eyes searched back in time to a better place. "Raiders attacked our village. We fought. Then the nomads came. They killed the raiders. We came out to thank the nomads, and learned we'd exchanged the wolf for the tiger. Our village, my people, are all gone."

"You survived. How many others?"

"Twelve. Women, children. All slaves now. They brought us here, told us we must swear loyalty to Moonpriest."

"You did the right thing. You're still alive. Hope only ends with death."

Her smile was like a fissure in ivory, an ugly break that marred a lovely surface. "I was the first one asked to swear, being the oldest. You're right, Matt Conway; I did the right thing. I refused Moonpriest and his dark worship."

Conway turned away from the change in her. He grabbed his clothes, started to dress. More gently than ever, her lips almost touching his ear, she said, "Can you help us, Matt Conway? There are still seven of us captives alive. Some say Katallon fears Moonpriest, that he's jealous of Moonpriest's warrior, the Fox one you came with. You helped the Rose Priestess Sylah, and my people, too. Please, if Katallon and Moonpriest fight, help us escape."

Conway stood, pulled on his trousers. "I can't. Things will get better. Look, you rejected Moondance, and they didn't kill you. I wish you were still free, didn't have to work here, but you haven't been punished all that harshly."

She bent, felt for her basket of supplies. Rising again, she reached tentatively to touch Conway's chest. She said, "I understand. You have your own path. I hoped ... Never mind. But know this, before you judge my punishment. Before I spurned Moondance, my eyes were brown. And I could see."

Conway was still trying to catch his breath when she reached the door, walked through it, and disappeared.

Fox stirred on his cot. Conway called harshly to him, told him he wanted to get back to the tent. Amiably, still drowsy, Fox hurried with his dressing. Once Conway was outside again, he wanted to go back and stand under the shower, wished it could wash away the memory of the girl's words.

There would be no time for that, however. Not with Katallon

thundering down on them, his face drawn taut in fierce amusement. Karda and Mikka took place beside Conway.

Katallon dismissed Fox with a glance. To Conway, he said, "It's good you're clean and prepared to face the truth. The test is now. You and Otraz."

CHAPTER 84

The external walls of Moonpriest's tent were a double thickness of heavy felt. The outer layer of white reflected heat. Flaps on the roof permitted the quick creation of scoops to catch any passing breeze. Others acted as heat exhausts. The lower edge was rolled up ankle-high; cool air flowed in and rose as it heated, generating a draft. The interior enjoyed a soft luminescence that seemed to multiply where it picked out the many silver moon disks decorating the walls.

Conway stood alone in a room he estimated to be twenty feet square. Muffled crowd sounds filtered through the cloth walls.

The various clans and tribes of Windband were gathering.

A test. Another chance to prove himself.

To whom? More than that, why?

Conway knew killing had nothing to do with manhood. What, then, was twisting him so? When he'd rescued Nalatan, shot the raiders like so many paper targets, he'd exulted in that raw, almost omniscient power. Men had tumbled and fallen in the distance, more symbols than creatures of flesh and blood.

Now he stood in the flowing, changing light of this cult-heart and felt a savage, frightening eagerness. He wanted Otraz close. He wanted to see his face when death beckoned. He wanted to feel his own life swaying on balance.

Life wasn't so hollow for him that it had no value, Conway told himself. The core was rotten, with Tee gone, but the loss of her was the very thing that meant he had to live.

Lanta.

He thought of her and was angry with himself, because he'd let himself forget for a while that she was responsible. And, behind her, the brooding black hypocrisy of Church. He resolved to be more attentive to those facts. It was shameful that he'd stop blaming her, even under the influence of this trial's stress.

A sighing movement broke Conway's introspection. Moonpriest

swept into the room past a flap held aloft by a slave dressed in white blouse and loose trousers. A black diagonal stripe ran from the man's right shoulder to left hip, where another struck back across from hip to calf. When the slave dropped the flap, turning to leave, Conway noted that the pattern was repeated on the back of his clothes.

Moonpriest continued to wear his white, silver-streaked robe and his white turban. He smiled greeting. Tight, twisted, the expression shrieked of secret, knowing amusement.

The simple act of striding into the light-sodden room and flashing that suggestive smile put fear in Conway. He fought a need to swallow, to cough.

Pacing, keeping a distance of perhaps eight feet, Moonpriest moved in a measured semicircle. He said, "Things are revealed to me. Not everything. My mother won't let me fail, but she tests me, Matt. It wears me down. You can't imagine. Mother is as cruelly demanding as she is lovingly generous. The more you know of her, the more you'll love her. You'll see. One day, you and all the truly loyal will meet her." He stopped then, gazing skyward, beatific. "Paradise. Eternal life."

Suddenly suspicious, Moonpriest bent forward aggressively. "Are you loyal to me?"

"What? Of course."

Conway's minute pause didn't go unnoticed. Moonpriest's eyes narrowed. "You must be sure, Matt. I sense doubt or courage or thirst—anything and everything—in other men as easily as they sense it in themselves. Better, actually. Those who would trick me, I strike down. Above all, I'm compassionate. My mission can't afford interference from trifling people, however. I am steel in my resolve. Those who do not support me completely are doomed. It is the way."

Conway shivered. This wasn't combat, life and death. This was insanity. No logic, no reason. One survived as one could. "I sought you out, Moonpriest. I came to be with you."

Moonpriest shook his head. A pitying, disappointed smile worked his lips. He shook his head. "You came to use me, Matt. But now you've seen. Not everything. Enough. I hope. Your head jangles with questions; it hurts me to hear you think, it truly does." He stopped in front of Conway, extended a slow, languorous hand. Conway had the feeling it stalked him. It settled delicately onto his sleeve. "Questions are good. The sign of a good, working mind. I want that more than your weapons. In the world of my vision, there will be no need for weapons. Peace. Harmony.

Obedience." The hand snapped back, startling Conway. "We must be determined. Mercy is for those who earn it."

The swell of sound beyond the walls reminded Conway that he faced a trial out there, as well. He gestured at it. "I told the truth about Otraz. He killed the other men. If I must, I'll kill him. I hope that won't make trouble."

Moonpriest said, "I believe you. Wait here for Fox and Katallon. Remember, what is truly important is that my mother must be satisfied that you're worthy. Otraz has served me well. I can't allow one small failure to cheat him of his place beside me, and yet he must be punished if he's lied to me."

Moonpriest stopped at the door, turning for one last word. "You see the penalties? I was so happy to discover my godhood. Mortal foolishness. How I envy you. Godhood is grueling. I, who once feared death, now long to rest my burden. You appreciate the irony. No one else here can imagine it. For that alone, I want you with me."

The curtain slid silently across his exit. The last words hovered in the luminous air of the room.

Outside, Conway heard the braying of deep-throated horns. A prolonged cheer announced Moonpriest's appearance among his people. When that uproar quieted, the singing began. Surprisingly beautiful, the voices of Windband lofted a hymn of praise. It failed to soothe Conway.

Katallon threw aside the entry panel. Expressionless, he said, "Come," and left. Conway hurried after.

The dogs, waiting at the front entrance, rose to take position beside their master. Fox brought up the rear.

The crowd parted ahead of Katallon. For a moment Conway was surprised by the dire respect shown the man until it occurred to him that Katallon once ruled Windband alone. Conway had already fallen into an acceptance that Moonpriest controlled the nomads. Now he saw that was wrong. As the girl at the baths said, Katallon was the leader, a man of men. Moonpriest, as a god, held the power of life *after* death.

Then Conway saw Katallon look at Moonpriest. And turn away. For the briefest instant, Katallon's face revealed anguish and hatred.

The ramifications of that instant were overwhelming.

There was no time to consider them. They were moving to position directly in front of Moonpriest, who said, "Place the dogs and your weapons over there."

Conway moved to obey, then checked. Iron stakes, thick as leg bones, were driven into the ground at the edge of the crowd. Chain wrapped around the stakes. Conway said, "I won't chain them. They'll stay where I tell them."

Fox said, "Not if they think you're in danger. I know your animals of old. Chain them."

Conway opened his mouth to argue, and Katallon said, "Look around at all the strung bows. Chain the dogs now, or the test is finished. So are you."

Moonpriest was impassive, unreadable.

Slowly, skin crawling with the fact of his betrayal, Conway led the dogs to the posts, put down his armament, and tied the chain in ugly knots around their unresisting necks. They lay down on order, looking at him uncomprehendingly. As he left, they whined.

Behind Conway, a voice from the crowd shouted, "Fail, you lying piece of dung. Your dogs will be saddle furs for my sons."

Conway flinched, refused to turn. From the corner of his eye, to his right, he saw Otraz step away from the crowd. A cheer rose. It made Conway feel better to note that the crowd's enthusiasm didn't change the fright on Otraz's face. They arrived in front of Moonpriest together. Fox and Katallon were gone.

A horn blew, brazen, animal-like. Silence came over the crowd.

Moonpriest's sonorous voice projected over the throng. "Otraz is accused of turning against Windband and killing two of us. His accuser is a man I know of old, one who rode through many dangers to join us. If this were an ordinary crime, Katallon would judge. Otraz is no ordinary man. He has served me and my mother, as well as Katallon. Because I have not seen the Conway one for many moons, it's possible he's not the man I remember. Men change. The change can bring joy. Or sadness. So Katallon agrees to this test. If Otraz dies, we will know of his guilt. Still, he will be forgiven by me, blessed, to reside with my mother until the day we are all reunited. If Conway dies, we will know of his guilt. He will stand revealed as a liar and a murderer. My mother will have rejected him in this world. And in the Land Beyond."

The last resonated, thundered at the crowd. They cringed. Then sprang back, alive with eagerness.

Karda barked angrily. Chain clattered against steel.

Moonpriest extended his arms upward, looked to the sky. Gradually, he pulled his hands back, rested them at his breast. Beside Conway, Otraz mumbled. By straining, Conway could see him without turning away from Moonpriest. The warrior was palled with a fear that drew back his teeth in a rictus grin. Conway barely got his full attention back to Moonpriest in time to see him thrust his hands inside his robe.

The hands reappeared holding twin rattlesnakes.

Conway couldn't breathe.

Otraz's mumbling grew louder, faster. Conway heard "please" and "sorry." Then Conway had attention for nothing but the weaving, coiling snakes.

A chant started in the crowd. Stately, it spoke of truth and honor, of obedience. The fury of Conway's dogs ripped through it.

Tongues darting, the thick bodies of the snakes wrapped around Moonpriest's arms. He extended them toward Conway and Otraz, simultaneously advancing a full step. In concert, the snakes slid forward. Now at full reach, Moonpriest's hands, palms up, were a mere foot in front of the men.

Conway stared. He couldn't stop shaking, but he knew better than to move. The snake in front of him rose, rattling, its head at his eye level. The coarse scales seemed as large as roof shingles, the eyes bigger than plates. Dry, earthen colors made the glistening tongue seem even brighter by comparison, as though it glowed of itself. Brown, tan, black, the camouflaging patterns seemed to be running together as the deadly, questing head swung back and forth.

Otraz spoke. "Moonpriest." The word came with a stuttering explosiveness. "Your servants have spared me. This man lies. Send me back to my people. Please."

Both snakes struck. Conway wasn't sure he'd seen anything at all until Otraz screamed and staggered backward.

S-curved, the reptiles concentrated on Conway. In unison, rattling, tongues darting, they fixed diamond-hard eyes on his face and waited. Waited.

Moonpriest's arms were wearying. They trembled. The triangular, poisonous heads irritably edged forward. The pitch of the rattling rose noticeably.

Smoothly, swiftly, the snake directly in front of Conway reversed itself, sliding across its own body, disappearing back inside Moonpriest's robe. The second, after a slight hesitation, slipped in behind its twin.

Conway had to look. He turned away from Moonpriest's unwavering eyes to see Otraz clawing at two holes just below his right jaw, two more at the left temple. The stricken man staggered toward the crowd. A few steps short of the straining, backing front rank, he dropped to his knees. Imploring, he reached out. Those he sought stampeded like cattle.

The dying man painfully turned to face Moonpriest. Already his wounds were dark, swollen. Conway imagined the poison behind that blue-black discoloration, seizing the blood, turning it into a clotted mass.

Conway turned away, and found himself caught by Moonpriest's eyes. Moonpriest smiled. The same earlier, covert amusement lurked behind it. Moonpriest said, "You have been fairly tried before my mother, and she declares you innocent." He raised his arms, gesturing the rumbling crowd to silence. When the dogs continued to snarl and bark their rage, Conway managed to silence them. That left only Otraz, gasping and choking. Moonpriest ignored the disturbance. In the practiced, fluid voice, he intoned, "Otraz is now one of my brothers in the moon. My mother saw through his lies, so he is punished, but she grants him eternal life with me. He waits in paradise for all of us. Cheer for Otraz!"

The gathered hundreds cheered. Otraz writhed, the strangled whine of his breathing barely audible by then.

Moonpriest said, "Go to your dogs."

Conway rushed to them. Disregarding the wounds on their necks where the chains had bitten into the flesh, they leapt to lick his face, delirious with joy. On examination, the cuts weren't serious. That did little to relieve Conway's distress. Reclaiming his weapons, he ordered the dogs to position.

A heavy hand clamped on his elbow. Whirling, Conway pulled free of the grip, belatedly recognizing Katallon. The burly chief said, "Easy. The danger's past. I only want to talk."

Katallon moved away from the crowd. Moonpriest was nowhere to be seen. Conway followed, then said, "What do we have to say to each other?"

The nomad chief stroked his chin, studying Conway. He gestured at where Otraz still twitched feebly. "We of Windband believe some men live in the circle of a curse, the way some wasps live in small, dark burrows. The mother wasp puts a live spider in there, and lays an egg on it. I've seen this with my own eyes. The egg hatches, you understand? It's a worm. The spider's not dead, but it can't move. The worm eats it. Alive. We believe some men are like that wasp's egg. They eat the life of others. Without even understanding. Death seems to stand close to you, Matt Conway. First two of my warriors. Then Otraz. And the girl."

"Girl?"

"At the baths. The Small who massaged you. Children found her in the river. She drowned herself."

BOOK III

THE WAY
OF DISCOVERY

CHAPTER 85

Sylah reined in Copper and gazed out over a scene that was as heartbreaking as it was spectacular. After more than a moon of furtive, frightened travel through the ravaged lands of Kos, this different vision beckoned. In the unsullied air of a perfect day, the ragged crags and peaks of the Dry extended eastward as far as she could see.

Lost in that shimmering distance was the end of her quest.

The enormity of it was appalling. Crumpled, broken land in an unending variety of grays, washed with the softest of blues and purples, rose and fell in savage obstacle to her dreams. The fierce landscape was her enemy as surely as any human. The worst of it was, it was beautiful. She quailed at the thought of traversing those sere valleys, scaling those scorching slab-sided mountains, yet was awed and drawn by their cruel splendor.

Copper's hooves struck a clattering challenge of their own on the rocky ground of the pass. Sylah laughed. Alone, faced by terrain that daunted the hardiest, she was suddenly bursting with renewed purpose.

This place—here, now—was end and beginning.

She had allowed herself to dream of empire, of alliances and power balances. Those were not the stuff of her life. Pursuing such golden butterflies had led her away from her true goal.

She'd been tested, and proven weaker than her worst fears. She had erred. Grievously. Tee and Conway must be presumed dead. Only the One in All could know if Wal and his crew still survived on their trek north to Ola. Finding the Door wouldn't help any of them. It wouldn't help her overcome the remorse she knew would eat at her for the rest of her days.

But she hadn't failed. The quest continued, the bitter lessons of adversity well learned.

Primary was her understanding of what happened to those who sought power. The search made them ruthless; the finding made them vicious. She must be aware of the danger. The Door would cloak her in power. Not like the Chair or the Harvester. Instinct told her that what she sought would entail more responsibility than privilege, more duty than liberty.

Looking into the teeth of a land that dared her to leave the cool heights and plenty of the mountains, Sylah exulted at the onrushing contest.

Again, she laughed. It was a sound of joy, of fear, of delight, of desperation. She felt she could reach out with both hands and grasp the very substance of her own life.

She was quiet by the time Tate and Dodoy drew abreast of her, followed by Lanta and the infant Jessak. Lanta was also leading the most recent goat they'd stolen to provide the milk Jessak needed. It was a rangy, long-legged beast, its black coat splotched with white. So far, it had proven to be a surprisingly enduring traveler. Two others before it had been cut loose in precipitate retreats forced by large parties of roaming raiders.

Jessak rode strapped in a basket. He was lashed to the side of Lanta's horse for the present. The women traded him off. Every time Sylah handled him, she marveled at the tenacity of life in the tiny, helpless body. Both fists worked now, both arms appeared sound. In spite of his excessive size at birth, he seemed only slightly larger than average, further proof that his original size was more a condition than a bloodline result. And he was a good baby. If anything, he was abnormally quiet.

Nalatan, routinely assigned to rear guard, was excused from carrying the boy. Too often on their race away from the wolflike packs of Kossiars and the furious excesses of the freed slaves it had only been Nalatan's skills that kept them alive. They teased him mercilessly about shirking his duty when it came to Jessak. He took it in flustered good nature. He was as uncomfortable dealing with the infant as only a male can be, and his gratitude at being spared that job was pathetically obvious. Nevertheless, the truth underlying the jokes made him sweat.

As he rode up to join the rest, his attention was more closely directed north and west. He gestured sharply. "The Kossiar I questioned a few days back said the nomad camp was north and east of the Everchanging Lake. It's not that far away. The normal route from Church Home to Kos goes through that country."

"Which way is this Church Home?" Tate asked. Her dogs were nowhere in sight. Her horse carried a nasty scar on its chest, with two lesser, better healed slashes on its rump.

Nalatan pointed north and east. Anticipating her next question, he darted a pointed glance at the baby. "We'll have to travel fast. Distance and time aren't as great a problem as water and horses."

Lanta said, "What about the nomads? They'll want to stop us."

Nalatan's grin was apologetic. "I was going to let that go."

Sylah said, "You were going to 'forget' what the Harvester or the Chair can send after us, as well?"

"I didn't see any point in bringing it up. Our security is speed. We must hurry."

"They'll be looking for us." Dodoy was more gaunt than ever. He slumped in his saddle. "All of them. They'll make us slaves."

Tate worked her horse backward to be next to the boy, saying, "No one's going to catch us, no one's going to hurt us."

Dodoy's lower lip stuck out. "Sylah said she wanted to find the Door. I told her before we met him"—he pointed at Nalatan, as if accusing him of something—"there's a river. There's no river in the Dry. This is the wrong place. We have to go back to Gan Moondark. We were safe with him."

The comment rankled Sylah more than she dared admit. She was as capable of fighting her way through to a goal as any man. She couldn't use a sword or bow like them. She had to be more clever. And determined.

What must be borne, grasp.

The Door was her destiny. Hers to seek and to find.

Nalatan said, "As soon as we find a good campsite, I think you should all settle in. I'll ride ahead and scout. If I can, I'll get some packhorses."

Tate said, "Is that safe? I mean, what if the nomads have penetrated this far south? Are the people who live around here friendly?"

Sylah suffered for Nalatan when she saw the way the proud, hard warrior snatched at the crumbs of Tate's expressed concern. Pretending no more than a normal interest in the question, Nalatan answered, "I'll be careful. I'll be gone four days, possibly six. The people of the Dry can be very hard to find. Farther south, it's best not to find them at all."

Sylah asked, "They're all hostile?"

"Always. Fortunately, they're also poor." Nalatan jingled a sack of Kossiar coin. "This should get us horses and water. Without

501

coin, or something else they want, we'll have to steal water, or fight for it."

"Sounds like a great trip," Tate said. "This Church Home place must be wonderful."

"It is." Nalatan was perfectly serious.

"We should be looking for a campsite," Sylah said. "One can smell the heat from the Dry all the way up here. A few days to build up our strength won't be wasted." Having spoken, she urged Copper forward. A movement down the slope caught her eye. Tanno was patrolling ahead.

In the distance, a leopard coughed, long and loud, a noise like a huge, dull saw. Startled, Sylah searched anxiously. Leopards made no noise, usually, and anything unusual was to be feared.

Nalatan, watchful as ever, caught her momentary concern. He said, "That's a mating call. We can be pretty sure he's not interested in us just now."

She forced a smile while the thought of the cat crying for a mate transformed into memories of the night on the roof with the Chair.

Mindlessness.

No matter how often she told herself that she would never have betrayed her husband, she was forced to remember that fate made the final decision, not herself. She was pushing the Chair away when it ended. If he'd used his strength, there was little she could have done.

That wasn't betrayal, deceit.

But what did she call being there, how did she explain to herself that she deluded herself? Endangered herself and her quest?

There should have been no danger. An acid taste of guilt hung in her mouth. She clenched her teeth on it, spat it out.

Another layer of steel reinforced her resolve to succeed.

They found their way to a secluded level place, well shaded, with a clear spring only a short distance away. A welter of tracks indicated game—deer, goats, some wildcows—as well as leopard and one huge bear. The dogs stalked around the water stiff-legged, growling.

"Keep your dogs with you at night," Nalatan warned Tate. "There's no sense exposing them to leopards or that bear unless it's necessary. I think you should sleep over there, against those rocks. We'll cut logs for a lean-to, with an adjoining pen for the goat. Keep a fire going. You'll be all right."

"Promise?" Tate's humor was a bit shaky.

Nalatan grinned. "When the night hunters learn the Black Lightning's here, they'll run for the valleys."

She grinned back at him. "If there's any footracing to be done, you just keep those clumsy animals out of my way, and you'll see some *speed*."

Even Dodoy found that amusing. The work of setting up camp went smoothly.

The night passed quietly. The lean-to, with its cover of the apparently indestructible cloth from Ola, provided quite adequate shelter. Nalatan slept just outside. The dogs curled up in the doorway.

The following morning, as soon as he'd completed his sun-greeting prayers, Nalatan left.

Tate moped around the spring most of the morning, irritated that she worried about him too much. At first she told herself she missed him because he was the group's primary protection. That lie stung, and she substituted one that said it was natural to worry about such a fine friend. When she admitted why she was so afraid for him, the familiar, forbidden warmth returned. She jerked awkwardly to her feet, hurrying back to the protective comradeship of the other women.

Darkness brought worse times. Awake, when her mind sparked with forbidden imaginings, she could consciously extinguish them. Asleep, dreams came in unending, inescapable parade. She woke from them each time with a start and a small, anxious cry that brought her companions to attentive wakefulness. Tate, confused and disoriented by the reality of the dreams, could only mutter apologies and urge them to go back to sleep.

Jessak seemed to sense the tension around him. He fretted far more than usual, so that when Tate wasn't waking the other women, the baby was.

In the morning, when her friends returned from their prayers and washup bleary-eyed and wan, Tate was all the more chagrined.

Sylah and Lanta busied themselves working on their medical kits. When Dodoy saw Tate inspecting her badly frayed and worn reins, he showed her how to cut out the damaged sections and sew in patches. That done, he wandered off to practice with his chain axe. He attacked the tree trunks as if in battle for his life. Afterward, he carefully cleaned off the resin, then oiled and sharpened the blade.

Dodoy's preoccupation with the weapon was another source of anxiety for Tate. In her hope that he'd lead her to a place where she'd be among others who shared at least some of her ancestry, she imagined a society that probably didn't exist. She'd pictured a happy, peaceful culture.

On the escape they passed ruined villages, burned farms. Survivors. Sick, wounded, the human wreckage of the revolt saw salvation in Sylah and Lanta. The people held up injured limbs, bared wounds, displayed their infected children. The Healers did what they could. Nalatan and herself stood guard and chafed.

Some survivors attacked. Moondancers. Tate noted early on that the group was safer from ambush when they rode near abandoned buildings. It took a few days for her to understand why. They came across a group of seventeen former slaves huddled in the burned-out shell of a luxurious estate. All were dead or dying of disease. Tate realized then that plague must follow conflict, and where man lived in greatest concentration, sickness thrived.

Tate also began to seriously wonder why Sylah and Lanta used some medical terms that should have died hundreds of years ago, while their idea of germ theory was "unseens." Their medical knowledge was more stunted than simply deficient, as if their abilities were tailored to the tools available in their environment. Even in those areas where they were weakest, there was no attempt to invoke multiple deities or charms. Tate asked herself how their knowledge survived with near universality throughout Church, while in all other communities even the simplest arithmetic and reading were considered evil and dangerous.

Everything was so confused. This world was all violence and struggle. The idealized land of her hopes couldn't exist, Tate knew. She had to try, nevertheless.

When the word *obsession* picked at her mind, she rejected it. She knew her friends were all troubled by her restlessness. She wanted desperately to talk to the women about her dilemma, but how could they understand? They had no cultural or racial constraints built into their need for a mate. What could she tell two women of this world about the necessity to maintain an ethnic existence?

Over a smokeless fire of carefully selected dry branches, Sylah baked cornbread cakes and stewed the last of the dried beef. When the meal was done, she suggested they explore the surrounding area, specifically hunting for deer horns.

"Deer horns? Are you going to make buttons or something?" Tate asked.

Sylah shook her head. "We're going to grind them up, steep them. I'll make awakener."

Tate decided to wait and see what that meant.

Lanta stayed in camp with Jessak and Dodoy. Tate enjoyed getting out with Sylah and the dogs. They found several partial sets of antlers. Most had been nibbled away by mice.

On their return, Sylah set everyone to work grinding horn shavings to a fine powder. Little by little, the off-white pile going into the metal pot grew. When she had enough, Sylah added water and heated the mixture almost to boiling, then set it aside.

"Why are we doing this?" Tate said. "I know mice eat the horn. We're not going to drink that, are we?"

Lanta and Sylah both laughed. Sylah said, "The Dry's going to be very difficult, you see? A few drops of awakener in drinking water is stimulating."

Tate was dubious. "Stimulating? Deer horn soup?" She bent to sniff the pot. She straightened immediately, shocked. "What in the world? That's *ammonia*."

Sylah cocked her head to the side. "An odd word. How was it? Ah-mo-nya? Is that what you call it?"

Stunned, Tate shook her head. "That's it. We call it that. Always did. Ammonia. You made it from a deer horn. What will they think of next?"

"Next? All I can make with deerhorn is awakener. Did you expect something else, too?"

Tate threw her hands in the air, turned away from the fire. "Plutonium, at least." She whirled. "Never mind. An idle thought." She wandered off, talking to herself.

Sylah and Lanta looked at each other, made faces expressing resignation. Then they returned to the housework of the camp.

It was Tate's turn to feed the baby. As she held him, she admired once again the feeding device Sylah created. The container was a small ceramic bottle, which was carefully cleaned and boiled before each use. The end, tied off with rawhide, was a cone-shaped soft leather nipple. Its holes were minuscule, the size of porcupine quill-tips. Sylah insisted that the leather also be cleaned faithfully. Jessak made hard work of sucking on something so alien, but he did it. He seemed to understand he was being deprived of a normal breast, and he attacked his meals with astonishing determination, if not outright resentment. His feedings and burpings were times of fascination and involvement. Despite all the hardships and dangers of the escape, Jessak was well launched into being spoiled.

Feeding him was Tate's most peaceful time. Her concerns about Nalatan and the power of his attraction were forgotten. Her dogs

505

lay beside her where she sat with her back against the pole wall of their shelter. Oshu stirred, pressing harder against her mistress, and sighed, a confiding, contented sound.

Not even the dogs were aware of the massive beast above them, limping from cover to cover with a stealth unbelievable for something so large. When it raised its striped-mask face to test the scent of the group huddled in their camp, it snarled in silent grimace. It twitched its tail, the snarl diminishing in repetitive jerks.

The tiger was angry. First the impertinent leopard and its intended mate invaded hunting ground it was just claiming for itself. The pair saw the tiger's stalk and fled. Now there was this disturbance. Horses. Dogs. Even a goat. The tiger growled softly; goat was a delicacy. Easily killed.

So were humans.

CHAPTER 86

Tanno and Oshu quickly discovered that the tiger was in the area. Patrolling with Tate they fanned out away from her with visible reluctance. Dodoy, swinging his chain axe like some macabre toy, sneered and called them fat and lazy. Tate tolerated the carping until her sense of fair play required comment. "Stop it. The dogs kept us warned for almost two moons when everyone was trying to kill us. Don't criticize so much. It's irritating."

The boy's face closed.

Soon the animals stopped. The forest was silent. No birds called. No breeze stirred the trees.

Tate and Dodoy made their way to the ground seep where the dogs waited. Water oozed to the surface, not strong enough to create an actual spring, but sufficient to make mud for several yards downhill. The prints were huge. Tate's skin crawled. She traced the tracks.

The tiger had stopped at the limit of the wet ground. Downhill from that point, perhaps twenty feet away, was a boulder. Tate read how the cat tested the footing, then leaped to the sun-baked rock. It was as if the animal deliberately walked through the mud to be sure its presence was noted. Then, to show off its strength, it vaulted to the boulder.

The prints were still filling with water. Tate hurried to the rock. Moisture remained where the cat landed.

There were no unsupervised tigers in the world she'd left behind, but people made movies about the ancient days when such beasts roamed free. There were even books about such things. They emphasized that tigers rarely hunted man, unless they were so old or crippled they needed easier prey. Re-examining the tracks, Tate discovered a malformation of one hind foot.

Back at the camp, telling the other women what she'd seen, Tate finished by saying, "We'll have to be careful, but I doubt if he's a menace."

Sylah said, "No one goes anywhere alone or unarmed. No more night patrols for the dogs. I want them close so they can warn us. We can protect them, and they us. I don't think you want to match them against a tiger, Donnacee."

Nodding agreement, Tate extended a hand to rest on Oshu's back.

That night Tate opened their last bottle of wine, and was dismayed to find it was vinegar. Oddly, Sylah was delighted. Tate's own reaction was as sour as the liquid. "What's so wonderful? It wasn't very good wine, but it beat swill." She moved to pitch out what was left in her mug, and Sylah grabbed her arm. "We need that."

"Blah." Tate made a face.

Smugly, Sylah said, "Wait until morning. I'll show you."

True to her word, Sylah called to Tate as soon as she'd finished milking the goat. "Come see," she said.

Tate watched skeptically as Sylah placed the copper pot holding all but Jessak's share of the milk on the fire. After constant stirring and several finger-dipping tests, Sylah said, "You know how much milk we've wasted because Jessak doesn't need it all."

"So how's heating it going to help?"

With a teasing smile, Sylah held hands apart a bit more than shoulder width. "I'll need a piece of cloth about so square. Is that white cotton blouse of yours clean?"

Tate sniffed. "I wouldn't pack it away dirty, and I'd hardly wear white while we're trying to hide from everybody in the world." Moving away, she asked over her shoulder, "What're you going to do to it?"

"And some cord," Sylah said. "Rawhide's as good as anything else."

Tate said, "You're enjoying your little mystery, aren't you?" when she handed over the articles.

Laughing, Sylah tested the heat of the milk once more. Then she took the pot off the fire and opened the bottle of vinegar.

507

Pouring a thin stream into the heated milk while stirring, she said, "Watch."

"It's going to curdle. Even I know that."

"Exactly. And that means cheese. No more wasted milk. At least, not until we use up our vinegar."

Surprisingly quickly, the curd separated. Sylah lined another pot with Tate's blouse and poured in the mix, wringing loud dismay from the owner. Sylah assured her everything would wash out.

Dodoy was detailed to hang the pendulous sack from a tree limb over the original pot to catch the dripping whey.

"Don't you have to age that stuff?" Tate asked.

"It'll be ready in an hour. We'll eat it tonight."

"Just like that? Yummy."

"Oh, you. You'll like it. We can cut it up and fry it, use it in soup. It's good for you. Best, it'll stretch out our meat supply. We won't have to go out there to set so many snares."

"The tiger." Tate nodded thoughtfully. "I'd forgotten him. I feel a terrible craving for cheese."

Sylah laughed. "Taste's a peculiar thing, isn't it?"

The day passed peacefully until late afternoon. They ate before dusk, as usual, unwilling to chance a night fire. They were cleaning up when the goat scented the tiger and bleated anxiously. The women whispered the stalker's name in chorus, instinctively identifying the threat. The dogs crowded close to Tate, hackles up, threatening the deep-shadowed forest.

Tate moved forward, wipe in hand. "I'll get the goat. Jessak has to have that milk. The tiger won't come after her if she's here with us."

Sylah's voice was tremulous. "It may be out there, just waiting." Her gesture was a soft, fluttery thing. "This can't be happening. We've come so far, escaped so much. Now this. What can we do?"

For a long moment, her companions were struck dumb. A crack in Sylah's resolve was incomprehensible. They stared. Tate felt the poison of despair surge in her own heart. Forcing confidence, she pretended Sylah's question was routine. "We can do what we have to do. You said it yourself: We've come so far. No cat's going to ruin that."

Sylah seemed not to hear. Wide, wild eyes searched the lowering dark.

The goat erupted into a frenzy of fear, choking on its tether, squalling terror. Tate hurried around the corner of the rock formation, her dogs racing ahead. She stopped immediately at the sight

508

of the crouched, snarling thing facing her and the raging dogs. Her command to Tanno and Oshu to fall back was a scream, a plea.

The tiger's tail thrashed. Its head was extended, low to the ground. Bent legs tucked in tight to the body. They pistoned slowly, almost delicately.

Fascination overrode fright in Tate's mind for a moment, and she imagined the huge cat savoring the strength of its own muscle and sinew. She looked into its eyes, saw nothing but savage, free purpose. For that merest fraction of time, she envied the beast.

The dogs gave ground. Every step allowed their enemy greater access to their master. Shrill frustration broke through their sustained barking.

The tiger lurched forward perhaps a third of its body length. It was still settling, intent on Tate, when Oshu broke under the strain. Her attacking growl rose to a ululating scream.

Rising on his haunches, the tiger met Oshu's charge with forelegs extended out to the sides, as if balancing. Oshu held her attack low, slashed at her foe's flank. The tiger pivoted. Oshu's jaws clamped down on soft flesh just below the rib cage. The tiger roared pain and rage.

A huge, taloned right paw hit Oshu directly behind the ear. The left ripped open her chest. Dropping forward, the cat crushed the dog's backbone with one shaking, snapping bite.

In the same movement, it charged a screaming, horrified Tate. Tanno bolted at the airborne tiger.

Tate held her fire when Oshu charged because she feared hitting the dog. Now she hesitated because of Tanno.

The impetus of Tanno's charge knocked the tiger off course. Tate had no sensation of firing, no way of knowing if the flechette struck. Tanno fastened her teeth in the tiger's throat. Tate saw the cat's slitted, fixed eyes and a red, wet maw ringed by teeth. Incredible details burned her mind. One fang was broken, rotten. There was a yellowed line at its base. Stiff whiskers stuck straight out from the muzzle.

A paw swatted Tate flat. The wipe went spinning. Scrambling to all fours, dazed, Tate saw Tanno rolling, rolling, yelping in pain. The tiger turned, faced its human prey. Fluidly beautiful, it soared into another leap. Tate put up pitiful, useless hands. She screamed.

Something swirled to a stop in front of her. Black. Indistinct. The tiger flew, roaring. Dropping.

Sylah. The thing in black. Sylah, planting the butt of Nalatan's puny lance in the earth, the makeshift metal point waiting for the approaching fury.

The tiger fell on her. Both rolled onto Tate.

The world exploded in a tornado of weight, screams, roars.

Tate opened her eyes. A rock poked her back. She reached to push herself up. Her hand slipped on wetness. Pain poured through her.

Claw marks furrowed her left arm from elbow to shoulder. Her blouse was gone. A gash bled on her chest, barely missing her breast. With her right hand, she traced a wound under her ear.

Lanta's face swam into view overhead. "You'll be fine. It's all right." Unutterably weary, Tate surrendered.

When she woke, she was looking past a watchful, recumbent Tanno at the sprawled tiger. The lance head protruded from its neck. The devouring, jewel eyes were mere glass, disinterested. A sagging jaw exposed the broken, brown tooth. Beyond, Lanta spoke to an ashen, bloodied Sylah. Tate called, wincing at the pain. The other women rose—Sylah rather shakily—and came toward her.

Lanta said, "You must hurt terribly. I'm so sorry. No blood carriers were severed. Everything's sewn. You'll heal well. Rest." She drew a black, blood-stained sleeve across her exhausted features.

Tate said, "Thank you." She looked to Sylah. "The lance. You saved my life."

A livid bruise covered the right side of Sylah's face. Her right shoulder was bandaged. She said, "It was dying when it leaped. The lightning hit it."

"You didn't know that. You finished it. Saved me." Tate stopped. Her eyes flew wide. "Oshu? Where is she?"

Sylah and Lanta exchanged glances. Sylah said, "I'm sorry."

Tate forced herself up, rolled onto hands and knees, holding up the injured left arm like an animal's wounded limb. She moaned, an unending, tearing elongation of the single word "no." Inching forward, she pushed off Sylah and Lanta. Tanno came to her, whining anxiety. Tate said, "Tanno, find Oshu. Help her. Please, please; someone help her."

She slumped face down in the litter.

Sylah was right there. She lifted Tate, rocked her like a baby, consoling. She was looking down into Tate's still, sad face when the dark eyelids trembled open. Tate's chin rose. "I told you."

Sylah understood instantly. She smiled. "And I'll never forget.

Be sure of it. 'We can do what we have to do.' You saved me, too. You and good Oshu. Thank you. Dear friend."

Together, sharing heartache, sharing triumph, they helped each other cry until Tate slept soundly once again.

CHAPTER 87

After assuring himself the rider with the train of three pack-horses negotiating the steep climb toward him was Nalatan, Dodoy ran for camp. "Nalatan's coming," he called to Lanta. The small priestess looked up, deerlike in her surprise, from where she was sewing a tear in her robe. Dodoy puzzled over that; he'd noticed her working on the same one before. There were tears in her eyes the other time.

Lanta said, "How long before he gets here?"

"He's down by the big tree with the broken top."

"Practically here," Sylah said, as she hurried out from behind the new shelter off to the side. It was wind protection for her and Tate while they exposed their sewn-up wounds to sun and fresh air. Tate followed, smearing ointment on the swollen flesh of her arm, tugging at her blouse. The out-of-place sea smell of the medicine tickled Dodoy's nose. Sylah put a pot of water on the stove. "He'll want some tea."

From the rocks above the shelter, Dodoy watched Nalatan's approach first. Tanno rose fluidly, positioning herself between the oncoming horse and Tate. When Nalatan skidded to a stop, the dog's head dropped, reached forward as far as its neck would stretch. A low, steady rumble boiled in its throat.

Staring at the bandaged women, Nalatan dismounted slowly. He approached Tanno first, hands out in fists, backs presented, letting the dog get reacquainted. Sylah smiled at the way the animal's eyes never left the man, while the man's eyes never left Tate. Nalatan absently stroked Tanno's head, stepping past her. Then a thing happened that Sylah could hardly believe. The dog wandered off a few steps, and for the first time since the tiger's attack, she lay down on her side. Gusting a massive sigh, she closed her eyes. Sylah would have sworn she was asleep instantly.

Still unspeaking, pale, Nalatan touched Tate's bandaged arm. He stroked the thick, lustrous hair around the stark whiteness of the bandage by her ear. After a quick glance at Sylah, he looked into Tate's eyes, asked, "How?"

All three women talked at once. He waited patiently for them to organize the telling, drinking herb tea, nodding. When Tate defiantly said they'd burned Oshu "in a proper warrior's fire," Sylah and Lanta watched him apprehensively. He smiled. They relaxed. At last, Tate said, "Aren't you going to say anything?"

For some time, it appeared he might not. Finally, he put down his tea mug. He addressed Sylah. "I swore an oath to protect you on your quest for the Door. Now you've saved the life of someone I care about. Very much. You risked your life for her. I'm in your debt forever."

Sylah blushed. "I told you: the tiger was dying."

Lanta said, "I wish you could have seen them, Nalatan. They were wonderful, both of them."

"And the dogs," Tate added. Her eyes gleamed with repressed tears. "So brave."

Sylah coughed. Her words had a rough, forced quality. "What did you find on your scout?"

He answered as he hurried to the packhorses. "I ran across a camp. A man and his family. He wanted to sell me camels, but I held out for the horses. No one should deal with camels. Ugly. Mean."

On returning, he raised the flap of the boxy packhorse pannier. "A crib for the boy," he said proudly. The women crowded close for a better look. "The woman in the camp sold it to me. Her baby's outgrown it. The side and bottom cushions come off and unbutton. You can stuff them with whatever you want to keep it sweet smelling. The Dry woman used mint leaves, fresh. It's better than that basket. And look at this." He pulled a square box out of another pannier. When he flourished the top off, Tate's disappointment was immediate. "Straw? A box of straw?"

Smugly, Nalatan pulled straw from the box, putting it aside. There was a ceramic lid under it. If the straw had been a surprise, the marvelous aroma that wafted from the clay pot hidden in it was an astonishment. Nalatan posed like a successful magician. "Stew. Grouse, rabbit, vegetables, herbs. I watched the woman do it. She boiled everything in the pot, then picked it up with thick gloves, put it in the straw in the box, covered it, then put in more straw. With the wooden lid on, it cooks all day. She made this yesterday. It was still warm this morning. We can do the same thing. We won't have to light any fires at night."

512

The last line brought Sylah's head around. "Are we that concerned about being seen?"

Enthusiasm fading, Nalatan nodded. "The family said they've seen nomad patrols. The new siah calls himself Moonpriest, as if the whole religion was his. He says he's going to destroy Church Home."

Sylah and Lanta executed three-signs. Sylah said, "That means war beyond anything anyone's ever seen."

With a sick feeling in her stomach, Tate resisted the urge to correct her. Instead she asked Nalatan, "Has any word from Kos reached the people you talked to? Any news of Conway or Tee?"

"Nothing."

After a pained, thoughtful silence, Sylah said, "The Harvester's heard of this Moonpriest's threats. Be sure of it. She'll ride for Church Home."

It was Lanta who put words to what they all feared most. "The Chair will send all the help he can spare. He can't afford to have a stronghold like Church Home in Moondance hands."

Sylah nodded, silent.

Jessak's fretful crying interrupted them. Everyone pointedly avoided looking at each other. Nalatan said, "I'm not sure we can move fast enough with the baby. It's the goat. It's got to browse."

"I know, I know." Sylah gestured wearily, put a hand to her brow. "I can't abandon him."

Nalatan coughed delicately. "The family I bought the horses from will take him. If we pay coin."

Sylah looked up questioningly. "You'd trust them?"

Nalatan's eyes went to Tate before he answered. "I was only presenting alternatives, Sylah. Myself, I wouldn't trust them with dirt. But if the Harvester's racing us for Church Home, we can't run and care for Jessak at the same time."

Tate said, "The only game in town, trooper." He looked at her with a puzzled affection that was becoming an almost chronic expression. She said, "If it can be done, you'll do it. The thing is, we don't give up on our Sylah. Or Jessak. Or anything." She turned to Sylah. "I can ride if you can. Tomorrow?"

Lanta said, "I'll take care of the camp chores. You two just get well." Sylah's voice trembled on the edge of control when she spoke. "What fools my friends are. What wonderful, precious fools. What have I done to deserve you?"

Tate's voice was as uncertain as Sylah's when she answered, but she managed to give it her own irrepressible twist. "The truth is, you don't deserve us, but we don't have anything better to do just now. First good offer we get, we drop you like something nasty. Just so you understand." She put her good arm around Sylah from one side, and Lanta did the same opposite her.

Nalatan watched them walk off toward the fire, scratching his head.

They were a fugitive-looking group. Nalatan insisted they be under way before first light, and so it was they began the descent toward the Dry with much sleepy stumbling and muttering. Jessak slept through all the packing and loading of horses. The women barely had time to remark on it before they were in the saddle. Under the dim touch of starlight, the narrow game trail was a thread of lighter-colored earth, barely distinguishable. Nevertheless, Nalatan followed it unhesitatingly.

The first soft rose of dawn found them in a new landscape. The trees, smaller in all dimensions, had a spare, constrained look. The leaves of shrubs, even blades of grass, faced the day with tough, grim determination. Sylah thought of patients whose bodies lost fluid faster than it could be replaced; they acquired the same strained appearance. Later, she caught her first glimpse of camels. They blended perfectly with sere landscape. Four of them watched the train of humans as intently as she watched them, their lower jaws working up and down, side to side, in almost perfect unison. Then, magically, there was only one. Somehow, the other three had melted into the scrub. When Sylah saw how ungainly the last one was as it walked away, she was even more amazed by the disappearance of its mates. The unimaginable hump flopped like an understuffed pillow.

The experience put Sylah in a very thoughtful mood. It came to her that this was a country where adaptation was paramount. In her experience, men used the forests and rivers, they used the prairies and harbors. The Dry would not be used. What it had, it would share, but only as a partner. Man, like everything else, adapted or perished. For a moment, that struck her as unswervingly hostile. On reflection, however, she decided that was too harsh a judgment. The Dry was independent. Eternally so. Whatever survived in its embrace would be the same.

By late afternoon they were on the bank of a small, deliciously cold stream. Dismounting, drinking, washing off the dust of the trail, the women and Dodoy exclaimed happily over it. Nalatan said, "Enjoy it to the fullest. By this time tomorrow we'll be entering the real Dry. I know where to find water, but we'll see none like this until we're near Church Home."

514

Tate said, "You mean there are no streams, no springs, in all those mountains ahead?"

"There are a few. What you must understand about the Dry is that no one drinks without permission."

"Whose permission?" It was Lanta, worried.

"Whoever has the rights to that particular water."

Tate snorted disgust. "How do we know who to ask? What if we drink without permission? They make us spit it back?"

"It's a killing offense." Nalatan was grim. "The people of the Dry live in very loosely organized tribes, made up of large family groups. Most are strong Church believers." He stopped, looked to Sylah guiltily, then plunged ahead. "The family I bought our horses and equipment from supports the Harvester. They told me most of their tribe does. They believe she's the strong leader the times require."

Lanta was indignant. "The woman's the exact opposite of what Church is supposed to be. We must tell them the truth."

Nalatan pushed pebbles around with a finger. "I told them we were the Harvester's advance, returning from Kos to make things ready for her."

Sylah spoke over Lanta's furious sputterings. "The situation's so bad as that?"

"They're ordered to capture the Flower, to hold her for the Harvester."

"They believed you?"

Nalatan grinned. "They believed I had coin to pay for what I wanted. More than that?" He shrugged eloquently.

Sylah nodded. "Two nights, and we have a full moon. We can travel."

Nalatan beamed approval. "It's cooler at night, too."

"Cool. An important word." Sylah rose smoothly. "I intend to bathe while I can. Lanta? Tate?" The other women got to their feet. Sylah reached for Jessak and his bottle, transferred the two smoothly from Lanta to Nalatan. Smiling sweetly, Sylah said, "You haven't had a chance to hold him all day. We'll take him when we get back. Thank you."

She couldn't help thinking his jaw worked almost exactly like the camel's.

In the softness of dusk, grass swayed gracefully on the banks of the stream where the women chose to bathe. Far away, coyotes sang of the night's hunt. Swallows and bats wove across a muted sunset.

The water was startlingly cold, and barely rose above the navel when they lowered themselves, gasping and exclaiming, to sitting positions.

Tate was first to immerse herself, leaning back, testing the injured left arm. It satisfied her. Arching back in a spine-cracking stretch of sheer exuberance, she settled onto her elbows until only her head, breasts, and kneecaps were exposed. Water swirled and eddied around her in mock rapids.

Sylah followed Tate's example, facing upstream, letting the current tug her hair in a rippling cloak behind her. Lanta paddled about, pretending to swim. Her waves washed across Tate's face, who burlesqued drowning, then slapped water at Lanta. Sylah, showing no favoritism, doused them both. Splashing and giggling like children, they gave themselves to the moment, rejecting the world as it was for life as it should be.

Later, clothed, clean, and dry, they scurried about in the fading light, harvesting the soft, furry leaves of a plant Lanta called "mull." She explained it was excellent diaper material for Jessak. That done, they all lay on the streambank, watching the first stars.

Tate sat up, positioned herself to face her friends. She said, "Can I ask you all a question? You won't think I'm crazy?"

Sylah laughed. "That depends on the question." When Tate failed to smile, Sylah sobered. "What's bothering you?"

"I had a dream. Often. The same one."

Lanta said, "Many believe dreams bring us into other times, places. I do." She glanced at Sylah. "Church says we mustn't, but Church claims all Seers, and some of us dream."

Sylah said, "I agree. We shouldn't be afraid of something just because we don't understand it. You fear?"

Tate nodded, face pressed in a confused frown. "I don't know why; it's not that scary. It's a burning hot day, and I'm in the cool shade of a tree, with a horse. It's thin, skin and bones. That makes me terribly sad. The tree grows a face, then, says I should feed its leaves to the horse. I gather what I think are the very best, but when I offer them, the animal hits me with its muzzle, sends the leaves flying. Then I look around, and all kinds of horses are running to get them. They love them. Then the tree talks to me again."

She stopped, moving close in the failing light to peer suspiciously at her audience. "You two aren't laughing?"

Reassuring her, the others urged her to continue.

"Well, anyhow, the tree says, 'You must cut me down, burn me. Only that way can I serve.' At first, that makes sense. Then I step back—one step, but it takes me far, far away—and I see the

516

whole tree, how pretty it is. I say, 'The horse will eat now. I understand it. It trusts me. I don't need firewood.' Then I have to say something else. Have to. I say, 'The comfort you give will last forever, like the shade of trees cools the summer.' And that's when I wake up, so sad I want to cry, and so frightened I'm shaking."

Lanta hugged herself, rocked back and forth. "It's a powerful dream."

Sylah said, "Neither of us interpret dreams, but in yours, you're alone. Here, you're not. Never will be."

Softly, musing, Lanta said, "It's more than that. I feel it. The dream speaks of mistakes. I feel the sorrow. It frightens me, too." She refused to look at her friends.

CHAPTER 88

The raid came the second day during the midday halt.

As usual, the packhorses were hobbled downwind. There seemed to be nothing to offer cover to anyone approaching them. Nevertheless, when Sylah looked up from her meal, the three of them were moving off through the brush, single file. She yelled alarm. Nalatan and Tate were mounted and after them instantly.

Tate and Tanno bowled straight ahead until Nalatan overtook her, physically forcing her to the side. Tate's Dog war-horse reacted angrily, biting at Nalatan and his horse. Confused, but deferring to Nalatan, Tate wheeled sharply away, calling Tanno to follow.

Almost immediately, Nalatan's reason became clear. To the left, four men draped in camouflaging branches rose, bows bent, arrows drawn to the head. Tate's straight-line pursuit of the pack animals would have sent her directly in front of them. Beyond them, four more men appeared, distance softening their leaf-mottled outlines. Nalatan had shouldered her away from a deadly tunnel.

The arrows from the nearest four darted past harmlessly. Tate, in her excitement, flipped the wipe to automatic. A quick burst of six rounds dropped one ambusher. Bemoaning the waste of ammunition, she repositioned the switch. By then, the other men were gone, shaking brush betraying their departure.

Ahead of Tate, Nalatan was about to ride over the top of a low ridge where the pack animals had disappeared. Inexplicably, he piled to a stone-spraying, skidding stop, reversing his field, thundering back toward camp. He'd covered no more than twenty yards when the first camel's head poked over the crest. The animal and its rider, with at least twenty more flanking them, came with startling speed. Arrows flew after Nalatan.

Tate sighted carefully. It was the easiest sort of shot, straight ahead at an advancing target. A flechette lifted a rider off his high perch on the camel's back; he plowed into the ground in a rolling, dusty heap. The remainder wheeled about and retreated as fast as they'd come. The riderless camel slowed to a walk. It clumped about with an air of offended superiority for a few paces, then ambled after its fellows.

Nalatan stopped beside Tate. Dust roiled in the wake of the retreat. Nalatan's face was scarred with concern. "That leaves us with one waterskin."

Tate continued to scan around them, despite Tanno's gradual relaxation. She said, "Are we that far from water?"

"We can reach the next waterhole I had in mind. The problem is, they'll know that's where we're going."

"Is there someplace else? In a different direction, maybe. We can do that, go a different way."

"I'll have to dream."

Before the dumbfounded Tate could respond, Nalatan was on his way back to camp. She followed, frown darkening with every passing yard. By the time they arrived, she was a breaking storm. She kept quiet while Nalatan described what had happened. He finished by saying, "Twenty to thirty men is a very large, very unusual number for the people of the Dry to concentrate. The Harvester wants you very badly, Sylah."

Sylah accepted his evaluation with a quiet, "Will they attack? What do you suggest we do?" She was unprepared for Tate's explosive sarcasm.

"He says he's going to dream a waterhole."

Nalatan flinched angrily, coloring. Then, as quickly, he laughed aloud. "We won't be attacked as long as we appear ready. They know about Tate's weapons. Their style is more surprise than assault, anyhow. As for the waterhole, yes, I'm going to dream it, as Donnacee puts it."

He stepped away from them, sat in the best of the mottled shade available. Cross-legged, hands in his lap, he looked up at Tate with a grin. "No man can know the entire Dry. The brotherhoods know it, however. All routes, all sources of water. One who knows sits before a student as I sit here. They sing the knowing song. The one who knows has a piece of obsidian on a chain. The other one watches the shining stone swing back and forth. When he sleeps, the knowledge is sung. Soon, both sleep and sing. The best dreaming makes the one who is to know see everything the one who knows has seen. Three men dreamed with me. Now I'll dream, and we'll know where to go."

Tate's head roared with words like hypnotism and thought transference. In a time and place where people were tortured and killed for learning simple addition, Nalatan's warrior monks dabbled in a psychic information exchange. Worse, Sylah and Lanta smiled and nodded like he was discussing the price of beans. Tate gave it up. She settled to watch.

The Priestesses edged back from Nalatan when he closed his eyes. His fingers curled. His body remained erect, although Tate noted how the visible muscles lost definition, flowed to repose under the skin. The unexpected onset of sound startled her; the quality of it raised the fine hairs on her arms and the back of her neck. Deep, throbbing, it emanated from him, as if his close-mouthed body were a sounding board. Pulse-rhythmic, it slowed. And slowed.

Tate wiped sweat from her brow, sweat that ran into her eyes and burned. There was none on Nalatan. His skin looked cool, comfortable.

The chant slowed more. Faded.

Grabbing Sylah's arm, Tate said, "Is he all right? We ought to wake him. He's scaring me."

Sylah nodded. "Me, too, Donnacee. We chant, use the trance. I've never seen one go so deep. If we wake him, though, it may be even more dangerous. Trust him. It's all we can do."

Tate blurted, "Trust him? Sylah, I love him."

Sylah covered the hand on her arm with her own. Lanta's smile was bittersweet. Sylah said, "Now that you've told me, think of the joy of telling him. Tell him. Be honest. For both your sakes."

"I can't. I never spoke, Sylah. Please. But don't let him die."

Lanta said, "You're making a mistake." Her following subdued "Believe me" raked at Tate almost as much as her own denial.

"I can't watch." Tate turned away. "I'm going up on that knoll, stand guard. Call me when he's normal."

Keeping below the growth height of the scrub, Tate scuttled up the nearby hillock with Tanno beside her. Prior to the crest, she broke to the flank. Crawling, she made her way to a good observation point on the forward slope. From there she could see much farther. The only sign of life soared overhead. Buzzards: black, drifting reminders of the Dry's ferocious patience. Death birds, Nalatan called them.

There were too many. Two, sometimes three, were normally visible. Tate counted five. A sixth swept into view from behind her, homing on the others.

Something had died out there. The buzzards knew. Nalatan said that what they didn't see, they smelled. They watched each other, too. Bright, single-purposed eyes saw across incredible distances. One dropped to feed, and another read the spiral. They brought each other from all directions.

Tate didn't mind them. She had no particular fear of death. She'd been a professional soldier in one world, and the one she inhabited now allowed no romantic notions about old age. What frightened her was the prospect of wasting her life.

So why did Donnacee Tate fall in love with Nalatan? Why did everything have to be so complicated?

Tanno perked up her ears and watched uncertainly as Tate slammed her fist into the ground, over and over.

A short while later, Sylah's sharp whistle called Tate to camp. The indecision and concern remained in her mind, but safely caged, so it could merely nag.

Nalatan was on his feet. Sweating. Tate touched his arm, assuring herself the flesh was warm again. She said, "Which way do we go?"

He pointed. "That way, I'm afraid. There's a good spring, about a day's ride. The trouble is, the Dry warriors know that's where we have to go. The water we have won't last more than a day, and they'll make it very hard for us to get there that fast."

Sylah said, "There's nothing else?"

"West of the spring. A waterhole. Bad water." He shrugged. "We'll have to take a chance on the good one."

Sylah sorted through her baggage, took out a fat leather bag. She held it up. "These crystals form on the side of wine barrels. Helstar got it for us. Tell me: this waterhole is the normal bad water of the Dry? It's not poisonous?"

Nalatan shook his head, watching Sylah with undisguised skepticism. Sylah grinned back. "We can use it, then. It won't taste very good, but it'll do. This makes it drinkable. A few drops of awakener makes it quite stimulating. So I'm told."

Skirting the edge of condescension, Nalatan said, "My brotherhood's been here for generations. We know the Dry's secrets. Whoever told you to drink bad water isn't your friend."

"Church has been here longer than your brotherhood, crossing

the Dry every time they left or returned to Church Home. Everyone knows their own secrets, it appears." Sylah opened the bag,
displayed the yellowish crystals. "This is how we fool the Dry
people. We're not as restricted as they think."

Lanta said, "They may not even be following us. Maybe they
only wanted our horses and belongings."

Nalatan said, "I wish that were so. They'll ride around us, try
to catch us off guard up ahead. They'll leave two or three men to
trail us, to report if we take a trail they don't expect. I'll have to
try to eliminate the followers. I don't want to have to fight
through an ambush just to get at some bad water. Not that I don't
trust your medicine, Sylah." He grinned, mischievous. She sniffed
at him, replaced the bag.

Tate looked at Jessak, tiny and pink in his pannier crib, his awning stretched over him. He looked past his bottle at her, the incredibly dark blue eyes wide and trusting.

CHAPTER 89

Sylah gripped the pommel of her saddle. It was burning hot.
She welcomed the pain. Anything that took her mind off the cruel,
bitter words that had to be said. "Nalatan goes alone, Tate." Seeing anger and betrayal flare in her friend's face, Sylah hurried on.
"He's right. We can't allow anyone to report which way we travel. Lanta and I dare not travel alone. That leaves you to escort us,
Nalatan to handle the back trail and free us of the trailers."

Furious, Tate said, "They won't just run away, Sylah. They'll
fight. He'll need help. No less than you do."

Inwardly, Sylah winced at the criticism. There was no choice,
though. Nalatan was a warrior, and he understood he must take
chances. Tate was no less a warrior; she had yet to learn that success of the mission was paramount. Sylah despised being the one
to provide that instruction. She pulled back her shoulders, hardened her gaze. "There's no time for discussion. Nalatan, are you
ready?"

"Yes." He made a three-sign. "You're sure you can follow the
instructions? You memorized the landmarks?"

"You made it very clear. We'll be all right."

Nalatan looked to Tate. He held her eyes for a moment, waiting. Sylah held her breath, wishing one of them would speak,

521

hoping one would find the courage to tell the other what everyone already knew. Under the weight of Nalatan's proud, near-hopeless gaze, Tate sagged in her saddle. Yet neither said a word. In a flurry of hooves, Nalatan was gone.

Tate half rose in her stirrups. Her hand lifted at the wrist, a wave that wilted to nothing as Nalatan never looked back. The expression she sent Sylah was poisonous. "No time, you said. Ready?"

Sylah said, "Donnacee, we—"

Tate jerked her horse around, the action cutting off Sylah. The others had to hurry to keep up.

As they rode, the sky heated to a silver-blue that made Sylah think of overheated steel keening on a grindstone. Scrub growth reached for her ankles, her knees. Hard, tough leaves and wiry little branches clawed at her. The unending harsh whisper of the foliage was even worse. Sometimes she heard it as mocking laughter, other times as muffled weeping. The truly bad moments were when she thought she heard the voice, the mind-words that drove her, led her, insisted on her quest.

She looked back at the crib lashed behind her saddle. After tugging the underlying blanket free of a wrinkle, she lifted the tented cloth top to peek in at Jessak. He smiled, and the familiar melting sensation rolled through her midsection. She told herself it was sinfully proud to believe he recognized her, or smiled more readily for her. At the same time, she decided there was no reason to avoid the truth. He certainly seemed to smile more when she tended him.

Wrapped in a diaper stuffed with the last of the soft mull leaves, he kicked and wiggled pleased excitement. Sylah reflected yet again that the boy bore the heat with an almost eerie complacency. He jounced along with hardly any complaint, slept at night like a hibernating bear. He fussed when hungry, took his milk with unfailing eagerness.

Flicking sweat off her brow and turning back to the front, Sylah remembered Helstar's reaction to the boy's name, and his superstitious tale of its significance. She smiled. If he could be present to see how wondrously well Jessak behaved, he'd have to take back his words. Or, more likely, he'd bluster some foolishness about mysterious powers.

Lanta's call distracted her. Sylah looked back. Lanta was gesturing, fear twisting her features. Dodoy, beside her, caught the movement. He looked back, too.

In the far distance, a buzzard moved earthward in its sinister coil. Another, closer, flapped lazily, going to investigate. Between themselves and the birds, Lanta had observed someone riding out of a draw Sylah recognized as one they'd passed through some time ago. Dodoy hurried past her to be near Tate and the protection of her weapons.

The rider was alone. Sylah relayed the news to Tate, just as Dodoy arrived at her side. Tate slowed, letting Sylah and Lanta close on her. "I think it's Nalatan," Tate said. She opened the sniper rifle case, holding it open in her lap. Looking through the sight, she nodded. "It's him. We'll walk the horses, rest them a bit. He'll catch up pretty soon. Watch close, be sure no one's behind him."

Watching Tate move out to her point position, Sylah let her mind drift back to the desperate ride they'd taken together across the Enemy Mountains of the north. Snow and ice threatened there. Now it was heat and thirst. The major change wasn't climate, though. It was Tate. There was a confidence in her work now unlike anything that earlier woman could manage.

Hidden in the pride of accomplishment was the sad truth that Tate's fighting skills were necessary. Sylah wondered if her friend would ever have the opportunity to learn anything different.

Sweat ran in gleaming rivulets across Nalatan's skin, painted dark splotches on his clothing. His sleeveless vest, open for ventilation, revealed a wedge of black hair chained with droplets. He was on foot, leading his horse. When he released the reins, letting his hand fall to his side, sweat cut paths in the accumulated dust on his forearm, curved and deflected off the raised welts of scars.

Tate handed him the waterskin. After a large swallow, he said, "We're not being followed." His expression was peculiar. Sylah felt he wanted to accuse her of something. He went on. "The main body of the raiders is moving toward the spring, as I thought they would. They left three men to trail us."

Before Sylah could speak, Tate said, "Did you . . . ?" She let the sentence fall away.

Nalatan continued to watch Sylah. "I found them. They were all dead." He reached into a saddlebag, drew out the feathered half of a broken arrow. It was white.

"Protectors." Sylah and Lanta breathed the word simultaneously.

Quietly, Nalatan said, "Conway told me of the man who tried to steal Dodoy. He told of the white arrow and the protectors you just named. Those men wouldn't be here, in the Dry. Even if they were, they have no reason to help us. I will only ask this once: Is

523

there anything anyone wants to tell me?" He examined the faces of the three women slowly, individually.

Sylah thought of Helstar and immediately dismissed the notion as ludicrous. If he'd intended to follow them into the Dry, he'd have at least intimated it. But who else could it possibly be? The idea that it was actually a protector was even more insane than considering Helstar.

It was all insane.

Sylah wanted to draw away, think. Or forget. Forget everything, not worry or puzzle or suspect.

Nalatan was watching, patient. Sylah thought, deadly patient, then looked to the other women. They waited, as well.

When she finally spoke her words were as if from a stranger. Quick, almost blurred. "There's nothing to tell you. There can't be any connection. That's ridiculous. You said yourself the people of the Dry are in constant conflict with each other. It's one of them, that's all."

Nalatan's tight smile expressed his skepticism eloquently. He took another mouthful of water, then, "That's no Dry arrow, Sylah. Those dead men ask more questions than I can answer, and that makes me very uncomfortable. I don't know who's following us now, or why." To Tate, he continued, "Stay on point, please. I'll take rear guard."

Tate nodded. "I'm glad . . ." She coughed, tried again. "I'm glad there wasn't any trouble. For you."

He smiled. Her relief at having him back was suddenly almost overwhelming. It made her lighthearted. She called Tanno and practically leapt onto her horse to escape.

Riding to her position, thinking more clearly, she wondered why Sylah was so upset when Nalatan asked if anyone had anything to tell him. Very little frightened Sylah, and she'd looked terrified. Her answer was almost babble. There was something else, too.

A word popped into Tate's mind. Furtive. That was it. The last thing to show on Sylah's face was furtiveness.

Still and all, it was Lanta who reacted most strongly. Nalatan's question made her jerk as if she'd been stabbed, her eyes bulging almost comically and her hand flying to her breast.

Hanging off the saddle to ruffle Tanno's ears, Tate said, "Turns out our ladies of the black threads have been holding out on the troops, big dog. What d'you know about that?"

Tanno looked up, panting, grinning thirstily, wagging her tail. Tate accused. "Ah-hah. Won't talk, huh? Think you're tough."

She swatted the dog's hindquarters and sat upright again, talking to herself. "Better be tough, old buddy. Look at that country ahead. Hungry looking." She shook her head.

None of it did any good. The notion that Sylah and Lanta knew something they weren't willing to share wouldn't go away.

It was very disquieting.

It took only two days for Dry scouts to reestablish contact. For the next week Nalatan led the war party through a chess game played on the sere mountains and baked valleys of the Dry. The pursuit made no attempt to close. They approached at night to shout taunts and curses, always at such a distance that any attempt to come to grips with them was an exercise in triggering an ambush. During the day, they were an unnerving presence, perched on faraway overlooks in plain view, launching arrows or sling-stones from closer, but always hidden, positions.

The path to Church Home was always disputed. Tate's fire-power allowed them to force their way, but under galling, incessant sniping. Every horse had suffered at least one wound. Because the ranges were great, injuries were minor. Nevertheless, it was nerve-racking to march all day, every day, never knowing when a hissing missile, striking from no identifiable location, might send one's mount into a rearing, bucking fit of pain and fury. So far, none of the humans were hit, nor was Tanno.

One afternoon, Tate broke out the sniper rifle. A Dry warrior, confident in his distance from the small party dragging itself across a sweltering valley, perched on a dramatic overlook to watch them. In an act born more of frustration than of any hope of altering the situation, Tate exposed the arrayed solar cells, and settled into a solid sitting position. Through the powerful telescopic sight, she put the fine cross hairs on the man's chest.

Her finger stalled on the trigger. She remembered Conway, so ashamed of being seduced by the godlike qualities conferred by the weapon. She wondered what the man was like.

He smiled at her. It was impossible for him to imagine anything that would enable Tate to see his facial expression. Nevertheless, he looked directly into the tube and he smiled, a superior, cruel grin that anticipated torment and destruction for the people he watched. He gestured, an obscene suggestion. Laughing, he partially turned to speak to someone hidden behind his watch station.

In the sullen quiet of the midday heat, the report of the rifle was like an unexpected shout of repressed rage. A moment later the heavy slug slammed the warrior back against the mountain-

525

side. Limp, disjointed, he paused on the steep slope for a moment, then slowly moved downhill. Faster and faster he fell, twirling, arms and legs whipping like reeds. Soon he was leaving the ground, flying from contact to contact, exploding clouds of dust at every touch.

When the echoes ceased, Sylah's group was still watching the empty space. There was nothing to indicate that a man had ever existed, much less died.

Voice cracked by thirst, Nalatan ordered them to move again.

That night they camped near a hot spring. Sure they were observed, the women managed circumspect bathing. The spring water was drinkable, once cooled, but far too chemically saturated for making tea. Later, there were more threats than ever. Even though they'd moved to sleeping positions under cover of darkness, as they always did, arrows fell among them all night. Coming almost vertically, each one plunged into the ground with a sound like a fist.

On the morning of the eighth day, Sylah looked up from a routine wetting of Jessak's parched lips and saw a smudge on a distant mountainside. Or thought she did. It was too faint to be sure. She called to Nalatan. Squinting, he shaded his eyes and studied the distance. "A large group, moving fast," he said.

Tate set up the sniper rifle, offering it to Nalatan. He handled it reverently, clearly apprehensive about putting his eye to the scope. He almost dropped it when he looked through it, exclaiming aloud. He executed a three-sign heretofore unseen by any of his companions, a matter of kissing the knuckle of his right thumb, then touching it to forehead, lips, and both eyes. Then he peered through the scope again. "Forty men. Kossiars. The Harvester." He handed the piece back to Tate, his hand lingering lovingly on the stock. He licked his lips, swallowed to make sure his words would come clearly. Looking at Sylah, he said, "We can't go back to the hot spring; it's indefensible. If we go forward, we may not reach water before they're on us."

Sylah dampened her lips with Jessak's wet cloth. The tiny cracks in her flesh burned like sparks. She said, "Is there any chance they'll fight each other?"

Nalatan shook his head. "These coyotes have been waiting for the Harvester to arrive. We have to run, Sylah."

CHAPTER 90

Excited by the sounds of battle and the choking billows of smoke from the burning fortified village, Stormracer shivered under Conway's soothing hands. Nomads circled the walls like wolves slashing at crippled prey. Occasionally one of the fort's inhabitants leapt into view at a fighting port to shout defiance. There were fewer incidents of that since Conway blasted three in rapid succession. The war cries from within the wall were now shrill with the knowledge of defeat. Conversely, the shouts of the nomad warriors degenerated to taunts and threats.

The thought of the impending climax to the battle pulled Conway's attention to the grove of pines off to the right. Varnalal's war-painted assault unit sat their horses easily, poised to strike at their young leader's command.

Varnalal was Fox's creation, as was the assault unit, made up of men from every component of Windband. As a unifying measure, all were initiated into Mountain tradition as much as possible. The Mountain People were unorthodox believers, mixing Church with their own mystic beliefs. Even now, totally converted to Moondance, they clung to some of the old ways. One example was their war paint. A Mountain warrior believed he appeared in the next world as he left this one. They painted their faces in anticipation of death, believing that a warrior fought his way out of a state of nothingness into the Land Above. Or, conversely, was killed again, and became a lost spirit, destined to haunt the world of men.

The design was a stark white death's head, the eyes black holes. The mouth was painted red, a gaping, toothed maw with descending red streaks at the corners. Conway thought how chilling it must be to discover that face an arm's length away, the black-circled eyes inflamed with combat madness.

A warrior of the unit caught Conway's gaze. Across the intervening distance, he saluted, raising and lowering his ma, the Mountain short fighting sword.

Conway duplicated the move with the wipe.

Before the afternoon shadows lengthened much more, one or both of them might be dead. The idea touched Conway with a sad excitement. He wondered about the other man. For himself, he didn't want to die. He didn't expect to. That brought a smile: not many men did. The human mind was capable of infinite dissembling. Every warrior who saw his companions killed accepted their death as proof of their bad luck or mistakes. It also confirmed his own immortality.

That was particularly true of Varnalal and his unit. Blizzardmen, they called themselves, laughing about it, telling everyone that, behind their advance, even the ground was left dead. Throughout Windband, Blizzard was extravagantly admired. Fox and his warriors taught the men individual combat. Conway taught them how to support each other, how to maneuver by unit, small unit control, and effective communications. Iron discipline and constant training, imposed on men who'd fought since childhood, created a fearsome shock team.

The old Conway considered battles a part of history, war a social psychosis. The new Conway remembered details that had never consciously registered before.

A nomad war drum crashed into life.

That was part of the Blizzard assault plan. Each drum—there were seven on this campaign—roared individually, in sequence. The eastern drum always sounded first; the rotation went north around the perimeter, ending at the starter. Conway watched the one nearest him, a short distance to his left. Mounted on a cart, it was a man's reach across and perhaps half again that deep. Suspended by leather straps, it was a uniform tube of vertical wooden slats glued together and bound with braided leather. The leather striking surface was hauled tight by an intricate web of lines. Waxed and polished to the color of honey, the instrument rode perhaps five feet off the ground. The drummer perched on the cart, armed with unpadded sticks. When it was his turn to sound off, the drummer struck as hard and fast as he could. When he stopped, the next one rolled.

Thunder circled through the valley. Thick, ominous silence followed the last solo. As soon as the eastern drum set the new rhythm, all joined. The chorus hammered the village.

Conway next looked to the distant hill from which Katallon commanded his units. The pre-assault flag was still flying.

The flags were Conway's idea, as were the signal mirrors. The nomads had fought the Kossiars for years, yet not once had any nomad suggested using mirrors as their enemies did. During the argument over adopting the system, the obstinate resistance to change of some of the nomad leaders triggered a nostalgia attack that kept Conway in his tent for two days.

Varnalal galloped up, war paint spangled with pearls of sweat. Karda and Mikka tensed at the sight of him, watching Conway closely for signals. Varnalal's eyes were circles of excitement; he blinked continually. "Katallon's being too cautious," he said. The words were breathy. "I . . . my men tire of waiting."

Conway glanced back at the wooded draw. Horses shuffled and tiptoed. Many men had mas out, swinging them, loosening muscles. Smiling easily, he said, "Not even Blizzard can go through a wall. Patience. Look, there's a break already."

The palisade of vertical pine trunks was burning in several places. A thin, hungry smile split Varnalal's face as sparks cascaded upward from a collapsing section. Too small to allow a charge, the gap would widen as the fire consumed more logs. Varnalal turned back to Conway. "You're riding with us?"

"Of course. There'll be no more lightning weapons, though."

Varnalal sobered. "We all know you must conserve your strength."

Moonpriest told the nomads that he and Conway used lightning drawn from spiritual powers within themselves, that using those powers was dangerously draining. All had seen Moonpriest's moon altar kill. They saw the wipe and the boop kill. Moonpriest's assertions went unquestioned. It was just as well, Conway thought at the time. Every morning he woke with growing concern over his ammunition supply. It was still healthy, but there was no replacement.

A man galloping a white horse broke out of the trees shielding Blizzard. Varnalal said, "A runner. To tell Katallon of the breaks in the wall. The white horse runners are a good idea. Everyone knows they carry important information, everyone clears the way for them."

Another white horse appeared from the far side of the fortified village's hill. Varnalal soured immediately. Conway laughed at him. "Another runner doesn't mean another breach, Varnalal. Even if it does, you know Katallon depends on Blizzard to exploit first."

Irritably, Varnalal drummed his fingers on his saddle. "We've earned the right to be first." He glanced around. Assured no one could overhear, he nevertheless edged closer to Conway. "Katallon doesn't trust us. He thinks we're too much influenced by Moonpriest. And Fox."

Stiffening, Conway looked down his nose at Varnalal. "That's a lie. Who said it? How can you be sure the man wasn't testing you? What if he reports to Katallon that you said nothing? Or *agreed*?"

A shiver jerked Varnalal. "I didn't agree. Not really. All I said was, Katallon's our leader in life and battle and Moonpriest leads in life and in life after death." He brightened. "And I said, 'Moonpriest obeys Katallon, too.' I remember saying it."

The pace of the drums quickened. Conway and Varnalal looked to the fort, where the smoke and flame of burning buildings behind the palisade boiled fiercely. The wall was still too strong to attack. Katallon's warning flags remained furled.

Varnalal ignored the new tempo. Consternation twisted the painted death mask grotesquely. Conway relented. "Don't worry about it. It was just one fool exercising his mouth. Who was it?"

Varnalal's gaze dropped to his hands on his saddle. He squirmed like a boy caught in a lie. "One of my men. But he said he heard it from someone else." He looked up, beseeching, not wanting to continue. Conway insisted. "Who did he hear it from?"

"Man Burning."

Startled, Conway pulled back. Stormracer, already tense, responded with arch-necked prancing. When Conway had the horse settled, he addressed Varnalal with icy calm. "My slave said this?"

The younger man looked away. Straightening suddenly, he pointed. "The pre-assault flag! Katallon's ready." He turned back to Conway. "Today he'll see what loyalty is. So will you. I know you don't doubt me, but I did a foolish thing. See how I make up for it." Standing in the stirrups, Varnalal twisted his mount around almost by main strength, then sprinted for his Blizzard. Still upright, he screamed, a sound that combined a man's voice and an animal's ferocity. A similar sound broke from the one hundred throats of Blizzard. Varnalal never slowed. He sped across the tree-covered front of the unit until he was centered, arriving there just as the yellow pre-assault flag dropped and the black assault flag whipped up. Repeating his cry, which again echoed from the woods, Varnalal galloped for the breached wall. His men streamed after him.

Coming out of the trees, they looked ragged, no more than three streaming packs, much longer than wide. Within a few strides, however, they were forming into distinct columns, each one four men abreast. The center one was close-ranked, its head even with the middle of the columns on either side. The men of the flanking columns were spaced much farther apart, side to side as well as front to back. From the front, the charge looked like a fork with two long, thin tines and one short, fat central one.

Defensive reinforcements already manned the breach. Only twice the height of a tall man, the wall offered no overwhelming tactical advantage. Still, the archers on its battlewalk were protected, well armed, and desperate. They shrieked curses and war cries at the thundering Blizzard, raining arrows on them. Blizzardmen and horses fell, screaming, tumbling, some ridden down by those still coming.

The riders of the widely spaced flanking elements were perhaps seventy paces from the defenses when the first return fire lifted from the columns. Only the first rank shot, but they were incredibly quick to get off second and third arrows. With the third, the reason for their spacing became apparent. Each rider wheeled left, retreating parallel to the ranks they'd led moments before. Every man repeated the maneuver. A constant stream of arrows rose from the columns, spiking the walls, skimming over them, striking defenders.

The center column lifted shields overhead as they drove full-gallop at the flaming, smoking hole in the wall. Excitement, fear, bloodlust—all mingled in their howling cries.

Conway dismounted outside the wall. With his dogs, he hurtled through the gap with the center column. Varnalal was inside already, facing back toward the wall, directing his men. Half drove right, half left, forcing defenders back from the opening. Conway threw himself into the battle on his left side. Varnalal held up a red flag, indicating new arrivals should ride past him and push into the heart of the village. Soon the red was replaced by a black and white pennant. Men pouring through the breach saw that, dismounted, and sought cover. The colors told them they were now the counterattack force, to hold position until needed.

That need came moments later. Conway was busy with a gritty fighter wearing ill-fitting Kossiar armor when the first Blizzardmen from the penetration column started reappearing, forced back by a shrieking, raging mob. Armed with everything from scythes to the finest Kossiar swords, they fought with the abandonment of the lost. Varnalal's men cut them down like grass, but there seemed to be two to take the place of every one killed. Sheer pressure forced Blizzard back on itself.

Conway took a step back, half turned as if to retreat with those around him. His opponent, sensing advantage, struck quickly. Karda came from the side, taking the sword arm just at the wrist. The man screamed, the sound punctuated by the crackling of crushed bone. Conway finished him with a throat stroke, then resumed his hurried retreat.

Step by step, Conway's section backed until the still-fiery logs singed their clothes. Karda and Mikka were frantic.

The black and white pennant dropped, replaced by the red. The counterattack force, rising from various hiding places, hurtled into the flank of the ill-organized, overeager defenders.

An arrow struck Conway's leather armor, gouged a wicked furrow, and skipped off. The vibrating shaft twanged nasally on its way to dash itself against a stone wall.

Suddenly, something from behind nearly bowled Conway over. Whirling, sword poised, he looked up into the white-rimmed, walling eyes of Stormracer. Rearing, pawing the air, the horse literally demanded to be with its master. Laughing in an excitement that touched on madness, Conway swung aboard the animal. The man, the dogs, the horse, charged, transformed into a tempest of destruction.

CHAPTER 91

Slumped in the saddle, listening to Stormracer's racking breathing, watching the bloodied flanks of Karda and Mikka bellows in and out, Conway noted the shadows on the ground and marveled that time could have passed so quickly. His gaze went to his sword arm. Blood completely covered his right side, from ear to heel. Splotches on his left told of cross-strokes to that side.

He remembered nothing.

A murky sense of guilt seethed through inchoate thoughts. There was foreboding, as well, completely incomprehensible, since the battle was already fought and won. It was time to celebrate.

He closed his eyes, was assailed by dots of remembrance. Glint of honed edges. Low hum of clubbing wood. Jarring thud of blows absorbed by his armor.

Hooves crushing a man's metal helmet. Dogs snarling, teeth rending.

A tug on his trouser leg brought his eyes open. He ignored whoever was there, stared straight ahead. A building burned on the other side of what must have been a market. The heat bathed his face.

A voice came with the next pull on his trousers. Man Burning's scarred visage smiled up at Conway. "Everyone talks of how you fought."

Ignoring that, Conway said, "You've been saying Katallon doesn't trust Blizzard, that Moonpriest and Fox have too much influence over Varnalal."

Man Burning cringed. "Please, master, not so loud. Since you asked Katallon for me, I've served you faithfully. Don't endanger me like this. Who betrayed me?"

"It's your mouth that endangers you, not me."

Despite the ruined features, Man Burning's expression carried subtle nuances of cunning. "Truth can never be treason, master. Rulers may call it so, but truth is truth, nothing more."

Wearily, partially stifling a groan, Conway dismounted. Man Burning scurried to help Conway get out of his armor. He nodded approvingly at the cuts and dents, fingering them with a knowledgeability that picked at Conway's mind. He was too exhausted to concern himself with it. When the armor was laid across Stormracer's saddle, Man Burning took the reins. As Conway headed for the prominent well, where many of Windband were already gathered to wash and drink, the slave fell in beside him. Conway said, "Who told you Katallon distrusts Blizzard?"

"Katallon told priests, friends of Wippard, who challenged Moonpriest and died."

Sarcasm soured Conway's question. "And the priests told you?"

"A slave of Katallon's told me."

Conway stopped. The image of the Small slave girl who worked in the bath tent came to him. He'd assumed she drowned herself because he refused to help her escape Windband. But she'd spoken of friction between Moonpriest, Fox, and Katallon. If Fox was only pretending to doze while she talked, if he, in fact, overheard her, she'd probably been eliminated. Why killed, though? Why not exposed, used as an example to others?

Because the dissension was real, dangerous, and must not be revealed.

Assuming that—and Conway cursed his own steadfast refusal to be associated with any Windband factions—Fox was probably the killer. Fox would never make such a move without consulting Moonpriest.

Leaning against the circular stone wall of the well, Conway watched Man Burning crank the windlass. The wooden roller squealed as if lamenting. Warriors approached, grinning, laughing, complimenting Conway. He acknowledged them with pat, automatic responses. Inwardly, he considered the matter of conflict between Katallon and Moonpriest.

Sluicing water over himself from the moss-slick bucket, he handed it back to Man Burning for refill. Conway didn't care if either Moonpriest or Katallon lived. Windband was a tool and a refuge, a place to gather strength.

Revenge. Conway ate, drank, slept with that word foremost in his plans. Tee denied her love because she wanted the man who loved her to continue a full, rich life. Not like Lanta. A woman like that brought out the worst, the utter worst, in a man, then looked at him with sad, forgiving eyes.

Eyes like daggers. Cut into a man, opened his soul.

Man Burning pulled at the bucket. When Conway resisted, glaring, still trapped in his reverie, the slave stepped back quickly, gesturing over his shoulder. "Others are waiting, master. You weren't moving."

"Look at me; I'm filthy. Fill it again." He thrust the bucket at Man Burning.

Varnalal, joining Conway, said, "I promised you a show of loyalty today. You outdid me. You outdid everyone."

"You directed Blizzard correctly. I let myself get involved in the fighting. You deserve compliments. I deserve punishment."

Unobserved, Fox had come on them. He chuckled softly, bringing both Conway and Varnalal around to face him. Fox had abandoned the barmal of his people, now elected to wear chain mail. The links slid across each other with metallic sibilance, made Conway think of Moonpriest's rattlesnakes. Fox said, "No man who fights the way you did today gets disciplined. You have no unit to command; we've talked about that. You fight or advise as you see fit. I depend on your judgment."

It seemed a good time to test Man Burning's comments. Conway said, "Do you think Katallon would give me a command, if I asked him? Church Home is stone and mortar, not logs or dirt. Let's go to Katallon together, suggest you put together another unit like Varnalal's, one trained to attack Church Home. Or the fort of Kos."

Significantly, Fox's first reaction was to look at Varnalal. The younger man was so eager to be included in the conversation, and so afraid of saying something out of place, he was practically strangling on swallowed words. Conway shook his head at the incongruity of the thing. Varnalal's courage in battle was unquestionable. Now he looked at Fox with the beseeching expression of a starving puppy. Fox turned to Conway. "If you value your life, say nothing of your idea to Katallon. Or anyone else. If I decide your idea is good, I'll speak to Moonpriest. He controls Katallon, as he must control the world one day. Katallon would rather we all die than admit he's lost his position."

Conway said, "This is a dangerous subject. You know I'm Moonpriest's man, the same as you. The snakes proved that. I'm not sure I'm ready to help overthrow Katallon."

"Nor is anyone else." Fox was coldly disapproving. "Moonpriest admires Katallon. I want to work with Katallon. You've seen me train the scouts and the Blizzard. Are these acts of disloyalty? Moonpriest needs Windband to conquer. We must help Katallon, not fight him. Am I heard?"

"I hear." Varnalal snapped out the words. Conway, a bit slower, allowing himself a hinted smile, repeated the answer. He thought he saw a similarly covert expression from Fox.

Fox said, "I came to tell you we took some prisoners. One says he knows you."

"Me?" Conway was dumbfounded. "It's someone from Kos, then. What's a Kossiar doing here, with slaves?"

"He was fighting. Now he's dying."

It struck Conway that Fox could as easily have been saying, "He's blond" or "He's tall." He was already walking away.

Conway turned to Man Burning. "Walk Stormracer cool, bathe him well, then rub him down. Hot poultices for his legs, to draw out any soreness from today's work. See he gets cooked mash tonight."

The way to the collected prisoners was a hellish landscape. As part of Kos, it had never been fortified before the revolt. The rough wall loomed in the background now, save where it had been burned through. Bodies littered the narrow battlewalk. A defending archer slumped against a still-standing section, bow still in his dead hand.

The village appeared to have been tranquil once. Fire presently raged among its buildings. The forlorn street Conway walked with Fox and Varnalal was near the center of town, which meant shops. Broken, looted merchandise, smashed furniture, and half-eaten food were everywhere. Bits of cloth writhed in the wind.

Rounding a corner, the three men faced a stable. Windband nomads guarded the figures inside the holding corral beside it. Approximately thirty women and children crowded into one knot, squatting tightly to the earth. Cowering in the center of that group, several younger women tried to shield their nakedness with remnants of clothes. Conway averted his eyes quickly, but not before he saw the bruises, the expressions of shocked horror that defined those women's experience of Windband conquest.

Ten malc prisoners stood at the opposite side of the enclosure. Two held a wounded man whose head slumped to his chest. A gaping slash in his chain mail marked a deadly wound. Bent knees threatened to surrender.

As Fox pointed, saying, "That one," Conway was climbing over the fence. Ignoring the angry warnings of the guards, Conway walked to the stricken Kossiar and maneuvered him to a more comfortable position. He lifted his canteen to the man's lips, saying, "I never saw you before. Claiming to know me won't help you with these people, Lance. The best I can do for you is protect you from torture."

The man managed a smile. "I didn't think you could even do that. I only wanted to see you. They told me you were with Windband." His eyes wandered out of focus, settled on something far beyond Conway's shoulder. His lip curled in contempt. "You left your friends. For this scum."

"These men helped me revenge myself on Kos, on Church. Kossiars like you killed the woman I loved. And I've seen what happened to Kossiars when slaves got their hands on them. There was no mercy there, no difference between them and Windband. You tell me: Why leave your friends for this scum?"

"I'm inland Kossiar, the people of the Board. We have our own quarrel with the Crew. Many Board people joined the revolt."

"How can that be? I've seen villages after the slaves finished with them. Massacre."

"There were excesses. Most of us—escaped slaves, anti-Crew Kossiars, and a few anti-slave Kossiars—merely want free of Kos. Life in the Chair's fist is slavery."

Conway sneered. "Excesses. More like butchery. I saw."

The wounded Lance's sagging head rose in defiance that taxed his failing strength. Long pauses spaced his words. "No slave in Kos is without his story of children sold away, wives pulled from husbands, brothers separated forever. I can't excuse slave vengeance. I understand it. What of you? What injustice do you combat?" The young voice had risen in keeping with his passions. Suddenly he pitched forward, coughing violently. Groaning, he wrapped his arms around his wounded middle. A red stream trickled from his mouth. Using the hem of his shirt, Conway washed the man's face with fresh water, then offered him another drink. The Lance strained to swallow. He coughed again, renewing the bleeding. When Conway reached to clean him once more, the

536

man pulled away angrily, determined to say what was on his mind. "No one ever thought you like these ones. Sorry for you. Funny. I die. I pity you."

The Lance slumped against the rails, head lolling. His chest rose and fell in sharp, pained jolts as the dying body strained for air.

Conway studied his hands. One clutched his own bloody shirt. The other clenched the canteen. He threw aside the shirt, took a long pull of water before replacing the canteen.

The Lance stopped breathing. A pulse in his throat flickered, stopped. Rising, Conway turned to leave. He literally bumped into Katallon. The Windband leader absorbed the impact, unmoving, staring fixedly at Conway with a strange, disturbed expression. The only word that came to Conway to describe it was "frightened," which made no sense at all. Conway stepped back. "Sorry. Didn't know you were there."

Katallon grunted. "You knew that one?" He flicked the dead Lance's hand with the point of his sword.

"No. He remembered me from Kos. We never met."

Katallon put his weapon away. "I said before, death is where you are."

"It was a battle. Many died."

"The rest of us were strangers to our enemies. Only one man knew someone here. People who know you don't live long. Strange." He was gone before Conway could respond.

Standing outside the corral, Conway watched warriors herding away the women and children. Small, helpless cries rose from those who were hurried by the point of a sword. Children bawled. One boy, barely waist high to his tormentors, dodged a blow, but managed to keep protectively positioned between an old woman and the nomads.

Other Windband warriors dragged dead defenders into buildings in the path of the fire. That would be their burning. Nomads were carried to a pyre of structure timbers and wall logs. The Windband fire was touched off as Conway passed abreast of it.

He walked on, wondering how many of those men knew his name.

The Lance's face appeared to him, dissolved. What a fool; sorry for a man who was still alive. Fool.

The funeral pyre roared. Syrupy dark smoke flowed past Conway to settle in ground hollows, eddy and billow its slow way through strands of brush and trees.

It came to Conway that he'd never asked the drowned slave girl her name.

CHAPTER 92

Moonpriest leaned back into a corner of the new piece of furniture in his tent. It was his own design, a thing he called a 'sofa.' It was long enough for him to stretch out horizontally. Two white, cloudlike pillows nicely complimented the off-white sueded pigskin of its rounded, inviting seat and back. A stuffing of goose down conformed to the sitter's body. Moonpriest even had a name for the padding; he called it upholstery.

The nomads, who considered chairs effete luxury, whispered about the device. Most insisted that a god sat anywhere, any way, he chose. Some, much more covert, took the position that a god who demanded suffering, endurance, and deprivation in the name of conquest might do well to take part in some of those experiences with his followers. Those people said Moonpriest merely used Windband. They suggested he was more man than god, and possibly not very good at either. They smirked, and disparaged pampering the posterior. They hinted it was not warlike.

When Moonpriest heard the latter, he laughed. Briefly. The fact was, he understood the grave danger underlying jokes at his expense, and he was resolved to do something about it.

What?

Moonpriest fondled his turban. Accuse Katallon openly? Too extreme. There was no clear proof Katallon led the malcontents. Known, but not provable. And Katallon inspired a great deal of loyalty. Moonpriest sighed; after all he'd done to whip the nomads of Windband into line, many still exercised lingering allegiance to Katallon. They couldn't understand the man was a figurehead.

Even so, a prudent man didn't stand directly under a figurehead while pulling it down.

Moonpriest strode quickly to the hall, and then to the door to peer outside. He inhaled deeply. Dusk in the Dry was his favorite time of day. A promise of cooler air covered the earth, a shroud of relief. There were the smells, as well; the redolence of cooking, the almost tactile pressure of sage and lesser plants, the muscular force of livestock herds. He frowned, making his way back into the depths of his tent in a swirl of shining white robes. A slave, lighting candles, sank to the floor, forehead to the ground. Moonpriest ignored him. He turned into the main room and collapsed back on the sofa.

Darkness would come quickly. With that, his guest. Perhaps Katallon had a weakness. The guest might provide some insight. He permitted himself a small chuckle; insight, indeed.

Heaving himself upright, he walked to the baskets in the darkest corner of the room. The snakes watched. Dark, glistening tongues forked the air until his scent was tasted and recognized. Moonpriest squatted to look through the woven lattice, crooning softly. "Such beautiful, supple lengths of power. Deadly, deadly, deadly. All day, every day, I'm surrounded by braggarts and boasters. They flaunt huge muscles. Or weapons. They grimace, show us well-practiced fearsome faces. None of them approaches you, my expressionless, lethal children. Not one of them strikes so surely, so swiftly. *My* weapons. Be alert. Be ready. Moonpriest will come for you."

Together, eerily, both reptiles shifted. Each lazily circled the interior of its basket before coiling near the latched release door.

Moonpriest returned to his sofa. The hallway slave came to light the tapers in their ornate floor-standing holders. When barely half were burning, Moonpriest ordered him out. The slave hesitated, unsure of his orders, and Moonpriest rose, berating. "You think a god needs your miserable little flames? You've seen me call brighter fire than all the candles in this camp, just to kill one man. Can't you hear? Get *out*!"

Leaving so quickly his churning feet disarranged the carpet, the slave never looked back. Looking at the rumpled floor covering, Moonpriest paled with rage. Then, with no appreciable pause between emotions, he was riotously amused. He fell back on the sofa, flailing the air with his arms as if in flight. Eventually, he subsided. He was relaxed, smiling pleasantly into space, when Altanar peeked past the edge of the tent flap.

Moonpriest straightened. The smile squeezed out long and thin. Flesh pressed hard against bone. The nose appeared longer. Eyes drew to slits. What had been a soft, absent expression became feral eagerness. Under the weight of that look, Altanar chattered, "We're here, Moonpriest. No one saw us."

"Bring our guest here to me." Moonpriest pointed.

The figure Altanar ushered in was covered from head to below the knee in a coarse woolen blanket of wide gray and white stripes. Soft boots extended up under the cloak. Hesitantly, testing the ground at each step, the visitor let Altanar lead the way.

Moonpriest's hand signal stopped the pair. He stepped away from his sofa. Quickly, he reached out and whipped away the blanket. Unprepared, startled, Altanar froze momentarily before ducking out of reach. The stranger stood revealed as a woman. Tall, fair, full figure obvious despite loose-fitting blouse and skirt, she had a firm, handsome beauty. Stripped of cover, she raised graceful white hands in ineffectual seeking motions. The rest of her body remained absolutely still. Not even the loop of the braided hair slung forward over her right shoulder swayed. She stood with her chin slightly raised. Her eyes were firmly closed.

Moonpriest moved around her in a semicrouch. Stopping on her left side, he said, "You've worked in the baths a long time, Bayek." It was a statement.

"Yes." Her voice was melodious. Peculiarly, the sound of Moonpriest's voice released some of her tension.

Moving to Bayek's right side, Moonpriest grew louder. "You were there the afternoon your friend killed herself."

For a long moment, Bayek didn't answer. Moonpriest was frowning heavily by the time she did. "Zeecee was my associate, not my friend. I don't believe she killed herself. Yes, I was there."

"A blind slave contradicts *me*?"

"A god kind enough to assume a man's guise can't be asked to remember everything, yet every decision a god makes must have a proper end. I have a duty to provide you correct information."

"Smart. I like that."

"I am blessed." She spoke without inflection or intonation. Nevertheless, there was a wasp's sting in the words. Moonpriest pushed his face almost against hers. "There are worse things than sightlessness. Anger me at your peril."

"I know many of those things intimately. Am I to be tortured? Why?"

"Tell me what I want to know, and you need fear none of that."

"I do not fear. How could I deny a god's questions? Ask. You shall receive."

Coloring, Moonpriest pulled back to a more normal distance. He squinted suspiciously at this serene woman. He said, "Katallon was your husband."

Bayek nodded.

"He tired of you."

Another nod, neck muscles perhaps a shade tighter.

"You were gambled away to another man."

"Yes. That one raped me. I killed him as he slept. My punish-

540

ment was blinding. Katallon claimed me as his slave. I manage the important men's baths. All Windband knows this."

"Did you love Katallon so much then? Healer?"

Bayek's lips moved. A vertical line of pain slashed between her eyebrows for the briefest instant. "I thought I did. It's much the same thing."

"No, no, no." Moonpriest circled behind her, chuckling. "A mistake like yours breeds more than resignation. The other Church Priestesses were enslaved. Murdered. You were spared. Used, then discarded. You hate Katallon."

Color soft as pale rose bathed Bayek's temples, the full curve of her cheekbones. A silken shine of perspiration on her upper lip caught the candle light.

Moonpriest pressed close again, lips almost touching the back of Bayek's neck just behind her ear. He inhaled. The scent of her and her occupation already filled the small room. Up close, the aroma was insistent, compelling. Traces of oils and creams. Juniper and pine and eucalyptus blended with florals of rose and lilac and honeysuckle. And more. A feminine touch on the air, an individual signature. Her alone.

The heavy, soft rope of her hair flowed like honey. Moonpriest reached up to it, traced the air beside it. Delicately. Suggestively. The long, sensing fingers trembled away from contact.

Perhaps, Moonpriest thought.

He was, after all, in a man's body.

Now she must know only the god. Only his voice. In darkness. Total, abject dependence. Fearful mystery.

Whispering, exhaling slowly, he said, "The other bath girl, Zeecee, was blinded because she refused to reject Church and convert to Moondance. Long before her, you rejected Church, but refused Moondance, too. Tell me why." Stepping away, he studied her arm and grinned broadly at the gooseflesh his breath on her neck had created. Then he continued on to the snake baskets.

Bayek said, "I believed I'd found a better reason for my life. I thought I left Church. She never left me. Church was—is—my heart." For the first time, there was a hesitation in her voice, and she corrected herself. "My true heart."

Moonpriest squatted, reached into the baskets. Picking up a snake in each hand, he withdrew them slowly, allowing them plenty of time to find a good purchase on his arms. When he straightened they faced forward. They watched the woman, tongues busy, as he approached her in silence. Directly in front of her, he said, "Have you heard of the Flower?"

An infinitesimal pause. Then, perversely, the same aura of relief about her. "Yes. Sylah, Rose Priestess. She seeks the Door. Her Church companion is Lanta, Violet Priestess and a Seer. There is a stranger named Tate, a black woman who travels with a boy. And a warrior monk named Nalatan."

"Exactly. Who else knows of this?"

"What Kossiars or slaves have said is quickly repeated to all."

"Is that how you learned?"

"Yes. And in other ways. Slaves have other sources."

"Church sources?"

Bayek smiled. A beatific expression, absurdly out of place. The snakes, an arm's length away, lifted their heads and swayed gently. "There are those who hear things. Slaves bring the information to other slaves. Messages of hope."

Moonpriest was too puzzled to pretend otherwise. "You're very free to admit something that brings unpleasant death. The names could be tortured out of you."

"Unpleasant death? Me?" Bayek's quiet laughter was merry. Nevertheless, it shivered Moonpriest's spine. The snake's heads rose higher, the swaying more pronounced. "No pain will twist names from me. I speak knowing you are Moonpriest. You kill Church. I am still Church. I tried to throw her away, I scorned her. I cursed her. And she forgave me. I *yearn* for death."

Moonpriest watched the snakes subside. They looked practically torpid, despite the warmth of the room. It wasn't like them at all. He extended his arms, thrust the reptiles directly into the blind, chin-up face. Startled by the abrupt move, the animals reacted by tightening coils, poising to strike. The tongues whipped in and out, so close to the down-white skin they seemed to lick it. Yet neither rattled once. Moonpriest was fascinated. He said, "Then I must disappoint you. My wish is to save Church, to contend with Church honestly for dominion over souls. I don't want to destroy her. We must both exist, for the sake of all."

Twisting her head, Bayek lifted her chin higher. "What cruelty is this? You bait me. Even Katallon had the kindness to curse me when he daggered my eyes. Do what you mean to do. I forgive you."

"Then help me. Katallon means to find the Flower and kill her. I say Church and Moondance must contend for souls in peace. Let people choose, let them see how my mother can provide for them. War between us would be the ultimate evil."

"You've killed those who resisted you. They say you forgive nothing, no one."

542

"Until I can command complete obedience, how can I direct the people? Until all Windband knows the pain of excess, as children learn they cannot eat too much without suffering, they can never understand the path of love and moderation. Of forgiveness, complete and inclusive. Look into your own heart. You thought you loved Church, you thought you loved Katallon. Until Katallon taught you hatred, you couldn't appreciate love, give love. Think how you feel about Church now. *That's* love. That's what I bring Windband. Unquestioning, impervious love. Help me snare the souls of Windband, and I promise your name will live in Church forever."

"I was forgiven. I am forgiven." The woman's posture sent her words upward, past Moonpriest. Angrily, he realized he was bent aside in front of her like some superstitious suppliant, afraid his body might impede her statement.

He straightened to full height. She'd missed the whole point; her head was as vacant as her vision. He pressed the snakes close again. They shifted nervously, scales sighing silkily.

Dubious, fearful, Bayek asked, "If I helped reconcile Church and Moondance, I could go back to Church Home? Repent at Sister Mother's feet? You would speak for me?"

"Yes, yes. Haven't I promised you eternity?" He wondered if the woman was stalling. Behind that marble cool face she could be mocking.

The snakes hardened, compressed.

Bayek took a deep breath. "The people of Windband believe in you. They can't choose between faith in this world and faith in the next. By becoming both man and god, you provide too many alternatives. You or Katallon must be destroyed, and you can only truly triumph in their eyes by defeating his strength."

Moonpriest suppressed a wince. He darted a sharp glance at Altanar, made a hand gesture that sent him tiptoeing from the room.

The woman was brilliant. Her conclusions exactly duplicated his own. He resumed circling, ever more intrigued and attracted. He wondered how such a rare creature had ever been allowed to waste away in such a place. Then he returned to the important matter. "I would rather Katallon be my ally. I see into his heart, and I know there is some tiny point of goodness there. His lust for power smothers it. I wish to nurture that goodness. If I cannot, then he must go to my mother, await me in the moon."

"Katallon will worship you. He will order his people to worship you. He will never obey you."

543

Moonpriest dropped his voice to a threatening whisper. "He would dare disobey? He would challenge a *god*?"

"Katallon lives for challenge. What better end for such a one than to die fighting a god?"

It was the crux of the matter, and Moonpriest was chagrined to realize he'd never thought of it.

A dilemma. Katallon had his own plans for conquest, and intended to use Windband to execute them. If allowed to usurp the allegiance that rightfully belonged to Moondance, his popularity might overwhelm the true leader.

Plans. They could go wrong. They could be thwarted.

But Katallon was formidable. Intelligent. The woman, Bayek, said it: "Lives for challenge." Disgusting.

The whole thing was unendurable.

A challenge by a god made a martyr of Katallon if it succeeded and destroyed the god if it failed.

A challenge by the man-body that Moonpriest presently inhabited wasn't to be considered.

Katallon would never trust the altar.

Trickery was impossible; Windband would never accept a Moonpriest who tricked a Katallon.

Moonpriest twisted his turban, paced, thought.

Strength. Challenge. Uncaring, savage conflict, for its own sake.

Moonpriest smiled. Giggled. The solution was so plain.

CHAPTER 93

Windband waited. Conway couldn't remember the camp so still, so thick with expectancy. Hundreds of people were around him, yet a few feet away, where the utter blackness of night ruled, it was as if that mass didn't exist. They made no definable sound, had no recognizable form.

Somewhere to the front was an open circle of six woodpiles. The junior priests of Moondance had placed the fuel, then roamed all the camps to announce the ceremony.

Katallon's appearance would coincide with the rise of the full moon. Rumor insisted he meant to announce the attack on Church Home.

Conway thrilled at the thought.

He knew it was wrong to harbor such rancor. If Church resisted, many innocents would suffer. That was the ultimate horror of a clash of beliefs. People could believe in almost anything without harming anyone. When zealots insisted people *must* or *must not* believe one particular way, some inevitably resisted. After that came murder. Some called it war, some called it conflict. Others even twisted things to the point of calling it "resolving differences."

In the expectant darkness, Conway's thoughts arced across centuries. Dimly, as through fog, he saw a woman. Children. They smiled, recognizing him.

Weak, unsure images. He loved them, and didn't think he knew them any more.

They were innocent. They hadn't known they were to die to make a point.

A brassy trump blared.

Conway broke out of his thoughts to see the moon's first silvered edge cresting the eastern mountains.

The trump's two notes lanced the night. Conway recognized the instrument by its music; it looked as he imagined the first bugles must have looked. Brass tubing, bent in a loop, ending in a bell-shaped mouth. There were no valves. Windband used them for signals, in camp or on the march, although not in battle. This call was new to Conway. The first tone was low, so short it was essentially a grace note. The second, sustained, was at the higher limit of the instrument.

The musician knew his function perfectly. The paired notes of his second call were pitched a bit lower in tone than the first two. The latter call ended an instant before the echo of the first rebounded across the darkened camp. The combination of notes, the disparity between hard, present metal and distant, gentle echo, created an eerie harmony.

Conway's neck hair rose.

Sparks flew at the points where the firewood was stacked. Creosote bush, sage, and juniper, all well dried, caught fire quickly. Light bathed the encircling faces of the seated crowd. It flooded the empty circle where Katallon stood alone. He wore a leather vest and tight trousers fitted into calf-high boots. His headdress was a snarling leopard's head. Polished agates gleamed from the eye sockets. The skin of the animal's forelegs hung across Katallon's shoulders, the paws joined on his chest. The pelt trailed down his back.

545

Crackling fire underscored the restrained rustle of massed, crowded bodies shifting nervously.

Katallon raised his arms. "Windband!" It was a shouted challenge. The crowd mumbled, beastlike. Scattered voices spun upward in emotional explosions. Katallon shouted again, driving a fist skyward. "Windband conquers!" The night shivered with wild cheers and war cries. After the noise had run on for a while, Katallon gestured for quiet. When it came, he began to walk. To strut, actually, stiff-legged, chest out. In most men, the posturing would have been comical. No one smiled at Katallon. He displayed himself as other men flaunt weapons or horses or valuables. Turning full circle as he spoke, he praised the various tribes, then spoke glowingly of Fox's patrol and scout units. Lastly, he congratulated Blizzard.

By the time he finished, his every pause was extended by war cries and victory whoops.

Once again, he signaled for silence. Somewhere in the camp a drumbeat began, background for Katallon's next words. "As your leader, I have given much thought to Church Home. Stories tell of gold, silver, jewels, hoarded there for generations. The black robes go among the people and cheat them of their belongings. Everything goes to their hive, this Church Home. No one has ever captured it. Women laugh at us from their high rock fortress. But I—Katallon—I will break them, make them obey. Windband conquers!" The fist struck at the sky again, and the howling, roaring cacophony that followed threatened to crack the night.

When he could be heard, Katallon continued, "Our warriors have swept the sunset slope of the Enemy Mountains clear of Kossiars. Kos, the richest nation known, runs from our raiders." He raised fists, then, "Raiders. Not our main force, but raiders. Now, think of this Church Home with her major ally crushed. What if Windband became husband to Church, instead? Does the wife control the family's treasure? The husband does. So we ride to destroy Kos. When it is no more, Church Home is no longer a fort, but a prison. Church will acknowledge Moondance as the true faith. Windband will claim her treasure as dowry, as payment for protecting Church forevermore. You. And you. And all the rest of you. Every man here. You'll have wealth and horses beyond count. I, Katallon, say it."

The crowd erupted. Swords battered shields. Drums boomed. From the middle of the surging, yelling mass of nomads, a group of fifteen men carrying a variety of drums raced to the center of Katallon's fire-rimmed circle. Laughing, expansive, he stepped aside for them. The group set up quickly, facing the risen moon. At the first rataplan of the smallest drum, all drums outside the circle stopped. Inside, a tall, deep-throated instrument spoke next, providing a bass line.

Katallon signaled, and another group broke free, coming into the circle. This time it was costumed women, the majority dressed in extravagantly beaded blouses and skirts and wearing head-dresses, either antlers, horns, or feathers. Those in animal costume carried drums. When struck they made a metallic, twanging sound. Other dancers, outnumbered ten to one, were dressed as hunters, save for the bright beadwork of their clothing.

The dance celebrated the hunt. Stalking, charging, falling back, the hunters danced intricate patterns around the inner, or game, group. Most of the latter, Conway noted with a wry smile, prom-inently featured white fur flashes at the rear. What was a danger signal for fleeing animals or birds attracted equal—if different— attention to the dancers. Nevertheless, the women imitated animal postures and mannerisms with startlingly descriptive technique, all the while chanting a winding, minor-key story of chase and kill.

Conway turned away, the overt sexuality of the dancing women searing his mind with an inchoate firestorm of images, memories, emotions. He made his way through the crowd, distractedly re-sponding to smiles and greetings with curt, dismissing nods. The nomads were all too excited by Katallon's announcement and the celebration in progress to be offended.

Clearing the outer limits of the gathering, Conway turned toward his tent. Assuming the figure suddenly appearing before him was another celebrant, Conway angled to the side. The figure moved to block him. Conway stopped. Altanar grinned up at him in the pale glow of light filtering through a tent wall. "Exciting news Katallon gave us, wasn't it?"

Not caring if Altanar took it as an answer or not, Conway grunted. The smaller man wouldn't be put off. He fell in beside Conway. "It's a fool's move. Church doesn't need Kos. Windband doesn't need Kos' manpower to take Church Home. If you be-lieve anything he said, it only means a smaller share of loot for everyone. I say he'll never attack Church Home."

The last statement was so full of conviction it intrigued Conway in spite of himself. He stopped, scanning the surrounding night. They were well among the tents now, with enough light to assure no one eavesdropping. Moving closer to Altanar, looking down into the shrewd, amused features, Conway felt his pulse quicken. Instinct told him that talking to Altanar at this time, on

547

this subject, was a headfirst dive into conspiracy. Conway said, "I'm in no mood for a game. Say what you mean, then let me be."

Altanar's smile broadened. "It's all a game, my friend. The stakes are terrifying, but it's still a game. With moves, counter-moves, and pieces that outrank others."

"And you make the rules as you go."

"Ah. You've not played, but you've watched well."

Conway managed to keep a straight face. Altanar's unvarnished duplicity was amusing. Deadly, but amusing. "You'd never come to me with this sort of talk if Moonpriest hadn't sent you. Why didn't he simply ask me to come to him?"

"He imagines he's a great schemer, knows what everyone's thinking. And for protection. If I speak to you, and you report me, he denies any involvement."

"You say that as if you don't think he can escape it."

Altanar managed to look incredibly sly one moment and completely frank the next. The two expressions blended from one to the other so smoothly that Conway was questioning what he'd seen before Altanar answered. "I wouldn't even speak to you if I didn't know how you'd react. I take no such chances. You might want to remember that."

"He ordered you to sound me out, didn't he? What if you thought I'd be angered, report you to Katallon?"

"I'd lie. Tell Moonpriest I talked to you, and you chased me away."

"You tell me all this and expect me to trust you?"

"Trust is for idiots. Fear is what brings us all together. When you know I can bring you down, and you know you can bring me down, we can work comfortably to bring down someone else."

"Charming. What's our next move?"

"I take you to Moonpriest. He's in a rage, so be very careful. If he goes near those accursed snakes, ready your lightning weapon. And don't have *anything* to do with the moon altar."

Altanar's vehemence impressed Conway. "You're being very helpful. I appreciate it. You'll understand if I ask why?"

"My well-being is tied to Moonpriest. Anything that makes him happy, I work to provide. Simple."

"Anything, Altanar?" Altanar was already leading the way. Conway directed the question at Altanar's back.

Dim light caught Altanar's eyes at a peculiar angle, almost creating an animal's reflectivity. "Anything. You know I wasn't always servant to a . . . to anyone. Some day Moonpriest will raise me to the position I deserve. I serve for my reward at his hands." Having spoken, he turned his back again, and there was the message in his movement that he knew he'd said more than he meant to. The conversation was finished.

Conway was satisfied. There was much to consider before the confrontation with Moonpriest.

CHAPTER 94

Altanar ushered Conway into Moonpriest's shadowy receiving room. Moonpriest sat on the sofa, agitatedly stroking his white turban. Conway flinched. No matter how composed Moonpriest's outward appearance, the hand reaching to the ugly scar at the side of his head was incontrovertible proof of distress.

Candle flames wavered in the candelabras. Greasy coils of smoke swirled to the top of the tent, hanging in a noisome cloud. A rising wind moved the ceiling. Trapped smoke throbbed and boiled. It caught the candlelight in its depths, sometimes bright, sometimes dark. It had an aura of sentience.

Conway recognized a carefully staged scene. Moonpriest's normal candles were smokeless beeswax. He also kept his quarters well ventilated.

Glancing behind him, Conway saw Altanar edging toward the door. Moonpriest said, "Don't rush off, Altanar. I may have need of you. You're important to me, you know you are. Get Conway a chair."

Altanar scurried to a corner, returning with the chair, placing it where Moonpriest pointed. The gesture turned into a wave, and Conway moved to sit down. Moonpriest's right hand caressed the turban constantly. Conway found himself staring, remembering the collapsed skull where Sylah had removed bone and tissue.

Moonpriest said, "Do you enjoy being a dupe, Matt?"

Conway's cheeks warmed. The flesh of his throat was next, hot as sunburn. Knowing his anger was so obvious made him aggressive. "Katallon's decision to delay attacking Church Home wrecks some of your plans, as well."

"Plans." Moonpriest flipped a hand, dismissed concern. "I can make plans as quickly and easily as I can contact my mother. No, I was feeling sorry for you. I meant to anger you. Poor psychology. You're already angry. Life is different for you. Plans are more important. I hate to see yours ground underfoot so thought-lessly."

Conway laughed. He didn't feel amused, and he heard the acid bitterness of his falsity. "Katallon's cheated both of us. I want to crush the hypocrisy of Church for my own reasons, and he's checked me. You have to have Katallon's nomads attack Church Home, or there's no way for you to overthrow the existing system."

Casually, Moonpriest said, "You could be killed for guessing about my goals, my thoughts."

"You need me. I've got lightning of my own, remember? Lightning that reaches out."

Moonpriest was on his feet, roaring. "Enough! You discuss the sacred gifts given us by my mother in front of a slave?" Moonpriest leveled a finger at Altanar. "Leave us. My brother and I must talk."

Altanar backed out of the room. Moonpriest continued to stare at the swaying cloth door flap. Pointing at his own mouth, moving his jaw, Moonpriest indicated Conway should talk. The weather seemed a safe subject. Moonpriest stalked the exit. Pausing, he made a sound exactly like a rattlesnake. Then he screamed and leapt through the opening. Hoarser screams replaced Moonpriest's, followed by the repeated sound of flesh on flesh. Altanar yelled innocence, exclaimed between blows that he wasn't listening.

Conway was smiling crookedly when Moonpriest stormed back into the room. "What's funny?" Moonpriest demanded.

Placating, Conway said, "Why keep Altanar around?"

"I need amusement. Anyone else would find him a cunning challenge. To me, he's a diversion. No one can trick me." His face darkened. "I can be disappointed, however. And careless. My mother hates it when I'm careless. She works so hard. When her son lapses in his duties, I'm shamed." He hung his head in remorse.

Without looking up, the words aimed at his feet, Moonpriest resumed in a whining mumble. "They're not obedient children. They try to avoid my will. Mother's will. They know I'm her child. How many times have I proven it? And still they won't understand that I see everything, comprehend their scheming before they do."

Conway inhaled deeply, surprised by how badly he needed that breath. He said, "You knew Katallon's plans?"

Moonpriest grimaced faintly, an expression more of annoyance than danger. "Nothing is hidden from Moonpriest. My crime is refusing to believe anyone would plot against me. Don't you see? It's so fruitless, so pointless; I can't make myself take my mother's warnings seriously. She told me Katallon means to harm her. I listened and failed to act."

"He's offering no direct challenge to you. Maybe the Kos campaign will go more quickly than we expect. We'll crack Church Home, in any case."

"I'm glad you said *we'll* take Church Home. But we won't while Katallon rules Windband. Can't you see his intentions? He has no need of Kossiar manpower to conquer Church Home. The warrior monks who guard that nest of whores are formidable, but Windband outnumbers them at least fourfold. The close ties between Church Home and Kos are historic and helpful to each, but unnecessary to the survival of either." He stopped short, fixing Conway with a demanding look.

It was a test, and Conway knew it. He tried to meet Moonpriest's eyes. The glassy intensity of them broke Conway's composure. He looked away, saying, "Katallon's numbers aren't enough for him to attack Church until he's consolidated the conquest of Kos."

Moonpriest's smile was a blade. "Half right. There won't be any attack on Church Home. The Harvester will be the next Sister Mother. She craves power. Windband roams wherever a man on horseback can go. If the Harvester wishes to expand Church's influence, Windband is her vehicle. If she rejects Katallon's offer of protection, her Priestesses will be hunted down like rabbits by the same Windband. If he's clever, and we know he is, he'll control Church while still holding immense influence over the believers of Moondance."

"You forget Sylah and the Door."

"There is no Door. There never was." Conway blinked, shocked. Moonpriest continued. "I am what I say I am. I ask, and all is known. You concern yourself about the witch, Sylah? The Chair and the Harvester pursue her even now. Sylah's quest was pointless at its outset. Now it's finished." A dry, rustling laugh made its way past thin lips. "She and the other witch, Lanta, stole the Chair's firstborn son, if you can imagine. Presumptuous, self-important fool. This time Sylah will pay for her arrogance. In the hardest coin of all."

"Lanta? Stole a child?" Conway caught the swift mad-glitter of Moonpriest's glare. Furious with himself for being shocked by anything Lanta might do, as well as nervous about upsetting

Moonpriest, Conway spoke harshly. "It's like her. She knows what's best for everyone. Endangering others is what she does best. What did you hear of the others? What about Tate? Nalatan?"

"They chose to associate with her. They helped her. They earned whatever comes."

"There has to be a way to stop it. Give me Fox and twenty men. Ten. Tate's got the sniper rifle, another wipe, a pistol, ammunition. Nalatan's a fighting machine. The women are Healers. You can't let that all that just go to waste."

Moonpriest reached to put a hand on Conway's shoulder. It settled softly, fingertips first, spreading out as it lowered. Conway watched it from the corner of his eye, the way he'd watch a spider he was afraid to startle. When Moonpriest spoke, it took all of Conway's will to take his gaze from the hand and concentrate on the man's face. "Your concern speaks well of you. Don't think me unappreciative. Still, I have to say I'm disappointed in you. Can't you understand, I don't need anyone? Anything? My mother has tasked me to bring her worship to the world. She helps me, but the chore is mine. My first responsibility is Windband. She's told me I must have it. She *will* have it. I'm in a death struggle with Katallon. If I can't displace him, I'm an unfit son. You think that because I'm a god, I can simply strike him down. I wish I could. Because I'm on this earth in a man's body, my mother insists I surpass Katallon as a man. Eliminate him, subordinate him—she doesn't care. Her only concession is that I may defeat him through my superior intelligence. As a man, however, not as a god."

He bent to cradle his head in his hands, shaking it sadly. "I wish I could help you. I must deal with Katallon first."

Conway felt his control fraying, pictured himself, rapt with attentiveness, as this faker prattled about the unavoidable death of Sylah's entire group. The image sickened him. He wondered what could have possessed him to ever attach any credence to anything the man said. Unless he was as crazy as Moonpriest.

What he wanted—*had*—to do required the madman. "Get rid of Katallon. You can't just let one of us die. Tate came into this world with you and me."

Unctuous evasion rolled from Moonpriest. "Once I have control, ask me for anything. Until then, I must attend to my own priorities."

Conway spun away from the hand on his shoulder. The chair beckoned, a target. One step took him to it. One kick sent its shattered pieces bouncing across the room. Raging, he picked up one of the legs and threw it against the cloth wall. The soft plop only intensified his frustration. Drawing the pistol, he fired at the piece of wood. Cloth walls absorbed the sharper edges of the explosion, damping it to a crushing, dull boom. The chair leg shattered in the middle. Splinters shrieked away from the impact. The two halves leapt and whirred.

Moonpriest lurched to his feet, hands clasped to his ears, eyes shut. He staggered forward in tight, uncertain steps. A smoking hole marked where the bullet plowed through the carpet and into the earth underneath.

Turning back toward Moonpriest, Conway found the other man staring at him in round-eyed shock. Conway waggled the pistol at Moonpriest's middle. "You talk about death like it was abstract. It's real. It lasts forever. I'll make a deal with you: Help me get out of here so I can at least try to help the others, and I'll solve the Katallon problem for you."

Altanar burst through the flap entry. His first glance took in Moonpriest facing a crouching Conway and the seeking eye of the pistol. Color fled Altanar's face. He dropped, facedown. "I'm a servant, a slave. I came to serve my master. Please, let me go. I saw nothing. I want nothing."

"Shut your mouth and get out." Moonpriest's swiftly regained composure surprised Conway. He turned from it just in time to see Altanar dart back out the door. Moonpriest returned to his sofa, stiffly, as if his joints pained him. He sat the same way. "That was foolish. Dangerous."

Conway apologized. "My temper. It seems to get worse. I'm sorry."

"I understand. We're surrounded by barbarism. It shrivels the soul after a while. We must guard against it. Our problems are too subtle for gunpowder."

"I said I was sorry."

Chiding with surprising gentleness, Moonpriest said, "We're still of a kind. We must work together."

Conway was reminded of two cats. Until they actually tore at each other, fang and claw, they pretended cool unconcern.

Outside, the wind was stronger. It shoved and bullied the tent walls. The material sighed and groaned under the buffeting. Restraining support lines whispered, occasionally creaking sharper complaint. Inside, more and more of the candles burned out, lending greater menace to the graying weight of the trapped smoke.

Conway said, "We have to eliminate Katallon. Even if we humiliate him, he'll be a problem. Such men are never beaten. Destroyed, yes; beaten, no. If you order Katallon to attack Church Home, he'll balk. In your name, I'll challenge him. Swords."

"He'll cut you to pieces. I don't care if your vaunted dogs are by your side and you're riding that horse these savages drool over."

Bridling, Conway holstered the pistol. "I might surprise both of you. Instead, I'll settle for a sure thing. When you were putting together your moon altar, did the words *Faraday cage* ever come to you?"

Blankly, Moonpriest repeated the phrase, then, resuming his stern mien, he said, "My mother used no such language. What you said means nothing to me."

"It will."

Moonpriest sniffed disdain. Conway refused to be baited. "Insist Katallon strike directly at Church Home. Tell him your brother—that's me—demands he acknowledge his first allegiance is to Moonpriest. I'll be ready in three, four days at the most. I mean to see Church ruined. What you and your mother do after that is entirely up to you. I'm out of it. I have your word on this? Once I've finished Katallon, we drive on Church Home?"

"Fight Katallon and you'll die."

Conway's hand made an involuntary twitch toward the holstered pistol. "Your word. Let me hear you say it."

Heaving a histrionic sigh, Moonpriest capitulated. "You have my word. I'll say a special prayer for you."

"Wonderful. I'm grateful." Conway turned on his heel and left.

Alone, Moonpriest sat stroking his turban for quite a while. Only two candles still burned, creating tiny spheres of light where the flames swayed in the eddying pressures of the moving walls. Moonpriest clapped, twice. Behind him, a fold in the cloth wall slowly spread and a white, ghostly form slipped through the revealed doorway. Bayek, in a flowing gown, made her way to the front of Moonpriest. She turned her head from side to side, adjusted her position a step to her right, then bowed.

Moonpriest chuckled. "You amaze me. You knew exactly where I was. Magical."

She smiled, a gentle, soft expression. "No magic. Many blind people can sense others' location. In your case, the power is very strong. I hear you, a sound of rushing water. Wind. It's the sound of mountains."

Folding his hands across his chest, Moonpriest nodded appreciation. "Really? The mountains. You never mentioned that before.

What a nice thought." He gathered himself reluctantly, became serious. "You listened to my brother?"

Quick disapproval marred her features. "He speaks too boldly, even if he does have your best interests at heart. He's a cruel man, but a good man is dying inside him. Who has hurt him so badly?"

"All that matters is that he helps me. Us. Moondance."

"You were brilliant. But can he defeat Katallon? Kill him for you?"

Moonpriest rose to her. Hands on her shoulders, he stroked them as he spoke. "My brother is one who survives. It's his talent. Katallon will die. My mother has ordained it. Afterward, you and I will bring Church and Moondance together in peace."

Bayek reached to still his hands, holding them. Slowly, wearing the same soft, enigmatic smile, she guided them to her breasts, pressed them firmly to her. Her voice turned breathy. "I'm seducing you. I have a confession, and I want your forgiveness before I speak. I'm terrible, am I not?"

"Terrible." It was almost a croak. Sweat beaded Moonpriest's eager features. He tried to pull away, tried to lead her from the room. She held firm, drew his hands back into place. Bending her body to his, she said, "Forgive me. First."

He laughed, a strained, hoarse sound. "Temptress. What is this great sin I should know about? You know I can't deny you anything."

The smile disappeared, replaced by genuine concern. "The girl who worked with me, the one who was killed. Zeecee. I know who killed her. They didn't have to do that. She was a harmless little thing."

"Is that all?" The laughter this time was relieved. "I knew you knew. It had to be done. She was just a slave, and a spy, at that. Poor Bayek, poor little thing, troubled for no reason." He embraced her tightly, then stepped away to lead her toward the slit in the wall. "The man who is me needs the mystery of you. The god who is me knows everything about you. What woman can claim so much? And how lucky I am that my mother directed you to me."

Moving along beside him, Bayek hugged him with the arm she'd wrapped around him. "There are no secrets from you, are there? I look forward to thanking your mother in person. What a wonderful day. Will we really go to her in the moon together?"

"When I go, so shall you. I promise." He held the gap open, ushered her through. He was pulling off his robe as he followed.

Later, staring up at the blackness of his bedroom, he reflected on the evening. It had gone incredibly well, he decided. He stretched luxuriously, savoring. Power. Control. Sex. How marvelously, how wondrously, they mixed. Indistinguishable, really. The delights of one magnified the delights of the other.

Bayek. A universe of pleasures.

Clever. What was it she'd said? " . . . a harmless little thing." Nasty spy, that's what. Fooled Bayek. Easy enough: such a trusting nature. A tribute to her, considering all the abuse she'd suffered. Good of her to worry about a nothing like the other one. Nasty spy. Fox heard. Fox hears everything. Foolish woman, talking to Conway, his first day in Windband. Well, that'd be cleared up soon, too. Conway could join his little drowned friend. Whatshername.

Sighing, Moonpriest rolled onto his side, draped an arm across the soft, pliant body next to him. He was asleep as soon as he closed his eyes.

CHAPTER 95

Cautiously, Man Burning bent to the entryway of Conway's tent. "Master?"

He called softly. Since the fiery argument between Katallon and Moonpriest, it wasn't safe to be too closely identified with either group of supporters. Men had already died for declaring Katallon an unbeliever; others called Moonpriest an intruder and false siah, and died just as quickly.

A haggard Conway, face still full of sleep, peered out. He glanced about, then gestured Man Burning inside.

The slave squatted by the small cooking fire. Conway scooped stew out of the simmering pot into a bowl and handed it to Man Burning. The scarred man took it with both hands, holding it high while he smiled thanks. Head bobbing, he said, "I was near Katallon's tent before I came here. His slaves got no meat this morning."

"Why?" Conway ladled his own bowl full, sitting across from Man Burning. Karda inched closer, crawling, not actually getting to his feet. Mikka held her place, eyes fixed on Conway's hands. Conway absently admonished them to stop begging. The dogs dropped their heads to the floor, clearly mourning cruel starvation and neglect.

Man Burning said, "Some Moondance supporters crept close enough to Katallon's tent last night to sing hymns to him in the dark. Katallon didn't like it: 'They were close enough to sing, they were close enough to shoot arrows.' All the guards were sent back to their own camps with instructions to send better men as replacements. The slaves were whipped."

Conway's grin gleamed whitely in the dim tent. "Do more people favor Katallon than me?"

Shaking his head, Man Burning grew serious. "Most people won't speak. They wait."

"To see who wins?"

"Yes." Man Burning shifted awkwardly, studied his stew as if expecting something unpleasant to surface.

"Out with it." Conway bent forward, jabbed Man Burning's knee with stiff fingers. "What else?"

"Oh, they're waiting to see who wins. I speak true." He shot a quick glance at Conway's uncompromising glare and surrendered to full disclosure. "They expect Katallon to kill you without taking a deep breath. What concerns them is, what happens next? If Katallon can kill a god's brother, can he kill a god? Will the god strike Katallon dead? What about Windband? Will the god take revenge on everyone for his brother's death? These questions worry everyone."

Conway spooned up the last of his stew, rose stiffly, groaning. "I've got to get more sleep. I was up most of the night." He grinned wickedly at the glum Man Burning. "Why worry? I die tonight. Lots of rest, then."

Man Burning moved forward, putting down the bowl, rising onto his knees. He knelt, almost supplicating. "You treat me as a man, Matt Conway. In here, with you, I'm not a slave. I serve you because it's my work. Hear me now as another man, one who's seen too much tyranny. Use the lightning weapon. I've seen what it can do. Kill Katallon. You're too good a man to die for Moonpriest."

"I'm not dying for anyone." Conway busied himself rooting two huge wildcow thigh bones out of a leather sack. The dogs bounded to their feet to claim them, then drew off to the farthest corner. Loud cracking and crunching noises followed. Only then did Conway continue. "My fight is with Church. It ruined my life."

Man Burning rose to full height. "So you've said before. I find it hard to believe. Church was always good to me."

"Well, not to me. No more talk about it. When I've killed

557

Katallon, Moonpriest will take Windband and crush Church. If Katallon were willing to do that, I'd never have any argument with him. That's as much as you need to know."

Man Burning continued to stand in front of Conway. Nervous, uncertain, his hands flexed at his sides and he shifted his weight from foot to foot. His chin jutted belligerently. Finally, Conway could stand it no longer. Gruffly, he said, "Oh, come on. What is it this time? Are we going to spend the whole morning like this, you looking put upon, me trying to get you to say what's on your mind?"

The dogs suddenly fell silent in their corner. Ignoring that warning, or too emotional to be aware of it, Man Burning said, "It may be time to share some things. I'm not ignorant. Or stupid. I know about you." At Conway's quick step back, Man Burning hurried his words. "A Peddler stopped near the camp of the Long Sky People. Slaves and Peddlers have an affinity for each other. Despised people usually do. They gossip. Every slave in Windband, and most of the people between here and Harbor, know how you lost the woman named Tee."

Snarling, Conway reached for the man's throat. The dogs roared, leapt to attack. Their action shocked Conway back to reason. Still, he was almost too late to save Man Burning. Pivoting, he twisted him around, got his own body between the slave and the raging dogs. Simultaneously, he commanded the animals to lie down. They continued to growl even as they obeyed.

Man Burning backed away, licking his lips. "Someone has to tell you what the Peddler said: The small sister didn't betray you." Man Burning was bent at the knees, not quite crouched, poised to leap for the exit. The dogs rumbled like distant thunder.

Wearily, Conway said, "You know nothing. The Peddler knows nothing. Get out of my sight. Go back to Katallon's slave quarters, tell them I'm returning you. Come near me again and I'll let the dogs have you." Turning his back, Conway bent to fuel the fire.

From his position a few tents away, Altanar watched Man Burning's hurried exit, saw the nervous glances the slave sent over his shoulder as he trotted away. When Man Burning was almost abreast of the horses shielding Altanar, the latter moved quickly to block him. Man Burning stopped instantly, twisting away in defensive reaction.

Altanar's smile cut. "You told him you knew about the woman?"

Man Burning nodded. Altanar reached out, took the other man's hand in both of his. With his thumbs on the back, and his fingers curled under, he bent the hand down and back. Man Burning's face wadded with pain. He pulled away, not hard enough to free himself. Altanar said, "Never shake your empty head at me. I expect a decent answer. Not an intelligent one, but at least one I can hear." Letting go, he went on, "Did it bother him when you told him?"

Sullen, Man Burning hung his head. "He grabbed me. My throat. The dogs came. I almost died."

"Almost." Altanar repeated the word with a gay lilt. "Conway blames Church?"

"Yes."

"Good. That explains several things; apparently the Peddler's story was accurate. Now, when Conway fights Katallon, will he use the lightning weapons?"

"No."

"You're certain." It was a challenge, not a question.

"He said."

"Then we have nothing to fear. Katallon will kill him." Altanar angled forward, tapped Man Burning's aching wrist. "Never forget your manners. Broken wrists never really heal well." He left with a spring in his step, humming a tune.

Man Burning wiped a hand across his face. It left a mark across a sheen of fear sweat. Looking down at the hand, at its shaking, he shook his head angrily and resumed his walk. He mumbled to himself. "Conway's greatest ambition is to destroy Church. Moonpriest's greatest enemy is Church. Altanar, who is nothing without Moonpriest's protection, wants to eliminate Conway. That dangerously weakens Moonpriest, may even destroy him. Why? Altanar would hurt anyone, any time. Yes. I know about that. But Moonpriest is more clever than that. So why destroy Conway?"

Some distance from Katallon's slave pens, Man Burning looked up and took stock of his progress. There appeared to be no one following him. He stepped between two tents, hurrying past them, doubling back, alert for watchers. A few children laughed and pointed. A woman at the back entrance of her tent shouted at him to get away.

Breaking clear of the tents, he moved into the brush lining the banks of the stream running past the bath tent. From a point upstream, he worked his way near the facility. Assuring himself no one was nearby, he gave a loud hawk's cry. Then he dropped low and waited.

A flap opened on the tent. Bayek came out. She took a few

steps, shook the drying cloth she carried over her arm, then returned inside.

Following that all-clear signal, Man Burning crept forward, keeping well concealed. Adjacent to the tent, he darted across the open space between it and the untrimmed scrub. Throwing himself on the ground, he rolled under the cloth wall. Inside, he scrambled to his feet, crouched warily. Off to the side, soft laughter welcomed him.

"Bayek?" His eyes strained to adapt to the poor light.

"Of course. What happened?"

Man Burning related his morning's activities, ending with, "What are they planning? What possible benefit can either Altanar or Moonpriest expect to gain from Conway's death?"

Bayek was thoughtful for a long while. Finally, she shrugged. "If we're successful, it'll make no difference."

"What if we fail?"

The blond woman's laughter rocked through the twilight interior. Man Burning winced at the sound. There was departure in it, a resigned melancholy that made him think of endless roads, of campfires abandoned and gone cold.

Her seeking hand rested fingertips on his lips. From there they traced the lines of his scar with easy familiarity. "My dearest friend. How predictable you are to me, and how fortunate we are that no one else realizes what a devious schemer you really are."

Gently removing her hand, continuing to hold it in his own, Man Burning said, "I saw new chain mail in Conway's tent. A shirt long enough to reach below his knees. It'll make him slow. Katallon won't fail to realize that."

"Conway knows armor protection won't help him as much as loss of mobility will hurt him. Can it be we're not the only people here being untruthful?" She burlesqued shock.

Shaking his head, Man Burning said, "Sometimes your newfound peace of mind frightens." Her hand twitched in his, and he quickly tightened his around it. "I didn't mean that the way it sounded. I'll be with you through the whole plan. It just doesn't seem like a thing one laughs about."

Bayek was immediately sympathetic. "I keep forgetting it's not the same for you. I dearly wish you could share my peace, my joy. It's not an end, it really isn't. It's a beginning. Try to believe that."

"I believe it for you. If it's so for me, then it'll be a pleasant surprise. As long as I can put an end to this world for him, then I can meet my own time with no regrets."

560

"Such a terrible cost. I almost wish—"

"No, no, no," he interrupted, "we'll have no wishes, no what-ifs. Everything's decided."

"It's wonderful to be able to say that, isn't it? No more fear, no more pain, no more shame." Smoothly, flowing to him, she wrapped her arms around him, pressed her cheek to his chest. "An end to the darkness. I'll be clean, Man Burning. I'll be with my sisters. They'll forgive me. Church will, too."

"They all forgave you long ago, sweet Bayek. You paid for any mistakes, many, many times over."

She pulled back her head, turned her face up to his. He thrilled when the feeling that something superior to ordinary vision enabled her to see directly into his emotions. She said, "You suffered, too. And paid. Can't you find some happiness in knowing all the bad things are ending?"

"I can't even remember happiness. All I ask is satisfaction. More than freedom, I need that."

Nestled against him once more, she spoke in a quiet, musing voice. "Sometimes I worry about what we're doing. It's wrong. I don't like to think we're bad people. It has to be done, doesn't it? I'm not just being cruel, am I? Nights, when I'm all alone and it's quiet, I think about some of the things that have happened, and I want them to know pain. Like mine. I'm not proud of feeling like that."

Man Burning swayed back and forth, rocking her in his arms. "Hush. What we're doing is necessary. For ourselves, yes. For others, people we'll never know, yes. For Church, yes. We strike down evil."

CHAPTER 96

Black sky pressed down into the valley holding Windband. Directly overhead and to the east blazed uncountable stars. To the west, that light was restrained, the ragged outline of the looming mountains there obscured. Several Moondance priests had commented on it earlier, muttering about mystic hazes and the upcoming conflict between good and evil.

Warriors of Katallon's personal guard tracked down the speakers. The priests were given to understand that Katallon invariably represented good. There was no more talk of that comparison.

Nevertheless, like everything else about the contest between Katallon and Conway, the weather was abnormal. People wondered. Animals behaved erratically. Not only priests said strange forces were afoot.

From outlying camps, the people bearing torches flowed in rivulets, then streams, and finally in three seething rivers. They poured up onto a relatively flat knoll. The site offered an encompassing view of the entire valley. Any other time, the torchlit movement would have been a thing of beauty.

Conway, alone at the edge of the high ground, thought of fiery snakes. And of Moonpriest.

Tendrils of suspicion and doubt crept smokily across his mind. They left a residue of fear wherever they touched. The same foreboding he'd known after the battle where the young Kossiar died lodged stubbornly in his head. Worse, the guilt returned.

The people jostled along, buzzing with excitement. Dogs barked, racing along the edges of the winding columns. Despite the darkness, cocks crowed from every aspect of the camps.

There was a fluttery, twitchy edge to the merriment. When the dogs tumbled over each other, the quick snaps and snarls degenerated almost instantly into bloody, squalling fights.

Human laughter crackled with repressed tension. People, too, bumped each other in the dark, much like the dogs. Similarly, they seemed overeager to take those minor collisions to confrontation.

The cloth walls of Katallon's tent were no proof against the brittle atmosphere. The subordinate chiefs of the tribal groups sat in a rough circle. There was an unusual formality in this night's arrangement, in that every man managed a distance between himself and his flanking neighbors. It was as though the awareness of a surprise blow was the uppermost thought in the mind of all.

Katallon strode to his chair. He wore leather under chain mail that reached just below his waist. Hundreds of metal rings sighed music as he moved. Vertical metal bars sewn to leather trousers protected his thighs and lower legs from slashing blows. He carried his sword in a scabbard slung across his back. Pheasant tail feathers decorated the handle; which rose above his head. The vivid plumes dangled and danced in the wind of his passage.

Drawing a long, slim-bladed knife from a scabbard at his side, he drove it into the empty chair where the War Chief would normally sit. There was a sharp intake from the circle; no one bared weapons in Katallon's tent. The prohibition could have hardly been applied to Katallon himself, but he'd honored it as long as anyone could remember. He said, "I have spoken to each of you in private, asking advice and counsel. I was undecided until I entered this room. Some of you asked me to compromise with Moonpriest. You say, rightly, that I need only defeat the Conway one to prove Windband's leader can defy a god. However, I know that Moonpriest's challenge is aimed at control of Windband. I will die before I share command. If the Conway one chooses to take Moonpriest's part in this argument, then he should be prepared to die for him. All agree Moonpriest is holy. Is Conway? Must we believe that every man who comes to Windband with a piece of magic is a god? Moonpriest tells us he'll die the death of a man when his time away from the moon is ended. Who can say when or how that time will end? As for me, if I am not to be Katallon alive as I am, then I choose to be Katallon dead."

The chief of the Long Sky People rose slowly. He wore the four-colored jacket of his rank. Each color represented a point of the compass and a branch of the tribe. His trousers and boots were beaded with sacred symbols related to the tribe's wanderings before it became part of Windband. Before speaking, he placed the palm of his right hand over his heart in the gesture that meant his honor stood on the truth of his words. "The heart and courage and skill of Katallon has led us always to victory. Against men. We all fought beside him. We killed men. Enslaved men. If Katallon wants to fight a god, we can only hold our breath. None here have his bravery."

Katallon grinned. "None here have yours, either, or you wouldn't be the only one on his feet, arguing with me. You're all afraid of what will happen to you if I lose."

The Long Sky chief winced. "Or if you win. Kill Conway, and what of Moonpriest's anger?"

"Conway hates Church. Have you heard why? He blames a Healer for the death of his slave whore. It's said he loved· her. What god's brother would love a whore *or* a slave? For Moonpriest to do his mother's bidding, he must supplant Church in every place with Moondance. He can't do that without Windband. I aim to take Church Home my way in my time. Moonpriest hopes his 'brother' will kill me only because he wants to pursue his own goals. Mark what I say: after I kill Conway, Moonpriest will be much easier to deal with."

Stubbornly, the Long Sky chief persisted. "We can't help you. We won't stop you. You are Katallon. We support your right to live or die however you choose. But we ask you to speak to

Moonpriest. Tell him he must not include your followers in his vengeance."

"I'll do that." Katallon jerked the knife from the chair's wooden seat. "Moonpriest has cost me a good friend and many good warriors. I accept that, as all men accept the whims of gods. Conway is another matter."

Another chief got to his feet. Nervousness made his words rapid, his voice scratchy, in cruel contrast to the solemn dignity of the Long Sky man. "The dogs. The horse, Stormracer. What of the lightning?"

"Moonpriest promises swords only. And knives. If the dogs or the horse come at me, you kill them."

The speaker hurriedly dropped back onto his chair. The Long Sky chief sent him a chill glance before readdressing Katallon. "Why does Moonpriest have the moon altar at the place of the contest?"

"So Moonpriest and his new 'brother' can be in perfect contact with the moon mother."

Then, as if aware of him for the first time, Katallon looked at Fox. Bleak, cold silence grew between the two men. The tension in the room was a flame, waiting only the tiniest breeze to lift it to a consuming blaze. To Katallon, the Long Sky chief said, "We have spoken among ourselves of the Fox Eleven one. He has trained Blizzard as well as our best scouts and trackers. We respect him and trust him."

Katallon said, "We are much alike, Fox and me. Just as I am Windband, and Windband is me, so he belongs to Moonpriest."

Fox got to his feet, dressed in an elegant antelope-hide shortsleeved shirt and trousers, both entwined with decorative vine patterns of appliquéd rabbit skin. When he gestured, his bared arms were hard-muscled as ever, and the sense of waiting violence within him was undiminished. "Only Katallon can command. All agree. Moonpriest has never said otherwise. Moonpriest only says that Church is the enemy of all, and Katallon should attack Church Home first."

The gathering of chiefs focused on Katallon so intently they seemed turned to stone. Katallon laughed at them. " 'Moonpriest says.' Look at yourselves. All with one thought: What if Katallon dies? Well, Katallon will not die."

Katallon stepped outside his tent. A warrior immediately lit off a torch on a pole by the entry. Another seized Katallon's red and black battle standard on its shaft, taller than three men, ready to follow his leader. Katallon stepped off, making his way along a cleared path reaching to the testing ground. Every fifth step, another warrior lit another pole-mounted torch. Katallon's progress was punctuated by a march of flames, and with each new appearance, the approval of the crowd grew louder.

Beyond that natural, inevitable excitement, however, there was a tingle to the air, a suggestion of physical contact.

Conversation was too loud, too fast. Children, when not wide-eyed with excitement, cried fitfully, sometimes for no apparent reason.

There were thirty torches flaring in the strengthening west wind when Katallon and the chiefs reached the roped-off area. By then the cheering was a chant, three beats, *Kat-al-lon, Kat-al-lon.* The night shuddered with it. Drums gave voice.

Katallon took his standard, stepped alone into the area of combat. Several paces from the altar, he jammed the metal butt of the pole into the earth. Only one small torch burned in the arena, far off, beyond the altar. The torches carried by the people were doused as they formed their watchful circle outside the lines. Moonpriest had insisted. The people had concurred. This was a battle to test the power of the moon. It would never do to cheapen it with torchlight.

Then Moonpriest appeared. Somehow, he made his way through the crowd practically unnoticed, appearing almost magically under the lone torch. Dressed in solid white robe and turban, he posed for a few heartbeats, stern, vaguely disapproving.

Cheering faded. One by one, raggedly, drums ceased. The last to stop left the silence that follows a tasteless remark. Moonpriest strode toward the altar. His sweeping robe made him appear to flow. The massive silver moon disk on its silver chain rode in his outstretched hands. A beacon of his power, it caught the moonlight and shimmered with its same cold beauty. One hysteric ripped open his shirt and cried for its gleam to bathe his soul. A warrior, hair roached in a horse's mane, he threw back his head in ecstasy and shouted Moonpriest's name.

Now the enthusiasm was for the man in white. The drums began again, a two beat, hard and soft. Slower this time. Insinuating, rather than insisting. Feet pounded in cadence. Thunder born of hundreds of boots rolled through the earth, a menacing bass accompaniment to subdued voices calling *"Moon-priest! Moon-priest!"*

Conway's advance to the altar didn't start until Moonpriest was already there, standing on the lowest copper step. Two Mountain warriors in the seats turned their crank handles. The disk rumbled irritably, gradually picking up speed. The brushes hissed against the outer rim.

Moonpriest stepped onto the altar to inspect its workings.

The first laughter jerked him upright.

Walking as if his feet hurt, Conway headed for the center of the arena. Bareheaded, clad in a comically long, loose chain mail smock, he carried a heavy sword in thickly gloved, mailed hands. His boots were ridiculously oversized.

He looked far more clown-like than godly.

Giggles speckled the crowd, choked explosions of ridicule, cropping up here, then there. A child shouted, "What is it?" and the wavering dam of respect collapsed under a flood of amusement.

Moonpriest's fury threatened to topple him from the altar. Bending to Conway in order to keep the warriors turning the wheel from hearing, he said, "You've made fools of us both. My dignity, my prestige . . ."

"Your ass." Conway was pale, as grim as Moonpriest was angry. "I'm on the line here, not you. Hook this up the way I told you." He extended a copper wire to Moonpriest, careful to keep the action hidden from the crowd and the wheel turners. Grumbling, Moonpriest moved away. He stopped in front of the container holding the Man Who Is Death. When the end of the wire was joined to the metal, he stepped back and sent a surreptitious glance at Conway.

As Conway moved off, the wire fed off the loops at his back. It was a fine wire, and, in moonlight, invisible. To further obliterate any evidence of his deception, the rising wind blustered across the torch flames. Their light swayed, creating a fitful illumination of confusing shadows. Even the night helped in the deception. The high silken mist that had earlier shrouded the western stars now appeared directly overhead. It veiled the moon's brightness, turned it pallid.

This time when the people pointed at the eerily obscured sky and mumbled of omens and portents, there were curses and angry orders to stop frightening the children.

CHAPTER 97

Katallon drew his sword. Raising it over his head, both hands clasping the heavy hilt, he shouted his challenge. "I am Katallon! I am Windband! Who would test me?"

Indistinct in the shifting light, he was a threatening dark bulk surmounted by a mesmerizing steel blade.

At Katallon's first wild shriek, Conway instinctively stepped back. Flushed, he glanced around. All eyes were on Katallon.

All but Moonpriest's. Sly, snickering, he whispered, "Formidable, isn't he? Frightening. No one knows how many men he's killed, not even him."

Conway spoke from the side of his mouth. He nodded at the altar. "Is that thing charging?"

"Charging? If you mean is the sky path open to my mother, am I in contact with her, the answer is yes. When you need her power, it will come. Unless you offend her."

Conway turned away from Katallon, rattled by Moonpriest's response. The priest's eyes were dots in round, gleaming whites. Angular features thrust aggressively at Conway.

The desperation of his situation finally cracked Conway's wall of hatred. He'd convinced himself he needed this madman. Now he was entrusted to him, at his mercy.

Bitterly, Conway told himself he deserved Moonpriest. They shared a past, a present. Now they shared a future. Insanity owned them both.

Why?

The insistent throbbing of a small drum penetrated his self-absorption. The galloping tempo conjured flight. He saw Tee's image, her dying, a thing he'd refused to see again since the moment it happened. Now, with the possible instrument of his own death posturing before him, he remembered her courage and devotion.

The destruction of Church, revenge on Lanta herself—how would Tee react to those goals?

Would a man of honest courage ask himself that question now?

Would a rational man set himself to single-handedly destroy an organization as demonstrably good as Church?

Conway realized all was silence around him. Only the laughing flutter of the distant torch and the heavy whisper of the spinning moondisk behind him made sound.

"Too frightened to speak?" Katallon taunted. His sword point cut tight circles in the air. "Perhaps too frightened to move?"

"I can move." The answer felt poor in Conway's mouth. He tried to cover the weakness by swinging his sword in a flat, horizontal sweep. Katallon grinned hungrily at the sluggishness. He sidled forward.

Surreptitiously, Conway reassured himself his umbilical-like wire was firmly attached to his chain mail.

Moonpriest stood beside the revolving disk, steadying himself by holding onto one of the decorated posts. He smiled broadly at Conway.

Katallon slid forward with long, deceptively swift strides. The sword hissed downward in a skull-splitting stroke. Conway hurriedly raised his own blade, perpendicular to the oncoming blow.

The impact staggered him. His knees bowed.

And nothing else happened.

Moonpriest's screeching laughter was a cry of mad betrayal.

Fighting for his life in a combat that should never have happened, Conway's mind momentarily detached itself.

Lanta. I never told her I was sorry.

At the forefront of the crowd, pressed against the restraining rope, Fox struck out in peevish reaction against a body crowding him. Turning, he recognized Altanar and seized his arm in a grip that lifted the slave onto his toes in pain. Mouth nearly touching Altanar's ear, Fox said, "Where have you been? Do you see what's happening? What have you done? Moonpriest said his mother would strike Katallon dead if he so much as touched the Conway one. You must have defiled Moonpriest's tent. Or the altar. Something. What have you done?"

"Nothing! I swear. I wouldn't dare touch the altar."

"Then why does Katallon live? Look, Conway can barely defend himself. Katallon plays with him."

Altanar pried at Fox's fingers. Reluctantly, eyes fixed on the moonlit struggle in the enclosure, Fox let go. He continued complaining. "I was promised the lightning weapons. Command of Windband's warriors. Moonpriest himself said it. He cannot fail. Unless you've done something."

Rubbing his arm, Altanar said, "He has his plan. You were there, you heard him say his mother wants Conway dead. The lightning will kill Katallon and the sacred water will kill Conway." By way of confirmation, he pulled aside his cloak to

568

reveal the tightly lashed top of the hidden waterskin. "You were there, you heard Moonpriest tell me: 'As soon as Katallon dies, you run from the crowd and declare Conway unclean. Throw the water on him. My mother will claim him.' That's what he told us. You heard. Don't blame me for this." He jerked his chin at the continuing struggle, where the ring of Katallon's blows glancing off Conway's defense was the inexorable song of hammer on an anvil. The crowd roared excitedly.

Behind Fox and Altanar, two people edged backward through the crowd. Some spectators complained. Others ignored them or made room gladly, pushing forward to claim vacated space. It took little time for the pair to be free of the watchers.

Man Burning pulled back his hood. "We can speak, but softly. And keep your hair covered. What were they saying?"

"Fox is angry. They thought Conway would kill Katallon, but now they're worried. Moonpriest promised Conway's lightning weapons to Fox; I heard that clearly. Altanar said something about sacred water killing Conway. That's all I heard. Have I failed you?"

Man Burning frowned, deep in thought. When he spoke, he was firm. "I don't understand what's happening. If you're going to strike Moonpriest tonight, you'll have to wait in the tent. You were a great help. You hear like the owl."

She shrugged. "Not so well as Fox, I think. Anyhow, I fear I only added to the puzzle. What will you do now?"

"Kill him. One way or another. He's too dangerous to live."

"But what if . . . ?"

Man Burning took her elbow, turning her toward the tents with sure gentleness. "He dies. Tonight. Everything else will happen as it will. Hurry now."

Bayek resisted him long enough to rise on her toes and kiss his cheek. "The air is strange tonight. I feel it. It means we'll succeed, my faithful friend. I wish you luck." Together, arm in arm, they disappeared into the waiting darkness.

Moonpriest continued to howl amusement. Leaning out from the edge of the altar, literally hanging from a post, he waved his free arm in burlesque mockery of the fighting men below him.

"Stop!" Moonpriest's suddenly serious command shrilled above the roar of the crowd. All other sound seemed compressed for an instant. The tumult subsided.

Conway staggered backward. Panting, soaked with sweat, he appeared ready to collapse. Katallon, breathing deeply but easily, cocked his sword like a woodsman preparing to sink an axe in a log.

Moonpriest repeated his order. "Stop, Katallon. I demand."

Glaring, Katallon relaxed his pose. Moonpriest stepped down from the altar. Stately, flowing, he moved to where the two antagonists faced each other. Holding up a hand, palm toward Katallon, Moonpriest pitched his voice to the masses. "The first time we met, I gave your false priest, Wippard, one last chance to come to my mother. Now I give you that chance. You have fought Conway fairly. I tell you you are already beaten and unable to see it. Oppose me longer, oppose my mother, and Katallon will be no more."

Katallon sneered, the mask of battle clearly on him. "I don't believe you, priest. You have magic. I have my sword. Step aside." Under the chain mail Katallon's leather jacket stretched as muscles bunched.

Conway reached for Moonpriest, who swept out of reach with swift grace. His eyes widened in sudden fear, and Conway spat at him. Again, Moonpriest was too quick. He backed off farther. Conway, nervously shifting his attention from the leering Katallon to Moonpriest, directed his words at the priest. "You set me up. You cut the wire, or grounded it, or something."

Unbelieving, Conway watched Moonpriest's features split in a grin, the dusky moonlight shining on his teeth. Moonpriest said, "You thought to teach a god. I, too, know that Faraday's cage encloses the occupant inside the electrical field, unless the insulation fails or the current is grounded." Subtly, the madman slipped back into control. Evil displaced simple cruelty. "A god swears to you: Katallon dies."

Conway looked at Katallon, met his stare.

Moonpriest hurried back to the altar. The wind caught at his robe. It crackled and clung to his legs. He kicked at it irritably.

Conway said, "We're a pair of fools, Katallon. For what it's worth, you're the honest one."

Katallon slid his left foot forward, twisting his body for fullest leverage. His intent was brutally obvious. He meant to simply crush Conway's defense.

A cry of exertion. Half shout, half scream. Katallon's sword flew from his shoulder. Conway's rose to parry.

Sparks like obscene sapphires exploded into the air. A hissing whipcrack swallowed the clang of metal on metal. Katallon's death cry was a pathetic anticlimax, nothing more than the yip of a broken-backed dog. He crashed backward in a heap, jerking spasmodically.

Conway's weapon sagged. It appeared he might drop it, might even fall to the ground himself. Dazzled, stunned, he reeled away from his victim. Moonpriest's voice came to him, low-pitched, urgent. "Careful, my son. Beware letting wire or sword or anything touch earth. Someone else may attack."

Incredibly, someone did. Hearing a commotion, Conway turned that way. A clumsy, burdened figure ran at him. A shout, the voice familiar. "Unclean! Get away from our siah, Conway! Unclean!"

Altanar. Mind spinning, exhausted, Conway's reaction to this renewed, unexpected threat was berserk rage. Screaming incoherently, he lurched forward, readied his sword.

A second figure appeared behind Altanar. This one sprinted, far faster. The newcomer overtook Altanar just as he reached Katallon's banner. The faster man raised his knife. Conway braced to receive both attackers.

Instead, the raised arm dropped. Altanar stopped. He swayed. The waterskin fell to the ground. It gushed a large puddle at his feet. Then he screamed. "Moonpriest!" The cry rose hot, tortured, like one of the Dry's spinning dust spirits.

The man struck Altanar again, then continued past his stumbling victim to Conway's side. Conway stared. "Man Burning? Why?"

Recovering from the paralyzing shock of what they'd seen, the crowd stirred. "Who is that?" "Who was killed?" And, most dangerous of all, "Get them."

Man Burning said, "Seize Moonpriest. He set Altanar to kill you."

Stupidly, Conway goggled. Even the rising threats from the crowd failed to break through his incomprehension. He turned toward the altar. Moonpriest bellowed with fear. Recognizable words finally found their way through his raving. "Altanar! Rise! Fox! Come to me. Windband! Protect your siah!"

Like a closing fist, the encircling crowd squeezed inward.

Conway snapped erect. Behind him, the altar's moon disk was still, the men who were supposed to turn it gone. He broke the wire attached to his chain mail, preparing to run, although he had no idea where to go.

The next thing he knew, the universe was aflame around him, white hot. Air itself lived, sizzled viciously. Heat seared his exposed face, crackled like dry, breaking sticks. A noxious stench scorched his nostrils, sucked the moisture from his throat. He choked, fell to all fours.

Words drifted in careless languor across his mind, turned amazingly cool and rational. "Clear air lightning." Where had he heard that? How many centuries ago? No matter. It explained what was happening, though.

Moonpriest could direct the electrical energy of the generator. At the start of the duel, he'd amused himself by diverting the current to ground, instead of the Faraday cage. Tonight's high mistiness obviously carried a massive charge. On the knoll, with Katallon's banner pole as lightning rod, nature had combined all those elements to strike with real lightning.

Conway lost interest. It wasn't important.

Screams all around him were grains of sand thrown against his rock hard desire to be free of everything. The disappointment that was himself.

Never said he was sorry.

A second power of lightning, a terror of thunder.

Air flooded his chest. It stank. It tasted of a different, horrible world. It jarred him back to life.

On hands and knees, head swaying, he surveyed the scene around him. At the base of Katallon's banner, smoke curled up from piles of dead. Survivors, fleeing, knocked over torches. Tents erupted in flame. Beyond the knoll, panic was no less. In every camp, fires leapt to life.

Conway ripped off the immense boots. Clumps of dry straw spilled out. Man Burning looked at them in mute puzzlement. Conway said, "Help me. Hurry. Karda and Mikka; they're chained in my tent."

Together, they helped each other up. Man Burning pointed. Conway saw the soiled, stained robe of Moonpriest scuttling off toward the tents. Looping Conway's arm over his shoulder and trotting off in pursuit, Man Burning said, "I don't see Fox. Dead, I hope. They planned to kill you."

It startled Conway to recognize his own detachment at the statement. Not that he was beyond surprise, or wise enough to understand all the undercurrents and tangents of the situation.

He was too full of sick anger at himself to be bothered with hatred for anyone else.

CHAPTER 98

Katallon's massive tent was engulfed in fire. Sheets of flaming cloth from it and others ripped free, scattering panicked nomads. More dangerous than flames were stampeding horses. Several swept down on Conway and Man Burning when they were close to Conway's tent, pinning the men against the searing heat of another flaring tent. The animals raced off as quickly as they'd come.

The men continued.

Moonpriest's pure white quarters stood untouched. Shifting light, color, and wind imbued it with an eerie liveliness. Conway thought of the misshapen ferocities that dwelled, unseen, in foul water.

Something in the barking of the dogs checked Conway at the entry to his tent. Man Burning bowled into him, nearly tumbling both of them. With his sword, Conway pushed at the overlapped cloth of the doorway. An answering sword thrust from inside pierced the cloth, nearly reached Conway's hastily indrawn stomach.

Diving under the blade, Conway charged, knocking out the legs of the intruder. The two struggled until, for no apparent reason, the other man went limp. Scrambling from under him, Conway recognized Fox. Man Burning was grinning crookedly, massaging the edge of his hand. "As good as a club behind a man's ear."

Hurrying to the dogs, Conway wrestled with their frantic welcome, releasing them from the chains looped through the new, heavy leather collars. The iron anchor stakes driven into the ground were bent.

Man Burning said, "Your horse is still in the back. He's near to panic. You want me to finish this one?" Knife already in hand, he nudged Fox with his foot. Fox mumbled, blinked once. In the next instant, he was conscious, alert. Dangerous as ever. Conway's reflex was to jerk back. Man Burning did the same, extending the knife as he did.

Fox rose slowly. Conway marveled. An ordinary man would have remained bleary-eyed and nauseated long after consciousness returned. Fox's voice was clear, crisp. "Moonpriest has said I'll have the secret of your weapons. I'll command Windband for his glory and conquest. You cannot escape him."

Conway pointed at the dogs' chains with his sword, then at Fox. Man Burning moved to bind the confident, unresisting Mountain warrior.

A grinding chill raced along Conway's spine. Fox had said, ". . . the secret of your weapons." Heart pounding, he inspected the pistol and the wipe.

The firing pins were gone. The sound of pounding hooves passed outside.

Carefully, Conway said, "I have to find Moonpriest."

Man Burning's sinister smile was more for Fox than for Conway. "I hope you don't want him to speak."

Conway tensed. "What's that mean?"

Man Burning saw Conway's expression. Defiance tinged his answer. "The Moonpriest one is dead. Bayek waited for him in his tent."

Fox strained wildly against the chains. Conway bolted, calling the dogs. Man Burning followed, hanging onto Fox's bonds.

Watching the smoke and flame, revolted by the stink of human works and human flesh consumed by fire, Conway felt the strength drain from his body. Memories of his own suicide world mocked.

Directly ahead, a ghostly white figure moved close enough to stand revealed as Moonpriest. "Conway." He almost had to shout to make himself heard. "You're helpless. Come to me, and I'll forgive you."

Behind Conway, Man Burning moaned. Gesturing the distraught man to keep his place, Conway forced himself to proceed calmly toward Moonpriest. He scanned the area thoroughly as he went.

Moonpriest's tent still stood, some distance off to the left. In the midst of coals and fitful flames, it glowed softly, ironically, from candles within. To the rear of Conway's quarters, a few other scattered tents had escaped the fire. They were dark.

Conway stopped, shouted across the intervening distance. "Give me the firing pins. Don't make me take them from you." He waved his sword.

"You simply won't learn. You think me mad. I'd never come here alone." To Conway's right, three men armed with bows and arrows materialized in the midst of the seemingly flat rubble. Even as Conway's heart sank at being outnumbered and outflanked, he admired the ability of the Mountain warriors to disappear into whatever cover existed. To Moonpriest, he said, "I misjudged you. But I don't think you've made the same mistake about me. You know I'll smash these weapons before I'll turn them over to you." He unslung the wipe, clubbing it by barrel.

Moonpriest raised a hand. "Don't be hasty. We can compromise."

"Kill him." Man Burning's voice was a low growl.

Conway nodded. "No deals. Give me the pins and we leave. No fuss, no bother. If I have to, I'll kill your man Fox and then come after you. Mountain warriors aren't going to force me to kill their chief."

Fox dashed that hopeful threat. "Send me to your mother. Let them kill me."

"Idiot." Conway drove his elbow into the pit of Fox's stomach. The damage was done, however. The three warriors, arrows nocked, advanced warily.

"Don't kill them!" The startling command, from a totally unexpected quarter, stopped the warriors in their tracks, pulled all eyes in the direction of Moonpriest's tent. There, highlighted against the glow, was Altanar. He held Bayek. His encircling arm was a dark band against her immaculate white robe. His other hand pressed a knife to her throat. She stood awkwardly, head cocked away from the edge.

Man Burning made a sound like a sob. "No. *No*. I killed him."

Altanar shrieked glee. Twisting Bayek around, looking over his shoulder, he showed them his back. "See where you stabbed me? Here. And here." He yanked Bayek in front of him again, then, "Even this blind bitch stuck me. Thought I was you, Jones, when I came into your tent. Shows how clever you are. All-seeing. All-knowing. Fake." A sudden coughing seizure interrupted Altanar, and Conway tensed. The knife remained firmly in place, however. Altanar recovered, went on. "The lightning gave me life. It killed all around me, but I am reborn. See how my clothes are burned. Look, a hole right through my shoe. Yet I live. Stabbed three times. Yet I live. *I* am the reborn. *Altanar* is Moonpriest."

The warriors stood together, talking softly. Fox shouted. "No. There's only one Moonpriest."

This time Man Burning threw Fox to the ground and raised his sword over him. "Speak again, you die."

Altanar screamed. "Say nothing, Fox. I need you. Us, Fox. Windband is ours. The false Moonpriest stole the lightning weapon secrets from Conway, but I have them. My mother, the moon, told me where to look." Triumphantly, Altanar extended the arm heretofore wrapped around Bayek. Three slim bits of steel gleamed in his open hand.

Bayek ducked away from the knife. Seizing Altanar's gesturing arm, she sank her teeth in the wrist. The firing pins, like hard, heavy sparks, glinted as they spun into the darkness.

Altanar yelled, threw Bayek away. Shrilling, he raised the knife high in both hands.

Soundlessly, an avenging darkness, Man Burning covered the ground to Altanar in huge bounds. Intercepting the downward blow, he flipped Altanar over onto his back. In the same movement, Man Burning knelt to lift Altanar to a sitting position and jam a knee into his back. One hand pulled Altanar's head up and back, aimed his chin at the moon. The other held Fox's sword to Altanar's throat. In a matter of heartbeats, Altanar had gone from shielded to shield; his body protected Man Burning from the Mountains.

Bayek rolled and scrambled to curl up behind Man Burning.

Man Burning called to Moonpriest. "We have them both, now. Your warrior and your spy-slave."

Moonpriest laughed. "Fox is glad to die for me. Altanar? Cut the treasonous wretch. We'll see how immortal he is."

"Save me!" Altanar's plea ended on a yelp as the sword nicked him.

Man Burning said, "I've waited long, Altanar. Your orders took my wife's life, and I accepted that as the way of kings. Your orders made me foul my honor, and I accepted that as the way of an obedient soldier. When you took my hearing, I could take no more. Who'd think a ruptured ear would open one's eyes? Know me, before I kill you. I am Eytal, and I was one of your captains."

Altanar squirmed. "I don't know what you're talking about. I don't remember any Eytal. I never hurt you. I don't remember. I swear it."

Conway was staggered. To himself, he said, "The one who captured us, took us to Altanar when he was king of Ola. How could it have happened?"

Fox overheard. "You'll never know. When you and the slaves are dead, we'll find the secret things Altanar dropped. Moonpriest will be glorified. I told you."

Conway yanked Fox upright in front of him, knowing that protection would only last until the warriors closed.

Presently, Man Burning was oblivious to everything but Altanar. He roared disbelief. "You don't *remember*? You ruined my life." He jerked on Altanar's chin, pulled the flesh taut. Altanar screamed for mercy.

Bayek's voice rose in a demand for silence. She pointed behind her. "Horses. A stampede. Listen."

The others froze, senses straining. Moonpriest scoffed. "You lie. There's nothing."

Crouching, arrows drawn, the warriors advanced.

Until the noise. A rumble, gaining volume. Moonpriest jibbered commands to the warriors, urging them forward. Dragging Fox, Conway retreated toward Man Burning.

The first horses burst onto them with appalling swiftness. Man Burning's slash that cut Altanar's throat turned into a lunging attempt to grab Bayek and pull her aside. A horse knocked him sprawling. Altanar disappeared under the crushing, pounding hooves.

The warriors released arrows, broke, and were engulfed. The herd, a river of flesh, separated Conway, Man Burning, and Fox from Moonpriest.

Elation turned to horror when Conway realized Bayek was unaccounted for.

Then he saw her. The white robe shone like moon silver, marooned in the middle of the herd. She sank to the ground. Conway wrestled with a crazed Man Burning. When Bayek came erect, none believed their eyes. She raised a fist, triumphant.

Simultaneously, Conway and Moonpriest realized what she had to be holding. "The firing pins," Conway muttered, and then gasped as she chose Moonpriest, raised hand now extended in offer.

Inviolate, imperturbable, she walked toward him with stately grace. Horses brushed her, stumbled clumsily to avoid her. The white robe, the braided rope of fair hair, the calm face—she was an island of tranquillity.

When she raised the other hand, it held Altanar's dropped knife. She smiled, as if seeing Moonpriest's sudden fear.

Drowned in the thunder of hooves, Conway and Man Burning could only watch.

Moonpriest retreated. Bayek moved toward him, cleared the maddened horses. She held out the pins in her left palm. The right hand held the knife at her waist. When Moonpriest circled to her left, she paused, head cocked, then followed his move. Moonpriest edged toward the flow of animals. Bayek trailed after. The closer they got to the herd, the more uncertain and hesitant she became. At last, she stopped, casting about nervously, her acute hearing overwhelmed. Smiling, Moonpriest stalked her.

There were fewer horses now. Still, the noise and vibration were to Moondance's back, a curtain of deception. Bayek edged away.

Suddenly, with the speed that had several times before startled Conway, Moonpriest struck. He touched her shoulder, and when she whirled, slashing with the knife, he caught that wrist almost contemptuously. With his other hand, he clasped the one holding the firing pins so it couldn't open. A quick twist, and he had her back against his front. Her right hand, trapped in Moonpriest's, still held the knife. It was turned back, pressed to her abdomen.

Man Burning rushed at the thinning stampede. He was thrown back like a chip in a torrent.

Smiling hugely, Moonpriest held Bayek's fist enclosing the pins aloft. She wept. Features that had faced runaway horses with stoic reserve surrendered brokenly.

Edging toward his tent, Moonpriest dragged the unresisting Bayek with him. When Man Burning raged and pounded the earth with his sword, Moonpriest threw back his head and laughed. The sound died under the drumming of the horses.

Conway called the dogs and raced for Moonpriest's tent. Seeing the action, Moonpriest's confidence faltered. Frowning, he tried to hurry. Bayek resisted. Roughly, he jerked at her. She winced, and a slow, dark stain grew on the white robe.

On Conway's command, the dogs attacked the horses. He joined the fray, screaming, slashing with his sword. Karda and Mikka savaged the already terrified beasts, leaping high to snap at throats, falling back, then attacking legs. The horses went mad. Already exhausted, they strained for more speed to escape their tormentors, strove to veer away.

Thinned to stragglers, the herd turned reluctantly, tripping and stumbling. Inevitably, one hit a guyline on Moonpriest's tent. The peg pulled free, arced upward at the end of the cord. A section of the cloth sagged. The internal soft glow stuttered. Momentarily, it dimmed. Then the light blossomed, a red, ravenous flower.

Conway yelled triumph. His hand in the air mimed a snake, then pointed at the tent.

Moonpriest goggled, understanding. He dropped Bayek and raced for the entry.

Man Burning reached Bayek, scooped her up in his arms. She winced, hands involuntarily moving to her wound. Still, her first words were, "Conway? He lives? I have the metal things. He's here?"

"Right here." Conway took her extended hand. She opened it

578

into his. The pins were covered with blood. He shuddered at the symbolism, reacted with brusqueness. "Let's get out of here. Man Burning, we'll need horses for you two."

"I'll take Bayek down the draw behind the moon altar. You'll catch up quickly on Stormracer. There are corrals off that way. If there are any Windband horses still fenced in, that's where they'll be."

In a few moments, galloping past Moonpriest's tent, Conway spared a look for the man. The tent itself was a smoldering mass. For a moment, Conway was sure Moonpriest must be lying in the ruins. It was not to be. Barely visible, obscure in smoke and darkness, Moonpriest shrieked at him. Distance, rage, madness combined to render the words incoherent. Without breaking stride, the dogs growled response over their shoulders.

The route to the horse pens was free of dwellings, and the trio met no interference acquiring mounts. Bayek insisted she could ride; her wound was a superficial cut, albeit painful.

Soon, they came across a camp. The few unburned tents were silent, forlorn shapes. In the distance, the voices of the inhabitants, hiding from the wrath of the moon, rose in Moondance hymns and prayers. A stealthy foray into the abandoned tents provided the trio with saddles, rigging, food, and utensils. Bayek stole clothes more suitable for the trail, leaving her white, bloodstained robe.

Dusk of the second day of their escape found them still riding south and east. Close to hallucination from sleeplessness, Conway watched night pour an intense purple wine into valley depths, where it swelled up the sides of the mountain slopes. Just before the darkness drowned color, the greens, browns, and grays of the land shimmered in a moment of defiant vitality.

Man Burning waited for Conway to come abreast as they reached the crest of an undulating ridge running north and south. Pointing, he said, "The Dry And Church Home. Off there. Have you seen any sign of pursuit?"

Conway shook his head. His weary features were grim. "They're coming, though. Fox will see to it, even if Moonpriest doesn't."

Man Burning agreed. "Probably took most of a day to be sure of our trail. From here, they'll have to choose. Chase you or chase us."

"Where will you go?"

Bayek partially straightened. Tired, weak, she nevertheless

579

spoke with sureness. "West first. Then north, to the Empty Lands and the Smalls. I heard there are no Healers there."

In spite of his drawn, worn features, the smile Man Burning sent at Conway brimmed with pride, concern, and a sort of loving resignation. He said nothing. Nevertheless, Bayek chuckled aloud. "Man Burning's humoring me, isn't he? He wants everyone to think he's so hard. Did he tell you I thought you should die along with Moonpriest and Altanar? He argued against it."

"Me? Die?"

"You hate Church. You mean to harm her. I'm grateful to you for saving Man Burning and me, but I'm Church. Fallen and shamed, but Church. I live in the hope I can serve her. Protect her."

When Conway tried to speak, Man Burning's frantic gestures stopped him.

The last meal of the day was over and Bayek was asleep before Conway dared broach the subject again. When he did, he was bitterly blunt. "She still wants me dead, doesn't she? Don't answer. You'd lie. But tell me this: Why'd you defend me?"

"Hard question." Obviously, Man Burning meant to be honest. Conway prepared for unpleasantness. Man Burning poked at the faint redness left from their cookfire. "There's more to blindness than not seeing colors and objects. Hearts that can't see—or worse, won't see—makes the eyes useless. She won't let me touch her, you know? Sexually. She slept with Moonpriest. For Church, she says. Perhaps. For revenge; I'm sure of that, even if she'll never admit it. Katallon made her betray Church. Moonpriest is Church's enemy." He rubbed his temples with shaking hands. "She can't accept me. I know what's happening, I just can't explain it. So why did I tell her I wouldn't help get you killed, or kill you myself? Because you're the same as her. Both of you speak of love, but you live in hatred. You say Church and the Lanta one betrayed the woman named Tee. You live only to destroy what hurt you. Bayek's greatest dream is to see Katallon and Moonpriest dead. I don't believe the priestess hurt you. Moonpriest himself never hurt Bayek. Maybe I hope both of you will live to understand the truth about yourselves. Maybe I want you to live because I want her to live." Man Burning ground out the gentle glow on the end of the stick, then rose. His expression condemned. "I look inside you and see what's inside her. I pity you. I'll give Bayek love, try to bring her to life. I'm afraid you won't let that happen to you. If so, fool you, Matt Conway. I may have been wrong to save you."

Conway continued to stare into the coals long after Man Burning was gone.

The too-human failure of Man Burning to mention his own blind determination to avenge himself on Altanar didn't escape Conway. On the contrary, it emphasized everyone's capacity for rejecting any view of one's own weakness.

The ashes were cold and dead when Conway slumped over on his side. Fretful, the great hounds only dozed, unable to rest while the unaccustomed sounds came from their master. They had never heard him cry.

When he slept at last, both animals sighed relief. They edged up against him, seeking contact. It was the only way they knew to reassure him, and themselves.

CHAPTER 99

The smell of piñon pines excited the morning air. Sylah faced the morning sun, hands lifted in greeting. In truth, she dreaded the rising orb that would soon be a fiery torch, punishing them through yet another day of flight across the Dry.

Flight. A soaring hawk, an arrow, a lilting butterfly; those things meant flight. Plodding, slinking from hidden draw to winding canyon wasn't flight. It was misery.

A few paces away, Lanta finished her ceremony. Catching Sylah's eye, she held up her basin with its meager drops of water. "If the One in All seriously cares about us washing before morning prayer, He must hate the tiny sprinkle we're affording."

Sylah winked. "Drink and sing praise, or wash and choke on a dry tongue. Not even He can have it both ways."

Lanta's easy humor wavered. "You shouldn't be so brash. Things could be much worse."

Nalatan's saw-edged harshness cut across their conversation. When she turned to him, he was adjusting one of the cloth caps he'd crafted for himself and Tate. Rolled and tucked, it formed head protection, and its long tail covered the exposed neck. "Things are worse." Lifting his chin toward the ridge to the east, he explained. "Kossiars. Among the trees. There's no real need for them to hide, so they're probably waiting for the main body of the Harvester's escort to show itself."

Gathering up the hem of her robe, Sylah trotted toward camp.

Nalatan's sharp command stopped her. He went on, "There's no-where to run. I just came off watch. On my last scout of the area, I caught the main element moving forward. I suspect they have a blocking party out to the north, as well." He paused, spat. "She has her camp just over there, in that canyon. We'll keep to our high ground here, make them come to us."

Coldly, Sylah objected. "Make no decisions for me. You're only guessing we're surrounded."

"I'm advising, Rose Priestess." Stung, Nalatan was formal. "Ready for your orders."

"I'm sorry." Sylah belatedly let go of the skirt hem. It rustled sly laughter as it fell. "It's not easy for me to admit I'm beaten, Nalatan. You, Tate, and Dodoy slip away. You've done all you can."

"I can't do that. Tate never would. Anyhow, there's no reason to consider it."

The last demanded Sylah's attention. She cocked her head, waited. He went on. "There are over fifty men with the Harvester. We're surrounded. There's been no attack. That means she wants to talk."

"For what?" Sylah asked the question with an extravagant look around.

Lanta was more positive. "You're the Flower. She knows you'll find the Door. She wants a share."

"Look." Nalatan's interruption pulled their attention to the east-ern ridge. Men strolled about openly. Light glinted from bared weapons. Cookfires spiraled ridiculously thick smoke. "To startle us. Build fear," Nalatan said. "What's to the north? Ah. Look. There. And there. That break in the hills, see? The perfect block-ing position. The men manning it are either stupid or deliberately showing themselves." Nalatan was enthused over the moves in the game. Taking Sylah and Lanta each by the elbow, he started for camp. "The Harvester will make her appearance soon. All this is preliminary. To impress."

Sylah hurried, pulled away from him. More thoughtful than concerned, she mused aloud. "We'll receive her, then. If the Har-vester feels she must bargain, I can gain time. I must have it. If we fight and kill her, I don't know how I'll face my sisters in Church. By bargaining, for whatever reason, she gives me time. For my mission. I think I know what she wants. I don't think she knows what's involved."

Nalatan and Lanta exchanged mystified looks, hurrying to keep up.

The Harvester made a great display of her approach. War horns and trumps blared from just beyond the canyon lip. Then the Harvester led a double column of mounted Kossiars onto the flat ridge where Sylah and her group waited.

The man beside the Harvester raised the white cloth.

Sylah answered with a cloth of her own. Nalatan, booming voice rolling from ridge to ridge, shouted, "We've been waiting, Harvester. Come visit." The echoes were still recoiling from rock-slabbed hills and canyons when the man holding the flag bent to the Harvester and spoke. Nalatan chuckled. "See how the cloth-bearer's horse moves? And now the Harvester's, as well. The animals reflect the riders, Sylah. You've struck first. They're confused."

There was no uncertainty in the Harvester's manner when she arrived at the campsite. She reined in her mount with a hard tug on the reins and glared down at the relaxed group before her. Still, Sylah knew she was seeing no more than the Harvester wanted seen. It was the Kossiar Lance with her who was revealing.

The man couldn't keep his eyes off Jessak. The infant rested in Lanta's arms. Tate, practically lounging on a boulder beside the smaller Priestess, dangled a languid arm across Lanta's shoulder. Jessak gripped the hand with both of his, noisily sucking on Tate's thumb. When the officer cut his eyes away from the boy, there was a frighteningly guilty cast to his expression.

The Harvester said, "You've disgraced Church."

Nalatan, seated a few yards higher than Tate, and directly behind her, rose with a threatening swiftness that had Kossiars reaching for arrows and swords. Nalatan ignored them, concentrating on the Harvester. "Liar. Kos uses Church. You would make Church the Chair's whore."

The Harvester kept her gaze locked on Sylah for a long moment. It was as if Nalatan didn't exist. Then, slowly, menacingly, she lifted her gaze to him. Utterly expressionless, she spoke in a cold, flat voice. "Bark your loudest, dog. You, of all here, know what I will do to advance Church." Without waiting for response, the Harvester continued with Sylah. "We need not be enemies. Oh, we'll never be friends, but our dissension cripples Church. I will be Sister Mother in three days. You must be by my side."

"I've marked you. You've tried to kill me. My friends. Succeeded with Conway, I fear. I will never cooperate with you. Never."

At the mention of the marking, the Harvester's eyes shifted

briefly. By the time Sylah finished, however, she was as composed as ever. "Conway? He lives."

The news surprised Sylah.

Lanta's hand flew to her heart, her expression ecstatic. Sylah saw the Harvester react, and knew her friend was compromised. The Harvester knew love for the ideal weapon.

Sylah said, "You should be more concerned. He's no less your enemy than I."

"Ah, but it's you he hates. He lost the slave, you know. The Tee one. Captured Trader gang men told us he blames Church, but especially he blames you." Lanta blanched when the Harvester's cold smile fell on her. The older woman continued. "Unless you're safe within the walls of Church Home, he'll find you, won't he? He's with Windband now. Moondancers. They're very inventive where pain is concerned. Come with me, you and Sylah. Rest. Let me help you regain your powers. We'll find the True Stone, Lanta. We all know it's only a symbol, but it's the secret heart of Violet. Unless I possess it, I'll never control Violet. Get it for me, and you shall be Tender of all Violet. And the Seer of Seers."

The Harvester bent forward, pitched her voice to a near whisper. The illusion of confidentiality was so complete, Sylah shifted uncomfortably, as if she listened to something private. Lanta leaned toward the Harvester's honey-soft, honey-sweet words. "We'll find Conway. I know techniques, medicines. I can alter minds. We'll make him see the truth. Make him yours."

Beside the Harvester, the Kossiar had the look of a man trying to be somewhere else. He moved, and his saddle squealed protest. The Harvester glanced at him. "Take these warmen and get back. I have no need of you."

As soon as the warmen withdrew to the lip of the canyon, Sylah took the Harvester's reins, gestured to the campfire. "We have tea. Cheese. Some rice, perhaps?"

The older woman dismounted, shaking her head in a brisk negative. "Don't overdo it, Sylah. We're back on my terms. You're nearly out of food and water." She sat down by the fire, taking a queenly pose. Nalatan cleared his throat noisily. A small vein at the Harvester's temple writhed. She went on, "You know the Chair wants your head."

"Because of the child. What news of Yasmaleeya?"

"Dead. You must have known."

"We left her alive. He killed her, didn't he?"

The Harvester made a tiny show of exasperation. "Him. Child-

584

birth. What difference? She's gone. Selfish, willful thing. Tell me how you got her through delivery. Why was the child growing so huge?"

It was Sylah's turn to be surprised. "You didn't know?"

"The midwife hinted that she knew. She told me it would be a killing birth."

"You had the old woman killed."

Brushing at dust on her skirt, the Harvester said, "You've become very contrary, Sylah. It's boring. Now, listen closely while I tell you what must be done."

Sylah jerked upright, stood over the Harvester. "You don't tell me that. No one. Ever again. I'm going to find the Door, find whatever power is there. Something so strong our sisters were murdered to keep it from their hands, so strong they died without revealing what it is or where it is. My true mother, my Iris Abbess, raised me to seek and find the Door. I will. I won't let you control Church."

"An interesting pair, you and that lost monk. He barks. You hiss like a cat. I seem to be surrounded by animals." The Harvester rose. The proud head, hair a silver helmet in the morning sun, turned in slow survey of the group. "Very well. I offer you one last chance to acknowledge me. We shall not face your weapons. We shall wait. Your tongues will swell. Your eyes will grow gritty. Have you seen the cracked, burnt lips of those who die of thirst? The ulcerated mouths? Or heard the moans when they're too weak to cry out for water?"

The Harvester whirled, flaring the long robe. Blue and green trim swirled, the lush colors triggering unwanted thoughts of damp forest and clear, leaping water. She almost crouched in her aggressive intensity. "Tate. Join me. Live in luxury. Sylah, Lanta; help me. We can control the Chair, Gan Moondark, Clas na Bale, the Three Territories. Think of the power, the authority. Don't fight me. Not for some ridiculous treasure we all know doesn't really exist. I'll even give you time, a full year, to continue your search. I know how strong these dreams can be. I understand, truly I do."

Lanta, hand to her breast, took an involuntary step backward. No one else moved.

The Harvester sighed. "At least give me the child. For once, let's not make the innocent suffer. Hate me if you will. I don't harm children."

Tate said, "You'll bargain with them, though, won't you, you old sow?"

Nalatan's words were immediately behind hers. "You orphaned the children of my brotherhood."

Sylah nodded. "You meant for Yasmaleeya's child to die, and Yasmaleeya, as well."

Color swept the autocratic line of the Harvester's cheekbones. "You stole that child. I'll return it. Church will be allowed to preach, to heal, to save. The Dodoy one can come, as well."

Tate said, "Dodoy stays with me. We're not finished yet."

The Harvester's lip curled. "Really? When the thirst is on you, remember that proud rejection. You'll hate him more with each drop of water that goes down his throat instead of yours. He'll curse you for keeping him with you."

Sylah said, "Do I have your word the Chair will let his boy live?"

"It's a boy? Yes. The Chair wants a son."

"No one knew it's a boy?"

The Harvester looked away, refused to meet Sylah's suspicions. "Yasmaleeya didn't tell us anything."

Lanta clutched Sylah's arm. "She never got a chance to speak, you mean. Don't give him to her, Sylah. We'll escape."

Sylah said, "We can't if we're slowed down by an infant and a goat." Her words had an iron conviction. By contrast, the hand she placed on Jessak's tiny head was gentle, confiding. She faced the Harvester. "You'll keep the boy alive because you think to bargain with the Chair. How contemptible. Hear me. There's mystery in this child that neither you nor I understand. Nevertheless, he'll die if I keep him with me, so I must entrust him to your care. To your self-interest, actually. Something tells me his path is yours. For now." Looking past the older woman, Sylah raised her voice. "Men of Kos. This is the Chair's firstborn son. My blessing is on him. I declare the Harvester personally responsible for his safety. It is on your honor to guarantee that responsibility."

The Harvester stepped forward, fixed Lanta with a dominating stare, and took the child. Lanta's hands fell loosely to her sides. Her head drooped.

The voice was in Sylah's head again, then. Stern. Loving. *Find the river, the canyon. The Door. All else must wait.*

And there was response. Her own voice, excited, the words coming without conscious creation. *I hear, Mother. I know. So close. Don't leave me now. Not now!*

Settling in her saddle, the Harvester interrupted Sylah's thoughts. "As always, Sylah, you learn too late. Tate told you; the child's a bargaining piece. You might have saved all your lives."

She hauled on the reins, yanking her horse around. Walling its eyes, it reared. She controlled it easily, starting back to her escort. Stopping abruptly, she turned, holding the child in both hands, level with her head. "Did she name him?"

"Jessak." Sylah had to shout. Beyond the Harvester, Sylah saw the instantaneous flurry of action among the Kossiar warmen. There were three-signs. The Harvester stared at the squalling child as if considering throwing him to the ground.

Jessak stopped crying. He raised miniature fists to his fiery red cheeks, shook them furiously. It looked exactly as if he threatened the Harvester.

Pale, the older woman tore her gaze back to Sylah. Features contorting, she said, "You think you're clever, don't you? You, and that witch, Yasmaleeya. Damn you both." Vicious slashes of her riding crop sent her horse racing to her escort.

CHAPTER 100

The scorpion advanced slowly, its senses telling it that something large and warm was directly ahead. Insect eyes and primitive brains weren't designed to encompass or comprehend humans.

Unfortunately, Tate understood exactly what was in front of her. Her brain didn't register the creature's temperature. It did, however, absolutely identify it, and determine that it was a handspan from its nose.

Her brain told her this wasn't fair. Dirt and gravel abused her cheek where it lay on the ground. Her tongue felt huge. She ached everywhere. No one ever explained to her that thirst turns the entire body into a factory for pain. The additional prospect of that wicked tail driving its poisoned dart into her face was unnecessarily cruel.

Once again, she told herself the idea of breaking through the encircling Kossiar force was a suicidal farce. All it really had to offer was a certain valor.

The nasty scorpion would ruin even that. She knew she'd yell—scream, retch, *something*—if the scratchy-looking yellow-gray thing so much as touched her.

The bubbling snore of the closest warman was little more than an arm's length away.

The rising sun would send the scorpion into hiding. Under something. Right now, the predawn light was a soft hint. Every throb of Tate's racing pulse seemed to bring more brightness. There was nothing nearby for the scorpion to shelter beneath. Except herself.

Splayed little articulated scorpion legs seemed to vibrate; it was halfway to her face. Tiny lobster-claw pincers waved threats.

Infinitely slowly, swaying gently, something rose just at the edge of Tate's peripheral vision. Her first thought was *Snake*. Her stomach knotted. She remembered that Nalatan was on that side, her left. His hand appeared. Lunging, it pinched the scorpion's tail between thumb and forefinger. Hand and squirming creature disappeared.

Tate closed her eyes, filled agonized lungs. She wished she could close her ears to the faint crackle of the hard shell being crushed.

A pressure on her shoulder brought her head around, facing Nalatan. He pointed uphill to her right, drew a line across his throat. Residue from the scorpion's demise left a trace of wetness on his forefinger. She swallowed, and wild laughter welled in her throat at the foolishness of someone being sensitive about a squashed insect while tensing to kill or be killed.

The retreat from hysteria turned to depression. Fifty Kossiars. Twenty-five to one. Numbers like that weren't odds, they were arithmetic; two against fifty equals once is too often.

Behind her, Tanno put a foot on her boot.

That was when the hatred rolled in. In a few moments, warmen would be killing Tanno, trying to kill her. Tate welcomed the burning in her throat, so different from the draining heat of thirst. This was battle fury, bringing strength, concentration, will.

The hand on her shoulder pressed again. And again.

The signal.

Rising in silence, Tate and Nalatan struck. The first four men died asleep. Then one opened his eyes. Tate rushed at him through the soft dawn, bayonet leveled, Tanno beside her, teeth bared. In her mind, she saw herself as the warman must. Eyes like moons. Throat muscles ridged like steel cables. Mouth open with exertion, lips drawn back in the animalistic snarl of close combat. The man screamed. Tate answered, shrieked ferocity. Thrust the shining bayonet.

Shouts of alarm erupted. Orders mingled with curses. An arrow hissed past Tate and Nalatan.

But a hole had been cut in the Kossiar wall. Nalatan said, "The others come. Use the lightning now. Keep the warmen back."

Sylah, Lanta, and Dodoy broke out of their hiding place in the valley. The priestesses each led a horse behind the one they rode.

A warman charged Tate. Before she could bring the wipe to bear, Tanno shot past her. The man was brave. He kept coming, flailed at Tanno with his sword. The dog dodged, leapt at the Kossiar's exposed right side. Man and animal fell in a snarling, yelling whirl. The yelling choked off abruptly.

Nalatan shouted, pointing at a group of four more warmen, racing downhill to cut off the fast-approaching horses. Two rounds from the wipe put down one Kossiar and sent the rest to tight cover. In the next moment, Sylah and Lanta were beside Tate and Nalatan, handing over the reins of the horses they led. Dodoy raced past. An arrow struck Copper, setting off frenzied bucking. Sylah regained control as Nalatan yanked the missile free. The foursome galloped down the back side of the ridge after Dodoy in a rain of arrows.

From that point to the protection of some broken hills was a long ride. It was soon apparent that the strain of long travel, plus the diminished food and water of the preceding three days, was affecting the horses. They slowed dramatically. Looking over her shoulder at the pursuing Kossiars, Tate begged her mount for greater effort. Tanno glanced up at her with wise, troubled eyes.

Nalatan had warned of this. He applauded Sylah's plan to wait before attempting a breakout; he concurred that a show of weakness and despondence would lull the Kossiar siege to complacency. The problem he identified was that they themselves grew weaker every day. No matter how great a surprise their attack provided, it was still necessary to outrace the Kossiars to safety.

The very tactic that enabled them to escape at all might have doomed them.

Nalatan said the terrain beyond the first visible line of hills was designed for ambush.

Urging greater effort from her horse, it suddenly, and most inappropriately, occurred to Tate that no one had thought to ask him how he knew that.

There was a small gully ahead. Dodoy reined up, putting his horse into a skid that pulled its haunches down to the ground. Yanking the animal about, the boy slid down one side and then had to beat the horse up the other. Nalatan shouted to the adults that they must jump the obstacle.

Tate's horse stumbled. The break in rhythm slammed the wipe

against the back of her head. She ignored it, checking on the animal's stride. It was sound, but he'd shifted leads, and was on his left foot. He only jumped well off a right lead, she knew, and the gully was flying toward her. Quickly, she moved her weight to the left, hoping there was time, then jerked herself back onto the animal's right side. He balked slightly, but he was leading with the right foot when the gully was under his nose, and he soared. Beside her, Tanno stretched for the far side. Both animals landed solidly. Tate praised them. Looking around, she saw her friends made it, as well.

She also saw the Kossiars gaining.

Nalatan forged past her, leading the way into a canyon. They raced around a bend, and were confronted by jumbled boulders and a choice of narrow exits. Unhesitating, Nalatan plunged into one. The group followed. A little farther, he signaled to Tate. She understood. It was time to discourage the pursuers. Wheeling, she brought the wipe to bear on the last bend in the canyon.

The Kossiars poured around it.

The hollow sound of the boop firing was lost in the thunder of hooves. The round's ripping explosion wasn't. Red-orange flame flickered and disappeared in smoke and rising dust. Three Kossiar mounts and riders went down in a sickening, crashing tangle. Two more, unable to stop, slammed into the mess.

Tate raced off, shouting to drown out the screams of dying men and horses.

Darting around a bend, she bit off her own voice in a gasp of dismay. Perhaps fifty yards ahead, the draw split. Each fork stretched out ahead of her for another hundred yards. There was no sign of her companions in either.

Thoroughly frightened, she slapped the horse's rump for more speed. Beside her on both sides, the vertical walls imprisoned, the flat tops etched an empty sky. She drove ahead, searching for a clue, trying to decide which side to take.

They had to wait for her. Had to.

Nalatan's sudden appearance startled a shout out of her. He was in the right fork of the canyon. He waved, wheeled his horse to face the wall, and was gone.

When Tate arrived at the narrow crack where he waited, she was sure he meant to make a stand. Following him, she silently decried the choice. There wasn't even room to turn around. Then, completely unexpected, the narrow alleyway made an abrupt turn that was invisible from outside in the main draw. Signaling silence, Nalatan led her to a steep, crumbling slope rising to the plateau above. After the passage of the others, the ground was broken, treacherous. Nalatan took the reins, pulling, while Tate hurried to the horse's rear and pushed. They tumbled out of the narrow cleft onto the flat surface with barely any strength left. The horse stood with its head down, sides heaving, legs spread. The priestesses rushed to help. Tate shook her head, handing over the horse, then went to find an observation point at the edge of the plateau. Sylah and Lanta withdrew to where Dodoy waited, well back, securely out of view from the draw. Nalatan scrambled down into the escape alley.

Hurrying out into the open, he scuffed away signs of their entry. At Tate's whistle, he ducked back out of sight. Taking position just around the hidden corner, he drew his sword and waited.

Kossiars streamed into the draw. Reinforced, the original ten to twelve pursuers were at least twice that number. They stopped at the fork.

Tate watched them, her hat pulled down to her eyebrows, her head filling the gap between two similar sized stones. Another rock on the ground in front of her covered the left side and lower half of her face.

Nalatan was directly below her.

The leader of the patrol dismounted to examine the ground.

Tate turned slowly, saw Sylah edged up close, prone behind her. "They're looking for tracks," Tate whispered. "If they're any good at it, we're in trouble."

Sylah said, "Nalatan told us there are many wild horses here. He says the floor of the draw is very difficult to read."

"Let's hope so. You better get back now. They're coming."

Half the Kossiar force pushed up each fork. Concerned about another ambush, they kept to the sides of the canyon and scanned the overhanging rim constantly. The tactic offered them the greatest opportunity for quick cover if they came under fire. Dangerously, it meant one column would ride directly across the mouth of Nalatan's hiding place.

Tate examined the ground near that point, trying to see it as a searching man would.

The clear mark of a shod hoof glared up at her. Visible from atop the bluff, it would be a beacon for a mounted man. Pitching a pebble at Nalatan, she got his attention, whispered hoarsely. "Hoofprint. Outside, to the right."

He frowned, not understanding. "Iron. Horseshoe." She injected as much urgency into the word as she could. Nalatan sprinted to the exit. He dropped to his stomach and slipped out. Cover was

591

extremely sparse, and from Tate's overhead position, he seemed to be nakedly exposed. Flat on the ground, he could see nothing. He half turned, looking to her for directions. Gesturing with fingers to keep movement to a minimum, she directed him. Finally, as much by accident as design, he dragged an arm across the revealing mark.

By then, the troopers were only a few yards away.

Nalatan scuffed into the crack in the wall a heartbeat before the first rider stepped onto the small rise that would have revealed him.

The Kossiar stopped, dismounted. Calling across the draw, he said, "Far enough. They're gone."

From the other side, the lead man said, "The Lance said to be sure."

"I'm sure. If that crazy old woman wants those people, let her hunt for them herself."

"Careful. She's a big Church leader."

The tired trooper made a rude noise. Several man laughed. Encouraged, he said, "Anyone wants a drink, now's the time. Then we'll head back. We tell the Lance we went up this fork until it split again and we didn't' see anything. Everybody got that?"

There was an assenting murmur, followed by hushed, general conversation.

The trooper in the lead dismounted. Stretching and groaning, he handed his reins to the rider behind. For a while he walked around, working kinks out of his legs, rubbing his backside. Then he began to idly inspect the ground up the draw. Toward Nalatan.

Tate bit her lip.

Bending, the man picked up something.

Tate pulled the wipe close to her side. Below her, Nalatan's questioning gaze darkened as he looked up to see her tension increase. Turning back toward the abrupt turn in the narrow cut, he listened intently.

Flipping away the rock that caught his eye, the trooper turned to examine the canyon wall. He noticed the gap. Calling the man holding his horse, he said, "Look at this; it looks like a hall, or something. Maybe it's the way to that Door the old woman says the runaway priestess is hunting for."

The second man laughed, ambled up with horses. He looked into the passageway. "Where d'you think it goes?"

His companion shrugged. "It just stops. Nowhere it can go." He strode inside.

Nalatan crouched.

Tate thumbed off the safety.

The trooper unbuttoned his fly and relieved himself against the wall.

A body's length away, razor-edged sword raised, muscles drawn tight as steel bands, Nalatan's eyes flew open at the unmistakable sound of splattering water.

One more step, and the Kossiar had to see the angled exit to the top of the plateau. It would be the last thing he ever saw, but his friends would come behind him.

Finished, the man walked back out. "Handy. Private. Just like the officers' latrines at base."

His companion said, "Except for the rattlesnakes. It's probably full of them."

"That's not funny," the first man said, swinging up into his saddle. "Why didn't you say that sooner? Come on, we're heading back." They were arguing spiritedly as they departed.

For hours, the group on the plateau endured. Sweltering, taking water in dabs and sips, listening for the sound of renewed pursuit, they held fast.

Dodoy bore it longer than Sylah expected. He'd found a crevice between two boulders, and was cramped into it as far as he could get, hiding from the sun and anything else that might come. His cries for Tate finally grew loud enough to demand her attention. Pulling back from the edge, she crawled to him. "I'm here. We're all right. It's going to be all right."

"It's not!" The boy screamed in her face, shaking his head. Huge, rounded eyes looked through her, off into a vision of his own. "They'll be back. They're going to get me. We can't get away. I'm thirsty."

Tate reached for him. He squeezed farther into the crevice. The high voice rose to a screech. "Hide me. Pile rocks in front of me. Dirt. Get some bushes, too. Don't let them find me."

The chain axe lay on the ground where he'd dropped it. Tate pushed it aside with her foot. Dodoy heard the faint rattle, saw what she was doing. His desperation turned to cunning. "Get it away. When they come, they'll think I meant to hurt them. You carry it."

Tate sighed, detached her canteen, and extended it. He grabbed it, drank greedily. Wiping his face, he said, "How much longer do we have to stay here? Is that all your water?"

"We'll be leaving soon. We have to be careful. I have to go watch with Nalatan now. Just be calm, honey. We'll be leaving soon."

"Stay with me. I need you, not him. He's big."

Tate took her canteen back. When she reached for him, Dodoy drew away. Tate left.

Sylah had watched the byplay. Now she made her way to the boy. When she reached in to touch him he snarled. "You're blocking my air," he said, pushing at her. Sylah persisted. "Dodoy, we're all very tired and very frightened. It's not just you. Tate's afraid. She's more afraid for you than for herself, though. That's the way it is when you love someone. Being brave doesn't mean you don't think or you don't care. Being brave is when you care so much you forget about yourself and only worry about someone else. Being brave is love, Dodoy, and doing what you have to do because you love."

Dodoy turned his head away. Still, Sylah was sure she'd seen a touch of understanding. She couldn't know if he'd take it to heart.

Leaving to rejoin Lanta, she jiggled the few drops of water in her waterskin. The boy might not have time to learn.

CHAPTER 101

Risking movement without the protection of darkness, the group resumed their retreat from the Kossiars in the early evening. A solitary nighthawk provided accompaniment for a while, diving in ruffling explosion, riding sharp wings effortlessly across the sky. Tate, walking between Sylah and Nalatan, gestured at the bird. "I wonder where he gets his water?"

Sylah said, "Nalatan knows. Don't you?"

He smiled. His cracked lips made it look painful. "I know we won't reach any before tomorrow evening. At dawn we'll get you into some shade. I'll leave what water I have with you, and go ahead for more. I'll move faster alone."

Sylah was firm. "We're not separating." When Nalatan started to object, she spoke over it. "There's no need. We'll be all right. Aren't we on your people's land yet?"

Nalatan stopped. "How'd you know that? Lanta? Seeing?"

"Don't be sacrilegious. You said your village was near Church Home. When the Kossiars came, you moved us west, when you could have gone north. Then, this morning, you insisted we ride

594

west. And you knew exactly where that escape thing was. Do you think we're all fools?"

Attempting to look offended, Nalatan said, "I was going to tell you." His eyes went to Tate, an almost imperceptible move. Sylah had the impression he'd been compelled to do it, that he meant his words more for Tate than herself. He went on with no noticeable change in manner. "There are many things I wanted to tell you about my people, but there's been no time. I've been hoping hunters from the tribe would see us, help us. The thing is, there's no water—not even bad water you can fix—between here and my village. My plan is our only hope."

"I'm the Flower." Sylah imbued it with strength. "I've prayed. I told the One in All my friends have done all people can do. If He wants His Door found, He better do something about it. Told Him while we escaped."

Nalatan said, "On horseback? That's a *prayer*? That's making terms."

"Stating the obvious isn't terms. Anyhow, are things going to get worse?"

Shaking his head, Nalatan spoke to Tate. "I'm not sure I care if we survive. It might be worth dying just to hear what she has to say when we reach the Land Beyond."

Sylah smiled at Tate and patted her hand. "They really are undeveloped, you know. Men. When it comes to hard cases, they're still boys, and all they really have any faith in is their own muscle and whatever iron toy they're holding at the moment. Comical."

Laughing, Tate agreed. Nalatan moved ahead huffily. "It's getting dark. This *boy* will lead, so you more perfect people don't break a leg."

There was little other conversation exchanged after that. Nalatan picked his way through the night at a steady pace that covered ground with minimum energy. Nevertheless, all of them, people and animals, were at the thinnest edge of exhaustion.

Dawn found them in a huddle at the base of a forbidding mountainside that rose away in a jumble of boulders. Tate turned a silent, pleading expression on Nalatan. He understood, spoke resignedly. "Beyond that. Water. The village of my people. I'll be back day after tomorrow. Midday."

Sylah pointed. "Would that be one of your people up there?"

Stunned, Nalatan looked. Far above them, a man stood on a boulder. Nalatan waved, made a strangling noise. The watcher waved back. A weird ululation almost like coyote song cascaded down the mountainside. Grabbing a waterskin, Nalatan refreshed his mouth. He threw back his head to yip and yelp as wildly as the first man. When he stopped, his companions were staring at him.

"My people," he said proudly. "We're safe. There's nothing to worry about now."

From nowhere, men appeared on the mountainside. All but the one who originally made the strange near-coyote sounds were much farther downhill. They'd obviously been ready to attack, if necessary. Now they bounded down the hillside, brandishing double-curved bows, soaring from rock to rock so effortlessly, so swiftly, Tate was reminded of the whistling flight of the nighthawk. Dressed in cloth that matched the colors of the earth, their faces were painted in odd, asymmetrical designs.

One of them thrust a waterskin at Tate. Handsome in spite of his paint, he grinned at her. "It's fresh."

Tate reached. "All I need is wet. Thank you." The words came out rough and thick. The man laughed, an amusement that turned to more serious consideration when she first had him fill her cupped hands for the dog and the horse. Then she allowed herself a long, luxurious swallow and a deep, rib-stretching inhalation. The man was waiting when she finished. "My name's Canis Minor."

"Donnacee Tate. Pleased to meet you."

A man with a gray-flecked beard made his way through the gathered warriors. His step was solidly muscular, but lacked the acrobatic elasticity of the men who'd vaulted down the hillside. The younger warriors cleared a way for him. He went first to Nalatan. They touched fists in formal greeting. Nalatan indicated Sylah.

Stepping forward, she greeted the bearded man with hands, overhead, thumbs and forefingers joined in the sun symbol. At the man's return sign, she introduced herself and the others. The man smiled openly. "The Peddler said anti-Church Kossiars were planning to attack us, and might drive you in our direction. We've been looking for you. We are Starwatch People, and my name is Orion."

Sylah bent forward. "Anti-Church? Peddler?"

"Scum." Orion made a three-sign. "Normally, we'd have ignored him. They're all liars and thieves."

"He told you of the Kossiars?" Sylah's smile remained firmly fixed on Orion. "Why attack you? Why pursue us?"

"He said you're riding ahead of the Harvester, making Church Home ready for her. Kossiars need slaves."

Nalatan blinked, opened his mouth. Tate pretended to choke on a mouthful of water, spun, and slammed him. The resulting confusion allowed Sylah to control the conversation. "Did he say anything of the Flower?"

"No, but everyone knows of her quest."

Dodoy said, "That's her." Everyone looked at him, then where he was pointing. Sylah continued to watch Orion. Her smile swiftly turned apologetic. "I would have spared you knowing that. There's too much tension within Church; you shouldn't have to worry about it. If we can have fresh water from you, we'll be on our way."

"Absolutely not." Orion was grim. Tate saw the hurt surprise in Nalatan. She leaned away from his sword arm and lowered her own hand to her pistol. Orion went on, "Starwatch has supported Church since the beginning. We'll weather this storm, as we have all others. The Flower is most welcome in our tents."

The broken tension was more refreshing than the water. In minutes, everyone was on the way up the mountain.

Nalatan rode at the head of the column with Orion. The man who'd offered Tate water fell in beside her as they climbed up between huge rocks. She asked, "Are all you men named for stars or constellations or something?"

There was great surprise in his voice, and Tate was glad her face was averted so he couldn't see her consternation at the enormity of her mistake. "You use your word for star pictures? No one else does. Not Kos, not Church. We heard you and your friends came to the Dog people from an unknown land. Maybe your siah knew ours."

Tate mumbled. Canis Minor went on. "All Starwatch men are named for a star. It's our duty to watch it, in honor of the giants who flew there. Women only have woman names, of course, and men who go to First Star brotherhood, like Nalatan, get new names from the brotherhood master."

Gritting her teeth, Tate ignored "woman names." "You have legends of people who went to the stars?"

Canis Minor glanced upward as he answered. "Long ago, even before the beginning, the giants went beyond the sky. From the Dry. Here's where they'll come back."

Tate smiled over pain. A world Canis Minor couldn't imagine built a spaceport in Nevada. Tate couldn't even remember its name or the name of the nearest city. Canis Minor was saying, "Most tribes live in the Dry because stronger tribes forced them here. Starwatch chose. This is our land."

Tate looked into Canis Minor's face. In him she appreciated the hard strength and cruel beauty of his country, the awesome lure of vistas so vast they frightened the viewer. All at once, she understood the love of a place that dared mankind and revealed its beautiful heart only to those bold enough to accept its terms.

Before Tate could express anything, Nalatan turned and smiled back at her. His look at Canis Minor was less than friendly.

The reaction rankled Tate. Nalatan had held back all manner of secrets. He only talked when he had to, anymore. Who was he to act as if he had some claim on her?

Dodoy noted the reaction with a nervous frown. It only added to his growing conviction that something was seriously wrong with Tate. Sylah said she was afraid. Dodoy was sure the fear had something to do with Nalatan, but he couldn't figure out how it all worked. They'd both changed. Before, they looked at each other like they were hungry. They still did, in a way, but if Nalatan caught Tate looking at him, she turned her head. He behaved the same way.

Afraid. Maybe that was it. Sylah said being brave came from loving someone, but if you loved someone, you worried about things happening.

If Tate loved Nalatan and was afraid for him, she was that much less afraid for Dodoy.

An image of the Harvester floated across his thinking. She didn't love anyone. She knew what she wanted, though. Dodoy smiled to himself, thinking back to the way the Chair bullied her. Stupid. He thought he'd won. Even the mighty Chair couldn't understand a woman like that wasn't beaten unless she was dead.

The Chair and the Harvester. Tate and Nalatan. Lanta and Conway. No one really cared about anyone. In his own case, they all thought he knew something about where the Door was, knew where somebody like Tate used to live. If it weren't for those things, they'd have sold him long ago.

A frightening thought. Dodoy wrestled with it. He had to find a place where he belonged soon.

It was all very tiring. He sagged forward in the saddle, lay on the horse's neck. He never twitched when Tate rode up to lift him off his horse and onto her lap.

When they reached the mountaintop and the trail widened, Sylah rode forward to join Nalatan and Orion. As soon as she did, Orion said, "Actually, we had two Peddlers come to us. Within two days. Usually we don't see one twice in a year. Common as rats anymore. Said Windband may attack Church Home. Is there something behind the Door to stop them, Priestess?"

"I don't know. I believe I'm destined to find it, to open it, and claim its secret. But I don't know what the secret is."

"Power." Orion gave the word a peculiar pitch, made it almost obscene. "Everyone seeks that."

"And no woman has any. I mean to change that."

Orion's smile patronized. "When you're as old as I am, you'll have opened more than one door you'll wish had remained closed."

"The Door was a secret of the Teachers. I have no fear of anything they left us."

"Us?"

Bridling, Sylah snapped her answer. "Church. Women. Us."

"Power." Sadness replaced the earlier cast of the word. Orion clapped his hands, as if dusting them of the whole conversation. "But none of that need trouble us. We're in good company, living at peace. Isn't that enough to bring a smile to anyone's face?"

The following evening the column descended one last hill toward a pleasant valley. A clear, inviting river hurried busily past small pastures and fields. Herds of cattle, horses, sheep, and llamas moved across the valley floor all the way to the ranging hills beyond. Flocks of goats utilized the higher, sparser growth; a young herder shooed his charges out of the column's way. Once the goats were clear, the boy cupped his hands to his mouth and yelped the same way the warriors had. Far below, people paused in their activities to peer up the mountainside. Some waved. Most merely went back to whatever they were doing.

Nalatan told Sylah, "I should have explained earlier. The howling's a war language. We can talk without others understanding. All males know it. The goatherd just told the village we're coming. How many, how fast. He said we look tired."

Sylah thanked him. Her thoughts flew to Clas na Bale, remembering the silent hand language of his Dog People.

Square buildings marked the corners of the equally precise camp. At the center of the village's uniformly spaced conical dwelling tents, however, a taller building dominated the entire settlement. It, too, was square. Two stories, flat-roofed, it was a solid stone-and-timber construction that Sylah understood was the tribe's defensive heart. She thought of Kos, and wrinkled her nose in distaste.

After the hardships of the Dry, the Starwatch village was dreamlike. Orion introduced them to the chief and the elders. The people smiled and greeted them easily. Considerately, they were soon left to rest.

That first evening, following a massive dinner of spit-roasted turkey and fresh vegetables, the women sat outside, with their backs to the tent Orion had provided for them. Tate suggested they make up a fresh batch of goat cheese for breakfast. Sylah and Lanta took turns thinking up fitting torments for her.

When they were quiet once again, sharing the silent companionship of tested friends, Sylah closed her eyes and marveled at her blessings. Opening them, she realized she was facing the direction of Church Home.

She felt the Door now. The small, secret voice that drove was constant, indistinct, not speaking words, but muttering, letting her know it was there. It thrilled her to think of it.

Frightened her.

Orion's heavy voice broke her introspection. She looked to see him stepping into the circle of the firelight. It didn't surprise her that he was alone. She'd already noted that even the chief deferred to him. After some conversation about food and quarters, she asked, "How did your siah decide on this place?"

"He led our ancestors here from the west, but we don't know where they started. That's a secret that died with the ancients. We were here when Church Home was born, though; we know that. The first protective brotherhood started with Starwatch men."

"I never heard that." Intrigued, Sylah leaned forward. "Did Starwatch train the other brotherhoods?"

"Recruited them," Orion declared proudly. "Our men have always protected Church. The reason I know as much about this as I do; I'm Starwatch legender. I have three young warriors living with me now. They'll be the men who wrap Starwatch in the web of our legends. We're not like other people. We respect the ancients, and legenders know the way the ancients lived. Canis Minor's the best of my men. You met him yesterday."

Introducing herself into the conversation, Tate said, "I've got a goal of my own, aside from helping Sylah find the Door." She indicated Dodoy, barely visible against a distant tent. "I think he was stolen from the Dry. Is there any chance he could be from around here?"

Bitter memory darkened Orion's features. "All tribes lose children to slavers. How old is he? Ten? Twelve?"

Tate shrugged.

Orion said, "We were raided seven summers ago. We lost many women and children. I'll inquire."

Tate hurried to kneel closer to him. "Oh, yes. Please."

Startled by such fervor, Orion leaned away. "Understand, the family may have died then. We lost many lives, as well as prisoners. The river ran black for two days."

Sylah asked, "Ran black? Ashes from burned tents?"

"Pyres." Orion was grim. "We burn our dead, as all people do. We have another custom, however, and that is to consign the ashes to our river. The river brings us life. So, when we die, we ride the river's flow into the Land Beyond."

"From here all the way to the sea." Lanta murmured the words; there was something like envy or longing in them. Sylah turned to offer her a confiding, sympathetic touch, but Orion's next words turned her blood to ice.

"Not to the sea. This river joins another. The combined waters flow westward many days' journey. At the place we call the End, the Dry absorbs all. Our ashes disappear into the earth with the life-water. We call our river the Devourer."

Canis Minor appeared out of the darkness to walk beside Orion. "Did you learn any more, or was this entirely social?" The question carried a teasing edge.

Orion said, "I wasn't prying. She's the Flower, Canis Minor. That's a very powerful thing."

"She says she's the Flower. You've mentioned that old tale. Who will you send to tell the Harvester Sylah's here when the Harvester gets back to Church Home?"

"The Flower's appearance among us and her obligation is no old tale, as you put it. Which is why I don't think we should involve ourselves with a Church power struggle. Let them handle it themselves. We support whoever wins. It's beyond our authority to influence Church."

Canis Minor threw an arm around Orion's shoulder. "We've had this discussion before. I can talk to you better than my own father. Starwatch has always supported Church; I know that. Why shouldn't Church return the favor? If we give this so-called Flower to the Harvester, we'll be in a position to demand real privileges for the new First Star brotherhood. There are more Peddlers all the time. They should pay to cross the Dry. Water's worth a great deal here; we can control most of it. With the other brotherhoods, all of it. The opportunities demand us."

Orion was dubious. "We've offered our hospitality, Canis Minor. I told her and her friends they were welcome."

The younger man chuckled softly. "We wouldn't get much use out of them if we didn't, would we?"

"That's not worthy. You didn't mean that. One gives one's word."

"You never laugh anymore. Don't be so serious. If you have to worry about something, worry about the effect on our women of three females who wander around in the Dry with a monk. There's a moral problem for you."

"Priestesses. Women of unquestionable reputation. The black one cares only to find the boy's parents and support the Flower. You'd do well to note their character, their loyalty. Nalatan's beyond suspicion."

Canis Minor withdrew his arm. "I don't think they're that pure. I don't trust any of them, and I think we should take care of ourselves, first and always."

They were at their tent by then. The deep questioning call of an owl followed them inside.

CHAPTER 102

Clustered around a single candle, the three women shielded even that paltry light with consuming care. Finger to lips, Sylah raised her eyebrows while looking at Tate, then gestured at the tent entrance. Tate nodded. Stealthily, she pushed aside the hide entry flap to peer out, then slipped away.

Unspeaking, not even meeting each other's eyes, Sylah and Lanta waited. Rejoining them at the flame, Tate said, "There's no one out there. Tanno's watching."

"Good." Lanta's whisper was packed with relief. "Now, explain, Sylah. Orion said this is the 'devouring river' the Iris Abbess told about. Why did you pinch me? I wanted to ask him about the other things. Why so secretive?"

Sylah felt her face warm, and was glad for the dim light. "I don't know." Confessing made her feel a bit better. "It's Orion. The way he says things, not what he says. His eyes: he meets one's gaze, but his facial muscles tighten too often. When he was telling us how welcome we are, when we first met his pupils dilated, contracted, dilated. Confusing. Possibly stress, possibly lies. I just don't know. But I want everyone to be very careful. As for the river, the name's no proof. There could be more than one Devourer."

Lanta's face dissolved into complete disbelief.

Tate muttered. "And tomorrow we could wake up to the music of pigs flying overhead."

Lanta exploded, covered laughter with a hand. In amused exasperation, Sylah said, "Tate, I'm serious about this."

"Me, too. Believe. I agree with Lanta, though; why the big secret?"

"We're so close, Donnacee. Can't you feel it? We're nearly there."

"Nearly where?" Lanta challenged. "If this isn't the river, we've accomplished nothing. If it is, why are we sitting here in the dark, arguing?"

"Because we have to be certain. Not of the Door, or what the Abbess said. We have to be certain of Orion, of Starwatch. We're four against the world. If anyone actually knows where the Door is, they've kept it a secret for generations. That alone suggests caution's wise."

Tate sighed. "What's the plan, then?"

"We learn. Remember the rest of what the Abbess told us: 'Near Church Home, across a destroying desert and a devouring river, south of the country where the sun can kill and the place where the sun can never shine.'"

"There was more," Lanta said. "'. . . the giants decreed there should never be darkness.' And the thing about monsters that kill with their eyes."

Tate said, "You've got a point, Sylah. If there's a place Starwatch considers forbidden, it could be the site."

"Exactly. Tribal legends may be our best signs. We can't afford to be spied on, though. The Harvester must have informants here. Be alert. Please."

Her friends murmured assent. Sylah blew out the candle.

In the morning, Nalatan joined them at their breakfast. A trio of men waited in the background. All were mounted on handsome horses, interesting animals with slender, energetic-looking forelegs and massive hindquarters. Nalatan's accepted a sniffing inspection from Tanno with equanimity. Nalatan said, "I've been invited to go hunting. Do you mind, Sylah?"

"Of course not. It's wonderful to see you among your people."

Nalatan blushed. Not much, but enough to notice. He turned to Tate. "Would you ride with me later? There are places you should see here. People you should talk to." His glance touched Sylah and Lanta, slid away. He tried to ignore their presence. Drops of sweat glistened at his temples. "There are things I've waited to tell you. About Starwatch, I mean. Things."

Tate rose, walked to him. "Any time."

He grinned and led his friends away on the dead run.

An unofficial welcoming delegation of Starwatch women arrived soon after Nalatan's departure. Hospitable, friendly, they settled in for a chat.

The unofficial leader of the women's group was named Tida. Like the others, she wore a loose cotton blouse, shortsleeved, with embroidered designs of flowers, fanciful animals, and geometric figures. Skirts reached the tops of heavy, protective ankle boots. At least ten narrow steel bracelets adorned every woman's wrists. The women used their hands incessantly while they talked, filling the tent with sibilant metallic whispers. For some reason, it sent chills up Sylah's back.

After some preliminary introductions, Tida clearly worked up her courage before addressing Tate boldly. "We've been talking about you a lot, Donnacee. You're a puzzle to us."

Tate tightened, and Sylah readied herself to intercede. Tate's apparent reaction was deceptively mild. "You want to know about the skin color?"

"Oh, that." Tida dismissed it with a clattering flick of her multibraceleted wrist. "What we wonder about is your tribe. Did they really let you go, to just wander? Is it true no one at all holds you?"

"Holds me?" Tate rolled the words, still mild. Sylah and Lanta, disturbed by the seeming inference of the question, realized Tate was smoldering. Sylah moved closer, making body contact with her warrior friend. Tate went on, "I'm not sure I understand. Is holding something like marrying?"

"Much like, and more." Tida was pleased with Tate's perception. "You have such cleverly built weapons; that doesn't match up with a tribe primitive enough to let a woman roam about without a holder. Especially since our own Nalatan's been shouting your praises to anyone who'll listen. Does the Conway one, the White Thunder, hold you? In secret? Is that why Nalatan hasn't asked you to belong to him? Some say Conway may hold you as a sister, to keep the proprieties observed. Women in Starwatch were unheld once, generations ago. Before our men realized how much we really need cherishing and protecting. Now all females are held, from birth to death. I don't understand how Kossiar or Windband women just do almost anything without protection or even asking permission. And Church; you women are insanely brave. How do you bear it?"

Tida put a sympathizing hand on Sylah's knee. At the touch, the glinting bracelets slid forward, clinking to a stop. Sylah's earlier revulsion defined itself. Chains. The clashing steel made her think of chains.

Carefully, Sylah said, "Our customs aren't exactly as you imagine. Tate's not held by anyone. In any way. We'll talk about it later. As for Lanta and me, Church protects us as your men do you. Which reminds me: we must bathe, in order to make our prayers as Church requires."

At Sylah's mention of bathing, Tida insisted on showing them the women's facility.

The square tent abutted one wall of the central fort. More than a bathhouse, its interior walls were decorated with the sun and flower symbols of Church. In one corner, a pair of older women showed a cluster of girls how to do fancy beadwork using porcupine quills. When Lanta showed them a design from Ola, they crowded eagerly to copy it. Another group worked with leather, trimming and carving. The largest number of children gathered around a massive loom; small faces screwed tight in concentration, trying to understand the clacking of treadles, the shooting of the shuttle, the bang of the bar.

Considerable time had passed before the trio were finished bathing, drying, and socializing. Leaving the tent, they found Orion and Canis Minor coming out a door of the fort. Tida and her friends drifted away when Orion waved. Both men came over. Quickly, Sylah whispered to Lanta and Tate. "It starts now. Learn all you can. Carefully."

Tate went through the preliminary small talk with a practiced ease that startled her. The glossy social graces and artifices that carried her through hundreds of cocktail parties and officers' club functions were centuries out of use. Nevertheless, they worked well. Canis Minor left Orion's side, fell into step with her. She remarked on his necklace, hand-hammered silver squares, each centered with a shining opal. Blue, red, and green darts flared from deep within each stone's depths.

He slowed, describing the location of the canyon where the stones were found. The couple fell behind the others. The gap grew. Proportionately, Canis Minor moved closer to Tate. When he asked her if she'd like to see the rest of the village, she agreed. He led her off on a tangent.

Tanno, attentive, her long-legged gait a shamble at the slow pace of the humans, trailed.

Canis Minor was an entertaining escort. At first, Tate worried about his obvious interest in her. Anxious to please, he leapt between sexual aggressiveness and a peculiarly disturbing fear of offending. Despite the latter, Tate confessed to herself that he was exciting. She found herself thinking of Nalatan, his rigid refusal to be drawn into anything like a repeat of their evening on the island. The memory irritated.

She encouraged Canis Minor. She told herself it wasn't as if she was leading him on. There were things she had to learn. Once this conversation was ended, they'd go their separate ways.

They stopped beside a tent decorated with paintings. Crude figures engaged in everyday life. Women cooked, rocked babies, knitted. Men hunted, tanned leather, fought. There was even a weaver. And a potter.

Looking past Canis Minor and the paintings of the placid village, Tate felt a wash of envy. It passed quickly. Such a life wasn't unimaginable or impossible. Donnacee Tate had requirements, though. More than that. Obligations.

Canis Minor's hand was raising hers, placing it on a leather jacket. Preoccupied, Tate didn't even remember walking to the front of the tent. The jacket hung on a pole that ran through the sleeves. The leather was incredibly soft, so white it glared in the sun. The yoke, front and back, was fringed to carry off rain water, as was the hem. Each strand ended in a rounded, polished agate. Rust red and white, the stones were drilled. The fringe was threaded through the hole, then knotted. At each breast was a rayed yellow sun of beads. With her free hand, Tate lifted the jacket to see the back. It was decorated with a stylized lizard in varying shades of green. She praised it extravagantly.

Canis Minor smiled happily. "This is the work of the best tanner in Starwatch. He's working on an antelope skin of mine. If you stay with Starwatch long enough, I'll have a jacket made for you."

When she turned to look up at him, the faintest trace of suggestiveness touched his smile.

Tate didn't want the relationship to move that far. She said, "If we stay that long."

Satisfied, he said, "Want to see our horses? I'd like to show you my favorite. I don't believe anything can outrun Ramrod."

Tate stopped in her tracks. "What?"

Canis Minor's jaw jutted. "I said my horse can beat yours."

"The name, man. What'd you call him?"

Truculence tightened Canis Minor's features. "Ramrod. Our horses have traditional names. Like people. My father owned six Ramrods. Grandfather had even more. When one dies, the next one gets the name."

"Oh." Once again, Tate swallowed bitter disappointment. Once again this world, blood-cruel, reached out to her with memories of her own time, her own place. Then dashed whatever tiny hope it engendered.

Nevertheless, this most recent hurt made her all the more determined to pursue the matter of Dodoy's ethnic background. Tida inferred black skin wasn't worth mentioning. That had certainly never happened before. She launched her question head-on, asking him of legends about Starwatch's ancestry.

"Oh, yes." Canis Minor, opening a corral gate, missed Tate's shock. By the time he turned, her expression was mild interest. He said, "Nalatan's been asking people about that. Orion told him our legends speak of strange people. Different colored skin. Different hair. Even different eyes, if anyone can imagine that. When the Peddler said you were black, I thought he meant dark, like Canis Major or Lacerta."

Tate kept her voice well-modulated. "Canis Major and the other one look like me?"

Canis Major's glance was bold, his laughter a touch forced. "I think not. They're men." He glanced around, pointed at a horse. "The color of Ranger, there."

When he looked back at Tate, he changed. She felt the strength of him in the concern of his gaze. There was challenge in the new manner. He said, "Everyone knows you want to reunite the Dodoy one with his people. He's not so dark; why is it so important to you that they be dark? Would you love him more if he turned darker? Or less, if you were suddenly whiter?"

The questions were old ones. In plain fact, she'd asked them herself more and more lately. Perhaps it was true that one of the greatest dangers of the racism of her world was that it poisoned the minds of its victims with suspicion as surely as it injured them with insult.

But if unquestioning acceptance was the ideal, why was Nalatan asking? He wasn't that concerned about Dodoy. He was concerned about Donnacee Tate, though. Canis Minor said Starwatch had legends of racial diversity in the tribal legends. Could it be that Nalatan was curious about black people, their character, their reputation? Could it have been more than hope of

607

rescue that caused him to seek out the hunting grounds of his own people when pursued by the Harvester? Where else would he investigate for clues to her qualities? Or vices. What racial rumors existed here? Was that why that woman, Tida, brushed aside the reference of color? A *sensitive* subject. Another word for *not us*.

Saddling the horses, following Canis Minor through the camp and back onto the mountainside, was pure reflex. Her thoughts were elsewhere.

Canis Minor was aware of her distance. At the edge of a thick grove of piñon pine, he reined up, turning from his position in front to ride back. He stopped beside her, close enough that their knees touched. "You've gone away." His tone was humorous, gently accusing. It invited, rather than criticized. "No Starwatch woman would go riding alone with a man, but I think if one ever did, she'd talk."

Tate wanted to respond, wasn't sure how. "I've been denying things to myself. I want to be free of all the things people think I am or want me to be. Even my friends think all I want is loneliness. I hate it."

"I've seen how alone you are." She cut a hard look at him, and he took it without flinching. "I think you've been hurt. I thought you were afraid. That was wrong."

She smiled, knew how wan it must look, and turned away. He said nothing. When she faced him again, his expression was one she knew full well. It was male, acquisitive, aroused. It attracted her. She wanted to be consoled, reassured, to relax in another's strength. Just for a moment.

Nalatan. His face swam in her inner vision, a troubling image that had no constant form, but accused, nevertheless.

He had no right. He held back things he could have told her. He was the one who backed away.

He cared, though. Truly cared.

Nalatan.

Canis Minor leaned closer. His hand grasped her thigh. She was amazed at how brightly blue his eyes gleamed. The ruddy glow of his face suggested a light burning under the flesh.

She leaned back, braced by her hands on the horse's haunches. Eyes closed, she retreated. Surrendered.

The smell of the horses. The brittle tang of pines, of scorched, thirsty grass. Heat. Baking rock, earth.

His breath. On her cheek, her throat. Hands on her jawline, neck.

The heat of the Dry was inside her. Dazed, weak, she filled

with pleasure, with want. Muscles strained as she arched her back. Sun beat down on her face, touched her open mouth, drew breath from her in sharp, taut inhalations. Her breasts, bared to the sky. Canis Minor, stroking. She looked. He stared at her, eyes slitted, face suffused.

The horse, unused to Tate, reacted violently when she dug her heels into its flanks. It bucked forward. Tate's knee was driven under Canis Minor's. The momentum of the leap forced his leg upward. Off balance, he gave a startled yell and tumbled backward out of the saddle.

Tate controlled her horse with one hand, hurriedly buttoning her blouse. She continued to look off into the piñons for a moment, breathing deeply, settling herself. When she turned, Canis Minor was walking toward her. He had a puzzled, angry look. More than that, he still carried the lust on his face, and in his hunched, bear-like posture.

Holding up a hand, Tate backed her horse. "I'm sorry. I can't. I didn't want anything to happen. It just did."

His chin tucked closer to his chest. He peered up at her from under a ridged, animal's brow.

Frightened, Tate turned her horse broadside to his advance and called, "Tanno. Ready." The hound leapt to stand between her and the oncoming man. Legs spread, head down, Tanno growled. Bared teeth gleamed warning.

Canis Minor stopped. Hand on his sword, he considered. When he looked up to Tate, she had the wipe resting on her thighs, muzzle pointed at him. She said, "Listen. Nothing happened. Understand?"

Slowly, he straightened. His eyes lost their fixed stare. Finally, he smiled. It was weak, self-conscious. He said, "I'm not used to women who act the way you do. You'd better be careful with Starwatch men. None of us will 'understand,' as you put it."

"There won't be another time."

Canis Minor's smile was glaringly false. "We should go back now. People will wonder." He spoke with a teasing lilt. Its edge of anger worried Tate. The affability, the comradeship, of the earlier talk was completely gone. Anxiously, Tate wondered if any of it had been honest.

All the way down the hillside, she couldn't stop thinking about Nalatan. Half the time she was hoping he'd never hear any stories of this foolishness. The other half, she blamed it all on his lack of commitment.

CHAPTER 103

Lanta wept.

Alone in the tent, pinned to the surrounding darkness by the shaft of light streaming through the ventilation vent at the crown, she rocked in silent misery. The absence of any sound lent her sadness an eerie, premonitory quality.

Initially, she cried out of feelings of inadequacy. Here, in calmer surroundings, with time to finally think, her mind turned on her viciously. She envisioned herself alienating Conway. Even when the rational part of her mind insisted she'd done nothing to antagonize him, much less earn his brutality, a part of it wallowed in guilt, insisted she'd done something to deserve such treatment.

Emotionally, she was destroying herself. Logic was incapable of stopping her.

Her mind seethed with rejection, with belittlement.

Tee.

Yasmaleeya's insistence that Sylah deliver Jessak, rather than herself.

Now Tate was helping Sylah pry out information concerning the Door. Again, Lanta was a nothing, doing nothing.

Matt Conway was the dream that was going to change that. Being loved by one she loved would be identity. To be important to someone, not as a freak who read riddles about the future, or as a practitioner of mysterious medical arts, but as a person full of hopes and fears and everyday worries. That was to be alive.

Wife to Matt Conway. One of a couple.

She wished she could have remained a young, innocent Chosen forever. That, at least, was anonymity. Times of contentment. Children had their spites and meannesses, but nothing compared with the cruelty of seeing adult dreams trampled into filth.

The fear in Lanta's heart flickered to life when she considered how long since she'd experienced the Seeing. Had time healed the loss?

Seeing could help Sylah more than potentially dangerous questioning. What if it revealed the Harvester's plans? The Chair's goals?

Conway. Would she See him?

She still shuddered at every memory of him amidst those alien, terrible scenes of death and destruction.

Having used the Seeing wrongly once, what further punishment did Church hold for her if she did it again? How many times could she be thrown into the torments of the Land Under?

Could that place offer more unhappiness than this one?

Unbidden, the words of her chant crept into her mind, imposed themselves on the rhythm of her swaying. Muscle by muscle, nerve by nerve, she relaxed. She felt herself slowing inside. The arc of her rocking movement dwindled.

The sun moved. She sat in darkness. The oval impact of the light was a dazzling pool directly in front of her. Half-closed eyes fixed on its center. Mental vision replaced the shabby, unsatisfactory world. The pool became an abyss of molten metal. Things moved there. Dim, shifting shapes. She understood they meant to frighten. She dismissed them with a cool nonchalance.

Calm claimed her, excluded everything else.

This wasn't her normal refuge. This was violence surrounding confidence.

A mountaintop. All snow and ice. The wind roared like all the raging rivers of the world. But Lanta was warm. Steady. She stood on the very edge of a precipice, reveled in the endless waves of sun-brushed mountains stretching away from her.

The Seeing came.

The old way. Swift, total blackness. Words in golden flames.

You and you alone are to know the Flower did not grow without nurturing. She was brought to bloom by her mentor, not entrusted to the uncertainties of nature. Know, also, the Flower may yet fail. Her victory, the triumph of the black and the white, born of man-darkness and man-fire, awaits. Nor will her victory, if it comes, stop the struggle for peace and equality. Sweetest victories bring bitterest envy. Doors are not endings, but beginnings. There are more tests to come. Even the most wicked, she who suborns Church herself, must be appeased, if it is necessary so the Flower may succeed. In the end, the Flower that nourishes all feeds on that which nurtures and benefits the Flower. One will sacrifice, one will bear the unbearable that the Flower may succeed. Yet, of what purpose the Flower, but to bear the seeds? And having borne, what Flower remains as before? Lanta is chosen from all to know the music that shall sing the glory of Church forevermore.

The golden letters coalesced, melted together in one huge, fiery ball that grew, grew, then hurtled at her. Engulfed her. She screamed. Burned.

Opening her eyes, she couldn't remember where she was. Her first cogent awareness was of heat. She lay on her side, face pressed to the pounded earth. Forcing herself to all fours, she realized she was in the sunbeam. Sweat soaked her underclothes, her robe. Sticky, dank hair clung to her head. Strength returned gradually. She moved out of the light into the dark, struggled to her feet.

The villagers watched in awe, hands flashing in three-signs, as the small black-clad figure trudged to the women's baths for the second time in one morning. Many remarked on the wetness of her robe, the shining moisture on her face, barely visible inside her voluminous hood. Others commented on the strangeness of her eyes. When a boy laughed and remarked to his mother that she looked like someone looking at a ghost, she cuffed him. Then made another three-sign.

Sylah walked with Orion on the riverbank. She noticed Lanta's passage on her way to the bath and wondered at the second trip. She had no time to dwell on it. Orion was saying, "No one from Church has ever studied our legends. I've often wondered if other tribes have any similar to ours. So much was lost to us. The people of the beginning . . ." He paused, shook his head. "They left us nothing. Some names, some skills. How ignorant they must have been. If our siah hadn't come to them, they'd have perished."

"That's true of all tribes. Some, like the Mountain People of the north, divided when the siah left. It makes for a very confused history."

Orion agreed. He glanced around, then leaned closer to Sylah. "I sometimes wonder about what we accept as truth. We watch the stars, because we know someday the giants must come back. If giants could go to the stars, why can't I fly? Just across the river?" Straightening, he cleared his throat, frowned. "Of course, I don't disbelieve, understand. It's just that I don't understand. One wonders how it was done."

"Of course." Sylah was happy to let the matter slide. Questions like that weren't unique to Orion, she thought wryly, and she already had a glut of them. "That's why I'm interested. If Church can learn everyone's legends, perhaps we can establish a unity, a common link between some tribes. Even all of them."

Orion smiled, patronizing. "Leave it to Church to want to bring everyone under one roof. That's a stranger dream than men flying. And an unhealthy one, child. Tell a Starwatch man he's related to the animals from Long Sky, or the Salts, or the Hents, and you'll hear language Church shouldn't know about."

"The next time I take an arrowhead out of a man, you come listen; there aren't any words I haven't heard."

He chuckled. "You're deceptive. Like good leather, soft and handsome, but strong. Flexible. I'm not surprised you got away from Kos. I wish you could have kept the child. You'd raise him better than those fools in Church Home."

"I wish we could have, too. We were afraid he'd die. He thrived. Hardly ever cried. Amazing." She sighed. "Now I'll probably never see him again. Poor little Jessak; lost his mother, then his trio of self-appointed aunts."

"Who?"

Orion was behind her, stopped. His voice told her something was wrong. Apprehensive, she turned. His eyes were wide, unbelieving. Sylah said, "The baby? His name? It's Jessak. Why?"

"You named him that?"

Sylah laughed. It was an attempt to dispel his distress, but sounded nervous, nevertheless. Helstar's words returned to her. She said, "His mother named him, of course. The last thing she shouted at us as we fled. You know the name? I was told it was— inauspicious."

Orion watched her closely, tugging on his beard. At last, having come to a decision, he started to walk again, taking her arm as he came abreast of her. Together, they continued on. He said, "The child is a lever, Sylah. Whoever has him can bargain very effectively with the Chair. You should have thought more seriously about that. The Harvester did. You've strengthened her position regarding the Sister Mother contest. On the other hand, you've endangered her greatly. Some would say."

The last phrase had the ring of afterthought. Orion paused, considering his next words, then forged ahead. He took on a speculative, calculating manner. "The name is old in Kos. A legend, central to their tribal beliefs. You know Kos as a Church stronghold and ally. There are other beliefs, however. Not a religion, exactly, but beliefs in other things. Spirits. Ghosts. Animals that men identify with."

"Sharks." Sylah remembered the jaws on the walls and the mystical appearance of the creatures even before the wallkiller's victim fell into the sea.

Sharks came when Jessak was endangered.

"Yes. Sharks," Orion said. "The man who told me the legend of Jessak drew a picture of one. Horrible thing. I'll never travel to

613

the Great Ocean; if I did, I wouldn't get near it. At least a man can see a tiger or a snake." He shivered. "They believe sharks are the agents of a Demon King, who lives under the sea. His magic bow shoots flaming arrows. One can burn a whole village. The sharks protect the king, you see, so they're sacred to the Chair, as well. Sometimes the Demon King comes to the land. To sire a son. If the child grows to maturity, he's destined to kill his parents, who don't know he's the demon's son, of course. The child is beautiful. So wonderful, in fact, many hate him. And well they should, because under all the beauty and friendliness is foulest evil. Occasionally, the evil breaks through; the boy's life is jeopardized. Anyone who helps him, without knowing his true identity, will be greatly rewarded. Anyone who knows who he is, or suspects, and uses him or deceives him, expecting to benefit, earns his undying wrath."

Sylah tossed her head. "I'm safe, then. I didn't know the poor babe was part of a legend, and my faith in Church is too strong to accept demons and witched children."

"Ahh." Orion lifted a warning finger. "There's some truth in all the old tales. We have to be clever enough to catch it. Sometimes I think that's how the One in All sees our efforts to understand the world: like children chasing butterflies. Look at yourself. You believe a prophecy, a Church legend."

"Admitted. I'm near it, Orion. I don't know why I know, but I do."

The man pulled at his beard again, his smile enigmatic. "Many have heard the same legend, Sylah. None have found anything. Some have disappeared while searching; did you know that?"

"No." Sylah made the admission with a tingle of fear. The Abbess never mentioned anything about disappearances. She continued. "No one found the Door because I'm the one who shall. I'm the Flower, Orion. I am."

"Some have said so." He laughed quietly at her surprise, adding, "The Seer of Seers predicted the Flower would come soon. To gain glory through the black and white. Traveling with the ones called White Thunder and Black Lightning has added much to your argument."

"I never heard of the black and white. I swear it. How do you know of the Seer of Seer's visions?"

"We have close contact with the brotherhoods that protect Church Home. We exchange news."

They were at a swooping bend of the river. Across from them, a marsh backed away from the water's edge, hoarding what it

614

could glean of the passing flow. Blackbirds rose and fell in sharp explosions of black and yellow. Unimpressed, a huge, scraggly, blue-gray heron stalked the shallows. Tall reeds swayed in a steady breeze. A few feet out from the near shore, a boy stood with a small fish spear. Unmoving as stone, he waited. The crysalline current built dancing whirlpools behind his slim legs. Spinning lazily, they drifted downstream to be reclaimed by the more sedate movement of the river.

Sylah said, "My friends and I will leave here soon. We'll look east. Over there." She gestured weakly, knowing how vague she sounded.

Orion was concerned. "Be careful. There's forbidden country that way. No one lives there. Never has. A place even few animals inhabit. Terrible cliffs. Our legends tell of monsters and canyons so deep and narrow the sun never reaches the bottom. Fanciful tales, but as I said, there's some truth in all the old stories. I advise you to avoid that area. If you go, I beg you to be careful."

Pulse racing, Sylah warned herself to give no sign of heightened interest. She tried to read him, saw genuine concern in him, but it was so admixed with such potent agitation that she was more confused than informed.

There was deceit. She was certain of it.

Why? About what?

On the return to the village, she saw Tate and Canis Minor returning from a ride. Nalatan approached them from the opposite direction. Even at this distance, there was a stiffness in the warrior monk's posture that touched off prickling at the back of Sylah's neck.

CHAPTER 104

Tate refused to acknowledge Nalatan's repressed anger. Canis Minor, on the other hand, bristled with hostility. Tate flinched at greeting. "Nalatan. What luck did you have?" The accent was on the word "you."

Suddenly, everything was still. Tate tasted metal.

Swatting her horse, she angled forward between the two men. Her tight grin felt grotesque. She chattered, hearing the words, brittle, shallow. "You should see the view from up there, Nalatan. The houses are like little toys."

Nalatan looked through her, at Canis Minor. "We killed two wildcows. And a coyote. You know how they grin and sneak around in the brush while you're butchering, hoping to grab something when men aren't looking."

Canis Minor paled. His smile withered. "Boys kill wildcows. Smaller boys kill coyotes."

Tate said, "I've seen some beautiful capes made of coyote fur. The Dog people wear them all the time."

Nalatan flashed her an absent glance. When he looked to Canis Minor again, he appeared sleepy. Tate could think of no other word for the deceptively heavy-lidded features. She heeled her horse, making for her tent. Over her shoulder, she called to the men, neither of whom had moved. "I'm going home. Is either of you coming with me?"

Without a word, both men wheeled to follow.

It was a weird procession. Nalatan rode to Tate's left. Canis Minor on the right. Other riders saw the trio coming and made way. A few younger men, contemporaries of Canis Minor's, turned to trail behind. He spoke to them all. His attention remained on Nalatan.

Tate burned. What was it Sylah said? Something about boys and their iron toys.

They killed.

Canis Minor mouthed remarks to his friends that were clearly meant to irritate Nalatan. "Our young women should be more like Donnacee Tate. She can talk to a man. She's got lots of understanding. It's no surprise our tribesman relies on her advice."

Teeth grinding, Tate refused to acknowledge either Canis Minor, Nalatan's steaming silence, or the crude snickering from the oafs in the rear. She cut her eyes at Canis Minor, keeping her head still. He rode chest out, nose up. For a moment she felt sorry for him.

Sylah and Orion stepped from between two tents ahead. They stopped there, waiting. Tate wished she could yell at them to hurry, to come to her. The tension darting back and forth across her was unbearable. Muffled conversations and sniggers coiled up from the young warriors tracking the episode. Beside her, Tanno growled uncertainly. Tate reached down, soothed her.

Canis Minor seized on the act. "Did you see that, you warriors? She touches the animal, and it obeys. Do you think Nalatan does so well? Maybe he needs a stronger touch."

Nalatan rode ahead, arriving in front of the waiting Orion a few paces earlier than Tate and Canis Minor. When Orion opened his mouth to greet him, Nalatan spoke over the effort. "Orion, I won't ask why you never taught this snotnosed fool manners. Why discuss failures? I tell you this, though. He insulted this woman. I . . . care for her. We've shared too many dangers for me to see her cheapened. I tell you—not him, not his squat-to-piss puppy friends—but you, a man, with adult intelligence. If he speaks to the Tate one again, I'll teach him everything you overlooked."

Throughout Nalatan's quiet, almost phlegmatic speech, Orion went through a series of reactions. Openmouthed shock at being called a failure. Embarrassment at accusation of Canis Minor's rudeness. He ended with red-faced anger at hearing one of his prized students shamed in public.

Confronted by the true gravity of the situation, Canis Minor put on an indignant defense. "I said nothing improper. My friends will tell you." Murmured assent rose from a group that had grown considerably. More people were arriving quickly.

Rasping, Orion said, "You accuse Canis Minor of a wrong. How you do it is equally wrong. This complication makes it difficult to know who to believe."

"If you're saying I lie, we can forget the child. You and I can settle this."

Sylah stepped forward. "Nalatan. Starwatch saved our lives. We're indebted."

In the heat of midmorning, a dragonfly from the nearby marsh chose that moment to swoop into the middle of the tense drama. Metallic green, crystal winged, it needled back and forth between Nalatan and Orion. It turned abruptly, landed on the muzzle of Nalatan's horse. The animal snorted surprise, jerked its head, pecked at the ground in a rapid, forefoot dance. Nalatan calmed it. The movement changed something in him. Tate saw his chest swell at a massive intake of breath, then slowly subside. He bowed his head, raised it, a deliberate, obvious nod. "I apologize to Starwatch. I request you relay to the Canis Minor one my request that he avoid the Tate one."

Orion said, "A difficult position for me." He turned quickly, addressing Tate. "Is this what you wish?"

Caught off guard, Tate stammered. If she agreed, the entire crowd would think she was "held" by Nalatan. If she denied it, she opened herself to more harassment from Canis Minor. She felt caught in one of those terrible, consuming moments, when time seems to break apart. Of course she wanted nothing to do with

Canis Minor: Did they expect her to throw open her heart in public, declaim her love for Nalatan?

There it was. Love. Confession.

There were smiles around her. Muffled laughter. "I don't know. I wasn't thinking . . ."

Loud guffaws interrupted her. Aflame with consternation, she stammered all the more.

Canis Minor rode around her to face Orion. All stern nobility, he said, "I meant to create no problem. Let Nalatan hold her. I have no wish to take food off another man's plate. Especially a meal not to my taste and badly overcooked."

Tate backhanded him. Knuckles crunched nose cartilage.

Canis Minor yelled, clapped a hand to his face, yanked his horse sideways.

Nalatan dismounted so smoothly his speed was deceptive. He handed his reins to Sylah. To Orion, he said, "Now I owe you nothing. He owes me." As Nalatan turned away, Orion called, "The legends, Nalatan. He learns Starwatch."

Nalatan drew his sword. "Let someone tell of him, then. We should all learn from fools." Standing against Canis Minor's horse on the off-sword side, Nalatan said, "I warned you, boy. You should have stayed with insulting me. I wouldn't have called you out for that. Now it's too late. Get down. Die well."

Canis Minor, stiffly awkward, staring at Orion, inched out of the saddle. A woman shouted, "He's a boy. The monk will kill him." A second answered, "It's the monk's right. Anyone can see she's in his hold. Canis Minor should know better." Another contributed, "Nalatan's two years older. I knew his mother."

The younger men exhorted Canis Minor. "Show him how Starwatch warriors fight. Or maybe the black one wants to take his place. Does she fight at all?"

Nalatan stepped back from Canis Minor. Searching in the direction of the last remark, he settled on a red-faced belligerent. "You?" Nalatan asked. The man understood, drew himself erect. "Yes, me. If Canis Minor doesn't finish you, I'll challenge you myself."

Nalatan smiled. "Don't go away."

Coldly, the warrior monk ceased to be Nalatan. Muscles bunched in blue-veined knots only to release again. Both men made three-signs, backed away from each other to perform personal rites. When finished, they drew swords and settled into fighting posture.

Shuffling, poised for attack or defense, Nalatan advanced.

In contrast to Nalatan's stony calm, Canis Minor moved in quick, erratic jerks. Suddenly, screaming, Canis Minor struck. His blow drove Nalatan's blade to the ground, the tip actually digging into the dirt of the street. Before he could raise it to defend, Canis Minor's return sweep was coming. Unruffled, Nalatan stepped inside it. The only thing to contact him was Canis Minor's wrist. Using that force, plus his own strength, Nalatan spun away, out of range.

Excited by what he interpreted as Nalatan's narrow escape, Canis Minor pressed his attack.

On the sidelines, Tate clamped onto Sylah's arm. "Can't you stop them, Sylah? Please? Do something. If he's hurt, I'll die."

Sylah put her arm around Tate's shoulders. "If you have prayers in your country, use them now. If you're ever going to admit you love him, this is the time."

Tate looked at her with a stricken, sick expression. She said no more. Still, Sylah noted, her lips moved without cease.

Imperceptibly, Canis Minor's attack swung to defense. Nalatan's sword took on life. Until then, neither man was wounded. Suddenly, however, Canis Minor made a peculiar grunting sound and backstepped quickly. Nalatan was even faster. The point of his sword flicked left, right, left again. Canis Minor yelled pain, danced away with his weapon sweeping the air in front of him, finally deflecting the stabbing bite of the other blade. Nalatan slowed. Canis Minor looked down at the slash on his right shoulder, then at the two even deeper wounds across the left side of his rib cage.

He looked at Nalatan. Questioning. Slowly comprehending.

Canis Minor was brave. He attacked. There was desperation in it, but there was courage and determination as well.

Sylah ceased her prayers for Nalatan's life. Now she prayed with equal fervor that he'd see what she saw, a man who'd made a fool of himself. Sylah refused to believe Nalatan would kill such a man.

Canis Minor went down. The blow that did it was a deflected two-handed swipe. Had Canis Minor been a hair slower, it would have decapitated him. Instead, the blade was turning sideways as it rose. The flat side struck his temple. Barely conscious, he dropped like a stone. His sword fell in the dust with a muffled thud, spurting dust all along its length.

Still two-handing his weapon, still devoid of expression, Nalatan stepped forward. Canis Minor sat, hands knuckled down in the dirt, legs splayed in front of him. Blood soaked his vest, his lower arms. A bleeding flap of scalp draped over his left ear. Taking a wide stance, Nalatan raised his sword. Dead, hard eyes measured the back of the bowed head.

Orion's groan checked the downward stroke. Nalatan looked at him. Orion raised his chin, closed his eyes. Nalatan returned his attention to his aiming point.

"Don't."

Tate knew it was her voice, wasn't sure she'd actually spoken.

Nalatan was very certain. He lowered the sword, let it rest suggestively on the back of Canis Minor's neck. "No?" It was almost a whisper. There was no sound whatever from the crowd, now almost the entire tribe.

"Don't." It was all Tate trusted herself to say. She mentally pleaded with Nalatan to see inside her, to know all the things she couldn't say. She wanted him to see the woman who loved Nalatan, couldn't bear to see his honor demeaned by simple butchery. She wanted him to see the woman who loved Nalatan for what he was.

Nalatan turned from her, looked to the crowd. Carefully, he inspected the faces. He came to the red-faced blowhard. Stared at him.

The man forced his way backward through the pack.

Nalatan looked back to Tate. He lifted his sword from the groaning, shifting Canis Minor. "Have him. A gift."

Sword in hand, Nalatan left through a gap that opened at his approach. It didn't close behind him.

CHAPTER 105

Conway signaled across the narrow canyon for Karda to remain in place. The dog shook, as if it wanted to argue and didn't know how. Dust flew. Loose, flying hair glinted in the sunlight. Nevertheless, Karda stayed put.

On Conway's side, Mikka lay at his feet. Stormracer and the packhorse were a few yards distant. Conway had taken the precaution of giving them some grain in feedbags to help prevent any snorting or whickering that might alert the man he intended to ambush.

It was two days since Mikka came in from a backtrail search with her neck hair up and a warning growl that told of human pursuit. It surprised Conway to discover it wasn't a Windband unit.

The individual following him was a determined expert. Backtracking, trail erasure, circular patterns—Conway tried every trick he'd heard. Nothing discouraged the man. There was no choice but to kill him and have done with it.

If he was going to find Sylah and the others, he had no more time to lose.

A full mile away, the tracker plodded along. Conway wondered what he looked like. He almost felt he knew the man, after two days of testing each other. Right now was as close as they'd been.

Soon Conway could distinguish the horse. A dun, black mane and tail. It moved with stumpy, chopped strides that looked as uncomfortable to sit as hopping downstairs, but the man riding it sat as smoothly as pond water.

A slow-burning anger rose in Conway's throat. He could respect this man. He'd never get to know him, never have a chance to learn what possessed him to get on his trail. It wasn't right. Bushwhacking never was.

The fight with Katallon was even lower.

Conway admitted it, with the taste of bile in his mouth. Katallon was a savage, a killer, and a slaver. He fought his duel with Conway fair, though.

Like the man coming down the canyon, Katallon had had no idea what he was up against.

Matt Conway. "Thug From Another World."

Whatever Matt Conway had been before this world, he'd had no reason to be ashamed.

Before.

Lanta's accusation of cowardice shamed him, but only because he never gave her a chance to understand. If he'd taken a minute—half a minute—to explain to her that he was assigned to that helicopter she'd Seen, he might still have some pride.

After what he did to her, tricking Katallon came easy. So easy. What was the old story? After committing murder, one sinks rapidly to soaking uncanceled stamps from envelopes? Something like that.

Katallon was a warrior. Death and violence were his daily portion.

Lanta deserved nothing like the abuse she'd gotten from a man she considered a friend.

If he was ever to make amends, he had to find her.

No glory-hunting tracker was going to interfere with that.

Shadow inched across the canyon. Conway's side was in the shade. Across from him, in full sun, Karda's eyes were baleful.

Conway moved to a point where he could rest the wipe in the juncture of two boulders. From the north, his target would see only a small irregularity in the stone. In country such as this, that wouldn't demand attention.

Slowly, sight set squarely in the center of the man's chest, just below the full beard, Conway squeezed the trigger.

He almost fired just as the man dismounted. Cursing under his breath, Conway eased off.

His target moved to the off side of his mount, lifted the animal's forefoot. After a moment's inspection, the rider, clad in loose, terrain-matching tan blouse and trousers, led the limping animal to a place where he could sit on a large rock and work on the hoof. At one point, he took off his floppy gray hat to wipe his face, fanned himself slowly for a while, then resumed his work.

Conway continued to squint down the barrel. No matter how he twisted and squirmed, however, he couldn't manage a clear shot. Either the man was behind the horse or behind a rock or exposed for only a fleeting moment. As a final blow, when he continued south, the man led the horse from the wrong side. The only target was his lower legs.

Then, suddenly, magically, the dun horse was alone. It stood head down, ears flopping, tail swishing at flies. The reins dangled.

The rider was not to be seen.

Despite the baking heat of the canyon, a delicate, swift icicle of fear slipped along Conway's spine.

Men didn't disappear. Not in broad daylight, not in the Dry, where a man could literally see from one meal to the next.

Mikka rose, pressed against Conway. She whined.

Conway said, "Next time, I shoot whatever's showing. Never mind the clean kill."

The shadows sneaking across the canyon floor grew longer. Sweat soaked Conway's cotton shirt. The limits of the stain turned white with dried salt. Across the way, Karda's chest was slick with saliva from his painting. Stormracer and the packhorse, long since finished with the grain, pawed the ground and snuffled, doing their best to ask for water.

The little dun horse appeared content to spend its life in the same place.

Hollowly, echoing, a voice filled the canyon. "You've done a good piece of work, Matt Conway. Can't see you, know you're there. Read your tracks, saw where you slowed to pick a spot, saw where you stopped and looked back at the view. Up in those rocks somewhere, you and those huge dogs. I come to help."

Hunkering down well out of view, Conway shouted back. "Turn around and ride north."

"Can't do that. I've been two days catching up to you. Was headed for Windband camp to do some business. Ran into a bunch of them. Looking for you, don't you know. Out of sorts. Unfriendly. Took my burro. Everything. I was pretty sure I'd already cut your trail, so I turned back south after you. You knew I was there. Brushing tracks. Doubling. Riding hard ground. You could hurt a man's feelings, make him feel unwelcome. Not the way to treat a man who wants to help."

"Help what?"

"Find your friends. Where you're going, isn't it? Looking for the Flower, Tate, Nalatan. The Violet one, Lanta. Every man should help Church, right? Even a Peddler. You might even say especially a Peddler."

The man's smile put off Conway. It looked innocent enough, but there was something cunning hidden in it.

Resuming his firing position, Conway said, "Let's see you. Hands high, sun sign."

"Exactly what I had in mind."

Conway sighted on a likely area ten yards or so from the horse. A movement at least thirty yards south of that drew his attention. The stranger was walking toward him, down the west side of the canyon. Responding to some unseen, unheard signal, the dun horse limped to join its master.

Conway stepped into view. There was no reason not to; the man was looking directly at his hiding place, hands raised in a sun sign over his head.

It was embarrassing. Conway glowered. Stopping at the point where the canyon wall started its rise, the stranger looked up, smiling, oozing good fellowship. "Don't often get involved with other people's adventures. Everyone's so excited about this Flower, thought I ought to do what I could."

"Just who are you?" Conway said, jerking the wipe threateningly. The man ducked his head, looked sheepish. "Now, isn't that the way of it? Man spends too much time in the wilderness, all his manners just fly away. Name's Bilsten. Peddler. Like my father, his father before him." He stopped, cocked his head to one side. "Not a popular people, Peddlers. Bother you?"

"I don't care if you're a witch. What do you know about my friends?"

Bilsten looked around as if crowds of listeners lurked. "Don't say witch. Not loud. Never can tell. About your friends; the Harvester's after them. From Kos. With warmen. Didn't catch them. Yet."

Words flew out of the man like sparks from kindling. None of them meant anything. Conway controlled himself. "You said you could help. That means something's wrong. Tell me." Remembering Karda, Conway whistled. The dog lumbered down the far side of the canyon, heading straight for Bilsten on his way to join Conway. The Peddler skipped to his horse and swung up into the saddle. Such agility from a man of Bilsten's apparent years startled Conway, until he thought back on the remarkable disappearing act. It occurred to him that this Peddler was entirely too easily misjudged.

Bilsten's smile turned ingratiating. "Peddler's life's a hard one, Matt Conway. Always poor. Hand to mouth, as they say. Hand to mouth. Windband took my things 'cause what you did made them angry. Some might say you owe me. Anyhow, your friends, they're close. Moving slow, heading for southwest corner of Starwatch territory. Nalatan's tribe. I can send you right to the village."

"What do you want?"

"Direct. Businesslike. Oh, I appreciate that." After assuring himself that Karda was remaining next to Conway, Bilsten dismounted to sit on a convenient rock. He leaned back, hands clasped on a kneecap. "That packhorse of yours. Sound animal. You grain her. Quality. I'd settle for her. If you want to throw in the load."

"What?" Conway's outrage was a croak. "For a piece of information?" Suddenly cunning, Conway said, "You told me they're close. South. I'll find them myself."

Bilsten let go of his knee, jerked upright. "That's hard. Oh, that's very hard. Man tries to be neighborly, just us two, out here all alone. Makes a little conversation, gets taken advantage of. Hard."

Conway smiled. "Your own fault. You got greedy. Anyhow, if my friends are with Nalatan's people, there's no hurry to get there."

"May be. Hope so." Slowly, dejected, Bilsten moved to his horse.

There was a jarring note in his voice. Conway said, "What do you mean, you hope so? Is there something you're not telling me?"

"Me?" Bilsten was astonished. "Told you all I know. Except about Starwatch people. No point. Like you say, Nalatan's tribe. Except the legender—that's the man who keeps the tribe history, don't you know—people say he's not sure if he should back the Flower or the Harvester. Touchy situation. I wouldn't worry, though."

Conway ground his teeth. "Where are these Starwatch people? How do I get there?"

Bilsten mounted. "I don't think we can do business. I don't think I want to talk to you any more. You just seem to squeeze things out of me. No telling what this last conversation cost me. I had that packhorse in hand, till my mouth and your quick ear got the best of me."

"You greedy clown. My friends could be in danger. All right. The horse. Forget the load. I've got pots, clothes, extra rigging. I'm not letting that go."

Sadly, Bilsten spurred his horse forward a few paces. "Couldn't do that, Matt Conway. Be taking advantage of you. I take that packhorse, you got no way to carry all those things. Not and be light enough to run, if something goes wrong. But I'm a soft-hearted fool. I'll help you anyhow. South. East. Not too much, mind. You'll find somebody. Starwatch, probably. Or maybe Windband. If you see helmets, that's good. A clear sign. Run for your life; that'll be Kossiars. Good-bye, then. And good luck. You're a fine bargainer. Been good to know you."

"Wait." Conway shook his head. "I ought to blow you off that horse. Unpopular? You give the word new depth. Take the horse. Take the load. How do I find my friends?"

"Can I come for the horse? Will the dogs bite me?"

"Not you, you weasel. Not if you were fried in butter." Conway stepped back, jerked the lead line free of its brush tie-down, held it out.

The dun horse limped up the hillside. Bilsten accepted the line with smiles and nods. Back down on the level, he said, "Down to the end of this canyon. Big valley there. Mountains ahead, no pass there, so head west. Ride steady; today, tomorrow. About sunset, you'll come to a steep drop, looking out over another small valley running across your front." He wheeled the dun horse, started north. "Best camp near there that night. Not a good place for fires. In fact, might be well to come onto Starwatch as careful as you can. Know exactly what's going on. They expect a Kossiar raid, you see, so they're a bit frisky, don't you know."

Bilsten was leaving rather quickly. "How far is the village from the steep drop place?" Conway shouted at him.

Bilsten rode a bit farther. He turned to shout back. "I can show you." He fumbled at his side, straightened with a bow. A moment later he released an arrow. It arced down the canyon past Conway. Bilsten was moving north when it landed. His voice echoed. "About four times that far."

Unbelieving, Conway stared from the impact to the disappearing Peddler. He screamed. "That's all? A day and a half ride and then only four bowshots? I'd have found it myself. You cheat! You thief! My packhorse. My gear. You . . . You . . ."

The echo mocked him. Worse, the Peddler was laughing. Happily. For a moment—a spark of a thought—Conway was sure he'd heard that laugh before. Somewhere. A place of fear. Death.

He shook his head. There were too many of those places. Anyhow, what could an old man, a solitary Peddler, know of Church, of friendship?

Conway was fuming when he heeled Stormracer into a jarring trot past the white arrow stuck in the sandy gravel of the Dry. Snowy feathers vibrated in a searing hot breeze. Again, something picked at Conway's memory, tried to distract him from the important thing, the danger facing his companions.

Conway glared over his shoulder after Bilsten. In the distance, the little dun horse was stepping out quite smartly, limping not at all.

CHAPTER 106

Dodoy dodged behind the tent. Most of the rocks flew past harmlessly. The rest boomed off the taut hide, bringing Tate and Lanta outside on the run. Hearing the women scolding, Dodoy essayed a cautious peek. The children who'd chased him scampered off, laughing and whooping. Lanta, hands on hips, hurried them along with a poisonous glare. Tate saw Dodoy and ran to him.

He didn't resist her embrace, nor did he respond. She said, "They don't understand, Dodoy. The tribe's mad at Nalatan and me because they think we shamed Canis Minor. They should be glad he's alive."

Dodoy listened. There was little else he could do, all wrapped up the way he was.

He'd thought it all through, though.

If she'd let him go with the Harvester, like Jessak, he'd be happy, sitting in the cool mountains at Church Home, with lots of things to do, instead of hiding in a tent all the time, afraid to sneak out even to go to the latrine.

Tate said, "I know it's hard for you. It won't last much longer, poor baby. We're going to go look for the Door again. Then they won't pick on you."

At least he didn't have to look at her when he was squeezed up against her. Look for the Door, he thought. Just what the Kossiars want. Starwatch would send them straight to a trap.

Whatever happened to Tate or any of them, they deserved it.

They made him come along. Maybe he wanted to, at first, to get away from Ola and to find a place to live. Church Home could have been the place. Even Kos, if they'd been smart enough to be nice to the Chair. Always making trouble, all of them. Spoiling things.

His thoughts went back to the Starwatch children. Oddly, his hatred was gone. He envied them. They had homes. If they wanted to throw rocks at outsiders, they knew who an outsider was. People like Tate were outsiders. A person had to have the strength of a group to be someone. It startled him to realize how simple it all was.

He gradually disengaged from Tate's smothering affection. Soon she was busy around the tent. For a while, he pretended to help.

In order to ventilate the tent, its skirt was raised to the height of his knees. By lying on the ground at its center, Dodoy looked out into the bright sunlight while remaining practically invisible to anyone looking in. Only a knot of smaller children remained. Dodoy slipped away on the side opposite.

No one he hurried past afforded him any attention. A few paces from his goal, however, a hard hand caught his shoulder from behind. Startled, hurt, Dodoy yelled, trying to twist away. The grip tightened, became intensely painful. Dodoy buckled at the knees, squirmed to see who held him.

Canis Minor's mouth bent in a malevolent smile. "Lost, small rat? Did they send you to beg for extra time? Water? The answer is no."

Dodoy struggled as much from fury as pain. It was demeaning to be interfered with by a disgraced man. He shouted. "I have information for Orion. Let me go. You're in enough trouble already."

627

Factually, the statement was true. Tactically, it was a disaster. Canis Minor paled. He drew back a fist. Dodoy screamed.

Grunting, Canis Minor reeled off balance as strong hands clasped his arm, preventing the blow. He whirled to confront whoever restrained him.

Orion said, "The boy speaks rightly. Look around you."

Dodoy partially stifled a satisfied smirk as Canis Minor discovered several people watching the scene with undisguised disapproval. The cocked arm wilted, the balled fist opened. Releasing Dodoy, released by Orion, the man seemed about to stumble away. Instead, he stiffened. Hoarsely, head thrust forward at the watchers, he said, "I'll make no apology. My mind isn't right. Defeat is hard to live with. Soon you'll all see my vindication and my vengeance."

Without exception, the women in the crowd were frightened. Most men nodded, looking stern. Many smiled. Dodoy recognized the latter expression. People who enjoyed inflicting pain smiled like that.

Orion interrupted his wondering. "What are you doing here, boy?"

Glancing around, assuring that the curious were out of earshot, Dodoy answered. "There are things you should know. I'm sorry about the way the people I'm with treated Canis Minor."

The speech ended in a piping squeal as Canis Minor's hand closed on Dodoy's throat. The man said, "You crawly little insect."

Orion pulled Canis Minor away, ripping at the younger man. "Control yourself. Please, Canis Minor, we need information." He shoved the pair ahead of him into his tent, where he sat down to listen.

Dodoy said, "I hid outside Sylah's door once when she talked to the Chair." Canis Minor muttered something about a spy. Dodoy pretended not to hear, kept his gaze fastened on the important audience. Orion nodded for him to continue. "Sylah told the Chair that when she finds the Door she'll send a Messenger to the Chair. He'll send warmen. Sylah and him will rule everyone." Dodoy was sure he saw a flicker of interest. He gambled. "Sylah mentioned Starwatch."

Orion inclined forward to fire questions. "What did she say about us? About other tribes? Are the brotherhoods with her or against her? What did she say about the Harvester? Are the ones with you part of the plan?"

"I couldn't hear everything. I think the word she used about

Starwatch was 'eliminate.' Something like that. She used the same word about the Harvester, anyhow. Sylah and the others planned it all way back in Ola."

Canis Minor squatted so he could look directly into Orion's face. "Gan Moondark. We should have known. He sees himself as a conqueror. Imagine the ambition of that Dog."

Orion stood. Like an owl hearing a mouse, he hovered softly over Dodoy. "So the Harvester's Kossiar escort are intended to cut her down as soon as Sylah has the secret of the Door in hand. What obscene treachery. Then it'll be Starwatch's turn, and any brotherhood monks who don't cooperate. I thought the Harvester had no match for ruthlessness, but Sylah's worse. 'The Flower.' Pah! It makes me sick. My instincts warned me she was just another greedy female. You knew immediately, Canis Minor. I should have listened. All right, Dodoy, tell me: Why did the White Thunder one go to Windband?"

It was something Dodoy never thought about. Unexpected. He'd forgotten Conway. Dirty, *stupid* Conway. Cold rushed outward from Dodoy's stomach, clutched his lungs so he couldn't breathe. He stared at Orion, caught, too terrified to move.

The man's hand flew at the boy, seized his blouse, twisted it, pulled him to his feet. "That's their plan, isn't it? Tell me. You've gone too far to hold back now. The White Thunder and Moonpriest were sent to Windband to entice them into attacking Church Home, weren't they? Gan, the Dog People, Sylah and her unholy schemers—they want Kos and Windband to crush the small tribes like Starwatch, then fall on each other, like wolves fighting over a kill. Then King Gan thinks he can destroy the winner and install Sylah as undisputed Sister Mother of his Church. Isn't that his plan? *Isn't it?*"

"Yes." Dodoy whispered the word. His thought were dust in the wind; everywhere, nowhere. If he agreed with Orion, maybe they wouldn't kill him. Maybe he'd be allowed to go back to Tate. She'd hold him close. Protect him.

Tears welled, blurred his vision. He said, "Please, don't kill me."

Orion released him. Dodoy sprawled facedown. Hands lifted him from behind. Canis Minor. Dodoy howled, flailed wildly.

Canis Minor stroked his head. Dodoy howled louder. He knew. Canis Minor was feeling for the place to club him. His throat closed, pinched off his voice. All he could do was sob. His heart slammed against his ribs.

Orion said, "You did the right thing. Coming to us was very

brave, very honest. This is a more important moment than one such as you can imagine." "To Canis Minor, Orion said, "Get the boy calmed, send him back. We have to plan."

Later, Dodoy, face washed and clothes dusted off, returned to his tent from one direction just as the chief, the elders, Orion, and a huge crowd approached from the opposite end of the village. Catching sight of Dodoy, Tate rushed to sweep him up to her.

The chief wore impressive finery, bright blue vest with clamshell buttons, trousers of green and yellow stripes. Rows of tiny brass bells on wide leather knee bands jingled at his every step. He carried a heavy staff a full head taller than himself. It was surmounted by a golden-rayed sun.

Planting the butt of the staff, he said, "Rose Priestess Sylah. Violet Priestess Lanta. Donnacee Tate. Starwatch has graciously granted your request to leave us tomorrow morning. We fed you. Sheltered you. Saved your lives. You repaid us by seducing and shaming one of our finest, a future legender. Many here hate you. Hate births fear. You must leave us in the dark of morning. From this time, remain in your tent until escorted away. You are denied light and fire. Meals will be provided, so you can never say we mistreated you."

Orion gestured, and a woman hurried forward, bent under the weight of a large, steaming pot. She put it in the tent and rushed back to the safety of the crowd.

Tate said, "You have no reason to do this to my friends. They didn't reject your failed rapist. I did."

Orion's cheeks and forehead flamed. The beard bristled. "There are those who would harm you. Don't incite them." Proving his point, a rock hummed out of the crowd, thumped on the tent hide. After an initial surprised flinch, there three women drew closer in unspoken accord to stand proud and unintimidated.

When Orion turned back to them, after shouting down the incipient attack, he frowned at their solidarity. As he left with the other leaders, Sylah called after them. "Water. We'll need water."

The chief looked to Orion, who said, "You have soup. Among us, water is for friends. Take what you wish from the river in the morning darkness, before Starwatch can see you." With that, they were gone. In the space of a few heartbeats, the silence around the tent was that of the Dry, massive with the sense of waiting menace.

Tate remarked that the soup was, at least, delicious. Sylah and Lanta agreed. Even Tanno approved, wolfing down her share and looking up hopefully from her feeding dish for more.

Dodoy pleaded a nervous stomach. Tate insisted he take a nap. Smiling appreciation, he allowed her to fuss over him. Instead of going to sleep right away, however, he lay on his side, watching the women and the dog with bright, curious eyes.

CHAPTER 107

Soft wraps of sleep pinioned Sylah in the aftermath of a dream she still felt, but could no longer remember.

A lifetime of training invariably lifted her from bed; waking and movement were synonymous in her experience. Now, however, she was seized by a confused lethargy.

Deep in her mind, far outside logic and reason, something stirred. Tiny, venomous creatures. Not scorpians like the one Tate still muttered about in her sleep.

Sylah heard herself make involuntary pleading sounds.

She feared them. Ironically, the creatures feared everything. "Sleep on," the things said, "forever, if need be." Harmonious. Seductive. They couldn't fool her. She saw their jagged claws, their pointed teeth.

The voices grew shrill. "If you won't be intelligent and just sleep, then flee. Rise up running for your life. Scream for Clas. For mercy."

Sylah's eyes jerked open. An unuttered cry grated to a silent halt in her thirst-closed throat. Fiery sunlight poured into her eyes.

The panic-things ranted exultation, surged forward to claim her.

Sylah twisted to avoid the direct sun rays. Clearing vision revealed leather straps binding her hands. A connecting strap ran up her chest, circled her neck. A second strap ran to her ankles, which were bound in such a manner that she could walk, if she ever got to her feet.

A surge of horror broke against a lassitude that questioned the need to ever move again.

Struggling against that enervating impulse, wriggling against her bonds, she sat up, saw it was past midday. Her head threatened to crack into halves. Her stomach pitched and tossed.

Lanta stretched out on her left. Tate was to her right. Beyond Tate, the only one facedown, lay Nalatan. The back of his head was crusted with dried blood. Shallow breathing ruffled stubby blades of grass at his mouth.

Orion came from somewhere behind her, circling around Lanta. Sylah's first attempt to speak failed. She tried to swallow, choked. Orion looked at her with a controlled expression that failed to hide a stain of shame. Persisting, Sylah managed, "My friends. You said we could go. Drugged us. Lied."

A muscle twitched at Orion's right eye. "It's not immoral to lie to a deceiver. You tried to trick us. We tricked you, instead."

"We? How?" Her voice was returning.

"The uncorrupted boy. He overheard you scheming with your ally, the Chair."

Anger melted with resignation to create a sort of defeated amusement in Sylah's struggling consciousness. "Dodoy. Uncorrupted. The two words don't belong in the same *day*, you poor fool. Would I steal my ally's firstborn? Why were Kossiar warmen trying to kill us when you found us? Did the uncorrupted Dodoy suggest what I might gain from this nonexistent alliance?"

"Don't play innocent." He spat close to her feet. "Power. What women such as you always lust after. You almost made me believe your lies. What dregs you all are. The black one nearly destroyed Canis Minor. You plot at the overthrow of your own Church."

Helpless outrage sent Sylah's mind spiraling into a thundering void. Consciousness streamed out of her, a winding veil that slipped between her reaching fingers. Disoriented, she nevertheless felt answering words rise from within her. "You offend. You cannot lie to me. You know I am the Flower. Remember the Apocalypse Testament: 'The lie of an enemy may take a life. The lie in one's mouth can condemn one's soul.' You are the heir to a sacred trust. You dare not prostitute it. Consider the unspeakable eternity of your situation."

Clouded vision gradually cleared. She found Orion still before her, but stooped, ashen, a man aged to the end of his years. Fear crabbed his hands, twitched at his muscles.

Canis Minor strutted to Orion's side. "Threats. Woman's ways. The Tate one has hers, you have yours. We'll cure you. All of you." He kicked Nalatan's feet, earning a breathy groan from the monk.

Sylah dismissed Canis Minor's mindless tormenting. Like thirst and pain, she discovered she was able to retreat from it into a serene distance. Her self-possession inflamed Canis Minor. He slapped her.

Sprawled on her back, Sylah heard his words to Orion as from a distance. "And you wanted to execute them. That sort of arro-

632

gance alone should be called treason, coming from a woman. Now can you understand why the chief and council agreed with me that Nalatan's a traitor, and they're all equally guilty?"

Regaining her sitting position, Sylah told Orion, "You say you pass on Starwatch legend to Canis Minor. It seems he'd rather defile them."

Canis Minor poised to strike again. Orion said, "Stop. The rules are clear. No abuse."

Grudgingly, Canis Minor let himself be led away from the prisoners. Tate stirred, mumbled something indistinguishable. Canis Minor's smile at her was barbed. He spun on his heel and left.

Sylah said, "Well, Orion? What's to be done with us?"

Fetching a waterskin, Orion concentrated intently on filling a dried gourd cup. He handed it to her. Throughout, he avoided her eyes. She bent to sip. Only then would he answer. "We've sent for the Harvester. To witness."

Sylah poured out the scorn in her heart. "Of course. You grovel. For you, Church is only fear, so you'll use us for entertainment that terrorizes your people. You'll tell each other how powerful the men of Starwatch are. To prove it, you'll gather the tribe to watch us suffer. Nalatan, because he's truly brave, and you're not. And us. Three women. We challenged you. We defied men. That's our treason." She stopped, exhausted, but yet again, unbidden and uncalled words compelled her to speak them. Her voice took on a heavy, forbidding timbre. "Poor, poor man. To wait so long, only to be the one to poison the field again, before the seeding. False Orion knows the truth. He will know sorrow and punishment."

Orion sagged. His voice shook. "It's not true. You're trying to witch me." He backed away. Distance improved his nerve. "Witch. Leave off. Church—the Harvester—protects me." He almost ran away.

Sylah examined their location. A gray slope, dangerously steep, rose behind them. To the front was a large semicircular area cleared of plants or large stones. Its limits were defined by a waist-high rock wall. Beyond, brush softened a valley floor that extended another fifty yards before becoming the opposite slope. That one was gradual, and Sylah detected faint smoke rising beyond it; the village had to be over there.

Archers blocked any possible escape routes.

The waterskin lay nearby. Sylah fetched it. She dabbed Tate's lips, cleaned Nalatan's wound. Lanta appeared at her elbow.

Wordlessly, Sylah extended the skin. Lanta took a hearty drink, swayed, then took the skin to Tate, who was stirring.

Tate's recovery was hard. Her friends helped her up, supported her in an awkward shuffle to the edge of the natural amphitheater. Tate was sick for some time. At last, the three sat down together.

Lanta said, "They drugged us very heavily, to bring us here without waking. What will they do? Have you tested these straps? They knotted the leather wet. It's dried like iron."

Sylah summarized her conversation with Orion, omitting reference to Dodoy. Tate extremely agitated, screamed at the archers for news of the boy. They ignored her. Sylah and Lanta soothed her, assuring her Starwatch wouldn't harm him. Lanta watched Sylah shrewdly, careful to repeat only things Sylah said.

Wearying, Tate lamented. "It's all my fault." She looked to the unconscious Nalatan. "I did everything wrong." There was a gloss of soft wonder on her words, the bewildered regret of a cheated child. "It should have been so easy. I love him. I think he loves me. That's not necessary, though, you know? I want to hold him in my arms, make him know I love him. Why didn't I tell him? Do something about it? I'd at least have had something. Now I've caused all this." She searched the faces of her friends for the wisdom she lacked.

Sylah scuffled closer, took Tate's clenched hands in hers. A guard shouted from the ridgeline. "No touching! Leave the bonds alone. I'll shoot."

Lanta lurched to her feet. Amazingly loud defiance bellowed out of her. "Shoot! Shoot and be damned! You don't have the guts!"

The warrior disappeared.

Tate goggled. Laughed. "Guts? Be damned? Lanta. Where'd you learn such language?"

"You know very well where. Never mind. Are you feeling better now?"

Tate shook her head. "Stronger, anyhow. Thanks."

"Then tell him what you told us." Sylah tilted her head toward Nalatan. "Wake him. Tell him."

Consternation danced across Tate's features, set her eyes darting, looking for escape. Suddenly, she said, "Tanno. Have you seen her?"

Lanta was firm. "No. Now go to Nalatan. While you have the chance."

The last words brought Tate's head up. Very thoughtfully, she said, "It's down to that, isn't it? '. . . the chance.' "

Sylah said, "Whatever they do, we help each other. Sisters. Agreed?"

Lanta and Tate bent forward to kiss her cheeks. Tate rose, graceful in spite of everything, and went to the unconscious warrior monk with the water. Washing her hands first, she poured a few drops on her fingers, then moistened his lips. Tentatively, his surprisingly red tongue worked to touch the water, then retreated. She repeated the wetting, and he licked again, frowning concentration.

It was late afternoon before his eyes fluttered open. At the sight of her, he smiled. A hand instinctively sought to examine the wound at the back of his head, only to be brought up short by the bindings. He froze.

In the next instant, Tate was flat on her back. Nalatan stood over her, knees bent, wide-legged, poised to defend or attack. He pivoted in a series of turns that moved him in unpredictable arcs.

Tate scrambled to her feet. He whirled to face her. His face was a staring, inhuman mask. Tate's mind flashed to the past. The tiger's eyes. Glowing, lit by a compressed energy intent on the task of killing.

Tone would be as important as words. "It's me, Nalatan. Donnacee. Talk to me. Please. Let me talk to you."

His weight rolled from one foot to the other. Hands like blind animals clawed at his bonds. Tate cajoled, begged. Behind her, she felt the presence of the other women, prayed they'd keep away. Even more dangerous, the archers were watching. So far, they'd remained silent. If one of them startled Nalatan . . . She shut out the idea.

The muscles around Nalatan's eyes softened. His hands lowered. Tate spoke more quickly, urgently. Nalatan's stance closed. He stood taller. He looked down at the bindings in puzzled wonderment. His gaze went to Tate. Recognition smoothed his features. He raised his hands.

Tate said, "They drugged us. Someone clubbed you. Did you eat their food?"

"Water. It tasted strange." He drove the bound hands down against his stomach. "Fool!"

Running, tripping, Tate put her hands to his face, and cried out in dismay. The eyes that menaced only moments before rolled up in his head. He would have fallen if she hadn't caught him.

He recovered quickly, but Tate insisted he lie down. He agreed with a tired smile. "I'm sorry if I frightened you. We're trained to respond. When the energy stops, it leaves you empty."

She shushed him, sat next to him and cradled his head on her thighs. He looked up at her. Stroking the hair back from his temples, she said, "I'm here now. The way I should be."

He said, "I behaved badly. About Canis Minor, I mean. What he said. And then you seemed interested in him." His expression pleaded.

"Lots of men interest me. Always will." She watched disappointment touch his features before adding, "There's only one I want to interest. Ever. I should have said so a long time ago. That night on the island."

Nalatan sat up, looked away. "That was when I decided to bring you to my people, if I ever had the opportunity. With the Harvester herding us away from Church Home, I took it as a sign. Since we got here, I've been asking about the stories of black-skinned people in our tribe."

"You could have told me." Tate tried not to scold.

"I wanted to tell you everything at once. You're so concerned about Dodoy's past, your past. I wanted you to see that you shouldn't look at the present and the future—our present, our future—only in terms of the past. Sometimes things change only because they must, but even then, we can hold onto the best of what our forebears created. I don't know what you left behind. I didn't know if you wanted to be with me. I only knew that nothing new can be built without some change to what is old. You're not like the women of my people, and I didn't want to claim you. I wanted you to come to me because it was what you wanted."

Tate's mind swam with images, shameful memories of the abandoned, unattached feeling that made Canis Minor seem necessary. She remembered Sylah's comment, something about how Donnacee Tate wanted to dominate her surroundings. Even now, in this moment of hopeless tenderness, that penetrating analysis rankled.

Because it had been true. That Tate couldn't break free of a dead world's arbitrary social vision. That Tate wanted to marry, raise children, but only according to the dictates of that culture's perceptions. Nalatan couldn't imagine the base of the problem that kept them apart, but he had the wit to know that love would transcend it. He was willing to wait for her to come to him. In her own way.

Her way.

Nalatan reached to touch her. The strap checked him. She bent to his caress. With her chin cupped in his vee'd hands, he said, "I love you."

636

She kissed him. Lingering. Tender. It spoke of forever. And good-bye.

Lanta watched, ashamed of prying, too touched to resist. Her head roared with recollection of the Seeing. . . . *the Flower that nourishes all feeds on that which nurtures and benefits the Flower.*

Surreptitiously, Lanta raised a hand to her breast. Through her robe, she clutched at the True Stone. She asked herself if the Door was worth so much sacrifice.

If the Door was a source of some secret power, they'd never know. Not now.

The True Stone had a known power.

The Harvester would pay any price for it.

Lives, for instance.

The Seeing also said, "What Flower remains as before?"

What if the promised change the Flower must go through was bad?

Should they all die in order to nurture one whose future was so ambivalent?

CHAPTER 108

Shuddering across the darkness in resonant waves, haunting warhorn blasts announced the Harvester's party. There were three horns, each with a different note. Harmonizing, they filled the valley with an infinity of reverberations.

Sylah heard them as the forlorn lowing of beasts separated from their young.

The image reminded her she'd heard no encouragement from her inner voice since Starwatch drugged her.

Had it deserted its defeated listener?

Ignoring the aching muscles generated by what was now a full day and a half of being bound, Sylah straightened and threw back her shoulders. She'd done all she could. She'd fought hard. If the voice that brought her so close to the Door wanted her to succeed, it should have helped at the end.

Sylah ducked her head guiltily, peered about her into the darkness. Now she was scolding the One in All. Or the Iris Abbess, who was only a few steps removed.

She thought about that for a bit, and decided she had a right to scold. The Door was near. Practically at hand.

She shifted irritably. The braided leather line holding her to the post set in the ground brought her up short. For the moment, she'd forgotten that new development, just put in place that afternoon. She guessed she should be thankful Starwatch hadn't leashed them the previous day.

Nalatan explained the significance of the arrangement. At night, with the prisoners backed up against the steep slope behind them, the tribe would assemble in the cleared area to participate in the punishment.

Sylah questioned the word *participate*. Nalatan explained.

Starwatch stoned traitors.

The tears scalding her eyes weren't so much fear or disappointment as frustration. So much work. Faith. Not hers alone. Lanta. Tate. Nalatan. As far back as Gan, and that conniving, devious, wonderful Peddler, Bilsten. Helstar.

Above all, Clas. Clas, who believed in her enough to let her go. Who else could boast such a one?

All finished. Everything wasted.

Another tone soared through the mournful notes of the warhorns. Trums, the notes like brass arrows.

On the ridge between the amphitheater and the village, a torch crawled up into sight from the reverse slope. Another followed. Soon a cluster gathered on the crest. They paused, then plunged downhill in a confused welter. On the low ground, the torches gathered in a roughly round mass, waiting at the edge of the defined clear area.

Sylah wondered why they didn't simply move forward and settle in for the entertainment.

In answer to her unspoken question, a lone rider galloped onto the scene from her left. He, too, carried a torch, raised high in his left hand. Sliding to a halt, the rider dismounted smoothly. When he planted the pointed end of the torch holder in the ground, Sylah saw he was dressed in a tight vest, laced at front and sides. That, and his loose trousers, appeared to be gray. His headgear was a high-crowned affair with a crease down the middle and a wide brim. Small shining things dangled from the edge of the brim in a half circle running around the back from ear to ear. They glimmered, hanging by some sort of cord that also caught the torchlight. An unstrung bow and quiver of arrows were slung on his back, and a short sword at his belt was strapped to his right thigh. When he shifted position, moving past the front of the grounded torch, Sylah saw three vertical black lines drawn on the back of the vest.

Nalatan said, "A warrior monk. Opal brotherhood. See them on his hat? The largest brotherhood, over a hundred men. I know many of them."

Tate perked up. "Will they help us?"

"I wish they could. So do they, I imagine. They'll be neutral, so long as no one threatens the Harvester." Nalatan turned his attention to Sylah. "It's their oath, Sylah. It's not personal."

She found a smile. "I know."

Tate said, "They sound as smart as my dog. I'm worried about her. They wouldn't hurt her, would they?"

Her companions all shook their heads, made assuring sounds. It was Nalatan who said, "Starwatch puts great emphasis on freedom. I expect them to release her."

Tate clutched at the hope. "She'd like that. Even here in the Dry. To roam. You know how she loves to run. If I thought someone would be good to her, I'd give them the Dog word, give her to them."

Sylah shook her head. "It wouldn't do. She's yours now. She'd never accept anyone else."

"She'll die, then. Like us. Now that the Harvester's here, they're going to pull the plug."

Sylah said, "Plug?"

But Nalatan understood the context. "Don't think about it."

Bitterly, Tate said, "You spent your whole life waiting to die for your cause. I can't get enthusiastic about it, all right?"

They had no more time for argument. At the end of the valley, a string of torches appeared. Single file, at first, the column split, forming two lines. As the group came closer, the warriors of Starwatch set up their howling. Lanta winced, turned her face from the advancing unit. Sylah reached to take her hand. The smaller woman's grip was frigid, the pressure the strength of desperation.

More torches appeared on the other flank. Starwatch's leaders trailed in. The two groups met directly in front of Sylah and her friends. The Harvester dismounted with a swirl of her voluminous robes. The chief of Starwatch greeted her formally, flourishing three-signs. He gestured at a man carrying a large bundle. Opened, it revealed Tate's weapons.

Orion watched without moving, stiff and distant until the Harvester turned to him. Sylah strained to hear, but they were too far. A moment later, Orion lifted a torch and waved it over his head. More howling ululated through the valley. The crowd surged forward. Sylah recoiled. There were only men and boys. They'd filled baskets or nets with rocks. The dignitaries moved to the flanks, out of the line of fire.

The warhorns came forward. Slender, copper cones longer than a tall man from mouthpiece to flared bell, their burnished forms glowed warmly. Two men carried each horn. They halted on the edges of the stage area. They faced away from the prisoners. One of the team mounted the bell on his shoulder. The other put his mouth to the instrument. The three horns sounded.

Orion came to stand behind the left pair. When the echoes stilled, he said, "We are here to execute traitors to Starwatch, to Church. The Harvester is here to witness that Starwatch justice includes loyalty to Church. The prisoners shall be stoned. Men will pass among you to assure no one uses stones too large."

Tate pressed against Nalatan. "What's that mean? About the stones?"

He looked straight ahead. "A large stone can end a stoning too quickly."

Tate made a low moaning sound, and Nalatan drew her to him. He said, "We're taught what we call a mahn. It's like a hymn, in your mind. It gives calmness."

"The trance," Sylah nodded. "Tate hasn't had our schooling."

Hysteria flashed in Tate's throat for the brief moment that she imagined a commanding officer's face if she'd ever suggested Marines learn to chant so they could die with equanimity.

Nalatan said, "Sit by me."

Sylah and Lanta joined them, shoulder to shoulder. Even as she dreaded what was coming, Tate marveled at the serenity of her friends.

Friends.

Leaning into Nalatan, Tate indicated the milling, excited crowd. "This isn't the way I thought it'd all end, but I'm with the people I'd pick to go with. Except for Conway." Her face broke in a hardbitten grin. "I'd love to see what he does to this outfit when he finds out what happened. And Clas. Oh, my, yes. Clas. I hope the two of them do it together. Take a good look at them out there, Nalatan. Those fools are just a massacre that hasn't happened yet."

He chuckled. When she looked, he was shaking his head. "What a warrior you are. Too bad we can't make them pay. We can be strong, though. We can help each other."

Tate kissed him, closing her mind to the howling warriors.

640

Until the noise changed. Sharpened. She pulled back from Nalatan, turned where the eyes of the mob led her. And screamed.

Four men carried Tanno on a pole. Suspended from all fours, lashed to the sapling, her eyes darted in all directions. A boy threw a rock at her, and she lunged, snapping. The crowd roared. An adult pulled the boy back, although he was yards beyond the dog's reach.

Tate gripped Nalatan. She'd heard the sounds of death often enough to be inured. This was the sound of insensate killing. It frightened her as nothing else ever had.

The horns bellowed constantly. The crowd's screaming escalated.

Sylah put a hand on Tate's forearm. She had to shout to be heard. "They mean to break us, Donnacee. This is how it starts. Don't look."

"She's a dog, Sylah. A poor, loyal dog. They can't."

Aching, Sylah could only move to shield Tate's vision. Tate firmly pushed her aside.

Four warriors with long ropes fixed loops around Tanno's neck and waist. The bearers dropped her heavily to the ground. Other men slashed the lines binding her to the pole. Instantly, Tanno was up. Crippled feet betrayed her, made her clumsy. The four lines kept her centered, controlled.

A rock struck her. She snarled, redoubled her efforts to attack her tormentors. A second rock, larger, took her forelegs from under her. She sagged, choking, hung on the throat lines.

Incredibly, the sound level rose.

Tanno struggled for footing. More rocks flew. Many struck. Still she fought. The great, intelligent eyes watched her foes. She tried to dodge the storm of stones flying at her. There were too many.

Tate shrieked every curse and obscenity she'd ever heard. Flailing, she broke the hold of Sylah and Natalan. When she hit the end of her restraining line, the crashing fall dazed her. Nalatan pulled her back, held her to his side.

Although the movement was far behind her, Tanno sensed her master. She turned, barked once. Dragging the straining line handlers into the rain of missiles, she forged her indomitable way to Tate. The dog collapsed with her head in Tate's lap.

The handlers let the lines fall slack. The barrage from the crowd stilled while they got out of the line of fire. After they were clear, a strange pause continued.

Someone cursed. A rock hummed across the open ground,

struck Tate just above the eye. She exclaimed, reeled. In a strain ing bound, Tanno launched herself at the crowd. Bloody-mouthed one eye closed, a leg hanging uselessly, she charged. Hackle raised, roaring like lion, she hurtled massively past the limits c the forgotten restraining lines. The crowd crushed backward on it self in panic-sodden retreat.

The arrow came from the flank, a shard of light, silent an treacherous. It drove solidly into Tanno's rib cage. The great hea broke. The huge, loyal body tumbled to earth, forever facing he master's enemies.

An eerie hush settled on the valley. Darker than mere silence there was a feeling to the quiet, something foul and shamed When Tate rose to her feet there was a sibilant inhalation, a dam sound of collective guilt. Rhythmically, powerfully, Tate ap plauded. "Good dog," she said, and stopped clapping. Her voic cracked. "Oh, you good dog, Tanno. You steadfast heart. The fir and courage of you. There was never a one like you, my Tann My wonderful, loyal Tanno." She stopped, swept the crowd wit a slow gaze that stopped men, dropped their faces low so the saw only the dirt at their feet. Those who'd held the binding rope trickled away into anonymity among the tribe. Only the Harveste held Tate's eyes as the hating, shaming look crossed her.

Tate went on. "Look, brave Starwatch. Make your sons look, s they can remember forever the valor of their fathers. Where's you savior, the one of the last arrow?"

She caught Canis Minor pushing his bow behind him. "You Too weak to fight a man. You grow, from lying coward all th way to skulking killer."

A long, soft sigh rose from the tribe. The Harvester assessed i shoved into action with a whispered command. Orion spoke to flame-red Canis Minor, then hurried toward the prisoners. Stand ing beside them, he raised his arms.

"These traitors are to die in shame, denied the weapons of men Church demands they be stoned. Stoned. Stoned. Stoned." At eacl repetition of the word, he pointed at one of the foursome.

Canis Minor advanced, his movements oddly stiff. His fac gleamed with sweat and rage. Facing the gathering, he said, " will hold the black one. The oldest law of Starwatch says her lif is forfeit to the tribe, and I claim it. I will fight any for her."

Orion, shaking his head, stepped forward. Warriors along th front of the crowd shouted approval before Orion could speak Others took up the cry. In an instant, it was practically universal

A gesture from Canis Minor brought his friends on the run

Most struggled to restrain Nalatan. Others slashed Tate's bonds, spun her onto her back at Canis Minor's feet. He reached for her.

Tate let him lift her until she was standing in front of him. Quickly gripping his vest in both hands, she fell backward. Startled, caught unaware, he was drawn along. She rolled and lifted her feet into the pit of his stomach. When he was overhead, she straightened her legs, hard. By releasing his vest fractionally later, she sent him into a soaring midair flip. Dust billowed where he landed.

The crowd gasped.

Tate leaped to her feet, faced the gang of cronies. They hesitated.

Sylah's laughter pealed out across everyone. Even the Harvester swiveled to stare. Pointing at Canis Minor, Sylah stopped guffawing long enough to say, "Another show of manly skill, Canis Minor, mighty champion of Starwatch. You want her? Wait till you're a man. She'll beat you like a drum."

Tears of rage sparkled on Canis Minor's cheeks as he scrambled upright. He drew his knife.

Canis Minor's friends cheered and laughed. "Open her up," one shouted. "See what color she is inside." They moved in a group to seat themselves at the front of the stage area. Canis Minor moved toward Tate, who crouched, hands raised in defense.

"What have you done?" Nalatan demanded. "He doesn't mean to kill her, he wants only to cause pain."

Sylah's gaze remained locked on the maneuvering pair. "Get behind me and Lanta. For the first time since they drugged us, no one's watching us. Chew on your wrist bindings. And pray for Donnacee."

Nalatan didn't argue. Behind her, she heard him, gnawing and grunting.

Clamor encouraged Canis Minor. He postured. Played. Still, when he slashed at Tate, it was in earnest.

Soon, Sylah heard growing surliness in the crowd noise. Tate's clever defense frustrated them. Sylah knew it was a matter of little time before the stones would come. Or worse, intervention from one of Canis Minor's friends.

The watchers were recovered from their momentary embarrassment over Tanno. They wanted their new victim humiliated. Bloodied. Quickly.

CHAPTER 109

Pressed to the near-vertical slope, Conway watched Tate dodge Canis Minor's blade.

Behind Conway, Karda and Mikka scrabbled for purchase. Conway patted them. He needed them calm, confident; one misstep would send them bowling downhill.

Surprise was the only hope Conway had. He meant to get full use of it. Bile still burned his throat, the residue of watching Tanno die. Such sacrifice demanded retribution.

He and the dogs crept downward. Closer.

Tate blocked a thrust. It was a feint. When she made her move, he turned the blade, slashed upward. Reflex pulled her back, exposed her throat. Taut, sweat-gleaming, it seemed to attract the weapon.

Conway bit back outcry. The prisoners tied to the post shouted in horror. The crowd thundered.

Tate staggered back, windmilling. She caught herself, reached for the wound. Blood ran thickly between her fingers.

Conway exhaled slowly. She was cut, but it was her jaw, not her throat. Regaining her defensive posture, Tate concentrated on her enemy.

Nalatan huddled against the post, unimaginably quiescent, seemingly defeated. Only when Conway looked closely did he see him furiously tearing at his bindings with his teeth. Sylah watched the uneven duel with iron self-control. Lanta covered her eyes with her hands.

Canis Minor lunged again. Tate struck his right forearm inward with her left. Pivoting on her left foot spun her away from the blade. The turn continued to a full circle, ending with her beside Canis Minor. Off-balance, arm extended awkwardly, the man was already turning in pursuit.

Tate speared the point of her right elbow into his unprotected kidney area. He froze, paralyzed in a shock of agony. Pirouetting with deadly delicacy, Tate moved to Canis Minor's left side. Translating speed into force, she repeated the elbow blow. It crushed the other kidney.

This time he screamed. Staggering, arms clamped to his sides, the projecting knife in his hand was a passive barrier.

The crowd surged to its feet as one, shouting encouragement to Canis Minor, cursing Tate.

Conway scrabbled closer. Only a few yards away, Orion stood with his back to the hillside. Tightening his grip on the wipe, Conway steadied for his rush.

Tate punched at Canis Minor's face. The knife hand went up protectively. Tate's other hand chopped at his wrist. The weapon flew, glinting, beckoning. Canis Minor reached uselessly, pathetically, after it. Tate hacked him behind the ear on her way past him. When she had the knife in hand and turned back to him, he was stupefied, drooling, knees bent, hands at his sides.

Tate moved to finish him.

A warrior sprinted from the crowd, knife in hand.

Nalatan's shout warned Tate. Turning, dropping to a crouch, she saw the man's rush. Her decision was instantaneous. She whirled, leapt at Canis Minor. Disbelieving, he watched her stab past his imploring hands. She withdrew the blade. Stabbed again.

The attacking warrior was too close for her to free the knife and defend herself.

The report of the wipe altered time.

Tate remained bent, looking over her shoulder.

Nalatan strained at the end of the line.

Sylah was a statue.

Lanta cowered, peering through her joined hands.

The crowd was an unmoving forest.

The warrior's head twitched sharply right at the impact of the flechette, as if responding to some distant call. For a moment—so brief the mind doubted the eye—the skull expanded. Eyes bulged. Cheeks puffed. A faint red mist bloomed in midair by the man's temple, vanishing as he careered sideways on boneless legs and collapsed in an untidy pile.

The flechette, distorted by its passage through bone and tissue, shrieked over the heads of the gathered tribesmen. The insane wail reestablished the present. Men fell face down, dragging their sons with them. Many ran, screaming. Panicked Opal brotherhood horses reared, threw riders, galloped into the night.

Conway and the dogs raced past a dumbfounded Tate. He threw the wipe to her. "Here. You take this." In the next instant he held Orion from behind, knife blade snuggled under the beard, against the throat. Shoving his captive toward the dignitaries, Conway shouted, "No one moves or this one dies."

The Harvester rose in the stirrups.

Aiming the wipe at her, Tate preempted any speeches. "Stop.

You'll go first, I swear it." As she spoke, Tate hurried to shelter directly behind the helpless Starwatch chief.

Hatred trembled in the air around the Harvester. Even so, it was obvious she was weighing, judging. The stoicism of the bleeding, exhausted woman peering along the wipe barrel convinced her. Turning her head as far as possible toward her escort, while still keeping her eyes on Tate, the Harvester said, "Men of Opal. Whatever happens to me, do nothing. I order it. Protect Church Home." She settled back into her saddle.

Taking Tate's knife, Conway dragged Orion to the prisoners. He handed the weapon to Sylah. "Free Nalatan so he can get the lightning weapons." Conway looked to Lanta. She tugged at her wrists. The frayed leather snapped. Conway joined in her grin of accomplishment.

They gathered beside Tate. Lanta gestured at Sylah to attend to events while she went to work on Tate's wound. Tate's eyes narrowed and the corners of her mouth twitched at Lanta's ministrations; the wipe remained firmly centered on the Harvester's midriff.

The chief and the elders milled distractedly. The Starwatch warriors were restive. There were whispers, sidelong glances.

Nalatan brought Tate's weapons. Shoving both pistols inside his jacket, Conway replaced his knife, electing to control Orion with his wipe. Lanta took custody of the sniper rifle, standing on its case to continue her work with Tate.

Nalatan said, "They'll come at us soon. The moral structure of my tribe is broken, but they're not cowards." He spoke in great sadness. Conway had the feeling Nalatan never expected to see his people again after this night, live or die.

The Harvester said, "You can't be so foolish you hope to escape."

Conway said, "We've got plenty of hostages."

Sylah stepped forward, put a hand on Conway's forearm. Her training understood more than scornful warning in the Harvester's words. Sylah said, "You didn't come here just to see us killed."

The Harvester's smile was bitter. "Very shrewd. It would gratify me to see you die, but the experience wouldn't warrant a trip to this nest of incompetents."

"What would?"

"Saving Church Home."

Sylah grimaced, turned away. The Harvester continued. "You think you alone care about Church? You think me a monster because I intend to control it? What of you, then? Look me in the

646

eye and tell me you don't think you know what's best for her. Tell me your fabled Door doesn't mean ascendancy. You may tell yourself you're wondrously pure. I see into the cobwebbed crevices of your soul. Guidance. Influence. Authority. Call it what you will, you mean to dictate to Church. Our only difference is that I acknowledge it. You shrink."

"Liar." Fists white-knuckled in front of her, Sylah took a cramped step forward. "I seek peace. You leave a trail of death wherever you go. You kill."

"I kill. And what is that? Or that?" Languidly, the Harvester's pale hand drifted out of the end of her night-black sleeve, indicated the dead Canis Minor and the warrior.

"It's not the same. I'm sorry about what happened. It's not the same thing at all."

"They opposed you. They're dead. There are no variants in death. One is no more dead than another, no better or worse. None of us escapes. Institutions live forever, though. That's what brings me here." She broke off to point at Orion. "This sniveling fool knew. Only Nalatan and the Tate one were to die. You and Lanta were to be delivered to me. I need help to save Church."

Conway interrupted. "Who's going to save it from you?"

The Harvester's unflinching gaze never left Sylah. "I told you we must talk. Send those Starwatch idiots back to their hovels. I don't like the sound of them."

Sylah was embarrassed to realize she'd forgotten the tribesmen entirely. A glance showed the enormity of her mistake. The warriors were closer. Most had weapons in their hands. All carried stones. Conway, Nalatan, and the dogs watched them intently. Tate remained concentrated on the Harvester.

Orion broke his silence. "They'll go if our chief orders it. We are still Church; our men have no desire to kill priestesses, no matter who would have them do so." He looked at the Harvester as he spoke. Her glance touched him, and he turned away, shaken.

Lanta said, "Equipment. Horses. We want our possessions." Orion nodded miserably, then called the terms to the chief. The tribe's officials herded the sullen warriors toward the village. By the time the last torch disappeared over the ridge, a trio of youngsters was already returning with the things Lanta demanded.

Including Dodoy, trussed, bound to his mount.

Tate didn't see him until the escort was racing off. She ran to cut Dodoy's bonds, shouting outrage. Then she turned on Orion. "Why did you do this to him?"

Sylah said, "Please, Donnacee; we have Dodoy back. Let's settle things here. The warriors could come back."

Tate rejected the plea. "I'm talking to you, Orion. Answer me."

Orion looked to Dodoy.

"They made me do it!" Dodoy flung himself off the horse, embraced Tate. "They did terrible things to me. Don't let them get me. They'll hurt me again. Hold me."

Tate poked Orion with the muzzle of the wipe. Muscles jumped in her jaw. Fresh blood from the reopened wound soaked through her makeshift bandage. While Sylah rummaged for needle and thread, Tate said, "I ought to kill you."

Sweating, Orion struggled for courage. "Not for harming Dodoy. He came to us. He said Sylah had plans." He shrugged, defeated. "It doesn't matter. We wanted to believe him. You needn't take my word for anything. He's been boasting all over the village how he exposed you. Ask anyone. He's only bound because he refused to return to you."

Tate sneered. "You're the only Starwatch here. You'd do anything to save your life."

"The best of me already lies dead. The son I never had. Send me to join him, if it pleases you. I lied to him. To myself. To Sylah. I'm done with lies. Believe about the boy or not."

The Harvester's voice brought Tate back to her. "The riders Orion sent for me talked of nothing but this boy's revelations. Tonight the chief and the elders all said the same thing." The older woman leaned out toward Dodoy, predatory. "You are nothing, boy. Less than dust. But your lies complicate my life. I want an end to it. The Black Lightning will forgive you any sin. I give you one chance. Disappoint me, and I'm your enemy until you die."

Tate pushed the wipe forward like a spear. "Stop it. You're frightening him."

The Harvester remained fixed on Dodoy. "Be quiet, woman. You won't kill me. Certainly not before you know the truth. After that, you won't because we must talk. So speak, boy. One chance."

The wipe sagged in Tate's grasp. She turned to Dodoy. He refused to look at her. She dropped to her knees, put her hands on his shoulders.

Dodoy was aware of Tate only as a presence. The Harvester was in his mind, *inside* his mind. Images snatched him to the past, blurred his vision. The captain's woman. Her eyes bored the same as the Harvester's.

But the captain's woman mixed up pain and pleasure in her

head. Dodoy looked into the implacable depths of the Harvester's stare and saw utter disinterest. No love of pain lived there. No lust for pleasure.

He had no words for any of it, couldn't have articulated what he saw at any cost. He did, however, understand intuitively he was confronted by consummate ruthlessness, and his inner being swarmed to it as to a god.

Anticipation tingled on the flesh of his arms, his legs, his back. The Harvester understood his need to belong.

Softly, Tate said, "Why, Dodoy? I love you."

"No one loves me, because I'm little and ugly."

"So you lied to me. About me. To Orion. Everyone." Tate's bewildered forgiveness forced the others to turn away. Except the Harvester; she studied. Dodoy saw that, and began to shake. "Yes. I wanted . . . someone to want *me*. You all hate me. I hate you. You don't love me. You lied, too."

"I was lying to myself. I made myself believe you'd lead me to people who look like me. Like me on the outside. You see the mistake? I didn't look inside, where a person's truth is. I was looking too hard. Someday I may find what I wanted. I won't be blinded by it again. I learned. No one loves someone because they want to. Or should. They just do. You understand that?" She tilted his head with a finger under his chin, made him look at her. "I changed. You helped me. I think you changed, too. Just a bit? When we sat close together, and I held you tight—weren't those good times?

"Maybe." True pain moved the thin, averted face.

Tate took his chin in her hand, pulled his head around. "Oh, Dodoy. Poor baby. What am I going to do with you?"

"Leave him to me." Orion stepped forward.

Dodoy recoiled, sought the Harvester. She smiled quiet satisfaction, looked deep into his eyes. Revelation swept Dodoy. The Harvester knew. He would have a family, a tribe, a *place*. And all the while, he would serve the Harvester. She was giving him a reason to belong. He wanted to rush to her. But that would reveal the secret. Their secret.

Tate brought the wipe to bear on the legender. Orion blanched, held his ground. "As a second chance for both of us. We both have many things to atone for, many things to learn about ourselves. Who knows? Dodoy may be our next legender. He may be home at last."

The Harvester smiled at Dodoy.

Blinking back tears, Tate steeled herself. If Dodoy was willing

649

to trust Orion, how could she deny him? Yet how could she be certain she was finally thinking only of the boy's best intrests? Starwatch and Orion offered no more than a stable life. That was far more than she could provide. But there were dangers. "I don't know, Dodoy. Some bad things happened here. These people almost killed us."

Orion said, "The worst mistakes were mine. Dodoy and I need each other. We can forgive each other, support each other. He'll become the man Canis Minor—and I—should have been." He sent an edgy glance at the Harvester, but continued firmly. "A leader who speaks of good, but forgets that goodness concerns the least, not the greatest, of us has much to atone for."

The Harvester's gaze remained unswervingly on Dodoy.

Quick, antenna-like fingers meshing, unmeshing, racing the buttons of his leather vest, Dodoy turned toward Tate. Shyly, whispering, he said, "Everything's changed. I think I should stay. Can I? I'll be good."

Tate smiled, swallowing fiery hurt. "Only if you tell me you'll miss me. I have to be bribed." Dodoy threw his arms around her neck. Over the boy's head, she looked at Orion. In that repentant, hopeful face she saw herself. Orion feared, but it was the apprehension of one recognizing responsibility. Tate wanted to tell him she sympathized. They'd both lost. And won.

When Dodoy stepped back, pretending to look at the ground, he cut his eyes to the Harvester. She looked different. Pleased. Tate was smiling and crying at the same time. She kissed him on the forehead.

Not until he was walking toward Orion did Dodoy suddenly feel weak, unsure. He didn't turn to wave good-bye. Orion put a hand on his shoulder. Straining to match the taller man's stride, Dodoy walked off into his new life.

Tate stumbled into Nalatan's embrace. Her sobs rocked them both.

Feigning a loose stirrup, the Harvester bent away. Silent laughter twitched her shoulders.

Watching, Lanta muttered under her breath. "One will sacrifice most, confront the unbearable that the Flower may triumph." The words left a dusty, rotten taste in her mouth.

CHAPTER 110

The long, wavering wolf howl bothered the horses of the Opal brotherhood. They shifted nervously, stamping, whickering to each other in the darkness. The people gathered around a large mound of glowing coals paid no attention.

Tate stood tall, shunning Nalatan's offered support. Her cheekbones, tear-stained, gleamed like polished arcs of night itself. Still, her features were proud, stern, the skin hard-looking, as if Sylah's stitches under the clean new bandage stretched it tight.

Her mourning of Tanno was that of one warrior for another, a respectful taking of leave, and a sorrow for lost comradeship.

In the immediate background, the Harvester stood alone, either uncaring or unaware that Conway's wipe was constantly—if discreetly—trained on her. Momentary concern threw a shadow across her impatience as a drumbeat touched the darkness. Steady, solemn, it came with the insistence of heartbeat. A red glow limned the sky above the ridge between the group and the village.

Turning, Tate noticed the light. "Starwatch burns their fallen," she said. There was no sympathy.

The Harvester said, "They burn men. A holy rite."

"Tanno was worth more than both of them. Canis Minor killed her. I killed him. A poor bargain."

Sylah saw Conway and Nalatan share quick, conspiratorial smiles that mingled pride and a warrior's dark amusement. She gave no sign of her awareness, afraid she might offend. It was one of the things she envied Tate. Not the hard edge of her vindictiveness, but her inclusion in the most masculine of societies. Sylah knew in her heart that no woman ever loved a man more than she loved Clas na Bale. Yet Donnacee Tate, who didn't know him well at all, understood things about him that his wife could never comprehend. When Tate was her normal self, she was entertaining, considerate, helpful. A friend. Like Clas. When she was Black Lightning, she was violent, somber, deadly. Like Clas.

Sylah blushed, thankful for darkness; the truth was, she didn't fear for Clas' strength or his reckless courage. The irrational brute maleness of him thrilled her and she treasured it. The fear that never left her, that touched even their most intimate moments, was that those things must someday tear him from her life.

651

Donnacee Tate and Nalatan would share intense depths of understanding, more than she could share with Clas. She envied them both. Pitied them.

The Harvester said, "Priestess, are you with us? Your friends have retired. I spoke."

The remainder of the group was already sitting where Karda and Mikka watched over their equipment. Sylah walked away from Tate with the Harvester, joining the others in a circle that conformed to the nervous light of a nearly expended torch. Tate followed leadenly, took a place between Conway and Nalatan. She appeared unaware of her surroundings.

"I didn't hear," Sylah answered the Harvester.

"Obviously. I said I need help."

Sylah's barking laugh was bitterly humorless. "From me? You've tried to kill me."

The Harvester waved dismissal. "We've already discussed the why of that. Now we must unite, or sacrifice Church to our ambitions."

"I have no ambition. Not as you use the word."

"Can't you understand? I speak of the destruction of Church Home, the death or enslavement of all who reside there. You dither about definitions. Don't interrupt. Listen. I rule in Church Home. All have agreed." The silvered head turned away. A hand plucked at the opposite sleeve. "Almost all. Violet refuses me. Because of that, the Tiger brotherhood debates its loyalty. They are sworn to Church Home. I cannot trust them. I have only Opal and my few Kossiars to depend on."

Nalatan rose. His words scraped like metal on rock. "My brotherhood is no more. Your agents poisoned them when we said we'd never support your greed. Tiger and Opal should desert you."

The Harvester refused to react. She addressed Sylah. "Windband comes. Their patrols press ours closer to Church Home every day. I request a truce between us. Violet will acknowledge me if the Flower asks. More, Violet knows, as we all do, that Lanta should be the Seer of Seers. With the support of Opal, Tiger, and the lightning weapons, Church Home's impregnability continues."

Sylah said, "My fate is the Door. You split Church. If others had rejected you, as I do, Windband would be a source of converts, not a knife in our hearts."

Instead of the anger Sylah fully expected, the Harvester looked at her with speculation that slowly melted to musing regard. Sylah was sure she saw a glimmer of something else; sadness, the look of someone momentarily caught in a moment of reminiscence and regret. The entire manner was totally unlike the Harvester, and seeing it made Sylah very uncomfortable. She said, "You have nothing to say?"

Musing, the Harvester said, "Oh, I have much left to say, young Chosen. Oh, yes." She stirred, shaking free of whatever odd mental lapse had seized her, and continued with her normal sharp precision. "You speak of your fate. You know nothing of fate. Yours was decided the night slaves tumbled you out of a basket in front of my sister. Filthy. Mute." Suddenly vicious, the older woman pitched forward threateningly. Sylah's companions shifted, alarmed, but the Harvester went on, insulated from everything except her own thoughts and Sylah's presence. "Yes, Sylah. They dumped you on the floor like so much foul garbage. And my sister chose you."

"My Abbess? The Iris Abbess? She chose me?"

"No one else would." The Harvester sniffed, leaned back. A sticky, mocking smile bent her lips. She simpered. "You still hear her, don't you, sweet Sylah? The insistent voice that drives you to search for the Door, that braces you when all seems lost, that scolds when will falters? You think that's fate? It's the Abbess, you fool. Her voice, her determination, her will, all carefully planted in your mind through techniques she developed herself. Un-Church techniques. She had her confidential meetings with our dear, dead Sister Mother and that crack-brained hag who called herself the Seer of Seers. Whatever secrets they shared died with them. What should matter to you is that you never had a fate. You're a Chosen, a property. Worse. Your mind is the product of another's thoughts. You're a *thing*."

"No." The word drained all of Sylah's strength. She drew back, slumped into herself.

Lanta leaped to embrace Sylah, shielding her with her body. To address the Harvester she had to turn awkwardly, talk over her own shoulder. Like a small, spitting cat, she said, "You're the fool, old woman. Blinded by greed. Sylah was delivered to the Iris Abbess. The Abbess understood. She was loving enough, holy enough, to prepare her. She wanted the Flower. For Church. You want only power. Sylah is more complete than any of us. She has her own life, as well as the wisdom of others, lovingly poured into her."

Looking past Lanta's scowl into Sylah's wide, shocked eyes, the Harvester said, "Yes, Sylah, what of your life? Are you so

653

pure? The secret—is there no idea in your mind of how it may benefit yourself? 'I will not be owned.' Oh, yes, Sylah; I know about your precious motto. And much, much more. Try not to look so innocently scandalized. Are you willing to swear to your friends, to the One In All, that you'll share the secret fully, no reservations? Dare you swear, Sylah? Dare you?" She thrust her face closer, and Lanta hugged Sylah all the tighter.

Carefully, as if her bones were brittle, her muscles flaccid, Sylah disengaged herself from Lanta. Shattered by the Harvester's claims, terrified by the challenge of confessing the devouring self-doubt about her own incorruptibility, she rose. She took a step backward. Lanta was speaking to her, soothing, coaxing, yet the only words she heard came from her memory. Lanta had said, "Your will is not your destiny," and now the Harvester was saying that even that destiny wasn't of her own making.

She felt cold, damp. She thought she must be sick.

Lanta shook her. Startled, Sylah looked down. The elfin face turned up to hers pleaded. "Sylah, listen to me. The Harvester left out the most important fact. The prophecy of the Flower has existed for generations. Priestesses in hundreds have been born, lived, passed. None was the Flower. You were born to be named so. Try to find the Door. Search with all your heart and strength. Lead us. If you do that, and fail, your memory will still be honored and lovingly mourned for all time. Listen to this treachery, surrender to sly argument and weakness, and Sylah will be a name to curse, a title to put to the unspeakable." The pleading expression disappeared. Firmly, Lanta said, "I say no more. Decide. You are the Flower, or you are not."

Noise flooded Sylah's head. Low, heavy, it was the drum of distant storm waves hammering unyielding cliffs. Yet there was no fear. The horror of the Harvester's revelations was gone. Sylah wondered if that reaction was something else the Iris Abbess put in her mind, then decided she didn't care. In fact, she didn't care about any of it. Lanta was right. The Iris Abbess hadn't manipulated her, she'd perfected her. What difference did it make, in either case?

The Flower was chosen.

The Flower is Sylah.

Focusing her gaze deep, past the Harvester's eyes, Sylah said, "I swear I am she. I will succeed. I must, whatever the cost. Church needs the Flower, and the Door will only open to the Flower. I do what I must."

Turning away from the weight of Sylah's stare, the Harvester spoke in a tight, straining voice. "Church Home may fall. If she does, for the first time in history, unbelievers will walk our halls. Our sisters will be slaughtered in sanctuary. I will die there, if I must."

"As the One in All wills."

The Harvester faced Conway and Tate. "I am betrayed by my own. I implore the kindness of strangers."

Neither bothered to check with each other. Both refused her with a head shake. Conway added, "I'd fight you as readily as I'd fight Moonpriest."

Startling white teeth flashed in the Harvester's harsh laughter. "You'll get fighting. Windband will range the Dry, search every crevice, every peak. Church Home offers shelter, defense, survival. Outside our walls, Moonpriest will pursue you as cold-bloodedly as his snakes stalk gophers. He can keep us penned up with a fraction of his men. If Tiger brotherhood deserts, I fear he'll actually overrun us. Whatever numbers he can spare will seek you. And the Flower. With or without the secret of the Door, she is the focus of hope. He cannot tolerate her alive."

Lanta turned away from the silence that followed. She watched heat rise from Tanno's gray-cloaked pyre. Sinuous waves twisted darkness, gave eerie movement to the bushes on the mound's far side. Burned free of leaves, the scorched, skeletal branches stretched upward in supplication.

Sacrifices.

Tanno, dead. Dodoy, given up.

Conway, Tate; rejecting Church Home.

Violet, Tiger brotherhood; willing to abandon Church, rather than consent to the Harvester.

Lanta, who should be the Seer of Seers.

The True Stone.

One will sacrifice most.

Even the most wicked one, she who suborns the Church herself, must be appeased, if necessary, so the Flower may succeed.

Lanta faced the group again. For a long moment, she studied Conway, the line of his jaw, the way his hair curled at his collar. When he stirred, she looked away quickly, sought the Harvester. The imperious eyes met hers. Lanta said, "If Violet joined you, Tiger would defend Church Home?"

Speculation leavened the Harvester's bleakness. She cocked her head to the side, suddenly alert. "Yes."

Like an animal running an unfamiliar trail, Lanta felt the tug of a snare's set-string in that single word, knowing there was no turning back. She tried, hopelessly. "Without the Flower, is there anything, any other way, to attract Violet?"

Sylah interrupted. "Why pursue this with this murderess?"

Lanta forced herself to look only at the Harvester. "Our sisters must not die. If Church Home demands Windband's full attention, the Flower will be free to discover the Door."

"We can't do anything about it." Sylah was exasperated by Lanta's persistence. "Once Windband's beaten, Odeel will come after us. I marked her. Our struggle is mortal."

. . . having borne, what Flower remains as before?

Lanta said, "Our struggle is not with the good and innocent of Church." Probing inside her robe, she felt the True Stone on its golden chain. It seemed to vibrate in her grasp. A bitter image of Sylah surrendering the infant Jessak crawled across her inner vision. Dismissing that, she called to the Opal leader, demanding he come forward with his men. With her hand still on the True Stone, she looked up at the broken-nosed warrior monk. "Tiger brotherhood is sworn to Church, not to the person of Sister Mother. How stands Opal?"

The man frowned uneasily. Behind him, his companions were silent as the night. The man cleared his throat. "Opal answers to no Healer, small priestess. We . . ."

"We bluster." Lanta's stinging interruption shocked the monk into openmouthed wonder. She rushed on, firmer than ever. "I will know your answer and your soul now. Consider what you are. Speak. Commit yourself now. For eternity."

Straining, gaze rigorously avoiding the Harvester, the monk blurted. "Church, Sister. Opal lives and dies for Church. Not for any human."

"Good. Then you are witnesses. To save Church, not to serve the Harvester, a Violet Priestess, companion to the Flower, does this." Lanta withdrew the talisman. Extending the closed hand to the Harvester, she opened it dramatically, revealing the amethyst in her palm. "Church Home will survive. The Flower has made it so."

Even in the guttering light of the torch, the Harvester's swift blanch was shocking. She snatched the True Stone from Lanta, held it up to inspect the symbol in its depths. Clutching it to her breast, she closed her eyes tight, face a scrawl of pain. She keened a note so high the dogs shook their heads until their ears slapped like wet leather. She stopped bent over, chin almost touching her knees. She spoke, the words muffled, cavernous. "You mock. Burden my every moment by handing me Jessak of the accursed name. Give me the True Stone knowing its gift will cheapen my triumph. All will say Lanta, the Flower's friend, saved Church Home in her name."

Unsteadily, she rose. An Opal brother trotted to her side. She braced herself with a hand on his shoulder. Strength flowed back into her features, restored the familiar steely hardness. "You want Church to know I'm beholden to you. So be it. Understand, however, that Sylah was right; after Windband, you. All of you. I—Church—will pursue you to the death. Hear my promise."

No one around the torch spoke long after the rumble of departing hooves marked the Harvester's leaving.

The wolf resumed his song.

Nalatan pointed at the ridge. A wavering glow marked an advancing torch, still hidden from direct view. Tate said, "They finally worked up the guts to attack," and loaded a round into the boop.

Conway did the same. Everyone eased away from the light.

The glow enlarged. A flame appeared. Sylah called to Nalatan. "Only one person?"

"Or something to distract us."

Conway said, "Be back soon," and called his dogs to him. Scratching noises from the brush faded quickly, and the group heard no more from them.

It was Orion bearing the torch. The group watched him, remaining in covered positions. Orion, unperturbed, put his light down beside the sputtering old torch. "I'm alone," he announced to the surrounding silence. "I had a long talk with the most important men of Starwatch. You won't be disturbed."

He cringed at the ghostly materialization of Mikka in front of him, and failed to completely smother a yelp of alarm when he inched backward and ran into Karda. Conway stepped out of the darkness, wipe slung over his shoulder. "No one following him," he said, and sat down beside Orion. The others returned to their places.

Orion's eyes widened. "The Harvester. Gone?"

Sylah told him what had happened, and Lanta told everyone of finding the jewel. Sylah ended by saying, "Nothing could have meant so much to Lanta. My heart can't hold enough love and appreciation—and sorrow—for all my friends have endured." Taking Lanta's hand, Sylah looked around the circle at her companions. On seeing how Conway looked only at Lanta, she ached to tell him she understood the pain he shared with the small Seer.

Still, Sylah knew that any word, any hint, would be unwelcome intrusion. She could only hope.

Orion said, "What I've heard, what I've seen, is what brings me to you." He coughed nervously, addressed Sylah. "In the time of the Teachers, Starwatch was the most favored of tribes."

Tate groaned.

Wincing guiltily, Orion went on. "We prided ourselves on the equality of our society. Starwatch hated fighting, compromised when possible, was merciful in victory. We offered asylum to the oppressed of other tribes. Legend says Starwatch absorbed the beaten remnants of whole groups on occasion, making them part of Starwatch itself. Still, the pressure of constant warfare demanded a haven. Our siah brought us here, to the Dry, taught us how to irrigate, how to use this land. Church Home existed before we arrived here. As soon as we did, however, we aligned with her. Nalatan told you we supplied the first brotherhood defenders. Not even he knows that many of our women were Teachers."

Sylah and Lanta made three-signs. Confessed association with Teachers, even after so many generations, was suicidally bold.

Orion said, "As the purge of Teachers swept the world, the men of Starwatch failed. There were betrayals." He drew himself erect. "No Starwatch man participated in the exterminations, though. Not one. Starwatch actually hid a small group of Teachers. For years. Then they were betrayed. No one knows how, but the tale tells us that the men of Starwatch decided the tribe couldn't challenge the winds of the times. The Teachers fled to the hills. Only one man fought for them. He was killed. One Teacher secretly passed on relics to our senior legender. As she died, she told him someone would come for them. Starwatch legenders have waited since then. We—I—hold the relics in sacred trust. Not even the chief knows. The senior legender passes them on." He hesitated. "That was to have been Canis Minor. Someday."

Sylah said, "What are they? Where?" The voice was in her mind, ecstatic, laughing.

Orion held up a hand. "Few know how cruel the purge was. To avoid suspicion after sheltering Teachers, Starwatch changed. We treated our women as other tribes did. We became warriors for war's sake. The senior legender has always known the truth. None has ever fought for a return to the right ways. Until now. The wrong path has cost me the one I loved most. My people will change. I must see to it."

"The relics," Sylah jittered with impatience. "Tell me, please. Please. The relics."

Orion reached inside his vest, took out a rectangular leather packet bound with a stained, frayed cord. As he opened it, he said, "The Teacher said the one who came would bring a spring of rebirth to the world."

Sylah bit her fingers in a frenzy of suspense. The voice was pure happiness now, golden song, a simple melody of joy.

The packet held a folded, tattered sheet of paper and a polished steel object. The latter was as long as a man's forearm and hand, and looked like a fork with three long, unequal prongs. The central prong was longest. The polished wooden handle was only slightly larger in diameter than the metal fingers.

Orion unfolded the paper. Lanta squealed, retreated fast enough to stagger Conway in passing. She made a three-sign, then turned her back.

Sylah was transfixed. She reached to touch the paper, now revealed as a multicolored square. "Writing." She gave the word the power of holiness. "The Teachers owned writing. And numbers. See? There. And there. And here. Everywhere! Words. Numbers. Sacred things, all over. Oh, Teachers." Her voice broke. Reverently, she made her three-sign, then went to Lanta. "Don't be afraid. No one can hurt us. Only our friends know we're looking at paper from the ancient times. It's marvelous. Generations ago, a Teacher held these things. Read them. Shared them with other Teachers."

Orion carefully refolded the paper, replaced it. He closed the packet.

Conway sidled to Tate's side. "You saw?"

She nodded. "A one-to-fifty-thou satellite tac shot on resinated weatherproof paper. Computer-enhanced colorization and lasered contour lines. Somebody used it a lot; handwritten compass azimuths, some ranges from known points. The print legend identifies processing unit, issuing unit, tac headquarters ID, and security classification. The problem is, there's no way to locate the ground in the shot without reference data. Did you see any?"

"No. And I can't figure out what the weird-looking trident's all about, either."

Tate nodded. "Look at Sylah. The word is *beatific*, old buddy. What d'you bet we're looking for the hills in that tac map tomorrow morning?"

"No bets. You ready?"

She surprised him by turning to look for Nalatan before answering. When she faced him again, her word *beatific* repeated itself in Conway's mind, and he thought how wonderful it was that

659

someone so terribly abused could continue to harbor so much love. He heard her say she was as ready as she'd ever be. He smiled automatically, responding as he knew he must.

His thoughts had gone to Lanta. He knew they always would. Her back was to him still.

CHAPTER 111

Sylah hovered fretfully behind Tate and Conway. Tate held the photo map. Sylah peered over Tate's shoulder. Unable to stand the suspense, she clutched her shoulder. "Is this the place? It has to be. We're close, aren't we?"

Tate turned. Sylah was haggard, her eyes red. Tension pinched her features, aged her.

Tate nodded briefly. "I'm pretty sure. We're two days' fast ride from Starwatch; Orion said that's the legendary distance to where the Teachers said they lived. The major points look right." She pointed. "There's that mountain, with the saddle, and this one over here, with the hump. I don't know where your Door is, but we're right here." She put her finger on the map. Beside her, Conway nodded agreement.

Sylah made a face. "Now that you've told me what the paper is, it frightens me as much as it did Lanta. Why do those black lines tie up the land? Why those bright colors? Who can know how the world looks from the sky, from the Land Above?"

Tate said, "A gift from the Teachers can't be bad."

"What of the metal thing? I don't understand that, either." Her sidelong look at Tate and Conway challenged. She turned away quickly, however, ashamed of herself. Exhaustion was affecting her. What had started out as delight about the relics was becoming suspicion. Appreciation for her friends was giving way to criticism, eagerness souring to impatience.

The feeling of the Door was overwhelming. The voice was constant. No words. The same lilting music. When she managed to doze, she woke with a start, the inane happiness jangling in her head.

The thought of madness was a leering demon's face peeking at her from behind the musical notes.

She wanted to throw back her head and scream into the silent, disinterested hills. Why bring her so far, claim lives, only to shatter her mind?

Movement drew her eye. Karda's head rose, searching.

Nalatan wheeled his horse, trotted back the way they'd come. He dismounted, scrambled up a slope. Avoiding the skyline, he disappeared into a jumble of rocks. Coming back out, he sprinted to his horse, galloped to the others. "Nomads. Three, reading our tracks. Left at a run."

Sylah said, "Then there's no trouble?"

Patiently, Nalatan explained. "Orion said this is forbidden country. Windband wouldn't be sniffing around, if they weren't looking for something important. They saw the tracks of five riders and two dogs. They're after help."

Too sharply, Sylah said, "You can't be sure there are others."

"Yes, I can. They carry no supplies, have no pack animal. That means support somewhere close."

Sylah heeled Copper ahead. Such needless argument. Exactly what she had to avoid. She wished she had the courage to apologize.

Lanta caught up. "We all understand," she said, and smiled at Sylah's surprise. "Everyone knows we're close. It's very hard on you."

Before Sylah could do anything about it, all the stress and fear coalesced into a solid misery that blocked her throat, and the tears came. She slumped forward, unable to stop crying.

Lanta offered her shoulder to lean on. Neither woman gave attention to where they were going. The trio in the rear were preoccupied with the back trail. All ignored Sylah and Lanta's drift off the main valley floor and into a narrow canyon. When Sylah looked up, she realized they'd wandered through a narrow gap leading off the main valley and into a steep-sided dead-end valley shaped like a funnel.

Embarrassed, flustered, Sylah reined up abruptly. Startled, Copper jerked sideways. The move unseated Sylah. She grabbed Lanta, took her with her. Lanta's horse bucked wildly. Her medical kit flew forward.

It struck a large rock, tumbled forward and sideways. It burst into flame.

Granite shards crackled and leapt from the boulder with a huge sound of bacon frying. Blue-gray smoke coiled up from a glassed dimple in the surface. The stink of burned earth stung noses and eyes. The leather bag, on the ground, belched smoke and flame from the hole in its side.

The rear group hurried to the priestesses. Tate arrived first.

Even as she busied herself helping the shaken, but uninjured women, she absorbed the evidence before her. The men came skidded to a stop. "What happened?" Nalatan asked. "Why are we in here?"

"An accident." Tate grabbed Conway's arm, dragged him off his horse and aside. "Look at that bag. The rock damage. I don't believe it. It can't be."

Sylah was transformed. Assured. "A dragon tried to kill us, Lanta and me. Smell its breath."

Nalatan made a three-sign.

Tate unfolded the tac map again. "Look, see this circle? That's right here. Now here, on the edge of the map. Numbers. Azimuths, Matt. Bearings. Look at the first one. Look where it takes you. Up to that boulder there, see? Line of sight, right to the burn on the rock."

Dreamily, Sylah waved, the gesture sweeping the valley. "It's the place of the prophecy. I've come to the Door."

Conway said, "Laser. Right through the leather, the contents, into the rock. Impossible." He walked forward. Stopped, frozen. Several yards to the left of the smoking medical bag stood a tall clump of sagebrush. The old, twisted trunks rose amid scattered bones. A human skull grinned at Conway. Litter around the skeleton included smaller bones as well as a rusted shovel, a sword, and a pile of flint arrowheads.

Beside him, Nalatan said, "Old, old bones, Matt Conway." His voice wavered with awe. "Not just man. Coyote. Bird; buzzard, I think. A bad place. The legend is true."

Conway inched forward. Far away, high at the end of the valley, something moved. In a hushed voice, Conway said to Tate, "See that? Up there, past the shelf, to the left?" He pitched a small pebble forward. It arched to the ground, bounced about. Nothing happened. Frowning uncertainly he picked up a large rock and threw it high and hard.

Lanta screamed as something struck howling splinters from the flying rock's surface. When it landed, the blasted side facing the group fumed. They stood in silent amazement as the rock crackled and popped as if talking to itself.

"Laser, for sure." Tate said.

"Automatic. Sensor-controlled. Who?" Conway was mystified.

"A dragon." Sylah was serenely unconcerned. " 'Kill with the blink of an eye,' the legend says. The Iris Abbess didn't believe. She was mistaken. Everything else is as she said. Up there, somewhere, is the Door. Come."

She strode past Conway with a smile on her face.

He grabbed her, pulled her back just as the thing on the hillside moved.

Sylah struggled momentarily, then stopped. When she looked at Conway, he sensed a difference in her. He let go slowly. She flushed. There was a touch of mischief in her smile. "That was silly. Sometimes faith wants a dose of clear thinking, doesn't it?" She settled down with her back to the cooler wall of the draw. Legs comfortably folded, hands upturned in her lap, she repeated the chant that drew trance around her, submerged her in its detachment.

The foolish, repetitious music fought her, pushed at her will. At last, it faded. The return to slowed, normal body rhythms was delicious. She softened, relaxed.

She was alone in her grove, with the sun streaming through the magnificently tall cool-shading trees.

Her mind was hers again.

The valley wasn't impregnable. The Flower must open the Door. There was an answer. She hadn't discovered it because she was reacting, not thinking.

The Teacher left the relics with Starwatch to be used. The thing Conway and Tate alternately called a tac map and a photo map brought them to this place. Still, neither of them was the Flower; they could see, but not understand.

The power of the Door demanded faith. Answers were provided, not guarantees. To open the Door, one risked life itself. The Teachers provided the key, but only those with courage and understanding could triumph.

They key.

Sylah woke instantly, bolted to her feet. "The key!"

Her friends stared, fearing another slide into mental disarray. She flashed them what she hoped was a reassuring smile. Taking the three-pronged device from one of the deep pockets in her robe, she flourished it high. "The magic of the Teachers tells me this is the place of the Door. We don't understand all, but we will. With this. The key to the Door."

Tate was almost patronizing. "Maybe. First, where is the Door?"

Sylah was blissfully unconcerned. "I know. I just don't know I know." She laughed, wishing they could join in the gaiety, the carefree certainty, of success. "The answers exist. I'm too foolish to see them. They'll come."

Karda and Mikka growled, trotted together to the mouth of the canyon. Everyone fell silent. Nalatan closed his eyes, listened. "Many horses, ridden hard."

663

The music rang in Sylah's head, as full of rapture as ever. She hated it. She raised her hands to her ears. Lanta leapt to her, solicitous. Sylah smiled gratitude. Her voice, however, belied renewed concern. "Have we come this far to fail? Why has my Abbess deserted me now, on the last step before success?"

"A test. The most difficult. Not just for you. For those you enlisted to help you, too. We all succeed, or we all fail."

"And quickly." It was Nalatan again. "Time's short, Sylah. Your Abbess sets hard rules."

Conway and Tate loaded their weapons, the metallic clatter jarring in the ancient stone silence of the canyon. The noise emphasized the infuriating music. Sylah continued to Lanta. "A tune keeps dominating my thinking. I can't concentrate. It won't stop. It's destroying me. I should be hearing instructions."

... no man will know the music that will sing the glory of Church forevermore.

Lanta said, "Music? You hear music?"

"No. A simple tune. Notes. Dum, dee, dah."

Wide-eyed, afraid, Lanta held up three fingers. Mute, she pointed at the trident in Sylah's hand.

Sylah looked at Lanta, then through her, taut with growing comprehension. Suddenly, Sylah's pealing joy echoed up and down the valley. The sound triggered surreptitious movement and strange, hard glints of light completely inappropriate to the dusty, baked terrain. Conway and Tate exchanged nervous glances. Nalatan saw the things happening on the hillside. Hand on his sword, he stepped in front of Tate.

Confident, free-striding, Sylah advanced toward the invisible point of danger. She raised the key. "The key opens the Door, the way to the discovery of the Door." She struck the three prongs with a convenient stone. Separate tones braided themselves into a chord. In the bright sunlight, the vibration of each tine became a glittering dazzle.

The sinister glints and shinings on the hillsides stopped. Sylah marched forward, exorcising.

The others exchanged uncomfortable looks. Nalatan gestured at their back trail. "There's little choice. Many horses, many men come. We better follow her."

Lanta was more direct. "We will follow her because we're her companions. Because we must. She's the Flower."

Conway whistled up the dogs. Everyone grabbed the reins of a horse. Conway took Copper, as well. Single file, shoulders unched, heads down, with Conway and Nalatan as distant rear guard, they trailed the exultant Sylah.

"Fulfilled," Tate said, watching her.

Lanta looked back. "What did you say?"

"Nothing. Thinking out loud." Tate berated herself for not thinking how that word, of all words, would cut Lanta.

Lanta said, "I Heard. 'Fulfilled.' You meant Sylah. Of course." Lanta glanced back at the men. "I was thinking of you and me. The Door is here. We'll have its secret. Somehow, we'll escape the nomads."

Behind them, at the valley entrance, a shrill, triumphant war cry announced the arrival of Windband.

CHAPTER 112

Nomads poured through the valley's narrow entryway. Conway's heart sank. Blizzardmen. Windband's best—to his shame. The savage death masks had never looked so menacing before.

Conway handed off Stormracer's and Copper's reins to Nalatan. Two boop rounds broke the charge, sent the survivors scrambling for cover.

Ineffectively aimed arrows flew up at the slowly moving group. Sylah continued to lead. An arrow plunged into the ground beside her. She kicked it away. Ahead, the ground angled up sharply. Left and right, the slope was the same. There was nothing that remotely suggested a door.

Conway's wipe blasted. A man cried out. The number of arrows fell off dramatically.

Fear shivered across Sylah's back. Without turning, she knew from the increased noise that more nomads were making their way into the inescapable valley. What was a haven, a goal, moments before was quickly becoming a trap.

Tate shouted. Sylah was knocked aside, staggered. An arrow hissed malevolently, passed through the air where she'd stood. It hummed where it stuck in the earth. Tate said, "Find that Door. It's getting nasty."

Shots from both wipes quieted things again.

Remembering the crèche that had held him for centuries, Conway shouted up to Nalatan and Sylah. "Look for a rock that doesn't look exactly right. It'll be hidden."

Sylah wondered how he could be so sure. Off to her right, at the base of a sheer wall, she saw a patch that looked discolored. She pointed it out to Nalatan. Unimpressed, he merely grunted and moved in that direction. He'd gone only a few feet when he turned to her, smiling. "I see a line. It's a cover, Sylah." He yelled the news to the others. They dodged uphill.

The nomads realized something was happening. The archers increased their efforts. Slingers appeared. Fist-sized missiles soon buzzed and smashed around Sylah's group. Conway ordered the dogs to the best cover available. It was miserably sparse.

Nalatan examined the line marking the cover. Meticulously made, the object followed the most minute contours of the rock surface behind it. Straining, prying, Nalatan forced the tip of his sword into the gap. Little by little, he widened the opening. Suddenly, with a loud snap, the cover flew off.

The Door was revealed.

A ragged cheer went up from the group. Tate, Lanta, and Conway rushed to join Sylah and Nalatan.

Stainless steel, satin-finished, it gleamed in the sun. There was no knob or handle. The only mar on the immaculate slab was a series of holes. Three lines of three.

Sylah held up the key, striking it absently, distractedly. She measured it against the holes. It would fit vertically, horizontally, diagonally. Conway muttered grimly, took cover behind a rock, sent a boop into the nomads at the bottom of the hill.

Nalatan pointed. A group of men pushing a wagon ahead of them as protection advanced up the entry to the valley. They dragged something behind them. Conway swore. "We've got a problem, Donnacee. I can see what they're bringing. That's a catapult. This one's a big bow and arrow. It'll reach us easy. Sylah! Try the key. Get us out of here."

Continuing to ring the tines, she said, "I fear. I believe there's only one way the key works. I believe a mistake is dangerous."

"Conway!" The call filled the valley. The repeated name rolled through echoes. "Conway! Moonpriest would speak to you."

A white banner on a long pole poked above the wagon. Resplendent in polished fish-scale armor and shining steel high-crowned helmet, the warrior carrying it stepped out. Conway made a face. "Fox. Bad news."

Moonpriest stalked into view, gleaming in his all-white garb. Fox bent to the ground, lifted the abandoned medicine bag. Moonpriest examined it. A warrior called their attention to the skeleton. Moonpriest's head swung in a slow, contemplative arc, examining the looming walls of the funnel.

Conway groaned, drawing a questioning expression from Tate. He said, "Jones is crazy, but he's not stupid. He's adding it up, figuring out there's a laser working here, and somehow we got up the hill."

As if reading Conway's thoughts, Moonpriest shouted up to him. "Conway. I've got something for you." A man raced out from behind the wagon, loaded the emplaced catapult. The weapon made a loud, snapping noise. The arrow crashed to earth a few yards away from Conway.

Moonpriest gloated. "A taste of my power. Church Home is mine. Surrender. Join me. We can forget the past."

"I have to talk to my friends."

Conway called softly to Tate. "You heard."

Tate asked, "How're we doing for ammo, buddy?"

"Short. You?"

"Same. Save the boop flechettes for last. And the sniper rifle; those heavy slugs'll go through two, three people. And no prisoners, understand?" Tate's expression made it clear exactly what she meant. He nodded, saying. "Understood. Win or die."

Lanta called out excitedly. "Sylah, look. At the bottom edge of the Door. Tiny words."

Crowding next to her, Sylah said, "I can barely see it." She traced the words with a finger. " 'The way of discovery is yours. You face but one more challenge.

" 'If you would know what is beyond the Door, welcome; be direct, use whatever you can, and know.

" 'If you would learn what is beyond the Door, welcome, be direct, use what you have, and learn.

" 'Whoever you are, come in the name of the One Who Is Two, denied to woman, born of woman.' "

Both women rocked back on their haunches. Sylah was thoughtful. "There's danger in this. Someone warns. No—threatens."

The small woman agreed. "The key offers choices. There can only be one right one."

More active threat rang in Moonpriest's sharper tones. "Don't stall, Conway. An answer. Now."

"We need time." Conway rose to argue, just in time to see the catapult launch. He dropped behind his rock, yelling at Sylah and Lanta. The arrow struck the stone face several feet above the Door. There was a loud crack. Stone chips hummed away, along with jagged splinters of wood.

Sylah screamed, lurched to her feet. A piece of wood as long as her arm spired up from her back at a near-vertical angle. She clawed at it with both hands.

Moonpriest exulted, "Moondance conquers! Moondance!"

Nomads took up the cry, charged toward the group. Coolly, methodically, Tate fired. Two rounds dropped two men. The others came on, shouting, undeterred.

Until the visible death swept the slopes. From hidden ports on every face of the valley's walls, lasers seared anything that moved.

The splinter in Sylah's back was suddenly only half as long. The charred tip of what was left burned smokily.

Nalatan pushed her to the ground, simultaneously scooping up the key, rapping it sharply against the door. Over the blistering noise of the lasers and the screams of dying men, the incongruously melodic chord sang through the valley with surprising strength.

The Door's weapons resumed their ancient silence.

Sylah's friends rushed to her. Lanta wrapped the skirt of her robe around the burning end of the splinter, ground out the flame. Gripping Lanta's wrist, Sylah said, "Get it out. Pull it."

Lanta hesitated, then set her jaw, yanked.

Sylah smothered outcry deep in her chest, prayed this wasn't the wound to end her quest.

Suddenly, she knew the answer to the final challenge.

The way of discovery was clear.

Lanta saw the changes in Sylah's expression, her manner. At this last one, her own trepidation disappeared, and she filled with intuitive excitement. "You see something? The key?"

Nalatan still held it. Features bathed in the fearful sweat of the unknown, he struck its chiming chord with determined regularity.

Sylah took it from him. "Sunrise to east, sunrise to left. The path of the One Who Is Two," she said. She inserted the key, the prongs angled from upper right to lower left. Something scraped, the vaguely sinuous noise of polished metal rubbing polished metal. Sylah pushed.

The Door opened.

For one frozen instant, they stared.

A catapult arrow smashed into the wall, showering splinters and rock chips. The rush inside was unhesitating. As was the attack of Windband.

Conway and Nalatan brought up the rear, after hurrying to the horses and stripping off weapons and supplies. With the dogs, they dove through the narrowing gap seconds before the first nomads arrived. There was no time to wonder at the failure of the lasers to react. Swords clanged on the steel door as Conway and Nalatan threw themselves into the job of pushing it shut. Yells and footsteps warned of reinforcements on the other side. The women joined the men. They gained an inch. Two.

Then they lost all they'd achieved, and more.

Sylah looked over her shoulder, away from the losing contest, searching for help.

They were in a small room, perfectly square, save for an exit to her left. A table stretched along the wall at that side of the room. Sylah realized she could use it to block the door. Calling to Lanta, she ran to it. When they looked down the passageway that opened into the heart of the mountain, they both gaped, incredulous. It was full of light, light that came from pure white jewels set into the walls. They glowed clean, smokeless, steady as the sun. The wonder of them subordinated even the danger clamoring at the door for a moment.

The table was another marvel, made entirely of steel. In unison, they chanted the prayer against witchcraft as they dragged it toward the straining, slipping trio.

The door was too open; there was no way to wedge the table in place.

Conway leapt free, signaled Tate and Nalatan. They stepped back, let the door swing.

The boom of the boop in the enclosed room was deafening. The havoc of the flechette-loaded rounds was monstrous. Nomads were flung backward, torn, blasted.

Nalatan helped Conway shove bodies out. Tate's covering fire protected them until the door got in her way. The yells of a new attack surged toward them as the trio pushed against the door once again.

A sword blade fell between the door and its frame. Sylah and Lanta wedged the table between the not-quite-closed door and the wall. Nalatan, Tate, and Conway stepped back. The nomads were closed out.

Retreating to the hall leading into the mountain, the group gathered itself. At the door, swords poked through the narrow gap, slashing at the air. War cries and shouts threatened. The steel table held firm.

Tate said, "Why don't the lasers cut them down?"

Conway said, "It looks like the defenses don't work when the door's unlocked."

Nalatan looked down the passageway, frowning. "The

dragons—the ones you call lasers—live in here. If Windband can't get in, neither can we get out. We need another door."

Lanta said, "Sylah's wound needs tending."

The noise outside stopped suddenly. Moonpriest's voice slipped into the room, cold and venomous. "We're bringing up a battering ram. I'm giving you one last chance. Come out now. I promise you no one will harm you."

Conway forced laughter. "You can't sit out there forever. Your ram won't break steel."

Moonpriest's words pitched higher, tighter. Conway heard the madness, like a tear in fine cloth. "We have water. Food. The witch Sylah is hùrt, sure to die. What of your Seer? How can she claim to see the future, and be trapped in that hole with you? Be intelligent. Come to me. You served me well, once. Let me be your friend, let me save you."

"I'd rather be friends with your snakes, Moonpriest. I'm going to power up these lasers. Ask yourself how much time you've got."

Pale, pained, Sylah moved to stand beside Conway. Moonpriest spoke again. Eerily, he addressed Sylah. "I appeal to you, Flower. Your friends are too loyal to leave you. Would you have them die? I am the future. My mother, the moon, is the faith. We bring peace. My men lie dying here, horribly wounded in your name. They beg for help."

Sylah turned agonized eyes up at Conway. "Blood. Always. Even now, after so many generations, blood demeans the Teachers. It's so terribly, terribly wrong. Is is worth so much?"

He tried to answer. She reached to touch his lips. Turning away, she spoke to Moonpriest.

"I am one with the Teachers. I feel their presence. My life is a brief thing of no importance. But I will spend it in defense of those good women. Accept Church. Come in peace, or come to die. The choice is yours."

Moonpriest's scream was a paean of hate.

The hollow booming of the ram raised a contorted, a veinlike wrinkle in the steel desktop.

CHAPTER 113

Open doors yawned at the group as they made their way down the long hall. The rooms were universally bare.

The receding thud of the ram made Sylah think of a heartbeat in the stone. She knew this place lived. She ached with its weary age, trembled at the hope impregnating its secret caverns.

Tate stuck her head through a doorway, called excitedly. Rushing to her, Sylah gasped at Tate's discovery, her wounded back forgotten. The room glowed, shining metal spangled with jewels even more marvelous than the ones in the hall. Unimaginably, many winked; alive with incredible intensity one instant, the next they were lifeless. Only to glow again.

Green, yellow, red. Uncountable numbers. Noisy. The room throbbed with a beehive's steady, warming buzz. Sylah's head swam.

Conway walked toward a wall with myriad gems. When he reached for it, Lanta, Nalatan, and Sylah all closed together. Lovingly, Conway stroked the surface. There was clear glass there. Perfectly round, covering black needle things that moved. Square glass. Unbroken.

"Treasure." Nalatan breathed the word. "No one ever saw such things."

Tate spoke to Conway. "A generator room. No nuke symbols. What else could power this place for so long?"

Conway said, "I read about a solar technology before the crèche. Worked on temperature differential. I suspect the 'rocks' on the ridge line are receptors. As I remember, solar heat generated electricity. Almost no moving parts."

"Anything would wear out, Matt. Anything."

"Not if it was 'on-demand' power, loaded into high-retention capacitors. There'd be no need for anything to move for months, maybe years. A little juice to replace leakage, and the system's up to speed."

"The lights, then; no bulb burns for centuries."

Conway nodded. "That stumps me, too."

Sylah came to them. "The Teachers didn't die to protect magical jewels and glass. And the sound of the ram has changed. Listen."

Conway nodded. "She's right. We better move on."

The hall ended at wide stairs. The group descended into a cavernous auditorium-shaped space. Ghostly rows of desks, each surmounted by a blank video screen, stretched in precise curves, their stepped ranks from wall to wall. Worshipfully, the desks faced a huge, dead white screen at the narrow base of the room. Several open doors led off into dimly lit passageways. Tate grabbed Conway's arm, pointing. "There. Directly opposite us. Light, coming out from under that closed double door."

Sylah said, "The Teachers. They wait." It sent a chill up Conway's back.

Weapons ready, they set off. When they reached the door, Tate awkwardly shifted her wipe and reached for the handle. Nalatan eased her aside, took over.

A figure slumped in a large, winged upholstered chair behind a huge wooden desk in a small office. It wore the black robe of Church, with a golden T embroidered on the left breast. The hood was raised. Inside the soft, black depths was a desiccated, mummified head. Gray, filmy hair draped to frame leathered cheeks. Closed eyes slept eternally. Lips like old cord parted slightly to reveal a fine white line of teeth. Her crossed wrists lay in her lap. One hand was exposed. The bones were clearly visible through the near-transparent skin. The fingers were curled, talonlike.

There was a solitary sheet of yellowed paper and a black plastic pen on her desk. Sylah stepped past Nalatan to pick up the paper. The writing was a faded trace. Sylah examined it for a moment, then handed it to Tate. Ceremonious, her act was the gesture of one Priestess extending a holy artifact to another.

Tate read aloud.

" 'To you reading these words, greetings to the home of the Teachers. I am the last. None of my sisters has come home for several years now. Sometimes I think I hear their voices, but it's never true. Lately, it's been my own words, and I cry as I listen to the echoes race away from me and escape this dreadful loneliness.

" 'Once, I hoped a sister would return. Now it's my greatest fear. It would mean one of us failed, and revealed the secret of our home to those who conduct the Purge.

" 'Whoever you are, I pray you are truly the Flower.

" 'There are those in Church who know this place exists, but not where. Even I, the last living caretaker, don't know who holds the secret of our location. Those who dug these impervious caves and created these horrible killing machines are long dead. How they would groan to learn the use we have made of their monument. I only wish we had no reason to keep the lasers operational. What made the Teachers a threat, however, must be protected. It will be the greatest irony of our kind if our secret asset eliminates the need for their destructive power. Ignorance is such a trifling, temporary nuisance for man. His abiding malady is a determination to consolidate the condition into a permanent state.

" 'Generations from now it may be possible for the Teachers to be reborn. The wisest and most compassionate of Church shall de-

672

cide when and where the ground is properly prepared to receive he seed. The Flower will be chosen.' "

Tate paused at the sound of sobs.

Sylah wanted to tell Tate to continue, but she needed a moment to think. *Chosen*—that hated word, now revealed to mean so much more. The Iris Abbess—wisest and most compassionate, indeed. Teachers, reborn.

A true realization of the immensity of her responsibility began to reach Sylah. It was like the first view of a rising sun, the merest hint of what one knew to be the edge of indescribable majesty. And ferocity.

At Sylah's signal, Tate read on. " 'The forces of evil and ignorances are indistinguishable. The Flower will never be safe from either. Nevertheless, the tools to build a world are here. When I die, a sensor will turn off power to everything but the defensive sensors and weapons our scientists, engineers, and theoreticians emplaced. They say only the key can unlock the door, disarm the system, and turn on the lights. They say only the Flower can accomplish the deed. We shall see. It was the assurances and invention of similar authorities and their political trained apes that brought us to this situation.

" 'I shall die at my desk (Clean for the first time, clean eternally. My own little ecclesiastical joke.) with my most precious possessions, my set of Church's finest jewels. As my life dims, I shall fondle them (my eyes aren't what they once were) and pray that the Flower will compassionately bring to the world the wisdom I have been entrusted to safeguard. It shames me to say we've kept it hidden, because what we offer should be central to the life of everyone born.

" 'The Flower's duty is to see that our sacrifices serve a purpose. She cannot guarantee the crop. She must assure the planting.

" 'Behind me, everything.

" 'Before you, more.' "

Tate cleared her throat. "There's no name."

Lanta sobbed quietly. Conway moved to her. Her look was wary, but then she clung to him.

Sylah moved to the desk. Cautiously, avoiding the mummified body, she pulled gently on a metal handle jutting from the Teacher's side of the desk. She started as a cunningly fitted open-topped box slid out.

Tate came to look. She said, "Her most precious possessions. Conway, come see this." Reaching inside, she lifted out a rectangular thing. The top hinged, somehow, and when Tate lifted i Sylah saw it was all made of paper.

With words.

After a three-sign, hand to her breast, Sylah backed against th wall.

Unaware of her distress, Tate and Conway continued thei search. More of the objects came out of what Sylah hear Conway call a drawer. She accepted the word, in spite of neve having heard it applied to anything metal before. Working up he courage, she asked, "Those things you're taking out of there– what are they?"

For a moment, he was blank, then a great sorrow touched him Softly, he explained. "Books, Sylah. They're called books. You Teacher treasured these." He held them up, one at a time. *"Th Complete Mathematics. Civil Engineering: Theory and Practice* This one's a basic chemistry text. This one's physics. An last . . ." He paused, cleared his throat. *"Poetry of the Ages."*

Turning to Tate, who'd moved to the other side of the Teacher* body, Conway asked, "Is there anything over there?"

"Nothing."

Sharply, Sylah looked at Tate. The answer was equivocal. Tat had seen something she didn't want to mention. Sylah couldn' find it in her to pursue the matter.

The books were too important.

Words on paper.

Apprehension hammered at Sylah's sense of the holiness of thi place. Since the beginning, Church insisted that all words le from the time of the giants must be destroyed. The ritual calle the Return demanded their burning.

If the secret of the Door was somehow connected with word and paper, it was anathema.

But the Teacher was clear: "Behind me, everything. Befor you, more." Her most precious possessions.

No Teacher could be evil, the secret of the Door could never b evil. The Teachers died because they possessed the secret an were feared.

The Flower would live for the secret. Whatever it was.

"I'll carry the books." Sylah ignored Lanta's shocked intake o breath. "They belonged to one of our finest. Church will treasur them, and her, forever. It's my honor to carry them."

Without hesitation, Conway handed over all five. Sylah stowe them in the deep pockets of her robe.

Lanta and Nalatan, watching her, made nervous three-signs.

Sylah ran for the door behind the Teacher. The others followed. Stopped short. Tate broke the silence. "A library. Vidisk cabinets. Thousands of disks. Hundreds of thousands."

Conway was reverent. "The knowledge of mankind. Everything, everything, must be here."

In a quiet aside for Conway alone, Tate said, "This explains the medical expertise. Here's why the Teachers felt they had enough power to bargain for equality."

Conway pulled open a drawer. Vidisks gleamed softly.

Excitement jittered in Tate's voice. "Like the crèche. A source of power somewhere. Matt, we can bring scholars here from everywhere, anywhere. It'll be the greatest university the world ever saw."

Her enthusiasm infected Conway. He hurried from row to row, touching, stroking. Tate chased after him. They called the names of subjects, authors, sources. Tate gave a whoop. "Books. Hidden away over here on this end. More old fashioned, honest-to-goodness *books*. Thousands. Shelves of them. Geology. Hydraulics. Oceanography."

It was Conway's turn to run to her. Like children, they danced, hand in hand, shouting.

Sylah and Lanta exchanged disturbed looks. Lanta said, "I don't understand what they're saying. You're the Flower; what's all this mean?"

"I don't know." There was a touch of resentment in the confession. This was the Door, and its secrets were hers. Why should strangers understand what she couldn't? Why did the flat, gleaming disks mean so much? What did Tate mean when she said "A power source?" Whose power? It was all confusing. And their near-hysteria was frightening.

Sylah huddled with Nalatan and Lanta. Lanta whispered, "It's what I feared. Books are evil. They make people mad. The Teachers must have been evil."

"Impossible." Sylah reached out, squeezed Lanta's forearm hard enough to generate a soft cry of complaint. Releasing the arm, Sylah continued without apology. "Conway and Tate were all right until they read. That's what's dangerous. Don't you see? People must treat books carefully. Of course our friends are mad; they've absorbed more than they can tolerate, too fast. They need help."

Sylah hoped she looked and sounded more courageous than she felt. It was obvious how learning had turned the giants against their slaves. It was a lesson she vowed never to forget, never to allow anyone else to ignore.

Despite the lunatic gaiety of her companions, Sylah felt the haunted power of the things around her, the sheer intelligence involved. When she grabbed Tate and spun her around, she was elated to see the instant departure of the wild, wide-eyed excitement. In a few choking breaths, Tate was back in control of herself. Conway took a moment longer, but then he, too, was calm again. They both apologized profusely.

None of them heard the silence, at first.

"The ram." Sylah whirled, looked back toward the massive room. Yells ricocheted through the passageways.

Tate grabbed Sylah's arm. "Come on. We've got to get out of here."

"No!" Sylah tore herself free, backed against the wall. "You heard. I have a duty."

Bluntly, Tate said, "You can't carry it out dead. We can't help you dead. Now move it. That way." To Conway, Tate added, "Can you and the dogs hold them off? Nalatan can't help unless they're on us, but he can help me look for a way out. Any ideas?" Her alert, constrained expression and the glaring white bandage on her jaw combined to image her as a fighter, a person executing an ordained role. Conway thought how much she meant to him.

He said, "The lasers. They had to be serviced from the rear. Maybe we can slip out through an embrasure. If we can find one."

Tate nodded. "I'm on it."

"Right." Conway returned to the double doors. He checked his ammunition. Twelve rounds left in the pistol. Fifty wipe rounds. Ten for the boop, one of them armor-piercing, and two flechette loads. Twenty rounds for the sniper rifle. He braced against the doorjamb to cover the stepped command room.

The first two nomads out of the stairwell went down like target practice. When the wipe's rolling thunder quieted, dire threats boiled from the dark doorway. Conway smiled ruefully. The fight had taken a turn. Battling underground in a place of magic took all the courage the nomads could find. When they came again, it'd be with a bellyful of fear, the sort that generated an absolutely mindless courage. He set himself to meet them accordingly. He checked the dogs on their "stay." They were ready.

A group of five nomads burst out of the stairwell, sprinted for cover behind the desks. Conway wasted five rounds, only hit one man. Another group of five was even luckier, avoiding four shots without injury.

With a sinking heart, Conway heard a roar of voices in the distance. Reinforcements. Pointlessly, he recounted his ammunition.

676

Five more men bolted. Three fell, still. Conway cheered. An arrow flew at him, dropped short, skipped to a halt several feet from the door. Without thinking, he sent a round where it came from, then cursed his wastefulness.

Something new touched his hearing. Crashing. Breaking. A cry of pain. Then Moonpriest's voice. "No! No! You fools! Don't . . ."

There was no light.

Abyssal darkness. Across the room, nomads moaned, screamed, clattered about in panic.

Moonpriest was speaking, soothing. "Quiet. Quiet. Be still, my sons. Moonpriest is with you." The hubbub slowly subsided. Moonpriest continued. "My mother blesses us with this blackness. The lightning weapons need light to function."

Conway snapped off a boop round in the direction of the voice. Moonpriest yelped at the sound. Conway was congratulating himself at the prolonged silence after the explosion of the round when Moonpriest spoke, boasting. "Blind, my children. Our enemy wastes his strength. Remember, this is Conway, the false brother, the apostate who brought death to your wives and children. Silently, my ever-changing snakes of eternal life. Strike. Windband conquers." The sibilant last was elongated, a hiss.

CHAPTER 114

Conway reached out, touched a harsh coat. "Attack," he said, and thrilled at the way the two massive dogs drifted away like a puff of air.

In the distance behind him he heard occasional thumps as his friends stumbled in the darkness.

Suddenly, growls and screams blasted the black solidity. Then snarling, rending noises. As quickly as it erupted, the noise was gone. Anguished shouts followed. Men called friends. In the end, it was one voice, breaking: "Vidba? Vidba? Answer me! Where are you?"

A gruff answer came from Conway's right, so close it startled him. "Vidba's gone. Double up. No one alone."

Conway snapped a flechette in that direction. An arrow sizzled back, struck the wall off to his right. He jacked a boop flechette round into the chamber. The noise earned another arrow, this one closer.

He whistled in the dogs.

Tate's voice almost startled him into firing her way. She said, "Matt. Come on."

"Coming." He reaching out in the blackness. Touched a dog. Only one. Frightened, he clutched it to him, stretched out, seeking. The second was there. There was a catch in his voice when he commanded them to follow. He eased the double doors shut. With his heel, he crushed the open end of a boop cartridge, jamming the resulting wedge under them at the juncture. He pulled and pushed the desk against them.

Hands outstretched, he called to Tate. She snapped her fingers. "Come to the noise." A moment later, he touched her, fell in behind her.

Soon, Nalatan's hoarse whisper said, "Donnacee?"

"Right here. Any news?

Nalatan said, "There are stairs at the far end of this room, leading to a long hall. I looked both ways, saw no light."

Behind them, the metal wedge squealed piercingly as the double doors were forced. A dull, orange glow followed. Conway said, "They've got torches. I'm going to get one."

Lanta put a hand on his arm. "It's too dangerous. We can find our way."

"If they can see, and we can't, we're finished." Conway pulled away. Nalatan said, "I'm coming with you."

Calling the dogs, they made their way back. The vidisk cabinets and bookshelves were as high as Conway's shoulder, turning the entire library into a grid of passageways. At one intersection, Nalatan indicated Conway should hold fast. Nalatan leapt to the far side.

A nomad carrying a torch trotted along the perpendicular alleyway. Across from Conway and the dogs, Nalatan's anticipatory grin was spectral eye whites and teeth.

The man approaching was so intent on his progress that Conway's presence didn't fully register on him until he was already past. As he turned, Nalatan's parrying bar struck with a sharp crack. Conway snatched the torch from nerveless hands as the stunned Blizzardman dropped.

Conway and Nalatan were at the stairs before the man groaned and called for help. Pursuers gave immediate chase.

Tate's boop fired twice. There were screams and curses. Tate and Nalatan returned at a dead run, shouting ahead of their arrival. "A lot of them, Matt, down that hall there. Get up the stairs.

Now!" She whirled, fired the wipe. A torch fell. Wild, surreal light patterns scrawled the walls and ceiling.

Firing, falling back, the group surrendered distance for time. They found many doors. None offered escape.

An arrow penetrated Conway's chain mail. It was harmless, but it made everyone understand how close the race had become.

It was Nalatan who found the light. He questioned it, afraid of disappointment. "Is that a reflection of the torch?"

Tate ran into the room with him, reached out and grabbed Sylah. Conway scooped Lanta in with him, slamming the steel door behind the trailing dogs.

Footsteps pounded in the hall outside, then hesitated, wary of ambush. Tate wedged her knife under the door. "Let's hope that holds better than your boop cartridge."

The torch revealed a featureless room with a square metal box in the center and a metal cabinet, floor to ceiling, to the right of the door. Wires rose from the black box to disappear into the ceiling, and a black tube approximately a half inch in diameter extended from its side to the wall opposite the door.

"Laser port," Tate said. "Just what you thought, buddy." She patted the box, pointing at the place where the tube reached the wall. "A ball joint where the tube actually fits through the wall. See here; the box moves, as well. It only gives a few degrees of bearing or elevation, but it expands the field of fire a lot. Smart work."

Conway found it difficult to share Tate's professional appreciation.

The minute speck of light was at the bottom of the ball joint. Nalatan dropped to his knees, twisted, and worked to get his eye to it. When he straightened, his grin told everyone what they needed to know. "The valley. We can do it. Escape."

Sylah looked at the door, closed against her. "The Teacher. My duty." She faced her friends, beseeching. "The Teacher said my responsibility is to bring all the magic in that room to the world."

Lanta said, "The Teacher said you must plant the seed. We must leave."

Conway muffled a groan. The naïveté was heartbreaking.

Nalatan was already chipping at the hole with his sword. The material was as tough as the stone itself. Conway noted other places where it had been applied to the wall. He couldn't fathom their significance. Sylah and Lanta drew shortknives, squatted to help Nalatan. Lanta positioned Sylah so she could work with least stress to her injured back. Conway and Tate faced the door, waiting.

A voice Conway recognized instantly came down the hall. "Conway. I am Fox Eleven. You should know who killed you."

"You should know I'm not dead."

Fox laughed. "You'll die here, all of you. Moonpriest has decided. I'm ordered to repeat his words: 'Knowledge not held by me alone must not exist.' He said you understand the strange things we found here, that you will understand the meaning of the words."

"Go back to your master. Tell him I'll deal with both of you soon enough."

"It would be a pleasure to take you alive, Matt Conway. There are things you should see. Church Home is gone. The women there are learning what it costs to anger men. It also pleases me to tell you there is plague in the Three Territories."

Karda and Mikka seemed to understand. Both rose, whining. Heads high, they paced, bouncing off each other, distracted.

The level of noise in the hall increased sharply. A distant voice called. Others rose in response. Footsteps sounded. Then silence. The group in the room exchanged puzzled glances. Work continued at the hole, now as big as a fist.

The dogs came to Conway, nuzzling him. Sharply, he ordered them away. They went reluctantly, tails down.

Tate said, "I don't hear anyone outside anymore."

Conway said, "Open that door, you'll hear plenty."

Once again, there was only the chink of knives on stone and metal in the room. And the whining of the dogs. Conway shushed them irritably.

"What smells?" Nalatan pulled away from the hole, sniffing. Tate said, "Keep digging. Leave the nose work to the . . ." The phrase trailed off to thoughtful silence. Everyone tested the air.

"Smoke." Fear edged Nalatan's declaration. "Not torches."

"Poison." Tate spat the word. "Wires. Plastics. Paints. This place is a toxic palace." She turned to Nalatan. "Out. How long?"

The hole was barely larger. He shrugged. "Not soon."

A lacy, gray tendril wisped under the door. Everyone watched in fascinated horror as its sinuous delicacy flowed to the hole and outside.

Tate said, "Is there anyone in the valley now?"

Nalatan looked. "Horse handlers. Many horses. I can see the Door. Three guards there. Oh. Men coming out. Looking back. Talking to the guards."

Conway pulled Tate's wedge out of the way. "I won't burn to death. No way. Back me up." He threw open the door, leapt out to fall, roll, ended up aiming down the hall. A thin, sinister haze smudged the floor.

Wordlessly, the others joined him. Trotting, they retraced their earlier steps. At the head of the stairwell leading to the vacated library, they looked down into a well of smoke. Pulsing, it seemed to be trying to gather itself to lunge up at them. Far above, hardly visible against the high ceiling, a thinner, more nebulous veil roiled angrily. An orange glow poured through the door leading to the dead Teacher's office. Its illumination touched the bottom stair and the floor. As they descended toward it, a thudding explosion tumbled them in a heap.

Disembodied cries from the huge auditorium bored through the dust and smoke, clearer now that the wall between it and the library was breached. Through those gaps licked eager, exploratory flames. Men screamed for someone to open the stairwell, let them out. Others merely screamed.

Sylah got to her feet, ascended a few stairs, turned back to face her friends and speak. She carried the torch, and in its wavering light, she was pale with grim resolution. " 'Ignorance and evil,' the Teacher warned against. They're destroying the legacy, except for what we saved. The seeds will be planted. Come."

Conway and Tate exchanged despairing glances. The books were such a meager find. The vidisks and the electricity to make them viable were both gone. The only escape route from the underground complex was blasted shut and afire. Everyone was already coughing and tearing from noxious gases.

Nevertheless, Sylah's voice demanded respect. Her determination was impossible; it was equally irresistible. Nalatan was the first to shuffle toward her. Obediently, her group followed her.

At the top of the steps, Sylah turned for one last, yearning look at what Conway and Tate called the library. Her friends hurried past her, anxious to get back to their only possibility of survival. She grimaced at the eruption of fresh flame from the tumbled rows of vidisk cabinets. A rumbling sound distracted her. Apprehensively, she looked up, afraid the ceiling was giving way. Instead, she saw a solid black wall descending. Ponderously, it lowered, creating a barrier between the vidisks and the books. The fire, as if aware it was being denied part of its due, flashed across the intervening gap, lashing at the curtain. It stood firm, unassailable.

Raging heat drove Sylah after her companions.

The laser room filled with smoke. Its smothering presence generated desperate urgency. Tate's bandage hung loose, swinging. Irritably, she jerked it free, hurled it into a corner.

The panting dogs lay by the metal cabinet. Conway patted them, consoling. Looking up, he wondered if the cabinet held tools that might help the nibbling progress on the cement wall. He opened it.

"Tate! Look. Ammunition. Wipe rounds. Boop rounds. And a wipe. Why didn't we look before? That's what those cemented spots are; sealed gun ports. And why didn't we think of these AP rounds for the boop? Load up. Everyone." He distributed with both hands. When they had all they could carry, he said, "That's it. In the hall. Lock and load, Tate. We're going out."

Sighting the boop, he pulled back around the corner, saying, "I don't want any splinters. I'll just—"

Something moved down the hall. At his feet, coughing, choking, Karda and Mikka rose groggily. Conway shouted challenge. Nalatan and he filled the hall, side by side, crouched.

The smoke swirled, suggested a figure, obscured it. Something solid materialized, advanced in tiny, uncertain increments. Tate gasped, stepped back.

Conway took the sword from the man's unresisting fingers and helped him to sit down, back against the wall. Looking up at Conway, the man gestured for water. Most of it spilled past his ruined lips. Where it washed away soot and grime, the flesh was burned. Charred clothing still smoked. When he finished drinking, he spoke in slow, pained words. "Me. Blizzardman. Good you left. Moonpriest. Set fire to everything. Blocked stairs after fire started. Closed doors. Fox. Others. Left us. Sacrifice, Moonpriest said." His head dropped forward, shook slowly side to side.

Sylah saw a forlorn child in the gesture. She rushed to him, Lanta close behind. He sagged in their arms. Tortured eyes sought Conway. "Moonpriest. Kill him. Kill the evil one." He sighed. It had a satisfied sound. Sylah and Lanta checked pulses, reflexes. They lowered him gently. Lanta said, "He's gone. You knew him?"

Conway shook his head. "I don't know. A Blizzardman. I trained them." He paused, features hoarding hurt he tried not to show. "Stand back. I'm firing."

It took five earsplitting rounds to blow a large enough hole. Nalatan crawled out first, sword in hand. The women followed, then the dogs. Last, Conway. Trembling, scrambling, coughing, they got away from the smoke pouring out of the hole behind them.

Another explosion thundered and vibrated deep in the mountain. Smoke erupted from laser ports all over the valley. The Door leaned outward from its base, smoke roiling up its back side. It toppled forward. With a low rumble, the tunnel collapsed behind it, expelling smoke that jetted horizontally for yards, then bent to raise skyward. A moment later, the hillside slipped, covering the Door.

The next explosion rocked the entire valley. The laser ports vomited larger gouts of smoke and, in some cases, flame. The ground leapt upward and slumped massively down again. The smoke and flame almost stopped entirely as the complex of tunnels and rooms collapsed. For several heartbeats, the earth shivered and growled.

As soon as they cleared their lungs and vision, the group proceeded downhill. Conway sent the dogs ahead to scout. When the animals reached the mouth of the canyon without incident, he called them back. Still, the group passed slowly through the defile leading to the larger valley. They were at the joining of the Door's valley and the larger one when Blizzard charged out of their hidden draw.

Obviously, the attackers had banked on the dogs scouting no farther than the canyon entrance. Conway cursed himself. These were men he'd trained, men eager to die for a siah they didn't know had just consigned their companions to a fiery, suffocating death. Their eyes were fanatic in their death-mask war paint. Tate and Conway fired as fast as they could. Nalatan waited, sword and parrying weapon in hand. The wipes did terrible damage in the few seconds before the charge was on them.

The dogs attacked the horses, sending them into hysterical bucks and leaps. Riders were thrown to the ground. Those at the rear of the attack pressed forward, crushing the fallen, forcing others into the maelstrom off balance.

Nalatan's parrying bar spun and twisted like a live thing, smashing, stabbing. In his other hand, the sword sang destruction. Conway and Tate drew swords, handed off the wipes to Sylah and Lanta to protect the barrels from damage.

The trio was inexorably driven back. Screaming of life eternal, Blizzard's warriors gave up their lives in religious frenzy.

Mikka yelped, staggered to Conway with a broken leg dangling. A sword thrust caught Nalatan in the stomach. He stumbled. Tate leapt to his side, slashed the throat of the man who'd done it. Nalatan recovered; bloody, bent over in pain, he was back in the fight. Mikka stayed beside Conway, using her minimal mobility to protect his off-sword side. Karda continued to rip at the horses.

Moonpriest's voice rose from far behind the melee. "Kill the

Church witches! Get me those weapons! Quickly! Moondance conquers!"

A man broke past Tate, reached for Sylah. She raised her short-knife. Needlessly, because Mikka threw herself on the man. Sylah screamed, turned away from what was happening at her feet.

A headbutt knocked Conway sprawling. Dazed, eyes unfocused, he struggled to his feet. Mikka had the man who'd felled her master. Karda assured Conway had space and time to clear his vision. A howling warrior pressed in. Conway parried, slashed, felt the impact of his blow shiver up his arm, twist him sideways. There was no time to wonder about the effect. Another man filled the gap the last man left.

The battle was a dull, painful roar in his head. He couldn't make his legs work. Instinct took the place of thought.

A voice, calling his name. Lanta. The last dregs of adrenaline shocked his system, energized his last reserves. He withdrew toward the sound of her voice, desperate to catch her words. At last, he was close enough to understand, and when he did, despair fell on him like winter's breath.

"They come, Matt! They come!" She was pointing. So was Sylah. They grinned. He decided they'd gone mad.

When he faced forward again, slumping with exhaustion, there was only himself with his dogs. Tate and Nalatan. There were no Blizzard men left standing. Three stragglers on horseback raced up the slope of the smoke-filled valley. It struck Conway as odd they should leave in that direction.

There was no sound from the group but the rale of exhaustion as a wave of fresh horsemen trotted toward them. Bleary-eyed, leaning on each other, Conway and Tate readied the wipes.

Lanta grabbed Conway's weapon, forced the muzzle down. Tate staggered sideways until caught by Nalatan. Lanta was laughing, crying, kissing Conway in a transport of happiness and relief. "They're Dog warriors, Matt. Dogs. The Messenger Sylah sent home got through. To home. Where we're going. We're going home."

CHAPTER 115

The sound of soft voices from the surrounding camp filled a waking Conway with a sense of well-being that approached euphoria. Eyes closed, he thought back on the meeting with the rescuing Dog warriors. Only hours ago. It seemed centuries had passed. Details of the fighting were vivid, shocking fragments, their place in time uncertain, disordered.

Primary, though, was the memory of joy. In his mind, he heard again the racket of glad greeting, relieved excitement, the elation of being alive.

Analyzing the latter sensation, he sobered. The battle of the Door was different. For once, he was able to consider what he'd done and feel clean, as if this time he'd washed away guilt and unworthiness.

He wanted desperately for it to be so. This time he'd fought to protect, to further something good. There was more than survival involved. More than simpleminded proof of ability, more than a warped sense of vengeance.

Had he found in himself the man he hoped he could be? Was he strong enough to face savage strength without becoming a savage? Was he wise enough to compromise, capable of pride without arrogance?

No man perfected those qualities.

Matt Conway sighed, willing to be contented by the self-awareness that he was closer to those goals than he'd ever been.

Something touched his face. Gentle. Wet, deliciously cool, herb-scented. A soft cloth, drawn slowly across his brow.

He opened his eyes. Lanta sat beside him, legs curled under her, catlike, compact. She smiled her greeting, wrung the cloth into a bowl on the ground, then resumed wiping his face. The cloth whispered against coarse whiskers, and she laughed at the noise.

The simple pleasure of the sound rang in Conway's ears like pardon.

Still flat on his back, he looked into her eyes. He said, "At the Starwatch camp, when you were all tied to that pole—you know the one thing that I was thinking, coming down that hill behind you?"

She shook her head, cloth poised, waiting. The posture suggested a readiness for flight.

"I had to tell you," he said. "All the way down, I kept telling myself that whatever happened, I was going to tell you how ashamed I am. I didn't care if I died to do it; I wanted you to know. And then I was too ashamed to say anything. Now I can. I hurt you unforgivably. No one can ever know how much I regret what I did. I'm sorry."

Lanta resumed washing his face. He winced when she touched the left cheekbone, where he'd been butted. She paused, studying the cloth for a long while. Then she looked at him, almost questioning, even though she spoke in the affirmative. "Not unforgivable. I don't think anyone can ever forget something like that. A person can forgive. For a while, I tried to tell myself I was to blame, too, but I wasn't. Until I admitted that, I wanted to forgive you, but I couldn't. But it wasn't my fault."

"That's what I had to tell you. I'd never ask you to forgive me. All I wanted was to be sure you knew. My fault. My guilt."

Lanta was suddenly brisk. "It's all been said, then." Conway opened his mouth to continue the subject. A closer look at her changed his mind. She went on in the same manner. "Mikka chewed off her new splint while you slept, and Sylah had to do that all over again. Nalatan's doing well. Tate's tending him."

Conway sat up. Evening light, sultry with blues, lavender, resonant grays, streamed across the face of distant slopes. The sky above them was tenuous, as if exhausted by the sun's day and anxious for night's dark ease. A short distance away piñons collected light on stiff needles, so that each stood out, individual and stark. He was surprised to realize he remembered almost nothing of the trek to his high ground. Nalatan, lip curled in a grimace that was a sneer at his pain. Mikka, limping stoically. Sylah, straight and tall, imperiously denying any effect of the wound that bloodied her back.

Conway remembered Sylah talking to the Dog leader. Conway asked Lanta her name.

A strange voice answered from close behind Conway. "I know you, Matt Conway." The man who came into view was young, ruggedly handsome. Exposed arms bulked with muscle. His grin was open, uncomplicated. "We met briefly, after we crushed Altanar in Ola. I'm Darbannen Vayar, a Nightwatch of the Dog People." As he spoke, Darbannen lifted his eyes to someone on the other side of Conway. Conway turned to find Sylah, Tate, and Nalatan approaching. The latter pair were obviously as freshly awakened as Conway. After a smile for them, he greeted Darbannen with Dog formality, asked how Dog warriors found their way to this place.

With the easy brevity of a tale repeated, Darbannen said, "A Messenger from Rose Priestess Sylah came to Clas na Bale. We'd already heard Windband was moving against Church Home, and that's where the priestess was going. We found Windband's burned-out camp as they were leaving, and followed them."

Conway called the dogs to him. They came from where they'd been quietly watching, Mikka stumping unhappily on her splinted leg. Conway had her lay next to him, so he could sympathize. She sighed gustily. He would have sworn she smirked at the aloof, proud Karda.

Looking to Darbannen again, Conway said, "You saw the destruction of Church Home. How bad was it?"

Darbannen shook his head. "They stopped their attack, left the bulk of their force to besiege the place. Moonpriest and a small unit rode off, looking for you." He made a wry face. "We didn't know it was Moonpriest leaving, at first. By the time we discovered it and pursued, we were almost too late. As it is, Moonpriest himself and most of his men escaped."

Tate moved to Darbannen, put her hand on his arm. "Nothing to apologize for. You timed it perfectly. If you hadn't chased him and his crowd, we'd have finished off the whole bunch, and there wouldn't have been a speck of glory in this for you all. Now you can brag about how you saved us. We'll back you up."

Grimacing wearily at Nalatan, Darbannen said, "Is she always like this?"

Tate faced the warrior monk, smiling slyly. "Answer the man right, honey: you've got a lot riding on it."

Nalatan blushed, fiery red. He stammered. Darbannen laughed raucously. Swamped by opposing waves of pride and embarrassment, Nalatan smiled and sweated.

Suddenly, inexplicably, Darbannen's face fell. His unexpected seriousness ended the laughing. "There's other news. I didn't want to mention it until you were all rested. I'm ashamed for smiling, for laughing. I let the excitement make me forget. There is plague at home. At the same time, the Skan grow worse every day. Gan Moondark battles them constantly."

Sylah's voice was thick with unspoken plea. "The plague. Has it taken anyone I . . . we . . . Has it taken many?"

"Your husband was well when we left. The sickness kills only the very young, the old, the ailing. There's fever. Weakness. It lasts a long time, but most healthy adults recover."

The five who'd sought the Door looked at each other. None had to speak. All remembered Conway's sickness. The symptoms sounded very similar.

Darbannen was saying, "Windband has it. They were dropping around Church Home. The pyres burned constantly."

Sylah said, "Have you heard anything of inside Church Home?"

"No. But I think the plague will send Windband running."

"And us, as well." Sylah was definite, in command. "We rest here only until everyone's fit to ride. Darbannen, you arrange our defenses. My group will camp upstream, past that cleft rock. We have things to discuss. You understand."

"Privacy. I understand perfectly." Darbannen winked at Tate as he spoke, then affected a grotesque simper. It was Tate's turn to be flustered. Before she could collect her wits and respond, the sturdy Nightwatch was walking away, chuckling, vastly pleased with himself.

The separate site Sylah chose offered reasonable seclusion within the defensive perimeter. Soon there was a fire licking at several spitted rabbits. With the group gathered around, Sylah addressed the paramount issue in everyone's mind. "Conway. Tate. You know more of reading. What value is in these books we salvaged? From the little I understood of 'vidisks' and 'library,' I realized the treasures of the Door were vast. What we have seems pathetically small. Have I failed, then?"

Both Conway and Tate bubbled with cheerful reassurance until Sylah's cold pragmatism silenced them. "What is in the books?"

From an improvised bag made of a knotted Church robe, Sylah produced the five volumes. Bound in plain black, they were identical in size, save for thickness. Conway handled them with delighted tenderness, turning them over and over.

Impulsively, he dumped them all in Tate's lap, moved to embrace Sylah. Holding her at arm's length, he sobered. "All the prophecies of bringing power to Church can be realized through these. Everything needed to build a state, a people, a world, is here in black and white. Understand, though, any of this knowledge can be profaned. You'll do great good, Sylah. There are those who'll corrupt everything you accomplish. Be warned. But don't hesitate. Go ahead with your mission. You were chosen to be the Flower. You've succeeded. Magnificently."

Tate said, "There's something else you have to see." With a care that was little short of reverential, she handed Conway a slim, red-jacketed volume. There was no title, only a scribbled column of numbers on the plasticized cover. He looked at her quizzically, and caught the glitter of unshed tears. She looked away, saying, "It was in the Teacher's other drawer. When I saw what it was, I almost left it, but I guess we have to keep it. For the record, sort of. I don't know." She gave a helpless half-shrug and waved a hand as if to make him go away.

The interior cover sheet said: TOP SECRET (BORN FREE CLEARANCE REQUIRED).

Conway turned the page. He made a choking sound and sat down hard. Hardly audible, he said, "Crèche locations. Names of volunteers. Dates. Five sites. Ours, Arizona, Michigan, Georgia, New Hampshire. Thousands of us. Gone. Just us. All that's left."

The others respected the pained silence of their strange friends. They drew away. Tate eventually spoke. "We don't know we're all that's left. Any more than we knew about the Door."

Conway nodded, continuing to flip pages. "You're right." He sighed heavily. "Quite a day's work. What've we turned loose, Donnacee?"

In a transparently conscious effort to accommodate a dubious situation, Tate straightened, threw back her shoulders, lifted her chin. Conway watched bemusedly, waiting. She said, "You wanted to create your identity. I wanted to have something to say about the culture of this new world. We're getting our wish. God help us."

"The One in All help us," Conway corrected. His smile could have been mocking, could have been hurting. However, he added, "An elegant way to express a supreme being, actually." He got to his feet. Tate followed him to rejoin the others. He told them, "This book is about our people—Tate's and mine. It's extremely important. Can I ask all of you to forget it was found? Please. It doesn't exist." He tucked it under his shirt.

Three heads nodded unhesitating agreement. Conversationally, Sylah said, "That's settled. Now we must eat and rest. We're needed in the Three Territories."

They ate slowly, with infrequent, desultory bits of conversation. After the meal, Sylah watched Nalatan and Tate, hand in hand, walk uphill away from the firelight, drawing the gathering dusk around themselves. A few yards away, Lanta and Conway prepared for the night. Sylah had to smile at the prim distance they arranged between their beds, and how they automatically met at the center of that gap. Together, seated knee to knee on the ground, they joined hands and conversed with the earnestness of lovers building their years.

The four of them filled Sylah with self-pity. She battled tears, confessed her loneliness. Her bitterness.

Where was that musical, strengthening, cajoling, demanding voice now?

Alone.

If this was triumph, what harm was in defeat?

The Door. What was it Conway said? "Everything you need to build a world, here in black and white." Something like that. Simple words. Awful, awesome responsibility.

A life that belonged to everyone, with nothing left for herself?

I will not be owned.

The words rang in her ears until sleep brought relief.

Two days later Nalatan declared himself fit for travel, and refused argument on the matter. Yet again, Sylah marveled at her comrades. Tate, battered and scarred. Nalatan, vehemently denying pain, even as he bent to ease it. Conway and Lanta. Quite likely the worst casualties of all, with no scars to prove it. Eager to ride north.

For her. Because it was what she must do. Because she yearned so desperately to be with her husband.

On the morning of the third day they left off, scouts far ahead, main body clustered loosely around Sylah and her precious cargo. Mikka managed on her splint. She whined complaint when Karda strutted off with Conway, but Tate and Lanta quickly spoiled her into a martyred acceptance of her lot.

The sun was directly overhead two days later when the white banner appeared on a ridge to the east. Nalatan called to Darbannen. "You see him? Helmeted. Kossiar, or nomad with a trophy."

Darbannen grunted, then. "Now's when I wish we'd brought our dogs. We were afraid our pace across the northern Dry would kill them. We could use their scouting abilities. We're going so slow people can ambush us too easily."

Sylah interjected. "That's a peace symbol. Look, he's coming toward us, alone."

Darkly, Darbannen said, "The symbol means peace. I don't know about the man. We rode through a lot of nomad-conquered country getting here; we know what they do. There are three more people on that ridge now; who knows who's hidden behind the one west of us, Priestess?" He barked orders for security to deploy to cover. Then they waited.

The Kossiar rider stopped several yards away, acknowledging Sylah formally, then saying, "Sister Mother Odeel requests a meeting. Will you receive her in peace?"

Nalatan snapped his response before Sylah could. "Will she come in peace?"

The Messenger flinched, and Sylah let him dangle for a moment before giving her own answer. "Tell Odeel this: No bargains or compromises. The Flower has not forgotten that she put the mark on the Odeel one. Or why. The Flower says, 'Let the apostate come.' "

Wheeling his mount, the rider galloped to the ridge. The trio left him behind, advanced at a trot. Lanta moved away from Conway's side to be closer to her sister. Together, they faced their enemy, straightbacked, unhooded, defiant. Conway, Nalatan, and Tate drew up behind them.

Odeel wasted no time in greetings. "I come to collect what is mine. These men are my assurance of fair value." She gestured over her right shoulder. "The leader of the Opal brotherhood. The other's Tiger's leader."

"I have nothing of yours. If that's your only message, go back where you came from, and leave us to our journey." Sylah was imperious, as if Odeel had the capacity to annoy, but nothing more.

Undisturbed, Odeel flashed a sly, malicious grin. "All warrior monks know of the Nalatan one's oath to kill the one called White Thunder. I am here to see the honor of the brotherhoods observed."

"Why?" Lanta's interruption was a plaint of heartbreak.

"For the same reason I will destroy you, when the time comes, outcast Priestess. He is the ally of my enemy." Glaring at Sylah again, Odeel continued. "You marked me. To the death, then, sister mine." Suddenly, she rose in her stirrups, her pointing finger a raking, accusing weapon. "All of you. Doomed. Church denies the Three Territories until the evil one is disavowed. As your untended people die of sickness and injury, blame Sylah. As your unprotected souls are devoured by dark forces, blame Sylah. I stand ready to forgive. After you deny her."

Darbannen was pale. He raised his voice in a brave show. "My orders come from Clas na Bale, Chief of the Dog People. We know Rose Priestess Sylah as pure. We are hers, as she is ours."

Odeel made as if to answer, and Sylah kneed Copper forward, pulling the horse up just short of contact. To a startled Odeel, she said, "We have nothing for you. Conway and Nalatan are the best of friends."

Recovering quickly, Odeel said, "Nalatan must fight Conway. One will die."

Sylah backed Copper, looked to Nalatan, then Conway. Nalatan refused her gaze, stared fixedly at Odeel. Conway said, "I won't fight him."

Smiling, Odeel drawled. "Tell this man who changes sides so easily what honor is."

The Opal leader said, "Nalatan fights you to the death, as his oath said or he shames all the brotherhoods. We must kill him if he shows cowardice."

"Cowardice? He's the bravest man you'll ever see. You want a fight? Good. Nalatan and me—we'll take you two. Right now."

The Tiger leader shrugged. "It was his oath. We must see it respected."

"For the sake of this warped old hag? Forget it. I free him of his oath. I surrender to him. I'm afraid to fight him. I beg protection of Rose Priestess Sylah."

Small smiles pulled at the faces of the Dog warriors. Lanta's wide grin was triumphant.

Nalatan was ashen, trembling. His voice caught as he spoke to Tate. "Understand. I cannot live with that oath over my head. I cannot kill my friend. My words were a sin, and I must pay." Tate's shock was so great she made no response, didn't interrupt when Nalatan turned to face Conway. "I will die here. I can't make these men do it. All who were my brothers would be shamed. You will win. It must be so."

"Wait a minute." The icy control in Tate's voice demanded obedience. All looked to her. Sylah noticed how the black woman had turned, a small movement, but one that put the empty eye of the wipe in direct line with the Opal leader. Sylah said nothing, wondering if she could permit what seemed to be developing.

Tate went on. "You, with the opals. And you, Tiger. You're sworn to protect this Sister Mother, right?"

Offended, both men nodded shortly. Tate said, "I'm making you an offer. Release Nalatan. Acknowledge that a mistake was made, that the oath isn't binding. Give him some penance or whatever, but let him go. Otherwise, I'm going to ice both of you; that means kill you. Then I'm going to take this old woman to Windband and sell her. Think on that: the Sister Mother, sold into slavery on your watch. How's that for dishonor?"

Odeel made an elaborate three-sign. "I can't hope to touch the soul you no longer have. I can affect you, though. I cast out Nalatan. I declare him under your spell, witch."

Tate's gaze remained on the warrior monks. "Cast out? That means he's not a brother. His oath's canceled. That's right, isn't it? Brothers?"

Twisting in her saddle, Odeel snarled at the men behind her. "Agree at risk of your souls. I can cast you out, too."

"If you do, they're not bound to protect you," Tate said. "In fact, I think they'd like to avoid protecting you." Unexpectedly, Tate turned Nalatan. Her hard manner cracked. "Help me, Nalatan. Please. Tell your brothers you want to be free. Everybody knows your honor's beyond doubt. Don't leave me. I love you. Don't leave me, not to prove something that doesn't need proof. Please."

"Me, too." Conway spoke to Nalatan, despite the monk's refusal to look anywhere but into Tate's eyes. "This is how people

692

like Odeel beat people like us. They debase our integrity by using it. Don't let her do it."

Moving her mount sideways, keeping the wipe leveled at the warrior monks, Tate edged to his side. She put her free hand on his. "I love you. I can't say any more than that. I don't have any more than that."

Agonized, muscles straining against the weight of a lifetime of dedication, of centuries of tradition, Nalatan tried to speak. Scarlet, his throat worked convulsively. At last, hoarsely, he said, "I refuse my oath. I was foolish. I won't worsen that foolishness. Odeel. I refuse you."

Harshly, almost screeching, Odeel said, "Monks. Do what you must. Obey Church!"

The pair looked at each other. Closing together, they backed their mounts. Whispering, oblivious to Odeel's ranting, they deliberated. When they were ready, the Opal leader said, "The White Thunder is right. I've never seen such courage. Nalatan breaks his life because he's learned that to be right is vital to a true man. All brotherhoods may grant dispensation for necessary acts that benefit the brotherhood or Church or both. It was always so. Nalatan's first oath was to protect the Flower in her search for the Door. We believe that work is not yet finished. Until it is, Nalatan cannot execute his second oath."

Sylah and the others cheered, laughed, congratulated a dazed, surprised Nalatan. Like something losing force, however, the happiness slowed, stopped.

The brotherhood leaders waited, stonily patient. Odeel watched them with hopeful malice. Speaking to her, the Tiger leader said, "Sister Mother, we swear loyalty to Church, but we won't harm Nalatan. Nevertheless, he publicly disavowed an oath. That cannot be tolerated. Nevermore is he one of us. Even so, Nalatan, we'll sing of you as the bravest of the brave." To Sylah, the Tiger monk added, "We're Church's weapon. We'll pray to meet next as friends. If not, until then, may the One in All protect you." He paused, then, significantly, "All."

"I forbid." Odeel was livid. She shook bunched fists at Sylah. Frothy white spittle flew, flecked her black robe. "They cannot bless you. I am Sister Mother and . . ." She stopped. Eerily, almost inhumanly, she reasserted control. Features relaxed, became marble-smooth and cool and white, defied the hot sun. Eyes lost their slitted glare, turned calm and direct. Her entire body eased. When she spoke, there was a freighted, deadly calm in her words.

"I will win, Sylah. Whatever you scraped up from the destruction of the Door will do you no good. You stole Church secrets. Your mere death can no longer slake my anger. Your friends, your love—I'll foul them. Remember Jessak every day. He'll grow to manhood hearing how you stole him and abandoned him. Long before I'm willing to let you die, you'll beg for the mercy of oblivion. Go, cast out, with your mangy pack. Go, knowing that every power of Church follows you, waits for you, searches for you. Go." Slowly, haughtily, Odeel turned and rode away. Her escort unobtrusively slipped into trail behind her.

No one in Sylah's group moved until the trio disappeared over the eastern ridge. Conway broke the long, thick silence, suggesting to Darbannen that they should resume their march. Awkwardly eager, the young Dog gave orders. The loudness seemed to shatter a spell. Everyone talked. Take drew aside a still-troubled Nalatan, her every move consoling, reassuring. Lanta hurried to Conway, laughing, happy, eager to tell him of her pride in him.

Sylah fell off the pace, rode by herself. She decided she didn't mind being alone just then. Before, the lovers' closeness of her friends meant exclusion. Now it suggested promise. For them. For her.

She touched the saddlebags holding the books. Lanta had spoken of Seeing a successful quest. There was reticence in her narrative, a holding. Lanta had seen more than she was willing to tell. That was acceptable. There were things Sylah didn't want to know.

Odeel's words came back. Sylah shuddered, forced herself free of them.

Books. The problem would be in convincing men—and women—to accept learning. Of all things forbidden, that was the greatest.

It would happen. Men could be changed. She'd seen it that day, with Nalatan and Conway. Honor need not be blindness. Courage need not be mindless. She had seen it.

So had Odeel.

Sylah threw back her head, doffed the hood, filled her lungs with savory, singing air that suddenly tasted of cool, high pines. She was going home. Not as Rose Priestess. Not as Flower. Those names meant battles past, battles to come.

Sylah. Clas' wife.

Going home.